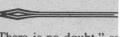

"There is no doubt," sa                          -
tion, "that there was a sp                          s
death; the traces of it remain. I suspect what it was, yet I
cannot—"

"Lady Aliera," said Khaavren, "if you would be good
enough to tell me what you are doing here, well, I should be
entirely in your debt."

"Why, I am investigating this body, in order to learn how
he came to die."

"Or," said Sethra, "perhaps to remove all traces of the
spell, so that nothing can be learned."

Aliera looked at Sethra for a long moment before saying,
"I don't know you, Madame."

The Enchantress bowed. "I am called Sethra Lavode."

Aliera bowed in her turn. "Very well, Sethra Lavode. I am
called Aliera e'Kieron."

Sethra bowed once more, and if she was surprised that
Aliera displayed no reaction upon learning her identity, she
gave no sign of it.

"Now," said Aliera, "that introductions are made, there remains the matter of your last remark, which sounded to my
ears very like an accusation. I must, therefore, beg you to
make it either more explicit, so that I may respond appropriately, or to recast it in such a way that no response is called
for."

"Perhaps you are unaware," said Khaavren, "that to find
you down here, engaged in I know not what activities with
respect to the bodies, puts appearances against you."

"Appearances, My Lord?" said Aliera, in a tone of voice,
and with a simultaneous look, expressing the greatest disdain.
"I have often heard that phrase, *Appearances are against
you,* uttered by those who wish to conceal an accusation.
Who are these people who believe appearances, My Lord?
Would you care to name them?"

"I am one," said Sethra, putting her hand on the dagger at
her side.

# BOOKS BY STEVEN BRUST

# FIVE HUNDRED YEARS AFTER

## STEVEN BRUST

**TOR**®
*fantasy*

A TOM DOHERTY ASSOCIATES BOOK
NEW YORK

This is a work of fiction. All the characters and events portrayed in this book are fictitious, and any resemblance to real people or events is purely coincidental.

FIVE HUNDRED YEARS AFTER

Copyright © 1994 by Steven Brust

Cover art by Sam Rakeland

A Tor Book
Published by Tom Doherty Associates, LLC
175 Fifth Avenue
New York, NY 10010

www.tor.com

Tor® is a registered trademark of Tom Doherty Associates, LLC.

ISBN: 0-812-51522-6
Library of Congress Catalog Card Number: 93-45291

First edition: April 1994
First mass market edition: March 1995

Printed in the United States of America

0  9  8  7  6  5  4

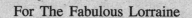
For The Fabulous Lorraine

# *Acknowledgments*

Thanks are due Terri Windling for helping me beat this one into shape, to Teresa Nielsen Hayden who did Many Fine Things for the manuscript, to Sam Rakeland for the nifty cover, and to Valerie Smith, for this 'n' that.

Thanks are also due Patrick Nielsen Hayden, who provided support, encouragement, and arguments.

I'd also like to thank Emma Bull, Kara Dalkey, Pamela Dean, and Will Shetterly, my coconspirators.

Special thanks to Ed Raschke, who supplied the leather.

Don't ask.

# Five Hundred Years After

*Being in the Nature of a Sequel to*

The Phoenix Guards

*Describing Certain Events Which Occurred*
*In the Year of the Hawk*
*In the Turn of the Orca*
*In the Phase of the Dragon*
*In the Reign of the Phoenix*
*In the Cycle of the Phoenix*
*In the Great Cycle of the Dragon*

*Or*

*The 532nd Year of the Reign of Tortaalik the First*

*Submitted to the Imperial Library*
*From Springsign Manor*
*Via House of the Hawk*
*On this 3rd day of the Month of the Lyorn*
*Of the Year of the Iorich*

## FIVE HUNDRED YEARS AFTER

*Or*

*In the Eleventh Year*
*Of the Glorious Reign*
*Of the Empress Norathar the Second*

*By Sir Paarfi of Roundwood*
*House of the Hawk*
*(His Arms, Seal, Lineage Block)*

*Presented, as Always*
*To the Countess of Garnier*
*With Gratitude and Hope*

# Cast of Characters

## Of the Court

Tortaalik I—*His Majesty The Emperor*
Noima—*Her Majesty the Consort*
Jurabin—*Prime Minister*
Rollondar e'Drien—*Warlord*
Countess Bellor—*Superintendent of Finance*
Nyleth—*Court Wizard*
Khaavren—*Ensign of the Imperial Guard*
Brudik—*Lord of the Chimes*
Lady Ingera—*Lord of the Keys*
Navier—*His Majesty's physicker*
Dimma—*His Majesty's Chief Servant*
Daro—*A Maid of Honor to Her Majesty*
Dinb—*Master of the First Gate*

## Of the Phoenix Guard

Thack—*Khaavren's corporal*
Tummelis e'Terics—*A guardsman*
Naabrin—*A guardsman*
Menia—*A guardsman*
Sergeant—*A guardsman*
Tivor—*A guardsman*
Kyu—*A guardsman*

Ailib—*A guardsman*
Heth—*A police-man*

### Of the Imperial Palace
Duke of Galstan (Pel)—*An Initiate into Discretion*
Lady Glass—*Chief of the Sorett Regiment*
Erna—*Master of the Order of Discretion*
Klorynderata—*A servant at the palace*

### Of Lord Adron's Company
Adron e'Kieron—*Dragon Heir*
Aliera e'Kieron—*Adron's daughter*
Molric e'Drien—*Adron's chainman*
Durtri—*A sentry*
Geb—*A soldier*
Dohert—*A soldier*
Eftaan—*A soldier*

### Of the Lavodes
Sethra—*Captain of the Lavodes*
Dreen—*A Lavode*
Tuvo—*A Lavode*
Roila—*A Lavode*
Nett—*A Lavode*

### Of the City
Raf—*A pastry vendor*
Leen—*A would-be assassin*
Greycat—*A ruffian and a conspirator*
Laral—*A Jhereg*
Chalar—*An Orca*
Dunaan—*A Jhereg*
Grita—*A Half-breed*
Baroness of Clover—*A Dragonlord*
Baroness of Newhouse—*A Dragonlord*
Count of Tree-by-the-Sea—*A Dzurlord*
Cariss—*A Jhereg Sorceress*

Tukko—*A Jhereg*
Mario—*An assassin*

**Of Others**
Aerich—*Duke of Arylle*
Fawnd—*Aerich's servant*
Steward—*Aerich's servant*
Tazendra—*Baroness of Daavya*
Mica—*Tazendra's lackey*
Sir Vintner—*A Lyorn delegate*
Lysek—*A Jhegaala*
Seb—*A messenger*
Theen—*A brigand*

# Preface

### In Which It is Demonstrated that the Works of Paarfi of Roundwood Display Both the Rigors of History and the Raptures of Fiction; With Examples Taken from Each of His Historical-Romantic Works.

*"Fiction, therefore, is more philosophical and more significant than history, for fiction is more concerned with the universal, and history with the individual."*
—Ekrasan of Sibletown

*"Truth is stranger than fiction."*
—variously attributed

WITH THE FOUNDERS OF OUR entire critical tradition expressing such opinions, it is no wonder that historical fiction, such as the volume you hold in your hand, occupies an uneasy position between scholarship and romance, and is pelted with opprobrium from both camps. When Paarfi of Roundwood published *Three Broken Strings*, those to whom he was responsible at this university's press asked him to use another name than his own, under which the press had occasionally published his historical monographs. He refused to do so, with the result that those who read his romance were in a position to purchase and read his historical monographs as well, and to put sorely needed money into the coffers of this institution.

This happy outcome did not prevent the repetition of that same request when *The Phoenix Guards* was about to go to press; but since by then Paarfi had already become engaged in various disagreements with the university press concerning the presentation of footnotes and maps for his latest monograph, he once more refused it; and once more, his ardent readers purchased his monographs as well. Some of them have written to the university expressing their disappointment in the monographs, but it may be assumed that those who were satisfied did not bother to write.

Writers of romance protest that there is no invention in historical fiction, no art, and no craft; writers of history protest that there is no scholarship in historical fiction, and furthermore that it is all, if not invention, at least that distortion which can be even more pernicious. Writers of historical fiction have so far kept quiet and gone about their exacting business.

Let us examine the works of this author with these protests in mind. It is well to note that while these romances do not purport to be history, they are read by historians, as well as by those who will learn their history in no other way. The first have always been concerned about the second.

*Three Broken Strings* was liberally accused of invention by several respected scholars, notably by the author of *Bedra of Ynn and Lotro: An Historical and Poetical Comparison*, and by the editor of *Mountain Ballads*. There is in fact no invention in *Three Broken Strings*, insofar as each of the episodes it details is attested to in at least three sources. Not all of these are reliable, as Paarfi clearly states in his preface; but none of them is his own invention. Where thoughts are attributed to the hero, they are taken from his own published words; dialogue is taken from the earlier sources, notably

*Tales of Beed'n, Mountain Ballads, Wise Sayings of Five Bards,* Vaari's *A Brief Consideration of Adverb Placement in the Colloquial Tongue,* and the unpublished letters catalogued as Yellowthorn MSS 1-14 and lodged in the library of this institution.

As for art and craft, *Three Broken Strings* was derided for possessing neither, notably by the honored author of the *Short Life of Lotro* and the three noble souls who kindly contributed their opinions, without giving themselves the credit of affixing their names, to *Literary Considerations.* But all of these protesters, historian and critics alike, are in fact deriding the book for not being a novel. It exhibits, if anything, an excess of both art and craft. The episodes of Beed'n's life are divided not chronologically, but by type: love affairs, political entanglements, artistic wrangles, travel, poetic composition, musical performances, and so on. The means whereby episodes are associated are often ingenious; the structure is not entirely successful from a narrative point of view, but one cannot deny that art and craft were expended upon it. It is true that no consistent portrait of the minstrel emerges. But as a collection of the available information, the book is valuable to the student; and as a collection of lively and affecting stories divided into types, it is, as its sales amply attest, of value to the lay reader as well.

Historians had nothing to complain of in this first effort, although complain they did. Lay readers did not, in fact, complain, but there is something to complain of on their behalf: the arrangement and unity of the book are scholarly rather than artistic. The subject chosen is so lively and so popular a figure that these defects are less serious; this perhaps accounts for the absence of complaint not only on the part of the readers, but on the part of the usual critics as well.

These defects are in any case remedied in *The Phoenix Guards,* which is a coherent narrative of the sort ordinarily associated with the romance. This circumstance has caused historians to complain even more vigorously that, the shape of the story being what it is, some liberty must have been taken with the actual events it depicts.

And yet when one considers the available sources, this alleged liberty has not much scope to exercise itself. In any scene involving more than one person, it will be found by the assiduous researcher that at least one of them wrote a letter or a memoir, or talked to someone who did. The activities of the villains in the case were throughly explored at their trials. The Teckla lackey Mica, whose overhearing of several interesting conversations was so important to history, told his own personal history at great length to his companion Srahi, who wrote all of it down, if in a less than organized fashion, and preserved it with her household accounts. Hence even the asides concerning Mica's state of mind cannot be called invention.

If one considers even the meals the companions are said to have eaten on their travels, one finds that the records of the inns they stayed at—and indeed made a considerable impression on—have been preserved. There is, admittedly, no actual record of what Khaavren's party ate on their journey from Adron e'Kieron's residence to the Pepperfields, but the food Paarfi puts into their mouths was in fact ordered by Adron's cook and steward and was therefore present in his kitchen at the time necessary, and was the sort of food generally carried by travelers.

In the interests of accuracy it must be admitted that one aspect of our author's depiction of these events is not, in fact, strictly in accordance with the actual practice of the times. The mode of speech employed by those at court, and by Khaavren and his friends as well, in casual discussion or when leading up to speeches actually recorded in history, does not represent, so far as can be determined, any actual mode of speech, past or present. It is taken from a popular anonymous play of the period, *Redwreath and Goldstar Have Traveled to Deathsgate*, where it is found in a game played by the principals to ward off unwanted inquiries. The proof of this is the exclamation of one of their executioners at the end of the play, "The Dog! I think I have been asking for nothing else for an hour!" This, or similar exclamations, are used several times in *The Phoenix Guards*, and more often in the book you now hold, to indicate that the time for empty courtesy is over.

But in the subtleties of its employment, the gradations of consciousness with which it is used, the precise timing of its termination, this mode of speech does in fact give very much the flavor of the old court talk without that speech's tediousness or outmoded expressions: it is a successful translation that does not distort anything of significance to anybody except a linguist.

So we answer the historians. But if they are silenced, the romancers rise up in their stead. Where are the art, the craft, and the invention, if every event, thought, and even meal is attested to in the records? Our three self-effacing critics all asked these questions, as did Vaari himself. They are readily answered. The art, craft, and invention reside in two places.

The first is in the structure of the story, in what Ekrasan called the arrangement of the incidents. Note that, while *The Phoenix Guards* might have begun by detailing the intrigues brewing in the imperial palace, and sprung wildly from person to person and room to room, gathering evidence as the historian must, it does not. It enters the city and the palace with Khaavren of Castlerock, and it stays with him while he finds and befriends the main actors in this history.

It may be objected that the main actors are rather Seodra, Adron e'Kieron, Lord Garland, Kathana e'Marish'chala, and various other important figures, many of whom do not make their appearance until late in the book. But this is precisely where the genius of our author shows itself. Here is the second place in which art and invention may be demonstrated: in the choice of viewpoint. When Khaavren enters the city, he is nobody: he must meet people, discover things, have matters explained to him. The lay reader, whose knowledge of history is imprecise, if not actually erroneous, is in just Khaavren's position. And the author does not carry this technique to extremes, but heightens suspense at the right moment by showing us those who plot against Khaavren and the empire, while Khaavren proceeds in blissful ignorance succeeded by bewilderment—a state, it should be remarked, in which readers, should they find themselves there for too long a time, are apt to become impatient. The events are historical, but the order in which they are presented to us, and the vantage from which we view them, are determined by the author.

*The Phoenix Guards* is a tale of adventure and intrigue, and has been so structured. The volume you hold in your hands is of another sort entirely. This is a tale of inevitable tragedy, and of the shifts and strange chances whereby some saved themselves, and others perished. It also tells of events that will be familiar to the most oblivious of readers. It is possible to be ignorant of what happened when Crionofenarr met Adron e'Kieron on the Pepperfields at the beginning of the reign of Tortaalik. But no one can be ignorant of Adron's Disaster.

The structure of the book you are about to read reflects this difference. It is not the role of the scholar to ruin a first reading of a fine book by tediously expounding on its scenes. But let us just glance at the very opening, in which a messenger arrives to speak to the Emperor. Our author stops to describe the messenger and her accoutrements, but when he has finished, he informs us that her progress has not been impeded by his own halt, and that while he has told us about her she has moved through the halls of the palace and stated her mission, and is about to be received by the Emperor. The author seems helpless before a moving sequence of events that cannot be halted or slowed, but proceeds to its fatal conclusion with the force of some catastrophe, a flood or thunderstorm, being presently experienced.

This is not, of course, the case, as an examination of the balance of scenes and viewpoints, the moments at which personages old and new to Paarfi's readers are presented, the arrangement, in fact, of the incidents, will amply demonstrate. But his work conveys a far different sensation than the earlier one, more complex and lasting, heavier of heart though not devoid of laughter. We leave the precise explication of these effects as an exercise for any reader so ungrateful as to continue in the mistaken belief that the writing of history demonstrates no art. Those who have been persuaded otherwise, or were too perspicacious ever to have fallen into such error, may merely enter into the stream of events and be borne along to its terrifying conclusion, while the scholar slips away unnoticed.

D.B.
Dean of Pamlar University
R2:1/2:1/2/12

# BOOK
## ONE

# Chapter the First

*Which Treats of Matters*
*Relating to the State of the Empire,*
*And Introduces the Reader to*
*The Emperor and Certain of His Court*

UPON THE FIRST DAY OF autumn, that is, the ninth day of the month of the Vallista in the five hundred and thirty-second year of the reign of His Imperial Majesty, Tortaalik I, of the House of the Phoenix, a messenger arrived at the Imperial Wing of the Palace and begged an audience with the Emperor.

Before delving into the source and content of the message, we trust we will be allowed to say two words about the messenger herself, because this will provide an opportunity to set before the reader some of the conditions which prevailed at this time and in this place, and will thus equip him to better understand the history we propose to unfold.

The messenger was a young woman of perhaps four hundred years, whose roundish face, stocky build, and straight, short brown hair without noble's point, all indicated unmistakably the House of the Teckla—a diagnosis easily confirmed by the roughness of her skin and the calluses on her hands. But far more interesting than her fallow state (if we may be permitted such a word to refer to her appearance as provided by nature) is her cultivated state, or the woman as she presented herself to those who guarded the Imperial Wing.

She was dressed in the yellow, green, and brown of her House, but the yellow was the pure, bright color of those flowers that grow in the lower valleys of Tursk, and took the form of a silk blouse embroidered with russet needlework of an exceptionally fine character. Her leather riding pants were also russet, and flared widely around her boots, which were dyed the bright green of new grass and had wide extensions in the form of wings emerging from the heels. She wore, as well, a woolen cloak of a tan color, with a clasp in the form of a dzur, wrought with fine silver wire.

These details now having been placed before the reader, let us make haste to follow her progress, which has not halted for our indulgences; while we have been describing her dress, the Teckla, whose name is Seb, after stating her mission, has been granted admission into the presence of His Majesty the Emperor, and we can, therefore, follow her and hear the delivery of this message ourselves.

Because, being a Teckla, she could not be given a safe-conduct badge, Seb was escorted by one of the guardsmen on duty, a certain Dragonlord called Tummelis e'Terics, who brought her to the officer on duty, who looked the Teckla over briefly but thoroughly before signifying, with an almost imperceptible nod of his head, that she could pass. This was all taking place, be it well understood, in the First Antechamber (or the Last Antechamber, as some have it, but we will hold to the usage of the historians of the period of which we write, and hope that our readers' perspicacity will surmount any confusion this causes), which connected to the First Lower Level Imperial Audience Chamber, to give its official title, or the Throne Room, as some historians have it, or the Portrait Room, as it was actually called.

At the point at which we begin our history, it has just passed the quarter-hour after the third hour after noon, and the Portrait Room doors are, consequently, standing wide open. Seb, notwithstanding her House, walked with full confidence among the nobles and courtiers who milled about the room, who in fact filled the room to the point of straining to the utmost the ingenious cooling spells that the Athyra Marchioness of Blackpool had set upon it.

At length, upon reaching a point directly before His Majesty, where waited Brudik, Lord of the Chimes, Tummelis, her mission accomplished, gave the messenger into Lord Brudik's care. This worthy, who had held his post for some fifteen hundred years, turned to His Majesty and announced, in his droning voice, "A messenger from Her Highness Sennya, Duchess of Blackbirdriver, and Dzur Heir."

His Majesty was just then amusing himself in a customary way, between bantering conversations with various courtiers: He was attempting to make himself angry, then sad, then happy, in order to make the Orb, which rotated above his head, change color. He was, as usual, achieving only indifferent success, wherefore the Orb glowed with the pale red of annoyance, which changed instantly to a delicate green as, at the Lord Brudik's announcement, he looked up with an expression of mild interest.

"Ah," he said. "From Sennya."

"That is it, Your Majesty," said Brudik.

"Well," said His Majesty, trying to remember if he had ever heard the name Sennya, and, if so, in what context, "then, let the messenger come before me."

As the worthy Seb steps up to address the Emperor Tortaalik, we will permit ourselves to quickly sketch the changes that have occurred in the outer, and, to some extent, the inner character of His Majesty since we last had occasion to bring him to the attention of our readers, which was at the beginning of his reign, in the history of *The Phoenix Guards*.

The Emperor, we should note, had changed but little in appearance. He had begun to paint his fingernails, forehead, and ears (all of which on this occasion were a bright red that set off the gold of his costume), and he now wore diamonds on all occasions, in the form of rings, bracelets, earrings, headdress, and necklaces; but neither his face nor his physique had undergone any transformation excepting only the addition of a few lines in the former and a bit of settling in the latter. Our readers will remember his delicate skin, of which he took greater care than ever, bathing every day in scented oils; his pale blue, narrow eyes; and his fine, yellow hair, which was of medium length and curled inward below his ears.

As for those aspects of his character which are not readily visible, we may say, with the perspective that only distance brings, that the fundamental shift in his personality had begun some four hundred years earlier, when he was forced to exile his sister for taking part in an attempt to introduce poisons into his drink through certain specially prepared goblets which were impenetrable to the mysterious powers of the Orb, although not, as it turned out, to the more mundane abilities of Gyorg Lavode. In point of fact, it is certainly the case that Tortaalik's sister had been the chief mover behind the entire affair, which information His Majesty did his best to suppress, although whether out of affection for his sister, a desire to limit the scandal, or for other reasons entirely, we will not speculate. But he had certainly changed since then, becoming gradually, over the course of the next few centuries, at once whimsical and morose, devoting much effort to idle amusements, and much time to doing nothing whatsoever, this pursuit being occasionally interrupted by sudden and short-lived periods of intense interest in the doings of the State of which he stood at the prow.

Of the many changes in the makeup of the court, the two most significant were the retirement of His Discretion, the Duke of Wellborn, and the appointment of Jurabin to the position of Prime Minister, which, in combination, gave His Majesty the inclination and the leisure to pursue his own amusements, such as they were. The reader may rest assured that, if these two changes have more far-reaching effects than we intend to describe at this moment, we will discuss them as occasion warrants.

The messenger, Seb, to whom we now have the honor of returning, performed the proper obeisance before His Majesty and said, "I bring you, Sire, greetings from the holdings of Her Highness, Sennya, and I bear her wishes that Your Majesty will deign to hear the message she has done me the honor to entrust to my care, and which she desires me to impart to Your Majesty."

"The greetings," said His Majesty, "are acknowledged. And we are anxious to hear whatever intelligence you bring us."

"Then, Sire, I will at once relay this message."

"And you will be right to do so. Is it written?"

"No, Sire, it was entrusted to me, by Sennya herself, from mouth to ear."

"Then you may deliver it the same way."

"I shall do so, Sire," said Seb. She cleared her throat and began. "This is it, then: Sire, Her Highness, Sennya, faced with a personal crisis of the most extreme character, begs to be excused from the Meeting of the Principalities. She hopes she has not too much incurred Your Majesty's displeasure by making this request, and hopes, moreover, that Your Majesty will do her the kindness of granting it."

His Majesty frowned, and the Orb took on a slight orange cast. He then looked around, and his eyes fell on the barrel-chested form of Jurabin, who was moving, or rather, bulling, his way through the courtiers to reach the throne. His Majesty stirred impatiently; Seb appeared quite at ease, although a few courtiers noticed that a certain amount of perspiration was evident at her temples.

Jurabin arrived at last, and leaned forward to allow His Majesty to whisper to him. His Majesty quickly explained what had transpired, and Jurabin, upon hearing the news, looked at His Majesty with an expression of mild surprise, and accompanied the look by pronouncing these words, "But, Sire, what question does Your Majesty do me the honor to ask?"

His Majesty flushed slightly, and the courtiers, who were unable to hear this conversation, noticed that the Orb darkened. "In the first place, Beespatch," said the Emperor, referring to Jurabin by title, as His Majesty always did when annoyed, "It was my opinion that you, as Prime Minister, ought to be made aware that yet another Delegate—in fact, an Heir—has backed out of the meeting. Other than that, I have not done you the honor to ask you a question, although, if I may make a suggestion—" His Majesty's voice was heavy with sarcasm—"you may want to consider whether we ought to no longer accept excuses of any kind. If this continues, no one will be at the meeting at all."

Jurabin perceived that he had, perhaps, annoyed His Majesty a little. He said, "Forgive me, Sire. My poor brain is straining to bear what is, perhaps, too much of a load, and so if I am brusque with my sovereign, believe there is no disrespect intended."

His Majesty relaxed, and signified with a wave of his hand that it was of no moment. Jurabin continued, "If my advice in the matter is of any use to Your Majesty—"

The Emperor signified that his advice was welcome.

"—I would say that by refusing to accept these excuses, Your Majesty would run the risk of being called a tyrant. Moreover, this is only the forty-sixth cancellation, which means we can still expect over two hundred delegates, which seems to me sufficient."

"Mmmmph," said His Majesty. "That depends how many more cancellations there are."

Jurabin bowed, but did not reply, seeing that he had convinced the Emperor, who then addressed the waiting messenger with the words, "Very well, the request is granted. Give your mistress my warmest regards."

"I will not fail to do so, Sire," said the messenger, who then backed away from His Majesty, bowed low, and left the room to return to her mistress. As she left, the Emperor turned to his Prime Minister and said, "I wish to have two words with you, Jurabin."

"Of course, Sire. I hope I have not been so unfortunate as to incur Your Majesty's displeasure."

"No, no, but this last messenger has brought to mind certain matters, and I wish to discuss them with you."

"As you wish, Sire. But allow me to point out that the time Your Majesty does your courtiers the honor of spending with them—"

"Is up even at this moment, Jurabin. Will you grant my wish for a few minutes of conversation?"

"Of course, Sire."

"Then attend me. We will go to the Seven Room."

"Lead, Sire; I will follow."

His Majesty rose, whereupon all of the lords and ladies of the court who had managed to find chairs rose as well, and the entire assemblage fell silent and faced his Majesty, who sketched them a perfunctory salute. He looked around for the officer on duty to escort him, and found this officer standing imperturbably at his side.

"The Seven Room," said his Majesty.

The officer bowed, and led the way through the throng, which parted before him. The Emperor and the Prime Minister followed at a leisurely pace; the Orb, a pale green, serenely circled His Majesty's head as he walked. Upon leaving the hall via the Mirrored Doors, which a servant hastily opened, the officer led the way down the Teak Passage, up the Green Stairway, and so to the room with seven walls where His Majesty most liked to hold private conversations. The officer himself opened the one door to this room, and, after satisfying himself that the room was unoccupied, stood aside for His Majesty and the Prime Minister to enter, after which he closed the door and placed himself in front of it.

His Majesty sat in his favorite chair—a gold-colored chair with thick stuffing and a small matching footrest—and indicated that Jurabin should sit as well. When the Prime Minister had done so, in a plain chair facing His Majesty, the latter said, without preamble, "What have you been doing, Jurabin, about the finances of the Empire?"

"Sire," said Jurabin, who appeared to be caught slightly off guard, "I have been doing all that can be done."

"And that includes?"

"Not a day goes by, Sire, that I do not endeavor to find some new economy. Today, for example, I—"

"New economies, Jurabin? Is that all that can be done?"

"That is all, Sire, until the Meeting of the Principalities."

"Ah, yes, the meeting. The meeting to which we have just

received yet another cancellation. Jurabin, if the meeting is to take place, the Princes and Deputies ought to begin arriving within the week."

"Perhaps, Sire," said Jurabin; who, while he seemed mildly startled at His Majesty's sudden interest in matters of policy, did not appear unduly concerned about the presence or absence of the Princes and Deputies.

His Majesty shifted impatiently. "Will you deny, in any case, that this rash of cancellations has the smell of conspiracy?"

Jurabin cocked his head. "There is a certain fragrance, Sire, but sometimes we think someone is cooking fish, when, in fact, we are only near the ocean."

"I usually know when I'm at the shore, Jurabin," said His Majesty.

"How is that, Sire?"

"Because my feet are wet."

Jurabin bowed at this witticism His Majesty did him the honor to share, and said, "Well, then, Sire, are your feet wet?"

"If there is a conspiracy around me, Jurabin," said the Emperor, "I am unable to see it."

"It is not, perhaps, a conspiracy, Sire," said the Prime Minister, "either around us here, or among the Princes."

"It is not?"

"Perhaps not."

"Then, you are saying that perhaps it is?"

"That is not precisely my meaning either, Sire."

"Well then," said the Emperor, "What is your meaning?"

"To speak plainly—"

"The Gods!" His Majesty burst out. "It is nearly time for you to do so!"

"I believe that many of the Deputies are, quite simply, afraid to appear."

"Afraid?" cried the Emperor. "How, Sennya, a Dzurlord, afraid?"

Jurabin shrugged. "The Dzur are brave enough when faced with battle, Sire; many of them have no special courage to face less tangible dangers—especially dangers they do not comprehend."

"Less tangible dangers? Come, tell me what you mean. Are they afraid of me, do you think?"

"Not you, Sire; rather, of each other."

"Jurabin, I confess that I am as confused as ever."

"Shall I explain?"

"Shards and splinters, it is an hour since I asked for anything else!"

"Well, then, this is how I see it."

"Go on. You perceive that you have my full attention."

"Sire, the Princes have been called, as is the custom, to determine the Imperial Allowance for the next phase, which begins in less than fifty years."

"I prefer," said the Emperor, "to refer to it as the Imperial Tax."

"As you wish," said Jurabin. "Though it can hardly be considered a tax, when, unlike the other Imperial Taxes, the Houses set their own portions, from a total amount which is, by law, determined by the Empire."

"Nevertheless, the term 'allowance' offends me."

"Very well, Sire. To continue, under Imperial Law, dating from the Sixth Cycle, the Princes will meet and come to some agreement about the portion each House must pay."

"Yes, yes, I understand that. Go on."

Jurabin cleared his throat and continued. "Yes, Sire. The issue, just at the moment, is difficult for the Princes."

"That's just it, Jurabin; what makes it so? Or, rather, what makes it more difficult than usual?"

"Well, in the first place, there is the House of the Dragon, which demands that its entire portion be waived, to offset the expenses of raising armies."

"Raising armies? For what reason do they raise armies?"

"There are encroachments of Easterners in the South, Sire. In addition, there are Teckla rebellions threatening in several western duchies. We have received petitions for Imperial aid from the Duke of Atwater, the Duke of Lonerock, the Duchess of Greatworks, the—"

"Well, but I had thought we had made peace with the Easterners."

"Sire, there are many Easterners, and they do not all speak with each other, nor do they adhere to each others' treaties. The agreement Your Majesty had of the kingdom east of the Pepperfields at the beginning of Your Majesty's reign still holds, but there are others—"

"Hmmph. A sloppy way to do things, it seems to me. They should be brought under a single banner."

"That, Sire, is what the House of the Dragon, through its Heir, Eastmanswatch, is proposing."

"How, Eastmanswatch is behind this?"

"According to my sources, Sire—"

"You mean your spies?"

Jurabin shrugged. "It seems that the Duke opposes such an action, but nevertheless brings it forward on behalf of his House, which favors it."

His Majesty shook his head, as if refusing to consider the internal politics of the House of the Dragon. "Well," he said, "and the Teckla? Has their House been asked about these uprisings, and warned that the Heir of the House may, under law, be held accountable?"

"They pretend, Sire, to be unable to meet the demands placed upon them, due to crop shortages, caused by general climate changes in the West over the last two hundred years, which has led to thirty or forty seasons of drought, which trend is expected to last well into the next phase. This same drought has caused their demand for a lessening in the payments they make to their landlords, and has also led to numerous uprisings, which seem to be continuing, perhaps even increasing."

"Drought? Haven't we sorcerers for that sort of thing?"

"The cost, Sire—"

"Ah, yes, the cost. Well, what of the cost?"

"The House of the Athyra has claimed that, should they call up the required sorcery, they would be unable to pay their portion."

"They have said this?"

"Yes, Sire, through their Heir, Tropyr."

"Well, that hardly seems unreasonable."

"Yes, Sire."

"And as for the lessening of the payments, can't this be done in an equitable manner?"

"Sire, most of those affected are of the Houses of the Jhegaala and the Lyorn, and the matter has been taken up by the Iorich, to study the legalities. But, as an Imperial matter, naturally the Iorich charge heavily for their services, and—"

"The Gods!"

"Yes, Sire. Especially as the Vallista are adamant on maintaining the full payments—"

"The Vallista?"

"Yes, Sire, most of the mines in the North are owned by Vallista, and they depend on trade with the West to feed the laborers, who have been growing restive, due to short rations. This has resulted in lower production, which, in turn, reduces the amount of shipping, so the House of the Orca is claiming extreme poverty among many of its nobles, and will have a great deal of trouble in contributing to the Imperial Allow—Tax."

"I see."

"Moreover—"

"How, there is more?"

"Yes, Sire."

"Go on."

"Various of the poorer Houses have banded together, to prevent the more powerful Houses from taking advantage of them."

"It is always thus."

"Yes, Sire. In this case, the Tiassa and the Jhegaala have formed an alliance along with the Dzur and the Iorich, while the Hawk, Tsalmoth, Jhereg and Issola are supporting the Orca and the Lyorn. The Teckla might have come to some sort of agreement with the Yendi; we are unable to be certain—one never knows what the Yendi are doing."

"Well?"

"It is very confusing, Sire, but it seems the alliances are

shifting a great deal, and everyone is trying to guess who will be forced to pay heavily, who will be able to escape paying heavily, and whether the Imperial Treasury will, in fact, be able to operate at all."

"I see."

His Majesty fell silent for a moment, then said, "These alliances—"

"Yes, Sire?"

"Can we break them up?"

"We have been trying to do so, Sire."

"With what results?"

Jurabin made a slight shift in his chair—almost his first movement of any kind since they had begun speaking. The Emperor was aware that this indicated that the Prime Minister was somewhat unsure of himself. "Sire—"

"Yes?"

"The alliances have been increasingly unstable, in part due to our efforts."

"Well?"

"The result is none of the parties are strong enough to stand against your will."

"That is good, I think."

"Yes, Sire. But it also means that many of the Princes and Deputies will be unable to avoid offending the Empire, or their own party, and in some cases, however things go, they will be certain to offend both."

"I see."

"And that is why many of them, either from fear or confusion, have been backing out of the meeting."

"I see."

His Majesty thought over all that he had heard. At last he said, "You ought to have brought these things to my attention years ago, Jurabin."

"I'm sorry, Sire, if I have erred. But—"

"But nothing! I would have settled it at once."

"How," said Jurabin, frowning. "Settled it?"

"Exactly."

"And, if I may be permitted the honor of asking a question—"

"You may."

"How would Your Majesty have settled it?"

"In the simplest manner, Jurabin. I would have commanded the Athyra to bring out their best sorcerers, and to solve this drought before it reached this stage."

"But, Sire, the cost—"

"Is nothing compared to the cost of ignoring the problem, Jurabin. With the drought removed—"

"So is the largest source of revenue for the Empire, Sire."

"The largest?"

"Yes, Sire. If Your Majesty had commanded them to bring the weather to heel, they would have been within their rights to refuse Your Majesty any contribution whatsoever, and, moreover, they would have done so. We then would have no funds for the Imperial Army, and would have to demand mercenaries to defend the eastern borders."

"But the House of the Dragon could pay heavily."

"Indeed they could, Sire, but they would not do so."

"They would not? Why would they not?"

"Because, Sire, if the House of the Athyra was not forced to pay, because they had provided services to the Empire, the House of the Dragon would demand the same right, and justly, too. If they didn't, the Athyra would gain economic power over them, and those two Houses are ever struggling with one another for much of the same land in the Northeast."

"And yet, there ought to be some money left in the Imperial Treasury."

"Very little, Sire. We will, by budgeting carefully, be able to survive to the end of the phase, until the new taxes are prepared, but—"

"But where has the money gone, Jurabin? I know that by the time wheat has been harvested and turned into flour, and the flour reaches the market, it has already been taxed four times, and—"

"Five times, Sire."

"—There has been no large war—"

"No large war, Sire? The war with Elde Island was not large?"

"Jurabin, it lasted a mere five years, and if our casualties were more than ten thousand, someone has deceived me. And, moreover, we won."

"Sire, there is no more expensive war than one fought on the sea, for each time we lose even a skirmish, at least one ship has been taken or sunk, and the smallest frigate in the fleet cannot be replaced for less than ten thousands of imperials. And in the Battle of Redsky Harbor alone we lost eleven frigates and two ships of the line, and we won that battle."

His Majesty paused to consider these statistics, then said, "But the War Tax should have seen to those expenses."

"Sire, that tax was necessary to raise money to prosecute the war, and there was little time to raise it, so we sold Bills of Taxation to speculators, mostly Phoenix and Dragons, who still own those Bills."

"Still? Well, we shall take them back, and use them to raise taxes for the Empire."

"Take, Sire? Your Majesty would invite civil war?"

"Well, then, we shall buy them back."

"With what, Sire? The least of them is worth twenty thousands of imperials."

"The Gods! Perhaps that war was a mistake, Jurabin."

"A mistake, Sire? But without it, the pirates of Elde Island would have utterly prevented our trade with Greenaere, Holcomb, and Landsight, which would have bankrupted the House of the Orca."

"Oh, the Orca!" said His Majesty scornfully.

"Yes, Sire, the Orca, who are politically allied with the Hawk, the Tsalmoth, the Jhereg, the Issola, and the Lyorn. Yes, Sire."

His Majesty shook his head, sighed, and looked thoughtful for several moments. Then he said, "Well, but surely we could survive, at least for a short time, without taxes from the Dragon and the Athyra."

"Sire? Without two of the three largest contributors to the Imperial Treasury? Perhaps we could, if that were all, but—"

"How, if that were all? It is not?"

"No, Sire."

"What more is there?"

"Well, Sire, we are of the House of the Phoenix, and you are Prince, as well as Emperor. What will be the contribution of our House to the Imperium?"

"I must ask our Deputy, who is the Princess Loudin, to whom I have delegated this matter."

"I have asked her, Sire."

"And has she given you an answer?"

"Yes, Sire. She has said that the House is on the verge of bankruptcy."

"Bankruptcy!"

"Those were her words, Sire."

"But how could this be?"

"Because, Sire, the House, in its own name, and many of us as individuals, have made certain speculations—"

"What speculations?"

"You know, Sire, that we are a small House, and none of us, except perhaps Baroness Highplane and Countess Nolanthe, have large holdings, so it is by speculation that, for the most part, we—"

"What speculation, Jurabin?"

"Primarily, Sire, to certain Dragonlords, counting on funds they will receive from the Empire for military operations, and to certain Athyra, counting on actions to appease the climate. These operations have been delayed, pending the Meeting of Principalities, and the—"

The Prime Minister stopped speaking, for His Majesty had stopped listening, but was, rather, sitting with his head leaning back, his eyes tightly shut. After an interval, the Emperor spoke, saying, "Jurabin, do me the kindness to summon my physicker."

"Yes, Sire. Is it the headache?"

"Go, Jurabin."

"Yes, Sire."

Jurabin rose at once and left to find the physicker, leaving His Majesty with his head in his hands, and the Orb an ugly brown as it circled His Majesty's head. The physicker, whose name, by the way, was Navier, though it is not our intention to fully introduce her at this point in our history, arrived in due time, bringing with her tea made with certain herbs that were used to cure the headaches with which the Emperor was afflicted on those rare occasions when he tried to understand the workings of the Empire he ruled.

After administering the treatment, the physicker remained to make certain His Majesty felt better, after which she took her leave, and a few minutes later, the Emperor, seeing that it was approaching his dinner hour, rose to leave. He opened the door, and found himself facing a familiar figure, that of the officer on duty, the Ensign of the Red Boot Battalion of the Imperial Guard.

# Chapter the Second

---

### Which Treats of an Old Friend,
### And His Conversations with
### Three Acquaintances from the Past.

To THOSE FAMILIAR WITH OUR earlier history, it should come as no surprise that the ensign to whom we have just referred is none other than Khaavren, who has now passed his six hundredth year—that is to say, he has achieved an age at which the energy of youth is lost, but is replaced by a calmness that comes with knowing one's position. In Khaavren's case, his position was at His Majesty's door—or, rather, at the door of whatever room His Majesty happened to occupy—and the centuries of waiting there, and making reports to his superiors, and making campaigns against enemies of one sort or another, had, to all appearances, entirely sapped the energy that had been the particular mark of his youth.

Where he had been wont to make wry observations and loyal outbursts, now he kept his observations to himself, and relegated his outbursts to those occasions when his duties required it (and, as a good officer, his duties seldom required outbursts). Where he had been quick to bring hand to sword upon any real or imagined slight, now he was more likely to chuckle, shake his head, and pass on. And yet, should anyone be foolish enough to insist on playing, there were, in the Empire, few with whom it would be a more dangerous pastime. Khaavren's wrist was as strong and supple as ever, his eyes were as sure, and his body as limber. If he had lost, perhaps, the rash exuberance of youth, he had gained far more in his knowledge of the science and art of defense.

As to appearances, the changes were fewer. The Khaavren of five hundred years before would, upon meeting the Khaavren of this day, have thought he was looking into a glass, were it not for a slight thinning of both face and figure, brought on by constant exercise, and a few faint lines on his forehead, brought on by responsibility—the implacable foe of all lighthearted natures.

Yet he took this responsibility gladly, for it was a mark of his character as it had emerged over centuries that he took great care and pride in carrying out his duties merely because he found he was good at them—that is, he no longer saw the service as a means to glory and accomplishment; rather he now saw it as an end in itself, and as his prospects for tomorrow faded, so did his resolve strengthen to perform to the very best of his ability. Whereas five hundred years before his motto had been, "Let there be no limit to my ambition," now his motto was, "Let my ambition carry me to the limit," which subtle change in emphasis, as we can see, bespeaks worlds of change in character.

This, then, was the person His Majesty suddenly found himself confronting—the same as he had accustomed himself to seeing for some five hundred and thirty years. The Emperor prided himself on being able to judge his fellow creatures (in fact, in one of his few surviving letters he wrote to his mistress of the time, Enova of Ridge, shortly before the infamous scandal of the Three Gibbets, "In spite of what they say, I trust Lord Capstra. Why? Because all of my instincts tell me to, and I'd sooner listen to my instincts than to all of the advisers in the Empire."), and, after seeing this officer, in the blue and white of the House of the Tiassa, with the gold uniform half-cloak of the Imperial Guard and the badge of an ensign—after seeing this officer, we say, for more than half a millennium, he realized that here was someone in whom he could confide. And his Majesty was taken with the need to confide in someone.

"Well, Ensign?" he began.

Khaavren's eyes widened slightly; he was unused to being addressed by His Majesty, other than to be given orders. "Sire?" said the guardsman, looking frankly back at him whom the gods had made his master.

It is worth noting that the Khaavren of a few hundred years before would have put into word and countenance all of his eagerness for glory and willingness to risk his life on His Majesty's orders; the Khaavren of today merely answered and waited, slightly curious. Faced with this mild yet confident look, the Emperor faltered for a moment, and covered his confusion by saying, "Well?"

"Sire?" repeated Khaavren.

"Have you nothing to say, then?"

Khaavren had, in the intervening years, become a soldier of few words, and those carefully chosen. On this occasion he chose six of them: "I am at Your Majesty's orders," he said.

"And I," said the Emperor, "am waiting to hear what you have to say."

"What I have to say, Sire?"

"Precisely."

"I beg Your Majesty's pardon, but I do not understand the question Your Majesty does me the honor to ask."

"Do you pretend you do not know what we were talking about just now?"

Khaavren's countenance remained impassive. "I assure Your Majesty, I have not the least idea in the world."

"And yet, you were outside of the door, and the walls are so thin that I can hear when anyone passes by, and I can even hear you explain to passersby in that soft, gentle lilt which still betrays your country of origin, that the room is occupied. How is it, then, that you cannot hear what is said within?"

"Sire, it may be that I have trained my ears not to hear what does not concern them."

"You have very complaisant ears, sir."

"That may be, Sire. In any case, they thank Your Majesty for deigning to notice them." Khaavren accompanied these words with a small bow.

Tortaalik made a sound that is the despair of the historian to render, but may be thought of as midway between a snort and a harrumph. After which ejaculation he said, "Then you persist in denying that you overheard our conversation?"

"I assure Your Majesty—"

"Would you say so again, standing beneath the Orb?"

For the first time Khaavren's expression changed; a light of something like anger gleamed in his eyes. He said, "It would not, Sire, be the first time I have been required to swear beneath the Orb."

"Ah—ah," said the Emperor. "You did so once before, didn't you?"

"I had that honor," said Khaavren.

"I seem to recall the circumstances," said His Majesty slowly. "It had something to do with a charge of murder, had it not?"

"A murder, Sire, of which the Orb acquitted me."

"Yes, and a plot that you uncovered, and a treaty that you arranged with an army of Easterners."

Khaavren bowed.

"And since then," continued his Majesty, "you have been involved in some eight or ten campaigns for us, have you not? Including the retreat from Watcher's Lake, where you distinguished yourself during the holding action?"

"Distinguished myself, Sire? I was not aware—"

"—That anyone had seen your actions after Brigadier G'aereth was wounded? But the brigadier saw, and he was pleased to tell me, in glowing terms, of the marvelous stratagem you devised which allowed him to reach the safety of . . . of . . ."

"Brickerstown, Sire."

"Yes, of Brickerstown. But I know of these things, Ensign, and of others, believe me."

"Sire, I am—"

"And, now that G'aereth is less and less able to fulfill his duties, it becomes my lot to consider a replacement. What do you say to that, Ensign?"

"Sire, I don't know what to say." Khaavren delivered this remark—as he had each remark since the inception of the conversation—with little inflection, no emphasis, and less emotion.

"What you should say, Ensign, is to answer my questions. I assure you, it will do you no harm."

"Questions, Sire?"

"Come, walk beside me."

Khaavren bowed, and they began strolling toward the Hall of Windows, an extension of the Imperial Wing that looked out of the Palace on five sides (including above and below), and where His Majesty was accustomed to dine on informal occasions. As they strolled, the Emperor said, "You are a military man, are you not, Sir Khaavren?"

"I have that honor, Sire."

"As a military man, what do you think of the state of the Empire, and of this Meeting of the Principalities that is to happen within the month?"

"What do I think, Sire, of the state of the Empire and the Meeting of the Principalities?"

"Yes, that is what I wish to know."

"What do *I* think, Sire?"

"That is, indeed, the very question I ask of you."

"Sire, we can arrest them all."

His Majesty stopped and stared at Khaavren, dumbfounded. Then he resumed his walk and said, "Do you, then, seriously advise me to arrest all of the Heirs and Deputies— that is, the Prince of each House—and the Deputies?"

"I, Sire? Not the least in the world."

"But then, I am certain I heard you say so."

"I beg Your Majesty's pardon, but I had no such intention."

"Well then, what did you mean when you said we could arrest them?"

"Only that, Sire. We are able to do it; and, at that, with little trouble. The Duke of Eastmanswatch will present a certain difficulty, but I am certain—"

"Sir, I still fail to understand. If you are not counseling me to arrest them, what *are* you doing?"

"Sire? I am answering Your Majesty's question. Your Majesty did me the honor to ask what I, as a military man, thought of the impending meeting. As a military man, which were Your Majesty's words, my thoughts at once fall to military questions. Now, as I recall, Your Majesty has, on one occasion, arrested one of them at least, and I doubt I am mistaken, for I believe it was I who had the honor to carry out the arrest of Her Highness the Princess of Bendbrook, of the House of the Tiassa—"

"Author of a play in which I am portrayed as a buffoon! She is fortunate I showed clemency, or she'd not have her head today, much less be free to attend this meeting."

"Yes, Sire, that is the lady to whom I refer. And you have caused to be burned certain pamphlets written by Lord Haymel, one of the Deputies of the House of the Hawk—"

"Yes, by the Orb! And I'd do it again! He not only proposed an end to the sales of judgeships, a not unreasonable suggestion, but that each House provide its own judges, which would have caused no less than rebellion from the Iorich, and then he went on to suggest unanimous approval for these judges by—me? No, of course not! By the Council of Princes! As if the authority of the Empire were not enough! He, too, is lucky he isn't a head shorter!"

"Yes, Sire. And then there is Lady Ironn, Deputy of the House of the Orca, whom you caused to be arrested some years ago on the occasion when she—"

"Publicly discussed matters of my personal history in terms that no gentleman could be asked to endure, then declined to apologize, and would not fight! Ah, then I missed old Lord Garland indeed, for he would have tracked her down and extracted either a recantation or her liver, instead of forcing me to use the powers of the state, which power ought, by rights, to have led her to the Executioner's Star."

"Yes, Sire. And that is how I understood Your Majesty's question."

The Emperor walked in silence for a while, and the Orb, which had been a foreboding red, cooled down. His Majesty said, "That is not, in fact, what I meant."

"Sire?"

"Sir Khaavren, Jurabin speaks of the state of the treasury and the correlation of the Houses; Countess Bellor tells me many things about the state of our treasury; the Princess Loudin, who watches over the interests of the House, speaks of the "humor of the Empire" as if there were only one; the Duchess of Pronfir, Trustee of Shipping, has much to say concerning the fall in trade; Brigadier G'aereth tells me of matters military; and Nyleth speaks of—or, rather, cackles about—matters arcane. There is not a one of them who agrees with another. And to me, whatever my inclinations, fall all of the decisions. Well, Ensign, I am asking for your opinion— what do *you* think I should do? Or, if you positively will not answer, then: To whom should I listen?"

Khaavren paused, and appeared to reflect for a space of time that lasted long enough for them to traverse the corridor that rose from the West Terrace to the Hall of Ferns, after which he said, "Sire, I think Your Majesty ought, without delay, find a Discreet to take the place of the Duke of Wellborn, now that he has retired."

His Majesty stopped, and looked at the guardsman, who returned his gaze with an expression of innocence. The Orb went through a rapid series of changes—beginning with a dull yellow of mild confusion, turning then to the orange of beginning anger, followed by the pale blue of anger contained, then mutating to a light green of consideration. At this point His Majesty began walking once more.

"I am most anxious," said the Emperor, "to learn why you make this suggestion."

"You wish to know the reason, Sire?"

"I more than wish to, I demand to."

"Well, then, Sire, it is because, if His Discretion were still here, and still practicing his trade, Your Majesty would have no need to confide in a humble ensign of the Imperial guard."

Together, they climbed the winding stairway up to the Hall of Windows, one next to the other, as if they were old friends engaged in pleasant remembrances. His Majesty broke the silence by saying, "You seemed uninterested in the advancement in rank which I did you the honor to mention."

"Sire, I am without ambition."

"How, a Tiassa without ambition? That is unusual. In fact, it is more than unusual—it is strange."

"Strange it may be, Sire, but it is true that I have none."

"Then you have, in fact, no interest at all in what I am offering?"

"Offering, Sire? I heard no offer. If Your Majesty were to do me the honor of assigning me new duties, of any form, I would certainly attempt to perform them with all the skill and energy at my disposal. But I heard no offer; I only heard that Your Majesty deigned to discuss certain matters of Imperial Policy—matters far too complex for Your Majesty's humble servant."

"My Majesty's humble servant," said the Emperor, "is not, I think, as humble as he pretends."

"That may be, Sire; yet I beg Your Majesty to believe that I have nothing useful to say, nor any opinions, about matters as far above my head as the complexities of Empire to which Your Majesty does me the honor to refer."

His Majesty seemed about to answer this, but they were arrived at the Hall of Windows, and Khaavren had to attend to his duty of inspecting the hall—a duty he carried out with a few quick glances at the half-dozen servers; the Consort Noima; His Highness the Prince of Ninehills, Tsalmoth Heir and Their Majesties' guest; and the two guardsmen. This being done, he bowed respectfully, and took his leave.

With our readers' permission, we will undertake to follow him; as he is an old friend, and one who has just had a conversation worthy of some remark, his path, and his thoughts, cannot fail to be of interest.

If, over the years, Khaavren had become positively taciturn, he had not lost his habit of carrying on lengthy conversations with himself; on the contrary, this feature of his character had, if anything, grown as if to make up for the decrease in his intercourse with others. And so as he strolled (strolled, be it understood, at a good martial clip) back to the Dragon Wing, he began to address himself on the subject of his recent discourse with the Emperor.

"Well now, my good Khaavren," he said, for he was in the habit of referring to himself in this ironic manner. "What do we have? His Majesty condescends to ask you for advice on the management of the Empire? Cha! Here we learn what happens to victims of fiscal irresponsibility! Come, Khaavren, we must look to our own accounts, if for no other reason than to make certain that we do not begin to show such signs if our needs become so much greater than our income. If they did, what would we do—find a silver polisher, and ask him how to manage the drilling of a corps? And, now that I reflect, why shouldn't I do so? Perhaps such a fellow would tell me how to make all of our cloaks flash so prettily that the Consort will notice, and cause me to be made Captain.

"But, no, hasn't His Majesty made just this offer? Well, what can this mean? Steady, Khaavren! What offer did His Majesty make? Why, none whatsoever. His Majesty said that with the Captain (Khaavren, out of habit, still thought of G'aereth as 'the Captain') become infirm, his duties must be assumed by another. Well, now this, as a piece of intelligence, is not worth the price of a cup of wine, even if it be the slop they serve to strangers at the Soup Kettle. But was there an offer, a promise, a guarantee? Not the least in the world. And if the promise of an Emperor—and this Emperor above all—is to be looked at as skeptically as Tazendra used to look at reasoned argument, then His Majesty's failure to give even a promise must have all the substance of the air.

"So, he has offered me the air. While I should not like to be without air, as it is reputed to be important to breathing, I seem to have enough of it, and it would therefore be ill-advised to risk life and limb in the pursuit of it. No, if His

Majesty wants something of Khaavren, he must make an offer worthy of Khaavren. Or, failing that, give a simple order—it amounts to the same thing, after everything to be said is said and everything to be done is done.

"Still, even two hundred years ago I might have made an effort to discover what His Majesty wanted of me, from curiosity if for no other reason. Well, we have lost our curiosity. We feel no lighter for its loss, nor weaker nor slower in body or mind. Therefore, whatever it is, we have no need for it, and have let it go the way the yendi leaves its excess skin to blend among the desert sands in order to frighten those whose eyes are sharp but whose comprehension is not clever. We didn't find out, and it is done, and there's an end to it.

"Or nearly an end to it. There are still, it seems, some tattered shreds of curiosity left to me, or I should not be asking myself what His Majesty might want of an ensign of the Guard that would have anything to do with the tangle of policy and finance of the Dragon and the Athyra, and alliances of the Teckla with the Orca, or whatever Jurabin was pleased to tell His Majesty. Cha! It's a wonder I didn't get the same headache His Majesty did, just from overhearing it all. And a pity that I didn't, for that should have made us equals for a time, and that would indeed be something to tell my children, should the cycle turn in such a way that I have any.

"No children, Khaavren, no promotion, and no curiosity. And, for that, no friends—at least, none that I can see. If they were around, would that conversation have gone differently? Would I have admitted to overhearing everything, whereupon His Majesty would have had me brought to the Executioner's Star, there to have removed those ears he was kind enough to notice, along with the head that supports them? Very likely. No children, no promotion, no curiosity, no friends, but, in exchange, a head, a pair of ears, and perhaps a touch of wisdom—which is the name we give prudence when we have become settled into our life with no hope or ambition."

With this thought, Khaavren had, after having passed into the Dragon Wing, and, in turn, the Sub-wing of the Imperial Guard, entered the antechamber of the Red Boot Battalion, to be greeted by the corporal on duty there. They exchanged no words, as it was Khaavren's opinion that words were unnecessary unless there was something to say, and he had instilled this tenet in all who served under him. On this occasion, as nothing unusual had occurred, the corporal saluted and Khaavren, nodding to acknowledge the salute, continued through the antechamber to his own office, where he sat down in the very chair that Captain G'aereth had occupied on that occasion when Khaavren and his friends had been questioned about their desire to join the Imperial Guard. Though he had sat in that chair thousands of times, it never failed to bring back memories, which were often accompanied by a fond smile.

"Ah," he said to himself on this occasion. "What would Aerich have said of the matter were he here? That is easy; he should have looked at me with that expression of sorrow, reproach, and affection, and said, 'My dear Khaavren, if His Majesty wishes something of a gentleman, what more is needed?' That is Aerich. And Tazendra, well, she would not have hesitated, she would have found the quest—for, to her, anything and everything was a quest—and charged out without another thought, hoping only that it was difficult. That is Tazendra. And what would our friend Pel have said? Well, that is, certainly, a mystery of the first order. Pel is a Yendi. One never knows what Pel might say, what he might do, what he might say he has done, or, above all, why he would say or do what he said or did. Still, one might have asked him. And, Cracks in the Orb, at this moment he is, no doubt, somewhere within this same labyrinth of Palace through which I have been walking, and yet I have hardly seen him five times in five hundred years, nor exchanged five words with him on each of those occasions.

"Such is the nature of friendship," he concluded morosely, at which point a corporal stuck her head in to announce, "You have a visitor, Ensign."

"How," said Khaavren, started out of his reverie, "a visitor? And who might this be?"

"He gives his name as Galstan."

"A Dragonlord?"

"I'm not certain, Ensign, yet I fancy not, for I do not see a sword. Perhaps he is an Athyra or an Iorich, for he wears the robes of a monk or a judge. He claims to be here on a personal errand."

"Indeed?" said Khaavren, trying to recollect the last duel he had fought, and realizing, with some surprise, that it had been more than a century ago. "Well, send him in, and we will see what he wishes."

The corporal nodded, and, shortly thereafter, a man, hooded and robed, entered, bowing. While it was hard to tell beneath the folds of heavy dark-brown fabric, he seemed to be small, and there was something athletic in his carriage. As the door closed, Khaavren studied his visitor, for there was something familiar about the way he stood and about the gleam of the dark eyes that peered out from the hood.

"Pel!" cried Khaavren suddenly, springing to his feet.

His visitor pulled the hood back and bowed once more, while Khaavren stared. If five hundred years can pass without a mark, then they had done so where Pel was concerned. He still had, or nearly had, the unlined face of youth, with the dark eyes we have already had occasion to mention, and the fine, noble chin and high brow, surrounded by black curls which made the color of his eyes all the more vivid. In other words, as far as Khaavren could see, he had lost none of the beauty of face that he had traded on so heavily years before. Khaavren stared, remembering how the Yendi had been accustomed to sorcerously change the color of his eyes from apparent whim, and change his opinions the same way, and how one could never know if there were a reason behind any of these changes. And yet, at the same time, he remembered a score of battles in which Pel's irrepressible blade and fierce humor had been instrumental in saving them all.

Khaavren stared at his visitor as these thoughts and their accompanying emotions flitted through his mind and heart, then he repeated softly, "Pel. And here I was, this very instant, thinking to myself . . . Pel."

"Most of him," agreed the other.

"How, most of him?" said Khaavren. "What, then is missing?"

"Why, the sword," said Pel, smiling inscrutably.

"Cha! You no longer carry one?"

Pel held his arms up, to show that he was, in fact, weaponless. Khaavren laughed. "Well, it is clear, then, that at least you do not come here to fight."

Pel's eyebrows rose. "You thought I came to fight?"

"My good Pel, when an unknown is announced as desiring to see one on a personal matter while one is on duty, well, has it been so long that you no longer remember what that is likely to mean?"

"I assure you, my dear Khaavren, that I had all but forgotten those days, and I thank you for recalling them to me. But when did I become an unknown to you?"

"Cha! When you entered by a name I have never before heard pronounced."

"What, you pretend you never heard my name?"

"Not in this life, my friend. But, come, what is this? I am leaving you standing. Sit, my good Pel, which name I use from familiarity and because curse me if at this moment I can remember the other."

Pel smiled easily and sat, without apparent discomfort, on one of the stiff, military stools that faced Khaavren's over his small writing table. "Galstan," said Pel coolly.

Khaavren shook his head. "The Duchy of Galstan," he said. "I confess, it escapes me."

"Escapes you? But, my dear Ensign, it is not running from you. Nor, for that matter, am I. Rather, I am coming to see you. In fact, I am here."

"Now this circumstance I had noticed, and even remarked upon, albeit only to myself."

"And, no doubt, you wish to know the reason for my visit, because, now that you are older, it would not occur to you that I might come to see you purely from friendship."

Khaavren shifted uncomfortably. "And would I be wrong in this?"

"Not the least in the world," said Pel. "And the proof is, I will tell you why I am here."

"I am waiting for you to do so," admitted Khaavren.

Pel smiled—a small, gentle smile that, on the one hand, brought back to Khaavren scores of warm remembrances, and, on the other, brought the realization that Pel might well be using that smile to evoke those remembrances. "I come to you," said Pel, "in all honesty, in the hopes that you will give me certain information."

"I will be happy to do so," said Khaavren. "Always providing, of course, that it is not information I am sworn to keep secret."

"Of course," said Pel.

"That understood," said Khaavren, "ask me anything. What do your questions concern?"

"The state of the Court."

"The state of the Court?" said Khaavren. "You? Asking me? One would think you an Emperor. No, do not ask me why I said that, but, rather, tell me why, of all the people in this Palace, you would ask these questions of me?"

"Well, and why should I not?"

"Because, my dear friend, should I have any questions about the Court, you are the first person I would ask."

"Ah, you have a good memory, my friend, but you seem unacquainted with my recent history."

"Your recent history? That is true, I know nothing whatsoever except that you have been studying the Art of Discretion."

"You know that?" said Pel. "Then are you unaware that, when one begins this study, one falls out of touch with the day-to-day goings-on in the world?"

"What?" cried Khaavren. "You mean you know of nothing that has happened in the Empire for the last five hundred years?"

"Nearly," said Pel. "Rumor reaches us of skirmishes in the North, and a war fought at sea in the West, but other than that—"

"Other than that—?"

"Why, we remain inside our walls, which are out past the Athyra Wing, barely in the Palace at all, and we rarely leave, nor does news reach us. You yourself know that we have hardly even seen each other in all that time."

"That is true," said Khaavren. "I had even remarked upon this fact to myself."

"So, you see."

"Yes. Well, my friend, ask your questions."

Pel studied the ensign in silence for a moment, during which Khaavren would have given a great deal to know what thoughts were passing through the Yendi's subtle mind. Then Pel said, "What do you think of His Majesty's humor of late, Khaavren?"

Khaavren frowned. "His humor?"

"Yes. You perceive that I am most anxious to know."

Khaavren nearly asked why, but he remembered his old friend well enough to realize that this question would elicit either a lie or an evasion. He said, "His Majesty has, I think, been pensive of late."

"Pensive?"

"So I would say, Pel."

"Do you assign a cause to this?"

"Do I? My friend, you speak as if I were a minister. I assure you, I am only an ensign in His Majesty's Guards—and, moreover, having been an ensign for nearly five hundred and fifty years, I expect to remain one for the next five hundred and fifty, after which I shall, no doubt, be promoted to Captain and given Orders of Nobility, after which I shall retire and marry the daughter of the mayor of some village in the Northeast, which will give me the income from two pensions and allow me to raise a family, which I will set about doing with the same thoroughness I formerly displayed in skewering anyone who looked at me in a manner not to my liking. When this happens, I will, no doubt, hear rumors of all that is passing in the capital, and, thanks to those rumors, I will know a great deal more of what is passing in His Majesty's mind than I do now—or, at least, I will think I do, which counts for just as much when one is as isolated from policy as a rural baron or an ensign of the Imperial Guard."

Pel listened to this monologue—which was, to be sure, the longest Khaavren had uttered aloud in scores of years—with a sad smile. When the Tiassa had finished, Pel said, "Come Khaavren, do you still care for our old friendship?"

"The Gods, Pel! As someone with no future, I already, like an old man, live in the past, and our friendship is the best part of it!"

"Well, then, for the sake of that friendship, won't you be a little more frank with me? You tap your heels at His Majesty's door for hours every day, and I know that your mind is not the slowest in the Empire; you must have some suspicions about what is passing in his heart. I do not ask for state secrets, Khaavren, only for as much as you can tell me without fault to your duty or your conscience. But, truly, I must know, and I can think of no one else who would both know and be willing to tell me. Open your heart, my old friend, and tell me what you know; or, at any rate, what you guess."

Khaavren heaved a great sigh. Hardened as he'd become, he could not hear such an appeal from one of the few who personified the happiest time of his life without being moved, and, more than moved, affected. He said, "His Majesty is, I believe, worried about the number of Heirs and Deputies who have withdrawn from the Meeting of Principalities, which is, as you may know, isolated though you are, to determine the tax allotments for the next phase."

Pel's eyes suddenly glowed, and Khaavren realized that this had been exactly the sort of information Pel was looking for. "Ah—ah," said the Yendi. "He is worried then."

"I believe he is, Pel. It is driving him to become interested in matters of state, and this is no small thing for our little Phoenix."

"Yes, yes," said Pel, as if to himself. "That is true. It must be true."

"Is that what you wished to know, my friend?"

"Yes. Much is explained, just with those few words, and I cannot tell you how much good you have done."

"And yet," said Khaavren, "I cannot help but wonder why it is today, rather than another day, that you have appeared here to ask these questions of me?"

"Why today?" said Pel. "Is there something about this day that is, in some way, unusual?"

"Of a certainty," said Khaavren. "You have come to see me. That is more than unusual—it is unprecedented."

"Well, that is true."

"And therefore, it is only natural that I wonder if something has happened to bring these questions to the forefront of your mind, good Pel."

"Oh, I agree that it is only natural."

"And therefore you will answer me?"

"Certainly I will answer you."

"Ah, you will?"

"Indeed, and this very instant."

"Begin then, for you perceive I am listening avidly."

"This is it, then: you understand, do you not, how the system of Discretion is worked?"

"In fact, my dear Pel, I understand it not at all."

"Then I must first say two words about our Academy."

"Very well, I am listening."

"Here in the Palace, there is a small building near the Athyra Wing, where, in the humblest of dwellings, live those who have undertaken the study of Discretion under the Masters of the House of the Issola. Periodically, some great—to you, Khaavren, I can even admit that this means *wealthy*—noble feels the need to have a confidant at his elbow—a confidant he can trust completely, and to whom he can unburden himself. On these occasions, a journeyman or, sometimes, a Master will accept this duty to the glory of the Academy and, I should add, his own advancement. But, however many nobles of one sort or another beg for our services, there is no greater need than by the Emperor himself. It is because the Emperor always has such a need that the Institute first came into being in the Fifth Cycle."

"And yet, good Pel, for the past half a hundred years, since the Duke of Wellborn retired, His Majesty has been without a Discreet."

"That is exactly the case, good Khaavren, and you can imagine that this has been the cause of no little interest among those of us—numbering, at the moment, forty-one—undertaking the arduous study, for it is possible that one of us will be selected for this great honor."

"Yes, I understand that."

"Well, and do you also understand that the Academy—for so we call it—is funded directly by the Empire?"

"No, I had not known that."

"Then, no doubt, you did not know that, mere moments before I arrived here, we received word that this funding was to be halved, which would necessitate dismissals among both staff and students."

"Hmmm. I see."

"Do you, then, understand my sudden interest in the state of mind of His Majesty, and my speculations over his concern with matters of financial?"

"I understand entirely."

"And can you offer any more insight?"

"I will say only one word, good Pel."

"One word from you, my friend, is as a thousand from another. What is this word?"

"It is—Jurabin."

"Ah—ah!" said Pel. "Is it he who controls the purse-strings of the Empire?"

"So it is said, good Pel, and so I believe."

"Well, well. And who controls Jurabin?"

"Ah," said Khaavren, smiling. "As for that, Pel, who controls the Court?"

"In the old days it was—the Consort?"

"You have answered your own question."

Pel nodded, then, abruptly, he stood, and pressed Khaavren's hand. "You have given me no little help, my old friend. If there is anything I can do for you—"

"Ah, but there is."

Pel's eyes narrowed by such a small degree Khaavren

hardly noticed. "What is it, then? If it is anything I can do without compromising—"

"Yes, Pel, it is that you stop neglecting your old friend, and come to me and visit from time to time, while I rot away to insignificance and you shine ever brighter, like a fire to which an invisible hand is adding log after log."

Pel smiled. "You may be assured that I will not neglect you, Khaavren. But I also assure you that, even if you believe what you have just said about rotting away to insignificance, I do not. There are some natures that are destined to rise to ever greater heights until they tower over all other mortals. The first of those I recognized was Adron e'Kieron, the Duke of Eastmanswatch. And, though I did not realize it at first, you are another. So have no fear."

"I agree about the first, Pel, but as to the second—"

"Remember my words, good Khaavren. And, to make them the stronger, I shall leave you with them, for I must be on my way at once."

And, after pressing his friend's hand again, Pel put his hood up over his head and left Khaavren, who was still standing, staring after him, a bemused smile on his lips.

# *Chapter the Third*

*Which Treats of Pastries,
And of the Care that Must
Be exercised with Regard to
Casual Correspondence.*

KHAAVREN LEFT THE DRAGON WING for home shortly after Pel's exit. Although the Tiassa, as ensign, had the right to quarters in the Dragon Wing, he kept as his own residence the house on the Street of the Glass Cutters, which we hope our readers will recall without further prompting. On the way, as was his custom, he stopped for a pastry from the vendor who took as his station the place where the Avenue of Seven Swans Park intersected with the Street of the Dragon.

The vendor, a Teckla named Raf, greeted Khaavren respectfully and said, "To-day, my lord, the pastries are venison, and have, in addition, a filling of mushrooms, both of which ingredients were left for some hours in a marinade of wine and tarragon before being cooked together and folded into the pastry."

Khaavren nodded and accepted one, for which he did not pay, as Raf was accustomed to give the Tiassa what he wanted out of gratitude for the way the latter had settled a territorial dispute with another vendor of pastries some ninety years before. Raf, therefore, not only handed over the pastry, which was deliciously warm from having been kept over the hot coals with which the cart was filled, but he also bowed as he did so. Khaavren wordlessly acknowledged the gift and the bow as no less than his due and turned toward home, when, being struck by a sudden thought, he turned back and said, "How is business, my dear Raf?"

The Teckla, startled by the onset of conversation where he had anticipated only silence, took a moment to gather his wits, after which he said, "Business, my lord? Pardon me, but does Your Lordship do me the honor of asking about my business?"

"You have understood me exactly, my dear Raf, that is what I am asking you."

"Well then, my lord, since you ask, I will reply, and frankly at that."

"That is what I wish."

"Business, my lord, is good. I have sold as many pastries today as I did yester-day, and because to-morrow is Market Day, I expect to sell even more to-morrow."

"And so you are surviving, Raf?"

"Indeed I am, my lord. In fact, I am more than surviving; I am positively flourishing."

"How, flourishing?"

"Yes, my lord. To such an extent, in fact, that my wife has been able to buy the best glazes, so that her pottery has begun to sell better than ever, which means, in turn, that I have been able to secure such fine meats as you find in that pastry which is, if I may be so bold as to remind Your Lordship, growing cold in your hand. This, as you may readily understand, increases my sales. The result is, my lord, that we will soon be leaving our quarters at Two Canals and moving to a fine set of rooms on the Street of the Monks, and have even been discussing the idea of having a child, which we have both wanted for most of this last century, my lord."

"Well, then, Raf, I ought to congratulate you, and I do."

"Thanks, my lord."

"I am pleased that, at any rate, the new tax has not harmed you."

"Harmed me, my lord? On the contrary, it has made me my fortune."

"The new tax has made your fortune? Come, how can this be?"

"In the simplest possible manner. Shall I explain it to you?"

"Yes, Raf, if you will do so, I assure you that I will happily listen."

"Well, this is it then, my lord. I had been selling each pastry for nine copper pennies—except, of course, to you. Well, between the new tax on wheat entering the city, and the new tax on meats, my costs have gone up, as nearly as I can guess, by about two copper pennies for each pastry."

"Well, and?"

"So, of course, the costs to all of my competitors also went up."

"Yes, that follows. And did you raise your price?"

"No, my lord, and that is the secret. I kept my price the same, where my competitors raised theirs."

"And so?"

"And so, my lord, now everyone comes to me. Instead of the loss of business, which, as I understand it, the other pastry sellers experience, I now have people walking miles for my pastries. Of course, I may say that this is due in part to the quality with which I invest each one—"

"I will certainly agree with that, good Raf."

"—but in large part I am getting the business that my competitors have driven away by raising prices. So, while I make less than they with each pastry, I sell many more than they—so much so, that each night for the past year, since the new tax has been passed, I have offered up prayers to Trout for the safekeeping of His Majesty. And that is how the new tax has made my fortune for me."

"Well, it is all clear to me now, and I thank you for explaining it so well."

"My lord, I am honored that you asked."

Khaavren nodded civilly, and left the street vendor to deal with the not inconsiderable queue that had been patiently (or, perhaps, prudently) waiting to buy pastries while Raf finished his conversation with the ensign.

We ought to mention that it was now early in the evening, at just the hour when tradesmen and merchants were returning from their labors, beggars and prostitutes were beginning work, and His Majesty would be rising from dinner and going to his gaming tables or to his evening of discussing the hunt with his companions. Khaavren returned to his home like any merchant, tired from the day, and ready to greet his family and partake of his evening meal.

But this similarity between our Ensign of the Guard and the tens of thousands of merchants, tradesmen, and Teckla, which similarity we are obliged to mention because it passed through Khaavren's mind every day at this time, ought not to be carried too far. For one thing, he had already had his evening meal, in the form of a pastry which he found, as always, delightfully flaky and perfectly seasoned. For another, the only family he came home to was the servant, Srahi, who had aged considerably and was now far more satisfactory than she had been—since, if she was no better as a cook or housekeeper, she was at least more taciturn.

And if this had been a day of remarkable occurrences in other ways, at least in this it was no different than usual: When Khaavren entered by the brass-bound door with the Tiassa crest, Srahi glanced up at him from her book, then returned to her reading without making any remark whatsoever. Khaavren walked by her, stopping only long enough to learn what absorbed her attention. He discovered it was a book of scandalous rhyme published by someone calling himself "The Poisoner," then he continued up to his own room without feeling called upon to comment. Lest the reader determine from this interplay (for certainly the lack of interplay is, itself, interplay) that relations between the Tiassa and the Teckla were strained, allow us to state at once that nothing could be further from the truth. Rather, they understood each other so well that no words were necessary, and they shared, moreover, an aversion to unnecessary talk.

Upon reaching his room, and hanging his sword-sheath on a peg at the top of the stairs, the first thing that caught Khaavren's eye was a letter he had begun writing to his old friend Aerich (the Lyorn to whom we have already referred and of whom, we dare to hope, the reader has some recollection) some weeks before, but hadn't yet finished. He picked it up and scanned what he had penned, which consisted of a few lines in answer to Aerich's last letter—lines that said little, because there was little to say. Aerich had written a short note asking after his health and his doings, and Khaavren had found himself unable to answer, wherefore he had left the incomplete missive on his desk as a reminder—the efficacy of which we have just proven.

The meeting with Pel caused Khaavren to resolve to, at the least, return his friend's courtesy, therefore he sat down at his desk, crumpled up the beginning he had made, and threw it into a corner where it joined a score of others like itself, there to await a season, which season arrived perhaps once each year, when Khaavren should be willing to have his sanctum invaded by Srahi at the same time as Srahi felt inclined to engage in such an invasion. Khaavren found a new sheet of paper (paper bleached to a pure white, so fine there was no grain, made in Hammersgate by the newest process) and began again:

My Dear Aerich [he wrote]: I thank you for your inquiry after my health and activities. My health, thanks to the Gods and the physicians (or, perhaps, thanks to the fact that I have intercourse with neither) is excellent. As for my activities—you may rest assured that they have in no wise changed from the last time you did me the honor to ask concerning them. I set the guards, I stand watch, and I hope for the diversion of battle, which seems unlikely, as His Majesty (whom the Gods preserve) has little interest, it seems, in assuming the personal command that is his right, but would rather trust Rollondar e'Drien, who, as you may know, became Warlord early this past century. Lord Rollondar is an easy enough master, if only because he has no interest in the Guards, and so leaves them to the Captain, who, in turn, leaves them to me. This is an arrangement that keeps me busy, and being busy keeps me happy, so there is no reason to be concerned on that score.

As for your own affairs, my dear Aerich, I am pleased to hear that everything is well. I had feared that rearrangement of the Imperial assessments might have created difficulties for you. We hear, now and then, murmurings of armed resistance, but, I am sorry to say, there has been nothing of an organized nature. Some days ago, His Majesty did me the honor to ask if I feared the people. I reminded him that I had been on duty in the two hundred and sixth year of his reign, during the food riots, and I had seen an angry populace, and an organized populace; and this one, for all their clamor, is neither. He seemed satisfied with the answer. I have no doubt, Acrich, that, if you were here, you would agree with me.

As for Pel, I can tell you little, save that I have recently seen him, and he is unchanged—secretive, mysterious, and always with one scheme or another running through his mind. I must confess that he hurt my feelings, Aerich, because he pretended, in order to get certain knowledge from me, to an ignorance that I know is impossible. Yet, that is only his way, and I forgive him for the sake of our old friendship.

And, speaking of friendship, I heard, some thirty years ago, from our old friend, Kathana e'Marish'Chala. She has married a Dragonlord of the e'Lanya line, whose name escapes me. I was invited to the ceremony, but was unable to obtain leave. Did you hear? Were you invited and able to attend?

While on the subject of friends, what of good Tazendra? I was pleased to learn that she was able to escape unscathed from the explosion at her home. I hope

she has learned from this, and will temper her studies
with care. What of her servant, Mica? Was he injured?
I should be saddened to learn—

Khaavren stopped, hearing a rattle over his head that indicated that someone had pulled the door-clapper. He carefully
blotted the last few words he had written, then prepared to go
down to see who was at the door. The route to the stairway
took him past the small window he was accustomed to leave
ajar to allow in the breezes—he had, in fact, become adept at
regulating the temperature in his room by gauging the opening on this window and the vent of his small stove. The reason we feel obliged to bring this window to the reader's
attention is because through it Khaavren realized that night
had quite fallen; he had spent more time writing to Aerich
than he had at first realized. With this thought, he also realized that he was tired, and that his bed was calling to him.

However, the door was also calling, and that more urgently.

Upon discovering, then, that it was in fact quite late at
night, he arrested his movements long enough to take his
sword from its sheath, which was, in turn, on its peg at the
top of the stairs, and bring it (that is, the sword, not the peg)
with him in order to be prepared in the event that at the door
might be one or more members of the Army of the Thorny
Rose—a battalion of mercenaries whose quarters were further
down the street, and who were not fond of guardsmen, nor of
officers, and all of whom were known to drink heavily.

Some three minutes after Khaavren went down to answer
the door, he returned to his room, returned his sword to its
place by the stairway, and returned his attention to composition.

I should be saddened to learn [he resumed] that anything
ill had befallen that good fellow. If you can learn something of this, please tell me what you can, and I shall be
grateful. You may be amused to know that I have just
killed a man who clapped at my door. He ascertained my
identity, and then attempted to discharge a flashstone at

me—perhaps writing letters is not as harmless an activity as I would have thought. Wherefore, prudence, as well as the lateness of the hour, dictates that I stop now, in addition to which I have just realized that I am bleeding, and I ought to do something about this, because replacing stained clothing is, as you may remember, difficult on a guardsman's income.

I remain, my dear Aerich, always your devoted friend,
Khaavren

At this point, we might venture to guess that our readers are, on the one hand, wondering how Aerich will react when he reads about this singular event, and, on the other, are themselves curious about any details Khaavren may have omitted. As for the first question, we must beg our readers' pardon, but it will be some time before the answer to this question reveals itself. We hope our readers will be satisfied if, at this time, we answer only the second of these supposed questions.

We can, in point of fact, reveal a little more than what Khaavren wrote to his friend. Upon arriving at the stairway, Khaavren had opened the door and seen there a gentleman in Imperial livery, holding a roll of parchment in his hand—parchment upon which an Imperial seal could nearly be made out by the luminescence from the lamp Khaavren had lighted on his way to the door.

The visitor had made a respectful courtesy and said, "Do I have the honor of addressing Khaavren, Ensign of the Imperial Guard?"

Khaavren saw nothing unusual about the visitor: It was by the merest chance that his naked sword was concealed behind the door, for Khaavren had, in fact, not thought of hiding it—it was only concealed because Khaavren was carrying it in his right hand and the door opened inward to the right. As it happened, however, it was a good thing, for when Khaavren admitted his identity, the visitor dropped the paper and revealed, in the palm of his hand, a smooth, flat stone—

the sort of stone Khaavren recognized from having used them himself on more than one occasion.

The Tiassa wasted no time, then, in putting a solid object between himself and the flashstone—the nearest solid object being the door, which he interposed by slamming it shut, after which he took a step back, let go of the lamp (which by chance neither spilled nor broke, which would have undoubtedly proved an annoyance) and assumed a guard position with his blade directly in front of his face and at a forty-five-degree angle to the sky. The assassin—for so we may call him—made the mistake of attempting to gain entry by charging into the door shoulder-first. The assassin was strong enough that this would have worked had the door been latched with the usual thin steel that kept it closed when the iron bolt was not in use. The door, however, had not been latched at all, but merely shut, and so it opened at once and the assassin stumbled through, his flashstone raised, and a dagger revealed in the other hand.

Khaavren had positioned himself so well that the discharge of the flashstone only grazed his cheek slightly while he, Khaavren, brought the edge of his sword down smartly onto the assassin's forehead, thus ending the assassin's attack and life, and leaving Khaavren to regret that he had not been able to leave the fellow alive for questioning. He did drag the body into the hall, however, and exchanged a few terse words with Srahi, who had been awakened by the discharge of the flashstone, to the effect that she need not consider removal of the body as part of her cleaning duties the next day. After that thoughtful remark, Khaavren cleaned his blade and went back upstairs to finish his letter.

This being done, in the manner we have already described, Khaavren quickly removed his shirt and set it soaking in a tub of water into which he poured a small quantity of lye, then set a cloth against his cheek, which was still bleeding slightly, after which operation he prepared the letter for the post, himself for sleep, and got into bed.

And yet, to his surprise, he found himself unable to sleep. Those who have spent several hundred years in uniform will be able to grasp at once how unusual it is for a soldier to have difficulty sleeping, yet Khaavren could not keep from wondering about the assassin whose corpse occupied a spot on the floor of his house. (We should note in passing that Srahi, the servant, had trouble sleeping for much the same reason, but in her case this is more readily understood.)

"Why," he asked himself, "would someone want to kill me? I have done nothing to make myself a special target for revenge, nor do I hold a position of any particular importance—at least, it seems to me that I could be replaced tomorrow by any of a dozen good soldiers and no one would notice the difference. Nor have I any possessions of special merit. It is, without question, decidedly odd." With these thoughts going through Khaavren's mind, the reader will readily understand why it took him over an hour to fall asleep.

# *Chapter the Fourth*

### *Which Treats of Several Others,*
### *All of Who May Have Been Engaged*
### *In Dangerous Correspondence.*

KHAAVREN AWOKE WITH THE SAME question on his mind that had occupied his thoughts before sleeping, and felt himself no closer to an answer. Srahi was still asleep, so he decided to break his fast at the Palace. He removed his shirt from the water, scowled on realizing that the shirt was soaking wet, and, opening up the single cabinet that contained his clothing, brought out his other shirt, and, at the same time, his old blue tunic, which, though the weather was too warm for such heavy wool to be comfortable, he hoped would cover the places on the shirt where the fabric had become thin.

He buckled on his sword, clasped his uniform cloak around his neck, examined himself in the full-length glass which he had had installed in the hall upon being made an ensign, and decided that his appearance would do. He then picked up the body of his visitor and slung it over his shoulder, took the letter to Aerich into his hand, and so encumbered, set off for the Palace. We can only speculate on the sight presented by this officer of the Guard carrying a corpse along the Street of the

Dragon; if there were any remarks made, Khaavren either didn't hear them, or chose not to hear them. In any case, there were no incidents.

Upon reaching the outer gate of the Palace, Khaavren gave the letter into the care of an officer of the post who promised to see the missive delivered with all dispatch, after which, in due time, Khaavren reached the sub-wing of the Imperial Guard.

He was greeted there by his corporal, Thack, who queried Khaavren with a raised eyebrow. We should add the reader might also raise an eyebrow upon recalling that Thack, when we met him in our previous history, was not one to inspire confidence; the reader might even be wondering how he came to occupy a position of trust under the command of our brave Tiassa. We do not propose to answer this question at any length, for the simple reason that our history does not require it; so, to put the reader's mind at ease on this question, we will say only that Thack, after transferring to G'aereth's command some eighty or eighty-five years after the close of the events related in *The Phoenix Guards*, had undergone sufficient transformation in character that Khaavren believed he could be depended upon. We will not take it upon ourselves to dispute with the worthy ensign on such a matter, and moreover, there is nowhere any evidence that the good Thack at any time proved himself less than completely deserving of Khaavren's trust.

Khaavren set his burden down in the antechamber and said, "My compliments to Gyorg Lavode, and I should be honored if he would grant me a brief meeting at his convenience."

"Yes, Ensign."

"Has the guard been posted?"

"Yes, Ensign."

"Then, I will assume my station, stopping on the way for a bit of bread and cheese."

"Yes, Ensign. And—"

"Yes?"

Thack cleared his throat, and dropped his eyes eloquently toward the corpse.

"Ah," said Khaavren. "Yes, you may leave him there. I do not believe he will be doing anything."

"Yes, Ensign."

Khaavren then set out, as he had nearly every day for the past five hundred and thirty years, through the corridors of the Dragon Wing toward the short ramp and the great doors which never closed that marked the beginning of the Imperial Wing (which was, the reader ought to understand, not a wing at all, but the innermost portion of the labyrinthine Palace). Yet he had not gone far before he was interrupted by a young gentleman whose costume indicated that he was a page and whose colors indicated that he was of the House of the Phoenix. This young man said, "My Lord Ensign Khaavren?"

"Yes, that is I," said Khaavren, arresting his motion.

"His Majesty is desirous of seeing you at your earliest convenience."

Khaavren frowned. "Well, you may inform His Majesty that I will be there directly. But, to do so, you must move quickly, or I shall be there before you arrive, and your message will be useless."

"I shall do so, my lord," said the page, and dashed back the way he had come, leaving Khaavren alone with his frown.

"Well," said Khaavren to himself. "This is no small matter. It has passed the seventh hour after midnight, and, in twenty minutes, I will be at the door of His Majesty's chambers, where I am at the same time every morning, in order to conduct His Majesty through the ritual that we are pleased to call 'Opening the Palace,' although the Palace is never closed. His Majesty has, I think, been awake for twenty minutes, and is still engaged in completing his morning toilet; and, at forty minutes past the seventh hour, I am always there. Why, then, does His Majesty feel compelled to instruct me to do something I have done for half a millennium?

"The only explanation is that something has happened to cause His Majesty so much distress that he is no longer thinking of patterns or habits, but wishes to see me about something extraordinary. In light of yester-day's conversation, and last night's events, this morning promises to be interesting indeed. Come, Khaavren, your master calls, and this is no time to hesitate. Breakfast must, alas, await a more opportune moment."

With these words sternly spoken to himself, he resumed his military walk, only this time putting himself out to arrive at the Imperial Bedchamber in ten minutes, rather than the usual fifteen. Upon arriving, he was greeted by a most remarkable sight. Two guardsmen stood outside the door, as usual, and saluted their ensign, and His Majesty, wearing his normal morning costume of rich gold silk and diamonds, was sitting in the chair next to a large, canopied bed, next to which was the tray which His Majesty's morning klava; but the Orb, which circled His Majesty's head, was showing a deep, lurid yellow, which indicated that His Majesty was both worried and upset. Furthermore, there were, also in the room, two figures Khaavren was unaccustomed to seeing there, these being Jurabin, and His Excellency Rollondar e'Drien, the Warlord.

Jurabin we have already met, and the reader, we believe, would rather learn the answers to Khaavren's questions than to waste his time learning about the Warlord, wherefore we will only say that Rollondar e'Drien was a very thin man of about eleven hundred years with straight black hair in a military cut, parted at his noble's point. Upon seeing him, Khaavren's first thought was, "Are we at war then?" But he said nothing, merely bowing to His Majesty and awaiting orders.

"My compliments, Captain, and you have arrived in a very timely fashion."

"My thanks—excuse me, Sire, but did Your Majesty address me as Captain?"

"I did. I have chosen to promote you, due to the death of Brigadier G'aereth, which occurred sometime last night."

"I see," said Khaavren, feeling—to his credit—a pang of sorrow more acute than the pride in his promotion. "I am honored, Sire, and I thank Your Majesty deeply."

"That is not, however," his Majesty added, "the reason for my summons, any more than it is the reason why these gentlemen are here."

"Yes, Sire?"

The Emperor cleared his throat. "You should know, for these gentlemen do, that, however old Brigadier G'aereth was, he did not die of natural causes."

"Sire?"

"He was poniarded as he returned from a ball given by the Count of Westbreeze."

Khaavren felt his eyes widen. "Sire! Who would wish to kill—"

"We don't know," said his Majesty, glancing at Jurabin and Rollondar, who shrugged. "And that isn't all," he added.

"What, there is more, Sire?"

"Yes, there was another murder last night, about which I was informed upon awakening."

"Yes, Sire?"

"A certain Smaller, an intendant of finance."

Khaavren frowned. "Yes, Sire, I believe I have seen him."

"Judging from the look on Lady Bellor's face, he was one of her ablest clerks."

"I can attest to that as well, Sire," said Jurabin.

"Sire, how did he—"

"He was found dead in his box at the Theater of the Orb, after a performance of *The Song of Vinburra*. We might never have known that his death was murder, save for His Excellency the Warlord, who grew suspicious of all the deaths, and thought to bring in a wizard to look for sorcery."

"It was a sorcerous murder?"

"Yes. His heart was stopped."

"I see. But, Sire, did not Your Majesty pronounce the words, 'all the deaths'?"

"I did."

"Were there others, then, Sire?"

"One other," His Majesty sighed. "Gyorg Lavode. He was in his bed, sleeping, when his throat was cut."

"What does Your Majesty tell me?" cried Khaavren. "The Captain of the Lavodes?"

"Himself," said the Emperor grimly.

Khaavren's mind fairly reeled with the news. "In that case, my message will, I suspect, not be delivered."

"Message?" said the Emperor.

"Yes, Sire. I had, just this morning, requested an audience with him."

"For what reason?"

"To consult with him upon a matter that, it seemed to me, would best be looked into by a skilled wizard who was also a warrior, and, moreover, one who had others of the same sort at his command."

"Well," said the Emperor, "that certainly described Gyorg Lavode. But what was the matter upon which you wished to consult him?"

"How, does Your Majesty wish me to explain?"

"Yes, and this very moment."

"Well, Sire, last night, an attempt was made upon my life."

Rollondar gasped, and Jurabin took a step backward, as if afraid that the odor of death might still cling to Khaavren's uniform. His Majesty stood up. "But this is infamous!"

"Yes, Sire."

"Who was the assassin?"

"I don't know, Sire." said Khaavren. "But I brought his body back with me, which body lies now in my antechamber. I had had the intention of asking Captain Gyorg what he could learn from examination of the corpse, but now ..." Khaavren punctuated his sentence with a shrug.

"But now," agreed His Majesty. "Now we must decide what to do. It is clear that there is a conspiracy afoot, and that, whatever the object of this conspiracy, the conspirators aim at the very top of the Imperium." His Majesty looked at those assembled before him. "How do we find them, and where do we look?"

"We look first," said Jurabin with a cold glance at the Warlord, "to the House of the Dragon, who may, perhaps, be desirous of seeing the cycle turn precipitately—that is, sooner than, in the natural course of events (if, indeed, any course of events in which men are involved can be called 'natural'), the cycle might turn."

Rollondar e'Drien glared back at him and said, "Dragon-lords do not employ assassins."

"That may be," said Jurabin, "but—"

"Please, gentlemen," said His Majesty. "You may bicker at a later time. It is clear that we must do something, and soon at that. I am already late for my rounds, and everything else will of necessity be late therefore, and today is my day for wine-tasting; I will not be pleased if that is delayed. So let us, right now, determine a course of action, and you gentlemen may pursue this course, and I will return to running the Empire."

"Sire," said Jurabin. "We must consider—"

"You may *not* consider," said His Majesty. "I will not have every activity of the day thrown into needless confusion, and have my schedule spoiled. I am willing to do what is necessary. Determine, then, what is must be done and then let us get on with our tasks."

Jurabin cleared his throat. "An investigation—" he began.

"Yes, yes," said His Majesty. "To be sure, an investigation. But who should investigate?"

"I will," said Rollondar.

"You?" said Jurabin. "Have you the resources—"

"With the help of the Captain, here," said Rollondar, indicating Khaavren. "I have no doubt—"

"Very well," said His Majesty. "Is that all? You will investigate, and you will tell me what you have learned."

"Sire," said Jurabin, "It seems to me that, at least, the Duke of Eastmanswatch ought to be summoned and questioned. As the Dragon Heir, he is—"

"Expected in the city within the week, in any case," said Rollondar coolly. "You forget the Meeting of the Principalities?"

"Well," said Jurabin, "that is true, I had forgotten."

"Your pardon, gentlemen," said Khaavren. "But it is clear to me that there is one person who ought to be summoned to aid in the investigation, if for no other reason than because, if we do not invite her, she will investigate anyway, but may not give us the benefit of her discoveries."

Rollondar evidently understood, because he suddenly turned pale. "Are you aware of what you are suggesting?" he said.

"I hope he is, said His Majesty. "Because I, for one, am not, and yet I am most anxious to be so."

Jurabin merely looked puzzled, and slightly apprehensive.

"I am aware," said Khaavren.

"Well," said Rollondar, "I tell you that I, for one, want no part of this idea."

The Emperor cleared his throat and said, "If you would be so good, Captain, to explain what is causing our Warlord so much distress, I assure you I will be grateful."

Khaavren bowed. "It seems to me, Sire," he said, "that with the death of the Captain of the Lavodes, we have no choice but to call on the old Captain, the Enchantress of Dzur Mountain, Sethra."

As if the very name carried a spell of great enchantment, nothing followed its pronunciation except silence.

# Chapter the Fifth

*Which Treats of Events*
*In a Part of the City*
*That the Author Visits*
*Only with Great Reluctance.*

IT IS WITH SOME REGRET that we must, at this point in our history, leave those who have, up until this moment, been the principal actors. In so doing, we also leave the well-known halls of the Imperial Palace in order to look in on an area of the city which has hitherto been entirely neglected. We assure the reader that this is indispensable, and that we would not abuse the power of our position to trifle with his sensitivities and interests.

Our journey does not, in fact, take us far from the Palace in distance, although it does in appearance and atmosphere. The Underside, as it was called, was the district directly to the north of the Palace, and bounded on the south by the Palace's north wall. It lay between the Street of the Tsalmoth and the Street of the Jhereg, with the Street of the Vallista running through the middle. Some say it went north as far as the Twostar Canal, but others maintained that nothing north of the Avenue of the Bridges could properly be considered the Underside. The reader will understand if, concerning this question, the historian remains neutral.

Its reputation has survived the Interregnum, and, in contrast to most such cases, its reputation, by all accounts, was well deserved. The White Sash Battalion (under the command of Baroness Stonemover, who does not, alas, appear in this history), who made up the police force of Dragaera City, never entered this district in lesser numbers than four; or never fewer than six or eight if night had fallen. There was, so far as is known, never an epoch when the area was well patrolled after dark, and at the time of which we write the police rarely entered even during the day. It had, in fact, become something of a jest—one might ironically suggest to a visitor who had outstayed his welcome that he run a footrace to the Bridge and return later for his prize. If one was suspicious of a business deal, one might say that it "smelled like the Underside." The reference to the district's foul atmosphere was quite literally true.

His Majesty, in the 183rd year of his reign, signed his Sewage Edicts, among the least remembered and most beneficial acts of a reign which the facts testify deserves far better treatment from history than it has received. There are surviving records of the efficiency and thoroughness with which the edicts were implemented, but nowhere is there any reference to any of the policies it details being put into effect in the Underside. The air of the Underside was filled with odors that we will not disturb our readers' sensibilities by reciting, save by remarking that, although the slaughterhouses of Baron Whitemill were located in this district, nowhere is it recorded that anyone noticed the fumes they produced. It is well known, also, that on those rare days when a north wind blew, all of the windows in the Jhereg and Vallista Wings of the Palace had to be closed, and there were even days when the stench would infiltrate as far as the Imperial Wing.

As to the class and condition of those unfortunates who actually dwelt there, well, this is a matter upon which we suspect the intellect of the reader may safely be turned with little worry that he will stray from the truth.

Let us, then, hold our breath and shut our eyes until we arrive at the relative safety of a small cabaret. We need not observe this hostel closely, for it looked like a thousand others; reached by walking down three wooden steps, it was dimly lit, with a large room in front and two or three small rooms curtained off in back. In the main room, there were four or five round tables, and plain, shabby benches at which to sit, and a long, high counter behind which stood the host, a burly Chreotha whose past must remain a mystery. The cabaret was situated on a street that may as well remain nameless, in a neighborhood like many others; it was a neighborhood populated by day-laborers, petty thieves, assorted malcontents—and one man in particular who was called, simply, Greycat, for reasons of which we must confess our ignorance.

Physically, we can sketch him in an instant. The first thing we might notice would be a pink, puffy scar just above his right eye—a scar as if a wild animal had attempted to remove this eye and only a dodge at the last instant, so to speak, had saved him. Far from being the only mark on Greycat's face, this scar was merely the most prominent, for there were, here and there, signs of other wounds about him, from forehead to neck, and even one on his scalp that ran alongside his noble's point—for he was, indeed, a son of the nobility. His right eye, because of the scar, was slightly squinting, and his left eye would at times match this squint, as if of its own volition.

He was by no means a large man, yet he conveyed the impression of great strength within his small frame—a single look would convince the observer that he was made up of bone and muscle and perhaps a small quantity of blood, and nothing else. He wore plain, dark clothes, and a floppy hat that would have been more at home on a buffoon or a beggar than on one with Greycat's countenance. For we should add that Greycat had an evil look about him—a look that, by itself, would have fully accounted for the fact that, even in this cabaret, peopled as it was by those used to surviving in the Underside, no one wished to approach him. In fact, there were additional reasons why he was left alone, not the least of which was his reputation.

To round off our sketch, we will add that he was armed. A long, heavy blade was at his side; and, judging from the plain, smooth hilt, it was a soldier's weapon. One rumor was that Greycat had, indeed, been a soldier, perhaps in one of the mercenary armies hired by the rebellious Duke of Hoarwall, and that he, Greycat, had deserted during the Battle of Irontown, at which the duke was captured and executed. If this tale was true, no one doubted that his desertion had been caused by something other than cowardice.

There were other stories about him. Some said that he had been the Consort's lover, and that His Majesty had had him tortured, and he had somehow escaped. At other times, it was said that he was a Jhereg assassin, and, in fact, some had promised him gold if he would beat or kill an enemy, but he had never accepted these offers.

Whatever his history, trial and hardship were clearly written there, and if he offered no explanation, neither did he make any effort to conceal them. It was known that "he never troubled anyone who didn't trouble him," and that, on those rare occasions when he drank, he only became quieter and quieter until he fell asleep. On one such occasion, a cutpurse with more courage than wisdom had attempted to ply his art; Greycat had come out of his stupor long enough to cut the thief's throat before resuming his interrupted nap.

This was Greycat; this was the man who, however distasteful we may find it, our history absolutely requires we observe, for, as evening falls on Dragaera City, he and certain visitors are about to hold a conference at which issues will be raised that are of no small importance to the subsequent events we must relate.

The first to arrive was the most harmless-looking—she was small and elegant, dressed in black pants, black boots, and black shirt with grey trim. She did not appear to be armed, but there was the emblem of a Jhereg below her left collar, and a ring with the same design on the third finger of her right hand, and these were sufficient to guarantee her safety—or, if not, they promised nothing good to whoever couldn't read the message they sent. She was called Laral.

She saw Greycat sitting alone at his table, and joined him there. As she sat, he stood in a gesture at once courtly and unconscious. She acknowledged his courtesy with a nod, and they sat waiting, neither speaking nor even drinking—which, considering the usual wines and ales at Underside cabarets, must be thought of as wisdom.

Next to arrive was one who would be called a gentleman only if one saw the noble's point peeking out from beneath his hood. The hood, we should add, was of the type used by seamen in heavy storms, and was attached to the appropriate oiled cloak. He was the largest of the group; his hands were heavily callused and there was hair growing on their backs—a sure sign, as is well known, of a bestial nature. He seemed ill at ease in the cabaret; in fact, he seemed ill at ease in general, to judge from the way he opened and closed his fists as he looked around for a familiar face. Beneath the oiled cloak could be seen enough of his pale blue and green garments to establish that he was, in fact, of the House of the Orca. His name was Chaler.

He espied Greycat and, after obtaining a cup of ale, sat down next to him, with a hesitant nod to Laral.

An instant later the fourth member of the party arrived. He wore no hat—indeed, it would have been difficult to find a hat that would not have looked absurd amid his hair, which was bright red, and, moreover, grew wildly and haphazardly all about his head, proving to be his most distinctive feature. Otherwise he had the sharp chin, long nose, and narrow eyes of a fox, on a thin frame that gave the appearance of being unable to bend, like a sword that has been poorly tempered, and so will, upon the application of pressure, break rather than bow. Even with his noble's point concealed beneath his profusion of hair, he was unmistakably an aristocrat, but neither his face nor his dress, which was dull black, though of a fine cut, gave any clue as to his House. At his side was an incongruously heavy sword, with a plain, leather-wrapped wooden hilt—a sword such as an elegantly dressed gentleman would never wear unless he knew its length. His name was Dunaan.

He sat next to Chaler, whom he ignored, after nodding to Greycat and scowling briefly at Laral.

It should be understood that, until this point, no words had been exchanged. Greycat said, "Let us retire." His speech was difficult to place, for it seemed, at first, like the refined accents of the court, but there were echoes of distant places in the way he drew out some of his vowels.

Dunaan's speech was of someone who had lived all his life in Dragaera City itself. He said, "Are we not missing someone?"

"No," said Greycat.

"Very well," said Dunaan.

They rose as one and followed Greycat into one of the back rooms, which he had reserved for their use. Chaler, who had finished his ale, left the cup where it was, making no effort to procure more, indicating that he was capable of what the natural philosopher calls, "learning behavior," which turn of phrase pleases us so much that we cannot resist making use of it.

It is worthwhile to wonder at the wisdom of moving into one of the private rooms. By doing so, they not only made themselves more conspicuous, but put themselves into a position where they would be unable to see anyone who chose to listen in on their conversation; the protection from eavesdroppers afforded by the thin walls of the room was negligible. Perhaps they chose this room because they had been given to understand that conspirators (and they recognized, as, no doubt, has the astute reader, that they were conspirators) always met in small rooms in public houses. Still, there can be no question that it was foolish, and the only reason their conversation escaped notice was because, in fact, no one in the cabaret actually cared what they said.

The room was small, lit only by a pair of lanterns in opposite corners, and, due to certain support beams that kept the building above from falling into the cabaret below, was crisscrossed with shadows, giving a sinister look to the place. In summary, then, we can say that it looked like the set of one of the Tenth Cycle conspiracy dramas so popular on the Street of Oranges at the time, and even gave the impression that those involved were playing at conspiracy, rather than actively involved in one.

We can only attribute this to a certain lack of experience, for the conspirators were, in fact, entirely serious about their intentions, and furthermore, considering their actions up to this time, there could be no question of joking at all.

Once they were all seated (in the same relative positions they had occupied before), Laral spoke, affecting the accent of the court. "What of Leen?" she said.

Chaler spoke with the twang of the Southern Coast—in other words, he sounded just the way he ought to, saving only that his voice was slightly higher-pitched than one would expect of a man his size: "He failed, my lady."

"Failed?" said Dunaan.

"Yes," said Greycat. "Chaler has already informed me. The Tiassa killed him."

"He was clumsy, my lord," said Chaler.

"I assume," said Dunaan ironically, "that you refer to Leen, not the Tiassa."

Chaler swallowed, as if Dunaan made him nervous, and said, "Yes. Leen was clumsy."

"I take it," said Laral, "that you were not?"

"I was not, my lady," said Chaler.

"Nor," said Laral, "was I."

"Nothing unexpected happened in my case," said Dunaan. Greycat simply nodded.

"What then?" said Laral.

"We must kill the Tiassa," said Greycat.

"If you like," said Dunaan, "I will see to him."

"No," said Greycat. "Leen was an Orca; let Chaler repair the error."

The Orca in question nodded, indicating that he thought this proposal entirely reasonable.

"What next?" said Laral.

Greycat smiled, and, in doing so, showed all of his teeth, which were exceptionally white and fine. "Surely you haven't forgotten," he said.

"Ah, yes," said Laral. "You are to pay us."

"Indeed I am."

"And do you intend to do so?" said Dunaan.

"I will pay you as I promised. And to prove it, here is the money. One purse for each of you. I trust you will find within the agreed-upon amount."

They accepted their fees, after which Laral said, "I will ask once again: what next?"

Greycat shrugged. "Next, we must embarrass Countess Bellor, which will not be difficult, now that the one intendant who knew the true state of the Imperial Treasury is dead."

"Pardon me," said Dunaan, "but I believe you said it would not be difficult."

"That is right," said Greycat.

"Then you have a plan?"

"No," said Greycat. "But I have confidence."

"How, confidence?"

"Yes, good Dunaan. Confidence that, before too much longer, you will have a plan, and a good one, too."

Dunaan nodded. "Very well, then."

"And I?" said Laral.

Greycat nodded. "You must know that Adron e'Kieron, the Duke of Eastmanswatch, is expected to arrive at court within a day or two."

"Yes, I know that."

"As the Dragon Heir, suspicion for these recent murders will naturally fall on him."

"Yes. And you wish me to help this suspicion along? Perhaps by putting a few words into the right ears, and a few clues before the right eyes?"

"On the contrary, Laral. Far from desiring you to increase these suspicions, it is my wish that you will remove them entirely."

"How, remove them?"

"Yes, that is correct."

"That will be more difficult."

"I know a way."

"And that is?"

"By removing Lord Adron."

Laral frowned. "Removing Lord Adron," she said, "will be no easy matter."

"If it were easy, my lady, I wouldn't need to entrust it to one as skilled as you are."

Laral laughed. "You attempt to flatter me, Greycat, but I think there is more truth than flattery in your observation."

"And then?"

"Very well. But the Duke of Eastmanswatch is worth three times as much as an intendant of finance."

"Agreed," said Greycat.

"Agreed," said Laral.

"And," said Dunaan. "What will you be doing?"

"Very little," said Greycat. "Because very little is necessary, just at the moment, to provoke a riot."

"Ah," said Dunaan. "A riot."

"For what purpose?" said Laral.

"You do not need to know that yet," said Greycat.

"Very well," said Laral, who seemed not at all disturbed by this.

"Will we meet again?" said Chaler. "And, if so, when, and where?"

"Let us meet here in four days' time," said Greycat. "That is, on the fourteenth day of the month. And I find this place congenial enough that I do not hesitate to use it again. Moreover, I will be here late at night on the thirteenth as well, should anyone have information to communicate to me. The night of the thirteenth and the early morning of the fourteenth should see—" he paused and smiled, "—certain activity."

"Very well," said Laral. "In four days, Adron e'Kieron will be dead."

"In four days," said Chaler, "Lord Khaavren will be dead."

"In four days," said Dunaan, "Countess Bellor will be discredited."

"And in three days," said Greycat, "this city will see a riot. Small, but, perhaps, a portent of great ones to come."

Dunaan shook his head. "I don't know how you can command a riot, my friend Greycat, but I do not doubt that you can."

"You are right not to doubt," said Greycat.

As he said this, he made a gesture indicating that the meeting was over, and, one by one, the others rose and departed, leaving Greycat alone in the room. He made no move toward leaving, however; rather he sat, utterly motionless, with a look of deep contemplation on his features. After several moments, he stirred and said, "Come over to the table, Grita; I see no reason to pretend I don't know you're there, so there is, you perceive, no reason for you to hide."

"I was not and am not hiding," said Grita, who still spoke from the shadows. "It is merely that I have accustomed myself to being seen as little as possible. You can, I assume, understand the reasons."

Greycat winced at these words, as if he were somehow affected by them. Then he recovered his blank countenance and said, "That's as may be, but please come forward now, for I dislike speaking to someone I can't see; it brings back unpleasant memories." As he said that, he chuckled slightly—a chuckle that would have sent shivers down the back of anyone who heard it and did not have nerves of iron.

Grita emerged from the corner and sat down opposite Greycat. If the reader had thought that her reticence was due to some grotesque aspect of her appearance, we must at this time assure him that nothing could be further from the truth. If Grita was not striking for her beauty, she had, at least, nothing of which to be ashamed. She was of middle years, certainly not more than six hundred, and small, with hair the color of new straw. The lines of her face were pleasing, if slightly sharp, with large eyes and a small nose. Her movements were, perhaps, a little hesitant, but not the less graceful for that. She had, to be sure, a small scar, as from a knife wound, above her left eyebrow, but it was faint, and made her face more interesting, rather than repulsive.

It was only when one looked closely, searching for those clues to identity that we notice almost unconsciously, that one began to be disturbed. She had a distinct noble's point—more visible because she kept her hair cut short and brushed back. If one looked at her cheekbones and her chin, one might think she was a product of the House of the Dzur. Yet the roundness of her eyes gave the lie to this conclusion, and, furthermore, her complexion (which was nearly the color of an unripe olive) and her size spoke of the House of the Tsalmoth.

At this point, the observer would suddenly realize, with horror and pity, that here was one of those unfortunates who, being the product of two Houses, belong to none, and go through life as will a ship that, with neither anchor nor mooring ropes, will be accepted by no harbor, but must instead weather every storm that comes her way as best she can.

It was one of the great shames of society of that period that such people as Grita could, through no fault of their own, be subject to scorn and rejection at every hand. And, we might add, in spite of the wishes of our own Empress, such treatment continues today, only moderately abated by the Edicts on Half-breeds which were signed into law within five years of the Empress taking the Orb.

If, as has been often said, many such people become beggars and criminals, how can this be considered their fault? If because of an excess of love or an insufficiency of precaution in the heat of a moment of passion, a child is born to lovers who cannot marry because one or the other (or both!) were born into the wrong House, surely, wherever the fault lies, it is not with the child. It is one of the marks of the civilized human being to separate the innocent victim from the guilty criminal; those who fail to make such distinctions fail to distinguish themselves from the tribes of Easterners who, to their misfortune, are never able to rise above ignorant prejudice.

And to those who say that such a birth is punishment from the Gods for transgressions in a past life, we say that we will hope for only misfortunes for those who make such claims, thus taking upon themselves the duties of Gods; and we can assure them that, whatever evils plague them, there will be few who show any pity. This historian, for one, will take unashamed delight in telling them that the loss of a loved one, or the collapse of a business, or a crippling or disfiguring injury, is punishment for transgressions in a past life.

Let no one claim to speak for the Gods who does not, in his own hand, hold the power to inflict and remedy that the Gods do. And such persons ought to consider, for their own good, if not from the kindness required of one human being to another, how the Gods will feel about those who dare to take on the attributes of Divine judgment by saying such things.

And yet, to our sorrow, we must confess that through no fault of their own many of these unfortunates do end as criminals, and, in some cases, of the worst sort. Such a one was Grita. We do not know what she was forced to do to live, Houseless and alone, in the Underside, and we will not lower ourselves by speculating, but she carried herself as one who has battled with the worst sides of her fellow creatures and emerged both victorious, in that she survived, and defeated, in that the sense of honor and decency with which we are all endowed at birth had, in her case, been entirely eradicated. Her countenance, as she sat with Greycat, was cool and confident—which says a great deal, because Greycat was one of the more feared denizens of that part of the city.

"We spoke before," said Greycat at last, "about producing a riot."

"That is right," said Grita.

"You still believe you can do it?"

"I can do it."

"How?"

"That is my affair."

Greycat shrugged. "It is my affair as well, because if I put into motion events that require it to take place, and it does not—"

"It will," said Grita.

"Very well. It need not be large. Just enough to—but why are you smiling?"

"Because you speak of a riot of the citizens as if it were a fire that is contained by a stove or a hearth. It is not. It is an open conflagration, and will only go out when all of the timber is consumed."

"And, therefore?"

"I can start a riot; once started, I can neither stop nor control it."

"Do you mean it will consume the city?"

"It may. And it may die almost at once. It may depend on the reaction of one man who sees his child threatened, or one woman who suddenly doesn't care if her shop is destroyed, or one soldier who does or does not strike at a certain time. It may destroy the city, it may turn into nothing. I suspect it will turn into nothing, because the people, while unhappy, are not desperate; while they despise the Emperor, they do not hate him. But I offer no surety. If you wish it done, it will be done, and after that, those boots will be on your feet."

Greycat considered these words carefully for several long moments, after which he said, "Very well. I will accept the risk. Carry out your plan."

"And when do you wish this riot to take place?"

"In three days' time."

"In the evening or the morning?"

"The evening."

"At what hour?"

"How, you can create a riot at a precise time, yet you cannot control it?"

Grita laughed—a laugh, we might add, as chilling as Greycat's chuckle of some few minutes before. "I know when I set off the flashstone; I cannot know what sort of charge it contains."

"Make it, then, at the eleventh hour after noon."

"It will be done. I would suggest that you go into hiding at that time."

"Me? Hide?"

"Where there is fire, there is water."

"Well?"

"Well, cats, I believe, are not overfond of either."

Greycat shrugged. "This cat knows how to use them both."

"For your sake," said Grita, "I hope so."

"Afterwards," said Greycat, "I will see you again."

"Yes," said Grita, looking fully into his face. "Whatever else may happen, that is one thing about which there can be no doubt: you will see me again."

There being no more to say, she stood at that moment, and took herself out of the room, leaving Greycat there alone, to consider what he had begun. For a while, his countenance appeared worried, but gradually, as he considered the details of his scheme, and the reward that awaited him, a small, wicked smile came to his lips.

Presently, he stood, left the small room, left the cabaret, and blended once more into the evening of the Underside of Dragaera City.

# Chapter the Sixth

*Which Treats of the Arrival
Of an Important Dignitary
At the Court.*

WE RETURN (WITH, WE CONFESS, some relief) to the Imperial Palace a mere thirty hours (that is, a day and a night) after we left it. In the intervening time, there has been constant activity amid the offices and secretariats of the Palace; messages have been sent and received, audits have been requested, post officers have been dispatched; but in spite of this, His Majesty's routine has, since the emergency meeting in his bedchamber the day before, been uninterrupted.

Before going on, we hope the reader will permit us to say two words about this routine. It was, first of all, invariant—more than invariant, in fact, it was unchanging. Each morning, he was awakened by the Orb at the seventh hour after midnight. At 7:02 a servant entered, bringing him, in a silver cup decorated with emeralds, klava with six drops of honey and a dash of cinnamon. He permitted himself only eight minutes to drink it, after which he began his morning toilet, finishing with dressing which, for reasons never revealed, he preferred to do himself. These procedures consumed thirty minutes, so that at precisely 7:40 he was ready to greet his ensign—or, rather, his *Captain* of the Guards, who conducted him on his "morning rounds," which consisted of walking by certain doors and commanding them to be opened—the official beginning of the day in the Imperial Palace.

The rounds ended back at his apartments (it was, in fact, because his walk described what was in effect a circle that they were called "the rounds") where, at 8:50, after dismissing the Captain (actually, until today, the Ensign), he broke his fast with klava, this time served in a silver cup decorated with rubies, and without the cinnamon; usually a smoked fish served at room temperature; dark or sour bread which had been toasted over a redwood fire and might have butter or goat's cheese on it; and some form of noodle covered with either goat's cheese or butter—the counterpoint, be it understood, to the bread.

After breaking his fast, he arrived at 10:00 in the Portrait Room, where he was accustomed to meet with any High Lords (meaning Dukes) and Princes (meaning Heirs) who had business with him. In fact, if there were any such, they usually met with Jurabin, who only interrupted His Majesty if it were necessary. The Emperor actually spent this time gossiping with the court gossips and jesting with the court jesters.

Visitors were asked to leave the Portrait Room, and its doors were closed, in time for His Majesty's Hour of Relaxation, which began at 11:45 and continued for an hour and a quarter. During this time, His Majesty might walk, or fence, or read, or even decide to cancel his afternoon appointments and go off to the Imperial Preserve to hunt the athyra, the wild boar, or other such game as might interest him.

Usually, however, the door would be opened at 13:00, and meetings with High Lords and Heirs would continue until the Lunch Hour, 14:15. When the weather was fine, His Majesty would eat his lunch on the terrace immediately adjacent to the Portrait Room (which caused a certain amount of difficulty for the staff, as there was no kitchen nearby); when the weather was poor, His Majesty would dine either in his own apartments, if he wished to be alone, or in the Table Room, if he desired the company of one of the Gentlemen of his Household (those to whom we have earlier referred, ironically but truthfully, as gossips and jesters). In any case, lunch would usually consist of assorted fruits (fresh in the summer and fall, dried in the winter and early spring) and possibly an omelet or some other dish made with hen's eggs, because His Majesty pretended that eating eggs every day was vital to maintaining his health and virility.

After allowing a mere forty-five minutes for lunch—in other words, at exactly noon—His Majesty would be back in the Portrait Room, which would now be open (at least in theory) to anyone who wished to speak with His Majesty on any subject at all. This was, in point of fact, his busiest time, and it was not uncommon for the press of Imperial business to actually impinge upon his banter and conversation with the ladies and gentlemen of the court.

At 1:30 he would retire to the Seven Room, or the Fireside Room, or the Glass Room, to meet privately with anyone Jurabin felt it necessary for him to charm (he could, indeed, be very charming when he put his mind to it), or to learn about the doings of the Empire when it came into his head to take an interest, or to speak with Jurabin if the inclination came upon him. Until fifty years before, this had been his time with the Imperial Discreet, but that post was now empty.

At 3:20, he would meet once again with—we may as well say his name—Khaavren, who would conduct him to the Hall of Windows for dinner, which began promptly at 3:30. Dinner was the largest and the most varied of the meals, and was often attended by guests of state. It was frequently lavish, always well prepared, measured at least six courses, and consumed two and a half hours. Lately, His Majesty had developed the affectation of wanting meals from every area of his realm. On one day the dinner might feature a kethna, roasted in the spicy style of the Eastern Mountains. On another, perhaps there would be anise-jelled winneasaurus steak from the North. On yet another day, perhaps a fish stew from the South.

At 5:45 began the evening recreation, which might involve

cards, or visiting a theater or a concert hall, or even quietly reading in his chambers. Depending on the activity, the Consort might be present; if so, this would be the first time they saw each other that day; if not, they would see each other at 9:15, which was when they had their supper together. Supper was the lightest meal of the day, and would often consist only of delicacies, perhaps preceded by a broth.

At 10:45 he would retire to his baths, often with the Consort, Khaavren, on those occasions when our Tiassa remained late at the Palace, would meet with His Majesty again at 11:55 and conduct him on his evening rounds of closing the doors as he had opened them—more often, Khaavren would delegate this duty to whichever guardsman had performed exceptionally well in some capacity or another. The Consort would sometimes accompany His Majesty on these rounds, which, in any case, would end at His Majesty's apartments at 12:55, which was the time scheduled for his Majesty's evening toilet, which would be completed by 13:10, which was the hour at which His Majesty would retire for the evening.

It is certainly the case that, on some occasions, Her Majesty the Consort, Noima, would accompany His Majesty into his bedchamber, and it is also the case that it is only Khaavren who would know how often this was done. Yet this is one subject upon which the Tiassa has never breathed a word, and so we are left to engage in unseemly speculation, or not. The fact that the Consort was delivered of a child must be held sufficient for our purposes. But we ought to add that, while court gossip was certainly divided about Their Majesties' domestic lives, most of those who held that moments of passion between them were rare and mutually unsatisfying were those who wished to pay court to Her Majesty, and were very likely engaging in the time-honored practice of confusing desire with truth. There were few, we should add, who desired to pay court to Tortaalik, for he furiously objected to any such familiarity, and his flirtations with mistresses were few and short-lived.

The astute reader will, no doubt, notice that, excepting only the briefest of remarks while discussing His Majesty's morning toilet, we have entirely neglected the subject of dress. Our reasons for doing so are twofold: We do not wish to tire the reader with needlessly lengthy descriptions; and the matter has been extensively elaborated upon in numerous scholarly and several popular volumes, not the least of which are Traanier's *Court Dress Before the Interregnum*, belonging to the former category, and the unfortunately named Baron Vile's *The Clothes Unmake the Emperor* belonging to the latter.

For those unfamiliar with these or similar works, we will mention that His Majesty changed his dress no fewer than six nor more than eleven times during the day, but rarely returned to his apartments to do so, rather instructing the chief servant of his household, Dimma, to procure what he wished so that he could duck into any unused room and effect a change in costume. The scandal caused by this Imperious disregard for his own dignity provides the basis for Vile's work mentioned above—a work whose careful attention to detail nearly makes up for the absurdity of its central premise.

Now that we have completed His Majesty's day in general, let us return to its beginning in specific; that is, we will return to 7:40 in the morning, when Khaavren has arrived to escort his Majesty on his rounds, exactly one day after the meeting with Lords Rollondar and Jurabin.

His Majesty stepped forth from his bedchamber. Khaavren bowed, and, although this was his first full day as Captain, he had no thought of changing his usual formulaic greeting to His Majesty, which was a bow made in respectful silence. His Majesty responded with a brusque nod, and Khaavren led the way to the White Stairway, which led to the Inner Door of the Portrait Room, the first door to be opened. As they walked, His Majesty said, "Is there news, Captain?" (It is to His Majesty's credit that, having promoted Khaavren, the Emperor never once forgot and referred to him by his former rank.)

"Yes, Sire."

"How, you say there is news?" (If His Majesty was astonished, it was because he invariably asked this question, and if

Khaavren heard something of interest once in twenty years, it
was very often indeed).

"Yes, Sire."

"Then, something has happened?"

"Indeed, Sire."

"And you know about it?"

"Enough, perhaps, to satisfy Your Majesty's curiosity, if,
indeed, Your Majesty has any."

"I assure you, Captain, I have some, and, moreover, it is
now jumping around in its cage like one of Lord Weer's
trained chreotha."

"Then, Sire, it is just as well that I can satisfy it."

"Do so now, Captain."

"Then, Sire, this is it: A messenger from the Lord Mayor
of Adrilankha awaits Your Majesty on an affair of some urgency."

At this moment, they reached the first door, and His Majesty nodded to the Lord of the Keys, who, at this time, was
a certain Athyra named Lady Ingera. Lady Ingera unlocked
the door and, as it was opened by the servants, she fell into
her accustomed position a step behind Khaavren and the Emperor.

"How," said His Majesty, continuing the conversation.
"The Lord Mayor?"

"Yes, Sire."

"I wonder what he wants."

"I think I know, Sire."

"You think you know?"

"Yes, Sire. In fact, that is the real news which I have for
Your Majesty."

"The real news is the reason?"

"Yes, Sire."

"And you can tell me what it is?"

"Yes, Sire."

"You will do so, then."

"Yes, Sire," said the Captain imperturbably. "I will do so."

"And this very instant, I hope."

"If you wish, Sire."

"If I wish? I think it is an hour since I wished for anything else!"

"Sire, Lord Adron e'Kieron, Duke of Eastmanswatch, and Prince of the House of the Dragon, has arrived at the city gates, and awaits the Lord Mayor's word to be admitted."

"Ah," said His Majesty. "Lord Adron is here."

"Yes, Sire."

His Majesty frowned, and spoke no more while they opened the next several doors. At last he said, "Captain, when you are finished here, if you would be so kind, please convey to the Lord Mayor my desire that His Highness be granted permission to enter the city. I understand that this is not, of course, your office, but if you would. . . ."

"Of course, Sire. I should be honored."

"Thank you, Captain."

"It is my pleasure, Sire."

As this is the only thing of interest to happen until after His Majesty's breakfast, and as we are rigorously opposed to wasting the reader's time with information not essential to the unfolding of the events of our narrative, we will now bring the reader forward in history a few hours, to the time when, in the Portrait Room, Lord Brudik droned, "His Highness the Duke of Eastmanswatch. The Countess of Limterak."

At this announcement, the space in front of the throne was parted as if by the prow of a tri-mast, and into the opening, walking as if he had never belonged anywhere else, came Adron e'Kieron and his daughter, Aliera e'Kieron.

Lord Adron had eschewed his identity as Duke of Eastmanswatch and even his identity as Prince of the House of the Dragon, appearing simply as a Dragonlord, clothed in black garments with silver trim—garments that fell barely short of appearing to be a uniform. But, let us recall, Adron was not only the Heir of the House of the Dragon, he was scion of the e'Kieron line—which meant that he could trace his lineage back directly to Kieron the Conqueror; that is, to the man who, if anyone did, fathered the Empire itself by gathering the disparate hordes into the world's first actual army. Looking at Lord Adron, one could imagine his fore-bear.

Adron was, at this time, past his thousandth year, and he was well known for his Breath of Fire Battalion, which had won its name in the Kanefthali Mountains, and proved its worth again in the War of Three Sieges, as well as in what is today called the Whitecrest Uprising, but was then referred to as "the unpleasantness along the coast."

Khaavren, observing him enter from his (that is, Khaavren's) place to the immediate left of His Majesty's chair, noticed that Adron's hair, in contradiction of Kathana e'Marish'Chala's portrait that hung in the Dragon Wing, was, in fact, thin on top, and it was so light in color that it almost appeared that he was losing it, like an Easterner, making Khaavren wonder with what sorts of spells His Highness had endeavored to keep his hair, or if, in fact, His Highness didn't care or hadn't noticed. Moving from Adron's hair, however, it seemed to Khaavren that, over the years, Adron's face had become even narrower, his jawline sharper and more pro-nounced, his lips thinner, and his shocking blue eyes colder and more distant.

Khaavren, no mean observer, would have, no doubt, no-ticed more about him, if he had not at that moment been dis-tracted by his first sight of Adron's daughter, Aliera e'Kieron, which sight affected him so profoundly that, for a moment, he quite forgot where he was, and nearly started forward in order to get a better look. Aliera had, at this time, passed her five hundredth year, yet to look at her, one would have thought her scarcely a hundred. Lest the reader think this an exaggeration, it may be pointed out that scholars, both of that time and of to-day, have proposed the most outlandish theo-ries to account for her apparent agelessness, such as the re-cent contention of the Baroness Fernway that Aliera had been held "loosely in space, but tightly in time" by a benevolent Goddess (naming, it should be added, a Goddess not known for benevolence).

But whatever reason we assign for her remarkably youthful appearance, we need go no further than any book of poetry written by any court poet of the time to find descriptions of her beauty. She has been, by various of these, compared to the glitter of torches reflected off the icicles that hang from Dynnep's Tower at midwinter; to the turning of the leaves of the plover tree in at least four different stages; to the gentle flow of Berrin's Creek; to the roar of the ocean in the Straits of Kurloc; to the stillness of the night in the Desert of Suntra; to the majesty of the Kanefthali Mountains; to the—well, in short, to every facet of nature that anyone has at some time or another thought beautiful.

We will not attempt to duplicate or better the work of the poets; we will only give the reader enough of a sketch to allow him to visualize the lady in question, wherefore we will mention that she was extremely short, sturdy without a trace of heaviness, had the blonde hair that is exceedingly rare in the House of the Dragon, the long narrow face that is associated with the House (but softened by delicate lines about her eyes, which eyes, we should add, were green or blue), and she had something like her father's chin without Adron's extreme sharpness. She kept her hair long and straight, brushed back so that her noble's point was prominently displayed. She wore a costume that was the match of her father's, and her only decorations were a medallion with a dragon's head, displaying a blue gem and a green gem for the eyes, and a fine silver belt such as one might hang a sword from, although, of course, only guardsmen could be armed in the presence of the Emperor.

As for her character, much less was known, and we consider it a sad comment on those court poets we have just had the honor to quote that they seemed utterly indifferent to this omission, as if Aliera's physical perfection were so great that it overshadowed any other concern. Yet she was known to be proud, quick-tempered, and impatient with anyone who denied her what she wanted. It is perhaps to her credit that she never cared, when annoyed, whether the individual who incurred her wrath was her social superior, inferior, or equal.

As to other aspects of her personality, we hope the reader will content himself with allowing these to be revealed by the progression of events that our history will unfold; for our purposes, we believe it is sufficient to say that Khaavren was, for a moment, caught off his guard, and had there been, at that moment, any threat to His Majesty, our Captain would certainly have failed in his duty.

But, in the lack of any such threat, Khaavren, after a moment, returned to himself, tore his eyes away from Aliera, and resumed his passive study of the room. Adron, meanwhile, said, "Sire, I beg Your Majesty's permission to present my daughter, Aliera e'Kieron, Countess of Limterak."

His Majesty bowed his head, while, to the delight of the court gossips, the Orb turned to a blue so light it was almost white—a color that indicated His Majesty was holding his emotions sharply in check. Several courtiers looked around to see if the Consort were there, but she was not present. Khaavren, though his quick eyes noticed His Majesty's reaction, noticed still more that Jurabin, who stood at His Majesty's left elbow, took some few moments to recover his composure.

His Majesty inclined his head, first to Adron, then Aliera, and then said, "We are pleased to welcome you to Dragaera, Your Highness."

"Thanks, Sire."

"And how are matters on your estates?"

"Peaceful, Sire."

"We are pleased to hear it."

Jurabin, at this point, leaned over to whisper into His Majesty's ear. The Emperor listened attentively for a long moment, then frowned, turned to Adron and said sternly, "Peaceful, you say?"

"Entirely, Sire," said Adron, who appeared completely indifferent to whatever the Prime Minister might have whispered to His Majesty.

"Then it is not true, the reports we have heard of wanton destruction by brigands of Your Highness's own game?"

"Game, Sire? Dare I ask Your Majesty to what game he refers?"

"I refer, Your Highness, to wolves."

"Wolves, Sire? In the mountains, wolves are sometimes considered dangers, and often pests, but are rarely game."

The Orb darkened and, with it, His Majesty's countenance. "Dare you address sarcasm to your liege?"

"Not the least in the world, Sire," said Adron so coolly that Khaavren was suddenly reminded of Aerich, which, in turn, reminded him of the warm feelings that had existed between Adron and the four friends so many years before.

"I could not help but notice," continued His Majesty after a moment, "that you use the phrase, 'are considered.'"

"Yes, Sire? And does not Your Majesty think it a fine phrase?"

"No, I do not. For it is very passive, and my preference is for more active phrasings."

"If Your Majesty would condescend to explain—"

"I mean that you say nothing about who does the considering."

"Ah. Well, Sire, I consider wolves in the way in which I have already had the honor to mention, and so do all who live among them."

"All? Does Your Highness, then, refer to peasants?"

Adron appeared to shrug without actually moving. "Peasants, yes, Sire, and others."

"But do not the wolves belong to you?"

"Yes, Sire, they do."

"And yet you countenance their destruction by peasants?"

"Sire, it is my opinion that if the wolves are allowed to destroy the little livestock the peasants possess, the peasants will hardly be able to render unto me my portion."

"And how long has Your Highness held this opinion?"

"How long, Sire?"

"Yes. I ask because word has come to us that you attempted to stop the slaughter of the wolves until the rising of peasants against them became too widespread for you to contain."

Once again, from where Khaavren stood, it seemed that Adron shrugged without actually moving. "There is," he said, "some truth in that, Sire, in that I preferred a wholesale slaughter of wolves, who destroy livestock, to a wholesale slaughter of peasants, who raise livestock."

"This is, then," said His Majesty, "what you mean by peaceful? That you, liege of one of the most important estates in the Empire, are unable to control your own peasants?"

"If Your Majesty will permit me to say so," said Adron, "there is a large step between the slaughter of my wolves and the slaughter of my person and retainers."

Khaavren glanced at Aliera, and remarked to himself, "She has some distance to travel before she learns to keep her emotions from her face; if thoughts were deeds, I should at once arrest her for attempted regicide." His Majesty, it should be noted, was doing scarcely better—he was plainly impatient with the answers Adron was giving him, and the Orb was not only giving off a reddish hue, but was moving about His Majesty's head at a noticeably faster pace—an infallible indication that the Emperor was agitated. "Perhaps," thought Khaavren, "I shall be called upon to arrest him. Well, if the order is given, I shall certainly carry it off without argument; for this Duke, Dragonlord though he is, ought to know better than to annoy His Majesty."

But no such order was given, at least yet. Instead, His Majesty burst out with, "And what, Eastmanswatch, of the reports I am hearing that you have dabbled in the sorcery of the ancients, that which was declared illegal at the beginning of the Empire?"

This charge seemed to catch His Highness by surprise, for his brows rose and his eyes widened. But he recovered himself quickly and said, "Sire, anyone who knows me at all could assure Your Majesty that such reports can only be lies."

"Indeed?" said His Majesty haughtily.

"Yes, Sire. As everyone knows, I never dabble."

There was something like a simultaneous gasp from the assembled courtiers; at the same time the color of the Orb darkened still more, and His Majesty, normally pale, darkened as if he wished to match it. He visibly trembled for a moment, sputtered, then croaked out, "This interview is at an end. Leave us."

"Yes, Sire," said Adron, and bowed, stepped back, and walked toward the door, his daughter matching his paces. Khaavren was taken with a desire to applaud, but restrained himself, and instead looked at His Majesty to see if the latter should give the order for the arrest of the man who had so annoyed him—which order, for a moment, to judge by the way His Majesty caught the Captain's eye; and by the corners of His Majesty's mouth, which trembled with agitation; and by the edges of His Majesty's eyes, which deformed his face with their squinting; and by the set of His Majesty's jaw, which nearly made Khaavren's ache to watch—which order, we say, it seemed the Emperor might be about to give; but the moment passed and His Majesty relaxed into his chair, while an inaudible sigh seemed to extend out from the throne to be picked up by each of the assembled courtiers, who then turned to watch the retreating backs of the two Dragonlords as they passed the guards and the doorway, and retreated into the comparative safety of the world outside of the Portrait Room.

His Majesty, meanwhile, after making a sign to Khaavren, rose so quickly that the courtiers scarcely had time to stand before he made his way out of the room through the hastily opened Mirrored Doors, the Captain at his heels.

"Sir Khaavren," said the Emperor as he traversed the long corridor.

"Yes, Sire," said Khaavren, matching his pace.

"He did not deny the charge."

"That is true, Sire."

"In fact, he all but boasted of his guilt."

"That is also true, Sire."

"And before the court!"

"Yes, Sire."

"Arrest him, then. We will see if he will give us an honest answer when the Orb is over his head. Practicing elder sorcery is punishable by death."

"Very well, Sire."

They walked a few more paces, bringing them to the foot

of the gently curving stairway of green marble that led up to the Seven Room. As they climbed, the Emperor said, "Well?"

. "Yes, Sire?"

"I nearly think I gave you an order."

"There is certainly no question about that, Sire."

"Well, is there a question about something else?"

"Sire, there is a question I would put, if Your Majesty will permit me."

The Emperor stopped just outside the door to the Seven Room. "Very well," he said.

"I would guess," said Khaavren, "that Your Majesty knew something about this already, before you questioned the Duke about it, else why would Your Majesty have brought the subject up?"

"Well?"      ·

"Well, Sire, I wonder why it is that Adron has not been arrested already."

"Why? Because he is the Dragon Heir, and his arrest would precipitate—" Tortaalik stopped in mid-sentence, and frowned.

"Yes, Sire?" said Khaavren.

"If he proves to be innocent," the Emperor began again, "to have arrested him would . . ." His voice trailed off, and he seemed, for a long moment, to be lost in thought.

"And," continued Khaavren, "if he is guilty?"

His Majesty stared angrily at the Captain, then took a long, slow breath. "If he is guilty, his arrest will precipitate chaos among the representatives of the Houses, and would delay the decision as to the allotment of Imperial funds." His frown deepened. "He plays a dangerous game, Captain."

"Yes, Sire. And the order for his arrest?"

"I withdraw it. For now."

"Yes, Sire."

His Majesty looked shrewdly at Khaavren. "Thirty hours have changed you," he remarked.

"Sire?" said the Captain, affecting a surprised expression.

"Yester-day, you would not have been so bold as to question my orders."

Khaavren bowed. "Yester-day, Sire, it was not my duty to do so."

The Emperor nodded slowly, then leaned against the door of the Seven Room and closed his eyes, as if he were suddenly very tired. "Do you know, Captain," he said softly, "that it is assumed by those learnéd in history that Emperors of my House will become, toward the end of their Reign, weak-willed, or addled, or silly, or power-mad, or that we will neglect the Empire, giving over our responsibilities in a quest for pleasures of the moment?"

"I have heard this said, Sire."

Tortaalik nodded. "So have I. All my life. And from the moment I took the Orb, I vowed that none of these things would happen to me. I have tried to keep my desires in check, and to find trustworthy retainers for all positions of importance, and to keep a close watch on my temper. And yet, Captain, at times like this, I feel that I am overwhelmed by my destiny; it is as if there were hidden forces that try to pull me into the abyss."

Khaavren looked at his master, as if seeing him for the first time, and, in a sudden return of the youthful loyalty that had been all but eradicated by the heartless years, dropped to his knee, took His Majesty's smooth, manicured hand into his own sword-callused one, and said, "Sire, only the fates know the final outcome of the battle, but surely there is glory in knowing one has not surrendered, and surely there is comfort in knowing one is not alone."

The Emperor nodded, and the Orb turned to a soft, gentle green as he straightened his back. "Yes," he said. "That is a kind of glory, and that is surely a comfort." Tortaalik indicated by a gentle pressure that Khaavren should rise. "Come, Captain. Go you and find Jurabin, and tell him that I wish to see him."

Khaavren stood, bowed, and turned hastily away, so that His Majesty wouldn't see the emotion that erupted unbidden in the soldier's eyes.

# Chapter the Seventh

*Which Treats of Our Old Friend Pel,
And His Recent Activities
Regarding Information, Deduction,
And Coercion.*

As KHAAVREN LEFT THE SEVEN Room, his old friend Pel, now called Galstan (although we, like Khaavren, will continue to call him Pel), sat on a large, amber cushion in a room some half a league distant, yet still within the Palace. This room was not overly large, and boasted two small but perfectly square windows, one looking out at the rounded towers of the dark and mysterious Athyra Wing to the north, the other looking out upon a walled terrace which enclosed a neat little flower garden, some distance below. The room was furnished with a plain bed, a simple writing table and chair, a bookshelf that occupied an entire wall and was filled with works on the history and philosophy of Discretion, the amber cushion we have already had occasion to mention, and a comfortable if unornamented chair against the wall facing the center of the room.

Pel was, we should mention at once, not alone; with him was the room's tenant—a handsome woman of middle years and dark complexion who wore the colors and features of the House of the Athyra and was addressed as "Your Discretion" and called only by the name Erna. Also with them was a pale young man (he had, to judge from appearances, scarcely seen his two hundredth year) in the brown and yellow of the House of the Jhegaala. His name was Lysek.

Erna was staring idly out one of the windows, seemingly indifferent to the conversation, or, rather, the interrogation Pel was conducting with Lysek. Pel's countenance was stern; Lysek's features were set in a stubborn expression.

"You must understand," said Pel in a tone of both patience and firmness, "that you are neither the first, nor the second, to come to us with such a request."

Lysek watched the Yendi, but made no rejoinder.

"Furthermore," said Pel, "you are neither the first, nor the second, to make the request for the same reason you proffer."

Lysek started slightly. "Reason?" he said. "You pretend to know—"

"Here now," said Pel. "Let there be none of this. You come to us, asking us to betray Confidence—which you ought to know we cannot do—in matters that concern personalities of the court, and you do not expect us to realize that there is only one lady who inspires such desperate measures?"

"I—"

"Are you aware that it is an Imperial crime to even ask us to betray such secrets?"

"You do not know—"

"What you are offering in exchange? No, I do not. Nor, young man, do I wish to know, for, in truth, I am weak, and can be tempted. That is why, when you asked to see me, I asked Erna, the head of my Order, to be here as witness, to keep me from such an error."

Lysek scowled and looked at the floor. Erna continued staring out the window, taking no part whatever in the conversation.

Lysek took a deep breath. "I have learned—"

"And yet you persist," said Pel.

"—of that which will cause the Empire itself to tremble, and within a space of hours. In exchange for this information, I merely wish to learn—"

"Bah!" said Pel, and rose to his feet. "There is no need to hear this, I know already, for your countenance betrays you as surely as if you shouted your desire through the halls of the Palace. You doubt me? Then attend: You want to know certain details about a certain highborn lady's personal life. You have seen her from afar, and though you were in the crowd or at a distance, you know that she looked at you, and you fell in love with her, and you are certain she loves you too, only you don't know how to arrange a rendezvous with her, and you wish to learn—"

"But this is impossible!" cried Lysek, who sprang to his feet, and whose voice trembled with emotion.

"Not in the least," said Pel. "Moreover, you have heard that we will exchange such information for other information. Where you heard this, I cannot say, but I know that such rumors abound. But there is no truth to them, and, to prove it, I will summon the Guard and cause you to be arrested for so much as asking us." With this, Pel turned and began walking toward the door.

"Bide," said Erna.

Pel turned back, a look of surprise on his countenance. "Yes, Discretion?"

"Well, I wish to hear him."

"Your Discretion wishes to hear him?"

"Yes, for I am curious."

"And yet—"

"Come, no arguments. We shall betray nothing."

"Well," said the Yendi, "if we betray nothing, why should he tell us what he pretends to know?"

"He will tell us," said Erna, "to keep us from summoning the Guard, as you were, in fact, about to do, were you not?"

"Indeed I was," said Pel. "So much so, in fact, that I am about to do so again."

"No, I wish to hear his story."

"But I," said Lysek, "will tell you nothing unless you tell me that which I wish to know."

Erna looked at him briefly, then shrugged. "You are right," she said to Pel. "He is useless. Summon the Guard."

Pel nodded, and walked to the door. He was, in fact, through it and into the hall before Lysek, still on his feet, cried, "Wait!"

Pel stepped back into the room. "Yes?" he said, in his melodious voice.

The Jhegaala sat down heavily. "Very well," he said. "I'll tell you what I know, and you may tell me, or not tell me, what you wish."

Pel caught Erna's eye, and they exchanged a look of satisfaction, "Speak, then," said Pel.

"I shall. But remember, this is for your ears; for you to act on as you see fit. The information I bring you is known to perhaps two others in the City, and yet it is of such import that His Majesty would tremble to learn of it."

"We will remember," said Pel. "Now tell us what you know."

"There is to be a riot in the city," said Lysek.

"A riot?" said Pel.

"Exactly. And within the week at that."

"Impossible," said Erna. "One cannot know when a riot will occur."

"Allow me," said Pel, "to disagree with Your Discretion on this."

"How, you think it possible?"

"At least," said Pel, "I wish to hear more."

"There is," said Lysek, "little more to tell. Someone is planning to start a riot, and seems convinced that she can do so."

"For what reason?" said Erna.

"That," said Lysek, "I cannot tell you."

"Then," said Pel, "tell us how you have discovered this infamous plot."

"You wish to know how I discovered it?"

"Yes, exactly," said Pel.

"Then I shall tell you. It was this way: You must know that I am employed at the Tricolor Theater, on the Street of the Curios."

"I know the theater," said Pel. "In what capacity are you employed?"

"It is my responsibility to keep the costumes clean and in repair, and especially all of the footwear of the actors."

"The footwear?"

"Yes. You perceive, it is important to the safety of the actors that their footwear remain clean."

"Well, I understand that, only what I fail to understand is how the footwear of the actors—and the footwear especially—becomes so soiled that a specialist is required to clean them."

"You say," said Lysek, "that you are familiar with our theater."

"Indeed yes."

"But have you ever seen a performance?"

"No," said Pel, "I must confess that I have not."

"Well, we specialize in the farcical costume dramas of the Late Fifteenth Cycle, which have never lost popularity, testifying to their quality by the only meaningful measure."

"Well," said the Yendi, who chose not to comment on this method of measuring artistic worth. "Go on."

"I am doing so. These dramas invariably feature a character, most often played by either Sir Crowlin or Lady Neftha, who takes the rôle of the villain."

"I understand that there is a villain," said Pel.

"Well, then, you understand that, for the drama to be successful, the audience must hate the villain."

"That is," said Pel, "the usual rôle of a villain in the theater."

"Well, it is customary for the audiences at our theater to express their dislike of the villain in certain ways—ways that, I must say, are so vital a part of our performances and our reputation, that I have often suspected they account for our continued success."

"And that way is?" said Pel.

"By pelting the villain with whatever vegetable matter they have brought for that purpose."

"And so?"

"And so, by the end of a performance, not only is the stage filled with such matter, but all of the actors' footwear is covered with it. If the footwear were not cleaned, why, a performance could hardly go by without someone slipping and hurting himself. There are others who clean the stage after each performance, but it is my task to ensure that the villain's costume is clean, and, moreover, that there is nothing slippery on the boots, shoes, and sandals that are to be used in the next show."

"And therefore, you spend your time cleaning rotten vegetables from the bottom of shoes."

"That is exactly the case," said Lysek.

"Well, if you will pardon me, it does not seem to be an enjoyable pastime."

"Oh, it is not, I assure you."

"It is, in fact, odious?"

"Odious is the very word I should use to describe it."

"But at least," said Pel, "the pay is good."

"On the contrary, the pay is so poor, I can scarcely live from one day to the next. I sleep in the theater, and if the actors did not, from time to time, take pity on me by allowing me the leavings of their meals, I should be perpetually weak from hunger."

"Well then, do you hope to someday rise to better position in the theater?"

"Hardly," said Lysek. "I have been given to understand that this is the only rôle to which I can ever aspire."

Pel frowned. "Well, then, why don't you find another position?"

"How?" said Lysek, amazed. "Impossible. I live for the theater."

Pel saw nothing to be gained by continuing this line of questioning, wherefore he said, "Very well, then, I understand that you were at the theater. What then?"

"Well, you must understand that, while the play is being performed, I am at liberty to watch it from a vantage point off in the wings."

"Yes, yes, I understand that."

"And from this position, I can see a portion of the audience, especially the boxes where the nobility sit."

"Yes, and?"

"Well, and that is where I saw her, just yester-day."

"How, yester-day? But the Consort did not leave the Palace yester-day."

"The Consort?" said Lysek, puzzled. "Who spoke of the Consort?"

"But," said Pel, "if not the Consort, whom did you see?"

"Whom did I see? Who else could create such an impression on the heart but the Lady Aliera?"

"What? She is in the city?"

"Well, she was masked, and so had not arrived as far as formalities are concerned, but it was she, nevertheless."

"You are certain?"

"Certain? Yes, for I had seen the portrait by Kathana that hangs in the Pavilion of the Dragon, near the theater. And, as you will soon learn, there was additional proof."

Pel exchanged a look with Erna, who (the reader may have noticed) had not spoken in some time. Erna still remained mute, and Pel continued.

"Well, then, you saw her."

"Yes. And, furthermore, she saw me, and I knew that the Gods had meant—"

"Yes, yes, I understand what you knew. But permit me to remind you that you were going to explain how you came to hear of this riot."

"Well, yes, and I am doing so."

"Continue then."

"When the show was over, I could not bear to let her out of my sight, while, on her part, though she remained discreet, she turned her head in such a way that I knew I was to follow her."

"You knew this?"

"Have I not said so?"

Pel and Erna exchanged another look, after which Pel said, "Go on, then. You followed her."

"Yes. She and another—I believe her father—"

"The Duke of Eastmanswatch?"

"Yes. They climbed into a coach. I—"

"Stay. Did the coach bear any arms?"

"Yes, on the side I could see, it bore the arms of Eastmanswatch, and, in back, was the e'Kieron sigil of the Dragon's head with blue and green gems for the eyes."

"You are observant," said Pel.

"I was, you perceive, fascinated by the spectacle."

"Very well. Go on."

"When they entered the coach, I sought for another, but there was none in sight."

"Very well, there was none in sight."

"I then began to follow it on foot."

"On foot?"

"It was not difficult at first, for the street was still crowded with those who had left the theater."

"I understand that. But later?"

"Later it became more difficult."

"Well?"

"Soon they reached Crier's Circle, and from there took the Paved Road toward the Gate of the Seven Flags, or else the Dragon Gate, which are, you perceive, near each other."

"I have seen the city," remarked Pel ironically.

"Yes," said Lysek, slightly flustered.

"Continue," said Pel.

Lysek nodded and said, "On the Paved Road they began to move more quickly—so quickly, in fact, that I could not keep up. But the thought came to me that the Paved Road makes a long circle to the Wingéd Bridge, whereas I could go directly by way of the Toehold Bridge, and perhaps I would be at the gate before them."

"Well, and was this thought a good one?"

"I don't know," said Lysek, "because I never made it as far as the bridge."

"How, you did not?"

"No. I made my plan, as I said, in Crier's Circle, and therefore I set out by the most direct route toward the Toehold Bridge. This route required that I reach the alley between the circle and the Street of the Fishmarket, which I did by stepping through a tanner's booth that stood open and unoccupied."

"Well?" said the Yendi.

"Well, I had not taken three steps before I overheard someone pronounce the following words: 'There they go—Adron and his daughter. Do you observe the Eastmanswatch crest on the side?"

"You heard this, you say?"

"Yes, from someone who was just on the other side and not five feet away from me, although concealed by the wall of the booth."

"So you stopped?"

"The Horse! I nearly think I did!"

"And?"

"They were not aware of my presence, for they continued talking freely, albeit in low tones. The one who had spoken seemed to be a woman, and, as I listened, she said, 'You must mark that device, for the passing of that very coach will be your signal.' To which the other, in a masculine voice, said, 'Well, I have seen it, I will remember it.' You can imagine how this conversation intrigued me."

"I can more than imagine it," said Pel. "I confess that I am nearly as intrigued now as you must have been when it occurred, wherefore I am even now impatiently awaiting your return to the narrative."

"Then I shall resume," said Lysek. "The man continued, 'But what if the coach does not pass?' to which the woman replied, 'In fact, if all goes according to plan, it will not pass, wherefore you will take as a signal the sound of the Old Tower Bell ringing the eleventh hour, which cannot fail to occur after dark.' 'I understand,' said the first. 'I am to look, first, for the passing of Adron's coach, and, failing that, listen for the eleventh hour on the Old Tower Bell.' 'Exactly,' said the woman. 'But,' said the man, 'I understand that if Lord Adron's coach is passing in parade, there will necessarily be soldiers; but if it is not, how am I to find soldiers with which to instigate the riot you require?' "

"Ah," interrupted Pel. "He spoke the word 'riot.' "

"Yes," said Lysek. "And, moreover, she didn't contradict him, as you will see."

"Go on, then," said Pel. "I am listening."

"The answer," said Lysek, "came in this form: The woman said, 'In the place we have selected, there will always be Guards, for it is on the very edge of the Underside, yet not within, and it is a well-traveled square, all of which cause it to be watched carefully by the police. At the eleventh hour, in particular, you will not fail to find two or three guardsmen, who should be enough to set off the disturbance.' 'Very well,' said the other. 'I understand.' 'Good,' said the woman. 'But,' said the man, 'when shall we meet when all is over?' 'In this very spot, the next day, if it is possible.' 'Then all is settled.' said the man. 'Then here is the purse.' 'And here is my hand.' 'Until then.' 'Until then.'

"And that," concluded Lysek, "was the end of the conversation."

"Did you see either of them?"

Lysek shook his head. "I came back around the corner, but they had already left. I realized that I had missed the chance to follow Aliera, but it came to my mind that I had valuable information, which I could trade for learning how I might have a chance to meet the lady, and I had heard that here, in the Academy of Discretion, information could be traded."

"You were misinformed," said Pel.

"So I perceive."

"Nevertheless—" said Erna.

Pel turned to the chief of his Order with an expression of some surprise.

"Yes?" said Lysek cautiously. "Nevertheless?"

"Nevertheless, we may be able to be of some help to you."

Pel frowned and bit his lip, but said nothing.

"I assure you," said Lysek, "that my attention is fully concentrated upon the words you are about to speak."

"You are, then, listening?"

"To nothing else."

"Well, then, it seems to me that there may be a way for you to meet the Lady Aliera."

Lysek nodded his head—perhaps unwilling to trust himself to speak, but he watched Erna's mouth with the intensity of a hound watching the soup bone in his master's hand.

"If you should leave by the Gate of the Dragon, and continue on that road for half a league, you will come to a wide road leading to the south and slightly east. If you take that road for two leagues, or perhaps a little less, you will see on your right a small house marked by a whitish stone, like a tusk, sticking out of the ground. Bear to the east, then, on a horse-path through the grove of trees you will see, and soon you will come upon the encampment of the Duke of Eastmanswatch, where you can, if you wish, ask for Aliera."

Lysek bowed his head, and, without another word, turned toward the door. He was, it should be noted, nearly running by the time he reached it.

Pel seated himself in the chair the Jhegaala had lately occupied and steepled his hands, assuming an air of contemplation. Erna said, "Well, you disapprove?"

Pel blinked and focused on her. "I? It is hardly my place to approve or disapprove of Your Discretion's actions."

"That is true, Galstan; I am pleased that you remember it."

"I could never forget, Discretion."

"We did well with the poor fool, Galstan."

"Yes, Your Discretion, we were successful once more."

"Once more, Galstan? You say that as if there were some doubt."

"It is a risky game, Discretion."

"But worth the risk, Galstan."

"As Your Discretion says."

She fell silent, then nodded brusquely, as if having reached a conclusion. "It is good you called me, Galstan, for this is certainly worthwhile to know."

"You think so?"

"Yes. Do you agree?"

"I more than agree, I concur. Yet I wonder what what be the correct steps to take."

"You need not concern yourself; I will consider the matter, and decide what is to be done about this forthcoming riot."

"Riot?"

Erna looked sharply at the Yendi. "Yes, riot. What, did you not hear him?"

"Yes, yes, I heard him. If Your Discretion will pardon my lapse, my mind was wandering."

"And?"

"And I assure Your Discretion I will not concern myself with this riot, but leave all matters pertaining to it entirely in Your Discretion's hands."

"That would be best," said Erna. "Leave me now, for I must consider the matter."

Pel rose, and bowed in the manner of his Order, with fists pressed together before his breast. Erna nodded briefly, and Pel left Erna's chamber and took the familiar route to his own—which in appearance and furnishing was nearly identical to Erna's, save for three factors: In the first place it was somewhat smaller; in the second place there was only one window, and that looked out upon the private garden of the Institute; and in the third place there was, in addition to the symbol of the Institute which graced one wall, a long rapier hanging by pegs on another.

Pel wasted no time, but sat down at the writing table, the twin to the one in Erna's room, and set before himself paper, quill, ink-pot, and blotter. With these he set to work composing two letters, the texts of which we are fortunate to be able to reproduce in full.

For the first, he wrote in a broad, careful hand, as of one accustomed to making sure that, above all, not a character will be lost. At the top, he wrote the date: "The twelfth day of the Month of the Vallista, in the 532$^{nd}$ year of the Glorious Reign of his Majesty Tortaalik I." We mention this because the reader may not remember that it was, in fact, only the eleventh day of the month.

This done, Pel continued in this fashion:

Lord Adron e'Kieron
Duke of Eastmanswatch
Dragon Heir, etc. etc.
Your Highness:

My Master, Calvor of Drem, has been informed that
you are to be among those who will speak at the ceremony to open the Pavilion of Kieron tomorrow. My
Master wishes you to understand that he feels greatly
honored to be allowed to appear before you, and that, in
your honor, he intends to read from his most recent
poem, "Morning in the Mountains," which has been so
well received here in the city.

My Master anticipates a splendid evening of entertainment, and looks forward to the chance to meet you in
person.

Until then, Your Highness.
I Remain,
Your Servant,
Dri, Scribe of Calvor,
Poet of the Streets.

This done, Pel sealed the letter and addressed it, then set it
aside to await the morrow; after this, Pel sat down once more,
with yet another sheet of paper. This time, when he wrote, it
was in a hand small, fine, and elegant. And, to be sure, he
used the actual date.

My Dear Temma [wrote Pel]: There can be no doubt
that our old friend, Adron, stands in danger of imminent
assassination. My reasons for believing this are sufficient to convince me, and my conviction will, I dare to
hope, be sufficient to convince you; yet I do not believe
these reasons are enough to convince the authorities (including, I must confess, our old friend Khaavren, who is
involved in investigating certain conspiracies and assassinations which have lately erupted about the Palace).

I am considering the question of appealing directly to
Adron, yet Dragonlords are often stubborn and foolish

with regard to their own lives, and, moreover, I have no clue about how or when the attempt is to be made. Or, to be more precise, I believe I have already foiled one attempt, but there can be no doubt that there will be another, and I am entirely ignorant of the form it will take.

In short, then, I am at a loss. And you should know, my friend Aerich (for so I continue to think of you) that whenever my thoughts are confused, I still, as I used, look about to see where you might be, for a word of advice from you is more valuable than all the tomes in the Zerika Library. Thus I write once more, hoping you will be able, from a distance, to give me the counsel that will allow me to see clearly what I ought to do.

I remain, old friend, your affectionate Galstan (Pel)

When he had completed the letter, he read it over carefully, then, with equal care, folded it, sealed it, and put Aerich's address on the outside, after which he summoned a page to deliver it to the post with instructions that it be sent to the Duke of Arylle with as little delay as possible, accompanying his request with a quantity of silver, and the promise of a like amount if an answer were returned within three days.

Then, convinced that he had done everything possible, he sat down in his chair, and thought deeply about the many things he had learned that day.

# Chapter the Eighth

**Which Treats of Sethra Lavode,**
**The Enchantress of Dzur Mountain,**
**On the Occasion of Her Arrival**
**At the Imperial Palace.**

ONE MIGHT THINK THAT His Majesty, after the meeting with Adron e'Kieron, deserved an interval of peace, quiet, and relaxation to recover from the ordeal; His Majesty was certainly of this opinion. Tortaalik was, then, not inclined to be gracious when Khaavren suddenly appeared before him near the end of his lunch and whispered, "Your presence is required, Sire." In fact, the Emperor was so distraught that he let go with a string of oaths sufficient to fill Khaavren, who had dwelt for five hundred years among troopers, with admiration.

When His Majesty's utterance of invective had reached its end, rather as a desert wash, after a sudden storm has spent itself, at last surrenders its torrent into the arid ground, he said wearily, "Well, what is it, then?"

"Sethra Lavode desires to be announced, Sire."

"What, here?" cried His Majesty, while the Orb, which had just begun to fade from its deep red, became positively purple.

"That is to say, yes and no, Sire. If by 'here' Your Majesty means this very dining room, then no. But if Your Majesty indicates with this word the Imperial Palace, then I am forced to say that she is, indeed, here."

"Impossible!"

"Sire?"

"The message can hardly have reached her yet."

"That may be, Sire; nevertheless, she is here."

His Majesty looked down at his plate, where a few lonely fish bones were floating in a sea of butter and lemon. He then wiped his lips on his sleeve and said, "I must change my dress."

"Of a certainty, Sire."

"Where is Dimma?"

"I am here, Sire," said the obsequious Teckla. "I have both your Afternoon Military and your Afternoon Imperial, with belt and scarf but no robe."

"Hmph. Military."

"Yes, Sire."

Khaavren stepped out of the room for the few moments it took His Majesty to alter his appearance. When the Emperor emerged, he wore knee-length shiny black boots, black hose, a dress sword hanging from a belt of gold chain, burgundy-colored split shirt with ridges forming a long "V" from collar to mid-chest, and a gold scarf around his neck. Such dress, while hiding his handsome calves, accented his graceful neck and proud head, and thus suited the Emperor admirably—garbed in this manner there were few cavaliers who could contend with His Majesty in appearance.

The change of costume seemed, as it often did, to have restored His Majesty's humor. He nodded to Khaavren and said, "It is too early to return to the Portrait Room, and I will not throw my schedule into more confusion than necessary. Dimma, cause her to be brought to me in the West Fireside room."

"Yes, Sire. Shall we light the fire?"

"No."

"Refreshment?"

"Wine. Something full and red." His face twitched into a

brief smile. "Make it a Khaav'n," he said, "in honor of our Captain."

"Yes, Sire."

Khaavren listened to this discourse without changing expression, then followed His Majesty down to the level of the Portrait Room, past the Hall of Flowers, and so into the West Fireside room. On the way, he caught the eye of a passing guardsman, and without a word being exchanged, the latter fell into step with Khaavren. When they reached the Fireside room, the guardsman, whose name was Menia, found a pike in a storage room nearby (one change Khaavren had made when he took charge of the Guards had been to place pikes at various points around the Palace, so there need be no delay for a guardsman assuming his station), and took up a position just outside the door, to one side, while Khaavren stood in the relaxed pose of attention by which the experienced soldier distinguishes himself. His Majesty, meanwhile, entered the room and seated himself in a cushioned chair facing a small stool, and in view of the cold fire. The Orb, Khaavren noticed, had calmed itself to the point where it was emitting a serene rose.

They had been waiting only a very few minutes when Khaavren heard the soft, tentative footfalls he had come to recognize as belonging to Dimma. Khaavren glanced at Menia—giving her a look that she, from experience, was able to translate as: *Something unusual is about to happen, do not make me ashamed of you.* Menia almost nodded and fixed her eyes straight ahead as Dimma turned the corner and appeared before them, leading the way (unnecessarily, in fact) for the Enchantress of Dzur Mountain, Sethra Lavode.

To understand the effect Sethra's arrival had on those of the court who beheld her—and, in fact, the reason for Khaavren's subtle warning to Menia—we must look beyond her physical manifestation, for her appearance was not, we know from several sources, unduly prepossessing. She was not exceptionally tall; she was neither remarkably handsome nor unusually grotesque. Her complexion was one of extreme pallor, her hair was dark, fine, straight, and, on this occasion, pulled into a tight knot on the back of her head, bringing her noble's point into sharp relief. She had the Dragon chin, slanted eyes and ears like a Dzurlord's, an angular jaw supporting a small mouth and thin lips, and a nose with a very slight hook. She moved with athletic confidence and, in soft lyornskin boots, without a sound. She wore the uniform of the Lavodes—black pants pulled tight around the boots, a sharp-collared black shirt tucked into the pants, and a wide leather belt with only a small pouch hanging from it—she had, presumed Khaavren, known that she could not appear before His Majesty armed.

So there was, in short, excepting only her unusually pale complexion, nothing about her that would cause her to be remarked in a public place, unless one knew who she was. And yet, who is there who has not heard of Sethra Lavode? She stands out in history, in mythology, and in folklore throughout the Empire and beyond. When one hears the word "enchantress" used in any context, one's mind immediately leaps to *The* Enchantress. No children's story is complete without an evil sorceress who is older than she looks and lives in a mountain fortress. And who can count the tales that speak of her either by name or by implication (the latter among those who believe—even to this day—that to name her is to summon her)? Had she actually done half of the deeds attributed to her, she would have to be as old as the Empire itself, and still could let scarcely a day go by without being involved in one or another battle, sorcery, or intrigue.

There are places, such as Moot County in Greenbough, where, in one town she is known as the wicked Enchantress, while five leagues away, in the next town, she is the hero who defeats whatever evil the storyteller creates for the delight of his audience.

What is really known of her? What are the drops of truth that intermingle in the cup of myth, legend, and folktale that flow from the Dark Lady of Dzur Mountain like wine from an augured cask? This is no simple question to answer. There have been convocations of historians, bards, and wizards who have gathered for no purpose but to address this question, and yet there is little they have been able to find that is unquestionably true; and we have no wish to add to the list dubious reports and doubtful anecdotes, wherefore we will confine ourselves to the little that is recognized as true by reputable historians.

The earliest authentic records of Sethra predate the founding of the Lavodes, and consist of a rough drawing of her device, which appears to have remained unchanged throughout her life, consisting of white Dragon's Head and Dzur's Claw against black—unquestionably the simplest device in use at the time, and the most unadorned on record from any time, saving only the Silver Sword on Black of the most ancient line of Kieron the Conqueror himself. In the oldest drawings of her device, a motto is shown at the top, but not only is the language one which no scholar has penetrated, there are even a few unfamiliar symbols, as if the very alphabet in which it was written were ancient and forgotten. This is certainly possible, and there has been endless speculation on the subject, though to no conclusion. Sethra has, by all reports, been silent on the subject, even to those few who have been close enough to be considered her friends.

Her lineage block, similarly, is in the form of a downward-pointing arrowhead or triangle, entirely self-contained, with no lines either entering or emerging, as if her maternal and paternal ancestor had appeared from nowhere at all, begotten her, and vanished. Lest this lead to uncalled-for speculation, we should note that, before the dawn of history, from which time Sethra almost certainly dates, there were no standards for lineage blocks, and Sethra was free to view and declare her lineage however she chose.

For it is beyond argument that she was (and, for all this historian can answer, may still be) the oldest human being the Empire has ever produced. How old remains a mystery, but there is no question that she was alive and living in Dzur Mountain during the Iorich Reign of the Fourth Cycle, for it is at this time that she appeared at the Imperial Palace and denounced the treacherous Warlord Trichon and was instrumental in turning back the invasion from Elde Island along with

Terics e'Marish'Chala, from whose memoirs we have our first verifiable accounts of her actions. As for the question of how she achieved her great age, we can speculate that it must have something to do with the nature of Dzur Mountain itself, but we can say no more than this, though we are entirely aware of how unsatisfactory this theory is.

It is also known, thanks to the work of Lyorn historian Taedra, that when she was Warlord during the Dragon Reign in the Fourteenth Cycle she was a living woman, but that when the Lavode Scandal broke, she was in fact undead, and had been for some hundreds of years. How did she die, how was she reanimated, and how did she manage the deceit for so long? These are not questions we can answer.

Allow us, for purposes of illustration, to pick one of the accurate stories to express Sethra's character. She was Warlord under the Lyorn Emperor Tiska during the Thirteenth Cycle, when rebellion broke out along the coast to the southwest, in response to the combination of wheat shortages from the north and the interdiction on shipping that Tiska had declared in response to piracy from the Longburry Islands. It seemed to Sethra, who was aware of all of the circumstances of the rebellion, that it would certainly continue to spread unless put down at once, so she set out at the head of the army just as it was—without waiting for additional conscripts or negotiating with mercenaries.

This quick mode of acting placed her, some few months later, at the head of some eight hundred cavalry and two thousand foot soldiers, facing seven thousand rebellious, heavily armed, and well-commanded Dragonlords, Orca, and Teckla on Bernen's Field. Sethra rode up alone to the enemy lines and, in full sight of her own troops, took from her brow the Warlord's Headdress, which had been the symbol of ultimate command since the First Cycle, and threw it into the enemy's line. The first reaction, of course, was great joy on the part of the enemy, and despair in Sethra's own army, but then she returned to her own lines and declaimed, "The enemy seems to have acquired a holy relic of the Empire. We cannot expect them to return it from kindness or duty, wherefore, my loves, I am about to order a charge, and if you care about my honor and the traditions of the Empire, you must not think of holding back or retreating until this relic is in our hands once more."

Three hours later the Warlord's Headdress was again on Sethra's brow, and the rebellion was broken and scattered. While we would hesitate to say precisely what this anecdote expresses about Sethra's character, we are certain, at any rate, that it ought to tell the reader something. Let us, in any case, pass on to other matters concerning the Enchantress.

The saying among the Teckla is, "By his home you know him," and we are not so foolish as to disdain wisdom because it emerges from beneath rather than descending from above; thus we will take a moment to discuss the little that is known of Dzur Mountain, Sethra's abode.

It is interesting to note that, while the records of the House of the Dzur document literally hundreds of Dzurlords who ascended Dzur Mountain with the reported intention of challenging Sethra, there is no reliable information on the fate of *any* of them—from which fact, no doubt, grow the innumerable stories purporting to explain the inevitable conclusion of any such journey.

The oldest verified report of anyone entering Dzur Mountain and returning date back to the Sixth Phoenix Reign, when a servant of the Warlord, Nilla e'Lanya, passed through the gates with a request for assistance during an uprising in the area. Sethra refused (there is some reason to believe she was, in fact, behind the uprising), but the messenger was treated well and came to no harm, returning with a confused report of pleasant, unpretentious furnishings, powerful wards, warm fires, and cold, grey walls.

Since then, there have been more than a score of confirmed reports from visitors, and what they (and many of the unconfirmed reports as well) tell of Sethra's lair is no less confusing, and very similar; they speak of an odd blend of the mystical with the practical, the impossible with the mundane, the powerful with the comfortable.

And what could be a better expression of Sethra, founder

and first Captain of the Lavodes, Lord of Dzur Mountain, warrior, poet, enchantress, natural philosopher, vampire? Who could meet her, in the flesh and for the first time, without feeling his knees to tremble, his mouth to become dry, and his heart to palpitate?

The answer to this question is not, we say with regret, Khaavren, who, in spite of having prepared himself for the encounter, fell victim to all of the symptoms we have delineated. Yet, to do him justice, we must add that not a shade of these sensations passed over his countenance nor was visible in his aspect; he remained expressionless as a Serioli and motionless as a hunting issola. We cannot, in all honesty, say the same for Menia, who, notwithstanding Khaavren's warning, allowed her eyes to widen and who twitched with some emotion upon realizing, by certain clues, who it was that stood before her.

Sethra, on her part, gave Captain and guardsman the most cursory of glances as Dimma led her past them into the room where His Majesty waited. Dimma, performing in this room the function relegated to Brudik when His Majesty was in the Portrait Room, then called out, "The Baroness of Dzur Mountain and Environs." We should add that she performed this office as if there were nothing in the least unusual in announcing the Dark Lady of Dzur Mountain before the Emperor.

Sethra bowed to His Majesty and took a step backward, seating herself, as His Majesty indicated she should, on the low stool that faced his chair. When Sethra had seated herself, Dimma poured wine for both His Majesty and Sethra, then left the room. Khaavren, meanwhile, acting on instinct, entered and took up a position in a corner which commanded a view of the entire room and was placed only a few steps from Sethra—although, as he admitted to himself, there was probably nothing he could do in the event that Sethra were to attempt treachery.

The oil lamps that illuminated the room—there were four of them—gave a slightly yellow cast to her features, and her attitude as she sat was that of a warrior: relaxed and confident. She studied the Emperor while giving him time to study her, then said, "Sire, I am informed of Your Majesty's desire to see me. I am here. What is Your Majesty's will?"

Tortaalik cleared his throat and sipped his wine—it seemed to Khaavren that His Majesty had not decided what to say, and wished to gain time. The Emperor then glanced around and drank more wine, as if hoping to find Jurabin at his elbow. Sethra also tasted her wine and, finding it satisfactory, swallowed a good draught.

"Madame," said the Emperor at last, "We have no doubt that you are informed of the assassination of Gyorg Lavode."

"I am, Sire," said Sethra.

"In addition," he added, hesitating, as if searching for words, "We do not doubt that you are as anxious as we ourselves to learn who has committed this act, and why."

"Your Majesty is not mistaken," said Sethra.

"That being the case, we—" he broke off. Khaavren, from his vantage point, was able to notice three things—first, that His Majesty's forehead was spotted with perspiration; second, that the Orb had turned to a bright, nervous yellow; and, third, that Sethra showed no sign of having noticed either forehead or Orb. His Majesty resumed, "we desire your assistance in learning these things."

"Very well, Sire," said Sethra, nodding.

His Majesty started, and his eyes widened, as if the campaign had proved successful before he had thought his forces to be so much as assembled. "How, you will assist us?"

"Yes, Sire. For I am, as Your Majesty has surmised, as anxious as anyone to learn who has killed Gyorg, and for what reason. I have no doubt that it is part of some deeper plan, and, while this does not concern me, I will certainly inform Your Majesty of anything I learn."

"Yes, very good," said the Emperor. His mouth opened and closed a few times. Khaavren cleared his throat slightly, calling for His Majesty's attention. His Majesty blinked, then said, "You may begin by speaking with my Captain of the Guard, Sir Khaavren, who will assist you in any way you desire."

Sethra turned her glance on the Tiassa, who withstood it, and bowed his head slightly. The Emperor rose to his feet, causing Sethra to do the same and, furthermore, to bow deeply to His Majesty, who returned the courtesy and made his way to the door as quickly as his dignity permitted.

Khaavren placed himself before the Enchantress, saluted, and said, "At your service, madame."

Sethra acknowledged the salute and finished her wine in a single draught. "I am informed," she said without preamble, "that an attempt was made on your life as well."

"Yes, Madame."

"And has the body been preserved?"

"Indeed it has. Or, rather, they have; all of the bodies have been preserved against a need to investigate them."

"That, then, is how I shall begin. Where are they?"

"In the basement, below the sub-wing of my company of the guards."

"Then, if you will have the goodness to lead me there—"

"I shall do so at once, delaying only to be certain that someone is attending to His Majesty."

"Very well."

Khaavren fulfilled this duty with his usual dispatch, using neither a word nor a step more than was necessary, reckoning, as was his custom, that a step wasted can never be recovered, an excess word can never be recalled. After five steps, then, in the direction of the corporal on duty, and after two words spoken to this worthy, Khaavren immediately placed himself, as he had said, at Sethra's service.

Sethra, like Khaavren, was not given to wasting words, wherefore in answer to Khaavren's declaration that he was prepared to render her any service she might require, she simply said, "Let us recover my dagger, then view the body."

"This way, Madame," said Khaavren, and directed his steps through the Imperial Wing, where Sethra's sheathed poniard was restored to her, and into the Dragon Wing, and so, eventually, to the basement level of the Sub-wing of the Imperial Guard. This level was reached through a large oaken door on iron hinges. On one side—the side, be it understood, facing up the stairs—the door was polished to a gleaming tan color and carved with an intricate dragon's head. The other side, however, marked the end of elegance and the beginning of cold utility, for the back of the door was hardly smoothed, and the walls it looked upon were barest stone, broken only by iron brackets to be used for torches, and the stairway, likewise, was of stone cracked and chipped, upon which great care was required to avoid an embarrassing or injurious fall. It is worthwhile to note that neither of these warriors appeared to give any thought to this danger, nor to make any accommodation in their stride to the condition of the steps, but simply walked down as they would have upon the finest marble stairway in the Imperial Wing, Khaavren holding aloft the oil lamp, Sethra following in silence.

After some thirty or thirty-five steps, Khaavren became aware that the temperature had dropped no small amount, and he began to wish that he'd worn his cloak, although he was careful to let no hint of this discomfort appear in word or gesture. Reaching the bottom, Khaavren passed through a wide room filled with sword-blades, pikes, chairs, and desks, ready to answer their call as soldiers in the Imperial Reserve might hold themselves ready for word of the outbreak of violence in the duchies. Beyond this was another room, which was filled with chairs awaiting glue, sword-blades awaiting a whetstone, pikes awaiting new hafts, desks awaiting nails, and other equipage of the guards in need of repair. After this, a passage off to the right led to a room where glue, nails, hafts, and whetstones resided, while one to the left would have brought them to a workshop where the contents of one room might be brought together with the contents of another, the result to repose in the first. They ignored both of these, and continued straight ahead for some forty or fifty paces, after which Khaavren stopped, murmuring, "Hullo!"

"What is it?" said Sethra.

"Light," said Khaavren.

"Yes," said Sethra. "I see ahead of us the flickering of an oil lamp. Is there, then, something in this sight that causes you distress?"

"Distress, Madame? No. But interest, certainly, and perhaps even concern."

"My Lord," said Sethra, "I am anxious to learn the reason for this interest and concern."

"That is easily explained," said Khaavren. "It is because there is no reason for a lamp to be burning down here, especially in the chamber up ahead, which is where the bodies have been placed."

"Well?"

"Well, if there is a lamp, then no doubt, there is someone with it, for I have never heard of a lamp which would ignite itself and bring itself into the basement where bodies lie. Moreover—"

"Yes?"

"That a lamp is burning implies a person who wishes to see."

"Well, I understand that, but could it not be the case that the lamp was left unattended and burning by whomever brought the bodies down here?"

"It is not likely," said Khaavren. "In the first place, I should wonder how this person found his way back up, or, alternately, why he thought it necessary to bring two lamps."

"That is true," said Sethra. "And in the second place?"

"In the second place, it has been more than a day since the body was placed here, and none of the lamps we use hold more than twenty hours of fuel."

"I understand," said Sethra. "Well, then, what do you propose? Are you going to call for assistance?"

"Assistance, Madame? Cha! When a soldier has a good sword by his right hand, and the Enchantress of Dzur Mountain by his left, he can hardly think he stands in need of assistance, whatever unknown circumstances may lie before him."

Sethra bowed to acknowledge the compliment. "Well then?" she said.

"Well then, let us pass on and see what we find."

"Very well."

They continued down the corridor, and, in short order,

stepped into a long room, which contained several tables, each of which held a body. There was, in addition, an oil lamp hanging from a peg on the wall, and a short female figure which stood over one of the bodies and appeared to be studying it, to judge from the thin glass rod she held over it. This person looked up as they entered, and, with no sign of surprise or embarrassment, nodded briefly to Khaavren before returning to her inspection of the corpse.

"Lady Aliera!" cried Khaavren, who had recognized the Dragonlord when she glanced at him.

"There is no doubt," said Aliera, as if in answer to a question, "that there was a spell laid upon this fellow before his death; the traces of it remain. I suspect what it was, yet I cannot—".

"Lady Aliera," said Khaavren, in a more normal tone of voice, "if you would be good enough to tell me what you are doing here, well, I should be entirely in your debt."

"You wish to know what I am doing here?" said Aliera.

"Yes, exactly."

"Why, I am investigating this body, in order to learn how he came to die."

"Or," said Sethra, "perhaps to remove all traces of the spell, so that nothing can be learned."

Aliera looked at Sethra for a long moment before saying, "I don't know you, Madame."

The Enchantress bowed. "I am called Sethra Lavode."

Aliera bowed in her turn. "Very well, Sethra Lavode. I am called Aliera e'Kieron."

Sethra bowed once more, and if she was surprised that Aliera displayed no reaction upon learning her identity, she gave no sign of it.

"Now," said Aliera, "that introductions are made, there remains the matter of your last remark, which sounded to my ears very like an accusation. I must, therefore, beg you to make it either more explicit, so that I may respond appropriately, or to recast it in such a way that no response is called for."

Khaavren cleared his throat. "My Lady, are you aware that

you are beneath the sub-wing of the Imperial Guard, and that this area is private—that is, reserved for those with Imperial business?"

"And," added Sethra, "you ought to be aware that you are doing—whatever it is you are doing—to the body of Gyorg Lavode, who was Captain of the Lavodes, and, moreover, my friend."

"Therefore?" inquired Aliera, assuming an air of curiosity, as if she could not imagine what these statistics might have to do with her.

"Perhaps you are unaware," said Khaavren, "that certain malicious gossips accuse your father of having had something to do with these assassinations."

"I know it so well," said Aliera, "that it, in fact, accounts for my presence here. I believe that only by learning who, in fact, committed these actions, will I be able to prove that my father had nothing whatsoever to do with the crimes of which he is accused."

"Well," said Khaavren, "but you have not contributed to the good of your cause."

"How not?" said Aliera.

"Because," said Khaavren, "to find you down here, engaged in I know not what activities with respect to the bodies, puts appearances against you."

"Appearances, My Lord?" said Aliera, in a tone of voice, and with a simultaneous look, expressing the greatest disdain. "I have often heard that phrase. *Appearances are against you,* uttered by those who wish to conceal an accusation. Who are these people who believe appearances, My Lord? Would you care to name them?"

"I am one," said Sethra, putting her hand on the dagger at her side.

Aliera set down the glass rod which had been in her hand, stepped back from the table, and drew a moderately long sword which was suspended from her hip by a leathern baldric. "Some," she said coolly, "might worry about the etiquette of drawing a sword against someone armed only with a dagger. Yet, as I know something of that dagger, and of the person who wields it, I do you the honor to believe I am not overmatching you. If, therefore, you would be pleased to draw—and instantly, at that—we can, I think, arrive at an accommodation without any further delay."

"I ask nothing better," said Sethra, bowing slightly. She made a movement as if she would draw, then frowned and appeared to reflect.

"Why do you not draw?" said Aliera.

"For the simple reason," said Sethra, "that I find this an unfortunate location for such games. Here we have the remains of several men who have died by violence, and who I intend, after having the honor of dispatching you, to investigate. I should, therefore, dislike to think that in our activities we should accidentally upset one, or in our excitement do something that will make the investigation more difficult. Let us, instead, go out from this basement into the open air, and, on the way, we can find seconds and an Imperial Witness—I have no doubt that Sir Khaavren will act as judge. Therefore, in addition to saving this evidence from damage, we will have observed all the forms, so no one can have any cause for complaint. Come, what do you think of my reasoning?"

"I find it excellent," said Aliera, replacing her sword in its sheath. "So good, in fact, that I will even tell you what I have discovered, so that if, in fact, you should prove victorious in our contest, I will have made your task less burdensome. It will only take a moment to inform you, and then we can adjourn upstairs and out of doors, where the weather is so pleasant, and settle our differences in the best way."

"You are very courteous, and entirely a lady. So much so that, if we do not slaughter one another, I have no doubt that, in the future, we shall have much pleasure in one another's company."

Aliera bowed.

Sethra returned her gesture and said, "What, then, have you discovered?"

"This man, in the corner—"

"Smaller," said Khaavren, "an intendant of finance."

"Very well," said Aliera. "This intendant was killed by the

simplest of sorceries; that is, the major vessel of his heart was suddenly constricted, causing a hemorrhage which resulted in a death that was almost instantaneous. As the simplest of spells killed him, so the simplest of spells would have protected him, and there is no evidence of concealment, from which I must conclude that he had no understanding of sorcery."

"Very well," said Sethra.

"This man—"

"Gyorg Lavode," said Khaavren and Sethra together.

"Yes. Although he was killed by a knife wound, there can be no doubt a spell was placed upon him to ensure he wouldn't awaken first. Look—" she picked up the glass rod she had been holding when they entered and handed it to Sethra. "You perceive the yellow coloring at the end? This was the result of casting the Mirror of Sandbourne above his eyes."

"It is," said Sethra, "only the faintest of yellow."

"He died more than a day ago," said Aliera.

"And yet," said Sethra, "why did not the rod become green, which is how the Mirror ought to have responded to a change in the mind's energies?"

"It is exactly this upon which I was musing when you entered," said Aliera. "My suspicion—"

"You have, then, a suspicion?"

"Very much so."

"Then I should be glad to hear it."

"This is it, then: The green appears, as you know, from a combination of the yellow, which indicates external energy having disrupted the workings of the mind, and blue, which is how the Mirror of Sandbourne signals the presence of sorcery invading the sanctity of the mind—or, at any rate, the brain. Yet if, instead of having been directed at the mind, the spell was placed about the area, the Mirror would not detect an influence in the mind, but only sorcery around it."

"Well," said Sethra. "There is some justice in what you say."

"And yet," said Aliera, "I should be glad to know where

there is a spell of sufficient subtlety to penetrate the Amulet of Covering that Gyorg wore, yet powerful enough to work on the area in which he rested—all, be it understood, without waking him up before putting him to sleep."

"That is easily answered. Do you perceive that, as I cast the Holding of Bren upon this instrument, the yellow dissolves and flows from one end to the other?"

"Well, yes, but what does it mean?"

"It means that the energies of the sorcery were not closely directed, but were dispersing even before the spell was cast."

"Which means?"

"It can only mean that the spell had been prepared some hours or days before it was cast."

"In other words," said Aliera, "the spell was placed in an amulet or a wand, and released, perhaps by someone with no knowledge of sorcery at all."

"That is correct."

"The Jhereg," said Aliera.

"That is most likely," said Sethra.

"But, if it is the Jhereg," said Aliera, "there ought to be about the body the marks of the sorcerous waves—the patterns of energy—which are so different from those left by the sorceries of the Athyra, the Dzur, or the Dragons."

"Indeed. Have you noticed them?"

"In fact," said Aliera, "I have not looked."

"Then let us do so," said Sethra. "I would recommend the Norbrook Threepass Test."

"Perhaps," said Aliera. "And yet, it has been more than a day. Perhaps we ought to attempt the Lorngrass Procedure at first, which has the advantage that, should it fail, it will not disturb the fields in any way."

"Very well, then," said Sethra. "I agree to the Lorngrass Procedure. But in that case, at the same time, we ought to look for these wave markings upon the aura from Smaller's remains."

"That should not be difficult," said Aliera, "provided we first prepare the area . . ."

And the two sorceresses, forgetting both Khaavren and the

duel they had all but agreed upon, proceeded upon a discussion that left Khaavren quite befuddled. He smiled, however, as he realized what had happened, or, rather, what would not happen, and, determining that he could be of no assistance to the two ladies, turned without another word and made his way back to the suite of rooms above, from which he was accustomed to carry out his duties.

# Chapter the Ninth

*Which Treats of Our Old Friend Aerich,*
*Certain Messages He Received,*
*And the Resolution He Therefore Undertook.*

WE OUGHT TO TAKE A moment to consider that, while to the pages of history (and to our own pages as well) a messenger may be a nameless figure, who carries dispatches, news, gossip, or letters, more or less important, from place to place—from the hand of one to the eye of a second—and that said messenger may appear in this brief rôle for only as long as necessary to carry out his function, after which he will vanish forever from the page and from history, yet to the messenger himself, he is the central figure of his own drama. What he thinks about this drama we can never know—whether he sees himself as a vital link in a chain of destiny the outline of which he can only glimpse, or whether he is concerned with his pay and promotion, or his plans upon returning from his mission, or his hopes, more or less specific, for his future, and thus cares not a bit for the broader issues at work—of all of this we must remain ignorant.

But if (as, in fact, we are about to do) we skip lightly over him, being more concerned with the personages on either end of our metaphorical chain, and with the message itself, still, let us, for just a moment, consider that these connections are made by a human agent, with his own thoughts, feelings, cares, and personality. Let us recall that someone has taken a letter (in this case) and secured it in some way against the elements and the chance of loss, and has brought it, by one means or another, to its destination, with what feelings of relief or satisfaction we can only conjecture.

That said, let us arrive shortly after the messenger at the lower door of Brachington's Moor, where are received such visitors who are above peasants and merchants, yet not, by rank, fully deserving the Upper Door, and observe a tall, thin man of the House of the Teckla who is richly though tastefully dressed in the brown and red of the House of the Lyorn as he carries the rolled-up parchment he has taken from the nameless messenger through the indoor terraces that distinguish the structure that is at once the chief residence of the County of Bra-moor, the seat of the Duchy of Arylle, and the home of our old friend, Aerich, whom we do ourselves the honor to trust the reader will not have entirely forgotten from his appearance in our earlier history.

Ah, but we have nearly been remiss in our duties, it seems, for we have been about to bring the reader through this manor house without in any way placing it either on the map, except in the most cursory way, or in the reader's mind; allow us to repair this deficiency at once.

The Duchy of Arylle is (that is, it was then, and, as it still exists, it still is), to begin with, an unlikely place. It comprises eleven counties of neat, elegant farmland, with the southernmost, called Groomsman, extending to a point abutting the Duchy of Luatha on the edge of the Great Plains. The westernmost county, called Pitroad, is separated from the Yendi River by the Collier Hills which, in fact, form something like a ring around the entire Duchy. It was settled during the Ninth Issola Reign by a privately funded expedition launched by a certain Lyorn named Corpet, who named it for the expedition's leader, a Dzurlord called, as our readers may have guessed, Arylle.

The area had been unsettled for countless years except for coal-mining not far away because, when viewed from the hills, the district had an ill-favored look, appearing at once marshy and barren. Yet when Corpet, who had been driven from his lands to the East by certain political and economic pressures which originated with the Emperor's desire to have a more direct control of the lines of coal in Corpet's old land (still known as Corpet County), the look proved illusory, and the region proved to be wonderfully rich farmland, at least as excellent as those lands on the Great Plains which surrounded the Collier Hills, with soil and climate ideally suited to wheat, maize, and various obscure but nutritious legumes.

The County of Arylle was raised to a Duchy by the Ninth Vallista Emperor in recognition of Corpet's daughter, also called Corpet, who assisted in the Siege of Blacktar by refusing passage of supply trains through her domain, and, furthermore, by refusing to sell her produce to the rebellious Baroness of Lockfree. Corpet the Younger, upon being made a peer, immediately raised each of her eleven baronies to counties, winning her much gratitude and friendship among her vassals and sowing the seeds of jealousy and resentment with her southern neighbor, the Lyorn Count Shaltre—seeds which were not destined to sprout for some thousands of years.

It should be noted in passing that the district between Shaltre and Bra-moor was given to the Dzurlord, Arylle, and within it was a barony called Daavya, which, our readers may recall, was the home of our old friend Tazendra.

Bra-moor County consisted of rolling hills, speckled with woods, streams, and ponds, and distinguished by a large population of curkings, whose bark could be hard from before dawn to well after dusk, and who could be found waddling in neat rows from pond to pond, occasionally venturing across one of the neat, tree-lined dirt roads that connected the cottages and villages of the district to one another and to the central estate of the duchy, a fine, four-story, thirty-room house called Brachington's Moor, which was reached by a wide road that ran from the hamlet of Moortown, some three leagues distant, up to the nine-foot hedge that concealed the gateway to the estate. The gate being opened, the road, albeit far narrower, actually seemed to continue, turning into a path that circled past the Duke's fishpond, the simple outbuildings of the estate, the gardens, and then met itself once more; in the course of which meandering it gave off shoots which led to each of the doors of the manor house itself, by one of which arrived, and would subsequently depart, the messenger to whom we had the honor of referring in the initial lines of this chapter of our history.

To resume, then: Aerich's tall, thin servant whose name was Fawnd, found our old friend Aerich sitting at a sort of desk in a corner room of the manor house, where he was re-reading a letter he had received some few hours before, and occasionally glancing out at the fishpond, as if in a reverie. Fawnd coughed delicately, and waited.

Aerich looked up, and took a moment to return his thoughts from whatever travels in time and space they ranged to, then said, "What is it?"

"A letter, Your Venerance."

Aerich raised one of his graceful eyebrows. "A letter? Another one? Pray, bring it here."

Fawnd delivered the parchment, bowed, and departed the room as silently as he had appeared. Aerich studied the seal, and his glance involuntarily darted to the letter he had been holding a moment ago. "Well," he murmured. "First Khaavren, then Pel. And on the same day. What is happening in the city?" With this, he broke the seal and scanned the top of the letter, noting that, whereas Khaavren's letter had arrived a short, but reasonable three days after being sent, Pel had caused his letter to arrive in rather less than two days, testifying at once to the Yendi's urgency. After forming this conclusion, Aerich read the letter, after which, frowning, he at once read it a second time. Then, after a moment's consideration, he reached for one of the ropes that hovered above his desk, and pulled it once. After another few seconds of thought, he reached for a second bell rope and pulled it twice.

An instant later Fawnd was back in the room, to be joined

almost at once by a small, middle-aged Teckla named Steward. Fawnd said, "Yes, Your Venerance?" while Steward contented herself with bowing her head and waiting.

"Is the messenger still here, Fawnd?"

"He awaits Your Venerance's reply."

"Very well, then."

He turned to his desk, and taking up a good quill, black ink, and strong, bleached paper, dashed off a quick note, which we will reproduce in full:

My dear Pel, I have never known you to err in such a matter, and I hope I retain enough of a sense of duty to respond in the proper manner, and in good season, wherefore I shall call upon you as soon as I can manage. Apropos, if you will find some means of letting good Khaavren know, that will be so much the better. I will be bringing Tazendra along, because there are no arms as strong nor a heart as loyal, and I fear that we shall have both of our strength and our loyalty put to the test in the months, weeks, or even days to come.

I remain, my old friend, your affectionate, Aerich

He sealed the letter, and handed it to Fawnd to deliver to the messenger, along with a small quantity of silver.

"Is that all, Venerance?"

"Not in the least," said Aerich.

The servant waited patiently.

Aerich considered for a moment, then spoke in this fashion: "Fawnd," he said, "be good enough to prepare for an expedition. Two horses, traveling and court dress, and my sword. Take ten imperials from the chest, most of it in silver. You will be coming along as my lackey."

"Yes, Venerance."

"Be ready to set out within the hour. You should, therefore, be dressed for traveling as well."

"Yes, Venerance," said Fawnd, with no change of expression. He bowed and set about his business.

"Steward, see to the residence. I cannot say how long I will be away, most probably some weeks."

"Particular instructions, Venerance?"

"Yes. I shall give them to you now."

"I am listening, Venerance."

"Here they are, then: Inform Goodman Loch that I will see to his dispute on my return; he must understand that he will disoblige me by taking any action on the matter himself. The same, of course, applies to any representatives of Goodman Handsweight who should appear."

"Very well, Venerance."

"Be certain Smith finishes the hinges on the lower door."

"I will not fail to do so."

"If the Petrose Brook does not clean itself—that is, if there are insufficient rains—those who live along the Seeming Road may fish my pond—but only they, mind; not all of their friends and acquaintances throughout the county."

"I understand, Venerance."

"Speak to Warder about keeping an eye out for poachers in the back woods."

"Yes, Venerance."

"The Westering Road may be opened for transport from the mines, and the miners are welcome in any of the markets, but only in groups of six or fewer. Apropos, any hardship cases among my tenants may be sent with maize and beans to sell to the mines; you know the rates."

"I do, Venerance."

"The rent-list is here, in this drawer; have Warder collect the rents as they come due, unless I have returned; and he may keep a twentieth part for his trouble. He is, however, to take no action in the case of default—all such instances will await my return, or the arrival of heirs in the case of misfortune."

"I will be certain he knows Your Venerance's wishes."

"Urgent matters may be forwarded to me in care of Sir Khaavren, whose address is in this box."

"I know the box, Venerance, and I will find the address should it prove necessary."

"Do you understand all of this, Steward?"

"Your Venerance may judge," she said.

"Let us see, then."

"The residence; Goodman Loch's dispute to be delayed, he to do nothing; Smith to see to the hinges; those on Seeming Road may fish the pond; Warder to watch for poachers; Westering Road for transport; miners to the market, but no more than six at once; hardship cases may sell maize and beans at the mines; Warder to collect the rents for a twentieth part; Sir Khaavren's address in the box."

"That is it."

"I hope I may be permitted to wish Your Venerance a prosperous and not unpleasant journey."

Aerich nodded; then, on a sudden idea coming to him, said, "Bide."

While Steward waited, Aerich turned back to his desk, and once more set quill to paper, writing a short note to which we will give the same courtesy that we gave his earlier literary endeavor:

> My dear Baroness, [said the note] I believe our old friends to be in some danger. We must, therefore, depart at once for the City. Pray make ready for a journey of some duration, which will commence upon my arrival at your door, where I hope to be not more than an hour after this message. Please have four horses ready, two of them equipped for you and a servant. Your Affectionate friend, Aerich

He read the note over once to be certain he had said everything that was required, then gently poured sand over it, making certain it wouldn't smear, after which he folded, sealed, and handed it to Steward. "For the Baroness Daavya, to be delivered at once," he said.

Steward bowed, took the letter, and left without delay—she had served Aerich long enough to understand that he would not thank her for standing on courtesy when he was in a hurry.

These matters attended to, then, Aerich repaired to his dressing room, where Fawnd assisted him into his traveling clothes, which consisted of his brown skirt and a loose-fitting but well-cut red shirt, over the sleeves of which he slipped his copper vambraces. Fawnd then clipped onto Aerich's belt the sword Aerich had purchased so long ago, upon the occasion of his joining the Imperial Guard, and opposite it hung a simple poniard. Fawnd had, by this time, dressed himself in dark garments suitable for the rigors of travel, with the Lyorn crest over the breast of his jerkin; he gave an appearance, to be sure, somewhat at odds with his demeanor—almost comical, in such informal apparel—but if Aerich noticed this he gave no sign of it.

"You have given the silver and the letter to the messenger?" asked Aerich when he had quite finished dressing.

"I have, Venerance. And he rode off as if Kieron the Conqueror were on his heels, which gives me to think that he is being well paid for speed at the other end of his journey."

"I don't doubt that you are right, Fawnd. You may go and attend to the remainder of your duties."

Fawnd left to finish the preparations for travel, while Aerich spent the time consulting certain maps and other documents, until, in rather less than the allotted hour, Fawnd returned to inform him that all was ready for their departure. Aerich nodded, rose, and, on sudden thought, opened a plain wooden chest in the corner of the dressing room, from which he brought out silk yarn and a crochet hook, which he gave to his servant along with orders that they be placed in the saddle pockets.

"Let us go," said Aerich. He led the way through the manor house, to the silent and respectful courtesies of the few servants he kept around him. Five minutes later he and Fawnd were on horseback, setting off down the road toward Daavya County and the Castle Daavya, which overlooked both a village and a river of the same name. After riding for some few minutes, Fawnd said (rather breathlessly, for he was by no means an experienced rider), "I beg your pardon,

Your Venerance, but may I be permitted to make an observation?"

"You may, Fawnd. What is it?"

"At this rate, will not we fatigue the horses unduly?"

"No," said Aerich. He could have added, "Speed is everything," and he could also have explained that they would be changing horses upon arriving at Daavya, but Aerich was not accustomed to offering unnecessary explanations to servants—or to anyone else, if the truth were to be told. Fawnd accepted the answer with nothing more than a muted sigh.

They presently came down the far side of a very long, gently sloping hill, forming the eastern side of the Daavya River valley, and so into sight of Castle Daavya, the largest structure in the Duchy, made of fine stonework and surrounded by a fourteen-foot wall above which could be seen the upper few stories and the single, square tower; over this tower flew the two banners—Arylle on top, Daavya beneath. They crossed the bridge (called, as one would expect, the Daavya Bridge) and made their way to the gate, which stood open.

Servants in Dzur livery rushed off toward the keep itself. Aerich dismounted gracefully; Fawnd dismounted. They waited beside their horses until a familiar figure appeared: a Teckla dressed in the livery of the House of the Dzur, with the Daavya crest apparent on both jerkin and hat. "Your Venerance!" cried the Teckla. "Welcome, welcome. My master the Baroness will be here in an instant."

"That is well, Mica," said Aerich giving the servant a smile to indicate that he was glad to see him. Aerich then added, "I observe that you are prepared for a journey."

"Yes indeed, Your Venerance."

"Good. But why do you not embrace your friend Fawnd?"

"Why, I will do so at once, if your Venerance permits."

Aerich signified that he had no objection to make, and Fawnd and Mica embraced as old friends will, and exchanged a few words of greeting, after which they set to work together to transfer the equipment from the horses on which Aerich and Fawnd had arrived, to the horses on which they were destined to depart. Meanwhile, in response to Mica's imperious command, other servants came forward to make certain that Aerich's horses were fed, watered, groomed, and sent back to his stables.

As all of this was taking place, the Baroness, Tazendra, appeared, dressed in her black travel garb (as distinct, the reader ought to understand, from her usual black garb, or her black court garb) and with a long sword girt over her shoulder; she at once rushed to embrace Aerich. "Ah, my friend," she cried. "It has been more than two years since I have seen you!"

"Indeed," said Aerich, returning her embrace with real affection. "And may I say, my friend, that you seem to be in the best of health."

"Oh, yes, tolerably good health," said Tazendra complacently. "I am entirely recovered from the accident of which you know, and, as you see, I am back at home, which has been repaired in all particulars."

"So I observe, my dear Daavya, and I present my congratulations."

"Oh, bah," said Tazendra. "But you—shards and splinters! as our friend Khaavren would say. You seem to be as well as ever. Come, let me look at you."

So saying she stepped back and studied Aerich with an eye that was less discriminating than affectionate. Aerich had, to be sure, aged—but he had done so in the most graceful of ways. His hair was rather longer than he used to keep it, and whether from age or from some other reason, had begun to curl, so that it now fell in rich, brown ringlets from a part of his noble's point all the way to below his ears. His face, though still thin, showed more lines, so that his mouth no longer appeared small. But his eye still had the calm that bespoke a man who was contented with himself, and was, moreover unlikely to remain anything but cool before whatever vicissitudes fate might send his way. He still appeared, in form, the picture of robust good health, and he moved with the grace one would expect of a trained Lyorn warrior who has continued his training for hundreds of years.

Tazendra, for her part, had in no wise lost the beauty that

she had traded on so heavily in days gone by. If her face showed a few more lines, these were nevertheless concentrated around her eyes and mouth, and made her seem more amiable than ever—and amiability, as everyone knows, is one of the hallmarks of beauty. Her form showed the signs of one who rode on horseback every day, and engaged in all manner of exercise besides, and, as what we call beauty is neither more nor less than the attributes of nobility combined with those of a good constitution, the Baroness was still in the full flower of her appearance.

"I am pleased to see," said Aerich, "that Mica is still in good health—Khaavren asked after him."

"Oh yes," said Tazendra, smiling fondly at her servant. "He is a good, faithful servant, even when there are no blows to be struck."

Mica blushed and looked at his boots, while Aerich said, "And, do you miss the blows?"

"Well, of a certainty, but I perceive we may about to deliver some more."

"That, and maybe receive a few."

"Bah," said Tazendra.

Aerich smiled. "Come," he said. "We have no time to waste."

"Yes," said Tazendra. "Our old friends, you say, are in danger?"

"Very much," said Aerich.

"But, what is this danger?"

"That, I cannot say, except that it concerns His Highness, the Duke of Eastmanswatch."

"How, Adron e'Kieron, our old friend?"

"Daavya, you must break yourself of this habit of referring as friends to those more highly placed than you in the eyes of society. Some would think ill of you for it."

"Bah, let them. And what of you; are you not a duke and a peer? And yet I do myself the honor to consider you a friend."

"Oh, that is different, as you well know," said Aerich, with a gentle smile.

"Well, then," said Tazendra with a shrug. We should point out that she had learned to shrug by watching Aerich, and had become proficient at this delicate art.

"But yes," said Aerich. "I do indeed refer to His Highness Adron e'Kieron, he who showed us so much courtesy and good will in days gone by. And, moreover, Khaavren is in the middle of it."

Tazendra shrugged as if to say, "Where else would he be?" Aloud she said, "And Pel?"

"Pel is, as usual, in the wings, observing, but I believe that the wings are not as stable as they were a hundred years ago."

"How, not stable?"

"The foundations have, I believe, shifted, and the wings may collapse before the curtain falls."

"Well, yes, certainly," said Tazendra, who had, in fact, become confused during the expansion of this metaphor.

She was rescued from embarrassment by Fawnd, who said, "The saddles have been transferred, Your Venerance, and all is ready."

"Then," said Aerich to Tazendra. "Have you anything left undone?"

"Not in the least," said the Dzurlord. "Upon reading your message, I turned everything over to my steward, who, I am forced to admit, maintains my holdings and household in any case."

"Then there is nothing keeping you here?"

"Nothing at all, my dear Aerich."

"Well, then, let us set off at once."

"So late in the evening? It will be dark soon."

"We will ride through the night," said Aerich.

"And the horses? Will they ride through the night as well?"

"We will use the post."

"Shards!" said Tazendra, in a voice which covered up the nearly inaudible moan that Fawnd permitted to escape from his lips. Tazendra said, "There is, then, no lack of urgency to the affair?"

"That's my opinion," said Aerich.

"In that case," she said, "Allow me to give you this," upon

which she handed him a pair of flat, grey rocks, smoothed until they were almost polished. "Each of them contains a good, strong charge—I prepared them when I received your letter."

"Had you time?"

"Oh, it doesn't take me as long as it used to."

"And have you kept any for yourself."

"I nearly think so," said Tazendra. "And I even have one each for Khaavren and Pel, should they express a desire for such arguments."

"That's well," said Aerich, putting the stones into his saddle pockets. "Then, as nothing more keeps us here, why, let us set out."

"To horse," agreed Tazendra, and, suiting action to words, she led her horse to the mounting block, and pulled herself into the saddle with no other assistance. (She was, we should add, so tall that she would not have required even the inanimate assistance of the block, but mounting directly from the ground would have a necessitated a certain struggle, and thus would have imperiled her dignity.) Aerich did not use the block himself, but mounted his horse with the grace that never deserted him under any circumstances. Then the two lackeys took to horse, and they turned toward the gate.

Tazendra took a last look at the grounds of her home, as if uncertain whether she would ever see them again, then turned her head and her horse's resolutely forward.

Aerich, looking over the lackeys, said to Mica, "I observe, tied to your saddle, the bar-stool I remember so well, and which you put to such good use."

"Your Venerance, my master the Baroness gave me to understand the affair might become tolerably warm, and, moreover, Your Venerance has just confirmed it in conversation with my master that I could not help but overhear."

"Well," said Aerich. "I don't say you are wrong."

"In that case," said Mica, "I thought to stay with the weapon I know best—although the wood has been replaced, it is the same weapon."

"And it was well thought," said Aerich.

"How far is the first post?" said Tazendra.

"I studied the map while Fawnd was preparing for the journey," said Aerich. "For the first post, we must travel north nearly twenty leagues. After that, we travel for sixteen leagues until we join Undauntra's Highway, where the posts are set every ten leagues."

"The Imperial posts? But, my dear Aerich, can you use the Imperial posts?"

"You forget that I am a peer, my dear Baroness. Come, it must be good for something."

"So it would seem. Well then, there is no need to spare the horses."

Fawnd moaned again, which sound was obscured by Aerich saying, "Indeed not, though we must not kill them, for then we should be delayed."

"That is true. When we shall be in Dragaera City?"

"With luck and good posts, by this time to-morrow."

"Amazing!"

"Well, the Empire has learned something from Lord Adron," said Aerich with a smile.

"Yes, certainly," said Tazendra, on whom this reference was entirely lost, for, although she was well acquainted with magical philosophy, and with the science of defense in all its branches, she knew little of history, politics, or the point where these two phenomena intersect, and which we are pleased to call, "news."

"And we shall make full use of it," added Aerich.

"Indeed we shall," said Tazendra. "Only—"

"Yes?"

"You set the pace."

"I will do so."

"Then I await you."

"Rather than await, follow me!" said Aerich, and set off at a good canter through the gates of Castle Daavya, to the respectful salutes of Tazendra's vassals, after which the horses turned north beneath the slowly darkening sky.

# Chapter the Tenth

*Which Treats of the Meeting
Of a Captain with a General,
And of the Various Suspicions
Entertained by Each.*

ALIERA AND SETHRA HAD STILL not emerged when the hour arrived at which Khaavren was accustomed to go home. He thought about inquiring after their progress, but, recalling a certain lieutenant under whom he had served during a certain action, who had the custom of pestering his subordinates as to the status of every order that was issued to make certain it had been carried out, Khaavren determined to avoid doing anything that resembled harassment (and there was, to be sure, the question of to what degree it was practical to harass Aliera e'Kieron and Sethra Lavode).

He resolved, at all events, to give them another hour, in case they had something of interest to tell him. When the sixty minutes had nearly expired, he added another thirty minutes onto the top of it, then another ten, after which he decided that, had they learned anything, they would certainly have informed him; and, upon reaching this perhaps dubious conclusion, he shrugged and went out to procure his dinner, which he did quite successfully, albeit at a later time than usual. He finished his journey home at almost the same moment he finished his pastry, and, after exchanging silent greetings with Srahi, he took himself to bed, where he slept prodigiously.

The next morning found him once more in his accustomed place, escorting His Majesty on his rounds, after which he repaired to his quarters within the Palace and sent to see if Sethra Lavode could be found. According to the previous watch's log—insofar as Khaavren could make out the nearly illegible scrawl—she and Aliera had emerged in the small hours of the morning and left the sub-wing, which was not sufficient information upon which to base a search or risk a conclusion; wherefore Khaavren, slightly but not unduly annoyed, returned to his customary duty, when nothing else was pressing, of attending personally upon His Majesty. He did, however, make certain that those under his command understood that he was to be informed at once should either Sethra or Aliera be seen.

The court was quiet, as if the excitement of the last few days—assassinations, attempted assassinations, the arrival of Adron, the introduction of Aliera, and the appearance of Sethra Lavode—had proved to be too much for the normally stately progression of events, and a breathing spell was therefore required. This gave Khaavren time to contemplate his introduction to and conversations with Sethra—events which had at the time appeared so fabulous that he had refused to consider them.

"Come then, Khaavren," he told himself as he observed the peaceful comings and goings of the court and His Majesty's formal greetings of the Deputies and Heirs who arrived in preparation for the Meeting of the Principalities. "You did not, if truth be known, fare too badly. It is not every day that a figure from legend appears in the flesh and presents herself before one, and a little confusion is not, therefore, to be held too strongly against one. She is, after all, powerful, mysterious, beautiful, and sinister; if these are not grounds for a certain confusion, then what could be? And if I held to my duty, and did nothing of which I ought to be ashamed, then what matters a bit of trembling in the knee, so admirably concealed by these light blue breeks, and a thumping of the heart, equally well hidden by this blouse?

"There can be no doubt, at any rate, that I concealed my feelings better than Jurabin—who, if he is not a Captain of the Guard, is at least a Prime Minister—concealed his reaction to Aliera. My word! It is a wonder that he did not tear grooves in the arm of His Majesty's chair, the way his fingers were clutching it!

"Ah, but that was a rare sight—to see Jurabin, who is normally so collected, in such a state! And over what? A pair of pretty eyes that are blue or green or some nameless shade that is neither one nor the other. Is it worth twisting one's baldric for? Not if one is Khaavren, it isn't. And look at him now, standing at His Majesty's elbow, yet staring above the heads of the courtiers—I'll be starred if his thoughts aren't upon her now.

"So, we have the Prime Minister, whose mind is taken up with a woman who—I should stake a year's pay on it—he'll never touch, and we have His Majesty, who cannot keep a thought in his head long enough for it to generate offspring. And they wonder at the state of the Empire! Cha! If I were the Dragon Heir, I should take it as a sign the cycle had turned, and march into the city with—"

He frowned and his soliloquy abruptly ended, as his thoughts continued for some few moments in a direction that he did not wish to express even under his breath. After these reflections had taken their course, during which time his face grew sterner and sterner, he made a signal to one of the guardsmen, who, being trained to respond to the least sign from his chief, approached directly.

"Yes, Captain?"

"My good Naabrin," said Khaavren, "please bring Thack here directly."

"At once, Captain."

Naabrin departed at a good, martial speed, and in a few moments, the guardsman Khaavren had designated arrived and inquired as to the Captain's wishes.

"You will take over my duties here, Corporal, for I am called away most urgently."

"Very well, Captain," he said, and stood at once to Khaavren's post, behind His Majesty, in a position where he could survey the court.

Khaavren, for his part, using the prerogative that was his right as Captain, interrupted the conversation in progress between His Majesty and the Lyorn Sir Vintner.

"Yes?" said the Emperor.

"Sire, I find I am called away. Thack, my most trusted corporal, will attend to my duties until I return."

His Majesty nodded and dismissed Khaavren with a wave of his hand. The Tiassa wasted no time in quitting the Imperial presence and making his way back to his own sub-wing, where he called for a horse to be prepared and brought to him. As this was done, he required one of his guardsmen to discover where the Duke of Eastmanswatch had encamped, and desired of another to learn if His Highness intended any public appearances.

"It is interesting that you should ask, Captain," said one guardsman, a willowy Dragonlord of the e'Terics line who had been given the unfortunate birth-name of Sergeant, leading to no end of confusion and embarrassment.

"How, interesting?"

"Well, the public scrolls spoke of his intention to speak at the dedication of Kieron's Pavilion, which is, as you know, to take place this evening, and, moreover, he has informed us of this intention."

"What makes this so interesting, Sergeant? Be laconic, I beg, for you must know that I am in a hurry, and will be setting off when my horse is ready."

"I shall endeavor to please you, Captain."

"His Highness has been, as I requested, keeping us informed of all public appearances, has he not?"

"Yes, Captain."

"He told us he would be at the dedication ceremony this evening?"

"Yes, Captain."

"And he still intends to be there?"

"No, Captain."

"How, he does not? He has canceled this appearance?"

"Yes, Captain."

"How has he informed us of this change in plans?"

"A note that has just this morning arrived by a messenger in his livery."

"Have you checked the seal?"

"I have, Captain."

"Well?"

"It is, indeed, his seal."

"But, does he give a reason for this change?"

"In a way, Captain."

"In what way?"

"Captain, he pretends that he is indisposed."

"Hmmm," said Khaavren, thinking deeply. "Very well."

At this moment, it was announced that Khaavren's horse was standing, saddled and equipped, by the door, where a groom was also waiting to help Khaavren in mounting. "I will be back this evening, my friends," said Khaavren. "You know your duties—attend to them."

"Yes Captain, we will," said all the guardsmen present, and Khaavren took himself out of the sub-wing, his long sword slapping reassuringly against his leg. Once mounted, he set off from the Palace, and, after making his way to the Gate of the Dragon, left the city at a good speed, still considering all he knew of His Highness and wondering what approach to take in order to confirm or deny the suspicions that continued to grow in Khaavren's mind even as the leagues fell before the feet of his horse.

At this same time, a short distance away, His Highness Adron, Duke of Eastmanswatch, Count of Korio and Sky; Baron of Redground, Tresli, Twobranch, Pepperfield, and Erfina; Knight of the Orders of Kieron, Lanya, and Zerika; Imperial Baron of Noughtfound, who was standing in the tent which served as his quarters, drew himself up with all of the dignity of the Dragon Heir to the Throne and the scion of

e'Kieron line of the House of the Dragon, turned to his chainman, and said, "Stuff."

The chainman, who was called Molric e'Drien, was, in the
first place, Adron's nephew, and, in the second place, a good-
looking, earnest young man who took his position very seriously indeed. He said, "I beg Your Highness to consider that,
not only had you said you would be there, and not only is the
pavilion to be dedicated to your particular ancestor, but the
Lord Mayor of Dragaera is positively depending on your appearance, and—"

"Stuff," repeated Lord Adron.

Molric opened his mouth, but Adron silenced him with a
gesture.

"Young man," said the Prince, "I will submit to battle, war,
uprising, insult, and even humiliation if my duty calls me to
it. But I will *not* submit to sitting for six hours listening to
the drivel that comes out of the mouth of Calvor of Drem,
whom I have heard before, and whose tiresome utterings, I
assure you, give me more bad dreams than the missed signals
at the Battle of the Arches. No. I have sent my apologies to
the Governor, informed the Guard of the change in my schedule, and even, though it may weigh against me in the Halls
of Judgment, rendered a thoroughly dishonest apology to the
pretended poet himself. It is done; there is no more to be
said."

Molric appeared to consult with himself for a moment before deciding that this battle was lost and his forces, such as
they were, ought to be preserved against some future engagement, which conclusion he communicated to his liege by
making a respectful bow.

"Is there anything else?" said Adron.

"Yes, General," said Molric, announcing by this form of
address that it was a strictly military matter to which he referred.

"Well?"

"A message from Turvin."

"And what does she say?"

"That she has treated for the three thousand horse Your

Highness wished for, and that the equipment is ready, and she desires to know if the horses and equipment should be placed in the manner Your Highness has described to her."

Adron considered for a moment. "Not yet," he decided. "Tell her to stable and hold them, and I will inform her when they should be emplaced."

"Very well, General. There are also chits to be signed for the expenses of transporting another month's worth of fodder to all posts."

"Leave them here, I will sign them later. Is there anything else?"

"No, Your Highness," said the chainman, with something like regret.

"Dismissed," said Adron.

Molric turned and left the tent in a manner thoroughly military. Adron returned to the activity which had been interrupted by his chainman, an activity which involved staring, first, at a small purple stone, like a gem, which he held between his thumb and forefinger, and, next, at a large, flat piece of smooth, brown wood into which several similar stones were embedded, forming a peculiar pattern. After some moments of contemplation, he picked up a sort of awl and used it to carve out another hole in the wood, into which he pressed the stone he held. Then he stepped back and considered the pattern thus expanded for some minutes, after which he gave it a grudging nod and turned to the papers Molric had left for him to look over and sign.

It was while he was engaged in these uninteresting but vital activities that he was interrupted by a clap from outside of the tent. Without turning around, he said, "Who is there?"

"General, I am Durtri, third sentry at the North Post."

"Well?"

"Lord Khaavren, Captain of the Phoenix Guards, has arrived, and requests an audience."

"Indeed?" said Adron, turning around and coming to the mouth of the tent. "I am only surprised he has taken so long. How many guardsmen has he brought with him?"

"None, General. He is alone."

"What, alone?" To himself he added, "He has some trust, then. That is, at any rate, a consolation." Then, aloud, he said, "Very well, I will see him at once."

Khaavren entered an instant later, and, removing his hat, bowed to the very ground. "I hope," he said, "That I find Your Highness well?"

"Tolerably well, sir," said Adron. "And I hope the same may be said for you?"

"Yes, I think so," said Khaavren. "And Your Highness does me too much honor by asking."

"Well," said Adron with a shrug, "if the message is not, I think, one I shall like, at least I may say the messenger does not displease me."

"Your Highness is kind," said Khaavren, "though I will admit to being confused by Your Highness's remarks about a message and a messenger."

"Confused, Sir Khaavren? Yet surely you must know that your errand will be, if not unexpected, at least in some part disagreeable to me."

"And yet I must confess," said Khaavren with another bow, "that I do not understand what Your Highness does me the honor to tell me."

"You pretend you do not understand?" said Adron, with a smile that was not unkind.

"I assure Your Highness that I am entirely bewildered."

"Well, then, what is the cause of your visit?"

"Why, the desire to see Your Highness, nothing more."

Adron laughed without mirth. "Bah, my good sir. Be frank. Do you retain any affection for me, from our experiences so long ago?"

"The Gods!" said Khaavren. "I think I do."

"Well, then, from that affection, do me the honor to answer my questions as honestly as I ask them."

Khaavren bowed. "Your Highness need but to ask; I assure Your Highness that you will not be unsatisfied with the truthfulness of my response."

"Well, then, here is my first question: You come on the part of His Majesty, do you not?"

"I come on the part of His Majesty? Not the least in the world."

"How, you do not?"

"By my faith as a gentleman," said Khaavren.

"Then you are not here to arrest me?"

"Arrest Your Highness? And for what?"

"For what? Why, you know that His Majesty was vexed with me at the end of our interview."

"On my honor, I know nothing about it."

"Impossible! Then you do not come to arrest me?" said Adron again, as if he could not believe it.

"Nothing like it," said Khaavren. "Oh, should that have been my plan, I beg Your Highness to believe I would not have traded upon your kindness this long, but should have at once said, 'Your Highness, I have the honor to arrest you in the name of His Majesty; please give me your sword and come with me.' And that would have been all."

"Well," said Adron, over whose countenance a slight shade had passed when Khaavren had pronounced the words he hadn't intended to speak. "You nearly convince me."

"And then?"

"Then it remains for me to place myself entirely at your service. Would you care for wine?"

"Wine would not be at all unwelcome, Highness, for there is no small amount of dust in the air between the city and the tent, and hang me if most of it has not taken up residence in my throat."

Adron rang a bell, and, in less than a minute, Khaavren was seated facing His Highness while the two of them drank to each others' fortune. "Apropos," said Adron when this ceremony had been thirstily brought to its conclusion, "how does your fortune fare, and that of your friends? That noble Lyorn, and the others. Do you still see them?"

"Alas," said Khaavren, "not the least in the world. I hear from Temma—that is, Aerich—from time to time, and he tells me that Tazendra is still thriving, and once or twice in a hundred years my path crosses Pel's, but I'm afraid our society is ruptured by the years, which, as you know, have neither pity nor empathy. And as to my own fortunes, well, you perceive that I am Captain of the Phoenix Guards, which would seem to be the zenith of my ambition—and not bad, Your Highness will allow, for the younger son of an impoverished Tiassa nobleman."

"Not at all bad," said Adron. "And please accept my compliments."

"And I hope Your Highness will allow me to offer congratulations for Your Highness's successes—the Breath of Fire Battalion has made a name for itself that will not soon be forgotten."

"Yes," said Adron, with a small smile. "We have not done too badly. Of course, you must take some of the credit yourself, my dear sir, for it would have been impossible to form the battalion at all if we had still to worry about invasions from the East, and, moreover, had it not been for your skill as a diplomatist we should have been unable to trade for the number of horses—the truly appalling number of horses, to be frank—which made the battalion possible."

"It is good of Your Highness to say so," said Khaavren. "Ah, but I regret those days! At any moment either a sword was in my hand or a beautiful woman was on my arm! Now, my sword remains at my side, and my arm touches nothing but the hilt, which hilt, allow me to tell Your Highness, has made a fine callus near my left elbow, which is not where soldier's calluses ought to be, and has besides worn out the sleeves of several blouses in the process."

"Is that what you remember of those days, my dear Captain?" said Adron, laughing. "Well, I remember other things. I remember a fugitive whom I was obliged to hide, and whose presence caused me to wonder if I should be led to the Executioner's Star. And I remember fear of—not an invasion of Easterners, but, rather, an invasion of Easterners that would force me to choose between duty and oath—that is, between honor and law. If there is a less comfortable choice, Captain, well, I don't know what it is."

"Ah, it is true what Your Highness says—that is a sad choice to be brought to, and, if Your Highness has no such choice to-day, well, so much the better."

"To-day? Bah! To-day my cousin is Warlord, and his younger son is my chainman, so that whenever there is an opportunity for glory, well, there is no question about who will be the first one called upon."

"Your Highness does himself an injustice in thinking that these opportunities are anything but the result of a well-earned reputation. Who else but Your Highness could have managed the Briartown affair with such dispatch? Ah, if Your Highness had been at court while that was going on! On one day comes the word of the uprising, on the next Lord Rollondar—your cousin—is preparing to march, and on the next we receive word that you have the matter in hand. I still recall the look on His Majesty's face! And a month later came the reorganization of the posts. His Majesty said, 'If Eastmanswatch can move two thousand soldiers four hundred miles in a day and a night, we should be able to move one post officer a similar distance in the same length of time.'"

Adron laughed. "Is that what he said?"

"I have the honor to assure Your Highness that those were his very words."

"And the expense?" said Adron, still smiling. "What did My Lord Jurabin say to the expense?"

Khaavren matched His Highness's smile with one of his own. "Neither more nor less than you would think," he said, "And yet, in truth, it could not be that bad. You are only one man, and you have managed the expense of maintaining the posts for ten thousand, if my memory is not at fault."

"Oh, you know I am tolerably wealthy," said Adron. "The diamonds from Sandyhome must travel through Pepperfield on the way to Dragaera, and the peppers from my own land travel in all directions, and so a part of each comes to me. In outfitting the Breath of Fire Battalion I have, to be sure, used up no small sum, but hardly enough to make me look to a surrender of debts, or to fear the loss of my daughter's inheritance."

"Well, then, can Your Highness doubt that the entire Empire, with all her resources, can be so much further behind, when there are even fewer horses to equip and stable?"

"There is some justice in what you say," said Adron.

"Indeed, I wonder, if Your Highness will forgive my curiosity—"

"Oh, indeed; you may ask anything you wish."

"Well then, I wonder at Your Highness's desire to bring the entire battalion along to the Meeting of the Principalities, which, as I understand it, is the reason Your Highness graces the city with his presence."

"Oh, you wonder at that?"

"Well, Your Highness perceives that I am but ill-informed about anything happening at the Palace that does not fall within the sphere of my duties."

"And yet," said Adron, with the ghost, as it were, of a smile playing about his lips, "do you not wonder if this battalion which now surrounds you might fall within the province of your duty?"

"How could it?" said Khaavren, affecting surprise. "My duty only involves the security of His Majesty and the integrity of the Imperial Wing of the Palace, as well as, to a certain extent, seeing to the general safety of the city and supporting Lord Rollondar's forces should he request such support. Not arduous, as Your Highness perceives, and entirely unconnected with anything Your Highness might do."

Adron, who did not seem convinced by this fine speech, still smiled. "And yet you are, you say, curious."

"Well—"

"Then allow me to satisfy your curiosity. I have brought my battalion with me for no other reason than because His Majesty requested that I do so."

"How, His Majesty?"

"Exactly."

"The Emperor, Tortaalik?"

"I know no other. You pretend you were not informed of this circumstance?"

"Not the least in the world. You perceive that, as I said, I know little that does not concern my duties. And yet I wonder—"

"Why His Majesty wanted the battalion at hand?"

"Exactly."

"I believe he is worried about disorder within the city."

"Ah, he worries about that, does he?"

"Exactly."

"And does Your Highness also worry?"

"On my word of honor, good Captain, I know nothing about it."

"And, yet—"

Here Khaavren was interrupted, for a sentry had arrived with a message. Khaavren fell silent while Adron accepted it. "Come," said the Captain to himself. "Either there is no treachery here and my fears are those of an old man, or Lord Adron is playing a closer game than any Dragonlord I have ever met would be capable of. But, what is this? He has gotten some news that puzzles him, for he is frowning. Perhaps he will tell me what it is, for I should be more than glad to know."

Adron, still frowning, looked up from the message, staring out at nothing. "This is decidedly odd," he said in a low voice, as if speaking to himself

"Your Highness?"

"Eh?" he said, looking suddenly at the Tiassa. "Oh, Sir Khaavren, I had forgotten you were here. I have just received the most unusual intelligence. Shall I tell you what it is?"

"If your Highness wishes."

"It is from a certain Calvor of Drem. Do you know him?"

"I must confess that I do not, Highness."

"No matter. He is a Phoenix, and a poet, and a colossal bore."

"Well?"

"Well, he has sent me a note in which he claims that he does not understand the reason for the excuses I sent him."

"How, excuses?"

"Yes; I sent a messenger to him, begging his forgiveness for canceling my appearance at the opening of the Pavilion."

"Ah, yes, I know something of that."

"He claims that he had no intention of being there."

"Well?"

"Well, I have here . . . now where is it? Ah! Here, what do you make of this?"

Khaavren glanced at the message, making sure his face remained expressionless, although he may as well not have troubled, for there was nothing remarkable in the note, save for its contents.

"Well?" said Adron.

"I assure Your Highness that I find it all decidedly unusual."

"As do I, Captain. In one note he says he will be there, and in the other he denies that he had ever intended to. I mistrust the unusual."

"Were I in Your Highness's place, I should do the same."

"So you think—?"

"There is some mystery here, that is certain."

"Indeed. Come, Captain, look at the first note, and at the second."

"The gods! The hands are entirely different!"

"And yet both are signed."

"With different names—this one, you perceive, claims to be from the hand of a scribe named Dri, whereas the name of the scribe according to this letter is Entoch."

"But then," said Adron, "why would he use two different scribes?"

"Perhaps, as a poet, he requires two. Is he a particularly long-winded poet?"

"He is indeed. And yet, I am not satisfied. There is, in any case, something unusual in all of this."

"I am entirely of Your Highness's opinion—I should think, in fact, that one of these documents is a forgery."

"Well, but which one?"

"Oh, as to that—"

"Well?"

"I confess that I am at a loss. And yet—" Khaavren looked at the first note, the one in which Calvor announced that he would be presenting his poetry. And, as Khaavren did so, he realized that he had seen that hand before—there was something familiar, although disguised, in the way the marks were laid upon the page.

"And yet?" prompted Adron.

"I can see no reason to forge the second note," said Khaavren. "And, as to the first."

"Well? As to the first?"

"It would seem an effective way to keep Your Highness from attending the dedication ceremony."

"Shards and splinters," said Adron. "That is true. But why should anyone wish to keep me away from the ceremony?"

Khaavren shook his head and confessed himself at a loss. "Will you, then, attend after all?" he asked.

"No," said Adron, frowning. "I have already made my excuses, and, further more, there is scarcely time."

"Then what shall you do?"

"I mislike mysteries," said Adron, in a thoughtful voice. "And shall take it upon myself to solve this one. Who can have done this and why?"

"Why indeed?" said Khaavren quietly.

"I have," said Adron, "every intention of finding out. Wherefore, if you will excuse me—"

Khaavren rose to his feet at once, and bowed deeply. "Of course. I thank Your Highness for receiving me, and for such pleasant conversation."

"It is nothing, nothing," said Adron who seemed to be so taken up by the puzzle that Khaavren had been dismissed from his thoughts even before being dismissed from his presence.

Khaavren, realizing this, made his way out of the tent, and found his horse, which had been fed, watered, and even groomed during the time he had been back visiting the Dragonlord. He saw to saddling the animal, and made his way back toward the Palace, saying to himself, "Ah, Pel, Pel! What are you doing now? And why? I will find out, if not in one way, then certainly in another!"

# Chapter the Eleventh

*Which Treats of Khaavren's Meeting
With Aerich and Tazendra,
Who Arrive in Dragaera
After a Journey in Which
They Make Very Good Time.*

KHAAVREN CONSIDERED VISITING THE DEDICATION ceremony, but his route did not take him that way, and,
moreover, he nourished a lingering fear that he had
made a mistake about Pel's handwriting, and that the second
letter was the forgery, and that therefore the poet Adron had
named would, in fact, appear; wherefore Khaavren returned
directly to the Palace. He left his horse in the hands of the
same groom who had brought it to him and who had, apparently, been standing in the same spot the entire time awaiting
Khaavren's return. The Captain left the reins and a silver orb
in the groom's hand, both of which the Teckla accepted as
natural, after which Khaavren adjourned to his quarters, stopping only to upbraid, with two carefully chosen words, one of
the guards who stood at the entrance to the wing and whose
attitude was more cursory than seemed appropriate to the
Captain.

Upon entering, he was saluted by those in attendance; he

acknowledged with a nod, and said, "Any word of Sethra or Aliera?"

"None, Captain," he was told.

He studied the log and found that nothing outside of the routine had happened, after which he ate a piece of bread with cheese and smoked kethna from the larder, then repaired to His Majesty's side (His Majesty was, at this time, just sitting down to supper with the Consort), relieved Thack, and resumed his duty.

"Well, my dear Captain," said His Majesty, who was, it seemed, in the mood for conversation. "I hope your day was fruitful."

Khaavren stepped up to His Majesty's elbow and bowed, first to His Majesty then to the Consort, after which he said, "Sire, I cannot say that it was."

"Oh?"

"Certain matters of security, Sire, led me to some investigations."

"Investigations?"

"Yes, Sire. Investigations that have proven my worries to be ill-founded."

"Well, Captain, I should rather you investigate when it is not necessary than fail to do so when it is."

"Thank you, Sire. That has always been my policy; I am pleased to find that it is agreeable to Your Majesty." He bowed and waited, sensing that His Majesty had yet more to say. Her Majesty seemed oblivious to the discussion, and concentrated all of her attention on a plate of sliced peaches, grapes, and rednuts that had been covered with a decoction of white wine and cinnamon mixed with sugar and sweet cream, all surrounded by tiny blocks of ice carved into the shape of trees. Khaavren, after noting it, turned his eyes firmly away, feeling uncomfortably like the family dog salivating at the bone on his master's plate.

Presently, the Emperor turned to him and said, "I wish that a discreet watch should be kept on the movements of the Duke of Eastmanswatch."

"Of course, Sire," said Khaavren, pretending surprise at the question.

"How, of course? You mean, you have already done so?"

"Why, yes, Sire, and the proof is that I can inform you of his activities, nearly minute by minute, from when he left the Palace."

His Majesty lifted his eyes from his plate to the Consort, who, although she attended carefully to her food, seemed ill-at-ease; Khaavren knew that she preferred matters of state to remain off of the supper-table, where they would, in all probability, clash with the decor and conflict with the comestibles. Nevertheless, the Emperor said, "Tell me briefly, then."

"Sire, he has returned to camp and remained there. Moreover, he has canceled a planned appearance at the Dedication of the Pavilion of Kieron."

"Canceled, you say?"

"Yes, Sire. A forged note is the cause of the cancellation; I am still searching for the agent of the note."

"I see. And he now remains at his camp?"

"Yes, Sire. Where there is a moderate guard, good discipline, and only the most minimal of training, consisting of post, dismount, and rolling attack drills."

"Rolling attack?"

"Exactly."

"I am unfamiliar with this term."

"Shall I explain it?"

"I would be pleased if you would do so."

"Then I shall."

"I await you." His Majesty assumed an attitude of great concentration.

"Sire, the troops are worked in companies of forty horsemen, who ride sometimes in ten files of four, sometimes in eight files of five, sometimes in other arrangements. At a word of command from the officer in charge, the soldiers dismount and cause their horses to lie down and form lines, either two or three deep, with one or two meters separating the lines and perhaps one meter separating the horses. The soldiers then draw sword and assume guard positions behind their horses. Then, at another word, they cause their horses to rise, after which they—that is, the soldiers—mount, ride, reform lines, and charge—all of which actions are accomplished in amazingly short length of time, and are, moreover, executed with great precision."

"Well, I understand," said His Majesty. "I perceive that you have, indeed, been keeping a close watch."

Khaavren bowed. "And yet, sire, I have a question, if Your Majesty will deign to permit one."

"Very well, ask."

"Did Your Majesty request that His Highness arrive with his battalion? For, if not, I confess that I am confused about why he should have arrived with them—they are, Your Majesty may perceive, a more formidable honor guard than one might expect of a Prince."

"Ah, ah. Yes, Captain, I ought to have told you, but I did make this request some months ago, when it appeared that the citizens were becoming unruly, and it appeared, moreover, that the army might be needed in the Holdfree Mines to the north."

"I remember the time, Sire."

"Well, is your question answered, then?"

"Entirely."

"Then, if you are willing, answer one for me."

"If I can at all do so, Sire, I shall, and without delay."

"This is it, then: Does this cancellation of His Highness's appearance at the Pavilion of Kieron seem at all odd to you, Captain?"

"It does, Sire. More than odd, it seems strange."

"Then you wish to learn the reason for it?"

"Very much, Sire."

"Well, so do I."

"Then I will address myself to the issue."

"How?"

"How? With Your Majesty's permission, I will attend the event myself, or, at least, the end of it, and see with my own eyes if there is any unusual occurrence. If there is none, I shall attempt to discover who forged the letter to His Highness, which will perhaps tell us who stands to benefit from His Highness's absence at the ceremony."

"Very good, Captain."

"Then, if I may retire—"

"You may."

"Until to-morrow, Sire."

"Until to-morrow, Captain."

Khaavren left at once, hastening to be out the room before he could overhear whatever remarks the Consort might choose to let fall before His Majesty in payment for the interruption of her supper. In fact, his exit was quick enough to miss Her Majesty's remarks, which included observations on the specific heat of ice, the nature of time, and other aspects of the physical world.

The Captain, though he had never given thought to the specific heat of ice, was well aware of the nature of time, and so wasted none of it while retracing his steps and calling for a horse, which was duly delivered. We should acknowledge, here, that we have, in fact, said little about the characteristics of the horses which have paraded across our pages. This is because Khaavren, though a good judge of horses (as every soldier who spends time on horseback must, to one degree or another, become), considered them nothing more than a means of transport, and gave no thought, except on the rarest of occasions, to any of the purely aesthetic aspects of the beasts. And, in fact, although Romances are often filled with long, loving descriptions of horses, it is the fact that to most of those who used these noble animals every day, transportation is exactly how they were considered; these literary descriptions usually represent nothing more than the desire of an author to extend, by a page or two, the length of his narrative. We wish to assure our readers that at no time will we indulge in this or any similar activity, and, moreover, if at any time we do stop our narrative to speak of the particulars of this or that horse, if it had a particularly fine gait, or held its head unusually high, or had the thin ankles that indicate speed or the proud chest that speaks of great strength, it will be for no other reason than that our history absolutely requires it.

This said, we will find Khaavren making his way at a good pace through the crowded streets near the Palace and the less crowded streets of the Hill District, where the newly begun Pavilion of Kieron was to be located. He was forced to slow down once he reached the Street of Ropes because of the traffic—foot, horse, and carriage—that began to come his way. He observed the colors of the House of the Dragon on several passersby, and concluded that he had, indeed, missed the ceremony. He wondered also at the lack of the parade which, he had been told, would begin at the end of the ceremony, and speculated whether the parade had been canceled when Adron had failed to appear. Khaavren determined, nevertheless, to continue on his route, hoping to learn something from those who, no doubt, still loitered at the site.

Khaavren was, to be sure, surprised at the size of the crowd, and wondered uncomfortably if he had dispatched enough guardsmen to manage it, although, in point of fact, there was no visible disorder. He looked around for gold cloaks, and was pleased to see two or three who seemed to be carrying out their tasks in a manner thoroughly professional. At length they saw him and saluted; he returned the salute and indicated by a gesture that they should continue their duty—which they did, though with perhaps a touch more alacrity, now that they were under the eye of their Captain. There were also, we should add, some number of policemen, who saluted Khaavren with the respect due an officer of a kindred corps.

With the subtlest of pressure from his knees—for he was a horseman of no small skill and had, moreover, arranged for the training of the horses—Khaavren directed his mount to bring him through the crowd, made up of Teckla who parted before him like water, bourgeois who parted before him like oil, and nobles who parted before him like sand or pebbles according to the rank, House, and disposition of the aristocrat in question. A widening in the street told him that he was approaching the market before the pavilion—an opening like the mouth of a river before the ocean leveled dirt where the lofty pavilion was destined to be erected. Amid a mass of humanity like drops of water in this sea was the wooden platform upon which the speakers had stood, and which now served as a gathering place for those who chose to depart by carriage. The tide, Khaavren observed, appeared to be ebbing; the area in front of the platform cleared as more and more of those who had assembled for the ceremony made their way down one of the three streets that came together in the wide circle which had been prepared for the construction due to begin on the very next day. Here and there he caught the flash of a gold cloak, which assured him that his orders had not been neglected.

He looked at the platform, lit by a number of torches against the onset of night, where some number of nobles, most of them Dragonlords, engaged in casual conversation, but he did not spot Adron. He signaled for one of the guardsmen to approach, and, dismounting, gave his horse into the care of this worthy. His plan was to make his way on foot to the platform with the intention of asking if any unusual incident had marred the presentation, and, moreover, if the poet Calvor had, in fact, appeared.

The astute reader will deduce from our careful use of the phrases *his plan was* and *with the intention* that, in fact, something unexpected disrupted both plan and intention, so that what next occurred was both surprising to Khaavren and important to our narrative (for the reader is by now aware that, were Khaavren's journey to the site of the Pavilion unimportant, it would have been summarily omitted from our history); any such deductions on the part of the reader are correct, as we are about to have the honor to demonstrate.

Khaavren had made his way through most of the crowd, and was only a step or two from the platform, which stood at about the height of his head, when his eye caught a sudden motion behind him and to his right, originating, it seemed, from under the platform itself. With the instincts and reactions acquired in five hundred years of training and battle, Khaavren moved sideways while turning and reaching for his weapon, yet he was keenly aware that he had been taken by surprise, and was certainly too late should the motion represent a treacherous attack—which, we hasten to add, is exactly what it represented.

From the corner of his eye he noticed what has so often been called "the glint of steel" that we dislike making use of the phrase, yet it is so descriptive of the phenomenon that we hesitate to forsake it. The realization that he was under attack and that, moreover, he had been caught sufficiently off guard as to be, in effect, helpless, occasioned in Khaavren neither fear nor anger, but, rather, annoyance directed against himself for having allowed the situation to occur.

Yet, in that peculiar space of time between Khaavren's sudden awareness of the attack and its culmination, another factor appeared, equally unexpectedly—this being a sharp sound as if a flashstone had been discharged (which was, in fact, exactly the case), which sound was followed instantly by the cessation of the attack. Khaavren, whose sword had come into his hand as if propelled from the sheath by its own will, now pointed at a body which was stretched out full length upon the ground, face downward, and which twitched and jumped as bodies so often will when the body has not realized that the mind no longer lives. At the same time, several onlookers, whose attention had been commanded by the sound we have already mentioned, looked toward Khaavren, the body, and the area in general.

All of these actions, be it understood, had happened so quickly that they were over, save for the twitching of the body and the appearance of Khaavren's naked sword, so that none of the onlookers actually saw what had happened—there had been a quick motion, a loud sound, and then the changed circumstance. A Teckla screamed. A voice said, "Well, my dear Khaavren, our arrival seems to have been timely." We should note here that, in fact, it was not a voice which spoke at all, but, rather, a person—yet as it took Khaavren some little time to identify the voice (and, hence, the person), we have chosen to use this locution to both indicate the unknown identity of speaker with reference to Khaavren, and fulfill our desire to delay, if only briefly, the revelation of the speaker's name to our readers, thus striking with two edges at once, as the Dzur say, and saving ourselves from the necessity of over-explaining, which could not but provide an annoyance to the discerning reader.

"Ah," said Khaavren turning his head in the direction from which the voice originated. "Is it you, my good Aerich? Was it you who discharged that flashstone to such good effect?"

"Not at all," said Aerich, emerging from around the side of the platform. "For here is Tazendra, who has come with me, and whose skill with such devices you know as well as I."

And, indeed, the Dzurlord appeared at that moment, the flashstone (still trailing dark blue smoke) in her hand. She smiled to Khaavren, made as if to bow, but instead rushed to embrace him—which embrace he returned in full measure, then greeted Aerich similarly, encumbered not at all by the sword still in his hand.

It was at this moment that three guardsmen, also with weapons drawn, rushed up, looking about for danger, disturbance, or, failing these, at least orders from their superior officer. "What has happened?" they cried.

"What has happened?" said Khaavren. "Indeed," he continued, as if to himself, "What *has* happened? Aerich, what did you see?"

"That person," said the Lyorn, indicating the body (which had, by now, quite stopped twitching) "made a treacherous attack upon you, which Tazendra,"—here he bowed to the Dzurlord—"managed to foil."

"I wonder who he is," said Khaavren, approaching the body. He turned it over with his foot and remarked, "Do you know, after all of these years I still cannot see a corpse—even the corpse of someone who has tried to kill me—without feeling sad. Isn't it odd?"

"I think it speaks well for you," said Aerich. Tazendra said nothing, but seemed perplexed.

"My dear Tazendra," said Khaavren, "would you be good enough to provide enough light to allow me to make an investigation?"

"Why, I should be more than happy to do so," said Tazendra. "In fact, I will do so this very moment, if you wish."

"That is exactly what I wish," said Khaavren.

"Well, here it is then."

"An Orca," remarked Khaavren as soft yellow light appeared above his head and began to brighten. "Though he has not been to sea for a score of years at least. He has never served forward of the catchhold, but was a maintopman of some skill. He has only handled weapons of the roughest sort—hardly an expert."

"You have good eyes," said Aerich. "And you have learned to use them."

"I do not see—" began Tazendra.

"He has been eating well lately, but was hungry for some time before that."

Tazendra began, "How can you—?"

"The fit of his clothes," murmured Aerich. "As well as certain lines visible on his face."

"He lives in the Underside," continued Khaavren. "Or, at any rate, has spent much time there recently."

"Ah," said Aerich. "I had wondered what that odor was."

"He uses dreamgrass extensively."

Tazendra said, "How ?"

"Stains," said Aerich quietly.

"And he is no longer addicted to murchin—"

"Which he took orally," added Aerich.

"—although he was within the last six weeks; he probably used the dreamgrass to combat his addiction."

"Which means," said Aerich, "that if you can find a murchin supplier in the Underside, you could perhaps learn more about this Orca, such as with whom he associates."

Khaavren shrugged. "There is no shortage of murchin suppliers in the Underside; half the Jhereg in the city use such enterprises to explain their income to the tax-collectors, and half of these are located in the Underside." He knelt next to the body and conducted a closer examination, which occupied some ten or twenty minutes, after which he remarked, "To the left, it helps to know that this particular supplier has a shop which lies next to a wax-merchant's or a candle-maker's, and faces directly onto the Street of the Jhereg, the Street of Vallista, or the Street of the Tsalmoth."

Aerich frowned. "I confess, my dear friend, that you have now mystified me."

"That is good," put in Tazendra. "For you know I dislike being the only one mystified."

"There is no mystery," said Khaavren, "when you recollect with what material those streets are paved, and if you know what happens to someone who has just ingested murchin orally, and you have looked closely at this poor fellow's hair and beneath his nails."

"Ah," said Aerich. "Now I comprehend."

"You do?" said Tazendra doubtfully.

"Therefore," said Khaavren, "we know what to do, and, for my part, I wish to begin at once—it may be that I will be able to discover a great deal by acting quickly, when nothing is known yet of the failure of this poor fellow's mission by those who sent him upon it."

"Mission?" said Tazendra.

"It is obvious," said Khaavren, "that he was set upon me— the signs are clear even if I had not had the experience of which I wrote Aerich."

"An assassin," said Tazendra, her brows drawing together in much the same way as the overcast will draw together and darken before the lightening opens a path in the heavens for the rain.

"A moment, if you please," said Khaavren. "I must speak to these worthy guardsmen who have been standing so patiently while I made my investigation."

Khaavren turned and beckoned to his subordinates, who held themselves perfectly still and awaited his orders. "My dears," said Khaavren, "duty forces us into the Underside, and you perceive that it is quite night. I am not unaware of the dangers associated with this course of action, and I should hesitate to ask it of you if I thought you to be any less brave and skillful than I know you are. But, as you are brave and skillful, and as duty absolutely requires it, I will lead the way, on foot as you are, into the Underside, where we will attempt to learn something of matters which affect the security of the Empire, as well as the health of him who has the honor to be your Captain."

The guardsmen bowed at once, impressed by this lengthy speech from their laconic Captain, though perhaps they wished at that moment that he entertained a slightly lower opinion of their courage and ability.

"May we accompany you?" said Tazendra.

"Why, I should like nothing better," said Khaavren. "For one thing, it will make us that much safer, and thus more likely to accomplish our mission, and for another, it will allow us to continue our conversation, during which I can perhaps discover how it is that you came to be here at just the moment I needed you, when I had thought you were far to the East in the Duchy of Arylle."

"Well, we were," said Aerich, and they began to walk toward the Underside with their escort of three guardsmen.

"Not long ago, at that," said Tazendra. "You would scarcely credit how quickly we came here—thirty hours ago we were leaving home."

"How, you came from Arylle in a day and a night?"

"Exactly," said Tazendra, proudly.

"You must be exhausted!"

"Not in the least," said Tazendra. "Oh, I confess that I was feeling a certain fatigue an hour ago, but it has quite fallen from me, so that now, why, I could charge into battle with no difficulty. And you, my good Aerich?"

"I must say that Tazendra speaks for me, too," said Aerich. "If we can be of help to you, why, you need only ask."

"I nearly think I already have," said Khaavren, smiling. He found another guardsman, and arranged for his—that is, Khaavren's—horse to be returned to the post.

"Well," he said after his horse—a fine-blooded animal with a fiery temper—had been attended to, "Tell me something."

"What is that?" said Aerich.

"You must have had a reason for coming to the city—the more so if, as you say, you came with all speed."

"Indeed," said Aerich. "You wrote a letter."

"Well, that is true."

"And then," he added, "Pel wrote a letter as well."

"How, Pel wrote a letter?"

Aerich nodded.

"Mmmm," said Khaavren. "Pel has been much given to writing letters of late. Perhaps it has become a habit with him."

Aerich shrugged.

"So it was my letter and Pel's letter, in conjunction, that brought you here in such haste."

"Exactly," said Aerich.

"Well, I know the contents of my letter, having written it, but I confess a curiosity about the contents of Pel's letter. So much so, in fact, that I beg you to tell me, without further delay, as much of its contents as you can honorably reveal."

"I will do so," said Aerich. "Pel wrote that he was concerned about an assassination attempt, which he expected would take place very soon."

"How, an assassination attempt?"

"Exactly."

"Then he knew what would happen here?"

"Not the least in the world."

"But he knew that someone was going to make an attempt on my life?"

"To the best of my knowledge, he did not."

"But then—"

"The attack he anticipated, my dear Khaavren, was not directed at you."

"Then it was directed at another?"

"Just so."

"Well? Who?"

"Lord Adron."

"How, Adron e'Kieron? The Duke of Eastmanswatch? Dragon Heir to the Throne?"

"The very man," said Aerich.

"Cracks and shards!"

"There is no doubt," said Tazendra, "that tonight's attack was an error, and the assassin took you for His Highness."

Khaavren and Aerich exchanged looks, after which the Tiassa turned to Tazendra and cleared his throat. "And yet," he said gently, "we look nothing alike, and I am dressed as a guardsman, and a Tiassa, rather than as a Prince and a Dragonlord."

"Well, that is true," admitted Tazendra. "Perhaps I am mistaken."

"Did Pel know anything about the nature of the attack upon Lord Adron?"

Aerich shook his head. "He said that he had already foiled one attempt, but did not know the nature of the second; only that he was convinced there would be one."

"I see," said Khaavren. "Yes, indeed, much is now explained. Ah, ah, Such a Yendi he is!"

"Well?" said Aerich.

"When we have discovered what we can in the Underside, we must speak with Pel, for I am certain he knows things that I would benefit from learning."

"That is not impossible," said Aerich.

"And yet," said Tazendra, "could there be *two* assassination attempts within the same day? It seems so unlikely."

"Well?"

"That is why I think the assassin attacked the wrong man."

"Well, yes," said Khaavren, and cleared his throat again. "Aerich, you have now explained why you are in the city; but what brought you to this place?"

"Upon arriving," said Aerich, "we wasted no time in asking after Lord Adron's whereabouts."

"Well, and?"

"It seemed that everyone knew, or, rather thought, that he was to be here at the dedication of the Pavilion of Kieron. It seemed that such circumstances would be ideal for a murderous attack, so we came with all speed with the idea of protecting him, only to discover that he was not here at all, which both mystifies and worries me."

"Cha!" said Khaavren. "He is not here because Pel arranged for him to be elsewhere, no doubt thinking, like you, that this would be a good place for the assassin to strike."

"And you perceive," put in Tazendra, "that the assassin *did* strike. Only, in the growing darkness—"

"Yes, yes," said Khaavren. "No doubt."

They walked in silence for a few minutes, then Khaavren said, "Whatever the reason, it is good you were there. Moreover, I am delighted to see you both, for it brings back a thousand pleasant remembrances to be walking beside you."

"If Pel were with us," said Tazendra, "it would bring back a thousand more."

"Well, that is true. But here now, if you were in such a hurry, you have no lodgings, have you?"

"That is true," said Aerich, with a smile, for the clever Lyorn knew in what direction this conversation was pointed.

"In that case, there is no reason why you cannot stay with me; you perceive your old rooms are still ready."

"We thank you," said Aerich, "and accept gladly. Indeed, if you will forgive my presumption, I even anticipated your invitation, for I have directed my servant, Fawnd, as well as Tazendra's servant, who is none other than our old friend, Mica, to go directly there when we found they could not keep up with us on the road."

"Ah, that is splendid!" said Khaavren.

"Do you know," complained Tazendra, "that I had quite forgotten the size of this city, and how long it took to get anywhere on foot."

"Well," said Khaavren, "you need not worry about that, for we are nearly there. Once we have reached the market square that you can see in the faint light provided by the glow-balls, we shall have entered the Underside, and from there it is not far at all to the place where we shall begin our investigations."

As he spoke, the bell in the Old Tower struck the eleventh hour.

# Chapter the Twelfth

### Which Treats of Social Unrest, Both in General and in Specific, And Discusses Certain Possible Responses, By Authority, to Such Occurrences.

IT IS INHERENT IN THE nature of riots that no one can be certain exactly how they began, who instigated them, or how, except in the most general terms, they might have been prevented this is, perhaps, the most significant difference between a riot and a popular uprising; it is also why the author hesitates to call the events of that evening a riot. Uprising is a more general term; disturbance a word even less specific; and with the lack of a precise word to describe the situation, the historian prefers the general word that, at least, does not mislead the reader.

It should be noted, however, that Khaavren made no distinction so nice, either then or afterward; his concerns lay in other directions entirely. The uprising, riot, disturbance, agitation, mutiny, or whatever term the reader prefers, which, by all accounts, took place on the night of the 13th and the early morning hours of the 14th day of the month of the Vallista in the 532nd year of Tortaalik's reign, began for Khaavren and his friends in the simplest manner: The Captain observed, in the very market that he was entering, three guardsmen running in the opposite direction—that is, into the Underside. Khaavren did not, we hasten to add, see this clearly, for night had quite fallen and there were few glowbulbs in this part of the city, but the three gold cloaks were unmistakable, as was the direction in which the guardsmen ran.

"Captain—" began one of Khaavren's escorts.

"I saw them. At a trot, now," and he led the way through the market, followed closely by Aerich, Tazendra, and his escort of guardsmen. He led them at a careful pace, thinking they might have to run for some time, but they had hardly left the market, stepping onto Backhoe Street, when he heard, from just ahead and around a corner, the familiar sound sword-blades make when acquiring notches and dents by being put to the use for which they were created.

"Hullo," said Tazendra, drawing her sword.

"This way," said Khaavren, taking his own weapon into his hand and leading them around the corner toward the sounds. Their escort of guards also drew their weapons. Aerich did not, but those who have read our previous history will understand that he had no need of such toys.

At points such as this one, the historian will always encounter the dangers of, to the right, assigning to those he is following a greater rôle than they actually played, and, to the left, failing to distinguish between what was witnessed by the characters through whose eyes the reader is watching the drama unfold, and the historian's own awareness, through whatever sources have come to hand, of the events as they actually took place. It is our desire to steer our literary barque carefully between these rocks, which we will do in this way: We will take the greatest possible care to inform our readers of the actual events, as they have come down to us from the memoirs and letters of those whose actions we have been following, while, at the same time, the deeds of our heroes themselves will be reported only insofar as they come from the recognized and reputable sources that have survived the Interregnum. In this way, we admit that certain trivial inaccuracies may, from time to time, enter our narrative; we hope, however, that on the whole, the foundations of our narrative edifice will remain strong, the edges sharp, the textures smooth, and the walls perpendicular.

With this clearly understood, we will say that when Khaavren came around the corner the first thing he saw, in the light of the glowbulb outside the Beescott Inn, was one of his guardsmen, stretched out upon the ground, his sword lying a few inches from his outstretched hand. Just past this fellow were two other guardsmen, who fought back to back (in the manner that Khaavren himself recommended for such circumstances) attempting, with indifferent success, to defend themselves against what appeared to be ten or fifteen opponents, all of whom were armed as soldiers, although no uniforms could be seen in the dim light, and from a distance of thirty or forty yards.

As they watched, one of the guardsmen fell to his knees; although he still maintained his guard, it seemed that he would be struck down at any instant, after which his companion would follow in short order.

"I believe," said Tazendra, "that you must order a charge if you are to save these fellows' lives."

"Well," said Khaavren, "I think as you do, my dear friend, only there is a matter which must be attended to first."

"How, first?" said Tazendra. "Before rescuing those guardsmen who, I believe, are your subordinates?"

"Yes," said Khaavren. "For there is a matter that will not wait."

He turned to his escort and pointed to one of them. "You will return at once to the guard-station on Narrows. You must run as fast as you can. You will have them send everyone at the station to this spot at once, and you will inform the sergeant on duty that I will break him if he fails to do so. You will then have a messenger sent to the Palace with orders for Baroness Stonemover to send three hundred horsemen to this spot. Emphasize, at all times, that haste is everything—an hour may well be too late. Lord Rollondar must be informed of what is happening so that he may put the Imperial Army on alert, in case our first efforts fail. Finally, you must reserve a hundred guardsmen to protect Their Majesties; these must be called up and Their Majesties taken to the Lower Square. Do you understand all of that?"

"You will judge, Captain: Return to Narrows, send everyone here; a messenger to the Palace for Thack to send three hundred horsemen; Lord Rollondar to be informed and his army put on alert; Their Majesties to be taken to the Lower Square and guarded by a hundred troops."

"That is it. Here is my ring in case anyone questions you. Give me your sword, it will slow you down and you have no time to fight in any case. Think only of speed. Now go!"

The guardsman left without another word. Allow us add, lest the reader wonder, that Khaavren had briefly considered alerting Lord Adron, but realized that bringing in the famous hero of the Battle of Briartown could enrage the populace even more than an intervention by the Imperial Army, and that, moreover, the Breath of Fire Battalion was but ill-suited—whatever His Majesty's opinion—to battles against insurgent Teckla. In any case, having now completed what he felt to be the most important part of his duty, the Captain turned toward the issue at hand—that is, the onslaught against his guardsmen. He raised his sword and cried, "Charge!"

We should remark that Khaavren's nerve was, in point of fact, at least a little shaken by what he saw; this must be so, for how else can account for the fact that, when Khaavren had covered the distance to the melee, he was holding two swords in his hands without being aware of it? Yet, upon realizing this, he took the opportunity to throw the sword in his left hand at one of his opponents, which startled this opponent long enough for Khaavren to use his other sword to good effect. In the meantime, Tazendra, at his side, was using her sword in her accustomed manner—flailing it about as if she had no control over its direction, yet making each stroke bite with deadly efficiency. Aerich, for his part, had lost none of his old skill, and, like the Lyorn warrior he was, used his hands, vambraces, elbows, feet, and knees as if they were bladed weapons. The two remaining guardsmen, we can be sure, comported themselves as befit their rank.

The result was that, in a matter of a few seconds, all of

their foes had either fled or fallen, and they—four guardsmen, Khaavren, Aerich, and Tazendra—held the field. "That
was bravely done," cried Tazendra, who, even in the dim
light, seemed flushed with pleasure.

"You think so?" said Khaavren. "Well, we must form ranks
for the night has just begun, and it promises to be a long one,
and full of hot work."

"How, you think they will be back?" said Tazendra.

"I more than think it," said Khaavren. "I am sure of it."

"Pah! Such rabble!"

"We will see," said Khaavren.

He returned to the guardsman they had first seen, a man
Khaavren did not recognize. He seemed to have taken a
wound in the face and another high in the side, but he still
lived, although the Captain, who had some experience with
wounds, thought nothing good of his chances to survive the
night.

Nevertheless, one of the guardsmen bound his wounds as
best he could, using material from the wounded man's blouse,
while another attended to the other wounded guardsman in a
similar manner.

We should apologize to our readers if too many of these
men and women who served so well remain nameless and
faceless, being referred to only as this or that guardsman;
where their names have come down to us, we do not hesitate
to supply them, but we are absolutely unwilling to fabricate
names when we do not, in fact, know them.

Of the three who had been the victims of the ambuscade,
then, one was severely injured, one slightly less so, and the
third was completely unscathed. Khaavren turned to this man
and said, "Come now, tell me what happened."

"Captain, that is easily explained," he was answered. "We
were patrolling the market and surrounding streets, for that
was our duty this evening as determined by our commander."

"Yes, I understand that. Go on."

"As we walked, I was—"

"Well?"

The guardsman, whose name was Tivor, seemed embarrassed, but finally said, "I was struck in the head, Captain."

"By what?" said Khaavren.

"By . . . that is to . . . by vegetable matter."

"I see."

"Well, Captain, we looked around, and spotted some young persons, who appeared to be taunting us."

"Ah. And you chased them?"

Tivor looked down and nodded.

"Well?" prompted Khaavren, who felt the need to understand what had happened, and determined that questions of discipline could be addressed later.

"Well, Captain, we chased them to this point, when Kyu was struck in the side by a bolt shot from we know not where. We drew the bolt, and were attempting to staunch the bleeding as best we could when we were attacked by the horde you saw, who came from two sides. Kyu, though severely injured, attempted to give battle but fell at once. We retreated to the wall, and, Captain, I will say that things would have gone ill for us if you had not appeared."

"There is no certainty," said Khaavren, "that things will not go ill yet, for everything you says confirms what I had thought from the first."

"Then you think—?" interrupted Tazendra.

Khaavren shook his head, and indicated where those who made up his small force should stand. He said, "Tazendra, have you any flashstones?"

"Why, I have three left, for you perceive that I used one at the pavilion."

"Well, I have one myself, that is four."

"I was issued one," said Kyu, who had regained consciousness and was propped against the wall.

"Five, then," said Khaavren. "We must use them sparingly."

"And yet," said Tazendra, "I do not see—"

"Be patient," said Aerich, who, like Khaavren, well understood what was about to happen.

And, indeed, it was scarcely a minute later that they became aware of a distant clamor, as of voices shouting, doors being broken down, and other sounds they could not identify save as being part of a general disorder; at the same time, they saw people running in small groups, gathering together and then dispersing, or breaking down doors with heavy instruments.

Tivor said, "Captain—"

"Be patient," said Khaavren.

And, at that moment, they heard tramping, shouting, and clashing that indicated a large body of armed citizens were making their way toward them.

As Khaavren prepared to face an angry populace (albeit a populace that had, as he had already determined, been aroused in accordance with the plot of scheme of parties unknown, rather than erupting spontaneously) in the streets of the Underside, we must run our attention elsewhither, for there was a meeting taking place scarcely a league distant. This meeting is, in point of fact, taking place at the same cabaret and even in the same back room at which we overhead the last meeting of certain conspirators, wherefore it should not surprise the leader to learn that some of these same conspirators, most particularly the one called Greycat, are again present. The other is the lady called Laral, and Greycat sat perfectly still as she stood before him and spoke.

"Chalar failed," said Laral. "He is dead."

Greycat allowed a hint of emotion to appear briefly on his countenance. "How, dead?"

"The Tiassa had some friends with him."

"I see."

"A professional would have noticed them."

Greycat stared at her. "Has the professional seen to Lord Adron?"

She stared back. "No."

"Well?"

"He canceled his appearance at the pavilion."

Greycat shrugged, as if to say, "These details are unimportant to me."

"I do not," said Laral, "go blundering about with the idea

of striking anywhere that looks convenient. That is the way to fail. And the proof is, that is what happened to Chalar."

"What will you do?"

"You will see."

"Very well."

"Is there anything else?"

"No. Have you anything else to say?"

"Yes. Be careful. There appears to be some sort of disturbance beginning some little distance away; the whole Underside may be burning by morning."

"Indeed," said Greycat. "It may."

"Then that is all."

"Remember that we are to meet again to-morrow night."

"I will not forget."

Laral rose and made her way to the door in a sinister stream of black and grey. She stopped there and said, "For your sake, I hope you know what you're doing."

"For your sake," said Greycat, "I hope so, too."

Laral nodded and left.

Grita emerged from the shadows and placed herself opposite Greycat. "So," she said without preamble, "you perceive that it has begun."

"Yes."

"Well?"

"Well, now we can only wait."

"You may also wish to reach a place of safety."

"I carry a place of safety with me at all times," said Greycat.

"Very well," said Grita. "If you will excuse me, I must be on my way."

"You wish to see how your riot is developing?"

"Not in the least. I wish to be out of the way in case the blaze becomes a conflagration; I do not have faith in my own invulnerability, and I know very well what sort of forces may be let loose to-night."

Greycat nodded, and Grita left the room. Greycat remained where he was, frowning, and wondering what the Underside, even the city would look like in the light of day. While he was doing so, some small distance away, in the Imperial Palace, the consort was frowning in almost exactly the same manner. If Greycat had known of the coincidence of expression, he would have been amused; Her Majesty would have been outraged.

But, if their expression were the same, we need hardly add that their thoughts were entirely different, saving only that the word on their lips was the same—in fact, it was the same word that was on Khaavren's lips, and is perhaps on the lips of the readers as well, that word being—*who*. The reader, perhaps, is wondering "Who is Greycat and what does he want?" Khaavren, at this same time, is wondering, "Who instigated this disturbance and why?" Greycat, meanwhile, is wondering, "Who will attempt to respond to the riot and how?" Her majesty, at this same instant, is wondering, "Who is this Aliera person, and why does everyone find her so attractive?"

We are aware that this transition—from worries about fire, death, and destruction in the city to the secret thoughts of the Consort—is abrupt. We are also fully aware that our readers are, in all probability, most anxious to learn about the former, and do not understand why they are being pulled against their will to the latter, while the city, not to mention the lives of people in whom we hope our readers have some interest, hangs in the balance. In our defense, we can only say that these thoughts (or thoughts very much like them) were, in fact, going through the Consort's mind at this time, and, as they are important to our history, we cannot fail to provide them to the reader in good season.

She stood, then, in her chambers, with her maids of honor in the next room and with her back to the glass, resolutely refusing to look into it—for she had the dignity of the House of the Phoenix, and in some matters she could not relax this dignity even in private.

"It has been two days," she said to herself, "since this Dragonlord has appeared, and in that time all heads have been turned to her—and from me. It is an aggravation. And yet, am I truly so bereft of pride, and, moreover, so frightened, that I allow such trivia to affect me? For beauty *is*

trivial—it is a surface, and inasmuch as the surface is a reflection of essence, that only applies to such matters as countenance, dress, and toilet; and I daresay mine are impeccable.
It scarcely applies to those accidents of form which were provided by capricious nature. And if—say it now, Noima—
nature has granted her a pleasingness of face and form greater
than my own, well, it is unworthy of me to allow the barest
hint of distress over such trifle to enter my deepest thoughts.

"But of course, that is not all there is to it. I am a simple
woman, in fact, only wishing to take from life those pleasures
and comforts it provides in the greatest possible measure;
and, in truth, was I born and bred for anything else? I,
who knew I would be Consort from when I was eight years
old? No. And, is it not also the case that, because of my position, I can only get what I want through the good will of
others? Surely, there is no one in the Empire with less power
than I have, if power be the facility to apply one's will directly to cause change. No, my power is only power through
those I can influence—my husband's first of all, then those
over whom I hold sway.

"And now this woman appears, and, by her appearing, my
sway is weakened, my power is reduced, my position is
threatened. No, the sting to my vanity, though as real as it is
ignoble, is not the issue here; what is at stake is my position,
which now trembles each time Jurabin's eyes turn to this
Aliera, where two days ago they had fixed on me.

"I must consider what to do. I have no wish to harm this
Dragonlord, who has never sought to hurt me, yet I must protect myself. Perhaps I can win her friendship. Perhaps. But
how? What is it she wants? She is a Dragonlord, and they are
unpredictable; furthermore, she is Lord Adron's daughter, and
he is thrice unpredictable. I shall have to—but what is that?"

Her thoughts were interrupted by a rustle of fabric and
footsteps in the next room (for so quiet was the Consort's part
of the Palace that one of her maids of honor moving to open
a door could be heard quite clearly). She heard the door in the
next room open, and someone she didn't recognize said, "I
must speak with Her Majesty at once."

"How?" cried one of her maids, a Tiassa named Daro. "At such an hour, my lady?"

"You may perceive by this pike," came the muffled voice from the next room, "that I am on duty. You may assure yourself that nothing less than strictest necessity could cause me to disturb Her Majesty at such an hour. Go, then, and inform Her Majesty that a guardsmen has come on an errand that will not wait, but that concerns nothing less than her safety."

"How, Her Majesty's safety?"

"Exactly."

"Well," said Daro, who sounded either hesitant or suspicious, "if it is so urgent as that—"

"I give you my word that it is."

"—I will inform Her Majesty that you are here."

"And you will be right to do so."

The Consort, who was wearing a white fur night-robe with a tall, gold-trimmed collar, came out and said, "I am here. What is it?"

"Your Majesty, I am Ailib of the Red Boot Battalion of the Imperial Guard, and I beg you to come along with me without delay."

The Consort stared at the tall Dragonlord, who held a pike so naturally in her hand, and said, "How is that? Come with you? And for what reason?"

"Your Majesty, there is a disturbance in the city, and it is His Majesty's wish that you be conducted at once to a place within the Palace that can be more readily defended."

At these words, there came a simultaneous gasp from all of Her Majesty's maids of honor (there were nine of them), and even the Consort herself felt slightly giddy, and put her hand to her chest, as if she were suddenly short of breath. "A disturbance?" she said.

"Yes, Your Majesty."

"Where is this disturbance?"

"In the Underside, Your Majesty. But we do not know how widespread it is, nor how fast it is growing, and so—"

"But the Guards!"

"Yes, they have been called out, and are, we dare to hope, restoring order. Nevertheless—"

"Yes, yes, of course. Come, ladies," she said, addressing her maids. "There is not a moment to be lost."

"Yes, Your Highness," they said, and prepared to follow the cool guardsman wherever she might lead.

Where she was leading them, in fact, was to a place called the Lower Square, which was far below the main level of the Palace, beneath the Imperial Wing, and consisted of eight or nine well-appointed rooms. It had been built under order of the Empress Undauntra, who anticipated (wrongly, as it happened) the need to withstand a siege or an attack, and so had wanted at least one place in the palace that could be defended, and that had, moreover, its own access to the outside world, which is why each of the rooms had a concealed exit leading into a labyrinth of tunnels.

The exact plan of the tunnels was known only to Undauntra, and thus to the Orb, and it had remained one of the most closely guarded secrets of the Imperium—Undauntra had passed an edict making it high treason to even ask about the labyrinth, ensuring that no one but the legitimate ruler would know its secrets. We should add that, although there are many stories that concern this labyrinth, it is our opinion that these stories exist because it is no more possible for a labyrinth to exist without attendant stories than it is possible for a flashstone to be introduced in the theater without, at some point in the production, its being discharged—in other words, to the best of our knowledge, there is no truth in any of the tales set within these tunnels, saving only the matter of Undauntra's whistle, which we will forgo discussing, as it has nothing to do with the history we have the honor to relate.

It was in this suite of rooms, then, that along with Jurabin, Countess Bellor, various advisors, companions, and a company of guardsmen, His Majesty abided, eschewing the comfortable if plain furnishings of the room set aside for his use, preferring to pace back and forth while awaiting word on the disturbances that had erupted in the very heart of his Empire. A hundred times he questioned Thack about what the messenger had said was going on, and a hundred times Thack had answered that the messenger had brought only orders, no information, except that there was trouble in the Underside.

"Trouble!" cried his Majesty. "Trouble! A fire is trouble; so is a flood; so is a windstorm. A thousand Teckla burning down a hundred buildings is trouble; so are ten Teckla burning down one building. An armed uprising is trouble; and so is a drunken brawl that has gotten out of hand. Which of these is it? How serious? What is being done?"

In point of fact, we should say that his Majesty could have used the magical properties of the Orb to reach out and question his Captain of the Imperial Guard. He could have, but he also knew that, if his Captain were in the midst of some critical operation, such contact could have the most disastrous consequences. So, with difficulty, His Majesty refrained and paced.

His disposition, to be sure, improved when the Consort arrived with her maids of honor, for he could then devote his energies to calming her fears—nothing relieves anxiety as much as helping relieve another's, just as wounds of the heart are best salved by helping another whose heart is wounded—for man has always lived best among his own kind, rather than alone, and there can be no doubt that when man was first forged, the need to help his fellow was mixed into the very alloy that went into his shaping.

So His Majesty sat with Her Majesty—Emperor with Consort, husband with wife—and they spoke together in low tones and awaited further news. The Orb rotated about them, a pale green, as the courtiers remarked in whispers that Their Majesties appeared to have achieved domestic harmony, and spoke in general terms of the usefulness of a crisis to show what was *truly* important and to help lovers past the trying times that they all faced now and then (although, in truth, none of these courtiers seemed inclined to give any details about any difficulties or tensions between Their Majesties of late, because, in fact no such difficulties or tensions existed, saving only a recent spat about interruptions at the supper table).

The courtiers began playing three-copper-mud, except for Jurabin who had brought a set of s'yang stones (made of ivory, in fact, with a board of cherry wood; the grooves were all hand-carved, and by a hand that knew its business), and became involved in a contest with Lady Ingera, who loved the game as much as he; the "tic" of the flat stones alternating with the deep rolling of the round ones were the loudest sounds in the room.

This was the state of things, at any rate, until there came a much louder sound—this being the rattling and knocking of wood from the next room. It is safe to say that everyone present was, to one degree or another, startled—His Majesty jumped, Her Majesty gave out a tiny screech, Jurabin missed his throw, several gamblers dropped their cards, and all of the guardsmen reached for their weapons. This was followed by an exchange of sheepish looks, when they realized that what they heard was only the sound they had been expecting—someone had pulled the clapper, announcing his presence at the door.

His Majesty drew himself up and walked toward it, as Thack, the senior guardsman on duty, called out, "Who is it?"

"Rollondar e'Drien," came the muffled answer through the door, "in company with Lord Khaavren." At the same time as this welcome response was heard, a guardsman looked through the peephole, then turned back to Thack and nodded.

"Sire," began Thack, "It is—"

"Yes, yes. Let them in at once."

"Yes, Sire."

The bolts were shot, the bars drawn back, and the door was opened to admit the Warlord, looking grim and dusty, along with Khaavren, who brought with him both the dirt and the smell of the Underside, along with rents and tears in his garb and numerous scratches and cuts on his person—his boots were scuffed and his shoulder-length hair flew wildly about, save for one spot in the front where it was matted down to his forehead by dried blood. If the Warlord, as we have had the honor to say, looked grim, Khaavren had the appearance of one who had been fighting for his life and would be ready to do so again, and woe to any who challenged him.

Khaavren resolutely forced his eyes away form the assembled and unanimously beautiful maids of honor, and dropped to his knee before the Emperor at the same time as Rollondar, executing a deep bow, said, "We can now report, Sire."

"Good," said His Majesty, making a gesture to Khaavren that he should rise. "Let me sit and listen to what you have to say, for, you understand, there is much that I wish to hear. I perceive that you have come directly from the streets."

"Your Majesty is perspicacious," said Khaavren.

Rollondar gave Khaavren a quick glance, but His Majesty chose to ignore the irony.

The Emperor sat down, then, with the two soldiers standing before him in attitudes of respectful ease. At his side was Her Majesty, who also listened attentively, a certain amount of disquiet on her countenance. Behind them stood Jurabin, and around them clustered the courtiers and the maids of honor.

When everyone was settled, His Majesty said, without further preamble, "What is the state of the city?"

Khaavren looked at the Warlord, who said, "For now, Sire, order has been restored."

His Majesty visibly relaxed, then said, "I wish to hear the details."

"Very well, Sire," said Rollondar, and nodded to Khaavren. "You ought to begin," he told the Captain, "for I was only called in later, and, come to that, at your orders."

"Very well. I can tell Your Majesty what happened," said Khaavren.

"Then I beg you to do so, and at once," said the Emperor.

"I will."

"I await you."

"Well, this is it. At the eleventh hour of last night, in the Underside, some children began to taunt some of my guardsmen."

"How, taunt them?"

"Yes, Sire."

"But your guardsmen did not respond, I hope. I should dislike to think that your discipline could be broken by children."

"At first, Sire, they did not respond."

"At first?"

"But the taunts turned into attacks—certain missiles were thrown at them."

"Ah, I see. And so they gave chase?"

"Exactly, Sire. They gave chase—into an ambuscade."

"An ambuscade?"

"Yes, Sire. Of the three, one was killed, another wounded."

"Hmmm."

"I arrived as the ambuscade was taking place, along with additional guardsmen and certain friends—friends you may recall from some years ago, during the Pepperfield affair."

"Yes," said the Emperor. "I remember them. They were involved, you say?"

"Sire, it was with their help that we—my guardsmen and I—succeeded in driving off the attackers."

"You drove them off, you say?"

"Yes, Sire. That is to say, we killed several, wounded several more, and the rest fled."

"How many were there?"

"Oh, a tolerable round number, I assure Your Majesty. A dozen, perhaps. Less than a score, at all events."

"So it was hot work, then, Captain?"

"Oh, yes, Sire," said Khaavren, laughing shortly and pulling his chin. "It was no cooler than a summer in Suntra, yet no hotter than the forges of the Serioli smiths." This speech was greeted by admiring gasps from the maids of honor, and a tiny shudder on the part of Her Majesty; Jurabin's face seemed set in stone, if we may make use of such a phrase, and the courtiers watched Khaavren carefully, not without a few traces of jealousy visible here and there, either because of the attention he was receiving from His Majesty, or the attention he was receiving from the maids of honor.

"Well, go on," said His Majesty, looking at Khaavren with respect and pleasure, for Tortaalik was enamored of all accounts of war and fighting, and the coolness of the Captain in recounting the battle pleased him.

"Sire, as I have had the honor to say, we drove them off, but we knew they would be back."

"You knew? How?"

"Sire, it was an ambuscade, hence part of a greater scheme, though I did not know—and still do not know—exactly what the scheme was. But we knew there must be more forces prepared."

"And so what did you do, Captain?"

"Sire, I dispatched a messenger to alert the nearest guard-post, and, moreover, to bring word back to the Palace; then we drew up what battle lines we could, and we waited."

"Well?"

"Well, Sire, the hottest work was ahead of us. We were not waiting a quarter of an hour before they attacked us—mostly Teckla, Sire, but Teckla armed with shovels and knives, and with leaders who knew what they were about. Indeed, we should not have survived were it not for my friend Aerich, who knew how to fight, and my friend Tazendra, who knew when to discharge a flashstone. I also have the honor to inform Your Majesty that my guardsman, Tivor, comported himself with great skill and courage."

"I shall remember that name, Captain, and he will be rewarded."

Khaavren bowed.

"But, come, what happened next?"

"Next? Well, Sire, we were holding our own, and inflicting certain damage on the enemy—"

"Damage?"

"We killed several, Sire."

Her Majesty allowed certain emotions to cross her countenance at the Captain's easy manner of discussing death. The Emperor, who had eyes only for Khaavren, said, "And your own losses?"

"Sire, another of my guardsman was killed, and yet another wounded severely, so that I do not know if he will live out the night."

"Well, go on."

"Sire, we managed to hold our position until we were reinforced by a detachment of some fifty or sixty guardsmen of the White Sash Battalion from the station on Narrows, under the command of Corporal Keen."

"You were reinforced, you say?"

"Exactly, Sire."

"And did that quell the disturbance, Captain?"

"Hardly, Sire."

"Well?"

"By this time, Sire, the planned disturbance had touched off a spontaneous riot, that threatened to grow in both length and breadth, and that in no great short time."

"Hmmm," said His Majesty. Her Majesty turned slightly pale, but strengthened her resolve as she recalled her duties as Consort, and that the Warlord had already said that the danger was in the past.

"Even with the reinforcements," continued the Captain, "there was little to be effected save containment, Sire, and so I broke what forces I had into groups of six or eight, and sent them around the edges of the disturbance, in the hopes that we could contain the amount of damage until the arrival of the army."

"And did this work?"

"I believe it did, Sire. It was thirsty work, and busy; yet when His Excellency Lord Rollondar,"—he bowed to the Warlord—"arrived, the riot had not spread beyond the ability of his forces—and forces most skillfully deployed, I should add—to quell."

His Majesty looked at Rollondar.

"Sire," said the latter, "When I arrived, Sir Khaavren,"—here he bowed to the Captain—"explained the situation in terms most precise and explicit. Upon consultation with him—in fact, upon his suggestion—we moved his forces to an area some half a league further into the Underside, while, with half of my forces—that is, with some three hundred troops—we drove the rabble into the arms of Sir Khaavren's command."

"Half of your troops, Warlord?"

"Yes, Sire. The other half remained back, and conducted a house-to-house search, to be sure we had missed none of the culprits."

"Ah, ah! I see. Well, and the results of this effort?"

"Sire, in two hours we had quelled the riot, and those responsible are now dead or imprisoned."

"How, all of them?"

"That is to say, Sire, if a dozen of them lived and are at large to escape Your Majesty's justice, well, I shall be surprised."

His Majesty beamed. "A complete victory!" he cried.

"That's my opinion," said Rollondar.

"And yours?" said the Emperor, addressing Khaavren.

"I am in all ways in agreement with the Warlord, save for one thing."

"And that is?"

"I am convinced that those responsible were not involved in the uprising, and thus are still at large."

"Hmmmm, hmmmm," said His Majesty. "Why are you so convinced that it was planned, Captain?"

"Why, Sire? Well, in the first place, there was the ambuscade."

"Well, yes."

"In the second, Sire, because of the pamphlets."

"How, the pamphlets?"

"Yes, Sire. As part of my duties, I keep track of the subversive material that is circulated within the city in general and the Underside in particular."

"Well, and of what does this material consist?"

Khaavren flushed slightly, stammered for a moment, glanced at the Consort, and said, "Sire, there is no need for Your Majesty to know the details."

"I see."

"But it is, for the most part, uh, humorous in intent."

"Humorous?"

"Yes, Sire. That is, these sheets poke fun at the court, and the edicts, and uh . . ."

"And me?"

"Yes, Sire."

"Well?"

"Sire, it is my judgment that, before a true explosion can occur, these circulars will lose their humor, and take on a tone of anger."

"Ah. And you, Warlord. What do you think?"

Rollondar bowed. "I am entirely of the Captain's opinion."

"I see. Then tell me, Captain, why is it these pamphlets are permitted to circulate?"

"Sire? Well, for two reasons."

"Two reasons? Let us see. What are they?"

"In the first place, because they would simply re-emerge elsewhere, and might be better concealed; hence we might not know when they began speaking with voices of anger rather than irony."

"That is not a bad reason. What else?"

"Because, Sire, to suppress them might well cause them to change their tone at once."

"Hmmm. Then you believe we should let them continue?"

"I am convinced of it, Sire."

His Majesty sighed. "Very well. Go on, then."

"Sire," said Khaavren, "there is little that I can add to what Lord Rollondar will tell Your Majesty of these things, and, moreover, I am overcome with fatigue."

"Ah, ah, good Captain. Yes, you must go and get your rest—you have well earned it."

Khaavren bowed, first to His Majesty, then to Her Majesty, then to the Warlord, after which he took his leave and, stopping only to give the necessary orders to his guardsmen for escorting Their Majesties back to their chambers, he made his way through the respectful looks of the courtiers and the admiring glances of the maids of honor, and so up into the Palace proper, out into the streets, and at last toward home.

# Chapter the Thirteenth

*Which Treats of Khaavren's Return Home
For Conversation with His Friends,
His Decision to Absent Himself
From the Palace for a Day,
And the Arrival of Guests.*

IN THE EARLY HOURS OF the morning, with the weight of darkness pressing silence onto the streets of Dragaera, which darkness was broken only by the occasional glowbulb or lantern outside a public house and which silence was broken only by the occasional lone footstep or call of the Watch, Khaavren made his tired way back home, his thoughts filled with scattered images drawn from the last several hours as he had experienced them; indeed, the Tiassa seemed to be in a waking dream, where hot faces and cold steel rose in ceaseless waves before him and carried with them all of the emotions—fear, anger, excitement, and even satisfaction—that, in the fury of the event, he had been too busy to feel. It was, then, with considerable relief that he came at last to his door, and it was with delight that he determined, from the low murmur of voices he heard as he opened it, that at least some of his friends were still awake, and so he need not face the loneliness of his bed just yet, while the emotions to which we have just alluded—the emotions of battle, and at times, it had seemed, hopeless battle—were still fresh in his memory.

Tazendra, who happened to be facing the hallway, was the first to see him. She rose from her chair with a broad smile and gleaming eyes, crying, "Khaavren! Ah, but it was fine bit of play to-night, was is not? Come, sit and drink a glass of wine with us, and help us as we tell the tale to our old friend Srahi. But come, you remember Mica, do you not? And this is Fawnd, who is Aerich's lackey."

Tazendra, and, for that matter, Aerich, who sat in the chair he had always preferred, still appeared to be awake and alert—a circumstance that amazed the Tiassa, knowing, as he did, that they had ridden for thirty hours and then fought for ten or twelve more. Mica appeared also to be rested and well, although the thin Teckla called Fawnd seemed, to Khaavren's experienced eye, to be stiff and in a certain amount of pain.

As it happened, Tazendra's enthusiasm was exactly the physick required by Khaavren's nerves, and, before he was aware of it, he was seated in his favorite chair, a glass of wine in his hand, laughing as Tazendra acted out in exaggerated detail a misadventure on the part of one of their antagonists of the battle; sang an old campaign song that mocked the exploits of certain generals who, though once of great repute, were now almost unknown; and recollected particulars of their past adventures.

Mica sat at the end of the couch, blushing with pleasure when Tazendra told how his famous bar-stool had been put to such good use during the ambuscade near The Painted Sign, which the reader may recall from our previous history. Khaavren observed with interest and amusement that, as this story was related, Mica made occasional shy glances at Srahi, who ignored him with such determination that there could be no doubt Mica's notice was returned.

"Well," said Tazendra, when she had for the moment run out of anecdotes, "but what of you, Khaavren? Was His Majesty pleased with your report on the night's work?"

"Pleased?" said Khaavren. "I nearly think he was. At least,

he smiled his most gracious smile, and had nothing but compliments to make us."

"Before the court?" said Tazendra.

"Indeed, before the court. And I should add that I caused your name, Tazendra, to sound in his ears, as well as yours, Aerich."

Tazendra beamed at this, while Aerich shrugged as if this were a matter of no concern to him (although, to be sure, Khaavren detected a spark of interest in Fawnd's eyes; this loyal retainer, it seemed, had more concern for his master's fame than his master did).

"Well, this is all very well," said Srahi suddenly, "only it seems that you, Sir Khaavren, must be awake at an early hour indeed, and you have had, if I am not mistaken, a long, hard night already, so that I should think sleep would not be unwelcome to you."

Khaavren's first inclination was to speak harshly to her, but then, with that perspicacity with which sensitive and intelligent natures are often endowed, he understood that she was, in her own way, displaying for Mica; and so, suppressing a smile, he simply rose and said, "You have the right of it, Srahi. The rest of you may continue your conversation, but, as for me, my bed is calling in a voice too shrill to be ignored, and I must placate it, and myself, wherefore I bid you all a pleasant evening."

"Indeed," said Tazendra; "I cannot deny that I have become weary myself; perhaps I am getting old."

Aerich shrugged, but he, too, seemed tired—and none too soon, thought Khaavren, wondering briefly if he were the one getting old.

Good nights were exchanged, and Khaavren took himself off to bed, where he slept long and deeply.

He awoke the next morning at his accustomed time, stumbled down to the kitchen, splashed water on his face, consulted with himself, then wrote a quick note, which said,

Sire, I find Myself in need of Rest after yester-day's Exertions. Should any Emergency arise, Your Majesty knows how to Reach me at Once. In hopes that my Absence does not Displease Your Majesty, I Remain Your Majesty's Humble Servant—Khaavren

He stepped out of the door, still in his nightclothes, and waited until a pair of guardsmen passed by. He called them over and put the note into their hands, enjoining them to carry it to His Majesty with all dispatch, after which he returned to his bed, where he slept several more hours, enjoying his rest as only an old soldier, who is perpetually short of sleep, can enjoy it.

He awoke the second time suffused with guilt, somehow aware that he should have been at his post. But then he recalled the events of the night before, and acquitted himself of any misdemeanor in allowing himself a day to recover, so he lay back against his pillows in luxuriant sloth until he became aware that the aroma of fresh klava was drifting up from the lower floors of the house, which in turn made him realize that his good friends were, no doubt, still present, and perhaps awake, wherefore he at once took himself from his bed, fairly leapt into his clothes, and dashed down the stairs with an enthusiasm he had not felt in centuries.

Nor was he disappointed; sitting in the parlor were Aerich, Tazendra, Mica, and Srahi, while Fawnd was emerging from the kitchen with a cup of klava, which he respectfully presented to Khaavren.

"Ah, ah!" cried Tazendra. "You have sharp ears, Aerich, for that was, indeed, Khaavren's step you heard. Good morning, my dear Captain—or, rather, good afternoon. We were just discussing the court, and who better to answer our questions than you? But come, you must, no doubt, first have your klava, which I'm certain will not be unwelcome to you."

"Far from unwelcome," said Khaavren, smiling. He sat down once more in his favorite chair, and inhaled of the bittersweet aroma before tasting it. He relaxed further into the chair, sipped again, and said, "But come, Tazendra, how long have you been awake?"

"Oh, not long, not long," said Tazendra. "An hour, perhaps, since I rose, and Aerich was only drinking his first cup when I emerged."

"Ah, well, then I have not been so lazy as I might have been. Did you sleep well? And you, Aerich?"

"Oh," said Tazendra, "I slept tolerably soundly, I assure you—I remember nothing after my head touched the pillow until I smelled the klava that Mica was making, and which pulled me from he bed as if horses were dragging me bodily from it."

"And I," added Aerich, "slept all the better for the warm remembrances inspired by this house where we shared so much trouble and happiness."

Khaavren continued drinking his klava from a large, black ceramic mug upon which his device and name were engraved on a silver plate affixed to the mug—a mug that-had been given to him by his command upon the date of the 500th anniversary of his promotion to ensign. He noticed that, although Srahi and Mica were not, in fact, sitting together, nevertheless their eyes often strayed toward each other, and that when their eyes met, Srahi would smile and Mica would blush and look at the floor. Khaavren, though tempted by memories of Srahi's sharp tongue to embarrass her, virtuously resolved to say nothing on the matter. Instead he treated it as a matter of course and addressed Tazendra once more, saying, "I'm afraid, however, that I must disappoint you in regard to your desires."

"How, disappoint me? In what way?"

"There is little, in fact, that I know of the doings of the court."

"What?" cried Tazendra. "You? Who live all of your life in the pockets of Their Majesties?"

"That is ·just it," said Khaavren. "In truth, there is little enough that can be seen from inside a pocket."

"Bah! So you do not, at this moment, know what gossip and scandal there is?"

"As I told Pel a week ago—splinters! Only a week!—if you wished to find anyone in the Empire who knew less of the gossip of the court, well, you would have a difficult search. When the courtiers gossip, I am on duty and cannot listen. When His Majesty does me the honor to address me, it is a matter of orders, not the reason for the orders. The guardsmen—who, as you recall, are always among the best informed—do not discuss such matters with me because I am an officer, whereas the other officers, such as the Warlord, do not discuss such matters with me because I have His Majesty's ear."

"Well," said Tazendra, who seemed to follow this speech only with difficulty, "that is a shame, for I had hoped to learn much that I could not learn in the duchies. You say you know nothing?"

"Not enough to satisfy you, my dear friend; although, to be sure, I know that these are trying times for many who make their homes at court."

"Trying times?" said Aerich, raising his eyebrows and putting into his expression an eloquent request for more details.

"Trying times of a certainty," said Khaavren. "Attend: Do you not know that, when the economy is troubled, intendants are dismissed? And, in addition, when war goes badly, generals are executed?"

"Well, yes," said Aerich. "That is the usual way of the world."

"Well, they have been executing intendants."

"Ah!" said Aerich.

Tazendra said, "But not, I hope, dismissing generals?"

"As to that, I cannot say."

"Well," said Tazendra, "so the economy is troubled?"

"Shards!" said Khaavren. "I nearly think so. His Majesty has no more money until the new Imperial Allowance is decided, the Great Houses bicker about how to avoid paying their share, the Teckla prepare to rise against the taxes, the revenue farmers prepare to revolt against the Empire if the Emperor decides to recall their tax-rolls, the mines are shutting down for want of food, ships lie idle in the harbors of Adrilankha and Northport, the armies and the wizards wait for negotiations with financiers before taking action to end the uprisings and droughts—in truth, the problems are better

suited to the reign of the Orca than that of the Phoenix."
Khaavren punctuated this speech with an elaborate shrug, as
if to say, "What matters any of this to me?"

Aerich gave Khaavren an indulgent smile, as if the Lyorn
did not for a moment believe the Tiassa's protests of uncon-
cern. Tazendra seemed about to speak, but at that moment
there came the sound of wood knocking on wood that indicated someone had pulled the door clapper.

Khaavren sighed. "I am needed at the Palace," said he,
"for some trivial matter."

"How, needed?" said Tazendra.

"How, trivial?" said Aerich.

"Why, yes. Who else could be calling on me but someone
from the Palace? And if it were urgent, His Majesty has faster
ways of reaching me than sending a messenger."

"Well, are you going to answer it?"

"Cha! Let Mica answer it. Lackeys are in fashion now; let
the messenger think I have one, and that he wears the livery
of the House of the Dzur; it will cause gossip and speculation, which will bring me a certain satisfaction in the contemplation, as I do not hear these things."

Mica rose and went to see who was at the door. From the
living room, they could hear the door open, then a murmur of
voices, and then silence. Khaavren frowned, suddenly remembering his last unexpected visitor and hoping that he had
not put Mica into harm's way. He was on the point of rising
to see when Mica returned, his eyes wide and his face pale.

"Well?" said Khaavren and Tazendra together.

The Teckla opened his mouth, closed it, swallowed, opened
it again, and said, "There are visitors, my lord."

"How, visitors?" said Khaavren. "Well, haven't they
names?"

"Indeed, they have names," said Mica. "And even, if I may
permit myself the honor of expressing an opinion, very good
names."

"Well?" said Tazendra. "What are these names? For you
perceive we are waiting for you to tell us."

"I am about to tell you," said Mica.

"Do so, ninny!" said Tazendra.

"They are," said Mica carefully, "Aliera e'Kieron and Sethra Lavode."

"The Horse!" cried Tazendra. "Adron's daughter, and Sethra Lavode? Here? Now?"

"Shards and splinters," said Khaavren. "It seems I was entirely wrong."

"Well," said Aerich, smiling. "Are they less welcome for your error?"

"Not in the least."

"Then, are you going to invite them in?"

"Cha! I nearly think so. Come, Mica, bid them enter."

Mica bowed and, not without some signs of trepidation, went to show in their guests. Everyone stood as Aliera and Sethra entered the room.

"Welcome," said Khaavren, bowing like a courtier. "Allow me to name the Tazendra and Aerich. Sethra Lavode and Aliera e'Kieron."

Courtesies were exchanged on all parts, after which Khaavren asked if their new guests would care for klava. This offer was accepted, and Fawnd stiffly brought in two more steaming cups, after which, still showing signs of pain, he vanished back into the kitchen to make more, along with Srahi to pulverize the beans and Mica went to accompany Srahi, leaving Sethra, Aliera, Aerich, Tazendra, and Khaavren alone in the room.

"Well," said Khaavren, "your visit is as unexpected as it is welcome. Do you know that I have been searching for the two of you?"

"How, searching for us?" said Sethra. "Impossible."

"It is a week since I have done anything else," said Khaavren.

"But then," said Aliera, "you must have a reason."

"I nearly think I do," said Khaavren. "You must know that I am anxious to learn the results of your investigations."

"Investigations?" said Sethra. "You mean, into the murders?"

"Well, and what else?"

"But," said Aliera. "We have learned nothing definite; you must know that we should have told you at once if there was an accusation to be made."

"Ah," said Khaavren, attempting to conceal his disappointment. "Well, but then, to what do I owe the pleasure of your visit? For you should believe that, delighted as I am by two such lovely and renowned ladies gracing my home, I cannot believe you have come to enjoy my society—especially when I recall that, had I not been overcome by my labors of yesterday, I should be at the Palace now and not be home at all."

"But we knew you were not at the Palace," said Aliera.

"How, you knew?"

"Of a certainty, and by the simplest possible method—we asked after you there."

"And," continued Khaavren, "finding that I was not there, you searched for me here?"

"We more than searched for you," said Sethra. "In fact, we found you."

"Shards! I nearly think you did. Well then, having found me, I hope you will do me the honor of explaining the reason for your search, for you must know that I am curious."

"Then," said Sethra, "we shall satisfy your curiosity."

"I shall be happy if you do."

"As will I," added Tazendra, who wished to call attention to herself before such illustrious visitors.

Aerich merely shrugged.

"We have," said Aliera, "something to report in our investigation into the magic involved in the death of Gyorg Lavode, and of the others."

"Something to report? But you have just told me that you had come to no conclusions."

"There are conclusions," said Aliera, "and conclusions."

"And what you say is true," said Sethra. "We have arrived at nothing definite. Nevertheless, we have learned certain things, and we thought you should know, in order to help your own investigations."

"Well, you are entirely correct, and I am pleased you have

done so. Is it safe to say that you have, at any rate, learned certain things?"

"Yes," said Sethra. "Or, that is to say, no."

"I beg your pardon," said Khaavren, "you must understand that this answer confuses me."

"She means," said Aliera, "that we have found answers to some of our questions on some matters, but none to which we can subscribe without room for doubt."

"Ah. Now I comprehend. Well, then, what are these conclusions, insofar as you can explain them?"

"I forewarn you," said Aliera, "that this concerns sorcery."

"Well, sorcery doesn't frighten me."

"And," put in Tazendra, "sorcery intrigues me."

"Then we shall explain," said Aliera.

"I await you," said Khaavren.

Sethra said, "The forms of sorcery that were used—that is, the patterns of tensions and energy about the affected area—are those of an unskilled sorcerer of the House of the Dragon, or a skilled sorcerer of the House of the Jhereg, wishing to disguise his hand."

"I had not known," said Khaavren, "that these patterns were similar."

"They are not," said Aliera coldly.

"They can easily be mistaken, one with the other," said Sethra. Aliera responded to this comment with a quick glare at Sethra, but did not speak.

"Ah," said Khaavren quickly. "I see your confusion. But, at any rate, it is hardly the work of your father—no one would say he is unskilled."

Aliera began to speak, then closed her mouth. Sethra said, "He is so skilled, my dear Captain, that, if he wished, he could make his hand look like that of an unskilled Dragon, or a skilled Jhereg."

"Oh," said Khaavren.

"We must look further," said Aliera, "for the proof of my father's innocence."

"We must look further," said Sethra, with a certain sharpness of tone, "to learn what actually happened and who is really responsible."

"The tasks," said Aliera coldly, "are identical."

"That remains to be established," said Sethra.

"But do you doubt the outcome?"

"I doubt everything."

"And do you doubt my word?" cried Aliera, rising to her feet.

"Your word, no," said Sethra, also rising. "But your judgment."

"So you said only yester-day," said Aliera. "And do you recall my response? I have not changed my mind, and I do not at this moment see a librarian arriving with ancient sorcerous tomes to distract us from the business at hand."

"Well, no more do I."

"Then, do you persist in your remarks?"

"This will be interesting," whispered Tazendra.

"Hush!" said Khaavren and Aerich together.

Sethra said, "I have seen you work, lady, and you are skilled in hand and daring in thought, but if you do not temper your opinions in the cool water of fact, the theory you forge may shatter the first time it is crossed with another."

"Then let us step into the street, oh lady of the tangled metaphor, that I might unweave it for you, and at the same time, teach you something of the tempered steel you discuss so carelessly."

"If you wish," said Sethra. "Do me the honor to lead, and —what is it?"

This last remark, so different in tone from those preceding it, was occasioned by a sudden change in Aliera's countenance: Instead of appearing cold and haughty, she now wore an expression of intense concentration, as if something she wished to remember were eluding her, or she were trying, like an actor of the Hantura school, to hold every muscle unmoving for as long as possible.

Khaavren rose to his feet. "Lady Aliera," he said. "Is something wrong?"

"Do not speak to her," said Sethra, who had understood almost at once what was happening. "She is involved in psychic communication—mind to mind."

"Shards!" said Khaavren. "With His Majesty?"

"With her father, I would think—for I know they communicate in this fashion from time to time."

"How, is this possible?"

"More than possible," said Tazendra. "Though I have never done it, I have been studying the art, and it is certainly possible between people who know each other well and are master sorcerers."

"Indeed," said Aerich. "It was thus, if you recall, Khaavren, that Garland kept in communication with Seodra; have you forgotten the famous disk he left behind?"

"Ah, yes, that is true," said Khaavren, remembering their old antagonist Garland and how he had communicated with Seodra. "Hang me, but I *had* forgotten it."

"It is exactly as this lady," here Sethra bowed to Tazendra, "has said. It is something a skilled sorcerer can sometimes do, although it works best when aided by a device, or between two people who know each other's minds very well indeed—such as a father and a daughter."

"Well," said Khaavren, "there are times when such a skill would be useful indeed. This may indeed be such a time for the Lady Aliera, as I perceive from her countenance that she is communicating on a matter of no small importance."

As he said this, Aliera's eyes suddenly focused on Khaavren—it was evident that the communication had ended. She bowed to her host and said, "I must leave at once. I have an errand that will not wait."

"Very well," said Khaavren. "We will, no doubt, see you again."

"No doubt," said Aliera over her shoulder as she left the room. An instant later the door was heard to open and close with a force that testified to the urgency of the Dragonlord's errand.

Khaavren drew a breath, then sat down. Sethra seated herself as well. Mica came in with klava; he had been standing in the doorway, afraid to enter, during the latter part of this conversation. Now he entered with some hesitation and poured klava from Khaavren's silver pot.

"Does this mean," said Tazendra to Sethra, "that you aren't going to fight?"

"Not at the moment, in any event," said Sethra, smiling a little.

"Well," said Tazendra, sounding disappointed, "perhaps it is for the best."

Aerich shrugged.

"You were explaining," said Khaavren, "that you have, in fact, been able to determine little about the spells used in the murder?"

"For my part," she said, "I am convinced that they were prepared by a Jhereg."

Khaavren frowned. "You are convinced of this?"

"Yes, I am."

"But then, why did you—"

"Irritate the Lady Aliera? Because I enjoyed it." She accompanied these words with a smile that made the hair on the back of Khaavren's neck wake up and stretch.

He cleared his throat to hide his confusion, and said, "I will take this information, then, and see what I can learn of the matter. I will say that I am nearly certain the murders are related to the riot yester-eve, though it is nothing more than instinct which tells me so."

Sethra nodded. "It is not hard to believe," she said. "It is clear that there is a conspiracy at work—a conspiracy that has laid its plans deep and subtle."

"Like a Yendi," murmured Aerich.

"Where is Pel?" said Tazendra.

"Who?" said Sethra.

"A friend of ours from long ago," said Khaavren. "He is a Yendi, and he now studies the art of Discretion. It was he who warned us of the attempt on Adron's life."

"Hmmm," said Sethra. "Could he be involved?"

Aerich shook his head. "If Pel were involved, we should not suspect a Yendi."

Tazendra frowned, as if trying to make sense of this, while, at the same time, Sethra frowned, shrugged, and rose once more to her feet. "Well, I have told you what I agreed to tell you. I will now continue my investigations, and do you do the same, and we will speak more of what we have found. Come, do you think my plan a good one?"

Aerich raised his eyebrows and shrugged at the word, "plan" while Khaavren said, "Entirely." Lyorn and Tiassa rose and bowed to Sethra, while Khaavren added, "For my part, I shall attempt to discover—"

He was interrupted by the rattle of the door clapper. Khaavren looked at Sethra, at Aerich, and at Tazendra, then watched the doorway. Presently, Mica came in and said, "A messenger from His Majesty has arrived, and desires Lord Khaavren to accompany him back to the Palace."

"Indeed," said Khaavren.

Srahi appeared behind Mica and said, "I'll fetch your sword and your uniform, Lord."

Khaavren began to ask why she wished to do this, but then changed his mind and simply nodded.

"What do you think His Majesty wants you for?" said Tazendra.

Said Khaavren, "Some trivial matter."

# Chapter the Fourteenth

### Which Treats of the Arrest
### Of a Superintendent.

WAS THE MATTER UPON WHICH Khaavren was summoned trivial in fact? This is not a judgment the historian is willing to make. The reader need not, of course, be reminded of the "Tale of the Smudged Letter," in which a drop of water causes the sinking of an island; and there can be no doubt of its basic, though apocryphal, truth: History is, for the most part, a recitation of paltry insignificant deeds that, taken together, or in sequence, reveal the complex workings of Man and how he came to the place he occupies. We cannot say if the single event for which Khaavren was ordered back to the Palace (which was, to be sure, of more moment than a love-letter to a cobbler's servant) was a vital link in the chain of events that we have chosen to narrate; we can only narrate it, and allow the reader to make this decision for himself.

Yet it behooves the historian, as one who has taken upon himself the task of relating historical fact and revealing causality and logic in the interrelationships of these facts, to consider the following: How poorly must this letter have been worded, that one drop of water could change its meaning so completely? How ignorant must have been the boatman to be unaware of the currents in a river he crossed every day? How foolish must have been the seer to mistake a broken oar for a sign from the Gods? How foolhardy must have been the wizard to exchange runes in a spell without testing the results? And so we may continue down the sequence of events related in the tale.

The lesson of the fable—which is, as much as anything else, to keep one's roof always in repair—is certainly a good lesson for those whose dispositions incline them toward laziness. Yet it would be a poor historian who would accept the mere relation of such a series of events as being good and sufficient explanation.

So, then—was the matter upon which Khaavren was summoned to the Palace trivial? This, we repeat, is not a judgment we are prepared to make. Nor, for that matter, did Khaavren make any such judgment; his only concern was whether it fell within his province as Captain of the Phoenix Guards, and it was to answer this question that, upon arriving at the Imperial Wing, Khaavren went at once in search of His Majesty.

While Khaavren had been speaking with his friends, an entire day had passed at the Palace (and Khaavren's absence, while noticed, had not impaired the functioning of the offices or ceremonies of the court in any way), so that when our worthy Tiassa—that is to say, Khaavren—arrived, His Majesty was at supper with the Consort.

Khaavren caused himself to be announced, and prepared himself to endure Her Majesty's stony glare while Imperial matters were transacted at supper for the second time within a week. However, he was not brought into the room—instead he was given a note with the Imperial seal.

He frowned, broke the seal, and, standing just where he was—without the Hall of Windows—read it. It was short and left no room for questions or interpretations: "Order for Khaavren, Captain of the Imperial Guards, to arrest the Countess Bellor, Superintendent of Finance, and confine her in my prison in the Iorich Wing of the Imperial Palace." It was signed by Tortaalik.

"Well now," murmured Khaavren, recalling his words of just a few hours before. "I spoke better than I thought if it has really come to this."

He addressed the servant who had handed him the message, saying, "How are His Majesty's spirits today?"

"His spirits, My Lord?" said the servant, a young Teckla with a clear eye and large ears.

"Yes. His spirits. Is he angry, distracted, cheerful?"

"Well, My Lord, it seems to me that he has had a sour disposition for the entire day."

"Ah, ah! And do you know anything that might be the cause of His Majesty's unhappiness?"

"My Lord, I know that he spent some time closeted with Jurabin, yet he seemed to be in an ill humor even before this occurred."

Khaavren shrugged. "I would be in a sour mood if I knew I would be forced to spend time with Jurabin," he thought to himself, "but I suspect there is more to it than that. But, still, no doubt the minister gave him news that displeased him, and the blame fell on poor Bellor, and that is the whole story." Aloud he said, "Tell me, if you would, did anything unusual happen at court today?"

"Unusual?" said the Teckla, frowning. "Well, My Lord, there was the fish discovered in the bathing pool. No one yet knows who put it there, yet the gentlemen of the court all laugh whenever—"

"What else?"

"What else? Two Teckla demanded to see His Majesty at different times during the day, which is, My Lord, the first time I have known two to appear on the same day."

"And was His Majesty disturbed?"

"Oh, not in the least, My Lord; Dinb was able to discourage both of them with no trouble. But it is unusual that, in one day—"

"Yes, yes. Pass on. What else of moment happened today?"

"Well, there was a petition from the Academy of Discretion, but I do not know its substance, for it was delivered in private."

"Ah, ah," said Khaavren. "A request for funds, no doubt."

"That is possible," said the servant. "And even likely. For immediately after the petition was presented, Countess Bellor was sent for."

"Indeed," said Khaavren. "Well then, perhaps that goes some way toward explaining things."

"Explaining things?" said the servant.

"Nothing, nothing," said Khaavren. "It doesn't matter. I am wondering aloud. Thank you for the information you have given me, my dear fellow. Here, take this to drink my health, and I will take another and drink yours."

"Willingly, My Lord," said the servant, pocketing the coin, bowing, and going about his business.

Khaavren spent a few more minutes thinking over what he had learned, then he shrugged philosophically, knowing that he might never know the full and exact reason for the order, and that knowing it made no difference to the execution of his duty. Khaavren, like a good officer, was rarely more content than when he had a clear, unambiguous order to carry out, and an order, moreover, that he knew to be within his powers to fulfill. Hence he put the letter into his belt next to his gloves, adjusted his sword-belt, and set off for the offices of the Superintendent of Finance.

The Superintendent had, in fact, two offices. The first was on the fourth floor of the Imperial Wing. It was large, elegantly appointed, lavishly furnished, and never used except for entertaining official visitors. The second, to which Khaavren at once took himself, was in the Phoenix Wing, on the first floor but far, far back, nearly abutting the Imperial Wing (although, except for any secret passages of which Khaavren was unaware, there was no direct route). Khaavren had no need to ask directions, and he found himself in front of the door, at which he clapped twice, strongly.

A clerk, a Lyorn Khaavren had never seen before, opened

the door, peered out, then opened the door wider, at the same time blocking it.

"My Lord," said the clerk. "May I perform some service for you? If you are here concerning pretended arrears in pay, I assure you that no one can help you until to-morrow, when you must present yourself between the twelfth hour after midnight and the third hour after noon, and you must, moreover, bring with you papers indicating—"

"Is the Countess Bellor within?"

"Why yes, My Lord. She is indeed. And yet, I am sorry to say that matters relating to arrears in pay, or," here the clerk looked at him shrewdly, "advances, are not to be addressed at all except—"

"Then if you will be pleased to announce to her that Khaavren, Captain of His Majesty's Guard, wishes to pay her a visit, I will be grateful to you."

"Nevertheless, My Lord, I must insist that—"

"A visit, I should add, on Imperial business."

The clerk hesitated.

"You will do well not to waste His Majesty's time," said Khaavren.

The clerk blanched at the cool, official voice of the Captain; he licked his lips, hesitated for another instant, then nodded and said, "My Lord, I will be honored to announce you at once."

"That would be just as well," agreed Khaavren pleasantly.

The Countess Bellor appeared with almost no delay, an expression of curiosity on her sharp-featured face. She wore purple and red of the finest silk, with gold over all, and had painted a red streak down the middle of her hair. She carried herself with the air of one accustomed to being polite out of duty, who knows herself to hold one of the highest posts in the Empire. She did not, in either dress or countenance, have the look of quiet skill and intelligence that Khaavren had always thought should mark the Superintendent of Finance for the Empire. Khaavren shrugged off these thoughts, for, he admitted to himself, he had never had Tazendra's knowledge of fashion, Pel's impeccable taste, or Aerich's ability to wrap himself in such dignity that whatever garb he affected appeared to be the height of elegance.

He bowed deeply to the Phoenix noble and said, "Countess Bellor, I am here on behalf of His Majesty."

"Well," said the Countess. "You are then doubly welcome. Please come in, and tell me at once how I can make myself agreeable to His Majesty my cousin."

Khaavren took a step into the room and bowed once more. "You can make yourself agreeable, Madame, by doing me the honor of putting your sword into my hand."

"Your pardon," said Bellor. "You wish for my sword?"

"Yes, madam, you have understood me exactly."

"I am to give you my sword?"

Khaavren, who was used to having his speech, normally so clear and precise, questioned at such times, merely nodded gravely.

"But, what use could you have for my sword?"

"None, in point of fact," said the Captain conversationally. "Nevertheless, I must have it."

Bellor stared. "How, am I arrested, then?"

"Yes," said Khaavren, bowing slightly. "That is it exactly. You are arrested."

There was a slight commotion behind Khaavren, but, when he looked around, he discovered it was caused by the clerk who had first admitted him, and who, upon hearing the word *arrest*, had sat down suddenly and without first being certain of the location of his chair.

Bellor, who seemed oblivious to her clerk's discomfiture (being, no doubt, too concerned with her own), said, "His Majesty has ordered my arrest?"

"Your arrest, madam, and even your confinement."

"My confinement? In prison?"

"Yes, Countess. Your confinement in prison. I am, in fact, to escort you there at once, as soon as you have surrendered to me your sword."

"But . . . but this is impossible!"

"How, impossible, madam? Not in the least. I assure you that I have carried out such orders before, and they are entirely possible. In fact, only rarely do they present any difficulty. I would hope that you shall not be one of those who present such difficulties, for you perceive it could only be unpleasant for us both, and the result will be no better than if you had remained agreeable."

Bellor stared openmouthed at Khaavren, so that her costume, which had appeared to him silly before, now, stripped of its wearer's confidence in herself and (hence) her appearance, seemed positively absurd.

"Come, madam," said Khaavren. "You perceive there is no reason to delay."

She looked at him as if he were a sort of impossible and inconceivable animal, then said, "May I be permitted time to write a short note to His Majesty?"

"You may," said Khaavren. "And, moreover, I will undertake to deliver it into his own hand, if you wish."

"I assure you, you will make a friend for life if you do so."

Khaavren shrugged. This was not the first time he had made a friend for life of one he was escorting to the Iorich Wing.

"And," she continued, "may I be allowed to change my clothing? For I am hardly wearing appropriate garb for prison."

"Better than that," said Khaavren, "you may take time to pack a small valise, so you will have some choice of what to wear while you are confined. However, I must watch you pack, to ensure that no papers are accidentally taken or destroyed, as sometimes happens when one packs in an hurry."

Rather than being insulted by this insinuation, Bellor gave a distracted nod as if she could not understand how any papers she possessed could matter to anyone. "Come, then," she said, "and we will fetch my sword."

"I ask nothing better."

She led the way past several plain desks at which sat clerks and intendants, all of whom wished to give the appearance of being hard at work and oblivious to the drama taking place. They went back into her office, which was filled almost to overflowing with pictures on the walls, chairs on the floor, and jewelry suspended from the ceiling, and in which a small desk covered with dust and documents was hidden in a far corner. After searching for some little time, she found a be-jeweled rapier in an even more bejeweled scabbard. Khaavren took this weapon with a bow, hiding his distaste as well as he could. He need not, in fact, have troubled himself, for Bellor was entirely oblivious to everything except the shock she had just received.

Khaavren did her the courtesy of turning his back while she changed into a pair of white breeks and a blouse that was also white and decorated only with a bit of gold lace, along with simple, comfortable brown boots. When she announced that she had finished changing her dress, Khaavren escorted her up a stairway in back which led to her quarters, and watched while she summoned a servant to pack a valise and to carry it for her. This operation took some little time, during which the Countess asked if Khaavren knew anything of why she was being arrested.

"I assure you, madam," said the Tiassa, "that no word of any reason has reached my ears."

"It is strange, then," said Bellor.

"Indeed," said Khaavren. "You are, then entirely ignorant yourself?"

"I feel as simple as a cow-herd," she said.

"So, then, you have done nothing to offend His Majesty?"

"Nothing at all, I swear it."

"You have not, for example, refused him funds he re-quested for some purpose or another?"

"How, refused him funds? Oh, Captain, it is true that he requested funds for the Academy of Discretion."

"And did you supply them?"

"You must understand, Captain, that there were no funds available, which I hardly think is my fault."

"It is not your fault?" said Khaavren. "You, the Superin-tendent of Finance?"

"Well, it is true that I am Superintendent of Finance. But in that rôle, I only keep watch on what money there is—I cannot create it."

"Well, and did you explain this to His Majesty?"

"Of a certainty I did."

"And did he seem satisfied with the explanation?"

"As to that, I could not say. At any rate, he asked me to show him the records."

"Well?"

"Well you understand, Captain, that I could not do so. The intendant who kept track of such things is scarcely cold. He was murdered, you perceive—"

"Yes. Smaller was his name, was it not?"

"That was it exactly."

"And he was the one who knew the state of the treasury?"

"As well, Captain, as you know your sword."

"You must miss him."

"To be sure, there has not been an hour since his death when I have not mourned him."

"What sort of fellow was he?"

"Oh, as to that, I couldn't say. We hardly exchanged ten words in the scores of years he has been employed by me. Yet—"

"Forgive me, madam, but I believe your valise is ready. Come, allow me to escort you."

On the way out, they walked past the Lyorn clerk, whose mouth had not yet managed to close, and to whom Khaavren remarked, "Perhaps I will see you soon about an advance in pay," to which the clerk could find no response. The servant closed the door behind them. As they left, Khaavren and Bellor walking together as if they were old friends, and the servant trailing behind with the valise, the Tiassa said, "I have the authority and the freedom, madam, to take any reasonable route to our destination, which is, of course, the Iorich Wing. Since I have this freedom, why, I give it to you. Have you a preference?"

"A preference?" said Bellor. "Why should I have a preference?"

"Well, you perceive that you are arrested."

"Indeed, sir, you have my sword."

"Exactly. Now some, upon being arrested, prefer that as

few people as possible see them. Others, for fear of vanishing without a trace, prefer their arrest to be witnessed by as many as possible. I, having received no orders on the subject, will be happy to guide you in whatever way you wish."

"You are most courteous."

Khaavren shrugged.

"Well, the answer to your question is that it matters to me not at all, wherefore you may choose whatever path most pleases you."

"Very well. In that case, we will take the shortest route. We ought, in that case, to turn here, descending these stairs, which will take us all the way down to the Blue Corridor, which leads directly to the main floor of the Iorich Wing."

"As you wish, Sir."

Khaavren had, by one route or another, arrived at the Imperial Prisons beneath the Iorich Wing perhaps a hundred times, yet on each occasion he was reminded of the first, when he came as a prisoner rather than a captor. This memory awakened several emotions within our Tiassa: a certain irrepressible fear of confinement; a sad longing for the simple love he had felt for Illista, who had proved herself false within these very walls; and a certain pleasure as he recalled the triumph which had followed on the very heels, as it were, of his disgrace.

None of these thoughts, be it understood, caused Khaavren to hesitate in the least in carrying out his duties. He said nothing as he led the way, until Bellor herself, who had appeared deep in thought for some time, broke the silence, saying, "Captain, did His Majesty say anything to you which might give me a clue as to why he has ordered my arrest?"

"No, madam, I must confess that he did not even speak to me on the matter, but he merely gave me the order through the hand of a servant."

"Would you like to know why I have been arrested? For I believe that, after thinking about it for some moments, I could tell you."

"If you wish to tell me, well, I will be happy to listen."

"I do wish to tell you, for I have no one else to tell, and, moreover, because you are someone who may be able to act on the information I am about to impart."

"In that case, madam, I assure you that you have my entire attention."

"That is well. This is it, then: His Majesty has ordered my arrest because I have failed to provide a proper account of the state of the Imperial Treasury."

"I see."

"It seems reasonable, don't you think?"

"Madam, I must take your word for it, for none of these matters fall within my province."

"I give you my word, it is reasonable."

"Very well."

"Only—"

"Only?"

"Only the reason I have been unable to provide these accounts, is because, as I have explained, my best intendant has been killed."

"Yes, you said that Intendant Smaller was killed."

"The very man."

"Well, go on."

"I have been thinking about this matter, trying to understand."

"What is it that is puzzling you? For you perceive that I wish to know."

"I have been trying to understand why anyone would wish to kill Smaller, who was, by all accounts, an inoffensive man, and entirely devoted to his duties."

"Ah. And have you a theory?"

"I do indeed."

"Well, I am listening."

"I will tell you then. I believe he was killed in order to precipitate my arrest."

"How, you think so?"

"Splinters, can you doubt it?" said the Countess. "For, within days after his murder, here I am, arrested!"

"Then you believe," said Khaavren, "that the object of

murdering Smaller was to manage your arrest and removal as Superintendent of Finance?"

"That is exactly my belief."

"Hmmm," said Khaavren. "It is possible." Khaavren allowed no trace of his opinion of this theory to appear on his countenance; he merely nodded somberly and encouraged his prisoner to continue speaking.

"And of course, the only reason to arrest me, is to throw the treasury, and hence, the Empire, into confusion."

Khaavren reflected that the murder of the intendant had accomplished that, and that the arrest of the Countess made no difference whatsoever, but he merely said, "That is, of a certainty, an interesting thought."

"And a true one, I am convinced of it."

"You may be right," said Khaavren.

"Good Captain, you must explain this to His Majesty."

"Hmmm," said Khaavren.

"It is not for myself I fear, but for him. Perhaps you can find the names of those who are behind this conspiracy against me—that is to say, against His Majesty—and what they plan to do."

"Indeed," said Khaavren. "I will consider carefully all that you have told me. But for the moment, we are now arrived at the prison, and I must leave you in the care of this gentleman, who will see to your comfort while you are his guest."

Bellor turned her eyes to the jailer, an Iorich named Guinn with whom Khaavren had had numerous dealings in the past. Guinn bowed politely, and, after signing the paper Khaavren presented to him, turned his attention to the Countess. Khaavren bowed and took himself hastily away from the Iorich Wing, and retraced his steps to the Imperial Wing with the intention of interrupting His Majesty, who was presumably engaged in his evening toilet, and of reporting to His Majesty on the results of the commission.

As he walked, he considered what the Superintendent had told him. "Certainly, from all evidence, there is no reason to conspire against *her*. Yet there is this much truth in what she says—the murder of Smaller must, indeed, be part of something bigger. And, the more I think about it, the more worried I become.

"Ah, Khaavren, this is a matter of the security of the Empire, and that is exactly your province! You must discover who is doing what, and why, and you must waste no time.

"But how to do it? Well, there is a clear answer to that: When there is a war, one finds a Dragon; when there is corruption, one goes to a Jhereg; and when there are conspiracies afoot, one goes to a Yendi—and there is a Yendi I claim as a friend. I will unburden myself to him, telling him all I know and suspect, and I will listen to his advice. So, as soon as I have reported to His Majesty, I will discover his quarters and return the call of courtesy with which he honored me just a few days ago. Ah! And here we are already at the Imperial Wing. Let us finish this business as quickly as possible, and so on to other, more important issues."

Yet, as Khaavren set foot into the Hall of Duchies, where those of the court often gathered for conversation after Their Majesties had retired, he realized that something unusual had happened or was happening. The entire court, or as much of it as was gathered in the Hall of Duchies, which seemed to Khaavren to be a great deal of it, was in an uproar of scandalized courtiers, frustrated ministers, and baffled guardsmen.

Khaavren frowned, touched his sword, and strode forward into the hall to discover the reason behind the excitement and commotion.

# Chapter the Fifteenth

*Which Treats of the Transformation
That the Duke of Galstan Undergoes,
And the Return of Our Old Friend Pel.*

KHAAVREN, AS WE HAVE SAID, entered the Hall of Duchies with the intention of learning what had caused the commotion and disturbance so apparent therein. Some of the guardsmen knew some of what had happened, and some of the courtiers knew more; the process of putting the story together from these pieces took Khaavren some twenty or thirty minutes. The reader will be glad to know that he will be saved this time; some of the value in reading history must lie in the ability of the historian to quickly summarize events that took the participants hours, days, or even years to understand; in fact, it is as much in efficiency—that is, in the saving of the reader's valuable time, as it is in the drawing of lessons and conclusions, that the value of written history lies.

Khaavren, upon seeing the commotion, had at first assumed that either Bellor had more friends than he had thought, or that some aspect of the arrest had been remarked upon as unusual or disturbing; he was as surprised as, perhaps, the reader is to learn that this uproar had nothing (or, at any rate, nothing directly) to do with the dismissal of the Superintendent of Finance, but rather followed a drastic breach of etiquette on the part of Aliera e'Kieron, who had demanded to see His Majesty while His Majesty was concluding his evening rounds. To be more precise, we will say that, at a certain time, Aliera had entered the Palace through the Dragon Wing, passed the Warlord's quarters without even acknowledging a challenge (Khaavren, if he had time, would no doubt have words for those who let her through!), and, after demanding answers of certain courtiers who ought not to have supplied them, discovered that His Majesty could be found, at this hour, walking through the Hall of Ballads, escorted by Corporal Thack, in lieu of Khaavren, whose duty this normally was, and the Lady Ingera, Lord of the Keys. Some of these courtiers were even indiscreet (or, perhaps, mischievous) enough to tell her how to find this hall in the labyrinthine Imperial Wing. By all accounts, when she arrived she burst into the hall just as His Majesty was commanding that it be locked; in fact, Aliera very nearly overturned Ingera, who was at the point of inserting the key into the lock when Aliera made her spectacular and unseemly entrance.

Thack, for his part, though startled, noticed at once that Aliera had a sword at her side, and knew very well that this was not allowed in the presence of His Majesty, wherefore he interposed himself between Aliera and the Emperor and drew his own sword, taking on his most threatening aspect. Aliera appeared quite unconcerned; she merely unbuckled her sword belt and offhandedly tossed it to Thack, while saying, "I beg leave, Sire, to have speech with Your Majesty," in a tone quite in conflict with her well-chosen words, but entirely in accord with the time and manner of her arrival.

Lady Ingera recovered her dignity, Thack stared at the sword-belt which appeared to have suddenly grown from his left hand, and His Majesty stared down at Aliera (who, the reader ought to recall, was exceptionally short) as if he couldn't quite think what sort of beast she was, but knew that it was one he'd seen before.

At last he said, "This is hardly the time for speech. Should you return to-morrow—"

"Sire, a most urgent matter has come to my attention, wherefore I humbly crave a moment of your time." Need we add that, even now, the tone of her voice and the attitude of her person made a marked contrast to her words? Need we add that the Orb, which, upon her entrance, had flashed to a startled white, was now turning red, and becoming ever darker?

Nevertheless, His Majesty, matching Aliera's angry gaze, said, "Well, then, if the matter is so urgent, you may speak of it," in a tone that said plainly, "It will go hard with you if you haven't sufficient cause for this outrage."

"Sire, it has not been an hour since, in accordance with Your Majesty's orders, my quarters were entered and one of my possessions taken."

The Emperor's face darkened and he bit his lip. "Impossible," said His Majesty.

"How, impossible? You say—"

"I say that nothing has been removed from your room that could possibly be your possession."

Aliera's eyes narrowed. "Would Your Majesty do me the honor to explain? For I confess that I am entirely bewildered." The reader ought to understand that these words, like the others which issued from her lips, were, if we may be permitted to use the expression, bitten off—that is, each was pronounced carefully and precisely, conveying, by tone, Aliera's exasperation as the words themselves conveyed her unfailing courtesy.

"I will more than explain!" cried the Emperor. "I will tell you exactly what has been removed from your chambers, and why."

"I ask for nothing better."

"What was taken was an object of pre-Empire sorcery. Do you understand me, Lady Aliera e'Kieron? An object of the sort that has been forbidden since the creation of the Orb itself!"

"Which is odd," remarked Aliera, "when one considers how the Orb was made. Nevertheless, Sire, I must protest—"

"You protest? *You* protest? You *protest*?"

"Indeed, Sire. But only once."

"Possession of such an object is punishable by death!"

"Is it, Sire?" said Aliera, in a tone of cool inquiry. "But what is the punishment for violating the privacy of a lady's chamber?"

"I think you do yourself the honor of questioning me!"

"Do I commit an impertinence, Sire?"

"An impertinence? I nearly think you do!"

"Well, but how does my impertinence in questioning Your Majesty compare to Your Majesty's impertinence in causing your guardsmen to enter my private chambers and conduct a search of my possessions?"

"You dare accuse me—*me*, of impertinence?"

Aliera looked at him coldly, and, though she was considerably shorter than he, seemed almost to be looking down at him. "The Orb and the Throne, Sire, are given when one becomes Emperor. Stewardship of the Empire must be earned." With this comment, she bowed, took several steps backward, and recovered her weapon from Thack, who still held it as he watched, dumbfounded. Then she turned and made her way out of the Hall of Ballads.

This was what had occurred, and was what Khaavren learned as he listened to and pieced together different stories and rumors from those assembled in the Hall of Duchies. When he understood enough, he paused and consulted with himself. "I must now," he said, "come to a decision. If I return home, or to my offices, there will, without doubt, be a message for me to find His Majesty, who will then order me to arrest Aliera, who is not a Superintendent, and is not, furthermore, someone I have any desire to arrest, as she is the daughter of someone I do myself the honor to consider a friend. If, instead, I continue with my plan and go to visit Pel, then I will avoid this order at least long enough for Aliera to have a good start on me. No one would accuse me of neglecting my duty when I had no duty to neglect—I am, after all, on my own time, now that the hour at which His Majesty retires is at hand."

Then he sighed. "I would, however, accuse myself. No, Khaavren, you cannot escape so easily. Your conscience will follow you, and it will whisper in your ear, and it will disturb that sleep which you value so highly, and cast a pall over that discourse with your friends, and especially with the noble Aerich, that you take such joy in. No, His Majesty wants me to arrest Aliera, of this there can be no doubt. Therefore, I will be as good a servant as I can, and I will seek him out in his chambers. If he has retired for the night, and left me no message—well, so much the better. If, as I suspect, he has left orders, or, more probably, he is waiting up to give them to me, then I will carry out those orders with as much dispatch as if I were arresting a Teckla or an Easterner or a Superintendent of Finance."

Having reached this decision, Khaavren made his way at once to His Majesty's bedchamber. The two guardsmen on duty informed him that His Majesty had only lately retired, and was, in all probability, still awake; an opinion Khaavren confirmed after passing into the antechamber by noticing the light which leaked out beneath the door of the bedroom. He positioned himself in front of this door and clapped sharply.

"Who is there?" called His Majesty.

"Khaavren."

"Ah, ah! My Captain of the Guard! Please come in, my dear Khaavren, for I desire nothing more than speech with you."

"I am hardly surprised," said Khaavren under his breath. He entered the room and bent his knee to the Emperor, saying, "Sire, I am here to report on the commission you have given me."

"Yes, exactly. Did the matter go off well?"

"Entirely, Sire. Countess Bellor is now confined in the Iorich Wing. Here, Sire, is the receipt I had of Guinn."

The Emperor took the receipt, read it, and nodded. "So much the better," he said. "Did she have aught to say?"

"Oh, Sire, she said one thing and another, as prisoners will on their way to prison."

"Ah, she protested her innocence?"

"Precisely."

"And claimed a conspiracy against her?"

"Exactly."

"And even against me?"

"Just so."

The Emperor smiled. "Well, you and I know of such things, do we not, Captain? Bellor was not the first to be arrested, nor shall she be the last."

"Now we come to it," thought Khaavren, but he only bowed to acknowledge His Majesty's words.

"Well," said His Majesty. "Is that all?"

"That is all, Sire."

"Very well."

"Sire?"

"I said, very well. If that is all, you may go, and I will see you in the morning."

"I—"

"Yes?"

"There is nothing else, Sire?"

His Majesty frowned. "Something else? What do you mean?"

"Your Majesty has no other orders for me?"

"Why no, Captain. There are no other orders."

Khaavren bit his lip, trying to keep the surprise from his features. "Nothing at all, Sire?"

"Why no. Is there something you expected?"

"That is to say . . . not in the least, Sire. I was simply making certain nothing had been overlooked."

"Nothing of which I am aware."

"Very well, Sire. I shall see Your Majesty in the morning."

"Yes, Sleep well, Captain."

"And may Your Majesty do the same."

Khaavren made a courtesy, and left the Emperor's chambers, puzzled. Not only had there been no order to arrest Aliera, but there was no trace of ill-humor on His Majesty's countenance. Had he, Khaavren, been misinformed? He considered the sources of his information and decided this was unlikely. So what could it be? Had something else happened? Was some part of someone's plan working, even now?

If so, there was one man who knew how to unravel such schemes, and there was no time to lose before finding him. Khaavren, without further delay, went back down to the main level of the Palace, out through the Silver Door, and so into the Painted Tunnel, which led to the Athyra Wing. Once there, he had three times to ask directions through the dark and twisted corridors of the Wing, until at last he emerged into a section of the third floor of the Palace, where a woman, seated on a plain, three-legged stool, guarded an entryway (or, at any rate, seemed to guard it, though she had no weapon) into what seemed an unlit corridor. Here Khaavren stopped and said, "Is this the Academy of Discretion?"

"It is, My Lord. May I be of service to you?"

"I hope so. I am looking for the Duke of Galstan."

The woman, whose features could barely be seen beneath the hood, raised her eyebrows and said, "My Lord? You wish to see him at this hour?"

"I am Khaavren, Captain of the Imperial Guard, and I assure you that my business will not wait."

The woman frowned and said, "Please have the kindness to wait here. I will inquire."

"I will not move from this spot," said Khaavren.

She disappeared back into the darkness of the hall. As her footsteps faded, it seemed to Khaavren that silence had descended on the entire Palace, as if there were no other living person within it. He shivered, though he was not cold.

Although the wait seemed long to Khaavren, it was, in fact, only five or ten minutes before she returned, appearing from the darkness as suddenly as she had vanished into it. She said, "He will be down directly, My Lord. If you wish, you may come with me to a place where you can sit while you await him."

Khaavren looked into the gloomy corridor and said, "I will wait here."

"As you wish."

Khaavren passed several more minutes alone—we say *alone* because the woman, after seating herself on the stool where we and Khaavren first found her, fell silent and motionless, so that it seemed to Khaavren his only company was a statue, and a statue less lifelike than many of the sculptures that adorned the Hall of Ballads which had, earlier that evening, been the scene of the very events which so mystified him now. Eventually, however, he heard soft footsteps and Pel appeared in the same robes he had worn when he had paid his visit to Khaavren, only in this place the apparel seemed entirely congruous with the surroundings. Khaavren was able to see that the Yendi was smiling within his hood. Pel took Khaavren by the arm and escorted him some forty or fifty feet away from the dark corridor and out of earshot of the lady who stood guard.

"My old friend," said Pel in a quiet voice.

"I'm sorry to have awakened you," said Khaavren, also attempting to speak softly, though he was not certain why it mattered.

"Awakened me?" said Pel. "I was not sleeping—I was merely meditating, and that only lightly, so that your interruption, if it can be called such, brings me nothing but pleasure, especially if it affords me the opportunity to be of some service to you."

In fact, Khaavren saw no trace of sleep in the Yendi's veiled but alert eyes. "So much the better," said Khaavren. "For I am, indeed, asking for your help."

Pel nodded. "Then let us find a place where we can not only speak, but allow our voices free play, which, out of respect for those who are sleeping or meditating, we cannot do here."

"If you wish," said Khaavren, "you may come back to my house, which is at the same place you remember. Even better, Aerich and Tazendra are there, for I believe it was you who sent to them."

"And they arrived?"

"In good time," said Khaavren, laughing. "Such good time

that—but I will tell you the entire affair when we are sitting down."

"I ask nothing better," said Pel. "But first, have you any errands about the Palace?"

"Why, yes, there are one or two matters I could attend to. Why do you ask?"

"Because I do not choose to go out in the world dressed as I am, so I would ask that you take care of your errands, and I will meet you in your offices, and you can escort me back to the house of which I retain such charming memories— though hang me if, at this moment, I can remember how to get there. Come, do you think my plan a good one?"

"I can think of none better," said Khaavren. "I will await you in my offices in the Dragon Wing."

"You will not need wait long," said Pel.

"So much the better," said Khaavren.

"Until then."

"Until then."

With these words they parted, Pel disappearing back into the gloom of the Academy of Discretion, Khaavren making his way as best he could into the Dragon Wing, and so to his offices, where he took care of certain paperwork that had accumulated during the day he was absent. When he was finished, he reviewed the log of the day's events, where two items seemed to him especially interesting. The first, in Thack's careless hand, was an account of orders received that afternoon to allow certain guardsmen belonging to the White Sash Battalion into the private chambers of Aliera e'Kieron in the Dragon Wing. It was, of course, the White Sash Battalion who would have conducted any searches; Khaavren would not allow his own guardsmen to soil themselves with such matters, nor had his battalion any business in the private areas of the Dragon Wing. In fact, there was some question whether Stonemover's guards ought to have been there, but, as this was outside of Khaavren's province, he gave it only passing thought.

The other entry that Khaavren noticed with interest, amusement, and a certain amount of annoyance, was that His Majesty's altercation with Aliera was recorded in this way: "Adron's daughter gained entrance to the person of His Majesty in the Hall of Ballads and had a conversation with him, after which the evening rounds continued."

Khaavren determined to speak with Thack on the matter of the log, as well as speaking to those who had let Aliera past— although Khaavren had a certain amount of sympathy for anyone who was required to stop Adron's daughter from going anywhere she wished to go.

It was while he was considering this matter that the night door-ward said, "The Duke of Galstan to see the Captain."

"Ah!" said Khaavren. "Come, that wasn't too long a wait. Bid His Venerance enter, by all means."

The Duke entered, and Khaavren sprang to his feet. "Pel!" he cried.

"Himself," said Pel, smiling and bowing.

Gone were his plain dark robes; instead he wore a bright white blouse with fine gold embroidery in wavy lines down the breast. The collar of this blouse was long, and pointed like arrows at the shoulders, which were covered by a sort of bright red vest with black embroidery. The vest, we should add, had also black borders, which formed twin lines down the front of his blouse, which worked to set off the gold embroidery we have already mentioned. At his waist was a wide leather sword-belt, with leather designs cunningly embedded, and in which reposed a pair of elegant grey gloves. Also from the belt there hung that sword with its slender blade and dueler's grip that Khaavren remembered so well, and that had been put to such good use in days gone by. Below the waist, Pel wore loose-fitting breeches, and shiny black boots which came almost to his knees. There were small silver spurs on the boots.

"Pel!" cried Khaavren again. "Shards, but it is good to see you back again!"

"Ah, then you approve of my costume?" said Pel, smiling.

"Approve? I nearly think so!"

"Well then, there is no more to be said. Let us go to your home, where we will greet our old friends, and you will discuss with me this difficulty you have encountered and about which you do me the honor to consider my opinion to have some value."

There being nothing to say to this, Khaavren rose and escorted Pel out of the Dragon Wing and so out onto the Street of the Dragon, where they walked arm in arm toward the Street of the Glass Cutters.

"It is a long time since I have made this walk," said Pel. "Yet it is all coming back, and bringing with it the sweetness of youth."

"Our friends will be pleased to see you, I think."

"Oh, yes. And the good Srahi? Will she remember me?"

Khaavren laughed. "It is unlikely that she will remember her own name; she is thinking only of our old friend Mica."

"Oh ho!" said Pel. "That is something I had not expected, though perhaps I should have."

They arrived in due time at the house, where Srahi let them in, only to inform them that Aerich, Tazendra, and Mica and Fawnd—the latter now somewhat recovered from the exertions of his journey—had left with Sethra some two hours before, appearing to be in a great hurry, though she, Srahi, did not know why. The Teckla appeared to be put out by this—so much so that she scarcely greeted Pel at all, although she did consent to bring him, and Khaavren, a glass of wine as they seated themselves.

"So," said Pel, "our reunion appears to be delayed. Nevertheless, you can tell me of this matter that has you puzzled, and I will, I assure you, put my entire mind to solving whatever the problem is."

"I will do so," said Khaavren. "Only I must first tell you that this is an Imperial matter, and if word of it reaches the wrong ears it may have the gravest consequences, both for me and for the Empire itself."

"Ah, Khaavren, you wound me," said Pel. "When have I ever been indiscreet?"

"Never, my friend," said Khaavren. "And I do not accuse you; I merely wish to inform you of the gravity of the matter we are about to address."

"Very well, I am informed."

"Then I will begin."

"I await you."

With this, Khaavren launched into the details of the various assassinations, the arrest of Bellor, and the peculiar situation with regard to Aliera and His Majesty. Pel listened to the story with careful attention, but with no change of expression at any point during the recital. He made no comment, nor did he ask any questions until, at length, Khaavren had finished, at which point he said slowly, "On some of this, my dear friend, I will be able to enlighten you."

"In that case, you have my complete attention."

"In the first place," said Pel, "you are correct—the Academy did, indeed, petition His Majesty for funds, and I think it was this that precipitated the arrest of Bellor. We did not wish to have Bellor arrested, or even removed from her office—rather, we hoped to secure the funds we need to continue our curriculum. You, who have dealings with His Majesty every day, must understand the importance of our rôle, and you must have perceived the changes in His Majesty's character since Wellborn retired."

Khaavren, not wishing to say too much to this point, contented himself with nodding.

"The matter of Aliera's confrontation with His Majesty, and His Majesty's peculiar lack of outrage, is, indeed, mystifying, and in two different ways."

"Two ways?"

"Indeed. The one you have noticed—how could His Majesty permit himself to be so insulted without responding?"

"Well, and what is the second mystery?"

"The second mystery is: How did His Majesty know that there was an item of pre-Empire sorcery in Aliera's chambers? Surely he would not have dared to order a search within the Dragon Wing if he hadn't been entirely convinced—certain, in fact."

"Well, that is true. And so?"

"And so, how did he come by this certainty?"

"Indeed," said Khaavren. "I had not thought of that."

"I do not know the solution to either of these mysteries, but I know where to begin looking."

"And that is?"

"The Prime Minister."

"Jurabin?"

"Exactly."

"But, Pel, why Jurabin?"

Pel smiled. "Because it is a matter that involves the Lady Aliera, and word has reached my ears that Jurabin has conceived a fondness for her that is so strong it clouds his eyes—eyes none too clear, perhaps, to begin with."

"Hmmm. I must consider what you say."

"As to the conspiracy itself, well, I am forced to say that I agree with you, Khaavren. This has all the odor of a well-laid plan. Too well-laid, in fact, for I have no idea where to begin looking."

"It is as I feared," sighed Khaavren.

"Although," Pel added suddenly, "now that I think of it, there are two places to try first."

"Well, and tell me those two places, and I will begin looking there."

"One is Jurabin, for the reasons I have already mentioned."

"Yes, Jurabin is one."

"The other is the Consort, because all intrigues involve the Consort, sooner or later."

"That is true," remarked Khaavren.

The Captain considered for a moment, then said, "Well, you have pointed out some directions in which I should look. I will begin investigating these matters in the morning." He spoke, we should add, with more confidence than he felt—Khaavren knew how to interrogate prisoners, but he knew little about how to conduct an investigation of the type he was about to commence.

Pel said, "With which of them will you begin?"

"Which one? I have not considered this."

"Well, let me know, because then I will begin with the other."

"How, you?" cried Khaavren.

"Indeed, and why not?"

"You are then, willing to assist me in the investigation?"

"More than willing, my friend, I am even eager; for it appears to be a serious matter, and I am anxious to do my part. Moreover," he added with a smile, "our friendship is not one lightly forgotten. So, will you have me?"

"I can think of nothing that would make me happier," said Khaavren, with perfect frankness.

"Well, then, with which of them do you wish to begin?"

"For my part," said Khaavren, "I will begin with Jurabin, whom I know a little better than I know the Consort. This will leave you with Her Majesty, and I know that you have certain skills in dealing with ladies—skills that I have never acquired."

Pel blushed slightly at this remark, but said, "Very well, then, it is agreed." He frowned then and said, "I wonder where our friends are?"

"I don't know," said Khaavren. "I, too, am curious." Then he sighed. "There is, I'm afraid, yet one more thing you ought to know."

"Well? I am listening, my friend. I perceive by the expression on your countenance that it is a serious matter."

"I'm afraid it is, dear Pel. Here, what do you make of this? It was in the bundle of correspondence that I was looking at while I was waiting for you in my office." He took from his pocket several pieces of paper which had been folded together, all of which he handed to his friend.

"It is," said Pel after studying it for a moment, "a poorly printed pamphlet, consisting of bad drawings of figures at court, gossip, and ill-executed rhyme."

"Have you seen such things before?"

"Indeed yes, Khaavren. And I tell you are wrong to be upset. When they mock—"

"You have not looked it over carefully, my friend."

"Indeed? What is it that catches your eye?"

"Do you see the drawing on the inside page, on the far left?"

"Yes. It appears to be an attempt to draw His Majesty engaged in a function which, while he no doubt performs it every day, belittles the dignity of the Imperium to contemplate. Yet I fail to see—"

"Look at the item below it."

Pel quickly read the indicated paragraph, then he frowned, looked up at Khaavren, and said, "Ah."

"Then you, too, see what I see?"

"Yes. The humor is coarse and the language execrable, but the implication is that Her Majesty is conspiring with merchants to rob the people."

"Exactly."

"It is the first such implication I have seen."

"And you think—?"

"As you do, Khaavren. It is a bad sign."

"And yet, to suppress it—"

"Exactly. Would only make it worse."

Khaavren nodded. "We may be in for difficult times, Pel."

"Indeed. I do not envy you your job."

Khaavren sighed. "Perhaps it will blow over."

"Perhaps," said Pel. "And yet, when the people whisper of conspiracies by the merchants and the aristocracy—"

"Yes. They are facing harder times than I had thought, and it may be that disorder will follow."

"Well, there is nothing to be done on that score," said Pel.

"Indeed, that is true. And yet, there is something that remains to be done right now, for the evening is not over. Although we must get an early start to-morrow, yet there is still something we must do to-night."

"Is there?" said Pel. "Then tell me what it is, and if I can help you, I will do so."

"Oh, indeed," said Khaavren. "I can think of no one who will be of more help than you."

"Then I am listening."

"Here it is, then. Earlier to-day, I had a discussion with a Teckla who gave me certain information. I promised him that I would go out and drink his health. Now this is something that, it seems to me, would be better done in company, and I can think of no company I would prefer. So, if you are willing, we will drink to the health of this nameless Teckla, and then—cha! we will drink to each other's health as well. Come, what do you think of this plan?"

"My dear Tiassa, I can find no flaw in it."

"In that case, my dear Yendi, let us find the Hammerhead Inn, which still stands, and which brings back such pleasant memories, and put our plan into operation at once, with the intention of being as successful with this one as with the one we will initiate on the morrow."

"After you," said Pel.

"I am leading," said Khaavren.

And they made their way out the door, where they acted on Khaavren's plan with all the enthusiasm two old friends could bring to such endeavors, and where they met with no small success.

# Chapter the Sixteenth

*Which Treats of a Busy Night
In Dragaera City,
As Greycat Unfolds His Plans,
And Adron e'Kieron Struggles
To Control His Temper.*

WHILE HIS MAJESTY, AND, INDEED, most of the population of the city slept, there was a great deal of activity taking place, as it were, beneath the surface. This was to be one of those nights with which history is here and there dotted; a night when plans, discussions, and ideas were first planted: plans, discussions, and ideas whose fruit would not emerge on the tree of history until after some as yet undetermined springtime should arrive to melt the snows of apparent quiescence and somnolence and awaken every mind to the light of day, open every eye to witness the passing of the season, and cause every heart to leap, in joy or terror according to its nature, at the wonder of the sudden blossoming of new growth which would appear, fully ripe, in the hazy dawn of a new era of history. This literal and metaphorical night, then, though passing unnoticed by all but a few, was pregnant with a day that would literally and metaphorically shake the Empire itself upon its birth.

We will attempt, therefore, to insure that the reader will remain cognizant of every seed that is sown on this night—the night following the 14th day of the month of the Vallista in the 532nd year of Tortaalik's reign. We hope that we have fulfilled our duties in keeping the reader informed of every significant development in our history up to the present point, and, with the Gods to guide our pen, we shall do our utmost to continue as we have begun.

As the reader might expect, our next stop on this journey through times and places, via the medium of the printed word, one of the most effective means of travel yet devised, is to a tavern. But it is not, in fact, to the tavern to which our friends Khaavren and Pel are directing their attention, for at the same moment they are off to renew their old friendship, there is a far more sinister gathering in an entirely different part of town—in fact, in the Underside, in the same cabaret to which our duties as historian have brought us on two previous occasions, and to which our duties may, we are forced to admit, bring us again before our tale is told.

On this occasion, there were three conspirators present, these being Greycat, Laral, and Dunaan. They sat in the same back room, and spoke quietly.

Laral said, "I have learned something of interest."

"Well?" said Greycat.

"You recall that His Highness, the Duke of Eastmanswatch, did not appear for his two appointments—that is, his appointment with the public, and his appointment with me—at the Pavilion of Kieron."

"I remember very well," said Greycat. "Do you now know the reason?"

"I do indeed," said Laral. "And, if you wish, I will tell you."

"That is exactly what I wish," said Greycat. "Why did he not appear?"

"Because he was warned," she said.

Dunaan seemed surprised, and looked an inquiry at her.

"Warned?" said Greycat.

"Exactly."

"By whom?"

"I don't know yet."

Greycat frowned. "If someone has learned that an attempt was to be made on his life, we may all be in danger."

Laral nodded.

"We must find out how he came to be warned."

"I will attempt to do so."

"Very well."

Dunaan said, "I am pleased to report, at any rate, that Countess Bellor has taken up residence in the Imperial prisons, and His Majesty is, at present, without a Superintendent of Finance."

"Excellent," said Greycat.

"What was your method?" said Laral.

"I have friends in the Academy of Discretion," said Dunaan.

Laral nodded.

"For my part," said Greycat, "the riot went off as planned, although it was ended sooner than I had hoped. Still, it accomplished what it was intended to accomplish."

"Which was?" said Dunaan.

Greycat shook his head but didn't answer. He then turned to Laral and said, "Now I must ask you a question."

"Very well, ask."

"Knowing that you had not succeeded in removing Eastmanswatch, did you then attempt to remove him in a different way?"

Laral frowned. "Speak more plainly," she said. "For you perceive that I don't understand your question."

"An effort was made to discredit His Highness, through his daughter, Aliera. This is not what I wish. It would be better if—"

"That was no doing of mine," said Laral.

Greycat sighed. "I was afraid you would tell me that. It means there are other players in the game."

"Does that startle you?" said Dunaan, smiling a little.

"Just what *is* the game?" said Laral.

Greycat hesitated, then shrugged. "I am attempting to gain

a position at court," he said, "as well as a certain measure of revenge, although that is secondary." He smiled slightly. "You two will not, I take it, object to having an influential friend at court?"

The two Jhereg matched his smile and saw no need to otherwise answer the question.

"How do you hope to accomplish this objective?" said Dunaan.

"By creating a crisis which I will be able to solve."

"A good plan," said Laral. "If it can be done."

"In spite of certain setbacks," said Greycat, "it is progressing satisfactorily."

Dunaan shrugged. "What needs to be done now?"

Greycat considered. "We must not make another attempt on the life of His Highness. If he suspects, then it will be too dangerous."

Laral started to object, but Greycat held up his hand. "No, we must concentrate on other things. If all goes well, there will be ways to make certain he is put out of the way."

"Does the same apply to the Tiassa?" said Laral.

"No," said Greycat. As he spoke, there was a certain narrowing of his eyes and curling of his lip that suggested that, to Greycat, Khaavren was more than an impediment to his schemes.

"Well?" said Dunaan.

"No," said Greycat, answering the Jhereg's implied question. "Laral will take care of the problem, since we are going to leave His Highness alone."

"I will do so," said Laral in a tone of finality that spoke nothing good about Khaavren's future.

"And I?" said Dunaan. "Toward what task ought I to set myself? For I assume you have something in mind for me."

"I do," said Greycat. "You are to find me an assassin."

The Jhereg frowned, then looked significantly, first at Laral, then down at his hands; then he sent Greycat a look of inquiry.

Greycat smiled and shook his head. "An expendable assassin."

"Ah."

"One who is skilled, and who will follow orders, and who is either stupid or naïve."

"How," said Laral. "A stupid assassin? A naïve assassin? It is unlikely."

"I am forced to agree," said Dunaan.

"Are you certain? Is there no one you can find who is skilled, yet not wise in the ways of deceit?"

Dunaan said, "Then you plan—?"

"Let us not discuss it."

"I see."

"Can you find one?"

He thought for a moment, then abruptly nodded. "I believe so."

"Good. Then there is no more to say."

"On the contrary," said Laral. "There is, indeed, more to say."

Greycat questioned her with a look.

"The riot."

"Yes, what of the riot?"

"Exactly what was that intended to accomplish?"

"That is my affair," said Greycat.

"No, it is now all of our affair, for, not only have you revealed much of your plan, but you must perceive that Dunaan and I are now far too involved to escape any repercussions of this plan should it fail."

Greycat looked at Dunaan, who, notwithstanding his apparent dislike of Laral, said, "I am forced to agree. I, too, wish to know, and you ought to tell us."

Greycat shrugged. "Very well," he said. "It was intended to make the court fearful of the people, and to heighten to the crisis."

Laral nodded. "Are you aware that it did more than that?"

"To what do you refer?"

"You may have convinced the court that it was a genuine riot, or you may not. But you have certainly convinced the people. There are whispers of revolt in the streets."

"Let them whisper," said Greycat. "Let them, in fact, shout

if they choose. They are rabble, which you know as well as
I. What can they do?"

"They can send the Empire up in flames if you aren't careful," said Laral. "Then where will you be?"

Greycat smiled in a way that only he could smile—a peculiar, feral expression. He said, "I will then be exactly where
I wish to be. For, because I create the unrest, I can quell it
the same way."

Laral watched him for a moment, then said, "For your
sake, as well as for ours, I hope so."

Dunaan nodded, silently echoing her sentiments.

Greycat shrugged. "Let us review, then."

"For my part," said Laral, "I am to kill the Tiassa,
Khaavren, and also to learn how Prince Adron was warned
about the attempt, and, furthermore, how much the Prince
knows, and how much is known by whomever warned him."

"That is it," said Greycat.

Dunaan said, "I am to arrange for you to meet an assassin
who is either foolish or naïve, but who is, nevertheless, a
skilled assassin."

"Precisely," said Greycat.

"Then," said Laral, "there is *now* no more to be said; I will
be about my business."

"As will I," said Dunaan.

Greycat nodded, but did not otherwise move as they departed the room and the cabaret.

When they had gone, Grita, her dzur-like eyes narrowed
and her hair sleeked back like a veritable tsalmoth, emerged
once more from the shadows. "Well?" she said.

"Well?" said Greycat.

"I think the lady from the Jhereg speaks with more wisdom
than you. I, too, wonder if you can put out the fire you are
so willing to start."

"You are not privy to all of my plans, nor to all of my secrets," said Greycat.

"Enough of them," said Grita, catching his eye.

Greycat turned away.

"Have you a task to assign me?" she said after a moment.

Her tone, we should add, contained a certain amount of irony, as if she thought it amusing that he should give her instructions.

He either didn't notice or chose to ignore the tone, simply saying, "Yes."

"Well?"

"Make your way into Adron's encampment, however you can, and—"

"However I can?"

"That is correct."

She laughed humorlessly. "You know, I take it, what you are implying I should do?"

Though still facing the wall, he blanched, as if he could not bear the look she gave him, even though he could not see the expression on her face. "I imply nothing," he said.

"Hypocrite."

He turned back to her suddenly. "You—you of all people will not address me in such terms. You know better than anyone what I am doing and why. And don't forget what you stand to gain from this. As for your scruples—if you have any—they are your concern. You are welcome now, or at any time, to back out of the entire affair. But until you do, and as long as you ask me how you can be useful, I will tell you. The details are hardly my concern."

She laughed, but did not otherwise answer him. "And once I have entered His Highness's encampment, what then?"

"Then you will stay with him, as close as you can, watching everything he does. Do nothing for the moment, but be prepared for anything."

"And yet, you are aware that my talents are best employed in the city, among those you call rabble?"

"I know," he said.

"Without me, how will you control this rabble, and set them off when and how you wish?"

"I have made arrangements."

"Ah! So I am no longer needed. Is that what you tell me?"

"As I said before, you do not know all my secrets, nor are you privy to all my plans."

Grita made him an elaborate courtesy. "Very well. I will go to join a host of Dragonlords."

"Good."

"Until later, then—Greycat." She laughed as she pronounced this name, as if she thought it funny; if so, she was surely the only citizen of the Underside who thought so. When he did not respond to her baiting, she turned without another word and walked out of the room, leaving Greycat alone with his thoughts, where we will also leave him, but only after, with the reader's permission, saying two words about Greycat as he appears on these pages.

We have endeavored to remain true to history regarding both the appearance, character, and intentions of this fascinating if distasteful figure. We are not unaware that there may appear to be a certain mystery about him—in fact, we should go so far as to say that if there is no mystery about him, we have failed in our duty as historian. Yet it has come to our attention that some readers may wonder if the historian is, as it were, playing games—and that Greycat may, in fact, be the alias for an entirely different person—Jurabin, for example, or even Pel.

This is a point on which we must insist: We are endeavoring to relate historical fact, and, in the course of doing so, to entertain and enlighten the reader, but only insofar as we can entertain and enlighten without compromising our integrity as an historian. We now give the reader our word that, in general, if we are withholding information, it is only because that information was not then available to any of these through whose eyes we are witnessing the unfolding of this history; and in specific, Greycat has not and will not appear anywhere in these pages under another guise.

With this firmly established, let us now move on. It is hardly coincidental that our next stop is identical to Grita's— that is, the encampment of the Duke of Eastmanswatch and his Breath of Fire Battalion, located outside of the city. Here we will catch up with several of our friends at once; for not only is the Duke Adron himself present, but so is his daughter, Aliera; as well as Sethra Lavode, the Enchantress of Dzur

Mountain; and, lo and behold, our missing friends, Aerich and Tazendra. Mica, we should add, was outside of the tent, near the entrance, sitting on his faithful bar-stool and awaiting the end of the discussion within. Fawnd, who had still not entirely recovered from the journey on horseback, had been given permission to retire for the evening, and was sound asleep not far from the tent.

These five were gathered, as beneath a dark, threatening sky, within the large tent that was Adron's home while he was with his battalion. In the back of the tent—which was big enough to hold a meeting of fifty captains—was the board covered with the peculiar mosaic of purple stones that we observed earlier, only it was, at this moment, entirely covered by a cloth, so that nothing of its nature could be divined. There was a small table off to one side, covered with the papers Adron had been perusing when the visitors arrived, and there were cushions thrown about the tent, on which cushions were seated four of our friends—that is, all of them except Adron himself, who walked back and forth, back and forth, between the table and the covered board.

Of the others, Tazendra appeared determined to remain plussed in spite of any vicissitudes in her environment, though her eye strayed constantly between those two giants of history, Adron and Sethra. Aerich, though he watched Adron closely, maintained his natural and habitual calm. Sethra was seated facing Adron, and the expression on her countenance was troubled, as if she heard the thunder and understood the lightning. Aliera seemed grim, as if she were determined to remain standing in spite of the ferocity of the wind. Thus we see that, to judge by at least four of those present, there was something disturbing at issue.

But to look upon Adron was to look upon the storm—for every muscle in his face was taut, his hands were clenched into fists, and he appeared to be having difficulty in preventing himself from exploding into a fully fledged rage that would make him a danger to everyone present—for there is nothing more terrifying than a Dragonlord wizard who has lost his temper and has no good place to direct his anger.

The reader will know from his own experience that it is no unusual trait to shout, rage, and shake one's fists when angry—it is as easy to find a person who acts this way as it is to find acorns in the Traveling Wood. But there is more than one reason behind such behavior. Some throw tantrums to frighten those around them into taking shelter, or negotiating with the lightning. Some, with no such plans, find it the only way to express their frustration at the uncaring climate. And some, like the Duke of Eastmanswatch, know that, when anger threatens to engulf them, to cry out their exasperation is the only way to prevent themselves from losing all control and engaging in undirected violence against anyone and everyone unfortunate enough to be within range of the lightning bolts of their rage. Where such people are concerned, we can only be thankful when they know themselves well enough to direct their tempers into a channel more or less harmless.

With this firmly in mind, we will observe the rage of his Highness Adron e'Kieron.

"Who is he, anyway?" cried Adron to anyone who would listen. "Did you know that his mother attempted to enlist in the Imperial Service during the Reign of the Orca, and was thrown out of the Navy because she could not learn to navigate? Did you know that his father, before his marriage, lost all of his wealth investing in a device that was supposed to clear the sky of its overcast—a device that never existed, wouldn't have worked, and, if it had worked, would have made no money because no one cares anyway? Did you know that his education stopped at the age of one hundred and ten because he was so arrogant his tutors, one at a time, gave up on the notion of teaching him anything? Did you know—"

"Father," said Aliera.

Adron stopped. "What? What is it? This fool, this spurious Emperor, this false commander, dares, *dares* to have searched the private chambers of my daughter, and then expects to be served by gentlemen? He expects to command the loyalty of—"

"Father!" said Aliera.

"What? The very idea that he could—"

"Father, you must stop. You must know that all of your troops can hear you."

"Let them hear me!" cried Adron, still rapidly pacing back and forth. "Do you think it matters to me if they know what sort of man—I say *man* not Emperor because, may the Gods hear me and weep, we cannot deny him his species, but he has never proven himself to be an Emperor—what sort of man we find ourselves in the service of?"

Aerich said calmly, "It is unseemly for a gentleman to belittle one whom the Gods have made his master in the presence of those of whom the Gods have made him master."

This stopped Adron, if for no other reason than because he had to think for a moment to work out what the Lyorn was saying. From anyone else, such a remark would almost certainly have been the "drop that broke the dike" as the saying is, but delivered by the Lyorn, it caused His Highness to pause and consider, and, in this consideration, he began to cool down.

"Perhaps," he said at last. "And yet the idea of this pipsqueak Phoenix having his ruffians enter—"

"Father," said Aliera. "I've spoken to His Majesty, and I assure you I said everything that was necessary. I think we should now put this matter behind us, and—"

"I beg your pardon," said Sethra. "But the last thing we should do is put it behind us—at least until we have stared at it from the front a little longer."

Aliera turned a puzzled glance her way. "You think so?"

"I am certain of it."

Aliera frowned and addressed Aerich, saying, "And what is your opinion, my dear Lyorn?"

"I am entirely in agreement with Sethra Lavode," said Aerich.

"Explain, then."

"I will do so," said Sethra.

"Come, let us listen. You too, father."

"Very well," said Adron gruffly, and sat down on the cleverly constructed collapsible chair that he always brought with him on campaigns so he could sit without undue strain on his back.

"This is it, then," said Sethra. "Before we move on, and put this unfortunate affair from our minds, it is well for us to consider several questions which spring from it."

"What questions?" said Aliera.

"In the first place, we must ask ourselves how His Majesty knew to search your room for this object."

"That *is* a good question," admitted Aliera. "And next?"

"Next, we must ask ourselves why you, Aliera, have not yet been arrested."

"Arrested? Bah. We came here directly. Who would dare to attempt to arrest me here, in the midst of my father's encampment?"

"Would you resist?" said Aerich. "If so, it would be open revolt against the Empire, as I hope you perceive. Moreover—"

"Yes? Moreover?"

"The answer to your question is our friend Khaavren. For I assure you that, if he had been given the order to arrest you, he would be here by now, though every warrior of the House of the Dragon stood before you."

Adron chuckled at this, and said, "I nearly think you are right."

"That was," said Sethra, "exactly the impression I had of him from the time we spent together."

"Well then," said Aliera. "Why has the order not been given? Have you any theories?"

Tazendra, who had been silent during this entire discussion, said, "Yes. Are there any theories?"

This produced an embarrassed moment of silence, during which Adron and Aliera looked at her quizzically, Aerich grimaced, and Sethra favored her with an amused glance. Tazendra blushed and looked away.

Sethra said, "It is clear that someone intervened on your behalf."

"Ah!" said Aliera. "Yes, that is possible."

"But who would have done so?" said Adron.

Sethra shrugged. "My own guess would be Jurabin, for he has His Majesty's ear, and it is obvious to everyone that he is much taken with you, Aliera, especially as you were, according to all the court gossips, eyeing him most indiscreetly during your introduction to His Majesty a few days ago."

As quick as an indrawn breath, Aliera was on her feet, crying, "I was *what*?"

"It does no good to be angry with me, my dear girl," said Sethra. "I only repeat what I have heard from my sources at court."

"You heard that I was—how did you put it? *Eyeing* this . . . this . . . this *minister*?"

"Exactly."

Aliera seemed to control herself only with difficulty. Then she said, "I am not angry with you, nor do I hold you to blame. If you will give me the name of whoever made this preposterous claim, I will say no more about it."

"How?" said Sethra. "Give you the names of my informants at court? It is unlikely."

"I must insist," said Aliera coldly.

"Insist?" said Sethra, in tones of amazement. "You?"

"You find it amusing?"

"Aliera," said Lord Adron.

"What? Am I to stand here and allow myself to be accused of such conduct while I have sufficient steel at my side to insist on the respect due my rank and lineage? I will not allow this woman to—"

"Aliera!" said Lord Adron.

"What? You must understand that this woman is implying that I have been playing the coquette—and, moreover, doing so with someone with whom I wouldn't so much as—"

"Aliera, recall where you are, and what we are talking about. We have no time to—"

"Bah! Time! It will take only moments to dispatch this haughty—"

"I should point out," said Aerich coolly, "that should the two of you slaughter each other, it will be much more difficult for us to learn what has actually been taking place at court—and, whatever is taking place, it is clear that it has more far-reaching consequences than who has insulted whom. I suggest the two of you delay your quarrel for at least long enough for us to come up with a plan of action. For my part, I think Sethra's point ought to be considered—it may well be Jurabin who has been involved in this, however much the Lady Aliera may have encouraged or failed to encourage such emotions as he may be experiencing."

Silence fell in the tent, then Aliera said, "Well, there is some justice in what you say."

The Lyorn bowed his head.

"Then how ought we to begin?" asked Adron.

"I wish Khaavren were here," murmured Tazendra.

"Well," said Aerich, smiling. "I think our clever Dzurlord has hit on it."

"How, I have?"

"Indeed, my friend. Our first step ought to be to find Khaavren, and let him know all that has occurred. Next, perhaps we should find Pel; the clever Yendi may be able to shed some light on these things—he certainly knew that Your Highness's life was in danger; who knows what else he has knowledge of?"

Adron shook his head. "No, we cannot involve Khaavren in any of this."

"Your Highness?" said Aerich, surprised.

"He is the Emperor's creature."

"Well? And if he is, he is nevertheless our friend."

"And therefore, can we ask him to help us in a matter which could bring his duty into conflict with his friendship?"

"Ah," said Aerich. "I had not considered that." He frowned and seemed troubled.

"Well?"

"Perhaps you're right. But Pel—"

"Is he not in the Academy of Discretion?"

"Yes," said Aerich.

"And is not his Academy supported by the Emperor?"

Aerich shrugged. "All of the nobility is supported by the Emperor."

"In fact," said Adron grimly, "it is the other way around."

"No, Your Highness. We support His Majesty with our gold; the Emperor supports us with his majesty."

"So it should be," said Adron. "It is rarely so."

Aerich shrugged.

"Khaavren is a good friend," put in Tazendra. "And so is Pel. If they were having difficulty in which we could help, they would not hesitate to tell us."

Adron bit his lip. "Nevertheless," he said, "for now, we should keep this to ourselves."

"Father," said Aliera.

"Yes?"

"What are you planning?"

Adron smiled at his daughter—a smile in which there was a certain degree of paternal fondness, odd as that may be to think of when discussing Adron and Aliera e'Kieron. Yet it was true, as all the accounts of the time agree, that these two giants of history, father and daughter, cared for one another even as fathers and daughters among commoners might. Adron said, "You are not easy to deceive."

"Well?"

His eyes strayed to the covered board in the back of the room, then he said, "I am planning nothing that I wish to discuss, Aliera."

"Very well," she said.

Aerich's eyes narrowed; Sethra's lips pressed together; and Tazendra's eyebrows rose.

"Then our plans?" said Aliera.

"Someone must speak with Jurabin," said Adron.

"I will do so," said Aliera.

Adron nodded. "You must attempt to learn what he knows

of the search of your room, and do not stop until you are certain you have emptied him of this knowledge.

"And I will try to learn as well," said Aliera, "what His Majesty's intentions are toward you."

"If you wish," said Adron, shrugging his shoulders.

"And I," said Sethra, "shall accompany the Lady Aliera, lest anything untoward happen to her while she is at the Palace."

"I will remain with His Highness," said Aerich, not saying anything more—to put into words that he feared for Adron's safety would, of course, have been an insult.

"And I," said Tazendra. "I will . . ." she frowned. "I'm not certain. What ought I to do?"

Aerich thought for a moment, then said, "You and Mica return to the house, and tell our friends that we have been in conference with Lord Adron. Of course, you must mention nothing of our plans, or of our concerns about Jurabin."

Tazendra nodded brusquely. "Very well," she said.

Sethra's eyes appeared to twinkle for a moment as she looked at Aerich, but if he noticed this he gave no sign of it. Tazendra rose and said, "If we are to go, we ought to take our leaves of Your Highness."

"Yes," said Adron, who seemed distracted, but came back to himself long enough to say, "Though I am not undisturbed by the news you have brought, still, I am delighted to see you, my friends, and I could not ask for better companionship for my daughter."

Tazendra and Aerich bowed deeply to Adron, after which father and daughter embraced. Then Sethra and Tazendra called to Mica, who appeared in the doorway, his faithful barstool slung over his shoulder.

"We are ready to leave," said Tazendra.

"Yes, my lady. I shall bring the horses."

"Aerich will be remaining here with His Highness."

"Yes, my lady."

As Mica went to fetch the horses, Aerich suddenly turned to Aliera and said, "My lady there is one question that I wish to ask you, for there is a matter upon which I am curious."

"How, you are curious about something?" said Aliera. "Well, you may ask."

"Then tell me this," said the Lyorn. "What exactly was this object that His Majesty discovered in your chambers, and that justified the search?"

Aliera shrugged. "Nothing, really. Just a small purple stone."

# Chapter the Seventeenth

*Which Treats of Small Purple Stones,
And of Irregularities in Dress.*

THIS IS NOT THE FIRST time the astute reader will have noticed these purple stones appearing in our narrative. Those with a knowledge of magical and natural history will, of course, have recognized them long hence, and be aware of their significance, and the threat posed by their very presence. It remains, then, our duty to assist those who have not had the privilege of making these studies, so that all of our readers will be, as it were, at the same place from this point forward, when those events which shape the conclusion of our narrative begin to coalesce into the patterns from which the final form of our history will emerge—or, to put it more simply, we must now ensure that all of our readers have the knowledge necessary to understand why those matters we are addressing fell out in the exact manner in which they did.

It has been theorized, and by such learned scholars as Richor of Mountcalm, that these stones were first created by the Jenoine—those mysterious, powerful, half-historical, half-mythical earliest dwellers on the world, who at last faded into the primal mist from which they emerged, or blew themselves up forming the Great Sea of Amorphia, or vanished to another plane of existence, or whatever theory the reader holds dear. It has also been theorized that the first of these stones occurred naturally near the edge or the "shore" of the Great Sea, although this seems unlikely.

Whatever their cause, the secret of creating them was discovered by wizards of the House of the Athyra late in the Ninth Cycle, and they were put to devastating use by sorcerers of the House of the Dragon early in the Tenth, for which reason the Lyorn Emperor Cuorfor II passed edicts forbidding their use or creation—edicts which have at times been rigorously enforced, at other times all but ignored. We should note that elder sorcery had been outlawed from the beginning of the Empire, and many believed—and still believe—that use of these stones was nothing more than a particular form of the sorcery that predates the Orb and the Empire; on this subject the historian will take no position.

It would, without doubt, require the services of an Athyra or a Dragon to reveal the details of their working—and it should be pointed out that such knowledge is available to those willing to look. Yet this history does not require such explicit detail—it is enough to say that to carry one of these stones about one's person will, over time, give one some understanding of the uses of that queer and dangerous branch of science called *elder sorcery*, and that these stones can also serve as a means of calling, storing, and dispersing the energies, taken from the very ether in which we live, that this sorcery calls upon and manipulates in its workings.

Where the sorcerer achieves his effects through the careful and subtle control of the powers were are granted, by the grace of Her Majesty, from the Orb, which controls and channels the energies from the Great Sea, elder sorcery, by its nature, eschews subtlety, instead relying on the sheer power of the amorphia. Is it any wonder that its use had been outlawed? Is it any wonder that no one save the crazed or the desperate will touch it? The difference between using these techniques—epitomized by the purple stones which we have now seen several times—and using the raw, naked power of the amorphia itself, is one of degree, not of kind.

And yet we must, for the sake of honesty, add that the Orb itself was fashioned (by Zerika the First, according to legend; by the Jenoine, according to myth) by this same pre-Empire sorcery. If so, then what power could be unleashed, what dreams of man could be fulfilled, if it were possible to achieve nice control of these powers, such control as the creators of the Orb must have had?

There is no answer to this question, so let us instead ask another: What sort of man might set himself the task of finding out? Who might take upon himself all of dreadful risks of unleashing such energy, wild and uncontrolled, in order to harness this power for mankind, or in order to further his own aims?

The answer, as the reader will already have surmised, is Adron e'Kieron, who had devoted more than four hundred years of his life to the study of this illegal and dangerous science—devoted those years to studying in the same fashion he did everything: with the enthusiasm of a Tiassa, the courage of a Dzur, the subtlety of a Yendi, the ferocity of a Dragon, and the thoroughness of a Lyorn.

What were Adron's aims in harnessing this power? This is a difficult question to answer, for he, himself, did not know. In all probability it began with simple curiosity—he wished to understand the nature of sorcery, which led him naturally and inevitably to a study of amorphia. Later, in all likelihood, he became aware of the potential in such power, and became, therefore, enamored of it as a tool he could unlock. Nowhere in his diaries is there any evidence of a lust for personal power, yet there are hints that he wished to have his name remembered, and he had, it is certain, a burning desire to create. We might even say that the same drives which led him to organize and lead the Breath of Fire Battalion led him to study ways to release and control the energies of the amorphia. While he had been growing steadily less happy with the court since observing Tortaalik's mismanagement of the White Goblet affair, had he had been livid about the debacle along the coast that had left an entire district, and one critical to Imperial trade, without a liege, there is no reason to believe he had ever contemplated revolt—and certainly no reason to believe that it ever entered his dreams to use the power of amorphia, or of elder sorcery, or of the purple stones, in any sort of bid for personal gain.

But here can be no doubt that, when His Majesty went so far as to deliver a direct insult to Adron's daughter, who was, in Adron's mind, doing nothing more than entering a study of one of the more esoteric (and, therefore, worthwhile) branches of magic, Adron's motivations, goals, and methods underwent a drastic, abrupt and irrevocable change.

It is possible that Aerich sensed some of this, and that it was in the hopes that the Lyorn's gentle wisdom would temper the fire in the Dragonlord's heart that Aerich wished to remain in Adron's presence, as much as to protect His Highness, toward whom the Lyorn felt some sense of duty and no small degree of affection. It is not impossible that Aerich realized this, whether aware of it or not, and this was why Adron welcomed Aerich's company.

Now that the reader has some understanding of these artifacts which have caused such a furor, let us look in on our various friends in the early morning light of the fifteenth day of the month of the Vallista in the 532nd year of the Reign of Tortaalik the First. We will begin with Pel, for, after a night's drunken debauch with Khaavren, he returned to the Institute of Discretion, and, at the time of which we write, he is doing nothing more than sleeping soundly. The reader ought to appreciate this moment, for it is rare indeed that we will have the opportunity to come upon our Yendi when he is not doing three, four, or five things at once!

Next is our Tiassa, Khaavren, who, notwithstanding the rigors of his night's feast of wine, nevertheless rose at his accustomed time, feeling, thanks to his iron constitution, none the worse for the debauch to which we have already alluded, and made his way as usual to the Dragon Wing of the Palace, and so on to meet His Majesty in time for the morning rounds.

Sethra, Aliera, and Tazendra, who had all returned to the house on the Street of the Glass Cutters before Khaavren and Pel had taken themselves to bed, were, in fact, awakened at about the time Khaavren was reaching the Palace. They were awakened, in fact, by Mica and Srahi bringing them klava. Of all the pleasures brought by riches (and we, unlike certain desert-born mystics we could mention, will not deny that riches can, in fact, bring pleasure), there is, perhaps, none to compare to being awakened, while still in bed, by a lackey bringing hot klava to which honey and cow's milk have been liberally applied, and realizing that one has the leisure to enjoy this first mug before arising. It was this pleasure which our friends Tazendra, Aliera, and Sethra experienced—we shall not, therefore, disturb their happiness by watching them, but will allow them their klava in peace; we will return to them again when they have arisen and are ready to begin their day's activities.

This brings us to His Highness, Adron e'Kieron, and to Aerich, both of whom began the day in military fashion—that is, at exactly the same time as Khaavren. Aerich accompanied His Highness on the morning inspection of the battalion, after which they broke their fast together on fresh, warmed bread with butter, both of which were purchased, at a good price, from nearby peasants. Aerich could see that the Prince was distracted, and that he had certain ideas frothing through his mind, but the Lyorn could not fathom what those ideas might be. He therefore watched gravely as Adron stood before the wooden board on which strange patterns were formed of purple stones; Adron worked hastily at first, removing stones and replacing them so that entirely different though equally abstract patterns appeared; then Adron began to slow down, until he spent long minutes staring at the design before moving a single stone. Aerich, while he did not understand precisely what the sorcerer was doing, nevertheless felt a deep disquiet as he watched the process.

Khaavren, after finishing the rounds with His Majesty, who appeared to be in excellent spirits, went off to find Jurabin in the hopes of learning from him something of what had passed, and what had not passed, between Aliera and His Majesty. Jurabin, however, was, it seemed, busy in one of the meeting rooms with which the second floor of the Palace abounded, and could not be disturbed. Khaavren shrugged and returned to his offices, where he discovered that he had a visitor, and an unexpected one at that. "Tazendra!" he cried.

"Ah, my dear friend," said the Dzurlord.

Khaavren rushed forward to embrace her, after which he insisted she come into the office that had been Captain G'aereth's but was now Khaavren's, and that she sit and converse with him.

She sighed happily as she sat down. "You cannot know what memories it brings back to be here again."

"And," said Khaavren, "what memories it brings back to see you here."

"Yes, but, Khaavren, do you know, there is hardly anyone that I recognize?"

"Well, but what would you have? There aren't many who wish to make a career of the Guard. You, yourself, are a splendid example of this very fact."

"How, am I?" she said, smiling proudly, not entirely sure what Khaavren meant, but convinced that he had paid her a compliment.

"Entirely," said Khaavren. "There is no one who is a better example than you."

"Well, it is kind of you to notice."

"Not at all."

"I have worked hard to become so."

"Yes, I perceive that you have."

"But enough of this, what of your own affairs?"

"My own affairs? Cha! Of what affairs are you speaking?"

"Why, I haven't the least idea in the world," she said. "Yet you were out last night very late."

"Oh, as to that, I was drinking with our old friend Pel."

"With Pel?" cried Tazendra. "Drinking? Does he still drink then?"

"Like the sea drinks the river, my dear friend. And you should have seen him, for he was dressed like the Pel of old.

Ah, what a fine companion he was! The innkeeper brought us the coals and tongs, but Pel would have none of it. In a motion as graceful as a dancer's he broke the neck of the bottle and, spilling not a drop, filled our glasses in the same motion."

"And was he still as graceful at the end of the night as he was when he began?"

"Shards, I nearly think so! My head was all in a spin, and the lights of the tavern replicated themselves behind my eyes, yet Pel was as cool as if he had not touched a drop, though I will swear he kept pace with me glass for glass."

"Well, I wish I'd been there, for I assure you it was wearying enough where I was."

"And where was that?"

"Where was that? How, you don't know?"

"If I knew, I would not have asked," Khaavren reminded her gently.

"Ah, that is so, that is so; you were always economical with questions."

"And so I still am, my dear Tazendra. And yet I find I must ask you again: Where were you?"

"Where were we? Oh, we were at Lord Adron's encampment, as the note said."

"Note, my dear Tazendra? I received no note."

"Bah! You did not? You received no letter explaining where we were and saying that you ought to join us?"

"No, for if I had, well, I should have done so."

"The Horse! That is true! And yet, I was so certain that I had written a note. And, look! I did write a note, for here it is in my pocket."

"Well, Tazendra, if it is in your pocket, that is why I did not get it."

Tazendra laughed. "Ah, ah! I wrote it, yet I did not remember to put it where you would find it. The fault is mine, good Khaavren, and I apologize."

Khaavren signified that it didn't matter, and added, "But I hope Lord Adron is well?"

"He? Well, yes and no, I think."

"How, yes and no?"

"He is healthy, yet he is not happy."

"He is not happy? Has, then, something happened to make him unhappy?"

"Something happen? I nearly think so! Did you not hear that His Majesty had a search made of his daughter's quarters in the House of the Dragon, or the Dragon Wing, I forget which?"

"Well, yes," said Khaavren. "It seems to me that I did hear something of that, now that you mention it."

"Well," said Tazendra.

"Were you able to cool his temper?"

"Oh yes," said Tazendra. "I spoke most soothingly, and he listened to everything I said. And of course, our friend Aerich was of some help."

"So that he was no longer angry when you left?"

"He was as gentle as a winneasaurus, content to let us make our investigations and do nothing until he learned what the results were."

"Investigations, my dear Tazendra?"

"Yes, certainly." Then she stopped and her eyes grew wide. "Ah, fool that I am, I was not to mention that to you."

"How, you were not to mention that?"

"Exactly."

"What were you not to mention?"

"That we have determined to investigate."

"Well, then I will pretend that you said nothing of any investigations."

"Oh, would you do that?"

"Cha! It is nothing. Though I confess that my self-love is a trifle damaged, Tazendra, that His Highness felt I could not be trusted."

"Oh, it wasn't that, I assure you."

"Well, but then, what was it?"

"He merely wanted to avoid putting you in a position where you must choose between your duty and your friendship."

"I see. Then it was a noble gesture."

"Was it not? I've always thought Lord Adron every inch a gentleman."

"Oh, certainly. Yet, I fail to see how an investigation you are conducting could cause a conflict between my duties and my friendship."

"Well, would you like to know something, Khaavren?"

"Certainly, my friend."

"I don't understand either."

"How, you don't understand?"

Tazendra solemnly shook her head.

"Then," said Khaavren, "it must be a deep matter indeed."

"Oh, the deepest."

"It must involve intrigue."

"I think it does," said the Dzurlord, her voice dropping to a whisper.

"And the court," said Khaavren, lowering his voice to match hers.

"Oh, of course, the court," said Tazendra. "Why else mention Jurabin?"

"Ah, that is who they wish to investigate?"

"None other."

"It is, I suppose, Aerich who is investigating Jurabin?"

"No, no. Aerich has remained with His Highness. It is Aliera and Sethra who are speaking with Jurabin." Then she winced. "Bah! I cannot keep my tongue under control. I was not supposed to mention that, either."

"Think nothing of it," said Khaavren who was, meanwhile, thinking of it a great deal.

"Ah, I am vexed with myself."

"But what *were* you to tell me?"

"Only that we saw His Highness, and passed the evening with him."

"That is all you were to tell me?"

"Not a word more."

"And whence came these orders?"

"Bah! From whom would these orders come except from His Highness?"

"But, then, who told you to pass on that you had seen him and that he was well?"

"Oh, that was Aerich."

"I see," said Khaavren. "Yet it seems to me that you have done just what you were asked to do."

"I have?"

"Why, yes, You have told me that you spent the evening with His Highness. So, you perceive, you have done what you ought to have done."

"Have I?" said Tazendra. "Well, then I shan't worry about it."

"And you will be right not to."

They continued speaking for some little time then, as old friends will, but they confined the discussion to reminisces and to praise for their friends and for each other.

"Well," said Tazendra, after a certain amount of time had passed, "I have seen you, and seen once more these rooms that were so important to me, and I have told you what I came to tell you. Now I shall be off, and I will, no doubt, see you at home this evening."

Tazendra stood up, and Khaavren did the same, and they embraced once more and parted with compliments. Khaavren returned to his duty of inspecting his guardsmen and reading the reports of the previous night's events, and was on the point of leaving to see if His Majesty required anything when he was informed that he had another visitor.

"Well, it seems to be the day for it. Who is this?"

"The Duke of Galstan."

"Ah, ah! Send him in!"

Pel came in, once more dressed as a student of the Art of Discretion: fully covered in plain robes the color of the mud that formed at the edge of the Dragaera River. "Pel, my friend! Sit down, sit down. Do you know, you have not missed our friend Tazendra by more than an hour."

"How, she was here?"

"In the very chair you now occupy."

"Well, but did she have a reason for her visit?"

"Oh, indeed yes. Aerich sent her to tell me that Adron is

furious, and may be contemplating doing something rash, and is, moreover, investigating Jurabin, because they suspect, as we do, that Jurabin may, for his own reasons, have prevailed upon His Majesty to be lenient toward Aliera." He frowned. "Our dear Jurabin cannot have had an easy time of it."

"I should think not," said Pel, smiling.

Khaavren shrugged. "Now you know what I know."

"That is true," said Pel, "but you do not yet know what I know."

"How, you have learned something since last night?"

"Indeed yes, and I will tell you if you wish."

"I wish for nothing else in the world."

"This is it, then: We were right about Her Majesty. She was behind the search of Aliera's quarters."

"Ah," said Khaavren. "How did you learn this?"

"I spoke to her, in my rôle as a student here. I asked if she had anything she wished to speak to a Discreet about."

"And yet, if it was told you in confidence—"

Pel laughed. "Not in the least. She denied requiring a Discreet, after which we had a pleasant conversation together, during which I learned much from her."

Khaavren nodded slowly, recognizing Pel very well in this tale.

"So, now what, my friend?"

"Now what?" said Pel. "I am not certain. Yet if, as seems to be the case, there is trouble brewing between the Consort and the Prime Minister, and at such a time as this, well, nothing good can come of it, Khaavren."

The Captain nodded, for he had been thinking exactly the same thing. Then he sighed. "I must think, and you do too, and we will see if, together, we cannot formulate some plan. For I will tell you, Pel, that I am frightened of this situation; and you know, I think, that I am not easily frightened."

The Yendi nodded solemnly and could think of nothing further to say. Khaavren rose and walked with Pel back to the Imperial Wing, after which Pel turned toward the Athyra Wing, walking at a slow, dignified gait so at odds with the spring in his step when he was garbed as a cavalier. Khaavren watched him, smiling. "Ah, my friend," he said softly. "How many of you are there? Do you even know anymore? And how do you keep them all distinct in your mind?"

He took a step toward the Portrait room and His Majesty, when, on a sudden impulse, he changed direction and made his way up to the suite of rooms belonging to Noima, Her Majesty the Consort. Now this suite, located on the east side of the Imperial Wing, featured an extension which had been grafted on above the Jhegaala Wing to provide a sort of balcony or parapet or porch where Her Majesty could sit on fine days and look down on the Dragaera River or the hills of Eastend. This balcony, for so we will call it, was entirely secluded from the rest of the Palace, and could not be reached except through the Consort's own bedchamber, which was always watched by a pair of guards (not to mention the other three pair who guarded the different entrances to the Consort's suite). All of this, in addition to providing an excellent setting for Luin's farcical murder drama, *Who Dropped Her First?* had the result that, if the Consort wished for privacy, all she need do was inform the guards to her room that she did not wish to be disturbed, and these guards would let no one, not even His Majesty, pass without word from the Consort.

No one, we should say, except their superior officer, Khaavren of Castlerock.

We ought to mention that it was not, in fact, Khaavren's intention to eavesdrop—his plan was to speak openly and frankly with Noima in hopes of pleading with her on Aliera's behalf. But when his clapping produced no response, and when the two guards informed their Captain that the Consort was, in all probability, taking the air on the balcony with her maids of honor, Khaavren simply shrugged and walked through the door, thinking nothing of it.

The Consort's bedroom was large and furnished mostly in white, with an imperial-size canopied bed, a white couch, and enough chairs for her attending maids. In the back of the room was the door which permitted access to the balcony to which we have felt obliged to call the reader's attention.

Khaavren was, in fact, setting his hand to the doorknob when he was caught up short by the sound of the Consort's voice, speaking in tones that were severe and left no doubt about the seriousness of the matter under discussion.

"Oh, ho," said Khaavren to himself. "Her Majesty is upbraiding one of her maids of honor. Perhaps, then, this would be a poor time to ask her for clemency, and it would be best to leave them alone and wait for Her Majesty's disposition to improve. And yet, one cannot help but be curious about the subject of Her Majesty's anger, for there is no doubt that what makes someone, be it Consort or courtesan, angry, tells us as much about her, or him for that matter, as what brings her pleasure. Let us, then, listen for a moment, and then we will steal away as silently as we have arrived, wealthier in knowledge and richer in experience."

As Khaavren listened, then, so shall we, and we will hear the Consort speaking in these terms: "Daro," she said, addressing a maid of honor whom Khaavren remembered as an elegant and haughty Lyorn, "you take liberties. I warn you that your position at court is in doubt if you continue speaking and behaving in this manner."

"Come, that's not badly said," murmured Khaavren. "What will be the reply?"

The reply, delivered in a feminine voice both strong and melodic, took this form: "Madam, I do take liberties, for which I hope Your Majesty can forgive me, yet my self-love speaks louder to me than my love of pelf, and if I must sacrifice one, why, there is hardly a choice. Your Majesty contemplates an injustice; I cannot remain quiet—"

"An injustice!" cried the Consort. "How, you are weeping for this poor, helpless, defenseless girl, who happens to be a Dragonlord, and, moreover, daughter of the Dragon Heir to the Throne? If you hate injustice, you might look to the injustices committed daily against those who have fewer means of defense than Aliera e'Kieron!"

"Ah, ah," said Khaavren. "What is this? They are talking of the very subject that interests me! Come now, this is fortunate; we must listen more closely than ever, that not a single note of this concert should escape our critical judgment."

"Madam," said Daro, "What Your Majesty does me the honor to say is full of justice. Nevertheless—"

"Yes? Nevertheless?"

"Weak or powerful, she is still a woman, which means she is human, which means she is able to feel pain, and Your Majesty has already subjected her to the humiliation of having her rooms searched, and this only for the crime of attracting attention that has previously gone to Your Majesty. Now Your Majesty contemplates crushing her beneath the weight of Imperial displeasure by bringing to bear all the weapons of the law—"

"The law she has broken!" cried the Consort, whose voice was beginning to sound shrill."

"—upon her head. Yes, madam, she has broken the law. An ancient law. A law some feel is unjust, and a law some feel is useless, but, nevertheless, a law. But I beg leave to point out to Your Majesty that it is a law no more ancient than those unwritten laws which regulate honorable behavior and use of power—laws designed to protect—"

"You are in danger, Countess," cried the Consort. "I warn you, take care!"

"Madam, I have Your Majesty's interests at heart, believe me. That which Your Majesty contemplates can result in nothing good for you, as well as those of us who have the honor to belong to you. I cannot stand by idly when Your Majesty engages in acts which cast shame upon you and on the court."

"How dare you speak to me thus?"

"I dare not keep silent."

"I believe I am condescending to dispute with you, Countess! Can you somehow have contrived to forget your rank, as well as my own?"

"You dispute not with me, but with Fairness and Justice, madam—two entities who know no rank."

"Shards and splinters," said Khaavren to himself. "It is a shame this girl is a Lyorn, for I declare that if she were a

Tiassa I should marry her in an instant, and then I should convince His Majesty to give me back the lands of Khaavren and we should have a fine daughter to rule my estate as Marchioness and a pretty son to rule hers as Count, after which we would retire together to Mount Bli'aard and let the Empire fall to whatever ruin it desires while we watched the golden lights dance off Redface in the morning."

If Khaavren was impressed with Daro's rejoinder, we can only say that the Consort was less so. She said, in a voice at once high and cold, "Countess, I think it is time for you to return to your estates, which, I suspect, stand in need of your firm and, no doubt, *just* hand to guide them."

"As Your Majesty wishes," came the answer, still in a strong voice. "Yet, madam, I have not surrendered. I assure Your Majesty that, before leaving, I intend to make certain that everyone at court knows——"

"You will do nothing of the kind!" cried the Consort in tones of outrage. "You will speak to no one; you will say nothing. You will be gone from here within the hour. If you fail in any way to do exactly what I have just said that is, if you disobey a direct order of your sovereign—you will be arrested for treason at that moment and you can spend the rest of your life in prison, remembering this day and all it has brought you. And if I were less merciful, I should not give you this choice, for you have hardly earned it. Now go!"

"Madam, I will follow your orders to the letter, yet I beg you to consider——"

"Go!" cried the Consort.

Khaavren suddenly realized his peril, and positively sprinted for the door, which he reached safely even as he heard the inner door open. He walked quickly past the guards, thinking to be out of sight before either the Consort or the Countess could see him. But then, on a sudden thought, he stopped where he was, in the Consort's sitting room, turned, leaned casually against the wall in the attitude of one who had been there for some time, and waited.

Daro appeared in an instant, her face flushed, but her eyes dry and appearing calm. She wore a floor-length dress of

Lyorn-red, gathered down the back, with puffed sleeves tapering to the wrist and a train that was also red save for a bit of tasteful gold embroidery. Her brown hair fell straight and plain to her shoulders, yet caught the light as if it had been brushed the legendary five thousand strokes. She appeared about to go straight past Khaavren as if she hadn't seen him, but he cleared his throat, bowed, and said, "Countess—"

She stopped, frowned, and said, "What is it, Captain? I am in a hurry."

"Well," he said phlegmatically.

"Yes?"

"If you will allow me to escort you whither you are going, I assure you I would look upon it as a great favor, and even as an honor."

Her eyes widened. "Surely I am not arrested!" Then she added in a low voice, as if to herself. "No, it would be impossible so soon."

"Arrested, madam? Not the least in the world, I promise you. Rather I am arrested. But that is neither one place nor another. No, there is no talk of arrest, merely a desire to escort you, for no reason other than the pleasure of doing so, for, if the words, however heartfelt, of a mere soldier can touch you, than be assured that you have interested me. Will you allow me the honor of escorting you?"

She laughed, though it seemed to Khaavren that she felt no great amusement. "What, Captain, after all these years have you become a courtier?"

"Ah, you wound me, madam. I—"

"Captain, I assure you that, as I said before, I am in a great hurry. I must see to my business with no delay. If you wish to accompany me, well, I have no objection to make, yet we must be about it at once. In fact, Captain, for reasons I dare not mention, it would ease my mind to have a strong arm to lean on just now, though perhaps it would be best for you if it were not yours."

"How, best for me? Yet—"

"No, do not ask why, and do not speak, merely allow me to take your arm, and let us proceed at once."

Khaavren bowed and held out his arm, which Daro took, and they walked down the corridor. Now we would not be faithful to our duty as historian if we did not admit that our Tiassa found himself confused by the tremor he felt in his arm when she took it, for he had been a soldier for five hundred years, and, after the heartbreak of his first love, had treated dalliance as the game that, alas! many soldiers do—forced to by the nature of their calling. Those who live with violence too often find that its opposite—love, becomes a matter as casual, and worth as little consideration, as swordplay. That is, to commit violence because duty requires it is to find one's self simulating hatred (for the best soldiers feel no real hatred for the opponent fate has placed before them); in the same way, then, it is all too easy to treat the acts of love—kisses, caresses, soft words—as mere simulation of love. One goes through the motions, and, indeed, takes certain pleasures from doing so, yet the touching of soul to soul that love brings to those who are blessed by it is denied by the very emotions that allow the soldier to take sword in hand, day after day, and commit acts which to most of us only accompany the most extreme passion.

In fairness, we must add that not all soldiers have this experience with love. Indeed, many of them, sickened by being constantly surrounded by thoughts of death, fall into love as an escape from the horror that surrounds them every day. Whether this is better or worse, we do not feel it our place to say, being merely the mirror upon which truth is, however imperfectly, reflected.

Khaavren had, also, fallen into the trap we have described, though he had never realized it. But now, when a gentle but brave hand was laid upon his arm, he became suddenly aware that he was not immune to such tender thoughts, and shooting through his soul were lances both of the pleasure that unselfish love brings, and the pain that comes with the awakening of emotions long asleep. Needless to say, he felt great confusion in his mind even as he felt a beating in his heart and a trembling in his limbs. Thoughts flitted through his mind too fast for his awareness to fasten on and pin down, yet they left their impressions in his clouded brow and shallow breath.

For her part, we should say that for years Daro had seen the Captain, and admired him from a distance—both his form and his character, insofar as she could see that he held himself apart from the intrigues and petty maneuvers of the court, and always carried himself with the relaxed confidence of a warrior, and had, moreover, a smile that, though rare, brightened his countenance, and made her think how pleasant it might be to cause the smile to appear. While she had never entertained serious thoughts in his direction, to find him there, a strong arm when she felt her strength exhausted, and a kind glance when she felt surrounded by malice, made her see him in a new way, and she was almost overwhelmed with bitterness at the thought that she had truly met him only now, when her life was ruined and she was to be ignominiously driven away. In addition, Khaavren had revealed a side of himself hitherto hidden—he had shown that he had a heart, and one that could be touched, and could open up to another in need.

The Countess endeavored to keep these thoughts concealed, and to recover herself as she walked, yet a part of herself cried out to reveal them, and so, as will sometimes happen when two souls develop a sudden sympathy, hints of her ideas communicated themselves to Khaavren via the hand upon his arm, which, in turn, accounted in part for the reactions that she felt from him.

By the time they reached the set of chambers where the maids of honor slept and kept their clothing, the Countess had recovered herself, and put up once more the barriers that prevent deep emotion from revealing itself too soon, before the heart is convinced that opening will not simply bring a fresh onslaught of pain without any likelihood of reward.

Daro's room was, by chance, unoccupied. She let go of Khaavren's arm with a bow, opened her wardrobe, removed a tall valise, and began filling it with her clothing.

"Tell me, Captain," she said as she haphazardly threw her

clothing into the valise (charmingly, thought Khaavren), "what brought you to Her Majesty's room? For it could not have been for the pleasure of seeing me."

"And why could it not?" said Khaavren. "Shards! I can think of few better reasons to walk a few paces, or even a hundred leagues."

She laughed. "You *are* becoming a courtier. But it could not be, because you could not have known I would be there."

"Well, that is a reason, at any rate, with which I cannot argue."

"Well then?"

"Madam, I came to see the Consort."

"Ah. Well, why did you not?"

"Because I saw you instead, and—"

"Flatterer!" she cried, although she did not seem displeased. "You said, 'and'?"

"And I heard you as well."

Daro stopped what she was doing, turned, and frowned. "You say you heard?"

"Every word, madam."

"I see. And therefore—?"

"I wished to pay you a thousand compliments, for I am a soldier, and soldiers know what courage is."

For the first time, Daro blushed, turning bright red for a moment and looking down. "Thank you, Captain. But you perceive, if you heard our conversation, that I have no time. And that is why it might be best for you not to be seen with me lest your light be stolen by my shadow. Indeed, I should not, for your sake, have allowed you to walk with me, but I was weak, and needed your arm. Forgive me."

"Cha," said Khaavren. "I will be seen with you whenever I can, madam, and hold myself honored."

She gave him a gentle smile and extended a soft hand, upon which Khaavren placed a reverent kiss. "You are kind, Captain. But it is the case that I am ruined, and your compliments, as well as the whisperings of my heart, are as nothing before the whims of the Consort."

"The whisperings of your heart, did you say?" cried

Khaavren, falling to his knees. "Ah, do not say aloud what your heart whispers, because if it speaks as mine, then, by the Halls of Judgment, I will cast every curse I know at the fates which decreed that I should be a Tiassa while you are a Lyorn!"

Has the reader ever found himself wondering, as he was engaged in some activity or another, "What else is happening in the world?" Or perhaps, upon hearing of some momentous event, has the reader ever wondered, "What was I doing at the exact moment when that occurred?" It is, without doubt, one of the charms of the historical account that these questions can be answered, at least for some people at some times.

By way of example, we will mention that shortly after the third hour after noon, a week and a day nearly to the minute from when we opened this history with a messenger asking to see His Majesty, another messenger was asking for the same favor, this messenger coming from none other than Adron e'Kieron.

At this same moment, the Consort, having positively run from her rooms after the interview with her maid of honor that we, as well as Khaavren, have just overheard, was closeted with His Majesty, and was begging of him certain boons.

Tazendra, who had been wandering the labyrinthine Palace for some hours, had at last managed to locate the Academy of Discretion, and was asking after Pel.

Aliera and Sethra, who had been closeted with Jurabin for most of the day were at last emerging, having learned what they wished to know, but still uncertain what to do with the knowledge.

Aerich was contemplating the Duke of Eastmanswatch while, at the same time, the Duke was contemplating his mosaic of purple stones and dreaming of inflicting countless humiliations on the Emperor in vengeance for those His Majesty had inflicted upon Aliera.

And, at this same time, Daro said, "How, a Lyorn? Not in the least, my friend. I merely chose these colors because they suit me, and I will not be bound by silly traditions. No, no, do you see my eyes, the shape of my ears, the form on this signet? I am as much a Tiassa as you, good Captain."

After which revelation our old friend Khaavren, unable to speak for the pounding in his ears, rose unsteadily to his feet and took Daro, Countess of Whitecrest, into his arms.

# B O O K
## TWO

# Chapter the Eighteenth

### Which Treats of Several Persons
### Who, for Various Reasons,
### Decide They Ought to Speak at Once
### To Our Friend, the Captain.

HISTORY IS NOT WHAT MEN could have done, or should have done, but, rather, what they did. It is unquestionably the case that, had the author chosen to write a romance, the ending of the last chapter would have been a rude and unpleasant shock to the reader. That is, the requisite element of classic romance—lovers of different houses finding each other at court but knowing their love is doomed—appeared, only to be set aside in a single, hasty moment of revelation, devoid of the intricacies of plot and counter-plot through which the author would cleverly prevent his characters from learning the truth about each other until either the last moment before the tragedy, or at the first moment after it was too late, depending on whether the author was of the romantic school of Lord Wrenchilde or the more ironic disposition of Lady Hopston.

But if history, though containing, we believe, enough true drama to satisfy anyone's cravings, rarely follows the formulae outlined by the subscribers to this or that school of history, still less, then, is she willing to follow anyone's notion of literature. She is a piece of wood afloat in the tide, and will go where the winds and waves bring her, caring nothing for the artist who stands, crayon poised, to draw her from the shore. Should he study her image as it is, she may be willing to fetch up near him long enough to allow some of the secrets of her form to be revealed by an honest canvas; if he insists she conform to his preconceived artistic laws, his work will never enfold her, and truth will always run before him, a step out of reach for ever, like the chreotha in Lady Neloy's fable.

We insist, then, that, the conventions of romances notwithstanding, we have related what actually occurred between Daro and Khaavren, and we have placed it in time and space as accurately as our meager talents permit. Furthermore, we believe the drama is stronger because it has the resonance of *truth*, rather than the artifice of fiction; yet the reader is, of course, free to draw his own conclusions about literature versus history, as about anything else we have discussed during the time when he has done us the honor to allow us to spend an evening with him.

With this understood, it is time to move on to the rest of the Palace, where events have not stood still while Khaavren and Daro discovered one another. On the contrary, the sudden and unexpected complication between Captain and Countess, though of great importance to this history (and, we dare to hope, to our readers), was so unimportant to the rest of the court as to pass entirely unremarked.

Lest the reader fear that, in following this "sudden and unexpected complication," as we have called it, we have lost track of the others whose actions we are obliged to follow, let us declare that nothing could be further from the truth. And the proof, if more proof is needed than the summary provided near the end of the previous chapter, is that we are now prepared to look in on Sethra and Aliera, as they leave Jurabin's council chamber.

"Well," said Sethra. "So, it is true that it was Jurabin who has saved you from arrest."

"There can be no further doubt on that score," said Aliera. "He confessed it with every gesture, every glance—"

"Every glance, that is, at me," said Sethra, smiling. "For, as you no doubt observed, he could not bring himself to look directly at your countenance."

"Well," said Aliera, shrugging, "there is some truth in what you say."

"And yet, we are no closer than we were to knowing who is behind the assassinations—both failed and successful—that have broken out like a plague over this last week and more."

"That is true," said Aliera. "For, though he was confused, and could conceal nothing, he gave no indication of guilty knowledge on this subject."

"And yet—" said Sethra.

"Yes?"

"There is one matter to which my mind keeps returning."

"Well, if you will tell me what it is, my mind will turn to it as well, and your mind shall have company on its journey, which will, no doubt, be as pleasant for our minds as the company we keep on our journey along this corridor is pleasant to us."

"You reason like an Athyra, my dear friend."

"Well, go on."

"This is it, then."

"I am listening."

"The way he spoke of the Consort. The quiver, if you will, in his voice, and the way his eyes shifted away from me."

"Ah! I had not remarked this! What do you make of it?"

"That he knew something he would not tell us."

"About the Consort?"

"Precisely."

"There is gossip about the two of them."

"That is certainly the case, my dear Aliera."

"Then you suspect—?"

"That she is your enemy? Exactly."

"And she has the ear of His Majesty."

"And His Majesty has his Guards."

"And the Captain of the Guards?" said Aliera.

"Khaavren," said Sethra.

"Yes, Khaavren," said Aliera. "The order for my arrest, as

we determined before, must go through him. But would he warn us first, if he were told to arrest me?"

"As to that, I cannot say."

"No," said Aliera, "but I can."

"Oh?"

"I need only a few words with him, and I will know if he has been given these orders."

"Well?"

"Then let us find him, and at once."

Sethra laughed. "How, you have not remarked the direction we are traveling? We are nearly to the Dragon Wing. Down these stairs, and we shall be at his offices."

"Then lead on," said Aliera. "And let us learn what we can from this Tiassa."

All of this took place in the Dragon Wing of the Palace, beginning on an upper floor and winding down toward the Sub-wing of the Imperial Guard. Some distance away, near the Athyra Wing (although not, technically speaking, within it) another of our friends had reached her destination.

Tazendra, as we have already mentioned, had, after several hours of diligent searching, finally located the Institute of Discretion. She asked to see Pel. The door-ward denied knowing any such person and persisted in this denial until, fortunately, at least for the door-ward, Tazendra remembered to ask for him as the Duke of Galstan, after which the Duke was sent for. After an interval of a few minutes, he arrived.

Tazendra gave a cry upon seeing Pel, and embraced him with an exuberance that simultaneously raised the door-ward's eyebrows and threatened the Yendi's ribs. He nevertheless returned the embrace as well as he could before disengaging himself and paying Tazendra a thousand compliments.

"So," he said at last, "you have been seeking me?"

"More than seeking you," said Tazendra. "I have found you."

"Well, you have," said Pel. "And yet—"

"And yet?"

"Well, I wonder—"

"Ah! I recognize you so well in that!"

"Oh, to be sure."

"But tell me what you wonder."

"Oh, I am about to."

"Begin then."

"I wonder why you have been seeking me."

"Why else, but to find you?"

"Yes, yes, I understand that, only—"

"Only you wish to know *why* I wanted to find you?"

"Yes, Tazendra. You have guessed it. I wish to know *why* you wanted to find me."

"Oh, as to that—"

"Yes?"

"I will tell you."

"And at once, I hope."

"Why, this, this very instant."

"Then I am listening."

"I wished to find you because I wish to learn what you know."

"You wish to learn what I know? But surely you must understand—"

"Ah, ah! You know that understanding is not something I do well."

"Oh, but this is something you *will* understand."

"I am skeptical."

"I know you are, Tazendra, and I assure you that it is a mark of intelligence."

"Do you think so?"

"I am convinced of it."

"Well, what must I understand, then?"

"You must understand that the secrets of Discretion are not to be divulged to anyone who is not an initiate."

"Oh, yes, I understand that."

"Well, you perceive I was right."

"Yes, yes. You are always right. Only—"

"Yes?"

"When I spoke of wanting to learn what you knew, I was not thinking about the secrets of Discretion."

"But, my dear Tazendra, what else could I, locked away in this tower, know? I assure you, it has been my whole life. No, no, don't answer yet. For I assure you that I desire nothing more than conversation with you, so let us find a place where we can sit comfortably while we speak. Here, turn this corner, and now this one, and so through this portal. Here, you perceive, is a room that is empty save for some chairs, and one that has, moreover, good, thick walls. Now, of what do you pretend I have knowledge?"

"Well, of the assassination attempt on Lord Adron."

"Ah! I admit that I had some concerns on that score, but they seem to have been misplaced."

"Not at all."

"How, not at all? Was an attempt made?"

"Yes, only—"

"Well?"

Tazendra dropped her voice. "They made a mistake, and attempted to kill Khaavren instead."

"How, Khaavren?" cried Pel, amazed.

"Yes. And they might have succeeded, except that, thanks to your warning, Aerich and I were there, and I was able to discharge a flashstone which, thanks to the Gods, did not miss its mark."

"Your flashstones rarely miss their mark," said Pel.

"You are kind to say so," said Tazendra magnanimously.

"Yet," said Pel slowly, "I cannot believe they would have made such a mistake."

"Oh, they did, although, to be sure, neither Khaavren nor Aerich seem to think it was a mistake."

"What do they think?"

"They think it was an attempt on Khaavren. But that would mean that you had erred in thinking that Adron was in danger, and I do not think—"

"When was an attempt made?"

"It was the evening of the riot. We had a hand in that, too, I should add. I mean, we helped to stop it; we did nothing to start it, I assure you."

Pel seemed to be considering matters deeply. "You say an attempt was made on Khaavren?"

"No, no. On Adron. Only—"

"An attempt was made, was it not, Tazendra?"

"Yes."

"And Khaavren was its intended victim?"

"Without question."

"Then that is enough for now."

Tazendra shrugged as if she, having done her best to open his eyes, would waste no more time pointing out the obvious. For his part, Pel did not seem distraught by this. He said, "Do you know who made the attempt?"

Tazendra frowned. "I must confess something," said Tazendra.

"Well, as a Discreet, at least in training, there are few to whom you could more safely make a confession."

"Listen, then."

"I am listening."

"I cannot remember what they said."

"What, who said, my dear Tazendra?"

"Khaavren and Aerich. They spoke at some length about the assassin, as if they knew him. Yet all I can remember is that he was from the Underside. You remember the Underside, Pel? We went in there one day, the two of us, when there was a disturbance in a private home, where eight or nine rogues seemed determined to plunder it. When we arrived, they were holding the residents hostage, and we had to—"

"Yes, yes, I recall, but—"

"Ah, that was hot work, that night! Some steel sang, and some blood was let!"

"Yes, yes, Tazendra. It was a fine night. Only—"

"Do you recall, after we had rescued the victims, they gave me a pewter goblet, with a ruby on the base?"

"I had forgotten that circumstance."

"I still have it, you know. I keep it on the mantel, near the dagger I broke when Khaavren and I were set upon by—"

"Your pardon, Tazendra my dear, but I must ask you this: You say Khaavren and Aerich knew the assassin?"

"No, no, Pel. They only seemed to. They spoke of his habits, and his House, and—"

"Well then, we need only ask Khaavren or Aerich who he is, and then we will know."

"Well, that is true. But what then?"

"What then? Why then, we will see if this information will help us track down those who are attempting to kill Lord Adron."

"Oh, I should love to get my hands on whoever hired the assassin!"

"Let us find Khaavren or Aerich, then, and perhaps you will get your wish."

"An excellent plan, Pel. You always have good plans."

Pel bowed to this compliment and said, "Where, then, is Aerich?"

"Do you mean, at this moment?"

"Yes, exactly. At this moment."

"He is with Lord Adron, protecting him."

"That is good. His Highness could not be in better hands."

"That is my opinion," said Tazendra.

"But what of Khaavren?"

"Oh, Khaavren would also protect His Highness, only he is not there."

"Yes, but, where is he?"

"Where is he? Where else but here, in the Palace?"

"With His Majesty, do you think?"

"There, yes. There or elsewhere."

Pel shrugged like Aerich. "In that case, let us go find him."

"Yes, let's. Only, I do not know this part of the Palace. I am not entirely sure how I got here, and I do not, therefore, know how to get back."

"But I do," said Pel.

"Well then, you lead."

"I am doing so."

And so, with this, Pel and Tazendra set off to find Khaavren. While they are thus engaged, we will take the opportunity to discover something of how His Majesty has been engaged.

The Emperor had been in jovial spirits for most of the day. He noticed the absence of his Captain, but assumed that Khaavren was involved, along with Sethra Lavode, in the investigations associated with the assassinations. His day went by as usual until, in the middle of the afternoon, he was interrupted by the Consort, who urgently requested a private audience with him, an audience he granted at once. They repaired, therefore, to the Seven Room, with Corporal Thack stationed outside of the door.

Need we dwell on the conversation? Can the reader not, from the information previously given and from his own imagination, supply the words, gestures, tears, and entreaties that fell, at first like flakes of snow, then like the floodwaters of the swollen Breaking River in spring, from Consort to Emperor, in an effort to see Aliera arrested and imprisoned? We can assure the reader that, for a least the first minutes of the conversation, there would be little deviation between the reader's hypothesis and the actuality.

Eventually, however, His Majesty ventured to say, "Madam, you have my entire sympathy, and yet—"

"Yes? And yet?" said the Consort, looking at him with reddened eyes.

"Surely, you must understand, there are reasons of state that make her arrest—"

"Reasons of state?" she cried. For a moment, she seemed about to launch an assault on his premise—that is, that reasons of state could take precedence over her desires. But then she calmed herself and said, "Well, then, Sire, let us look at these reasons of state which are so important they permit a dangerous criminal to walk free, and to laugh at the laws of the Empire to which all save Your Majesty are bound."

"Yes, yes," said Tortaalik quickly, for he had cringed when he thought she was about to lose her temper, and was grateful that she was willing to discuss the matter rationally. "Yes, let us look at these reasons of state."

"Well, what are they?"

"In the first place—"

"Yes, Sire, in the first place?"

"There is her father."

"What about him?"

"What about him? Well, he is the Dragon Heir."

"Very well, he is the Dragon Heir."

"A proud, arrogant, and powerful man."

"I dispute none of these things."

"A man with considerable support among the Princes and Deputies who are gathering to determine the Imperial Tax."

"I begin to see your argument, Sire."

"Do you? Then I am gratified."

"Well, Sire, go on."

"Very well. We have the issue of the Imperial Tax, upon which depends the stability of the Empire, not to mention our comfort."

"Yes, yes, I understand that."

"So much, then, for the question of Adron."

"Yes, I now comprehend the situation with Adron and the Imperial tax."

"Next, there is the matter of Aliera's friendship with Sethra Lavode."

"What is this?"

"I am told that they have become fast friends. And, you perceive—"

"Fast friends? And yet, Sire, I am told that they have threatened to murder one another no less often than once each day since they have met."

The Emperor shrugged. "Well? They are Dragonlords; wherefore does this means they are not friends?"

"Well, go on."

"Yes. Well, it is clear that there is some sort of conspiracy at work, which has resulted in G'aereth's murder, the assassination of Smaller, the—"

"Yes, Sire, there is a conspiracy."

"Sethra is helping to investigate it. Should we offend Sethra—"

"Then she will no longer help in the investigation."

"Exactly."

"I understand, Sire."

"Not to mention any other ways in which Sethra Lavode could exercise her influence to our detriment."

"Well then, I understand the arguments about Adron and Sethra. What next?"

"Next, the people."

"The people?"

"Exactly."

"You perceive, Sire, that I fail to see what the people have to do with this."

"Ah, then you have not been informed of Alicra's influence among the people? How they formed an attachment to her after the incident of the bakery?"

"The incident of the bakery, Sire?"

"Yes, exactly."

"But I know nothing of this incident."

"Then I shall tell you of it."

"Go on, then. I await you."

"This is it: Two days ago she saw a crowd outside of a large bakery on the Street of Six Fences. She became curious, and attempted to discover the reason behind the gathering."

"Well?"

"Well, the crowd had become angry because the baker had raised the price for bread, pretending that the new tax imposed on wheat entering the city had raised his costs. The crowd was debating breaking down the doors of the bakery and taking the bread."

The Consort frowned. "Were they serious about this, Sire?"

"As I am informed, madam, the only remaining question was whether, after taking the bread, they should hang the baker, or merely let him go with a beating."

"Rabble!" cried the Consort. "That an honest merchant should be treated so! Where were the Guard?"

"They had been sent for, but they were, as yet, some distance away."

"What happened, Sire?"

"You wish to know what happened, madam?"

"The Gods! It is an hour since I asked anything else!"

"Aliera, upon hearing the story, approached the baker and purchased his business."

"How, she purchased it?"

"On the spot."

"For a good price?"

"So I am informed."

"Well, and then?"

"And then she gave the bread away until it was gone." The Consort shrugged. "It is a solution for a day only."

"Not at all."

"Well?"

"She then gave the bakery back to the baker, on the condition that he return his prices to what they had been."

"And so?"

"And so the story has spread, and, no doubt, been exaggerated. The people love Aliera, and, if we should arrest her—"

"Bah! What can the people do, Sire?"

"What can the people do? And would you ask a sailor what the ocean can do?"

"No, for the ocean cannot be controlled."

"Ah, but it can, unless there is a storm."

"And you fear a storm?"

"A storm, or a flood, yes, madam. I am not ashamed to say that I fear it."

"Well, perhaps you are right to."

"So let us review."

"Yes, yes. Let us act like careful intendants, and be certain our accounts are in order."

"We have, then, first of all, Lord Adron, and the Princes and Deputies. Next, we have Sethra Lavode. Third, we have the people. All of these argue strongly that Aliera must not be arrested except under the most pressing of circumstances."

"I perceive, Sire, that you have been carefully advised."

"Yes, madam, and by Jurabin, whose business it is to know and understand these matters."

"Ah! By Jurabin."

"Yes, madam, exactly."

"Well then, I have no more to say about matters of state."

"Then you understand my position?"

"Entirely. Only—"

"Yes?"

"You might weigh these matters of state against personal matters."

"Personal matters, madam?"

"Exactly."

"I confess that I don't understand."

"Shall I explain, Sire?"

"If you would be so good."

"By personal matters I mean that, if you allow yourself to be moved by fear of the people, by fear of Sethra, and by fear of Adron, well, there are those who will think you a coward."

His Majesty frowned. "Do you think so?"

"Sire, I am convinced of it."

"And yet, if I do not, there are those who will think me a fool, and I will be the first of these."

"Then being thought a coward does not disturb Your Majesty?"

"Well, I would not say that it does not disturb me, madam. Yet ever since I was a child, I have—"

We do not know how His Majesty intended to complete this intriguing sentence; he was interrupted by a clap at the door, to which he responded—gratefully, to judge by the look on his countenance and the slight lightening of the Orb—by calling out, "Who is there?"

"Sire," said Thack from the other side of the door, "there is a messenger here who begs leave to speak with Your Majesty on a matter of some urgency."

"A messenger?" said the Emperor. "And for whom does he message?"

"His Highness, Lord Adron e'Kieron," said Thack.

His Majesty stared, half rose to feet, sat down again, and said, "Bid him enter."

"At once, Sire," said Thack, and the door was opened, admitting the messenger. Where the messenger with whom we opened our history was Teckla, this messenger was a Dragonlord. Where the Teckla was dressed in the height of style, the Dragonlord was dressed in simple military fashion. Where the Teckla was called Seb, the Dragonlord was called Molric e'Drien, and was, in fact, Adron's nephew and chainman.

His Majesty directed a look at the Consort, indicating that, this being in the nature of Imperial Business, she ought to quit the room. Her Majesty directed a look at the ceiling, as if studying the intricate floral patterns etched therein, indicating that she preferred to stay and hear whatever communication Lord Adron had for His Majesty. The Emperor frowned, thought about insisting, but in the end simply turned to the messenger and nodded for him to begin.

The messenger bowed and opened his mouth, when he, in turn, was interrupted by sudden footsteps appearing at the door. He turned as His Majesty looked over the messenger's shoulder at the still-open door.

"Ah, Jurabin!" cried His Majesty. "Your arrival is timely."

"Thanks, Sire," said the Prime Minister. "Word reached my ears that a messenger had arrived from His Highness the Dragon Heir."

"Exactly."

"If I may, Sire, I should wish to hear the message."

"You may indeed, Jurabin. Please come in. His Highness's nephew, Lord Molric, was about to begin."

Jurabin entered, bowed respectfully to His Majesty and to the Consort, and seated himself at the far end of the room, where he folded his hands on the table and assumed an attitude of careful attention. Excepting only the bow to which we have just alluded, Jurabin avoided looking at the Consort entirely—for her part, Jurabin may as well not have existed for all the notice she paid to his presence.

"Now then," said His Majesty, who appeared oblivious to the interaction, or lack of interaction, between Jurabin and Noima. "You, Sir, were about to tell us what His Highness does the honor of communicating to us."

"Yes, Sire," said the Messenger. "Here is the message."

"We are listening."

Molric began to recite the message, as if he had memorized

every word, pause, and emphasis, which, we do not doubt, is exactly the case.

He began, "To His Imperial Majesty, Tortaalik, Emperor of Dragaera, from His Highness, Adron e'Kieron, greetings."

"Well," said His Majesty to himself. "He begins well enough. Where he will go from there?"

The messenger continued, "Your Majesty ought to know that malicious gossips are spreading rumors injurious to Your Majesty as well as to me. In particular, Sire, there are those who claim that Your Majesty would so demean himself as to order searched the private chambers of my daughter, Aliera, the Countess of Limterak, on the flimsy pretext that certain outmoded laws may have been violated.

"Sire, I know this is impossible, yet these rumors abound, wherefore I, as a loyal servant of Your Majesty, feel obliged to bring them to Your Majesty's attention. Should Your Majesty wish to discover more details about these rumors, he need but ask his faithful and vigilant servant, Adron e'Kieron, Duke of Eastmanswatch, Dragon Heir to the Throne."

After the messenger, falling silent, had bowed, there was nothing to do except watch as the Orb grew darker and redder, and to speculate upon the nature of His Majesty's outburst. Even Jurabin, who was normally the one who could caution His Majesty against taking intemperate actions without thinking them through, dared not speak. And Her Majesty could think of nothing except that she had been the one who had cajoled and wheedled Tortaalik into having Aliera's rooms searched; she had no desire to call any attention to herself whatsoever.

At last the messenger himself, displaying, indeed, all the courage of a Dragonlord, said, "Sire, is there a reply?"

His Majesty stared at him, the Orb so red it seemed to be burning. "You may tell His Highness," he said at last, "that we have received his message."

Molric bowed low and backed away, taking himself out the Emperor's sight, and, no doubt, thanking his personal deity that none of His Majesty's wrath had been sent in his direction. Meanwhile, Tortaalik struggled in his mind to control the rage he felt. On the one hand were all of the arguments he had just outlined to the Consort, but on the other was a sting to his pride such as he had never felt.

Could matters have fallen out differently? Could someone have said something that might have had a different result, and could the course of the Empire have been changed thereby? In the sober judgment of this historian: No. Had His Majesty swallowed the offense, there can be no doubt that Adron, who had nicely calculated the insult, would have merely regrouped and, as he did during the Defense of the Gripping Ford, found a new line of attack, until he at last penetrated his enemy's position.

But such speculations, of course, are pointless, for history is not what men could have done, or should have done, but, rather, what they did. What His Majesty did was take a deep breath, let it out slowly, and turn to Thack, saying, "Bring me my Captain of the Guards."

# Chapter the Nineteenth

---◆===◆——◆===◆---

*Which Treats of a General and a Gentleman,*
*Or a Dragon and a Lyorn,*
*And the Interaction Between Them;*
*Comparing and Contrasting It*
*To the Interaction Between*
*Two Less Savory Characters.*

SINCE KHAAVREN IS, JUST AT the moment, unavailable, and it will be some time before any of those looking for our brave Captain manage to find him, we will take the opportunity to look in on Aerich and Adron, at the Duke's encampment outside of Dragaera. Following the departure of the messenger, whose errand Adron knew perfectly well and Aerich guessed, time had passed very slowly, though neither of these gentlemen gave any indication of impatience. Adron busied himself with dispatches and the seemingly endless paperwork of his battalion, occasionally breaking off to study his mosaic of purple stones, while Aerich worked with his crochet hook, creating a stylized Lyorn which he intended to put on a table in his library.

After some hours, a fine meal arrived in Adron's tent—a meal which combined the most advanced studies of the culinary arts as practiced by the military with the sensibilities of

Lord Adron, who had always believed in keeping a proud table. They were served by a young subaltern, who herself selected the wine and brought forth the dishes as they were required by her general and his guest, yet contrived to remain out of their way, and nearly out of their sight.

The two gentlemen set to work on the comestibles in their particular fashions: Adron attacked his food as if it were the enemy, and disposed his knife and his teeth as if they were the forces with which he intended to rout the roasted duck, drive back the hard-crusted bread, scatter the long-bean and rice, and force the confection of apple, cream, and plum wine to surrender unconditionally. Aerich, meanwhile, treated these same dishes as if each were an honored guest, and he did not so much devour them as hold conversation with them, treating each with the courtesy and respect he thought it deserved. It is difficult to say which of them enjoyed his meal the more, yet certainly Adron enjoyed his more quickly—he was sipping strong wine and wandering contentedly about the tent (if we may be permitted such unfortunate euphony) while the Lyorn was contemplating the whipped, frothy confection we have already mentioned, and wondering at the best way to address it with the sweet biscuits at hand.

"A most laudable repast," he remarked and looked upon the dishes, full and empty, and recalled their contents.

Adron bowed, and gave the subaltern an approving look that she would in due course take back to the chief of Adron's kitchen. When she had at last gathered up the dishes, napkins, and wine bottles, Aerich sat back contentedly, sighed, and said, "Will Your Highness entertain a question?"

"Gladly, my dear Lyorn," said Adron, looking up from the patterns of purple stones upon which he had, perhaps as an aid to digestion, begun working once more.

"I must apologize that this question is not related to the duck who has given his life for our palates, nor, indeed, to the elegant and thoroughly mysterious manner in which Your Highness's chef has managed to season and prepare it over the spit with only the tools of a traveling army at his disposal."

"Well," said Adron. "Pleased as I am that you have enjoyed the refreshment, you need not confine your conversation to it. Tell me, if you would, the subject that occupies your thoughts."

"What can it be, Your Highness, except politics, and the situation in which we find ourselves?"

"Ah," said Adron. "Yes, I understand you may have some questions on this subject."

"I do indeed."

"Begin then."

"Very well. How does Your Highness anticipate His Majesty will react to the insult?"

Adron frowned. "Insult? I must beg you to explain yourself more fully, for I do not understand the question you have done me the honor to ask."

"I refer," said Aerich, "to the insult contained in the message Your Highness has this morning caused to be dispatched to His Majesty."

"Do you pretend I have insulted His Majesty?"

Aerich returned him a look of inquiry. "I had not realized the matter was in doubt. Had Your Highness wished to convey some other impression?"

Adron's frown deepened. "Has Molric been indiscreet?"

"Hardly," said Adron.

"Then how are you aware of what I have said to His Majesty?"

"I have the honor of knowing Your Highness."

Adron's countenance cleared, and he very nearly smiled. "Ah," he said.

"And as to my question?"

"Well, what is your opinion?"

"Does Your Highness wish to know my opinion of this message?"

"Yes, exactly."

"I think Your Highness ought to follow it at once with another."

"Follow my first message with a second?"

"Precisely."

"And what ought this second message to contain?"

"An apology for the first."

Adron stared for some few moments at the Lyorn, as if deciding whether to become angry. Whether because Adron's anger was specific, and directed against His Majesty, or simply because Aerich had the natural dignity which permitted him to make such statements with impunity, the Prince in the end decided that anger was uncalled-for. He simply said, "And yet, why should I apologize, when the offense was given by the Emperor?"

"Because," said Aerich, "he *is* the Emperor."

"And therefore his subjects ought to accept whatever treatment he chooses to bestow upon them?"

"Yes," said Aerich.

Adron looked carefully at the Lyorn while he apparently considered this novel attitude toward the person of the Emperor. At last he said, "Why?"

"Because if the nobility fails in respect for the Imperium, what cause have the peasants to respect the nobility?"

"It seems that I have heard this argument before," admitted Adron. "And yet, it seems to me that if His Majesty fails to treat the nobility with the respect due our rank, then does that not also encourage the peasantry to do so as well?"

"Is it better to show an example of obedience and respect, or of rebellion?"

Adron took a step forward, planting himself in front of the Lyorn, and cried, "You go too far, sir! Who spoke of rebellion?"

Aerich remained seated and shrugged. "If one insults one's sovereign, one may be a fool who expects no response, or a martyr who expects to be arrested, or a rebel who expects to resist. I know Your Highness is not a fool; I doubt Your Highness is a martyr."

Adron looked at him carefully, for a moment, then laughed. "You are no fool either, Lyorn."

Aerich bowed his head.

"Well?" said the Duke of Eastmanswatch. "I have not rebelled yet, and His Majesty may still apologize."

"Surely Your Highness does not expect His Majesty to do so, any more than I do."

"Expect? Hardly, sir. And yet, I hope I am wrong. By all the Gods, he owes me an apology, or, at any rate, he owes my daughter one. To so treat the offspring of the Dragon Heir — but it is of no moment. You are right, I do not expect an apology from His Majesty."

"And then?" said Aerich. "Can Your Highness resist the entire force of the Empire?"

Adron smiled a little, glanced at the mosaic of purple stones, and said, "Perhaps I can."

"But," said Aerich, "does Your Highness truly wish to do so?"

Adron frowned but did not answer.

As these matters of morals (or, as the Demon of Knightsford would have us believe, ethics) were being hinted at, although never directly addressed, in Adron's encampment outside of the city, at this same time, within the city, other matters were being discussed; matters in which ethics (or morals) played no part, though there can be no question that any gentleman would have been outraged by the very subject, which was nothing less than cold-blooded murder, assassination, killing by stealth rather than skill.

Let the reader not think that this discussion is occurring in the Underside, or, indeed, anywhere that resembles in the least the cabaret where the conspirators have been conspicuously conspiring; rather, this meeting took place in a well-appointed public house on the Street of the Arches, between the Flat Circle, where the bourgeois gathered to buy, sell, and exchange their products, and Silver Exchange Square, overlooked by the graceful and slender Silver Exchange Building itself, frequented by bourgeois and nobility alike, and entirely avoided by Teckla except those servants, lackeys, and errand-runners whose duties brought them there.

The inn, called The Silver Shadow by virtue of its position below the Silver Exchange, was one of the proudest of this proud district, frequented by Dragonlords, Dzurlords, the highest Jhereg nobles, and even those of the House of the

Phoenix. There had never, in the thousands of years of its existence (it had, in fact, been erected just after the Silver Exchange Building itself) been a fight within the walls of the Silver Shadow, and even harsh words were rare. The proprietor, an Issola named Wensil, stood always at the door, and greeted every guest with a bow appropriate to his House and the cut of his clothing, except for those to whom he politely bur firmly refused entrance—and this he would only do if the individual's dress indicated someone who would stand out unpleasantly. It is a fact that, during the Teckla Republic, Wensil's ancestors had permitted Teckla within the walls, provided the Teckla in question displayed sufficient wealth.

Within, all was tasteful, and even somewhat reminiscent of Valabar's Restaurant in distant Adrilankha. There were four rooms, called the Big Room, the Oak Room, the Cherry Room, and the Long Room, each appointed differently, yet each blending harmoniously with the next. We will not try our readers' patience with descriptions of rooms we will never see, so we will content ourselves with briefly sketching the one in which we find ourselves, that being the Cherry Room, immediately to the right as one entered from the street into the Long Room. The Cherry Room, then, was distinguished by cherrywood booths, a cherrywood bar, and a large hearth in which burned, of course, cherrywood, filling the room with the gentle, sweet smell of this most prized of hardwoods.

The room was nearly empty as we look in on it; only one booth was occupied. This booth contained two Dragonlords and a Dzurlord, none of whom, we should point out, are those whom we have especially intended to look in on, and all of whom were sipping sweet wine and indulging in certain light, puffy confections which were one of Wensil's most renowned dishes. As they ate and drank, they engaged in conversation which, if it has no direct bearing on the events we have come here to witness, will, we are convinced, nevertheless be of interest to our readers. One of them, the sharp-featured Baroness of Clover, remarked to her companions, "I speak only for myself, for I am neither Prince nor Deputy, yet I should not give the Orb a penny."

"How then?" said the wiry Baroness of Newhouse. "You would bankrupt the court?"

"And why not?" shrugged Clover. "There is not only the Whitecrest Uprising, for which we received nothing, but there is this latest insult to Lord Adron. Moreover—"

"Yes? Moreover?"

"If we have any wish to preserve the integrity of the Empire—and I do not say of the Imperium, for I feel the cycle must turn soon—we will be needed again, and that with all our forces."

"Indeed?" said Newhouse. "Where do you pretend we will be needed?"

The third member of the trio was the Dzurlord, a tall, handsome man known as the Count of Tree-by-the-Sea, but whom we will call by his given name, Jaan, because his title is so unwieldy. He now spoke for the first time, saying, "In the streets of Dragaera, my dear."

Clover nodded, and felt pleased that Jaan agreed with her, for she found him not unattractive and was considering ways of arranging a liaison with him. "That is it exactly. The Underside is worse than ever, and the Teckla are grumbling in a way I have never seen before. Two of them pulled their ears at me today, and ran off into a side street. I am convinced that, if I had followed, they would have attempted an ambuscade."

"How, you didn't chase them?" said Newhouse.

Clover shrugged. "It would have meant abandoning my horse, which could not have negotiated the street, and I do not consider insults from Teckla worth responding to."

"Well, there is something in that," said Newhouse.

"And," added Jaan, "when Teckla dare to insult Dragonlords, there are dark currents in the stream."

"Exactly my thought," said Clover, looking at Jaan fondly.

"But," said Newhouse, who found Clover rather more attractive than Jaan, "what is the cause of their discontent?"

"What is the cause?" said Clover, startled. "Where have

you been that you do not know? I have received word from my steward that fifty Teckla had to be driven off my estate, where they had come from the city because there is no bread there. The highways are filled with brigands, and an appalling number of them are desperate Teckla who have left the city. After thousands of years of the city getting bigger and bigger, Newhouse, now the Teckla are moving away from it, because they cannot afford bread. And whose fault is this, except His Majesty's, who taxes everything to buy diamonds and—"

"Ah," said Jaan. "There I must disagree."

"How, His Majesty is not fond of diamonds?"

"Oh, to be sure, he is. But he has spent far less on this passion than many believe. I know this, because my cousin is in the Guard, and he has a close friend whose niece, also a guardsman, has spent a great deal of time stationed outside the offices of the intendant, Smaller, who has been killed, and this niece both spoke with him and overheard his discussions with his clerks. There can be no doubt that only the tiniest fraction of the Imperial Funds have ever gone to indulge His Majesty's whims."

"Well then," said Clover, who had no answer to this direct evidence, "what is the cause then?"

"As to that, dearest lady, I suspect a number of things at once. But if you will not think me a mystic, then I would say it means just what you have already suggested—it is time for the cycle to turn, and no more need be said. Lord Adron ought to do something, and if he were here, I would tell him so directly. He must act before it is too late."

"Yes, yes, I agree completely," said Clove, delighted at being called "dearest lady."

"And there is more," said Jaan. "My cousin spoke of the blockades set at the gates, where all wagons are searched. He said that they found that a wagon, which appeared to be full of Teckla entering the city, actually contained, in a hidden compartment, several sacks of grain."

"Indeed?" said Newhouse and Clover together.

"The Teckla were hanged at once," said Jaan. "But consider how desperate they must be to risk death to sneak grain past the tax collectors, not even considering what they must have done to acquire it." He shook his head, as if to say that there was nothing good to look forward to in the city, and, indeed, the Empire.

"And yet," said Newhouse, "if what you say is true, it would seem to be exactly the wrong time to bankrupt the Imperium."

Clover shrugged, as a pair of well-dressed Jhereg entered the room. "Let others supply the funds—we will have our work cut out for us." As she said *others* her eyes strayed significantly to the Jhereg we have just mentioned, and whom we will now, abandoning the Dragonlords, follow to the last booth in the room. One of these, the reader will recognize instantly as our old acquaintance, Dunaan. The other was a young, small, quiet-looking Jhereg, with regular, handsome features and nothing to distinguish him save for his countenance, which was marked by bright, sparkling eyes, and a peculiar expression resembling a faint smile that seemed to be permanently fixed on his features.

They seated themselves, and asked the obsequious waiter to bring them a good red wine, a dish of kethna sauced with green onions, mushrooms, and sage, and a bowl of fruit. Then they sat quietly, speaking only of such innocuous subjects as fashion and the weather, until the plates of food arrived, and the waiter departed. As they began eating, Dunaan said, "You have, Mario, acquired a certain reputation."

"Have I?" the one addressed replied mildly. "I had not been aware of it."

"It is, nevertheless, true."

"Well I hope, then, that it is a good one."

"I think so. It is, in all events, the reason I wish to speak to you."

Mario stabbed a piece of kethna with his skewer in a motion precise and graceful, acquiring both an onion and a mushroom at the same time. He lifted these to his mouth and nodded for Dunaan to continue.

"We have a task for which we believe you are qualified. I should warn you at once that it will not be easy."

Mario, having finished the piece of kethna, bit into a whitefruit, somehow contriving to eat it without, as usually happens to victims of this fruit, finding that it has exploded into his face or down his chin. He chewed thoughtfully, brought his napkin up to his lips and expelled a few seeds, then swallowed. "Very well," he said. "I understand. It will not be easy."

"In fact, it will be very difficult."

"It will be very difficult; I am warned."

"We wish you to kill someone."

"Well," said Mario phlegmatically.

"We are offering a fee that is, I daresay, more than anyone has ever been offered before."

Mario's forehead twitched in a peculiar manner, but he made no rejoinder.

"Yes," said Dunaan, nodding. "This is a very serious matter, and there is no question of joking. Our aim is high—very high, and we mean to hit what we aim at. Will you be our weapon?"

"How high?" said Mario.

"Very high," said Dunaan.

"Could you be speaking of a minister?"

"Higher."

"Of a Prince?"

"Still higher."

"Of the—?"

"Exactly."

"I see," said Mario.

"Well?"

"Yes, I perceive that there is no question of joking."

"Have you any interest?"

"Have you any assurance that such a thing is possible?"

"Anything is possible," said Dunaan.

"That is not assurance."

"What troubles you? The Guard?"

"I can elude guards, and I can strike before they are aware, and I can be gone before they can recover."

"Well then?"

"The Orb."

"Ah, the Orb."

"Exactly. Will it not act to save the life of the Emperor?"

"Not if the cycle has turned."

Mario considered this, then nodded. "Very well," he said. "You need only convince me that the cycle has turned, and no more need be said."

"Oh, as to that . . ."

"Yes?"

"I may not be able to convince you."

"Well, then—"

"But I can do something as good."

Mario nodded and waited patiently for Dunaan to continue.

Dunaan set a velvet pouch on the table before him, between a wineglass and a scrap-boat. Mario took the pouch, opened it, and a large pearl fell into his hand. He considered it, and, realizing that, though worth a great deal, it was still less than he should demand for killing His Majesty, turned a look of inquiry upon Dunaan.

"Bring it into the presence of the Orb, and crush it beneath your foot. For the next few minutes, the Orb will not act to save His Majesty's life."

Mario frowned. "How can this be?"

"The Orb will, for some minutes, believe that the cycle has turned."

"Shards!" said Mario, showing emotion for the first time. "This pearl you have shown me, when crushed, can deceive the Orb itself?"

"Exactly."

"How can this be?"

"How was the Orb made?" said Dunaan.

"I am neither scientist nor historian."

"And yet, you know that some are."

"Yes."

"The work of scientists and historians has gone into the design of this object, as well as the work of skilled sorcerers in producing it. How it was done, I know no more than you."

"But you are certain it will work?"

"I am convinced."

"Yet I must be convinced, too."

"Consider," said Dunaan, "that if it fails, you will fail. If you fail, the Phoenix Guards will almost certainly attempt to capture you alive; if they succeed in this, the Orb will be used to interrogate you, and if the Orb is used to interrogate you, you will, without doubt, reveal everything, including my name, appearance, and such other information as will allow the Phoenix Guard to find me. I am, therefore, staking my life as well as your own."

"That is sufficient," said Mario after considering this argument.

"As to the fee . . ."

"Well?"

Dunaan named a prodigious amount of gold, and stated that half should be rendered as soon as he, Mario, should agree to do what was asked of him, the other half when the mission had been completed.

Dunaan said, "Do you need time to consider this proposal which I have had the honor of making you?"

"A few moments only," said Mario. "A few moments that I will spend boiling these rednuts in this liqueur before spooning them onto the cold fruit, and eating them before the temperatures have evened out. I suggest, My Lord, you busy yourself in the same way, and, before the bowl of nuts has exhausted itself, well, I believe I will have an answer for you."

This plan was instantly adopted, and Dunaan applied his full attention to the rednuts, the liqueur, and the iced fruit, while Mario thought matters over.

We should explain that Mario, though he had scarcely seen his hundredth year, had already acquired a reputation within those hidden, illegal circles to which we have been forced to introduce our readers. We should add that, in these circles, reputation was of supreme importance, and it was rare indeed for the rumors of one's character or abilities to be incorrect. Mario was, by all accounts, as skilled in his trade as anyone could desire.

And yet, to be sure, he was also young, and coincident with youth is inexperience. His head was not turned by the amount of money, nor, indeed, was it turned by anything like the idea of glory (for glory is an unknown concept in the world-behind-the-world of a criminal organization), but he was susceptible to challenges, and his extraordinary reflexes, his ability to make quick decisions, to pay attention to every detail, and to carry out his plans with no hesitation or scruple made him, he knew, one of very few who might have a chance to carry out such a mission. He was well aware that the Orb had never before been defeated, but Dunaan's arguments were persuasive—at the very least, persuasive of Dunaan's faith in the magic of the pearl. And Dunaan had a reputation for being careful and not easily fooled.

It was, reflected Mario, the greatest challenge that was ever likely to fall in his way, and he knew that, if he passed it by, he would always wonder if he would have been able to carry it out.

So he was, we perceive, careful, thoughtful, and skilled well beyond his years—and inexperienced in the ways of the world, and even in the ways of the Jhereg.

That Dunaan was deliberately betraying him never entered his thoughts.

"Very well," he said. "I will do it."

# Chapter the Twentieth

*Which Treats of the Translation of Orders*
*By Teckla and by Captains,*
*And the Translation of Looks and Phrases*
*By Ingenious Yendi.*

IT WAS STILL THE MIDDLE of the afternoon when Khaavren took his leave of Daro, with soft words on both sides and a promise from the Countess that she would not leave for her estates before the evening at the earliest, but would, in fact, arrive at the house on the Street of the Glass Cutters to continue the conversations with the Captain that had provided them both with such great and unexpected pleasure. This established, she resumed her packing, which she finished with extraordinary speed. When each gown, petticoat, manteau, housecoat, scarf, wrap, glove, muff, boot, shoe, bonnet, hat, and various items we will not offend our readers' sensibilities by naming was stowed, or, more precisely, deposited in the appropriate satchel or portmanteau (there were no more than three all told), she caused servants to bring them to the Waterspout Door of the Phoenix Wing, where she came herself to wait until the carriage arrived. This it did in due time, and she gave the address of the house on the Street of the Glass Cutters.

She was, fortunately, preceded in her arrival at Khaavren's

house by a messenger who handed Srahi a note, which we will hasten to divulge to our readers:

"Daro, Countess of Whitecrest, has condescended to honor our house with a visit. The terrace room ought to be suitable. You may expect me at the usual time, if His Majesty's orders do not interfere. Convey my respectful courtesy to the Countess upon her arrival, and be kind enough to convey to her also my welcome to our home." It was carefully signed, "Khaavren, Captain of the Guard."

Now Srahi, though a Teckla, was, at any rate, sharp enough to cut dry wool, as the saying is. The first thing she noticed was that Khaavren did her the honor to sign his message with his title, and she knew that this indicated something of the importance he attached to this visitor. Furthermore, the phrase, "ought to be suitable" was significant, because there could be no question that this room, which had once been Pel's, would suit a guest; the only question was, would the room be ready. Khaavren, then, was informing her that, in brief, it had better be.

His remarks about being home at the same time as he was always home would seem to be wasted words, and Khaavren, as we have established, was not accustomed to wasting words in speech, and still less was he accustomed to wasting words on paper. This was an indication to Srahi that, when he returned, he would be looking at the state of the room in which this Countess was staying, and that he would tolerate no slovenliness in this case—this notion was underscored by the mention of His Majesty's orders, indicating that Khaavren expected his own orders to be obeyed as if they came from the Orb itself.

As a whole, then, the letter showed that this guest was important to Khaavren, and that this was one of those occasions when Srahi ought to spare no effort to see to it that his wishes were carried out.

Because of the excellence of her translation, and perhaps, because of the improvement in Srahi's disposition since the arrival of Mica, and, indeed, because Srahi had Mica's cheerful help in all the preparations, Daro, upon her arrival, was treated with smiling courtesy as well as efficiency. She settled into these rooms with the ease of a woman used to sudden changes in her situation, and, we ought to add, with the energy and joy of a woman suddenly and unexpectedly in love.

Speaking of those suddenly and unexpectedly in love, Khaavren, after sending this message, returned to those areas of the Palace to which his duty called him, and where he was immediately spotted by a page sent by His Majesty (it will hardly surprise our readers that, of those searching for Khaavren, it was His Majesty who found him first).

The Orb, when Khaavren saw it circling His Majesty's head in the Portrait Room, was a dark, brooding red; Khaavren thus prepared himself for his master's displeasure. He anticipated correctly, for, as the Captain made his way through the courtiers, Tortaalik's eyes fell upon him angrily, and he said, "I perceive you are here at last, Captain."

Khaavren bowed. "Yes, Sire; I have just received your message."

"You have been damnably hard to find to-day."

"I am sorry," said the Captain, "that Your Majesty has had trouble locating me."

"Well?"

"Yes, Sire?"

"What have you been about?"

"My duty, Sire," lied Khaavren, with a significant glance about him, asking if His Majesty really wished Khaavren to discuss the exact nature of his activities before the assembled court.

The Emperor harrumphed, and gave into Khaavren's hand a piece of paper, adding the words, "Please see to this at once, if your duties will spare you long enough."

Khaavren ignored His Majesty's irony, and merely bowed and said, "Yes, Sire," after which he backed away and retreated to the hall outside of the Portrait Room, where he broke the seal on the note and read it on the spot. As with Khaavren's note to his servant, we will reproduce the text of it here:

"Order for Lord Khaavren, Captain of the Guard, to Arrest His Highness Adron e'Kieron, Duke of Eastmanswatch, etc. etc., At Once and Confine him in a Secure Place within the Iorich Wing, taking All Necessary Precautions against Escape or Undue Disturbance."

Khaavren read the message again, and then a third time. Khaavren had had much experience in performing the necessary translation from the ciphers in which the most apparently simple order was couched—that is, he understood that a great deal could be conveyed in what was left unsaid, or in the precise wording of the orders His Majesty did him the honor to entrust to him, and what was said in this order was, indeed, enough to cause our Tiassa some unease.

By including his name, and even going so far as to use his title as well, Khaavren was being told that the responsibility for this order rested on his shoulders—he could delegate as much as he chose—but his position, perhaps even his head, would answer for the success or failure of this mission.

Next, there was the phrase, "At Once." All orders were to be carried out at once; that His Majesty deigned to make this explicit indicated something of His Majesty's state of mind, which would brook no delay for any reason.

Even more disturbing, however, was His Majesty's use of the phrase, "Secure Place." There was no reason to believe that any prison in the Iorich Wing was not secure—what this meant was that Khaavren would be held responsible, not only for arresting Lord Adron, but for seeing to it that Adron remained arrested; Khaavren had been given the responsibility that normally fell to the jailer. This was emphasized and even underlined by the remarks about escape and disturbance. His Majesty, then, feared an attempt would be made to rescue Lord Adron, or that social unrest might break out because of his arrest, and Khaavren was to be held responsible for all of this, as well.

It was, to be sure, no small task, and the phrase "At Once" compounded the difficulty, because it meant he had precious little time to make preparations for any trouble that might ensue.

He stood for a moment, thinking, then carefully folded up his order and put it in his pocket. After this, he continued, his contemplations. It was all very well for His Majesty to say, "At Once," but certain matters had to be considered. In the first place, how many men would he need to make the arrest? If Adron did not choose to resist, then none would be needed, but if Adron *did* resist, then, shards! all of his men at once, aye, and Stonemover's as well, would not be sufficient. Well, then, he would assume Adron would not resist. If he guessed wrong, why, Adron would have him, that is, Khaavren, killed, and Khaavren would then have fallen honorably, although his mission would not have succeeded.

"But, my dear Captain," he said to himself, "does that matter? Come, be honest, can you recall a mission you have set out upon with less joy in a hundred years? Arrest Lord Adron? Cha! I should more happily set him upon the—but stay, let us not contemplate treason, even in our most private thoughts. We have our orders, and we must carry them out, or fall nobly in the attempt; it is all one." He shrugged philosophically, "Still, it is, without a doubt, a shame that, if I succeed, I shall be jailing, and, no doubt, helping to prepare the execution of, one of the first gentleman in the Empire. And, by the Gods, as much a shame that, if I fail, I will be denied further company of my Lady Daro."

As he sub-vocalized this name, he felt a certain peculiar constricting in his chest, a sensation that all lovers will recognize at once; and which sensation, along with the thoughts it carried in its wake, brought a happy, if slightly dazed, expression to our Tiassa's countenance. This expression, however, gradually changed to a frown, as the thought he allowed to grow within himself became stronger, and he realized more fully what he would be giving up along with his life. This induced a certain melancholy, which our brave Captain checked as soon as he became aware of it.

"Come now," he told himself sternly. "Is happiness to make me craven? This cannot be allowed. No, no I must set about my mission directly, or resign my commission and become a hermit, which would be intolerable to one of my disposition.

"Well then, Khaavren my friend, onward, and meet your fate with your chin pointed forward, if not with your heart light. But what is this? More old friends approach. Ah, temptation steps onto my path!"

This was occasioned by the sight of Pel and Tazendra, who looked on him with expressions of unalloyed pleasure—pleasure which faded, or, as the sailors say, *moderated* as they approached, no doubt on observing that Khaavren appeared to be unhappy about something.

Nevertheless, Khaavren made an effort to be cordial. "Greetings, my good friends," he said. "What brings you to the Palace?"

"Why, you do," said Tazendra.

"You are looking for me?" said Khaavren.

"In fact," said Pel, "more than looking for you; we have found you."

"Come now," said Tazendra to herself. "I think I have heard that phrase before."

"And so you have," said Khaavren, speaking, we hasten to add, to Pel, rather than to Tazendra. "And yet," he continued, still speaking to Pel, "I confess, as much pleasure as your company brings me, I have little enough time to spare, for duty calls, and it is a duty that, if it affords me no joy, affords me even less time."

"Where does your duty take you?" asked Pel. "For if we can accompany you on its first steps, well, that will allow us a few moments to converse with you, and will cost you no time at all, while satisfying all we desire."

"It takes me," said Khaavren, "in the first place, back to my offices in the Dragon Wing, and I can think of no reason why you cannot accompany me at least that far."

"Then lead on," said Pel, bowing.

"Yes," said Tazendra. "For you always lead so charmingly."

To this, Khaavren had no rejoinder, so he began walking toward the Dragon Wing. As he did, Pel said, "Come now, tell me what you can about this poor fellow who made an attempt on your life just two days ago."

"Two days ago?" said Khaavren. "Is that all it was? Shards and splinters, but the days have been busy!"

"And like to become busier," said Pel.

"I have no doubt you are right," said Khaavren with a sigh.

"Nevertheless, I am interested in this circumstance, and, if you will relate all you know and have surmised about this fellow, well, Tazendra and I will have a look and see what we can learn about him."

"It is easily done," said Khaavren. "The more so because I was about to go to you and ask for your help in precisely this matter when I was interrupted, first by the outbreak of civil disorder, and then by other matters following quickly on the riot's heels, so I am now delighted that you will agree to look into the matter, and I am anxious for any enlightenment you can bring me." And he quickly related the observations and deductions he and Aerich had made with regard to the assassin, exactly as we have already had the honor of relating them to the reader, wherefore we will not take up the reader's time by unnecessary and redundant repetition.

"Hmmm," said Pel. "You have, in any case, given me something to look for."

By this time, they had reached Khaavren's offices, and the Captain said, "Here I must bid you farewell, for duty awaits, and it is a duty in which you cannot help me, nor, I think, would you wish to." He paused and looked carefully into Pel's eyes. "A very unpleasant duty. And I am certain you would not wish to help."

"I see," said the Yendi. "Yes, I see. Well, in that case, allow me to wish you the best of fortune, and we will be on our way."

As his two friends left, Khaavren sat down to begin considering and then composing the orders that might protect the city against any disturbance triggered by the arrest of Lord Adron. But he had scarcely begun considering, and was nowhere near composing, when he was informed of visitors.

"Who?" he said laconically.

"The Lady Aliera and Sethra Lavode," said the corporal on duty.

"Ah," said Khaavren. "Well, they may enter."

"My dear Captain," said Sethra without preamble, speaking even as she crossed the threshold a step before Aliera. "My dear Captain, you have led us a merry chase."

"In truth?"

"In truth. We have been here, and all the way back to the Imperial Wing, and around the rooms you are known to frequent, and once more to the Imperial Wing, and at last back here to your office, whence we started our search."

"I am sorry," said Khaavren, "to have discommoded you. Yet, as you know, my time is not my own. In fact, it is, at this moment, even less my own than usual, wherefore I'm afraid I can spare none of it for conversation, however pleasant that conversation might be."

"Oh, we quite understand," said Aliera. "Duty waits for no one."

"Exactly."

"Yet, it is duty that brings us here—in fact, your duty. Or, perhaps we ought to say, a certain duty you may have been assigned."

Khaavren felt the blow in his heart, yet he gave no sign of it on his countenance. "A certain duty I may have been assigned? Come, what can you mean?"

"We will tell you," said Aliera.

"I ask nothing better," said Khaavren.

"Then attend."

Sethra said, "We wish to know, insofar as you are allowed to tell us—"

"For," put in Aliera, "you may not be allowed to tell us, and if you cannot speak of these matters, we understand and will not press you."

"Yes, yes," said Khaavren. "Go on."

"You may have received certain orders," Sethra began again. "And we wish to know—"

"If you are allowed to tell us," put in Aliera, with a glance at the Enchantress of Dzur Mountain.

"—If you have been given these orders."

"Well," said Khaavren, still struggling to maintain his composure. "You perceive I am often given an order of which I am not allowed to speak—of which, in fact, it would be nothing short of treasonous to speak."

"Yes," said Aliera. "And if such is the case with these orders, well, we shall not require that you reveal them."

"That . . . that is well," said Khaavren.

"Nevertheless," said Sethra, a trifle impatiently, "we wish to ask."

"Oh, by all means," said Khaavren. "Yes, certainly, you may ask."

"Then we shall," said Sethra.

"Do so," said Khaavren.

"Have you then," said Sethra, "been given any orders that—"

"Yes?" said Khaavren, who began to feel that the clasp of his uniform cloak, which was exactly as he'd worn it every day for five hundred and thirty years, was too tight. "Orders that—"

"Orders that have something to do with the Lady Aliera?"

Khaavren blinked and attempted to stall for time, hoping to think of some means out of the uncomfortable situation in which he found himself. "How, with the Lady Aliera?" said Khaavren. "Why, any orders might have something to do with the Lady Aliera, for her interests could lie anywhere, and I cannot know what might have something to do with her."

"I meant," said Sethra sharply, "more directly."

"Well, that is—"

Aliera suddenly cut in, "Have you orders to arrest me, Captain? For, if so, I am here, and I have no intention of resisting, but will instead appeal, first of all, to my father, next to the Dragon Council, and then—"

Khaavren sprang to his feet. "Arrest you? That is what you think? You think I have been ordered to arrest you?"

"Why, we don't think so, Captain," said Sethra. "And yet, we know that Aliera has offended certain people, and we thought it possible—how, could it be, Captain, that you are laughing at me?"

Khaavren controlled himself and said, "Oh, not the least in the world, I assure you. And, moreover, I assure you that I have been given no orders to arrest the Lady Aliera. The Gods! If I had, I should have carried them out the instant you set foot in my office."

"Well," said Aliera, "I understand that."

"As do I," said Sethra.

"Then," said Khaavren, sinking back into his chair with a feeling of immeasurable relief, "there is no more to be said, except that, indeed, there is much that needs to be done, and precious little time to do it, wherefore I am forced, if you will excuse me, to bid you both a good day."

They bowed to the Captain, wished him well, promised to see him on another occasion, and took their leave. As the Captain turned once more to considering the orders he must write, and how to couch them in terms that would produce exactly the results he desired, allowing for the interpretations of Sergeant, subalterns, and corporals, we will follow Aliera and Sethra out into the wide hall before the entrance to the Guard's sub-wing of the Dragon Wing, where they exchanged words that cannot fail to be of interest.

"What did you think?" said Aliera.

"He would not lie," said Sethra. "Moreover, he was not lying. Nevertheless—"

"Yes, nevertheless, he was concealing something."

"Indeed he was," said Sethra. "And we should, no doubt, have discovered it if you had been less insistent on that point of courtesy to which you kept returning. Should such a matter come up in the future, you would be well advised—"

"Perhaps," said Aliera with a shrug. "And yet, you will admit that it was hardly a mere point of courtesy. To an officer—"

"I give you my word," said Sethra, "that I have been an officer, and I know what orders are. So, for that matter, does Lord Khaavren. He would have known perfectly well when to keep mum without—"

"Oh, of a certainty he would have known," said Aliera. "But it seemed to me that he must know we understood, and were not attempting—"

"To let him know," said Sethra. "Is one thing. Yet, by insisting, you prevented us from learning just what was on his mind, and I, for one, am curious. Just a few words from him would have been sufficient to have told me a great deal. I hope you remember this next time such a situation occurs."

Aliera, who began to grow somewhat warm, said, "Then, if I understand you, it was all right to mention it, but not to continue repeating it to the point of becoming tedious?"

"Exactly."

"As you are becoming tedious with your lesson?"

"You say I am tedious?" said Sethra coldly.

"The very word," said Aliera.

"Perhaps it is required when dealing with a pupil who fails to understand what is so obvious—"

"I do not recall asking you to teach me anything."

"Yet, my dear, you so clearly require it."

"Then perhaps you would care to give me a lesson on another subject entirely?"

"I take your meaning," said Sethra. "And I would be delighted."

"Take care, however, that your pupil does not surpass you—the embarrassment might kill you."

"I accept the risk. Come, there is a courtyard just through these doors, not a hundred meters from this spot, paved with flat stonework and altogether suitable."

"I know it; a charming place. Let us find witnesses and a judge, neither of whom can be far."

"I would think they'd abound in such a place."

"Indeed," said Aliera, "here are two acquaintances who will serve admirably. Greetings, my dear Tazendra. Pel, allow me to name Sethra Lavode."

For just a moment, the unflappable Yendi appeared taken aback. He recovered quickly, however, bowed, and said, "I am honored to meet you, madam. Indeed, I am."

"And I to meet you," said Sethra. "For all of your activities are not unknown to me, and those of which I have heard I honor."

Pel bowed deeply, and seemed about to speak, but Aliera broke in, saying, "Perhaps you could perform a service for us. If you, Pel, would act as my friend, and if the good Tazendra will stand for Sethra Lavode, we have a matter—"

"Alas," said Pel. "You have no time for such games; they must be postponed."

"How?" said Aliera. "*We* have no time?"

"You in particular, Lady Aliera."

"And yet, why not? I know of nothing that presses me so urgently that I cannot attend to the desires of my friend here for a few thrusts loyally given."

"You cannot?" said Pel. "But I can."

"Indeed? What is it, then?" said Aliera.

"Yes," said Sethra. "I am also curious."

"As am I," said Tazendra.

"Then I will satisfy your curiosity. But, before I do so, I must ask a question."

"If it will help," said Aliera shrugging, "you may ask ten."

"I have been waiting for you, Aliera, because, as I was leaving Khaavren's office, I noticed you enter, along with this lady," here he bowed, "whom I did not, I must confess, recognize."

"Well, yes," said Aliera, "we have seen Lord Khaavren."

"And—forgive me if my question is indiscreet, but I assure you I have no choice—he made no indication that he might have intentions toward you? Intentions, that is, that fall within his capacity as Captain of the Guard?"

"You are asking," stated Sethra, "if we are certain he has no intentions of arresting the Lady Aliera."

"You are perspicacious," said Pel, bowing.

"Shards!" said Aliera. "That is the very subject about which we spoke to him!"

"And?" said Pel.

"He denied any such intention," said Aliera.

Pel nodded. "I feared as much."

"How," said Sethra. "You feared it?"

"Exactly."

"Can you now," said Aliera, "explain why we have no time to spare?"

"It is simple enough," said Pel. "You must, without delay, return to your father and explain to him that, in just a very few moments, Khaavren will be arriving to arrest him in the name of the Emperor."

# Chapter the Twenty-first

*Which Treats of Khaavren's Mission
And How He Carried It Out,
And of a Conversation with a Noble
Of the House of the Phoenix;
With Notes Pertaining to
The Composition of Orchestras.*

KHAAVREN SPENT A FEW MOMENTS explaining to Thack the gist of his orders regarding the placement of troops, the calling up of reserves, the reinforcement of Guard detachments at the Iorich Wing, and the other measures he thought would be helpful. Then he put into Thack's hand these same orders, written out in more detail and signed, after which he called for a horse to be brought round to the door.

Though he was not happy about the delays forced on him by the interruptions and by the need to write out and deliver the orders to which we have just alluded, our Tiassa was not the sort of man to allow himself to tangle his belt over what was unavoidable. Nevertheless, he was keenly aware that time was continuing to flow at a rate of sixty minutes each hour, and so, without wasting a single one of these precious minutes, he mounted upon the roan mare that had been brought for him, and set off at a good speed for the Gate of the Dragon.

As always, it was difficult to negotiate some of the streets, but his urgency helped to clear the way—he charged groups of pedestrians as if he had no care about running them down, wherefore the pedestrians, somehow aware of this even when they were looking in another direction, hastened to give room to the galloping horse whose rider, head bent over his horse's neck, glared ahead with such a fierce expression.

Once past the gate and on the open road, Khaavren gave the mare her head, determined to reach Adron's encampment as soon as he could, even if it meant killing his horse. As it happened, his horse, though foaming and sweating, was alive when it reached the road to the camp. This was a long, narrow path, and at the midpoint, Khaavren remembered, Adron had set up his guard post. In fact, Khaavren's sharp eyes could distinguish three figures waiting there. With gentle pressure of his knees, he caused his horse to slow just the least bit, while he considered what it meant that there were three soldiers, instead of the two he had observed on his previous visit. He caused his horse to slow still more as he approached and considered. Though he arrived at no certain answer to his question, it did make him alert and watchful as he drew rein before the three Dragonlords in the uniforms of the Breath of Fire Battalion.

"I give you good day in the name of the Emperor," said Khaavren.

"And we give you good day as well," said one of the Dragonlords, a woman with short hair and sharply hooked nose, "in the name of the Emperor, and in the name of His Highness, Adron e'Kieron, Duke of Eastmanswatch, at whose camp you are now arrived."

"This is the camp of Lord Adron?" said Khaavren.

"None other," said the Dragonlord.

"Well, this camp is then just what I have been seeking, for I have an errand to His Highness that trembles with impatience and bites its lips with frustration at any delay; wherefore, good soldier, I ask that you let me by so that I and my errand can come to an understanding with each other. I am called Khaavren of Castlerock, and I have the honor to be Captain of His Majesty's Imperial Guard, and it is on His Majesty's behalf that I and my errand are come."

The soldier bowed, "I would like nothing more than to give you and your errand a good welcome, but, alas! His Highness has forbidden errands of any sort upon the site of our camp, and my companions and I fear that you would have some trouble leaving your errand behind, wherefore we hope that you will take no offense if we cannot give way before you."

Khaavren looked at her, and at her two companions, one being a tall woman who reminded Khaavren of Tazendra and had a short sword at cither hip, the other a great, burly man like a small mountain, with a sword as tall as Khaavren himself. The Captain then looked behind them, at the encampment half a kilometer further down the road, and he could not fail to notice, even at that distance, that the camp was being struck, and preparations were being made for the entire battalion to move, and quickly at that. He also noticed that, stretching out to both sides as far as he could see, was a tall, sharp-edged wire fence, of the sort that could be set up in mere moments, and which effectively prevented him from riding around the check-post—he would have to go through this place, which meant through those three determined Dragonlords.

"Nevertheless," said Khaavren, "I must have words with His Highness."

"I am sorry," said soldier. "My orders absolutely forbid it."

"Well, I understand orders."

"That is well."

"I have some, too."

"That doesn't startle me."

"Mine require that I pass."

"Ours require us to bar your way."

"Then we shall have to fight."

"Of that, there can be no doubt. Yet, before we do so—"

"Yes? Before we do?"

"I have been instructed to give you a message."

"To hear, or to bear to another?"

"To bear to another."

"You wish me to have a second errand before I have completed my first?"

The Dragonlord shrugged. "It is hard, I know."

"Well, what is this message?"

"It is to His Majesty."

"Yes. And the text?"

"His Highness will submit to arrest—"

"Ah!"

"—upon receiving an apology from His Majesty for His Majesty's lack of respect toward His Highness's daughter."

This time Khaavren shrugged. "What is your name," he said.

"I am Geb, and these are my companions, Dohert and Eftaan."

"Very well, my dear Geb. I hear your message, and will certainly undertake to deliver it, yet I can assure His Highness (and I will so assure him in person after you and I have finished our discussion), that His Majesty will not take kindly to being spoken to in such terms."

"You perceive," said Geb, "that, having done my duty, I have no concern for such matters."

"I understand."

"Well, in that case, unless you have more messages—"

"No, that was all."

"Nothing remains to be done, except for you and your cohorts to stand aside."

"It is impossible."

"Out of my way, in the name of the Emperor," said Khaavren. "You must stand aside at once or be ridden down!"

"Stand aside? Never in the world, my love. You perceive we were not ordered here so that we would step aside the first time we were asked."

"You will not be asked again," said Khaavren, preparing to spur his horse directly into them.

"So much the better," remarked the other woman, the one called Dohert, and as she spoke, she threw a short javelin into Khaavren's horse, which reared, stumbled, and fell. When the horse reared, Khaavren slid off its back and, after rolling once, came to his feet.

"I regret having to slaughter your horse," remarked Dohert.

"You will come to regret it more," said Khaavren, drawing his sword with his right hand while taking a flashstone into his left.

All three soldiers drew, but they had not even placed themselves on their guard before Khaavren discharged the stone into the face of the man called Eftaan, who was half a step ahead of his companions. He screamed and fell backward, and began moaning. At the same time as Khaavren discharged the stone, he also delivered a good cut at Dohert, forcing her to take a backward step.

Geb thrust for Khaavren's head in an attack so quick that Khaavren was only able to duck it in part—the point scraped along his temple, and for a moment his vision failed. He stepped back, crying, "If you are acting under orders, this is high treason, if not, it is low rebellion. Think of what you are doing!"

"It's all the same to me," said Geb, as she stepped in again, striking Khaavren's sword so hard that it was carried far out of line, as well as making his grip falter so that he nearly dropped the weapon.

"It is as well for me that my flashstone has a second charge," remarked Khaavren, as he set it off once more. Geb gave a sharp cry and then fell both backward and silent. The woman called Dohert, however, was now charging, and Khaavren, who had not yet managed to get a good grip on his sword, could think of nothing to do except throw the stone at her head.

She ducked, and, at the same time, gave Khaavren a good cut in his side, which he answered with a cut that nearly severed her sword arm. She stepped back once more, showing no sign of discomfort, but, rather, grinning at him as if she liked nothing better in the world than such a bloody battle, and said, "You ought to have brought along some help—in truth, My Lord Adron expected you to." As she spoke, she also dropped the sword from her right hand, though she still held the other in her left.

"Then he expected you and your friends to be killed?"

"We volunteered," she said. "And now, prepare yourself, for I am about to have the honor to charge you."

"Well," said Khaavren laconically.

She did, indeed, charge; Khaavren parried a vicious cut at his neck, but discovered that his legs felt weak, no doubt from the blow to his head, so that he was obliged to take a step backward. Dohert stepped in again, but Khaavren abruptly moved forward to meet her as she was preparing another cut, and found her unprepared for the sudden changes in distance and timing; he passed his sword through her body.

"Oh, well struck," she said admiringly, and cut once more for his head.

Again he ducked, and again it was too late: he felt a sick, horrid contact with the side of his head. Fortunately, his opponent was already falling, and, in falling, her arm twisted, so that only the flat of the blade struck Khaavren. Still, for a time he saw only darkness and was certain that he had reached the end of the time allotted him by the fates for this incarnation—he thought of Daro, and the thought brought him more pain than his wounds, until he realized that all of his foes were fallen, and that he was master of the field.

He sat down on the ground, breathing heavily. "I must bind my wounds," he told himself. "To die now, after surviving the battle, would be inconvenient. I must cut strips from my cloak, and . . . but what is this? The ground against my face? Rise, Khaavren, rise! Has time slipped by? Is it dark night already? And what sounds are these that bend my ears, so like the din of battle? Have I died in truth, and does Deathgate Falls sound like steel as it crashes? Are these smooth hands my friends and family, sending me over the Falls to my fate? I cannot recall my past lives, as one is supposed to in the River of Sleep.

"Ah, but surely these are the visions of paradise, for here, before my eyes, is my own beloved Daro, though stained with blood. Daro, Daro, if this be sleep, let me never waken, but let this vision remain before my eyes for eternity!"

"Hush, good Captain, and do not stir so."

"Daro! What? You? Here? Are you real, and not some phantasm conjured by my poor, wounded body and poor, weakened mind?"

"Yes, my dear Captain, it is I, and I am real, and you must not move so much, for you have lost nearly all of your blood, and, alas, I have not the skill of a physicker."

"But what brings you here? And, for all that, where is here?"

"You lie amid the slain, outside of the city."

"Adron's encampment? Then I am still here?"

"You are here, but there is no encampment. In truth, there are signs that a good troop was quartered here not long ago, but now we are alone, save for a few corpses."

"Three, are there not, and all Dragonlords?"

"All Dragonlords indeed, my Captain, but they number closer to five than to three."

"Five? Five? And yet I remember—"

"Hush now. Three of them are the work of your hand, the other two I will claim credit for."

"You? Two of them?"

"Bah. It was nothing. One at a time."

"Yet they were Lord Adron's picked men!"

"Well, what of that? I am a Tiassa."

"So you are, my sweet one. I had thought myself dead, and now I find—"

"Your wounds are bound as well as I can bind them; now we must see if you can stand, and then if you can sit in a saddle. To be sure, I will sit in front of you, and you need only hold onto me, and we will attempt to bring you back to the city, where you can be physicked."

"And yet, I still do not understand how you came to be here."

"You do not understand, my friend? Well, no more do I. Only, as I sat in your house, so charmingly filled with trinkets that called you to mind and allowed me to read ever more deeply of your character, well, it came to me that you were in danger, and that I should borrow a horse without delay."

"But how did you find me?"

"In the same way—I took the path that seemed right to me, and I found you at its end. And when I found you—up now, that's right. Here, let me . . . that is good. Now you must hold me about the waist, just so. When I found you, there was a Dragonlord standing over your body, as if he were wondering what to do with you. I called upon him to move, and we had a discussion, after which I began to bind your wounds, stopping only to attend to another Dragonlord who wished to converse with me as I worked."

"Then, I owe you my life."

"Oh, as to that—"

"Well?"

"Not in the least. Dragonlords do not murder their wounded enemies."

"Perhaps. But neither can they be relied upon to bind their wounds. And if, as I suspect, they knew why I was there, they—"

"We will speak of it another time. Is the motion of the horse uncomfortable?"

"Not in the least. In truth, I cannot have lost much blood after all; I suspect I was only stunned by the blow to my head, for I feel better with each passing minute."

"That may be, and yet, the ground around you, as you lay, was covered—"

"Cha! Let us speak of it, as you say, another time."

"Then of what ought we to speak?"

"Of you, my dear Countess."

"There is little to say on that score, my brave Captain."

"Whatever the score, let us play it, for I wish to hear every note."

"Even if the melody is wearying?"

"What matters the melody? Melody is but the means whereby the soul of the musician is expressed."

"And if the musician is only average?"

"The means are always an average."

"Ah, you are pleased to jest."

"You object to jests?"

"Not in the least; to make the patient happy is the desire of the physicker, and jests, which can lead the patient to a more cheerful and complaisant disposition, are often instrumental in that regard."

"There, you perceive that, having mentioned instruments, we are discussing music once more."

"If you like. But the instrument is not as important as the player."

"You think not?"

"I am convinced of it. An unskilled player—"

"Such an instrument as yours could bring forth no sounds but the most harmonious, and no themes but the most enduring."

"Yet, what is harmonious to one is dissonant to the next, and a theme you find enduring, another might consider trite and overused."

"What could be more enduring than love? Yet name a theme more trite. It is all in the rendering and orchestration."

"Well, and how would you have me orchestrate this theme?"

"Why, madam, you are the orchestra, as I will demonstrate, if you will allow me."

"Certainly, sir. You may attempt to prove your case, and I will listen closely to your reasoning, though I warn you that I will accept no shoddy logic."

"My logic will be as sharp as the sword with which you have lately delivered me from danger."

"We had agreed not to speak of that."

"Very well."

"Then begin."

"Listen: Your lips, first of all."

"My lips? Why do you mention my lips?"

"Because they are part of the orchestra."

"I perceive you are serious about this."

"Entirely."

"Very well, then, my lips. What part will they take?"

"They will be the reed pipes, with the humming of your voice as the reeds themselves."

"Do you think so?"

"I am certain of it."

"Then I accept my lips as the reed pipes, since you insist upon it. But is there a chanter-pipe in this orchestra, as well as the reed pipes?"

"There are chanter-pipes, reed-pipes, wood-pipes, and brass-pipes."

"What, then, are the chanter-pipes?"

"What could they be but your own sweet bosom, with the delicate, steady pulsing of each breath that so occupies my thoughts?"

"Did you learn such speech in the service of His Majesty? Well, what, then, of the wood-pipes?"

"Your eyes, my only. They flutter and trill the high notes, yet have a full, warm, deep timbre."

"I did not know you knew so much of music, Captain. What, then, are the brass-pipes?"

"The set of your chin and the lines of your face provide the music with its power, and make the forceful statements without which the sweet refrains would be insipid, but against which they are played with such beauty that all eyes moisten when the ears are so treated."

"I like these comparisons."

"I'm glad you do. And yet, you are laughing."

"That is true, but I hope my laughter does not wound you—you are already wounded enough. I laugh from pleasure, and because I must laugh in the face of such compliments, lest they turn my head."

"I am glad you are not laughing at me, at any rate, for my self-love could not stand the anguish."

"Be reassured."

"Well, what of the polychords? One cannot have an orchestra without them."

"Your hands will be the polychords, each finger ringing a different note."

"Well, what next? The idiophones, by which I mean the clappers, knockers, and cymbals?"

"These will be taken by the beating of your heart, which encloses my own in its gentle rhythms."

"Ah, ah! You are a poet, sir."

"And are there, then, membranophones as well?"

"But surely, madam, your legs are the membranophones, for they support the orchestra, and can as well exhibit grace, elegance, and beauty."

"You are making me blush."

"You do so prettily."

"It seems we have nearly completed our orchestra, except for the organophone, which must only be played by a master, yet which can produce music which excites, terrifies, strupefies, or calls up any of countless other emotions, all with the subtlest touch of the fingers."

"Oh, madam, no gentleman could be so crude as to detail the location of this most sacred of all instruments."

"Ah, now I am blushing and laughing at once, and my dignity is gone forever. I will never forgive you."

"But have I convinced you, at least, that you are worthy of discussion?"

"I assure you, I surrender fully. What do you want to know?"

"What else but everything?"

"Everything is a great deal. Where shall I begin?"

"Tell me of your family."

"My mother was Countess of Whitecrest; now she lives in Adrilankha and will become Dowager upon my return, for she has never loved governing. Still, we have interest in shipping, and in certain insurance companies, and even in a small bank. Mother saw to my training with the sword, and what little magic I know."

"Well, that is your mother. What of your father?"

"He was Baron of Fourleaguewood, but he gave up his title to wed my mother, and now he lives with her in Adrilankha. His father once performed some service—I do not know what—for Her Majesty, and it was upon this service that he called when I expressed a desire to spend a few years at court, in order to come to understand better the workings of the Empire, so that I could better govern my fief. A plan," she added, sighing, "which I must now abandon."

"Have you brothers, sisters?"

"None at all."

"I shall be pleased to meet your mother and father."

"And I, too, shall be pleased for you to meet them. But what of you?"

"Come, remember our agreement. We will speak of me later, though there is little enough to tell."

"You wish me to continue, then?"

"I should like nothing better."

"What else, then, do you wish to know?"

"What food do you enjoy?"

"Ah, I am from Adrilankha, which boasts Valabar's, with which even His Majesty's greatest feasts cannot compare."

"In truth?"

"As I live and breathe. Every wine worthy of the name, from the Empire, from the island kingdoms, from the Serioli, and even from the East—all are gathered in the cellars of Valabar's, and each is allotted its proper place as a companion to some specialty of the house, all of which are treats to the senses. In truth, Valabar's has spoiled me for most food, so you perceive it is a curse as well as a blessing."

"You must bring me to this house."

"I will do so."

"Tell me more."

"About food?"

"Or something else."

"What, then?"

"Your philosophy?"

"You pretend I have a philosophy?"

"Everyone has a philosophy."

"Well, you are right, but to describe mine would take more time than we have, for, see, here is your house before us."

"Ah, you are right, we are at our journey's end. Dismount, then, for I must return to the Palace."

"How, to the Palace? But you are wounded!"

"On the contrary, though a little lightheaded, I am feeling more alive than I have in years. I must see His Majesty and report on the results of the commission he gave me, after which, I promise, I will visit His Majesty's own physicker and return to you as soon as ever I can."

"Very well, I will not stand between you and your duty, but have a care for your health, for I do not wish my work to be wasted."

"I will be careful. And you, what will you do?"

"I? Oh, I will put the orchestra in tune in preparation for the next concert."

After leaving Daro at the door, Khaavren turned toward the Palace. A certain euphoria, with which all lovers will be familiar, remained with him as he rode. Yet as he made his way closer to the Palace, the realizations both of the failure of his mission and of his duty to His Majesty, gained pre-eminence in his thoughts, wherefore this euphoria, though still present, fell into the background, as it were, of his thinking, replaced both by a certain disappointment, and a feeling of urgency and even impatience.

We should say, in fact, that Khaavren's impatience upon leaving the Palace was nothing to his impatience upon his return, for, whatever was to happen, he knew that His Majesty must be informed at once. Therefore, when he heard someone say, "I beg your pardon, my dear Captain," even as he was dismounting from his horse, a brown gelding called Champer, he could not help but feel a certain annoyance, which at once transferred itself to the caller, whose voice Khaavren had not, we should add, recognized by sound.

He did his best, however, to hide his impatience and assume a pleasing countenance as he turned to see who beckoned him. It happened to be a certain Lord Vernoi, a Phoenix noble whom Khaavren recognized from having seen him at court. Khaavren bowed, saying, "Yes, my lord? I believe you have called out to me?"

"Yes, my dear Khaavren, I have called out, for I wish two words with you before you continue on your way."

"I will grant you two words," said Khaavren, handing his horse over to the care of the groom. "Yet, in good conscience, I can scarcely permit more. Not, you perceive, of my own will, but rather because of His Majesty's orders, which do not allow me any leisure, but, on the contrary, must be carried out without a moment's delay."

"I will be terse," said Vernoi, "for I have no wish to interfere with His Majesty's orders."

"Very well," said Khaavren. "Then speak, for I am listening."

"And yet—Captain, you seem unusually pale."

"It is nothing, a mere scratch."

"Is that why you are pressing your hand to your side, and have that bandage around your head?"

"The very reason. But, come, speak your question, for I promise you I can spare no time."

"Very well, since you will have it so."

"I will."

"This is it, then: Do you know the Princess Loudin?"

"That is your question?"

"Nearly. My question concerns her, which is why I ask."

"Well, I have seen her, if I am not mistaken. Was she not, some years ago, one of Her Majesty's maids of honor, and is she not now the Phoenix Heir?"

"The very woman. She resigned some eighty years ago, upon the occasion of our marriage."

"How, you married one of Her Majesty's maids of honor?"

"Why, that is exactly what I did."

"Allow me to congratulate you, my lord; for the notion of marrying a maid of honor has, in my opinion, a great deal in its favor."

Vernoi bowed and said, "It is, however, my wife who is causing me a certain measure of concern."

"How, concern?"

"Exactly. And it is this concern which has led me to bespeak you and, what is more, to take you into my confidence, if you will allow me to do so."

"Ah. You wish to take me into your confidence?"

"If I may, Captain."

"Then let us take two steps out of the door, and if you will speak in a low voice, well, I do not believe that anything we say will be overheard."

"It is good," said Vernoi as he followed Khaavren's advice, "that you are aware of the danger of being overheard—for much is overheard in the Palace, and most of it is overheard only in part, which leads to rumors, many of which are wrong."

"That is true," said Khaavren. "We breathe rumors every day, forsooth, and catch whispers of the air."

"Exactly. And, my dear Captain, some of these rumors are nothing short of terrifying to one in my position."

"In your position?"

"Yes."

"But, then, what is your position?"

"I should say, rather, in my wife's condition."

"Her—"

"She is with child, Captain."

"How, she is with child? I give you joy, my lord, with all my heart!"

"Thank you, Captain."

"But, these rumors—"

"Ah! Yes. I have heard rumors of possible disturbances in the city."

"Oh, you have heard that?"

"Exactly. And, Captain, if anyone would know, it would be you, and I fear for my wife's safety. I would not normally have such fears, Captain, for the Gods know there is nowhere a more deadly hand with a blade, or a woman more able to defend herself. Yet, she is not only with child, she is great with child, and may be taken to bed at any time. So, you perceive, if there is cause for fear, I wish to move her at once. Yet, I do not wish to disturb her with such a move if there is no reason. So, come, Captain, I trust you. Tell me what I ought to do."

Khaavren looked into Vernoi's honest face, and remembered the look of the empty encampment, and the orders he had given, and the broadsheets he had read, and even the faces he had seen as he traversed the streets.

Then he dropped his voice and said, "My lord, if you care for your wife and your unborn child, then lose not a moment, but send her out of the city at once."

Vernoi looked at him solemnly, then bowed once and walked back into the Palace. He was running by the time he reached the door.

# Chapter the Twenty-second

*Which Treats of How Pel Treats Investigation,*
*How Mica Treats Srabi to Dinner,*
*How His Majesty Treats with His Advisers,*
*And How the Physicker Treats Wounds.*

BY THE TIME KHAAVREN CAUGHT up with His Majesty, the Emperor had finished his supper, which Khaavren considered a stroke of luck; for the supper, and Her Majesty's annoyance, would not have prevented Khaavren from causing himself to be announced at once, yet must have led to an unpleasantness that Khaavren would, to say the least, not have enjoyed—the more so because, after overhearing her conversation with Daro, he feared that he would have no small difficulty in restraining his tongue should the Consort direct any ironic words in his direction. We should add, however, that this reflection, involving as it did the concept of *supper*, did make Khaavren realize that he had not eaten that day, and he resolved to remedy this omission as soon as possible. His Majesty, escorted by the Consort and by Thack, was on his way to the baths when Khaavren found him.

The Emperor, upon hearing Khaavren's gentle cough, turned, and cast his gaze over the Captain's grim countenance, dust- and blood-covered clothing, pale complexion, and trembling posture. "Well, my dear Captain," he said. "You seem to have met with some misfortune."

The Consort, turning at the same time as the Emperor, also looked upon Khaavren's worn visage and grim countenance, and she took a single step to the side, realizing, no doubt, that a matter of some urgency was about to be discussed, and that she should therefore stay out of the way; yet Noima was, for her own reasons, unwilling to allow whatever intelligence was to pass between Emperor and soldier to also pass out of range of her hearing.

Khaavren, we should add, paid no attention to the Consort except to bow to her before addressing His Majesty, which he did in these terms: "Yes, Sire, I have met with a most grievous misfortune."

"And that is? If there is a question of misfortune, I wish to hear about it at once."

"Sire, I have failed in the task you did me the honor to assign me."

The Orb darkened, and with it, His Majesty's countenance. "How, you failed, Captain?"

"It gives me pain to confess it, Sire."

"And yet, you have never failed before to my mind."

"Sire, everything that happens must, on some occasion, happen for the first time, and there is little that will never happen at all."

"You are a philosopher, Captain?"

"Yes, Sire, or a soldier, if it please you; 'tis hard enough to choose between them."

"How so? Please explain, for you perceive these observations interest me exceedingly."

"The soldier thinks with his sword, the philosopher kills with his pen, yet each is ruthless enough."

"Well, I understand what you are saying."

"In fact, Sire, I am saying that, to-day, Your Majesty would have been better off with a philosopher who could ride and fence, rather than a soldier with a ready wit."

"You say that because, there being an occasion for everything, on this occasion you have failed."

"Yes, Sire."

His Majesty sighed, as if attempting to calm himself, although the Orb remained a dark and brooding red. "Tell me how it happened."

"Sire, my thought was to proceed alone to effect Adron's arrest."

"Alone? And why alone, Captain?"

"Because, Sire, he is surrounded by an army."

"Well, of this I am aware. And so?"

"Sire, it seemed to me that, should he wish to do battle, all of my battalion together would be insufficient, and if he did not, well, I would not require anyone else."

"Well, I understand. Then I take it that he did not choose to be arrested?"

"He did not, Sire. He posted soldiers at the entrance to his camp, and they prevented me from passing."

"They prevented you?"

"Effectively, Sire."

"How many?"

"They numbered three."

"Well, I can hardly fault you for failing to defeat three of Lord Adron's best soldiery. And yet, it seems that if you had brought a good company, matters might have fallen out differently."

"That may be true, Sire. And yet, if I may be permitted to disagree with my sovereign, His Highness was expecting me to appear with support, and had posted the three Dragonlords there only to give warning—Your Majesty may recall that the Breath of Fire Battalion, above all else, is skilled in moving and attacking quickly. Moreover—"

"Yes? Moreover?"

"Your Majesty did me the honor to say that I could not be expected to defeat three of His Highness's soldiers."

"Yes, and if I did?"

"Alas, Sire, if my only goal was the defeat of these soldiers, I should feel naught but triumph."

"How is that?"

"Well, Sire, I still live, and they—"

"Yes, and they?"

"They do not."

"How, you killed all three of them?"

"I had that honor, Sire. Yet, in the course of the discussion, which I assure Your Majesty grew tolerably warm, they wounded me so that for several moments I knew nothing, and were it not for a friend who came to my aid as I lay on the ground, I do not doubt that I should still be there, dead or alive, as chance would have it."

"I see." His Majesty sighed once more. "So, we have been checked, and Adron is a rebel."

"Yes, Sire, Adron is a rebel. And it is true that we have been checked, although—"

"Yes?"

"I have only failed for the moment—the final throw has not yet been played."

"Indeed, Captain? Please expand on this statement, for you perceive I find it of great interest."

"Sire, Adron has left with his entire battalion, and, moreover, I was, as I have had the honor to explain, attacked as I attempted to carry out Your Majesty's order. What I have not yet told Your Majesty is that I was given, in his name, a message to deliver to Your Majesty."

"A message?"

"Yes, Sire."

"And the message takes what form?"

"Sire, His Highness will submit to arrest, he says, when he is offered an apology from Your Majesty for the insult he pretends you have done his daughter by having her rooms searched and her property seized."

The Orb darkened still further, and Khaavren noticed that the Consort, who had been listening intently to the conversation, took half a step backward and quickly drew in her breath, while simultaneously covering her lips with her fingers, as if she had committed an indiscretion at dinner.

"That is what he said?" demanded the Emperor, with a certain tone of amazed disbelief.

"His very words, Sire, as they were relayed to me by the

impudent soldiers who then proceeded to so effectually puncture my epidermis, though not without cost to themselves."

"Yes? And yet?"

"Sire, as Your Majesty has done me the honor to say, this is nothing short of rebellion; hence, it would seem appropriate to engage the Warlord, and to call out Imperial Troops. That is why I say the game is not yet over."

His Majesty pondered this for some few moments, while the Orb returned to a calmer hue. Then he said, "Give me your opinion, Captain: Does Adron think he can survive against the military might of the Empire?"

"Sire, His Highness is a military genius, and, moreover, a powerful sorcerer. I do not know what would be the final result of such a decision on Your Majesty's part, yet I cannot but believe Your Majesty would be unwilling to permit him to escape Imperial justice. He may well know this; in fact, he probably does. Perhaps it is to him a matter of principle, or perhaps he is merely stubborn, or perhaps he expects rescue from some source of which we are not aware, or perhaps he merely has such confidence in himself and his troops that he believes he can defeat the Empire. I do not know. And yet—"

"Yes? And yet?"

"If it is a matter of confidence in his troops, well, I do myself the honor to believe that we have today somewhat shaken this confidence."

"Yes, I believe you are right." The Emperor considered for another moment, then said, "You are exactly right about one thing at least, my Captain. He will not be allowed to engage in such blatant rebellion while I still have the power to bring him to Imperial Justice."

The Emperor waved to a servant, who attended him at once. "Find Jurabin and Rollondar, and have them meet me and Lord Khaavren in the Seven Room in an hour."

The servant bowed and hurried off on his errand. The Emperor turned to his wife and said, "My dear, I'm afraid—"

"Your Majesty need say no more," said the Consort. "I understand entirely, and I shall not look for you until you have appeared."

The Emperor pressed her hand, after which she departed down the corridor. As she left, His Majesty looked at Khaavren, frowned, and said, "But, Captain, are you in any condition to sit through such a discussion as we must have? You are wounded, are you not?"

"Yes, Sire, though not grievously. If I may have leave to find something to eat, I believe I will recover sufficient strength to survive two words of conversation on so vital a matter as we are facing, for, if we are to plan a campaign, there are things I must say that will not wait."

"Let it be so," said His Majesty.

Khaavren bowed, and hurried off as quickly as his condition permitted to find victuals with which to repair his long abstinence. He made his way to His Majesty's kitchen, a prodigious affair taking up three floors in back of the Imperial Wing. Here, after searching for only a few minutes, he found a servant, and, after making a few discreet inquiries, Khaavren was shown where to find bread and cheese, of which he availed himself with a fine passion.

"The bread," he remarked after swallowing the first bite, "is famous, warm as it is, though I admit that the color surprises me, and the cheese produces a sting upon the back of the tongue that I find quite pleasing."

"I am glad the food pleases you, my lord," said the pastry chef, who had done himself the honor of serving Khaavren personally, "for the bread is of my own fashioning, and uses, in proportions which are my particular secret, rednuts which have been ground to a powder mixed with the wheat flour; it is these that account for the color, as well as for the texture. As to the cheese, I can claim no credit save for selecting it. It comes from the vassals of Lord Dunn, and—my lord? Are you well? You seem pale and are pitching most alarmingly, and I beg you to—hullo? My lord? Help, someone! Help! The Captain has been taken ill!"

We cannot but think that the reader's imagination will adequately supply the confusion and consternation caused by Khaavren's unceremonious collapse—the running of messengers in search of His Majesty's physicker, the excitement in

Khaavren's offices caused by subordinates desperate to learn their Captain's condition, the annoyance of His Majesty who had counted upon the Tiassa's cool head and long experience in deciding how best to face the crisis brought about by Adron's abrupt rebellion. We will not, therefore, dwell on these matters, but will, instead, turn the reader's attention to certain events of which he must otherwise remain ignorant— that is, to our old friend Pel, who was, just as Khaavren was being carried to a chamber commanded by the physicker, emerging from the Underside in the company of Tazendra.

"And yet," said Tazendra as they walked toward the Palace at a speed that seemed entirely out of character for Pel, who was dressed again in his cavalier's costume, "I do not comprehend why our errand has such urgency."

"How, you do not?" said Pel, glancing at her in surprise without breaking stride.

"None in the world, I assure you."

"And yet, you were standing next to me when we entered the murchin-shop—"

"How, a murchin-shop? Is that what it was?"

"What you had thought it was, Tazendra?"

"Why, I hadn't any of my own thoughts; it was not, you perceive, my shop."

"Well, that is true," said Pel. "Nevertheless, you were there—"

"Oh, I do not deny that."

"—and you stood next to me while the shopmaster explained about the deceased assassin, whose name appears to have been Chalar—"

"Certainly, I heard that."

"—and where he might be found—"

"That puzzled me, because, he being dead—"

"—you perceive we followed on his trail—"

"—it follows that where he was could not be of interest to us—"

"—finding at last a place he has been known to frequent—"

"—and, in fact, we never *did* find him—"

"—where we also learned with whom he has been seen—"

"—which is just as well, for I have seen corpses, and have never enjoyed looking at them—"

"—and we received, eventually, very good descriptions of his cronies—"

"—so that I do not comprehend why we even went to those places—"

"—and learned that two of them were Jhereg—"

"—and spoke with Jhereg about I know not what—"

"—after which we spoke with certain acquaintances of mine—"

"—although you seemed to be on good terms with them, which I wonder at—"

"—and gave these descriptions to them—"

"—and then they said two words about each—"

"—and when we learned that they were both known assassins—"

"—after which we set off at this furious pace—"

"—we set off as fast as we could, because there is no doubt—"

"—with you claiming—"

"—that Khaavren's life is in danger—"

"—that Khaavren's life is in danger—"

"—and you still do not comprehend why?"

"—and I still do not comprehend why."

"Tazendra, were you listening to me?"

"I beg your pardon, my dear Pel, I was muttering to myself, for I am still tolerably confused. Attend—"

"Well, it is of no moment; you must trust me. Khaavren is in great danger."

"Bah! He? Impossible!"

Pel shook his head and gave up on the notion of attempting to convince his friend; on Tazendra's part, she knew, in spite of her protestations to Pel, that the Yendi had a subtle and clever imagination, and could see into deep matters that would baffle ordinary minds, wherefore she matched him step for step as they raced toward the Imperial Palace.

At the same time, some distance away, were taking place events that were not as unrelated to all of these other matters as the reader might, at first, suspect. In the Hammerhead Inn—which, as the reader may recall from certain events which occurred there in our earlier volume, was located quite close to Khaavren's house—the next step in a romance was being played out: To wit, Mica, after taking careful account of his personal treasury, was buying a good dinner for himself and for Srahi, to whose company he had grown more and more attached as the days went by.

Mica's generosity extended to roasted fowl, dripping with fat and positively smothered with mushrooms, short-grain bread baked with sweet peppers and half-garlic, and a bottle of sweet white wine; all of which were treated by Srahi with the reverence they deserved, both for their intrinsic quality and for what they cost (for, as the reader is doubtless aware, cost is not absolute, but relative—this same dinner, at the same price, would have been a mere trifle for Tazendra, yet it was nearly a fortune for poor Mica, who habitually lived on the leavings from his master's plate).

To complete the satisfaction provided by this veritable feast, Srahi endeavored to make pleasant conversation. We use the word *endeavored* because at first she had to make an effort to do so, yet we should add that, very quickly, because of the natural agreement in the character of these two individuals, no effort was required, but, rather, the conversation proceeded across the table as smoothly as the victuals proceeded in the opposite direction.

It is not our intention to weary our readers with details of this conversation—it is sufficient to say that it befit two worthy Teckla who were discovering, amid pleasant surroundings, how agreeable they found one another's company (far more agreeable, we should add, than the servants of the Hammerhead found their presence, for it is an invariable law that the most unpleasant sorts of patrons to an inn are, in the first place, those with so much wealth and power that they believe everyone ought to answer to their least whim, and, second, those who are so poor that they believe, as they are spending so much of their hard-won money on their repast, that it ought to be as important to the servants as it is to them).

As they neared the end of the meal, discussing their masters, those tasks they found most annoying as well as those they found most agreeable, the interesting color of each other's eyes and hair (all four samples of which were, in fact, a nearly identical nondescript brown), the value of white meat versus dark meat and the importance, in the case of the former, of insuring it was sufficiently moist, and so on, Mica gave a loud, imperious call for bread, with which he intended to soak the remaining juice from the broad, wooden platter upon which the fowl had been presented. A servant brought a loaf of coarse black bread, and accompanied it with such a resentful look that Mica could not help but notice.

"Bah!" he said. "Did you mark the servant, and his ill-favored countenance."

"I did," said Srahi. "Cha! What manners they have!"

"Had I my bar-stool, well, I assure you I should have words with him."

Srahi gave him a puzzled look. "Had you your what?"

"My bar-stool. Surely you recall the stories good Lord Khaavren told, of—"

"Ah, yes! Indeed, I do recall. I was merely startled, for I had not realized that you still thought of such implements as weapons."

"Well, I do not in general, but my own is different, for I am so used to it. Indeed, I assure you that, whenever I venture out upon a campaign, I would not think to leave it behind—it is, after all, the weapon with which I am most familiar."

"How, you bring a bar-stool with you?"

"Certainly. Have you not marked it, sitting in the corner by the door."

"Ah—ah! My dear Mica, I have done a terrible thing!"

Mica frowned. "What is it, my dear? Come you must tell me, for I perceive you are agitated, and I grow more so as you look at me with your countenance growing pale."

"I did not realize what it was, I thought it was only refuse from your journey, and in cleaning I—"

"Yes?"

"I threw it away!"

Mica, in his turn, became pale. "How, you threw it away?"

"Yes, onto the rubbish heap, to be removed every alternate week by those who are paid by the Empire to perform this service."

"Oh," said Mica, miserably.

"Will you ever forgive me?"

Mica swallowed, but, after several moments, he attempted, and managed, a pale smile. "Well, but it is only a bar-stool, after all. There must be others—"

"Bide," she said, suddenly sitting upright in her chair.

"Yes?"

"Something has occurred to me."

"And that is? I beg you to tell, for you perceive that I am most anxious to hear."

"The refuse will not be removed from its pile until to-morrow morning."

"Which means—"

"Unless someone has seen it, and decided to remove it—"

"It will still be there!"

"Exactly."

"Come, I will pay for our repast by leaving the exact amount required here on the table where they cannot fail to find it, and we will help our digestion by hurrying to the trash-heap."

"Which is, in fact, by the side of house, just outside of the kitchen window."

"Then, allow me to finish this last glass of wine—"

"And I, the same."

"And we are away. Give me your arm."

"Here it is."

His Majesty, meanwhile, had decided that, worried as he was about his Captain of the Guard, he must nevertheless come to a decision about Adron, and to this end he had Jurabin and Rollondar e'Drien brought to him in the Seven Room. By the time they were seated, the Orb had assumed a light, placid green. His Majesty gave them a brief summary of Adron's rebellion. While he did so, we should add, Jurabin remarked to himself (as, no doubt the reader has already remarked) upon the abrupt change in His Majesty's character in little more than a week: His Majesty, as he faced his councilors, appeared to be truly an Emperor, as if, whatever his responsibilities in allowing matters to reach this crisis, he was determined to see it through at all costs.

Jurabin wondered how it had happened that, in the blink of an eye, as it were, he, the Prime Minister, had become merely an adviser to the throne, whereas he had before been the true power and mover behind all decisions of the Empire (with the exception, of course, of those decisions affecting only His Majesty's personal life).

Does the reader wonder as well? If so, we are only too happy to be able to say, as proudly and humbly as those great philosophers of antiquity, Prince Tapman and Lady Tersa of Haynels, "Allow us to lay before you our theory on this question." We will not pretend to be philosophers such as those we have mentioned, yet, we too have a theory, and we hope our readers will allow us to lay it humbly at their respective and collective feet.

His Majesty, as we have already mentioned, had, over the course of his reign, become whimsical and morose, these alternating moods interrupted by occasional flurries of interest in the Empire of which he was the nominal ruler. The reader ought especially to note our use of the word *flurries*, as it forms an essential part of the theory we now have the honor to submit.

What, we wish to ask, is a flurry, except a mild rain-shower which encounters icy wind, and so freezes as it descends? Well, as the shower is to the flurry, so, then, is the downpour to the blizzard; in the same way, the occasional flurry of interest which we have just mentioned had become a blizzard of truly prodigious proportions.

For His Majesty the downpour was a combination of several factors, these being the disruption of his court by the entrance of Adron's daughter, the fears of financial collapse because of enmity and confusion in the Council of Princes (of whom Adron figured as a prominent member), and, above all, by Adron's rebellion. In simpler terms: by Adron e'Kieron.

But where was the icy wind that changes water into its light, flaky, crystalline equivalent? Wind is a more elusive element, blowing as it does hither and yon, leaving no tracks for the hunter to follow, and having no lair at whose mouth the hunter might wait; the wind is known only by its passing—that is, by its effects. The hunter—by which we mean the historian—then, must listen to the hissing leaves of rumor, look at the bent trees of letters and documents, and recall the lessons of the past winds as described by previous historians in order to judge the quarter, strength, and temperature of his particular quarry.

Let us consider that the court was disrupted, not so much by Aliera, but by the changes in the alliances of power and intrigue initiated by Aliera's arrival, and that most of these alliances revolved around—the Consort.

Let us consider that many, if not most, of the excesses so deplored by and worrisome to the various Heirs sprang from whims of—the Consort.

Let us consider that Adron's rebellion was instigated by an insult to his daughter and that this insult was delivered at the request of—the Consort.

In the opinion of this historian, then, although His Majesty didn't know it, it was the Consort herself who provided the blast of frigid air that turned the torrent of rain into a blizzard of snow, or, to abandon our metaphor before we ignominiously slip on it, that motivated the Emperor into assuming personal control of the affairs of the Empire.

We cannot know how much of this Jurabin knew, suspected, or felt instinctively, but to the extent that His Majesty was in control of himself and of the Empire, so, to that extent, was Jurabin puzzled and even put out by this change in his master's attitude.

Rollondar e'Drien, as it happened, knew little or nothing of any of this. He had been a soldier for nearly all of his one thousand and one hundred years, and matters military were his profession, passion, and recreation. He had married a few hundred years earlier the woman who had defeated him in a skirmish during the Shallow Valley Revolt, before he had been made Warlord, and there was no end of humor in the barracks about how the two of them spent their leisure hours—humor which we feel obliged to mention, but of which nothing could induce us to supply examples.

Rollondar sat stiffly at the table waiting for His Majesty to speak. The change we have mentioned in Tortaalik's character, so disconcerting to Jurabin, was of so little importance to Rollondar that, as we have said, he scarcely noted it at all, and would not have cared even had he noticed—Rollondar waited for the problem to be put before him so that he could suggest solutions.

As for His Majesty, he gave no thought to his own character, but only to the problem they now confronted. He had chosen to have only three advisers present: the one, Jurabin, who understood the political situation in the Empire; another, Rollondar, because any military action would necessarily fall under Rollondar's province; and the third, Khaavren, who was now under the care of His Majesty's physicker, but whom Tortaalik admired for his good common sense, clear vision, and occasional inspired suggestion. He was annoyed, then, that Khaavren was absent (and, to his credit, he was also worried about the health of his Captain), but, having made up his mind not to brook the insult offered him by the Duke of Eastmanswatch, he knew that no good could be accomplished by delaying.

"My Lords," he therefore began, "I have determined to punish the insolence of His Highness Adron e'Kieron, Duke of Eastmanswatch and Dragon Heir to the Throne. You should know that his Breath of Fire Battalion is within striking distance of the Palace, and we cannot be certain he will not carry his rebellion so far as to attack the Palace itself, in hopes of bringing about the turn of the cycle—which, as you are no doubt aware, would turn his action from rebellion to merely the working-out of destiny. It is not my intention to allow destiny to work out in this way at this time. We must, therefore, protect the city, and in particular the Palace, while attending to the capture of the Duke.

"Excellency, what is your opinion?"

"Sire," said the Dragonlord, "the Breath of Fire Battalion is known for speed as well as skill and ferocity in open battle."

"Well?"

"Well, they have neither the forces nor the skill to beat down walls."

"And therefore?"

"If all of the city gates are shut, and detachments of guardsmen are posted to watch for treachery, that should secure the city, and allow the Imperial Troops to concentrate on bringing in the rebel."

"Very well. Jurabin?"

"Sire?"

"Have you anything to say?"

"I have, Sire."

"Then I am listening."

"There are clear signs of a plot of some sort, against your Majesty, or the Empire itself. I refer to the assassinations of recent days, and to disruptions in finance, and—"

"Well, of these things I am aware."

"Sire, I wonder if it could not be the case that, as we earlier suspected, Lord Adron is behind it."

Rollondar drew in his breath sharply, seemed about to speak, but said nothing.

"It is possible," said His Majesty. "What then?"

"Sire, steps must be taken to guard us against attacks from within, as well as from without. Lord Adron has, by all accounts, a powerful and subtle mind, and I am not ashamed to confess to Your Majesty that I fear him."

The Emperor frowned. "What is your opinion of this, Rollondar?"

The Warlord shrugged, as if to say that this was an area outside of his knowledge and interest. Then he said, "I do not believe Adron is involved in any conspiracy, Sire. But, if

Your Majesty is at all worried about it, the solution is simple and easily had, at little cost."

"These are the sorts of solutions I like best, Warlord. Please explain."

"I will do so, Sire."

"I am listening."

"In the first place, do not let it be generally known that His Highness has taken arms against the Empire; this will delay the execution of any plot intended to coincide with the actual rebellion. Second, call out the reserve Guard; double or treble them in all vital areas. If the Lord Khaavren is healthy, so much the better; he has shown his skill in such matters. If not, his second-in-command will act as best as he can."

The Emperor nodded and said, "Jurabin?"

"I agree with the second, Sire. We can and should mount additional guards to secure the city and the Palace, and such other strategic points as the Warlord and the Captain might conceive of. As to the first, I doubt it is possible. The city is too large, and rumors fly too freely. It will be general knowledge within the day, if it is not already, that Lord Adron rebels against the throne. We must keep a sharp eye all around us, Sire, for I confess that, until we know who was behind the assassinations, and why, I will not sleep easily."

Rollondar bowed his head. The Emperor nodded slowly. "You are right, Jurabin, and we thank you for calling it to our attention."

Jurabin bowed.

The Emperor said, "Excellency."

"Sire?" said the Warlord.

"How long until you can field an army sufficient to destroy Lord Adron?"

"Sire, the Breath of Fire Battalion numbers about two thousand soldiers, all of whom are mounted, and all of whom are highly trained Dragonlords."

"I trust your intelligence," said His Majesty. Rollondar bowed his head. "What then?"

"Then," continued the Warlord, "To be certain of victory, I should require some eight thousand foot soldiers, most of whom can be Teckla, and another three thousand mounted, who must all be skilled warriors."

"Well?"

"Sire, Your Majesty need but give the word, and they can be gathered by to-morrow, and be ready to march against His Highness before dawn the day after."

"They can set off in two days, then?"

"If that is Your Majesty's wish."

"Well then, Rollondar, tell me frankly what you think of this plan."

The Warlord considered. "Sire, the more time Lord Adron is given, the more time he will have to bring the horses that provide the basis of his tactics into better positions, wherefore I believe that not a day—not an hour—should be lost in setting out after him. And, moreover—"

"Yes?"

"I intend to be careful in constructing a snare through which he cannot slip, and this must needs mean I will move slower than I should otherwise wish; thus, even more, we ought to hurry in setting out, to make up for the necessary delays in the forming of the attack. This is a case where, above all, speed is our ally, and we must treat with her with all the diplomacy we can muster."

"Then you favor gathering our forces this very night?"

"Yes, Sire."

"Let it be so," said the Emperor.

Rollondar bowed his head.

His Majesty continued, "We will see how fares the Lord Khaavren. If possible, he ought to give his orders for the protection of the city, but set out with you, Warlord, for it is his mission to arrest Lord Adron, and none but he should carry it out."

"Very well, Sire," said the Warlord.

"Have you anything to add, Jurabin?"

"Nothing, Sire."

"Then that is all."

Warlord and Minister took respectful leave of His Majesty, who sat alone in the Seven Room, reflecting. There was no doubt in his mind that he was doing what was necessary, and moreover, what was right—yet he regretted extremely the words of Khaavren, his wise Captain, and, moreover, His Majesty wondered if he had failed to account for something to which he ought to have paid attention.

After some few moments, he rose and, attended by the guardsman called Sergeant, went to look in on his Captain of the Guards, who was being attended in one of the spare bedchambers of the Imperial Wing. Attending him, we should add, was Navier, of the House of the Hawk, who was His Majesty's personal physicker.

His Majesty was announced, and then entered the chamber where Khaavren appeared to sleep peacefully, while Lady Navier stood above him, holding out her fingers for him to breathe on and then rubbing her fingers together with a thoughtful expression on her face. She was a woman of nine hundred or a thousand years, whose hair was the color of the Redbrick Inn (by which, lest the reader never have seen this structure, we mean dark brown); she had an unusually dark complexion for Hawklords, so that her face, blending in with her hair, was often concealed when her hair fell forward as she worked, and she had, moreover, the sharp angular face that Hawklords share with Dragonlords. She had studied blood-work directly under Burdeen, who wrote the famous monograph published by Pamlar University during the last Teckla Republic, had studied sorcery with the Athrya Lady Waxen, and had, in addition, worked with Lord Clir on his monumental and definitive work on anatomy, all of which, taken together, made her qualified as none other could be to be His Majesty's physicker.

Now she looked up and said in a whisper, "I beg Your Majesty to speak softly; above all else, he requires rest, and I fear to wake him."

"Very well," His Majesty whispered back. "What is his condition?"

"Sire, he has lost a great deal of blood, and, moreover, has received a sharp knock on the head. He is strong, however, and I have made him drink fortified wine to encourage his blood to replace itself as well as to help him sleep. Moreover, there are certain spells which I have made use of to ensure that the new blood is clean and in harmony with the old, so there need be no fear on that score. Of course, the wound in his side is nothing, for no organs were touched, nor even any ribs, and I have sewn it up and placed an enchantment to cause the skin to grow—it will itch like seven demons when he wakes, but it will knit with scarcely a scar."

"Well, but what of his head?"

"Sire, I have studied this wound, and I believe that there is no danger. His pupils do not seem to have changed size, and, in the few words we had while he was conscious, he did not complain of nausea."

The Emperor gave forth a sigh of relief and said, "Navier, you relieve my mind. When can I speak with him? For there are matters of state that make consultation with him urgent, though I would not willingly risk his health."

"Sire, I think Your Majesty ought to send him home in a coach—and a good one, mind—and allow him a night's sleep in familiar surroundings. Then, if he feels himself able to report for duty to-morrow, there is no reason why he should not be able to assume it, provided he regularly doses himself with the draught I am preparing for him."

"All will be as you say, Navier."

The physicker bowed.

Tortaalik made his way out of the room, and resumed his interrupted walk to the Imperial Baths. As he walked, he reflected once again on his discussion with his councilors, and how he wished Lord Khaavren could have been there. He resolved to speak with him as soon as could be on the morrow.

Khaavren, for his part, was aware of little of this. He was in a sort of daze, and through this confusion he was dimly aware that he was being sent home, but not why, nor yet that he had succumbed to his wounds—in fact, he did not remember being wounded. He did remember that there was something he had attempted to do at which he had failed, and even in his semiconscious state this grieved him; yet he was also aware that he would soon be seeing Daro, which cheered him.

And beneath it all there was the notion that there was something he ought to have done, or be doing, or have someone do, but he could neither concentrate his attention sufficiently to think of what it was, nor, had he been able to, had he the ability to wake enough for coherent speech.

He felt himself being placed in the coach that had been ordered for him, and by chance it was a good one, so that the rocking motion soon pitched him fully into a deep, restful sleep. At this same time, the Warlord of the Empire stood in his offices contemplating the maps of the terrain around the city, but thinking, instead, about Adron e'Kieron, about His Majesty, and about a thousand other matters that came to his mind. After some few minutes of this, he sat down, took out a good, sharp pen, and wrote a hasty note to his wife, which he lost no time in putting into the hand of a messenger, with instructions to use the fastest posts His Majesty had.

The messenger accepted the note and the instructions, bowed, and said, "Am I to await a reply before I return?"

Rollondar shook his head. "You will not be returning," he said. "Instead, you will bless me each day of your life, thanking me that you, and not another, had this errand of me. Now lose not a moment—you are to be there before dawn tomorrow day."

# Chapter the Twenty-third

*Which Treats of the Uses of Repetition
And of the Nature of Heroics;
With Implied Comments on the Heroism
To Be Found in the Lower Classes,
As Compared to Those of the Very Highest.*

**T**HE POWER OF REPETITION IS well known and highly respected among jongleurs, sorcerers, playwrights, and physickers, to name but a few; that is, it has long been known that frequent repetition of words or actions can elicit laughter, focus concentration, illuminate themes, or induce the painful and disabling Malady of the Tingling Hand.

The author of these words is not unaware that repetition occurs in literature as well, yet he would be saddened if readers believed that he was using the repetition of words, or, indeed, events, as a device to either entertain or enlighten—in fact, recurrences are so much a part of history in general, and Khaavren's history in particular, that it would be the most vulgar sort of dishonesty to leave out a vital exchange or interaction simply because something similar, or something reflective, had been earlier presented in the narrative. Should the reader choose to look for meaning, or, indeed, amusement in this repetition, we are powerless to prevent it (nor, indeed, would we wish to), but he is cautioned that such is in no wise our intention.

This being said, we may go on to explain that, as full darkness came upon the city, and as the carriage containing our brave but senseless Captain pulled up to the house on the Street of the Glass Cutters and, with the help of the coachman and a Palace servant, disgorged our ailing Tiassa, there was yet another attempt on his life.

It came about in this way: the carriage arrived, as we have already said, just as full dusk had fallen. The coachman, who had felt a great sense of urgency because of the money he had been given and because of the tones in which his orders had been expressed, did not even pause to light his lamps, but rather leapt down from his seat and opened the door to assist the servant in carrying our Tiassa to the door of his house, whose location the coachman had been given in explicit detail by the selfsame subaltern of the Guard who had transmitted His Majesty's orders in terms so clear and precise.

The coachman took one of Khaavren's arms, the servant took the other, and, with only that help Khaavren was able to render in his condition—which was, as we have said, on the edge of consciousness (or, if the reader prefer, the edge of unconsciousness)—they led the Captain two steps closer to the door, at which point the coachman let go of the arm he had been holding. Upon noticing this, the Teckla said, "My dear sir, I assure you that I cannot carry this gentlemen unassisted, wherefore I urge you to take the arm again before he falls to the ground and my back is called to answer for the failure of his legs."

The coachman did not answer, and the servant, upon attempting to discover why, saw that his companion was stretched out full length upon the ground and that, moreover, there appeared, in the uneven light cast by the nearest glowbulb, still some distance away, a stream of blood flowing from a not inconsiderable gash in his forehead.

Now this Teckla (whose name, we should add for the sake of completeness, if not euphony, was Klorynderata), had worked in the Imperial Palace for nearly all of his nine hundred years, and had often been assigned duties in the Dragon Wing of cleaning or carrying or fetching, and, hence, had heard no few stories featuring war, battle, blood, and death as either central themes or recurring motifs—yet he had never before encountered violence in such a close, and, we might add, intimate way. He responded, then, in a manner that ought to surprise no one: He loosed his hold on Khaavren's shoulder and bolted down the street as fast as he could, leaving Khaavren to fall helpless next to the prostrate coachman, who, being either dead or rapidly dying, could be of no assistance to him whatsoever. The horses stamped and shifted as if aware that something was wrong, and this sound, along with the jingling of their harnesses, was all that could be heard in the street.

Then it seemed as if a formless shadow grew from the larger shadow of the house and approached Khaavren's senseless body. A closer look would have revealed, in the figure's hand, a dull black rod, about a meter in length, of the type often used by sorcerers to concentrate, or even contain, particularly potent spells. A still closer look would have shown that the figure was, in fact, Laral, who quickly walked up to Khaavren, holding the rod aloft. There can be no question that all would have been up for Khaavren at that moment, except that, just then, the stillness was broken by Srahi, who cried out in her shrill, piercing, and abrasive voice, "What is this, a robbery in front of my master's door? Hey, you, what is it you are doing? Get away from there!"

Srahi had come around the corner, in the company of Mica, and seen just enough to know that there was a crime taking place on the street outside of her house. Now Srahi was no stranger to crimes of one sort or another—in fact, if truth be told, she had, before being hired by Khaavren, herself engaged in activities of dubious legality; she had no thought whatsoever of passing judgment in any moral sense. But she also understood that the space in front of her master's house was no place for criminal action, or violent crime in any case, and he Captain of His Majesty's Guard!

A sense of outrage not only filled her, but it positively carried her straight up to the amazed Laral, who could not believe that a Teckla would be so foolish, not to mention insolent, as to interfere with Jhereg business. We should add that, for her part, Srahi had no notion that this was a Jhereg before her, and whether she would have behaved differently if she had known we cannot say.

Locked up in the rod in Laral's hand was the embodiment of that spell called The Quick Road by those in the Jhereg who practiced assassination through sorcery—the spell was so named because it was reputed to be one of the quickest known paths to the afterlife: It acted by instantly freezing all of the liquids within the fairly small radius of the spell's effect, wherefore it was only necessary to direct it at the victim's heart for death to follow almost before the victim could be aware. For just the briefest of moments, it was directed at Srahi's heart, but Laral realized that it would be ludicrous to use the spell she had carefully prepared for Khaavren on a mere Teckla, who could hardly threaten her in any case. At the same time, however, she realized that this Teckla may have glimpsed her face, and thus had to die, and that without any delay. Her solution to this problem was to bring forth a simple flashstone which she had concealed in a convenient pocket, raise it, and discharge it fully into Srahi's face—a solution which she put into practice at once.

It happened, however, that instead of discharging it into Srahi's face, she rather discharged it into the space Srahi's face had occupied a moment before, for, just at that moment, Mica, who had seen such devices in action often enough to recognize one at once, pushed his own body into Srahi's in such a way that she was thrown to the side and the flashstone went off into the air above Mica's head—Mica having, fortunately, the presence of mind to duck at the same time that he pushed. The horses, already made nervous by the commotion and the smell of blood, took this moment to bolt, and, with no coachman to direct them, hurtled down the street (for the sake of completeness, we ought to explain what became of the coach, but, in point of fact, we have not been able to learn of it).

After ducking the murderous power of the stone, Mica straightened up and, doing his best to imitate the tones his mistress was wont to use on such occasions, addressed Srahi in these terms: "Now, my dear, you shall see the use to which I can put a good bar-stool, and we will both be grateful that we were able to find it in the trash-heap—it is true that it now smells of klava leavings, the peelings of vegetables, and the guts and heads of fish, but, what of that? The refuse before me will only feel more at home therefrom."

To Laral, he said, "Now then, you, defend yourself, for I am well acquainted with this weapon I bear, and if you are not at least equally familiar with your own, then, Shards and Splinters! I think you are a dead woman!"

Laral, for her part, felt no need to engage in conversation; moreover, she was far too angry to attempt words—the very idea of two Teckla happening by and ruining her careful plan filled her with outrage. But she was a sorcerer both powerful and subtle, as well as being a killer both fierce and heartless. She knew that, if she were to have any chance of completing her mission, she could waste no time with these Teckla; they had to be dispatched at once. She also knew that, with her flashstone having already sent its sharp, penetrating crack through the neighborhood, there was no longer any reason to be quiet, wherefore, with no hesitation, she now aimed her flashstone a second time.

Mica, looking at the flat surface of the stone only inches from his nose, realized, in the first place, that it must have been prepared with a second charge—he knew such things were possible because he had assisted his Master, Tazendra, in preparing such devices several score of times—and, in the second place, he knew that he was a dead man.

Or, to be more precise, we ought to say he *thought* he was a dead man, for he had reckoned without Srahi who, though weaponless, had no intention of standing by while Mica, who was well on the way to becoming her lover, and who had, moreover, just saved her life, suffered the very fate from which he had lately preserved her. Srahi let go an enraged cry that vied with the flashstone itself for volume, and threw herself on the arm of Mica's assailant.

This time when the stone discharged, however, it was not without effect; Mica, who had once been kicked in the left shin by one of his master's colts, with whom he had been disagreeing about the proper direction to move through the corral, felt for a moment as if this same colt had kicked him in the right shin; indeed, the crack of the flashstone even sounded in his ears very much as the crack of breaking bone had on that occasion, and the shock to the limb—that particular shock which resembles numbness but which promises pain to follow in short order—was nearly identical except that, on this occasion, it was accompanied by a searing heat which promised even more extreme pain and, half an instant later, by the smell of cooking meat—had he paused to consider that this smell came from his own tortured flesh, he may well have been so discomfited that he would have been unable to respond.

In the event, however, Mica did not pause to consider this, nor did he even pause to consider that he had been hurt, perhaps disabled, and that both he and his mistress might soon be left helpless before their unknown assailant; rather, the instant he felt the blow and the accompanying heat, he swung his faithful bar-stool with grim purpose and deadly aim. He was rewarded by the solid, satisfying feel of a good stroke well placed; Laral fell back three steps with a hiss of pain or annoyance at the same instant that Mica gave a scream that was, in fact, the loudest sound yet to ring out through that night, after which he fell, nearly senseless himself, next to Khaavren who slept, and the coachman who would never wake.

Laral, though stunned, was by no means finished; she dropped the now-useless flashstone and drew from her side a long, slim dagger, and, with this in one hand (the other, the reader ought to remember, still held that rod containing the spell with which she was determined to dispatch Khaavren) she advanced on Srahi with the intention of quickly finishing her, and then completing her business with the fallen Captain.

Srahi looked at the dagger, at the cold, heartless eyes behind the dagger, at her fallen lover, and felt a trembling in her knees and a weakness in her bowels the like of which she had never imagined, and realized, in her turn, that she was about to die.

And die she certainly would have, had not Daro, Countess of Whitecrest, aroused by the sounds of battle coming from outside of the house, emerged at that moment, dressed in a housecoat of brilliant Lyorn-red and holding a naked sword in her hand. The Countess, attempting as best she could to see through the darkness and the shadows, said, "What is this? Who are you to threaten an unarmed Teckla with a knife? And who are these people who lie, dead, dying, sleeping, or stricken, all about the doorstep of this good house?"

As Laral turned, Srahi gave a small sigh and sank to her knees. It is true that one might fault her for not having chosen that moment, when her assailant's back was turned, to launch an attack, but one ought to remember, in the first place, that she was weaponless, in the second that she was frightened out of her wits, and, in the third, that, when she had earlier launched herself at Laral's arm, even as the Jhereg was about to strike down her lover, she had already been far, far braver than one ought to expect of any Teckla. It is the judgment of the historian that Srahi be allowed a moment's collapse in relief at her delivery, without censure from the reader.

In any case, Laral did not hesitate, but threw her knife at this new intruder with careful aim and a strong arm. Daro had fought her share of duels, been involved in a few melees of one sort or another, and, on one occasion, had even been involved in what could only be called a battle (although, had Her Majesty known of this battle and the part the Countess had played therein, it is doubtful whether Daro would have been allowed any position whatever at court, much less that of maid of honor), but she had never fought with anyone who could use a knife in the way Laral did—that is, by throwing it. Daro had no means of repelling such an attack, and the knife struck her full in the body. Daro gasped and, like Srahi had the instant before, sank to her knees.

Her sword fell to the ground with a clang, and she stared, gasping, at the knife which appeared to grow from her stomach—nearly four inches of blade had penetrated, testifying to Laral's skill and strength. The assassin, however, did not pause to congratulate herself on the skill and strength to which we have just alluded; she knew very well that time, a most valuable commodity to an assassin, was quickly slipping away, and she must act at once if she were to complete her mission—or, indeed, if she were even to herself attempt the very thing that time was doing—that is, slipping away.

And so, once more, for the last time, she turned back to the prostrate Tiassa, raising the black rod in her hand; and once more, for the last time, she was interrupted, this time by Tazendra, who cried, "What is this, a massacre on Khaavren's very doorstep?"

"An assassination, more like," said Pel through clenched teeth.

"How! Do you think so?"

"I am convinced of it, my dear Baroness. And if we are too late, then, by all the gods of the Paths, someone will pay dearly for our tardiness."

Laral turned at these voices, and seeing two warlike figures silhouetted against the light from the slowly approaching glowbulb, decided that there was no longer time for saving anything, but, rather, she must use her most potent weapons at once, and hope only to escape with her life. She therefore raised the rod, directed it at the larger of the two, which looked to be a woman (and was, in fact, Tazendra), and cast the spell, while simultaneously drawing a rapier with which she intended to quickly dispatch the smaller (whom the reader will realize is Pel), after which she hoped to cut the throats of everyone present—certainly more of a bloodletting than she would have preferred; but, she decided, she had no choice.

Unfortunately for our Jhereg, Tazendra and Pel each had other ideas. Although Tazendra was not quick to comprehend the subtleties of intrigue, or the nuances of communication, or the feints and deceptions behind the schemes of a Yendi, she knew very well what the rod signified, and quickly cast a rune of protection over her and her friend, and such was her skill in the magical sciences that, although she felt a momentary chill, there was no other effect of the enchantment. Similarly, Pel had never in his life allowed anyone to pierce his skin with anything sharp if he could at all prevent it; in this case, he prevented it by drawing his own sword and neatly deflecting Laral's hurried lunge, a maneuver he followed at once with a riposte that cut her wrist, causing her to drop her sword.

We should say in Tazendra's defense that, had she noticed that the unknown sorcerer was weaponless, she (by which we mean Tazendra) would have held up on her own attack, but events proved too quick in the unfolding, and the light proved too dim in the shadows, so that Tazendra's massive sword was in her hand, and, indeed, the blade was embedded in Laral's skull, before the sound of Laral's own sword striking the ground had reached Tazendra's ears.

In the silence that followed the clang of the sword onto the stone walkway before Khaavren's house, followed, as it was, by the muffled sound of the assassin's body falling next to her own sword, Daro stared up at the two unknowns, grateful for their presence but wondering who they were. Pel stepped out of the way of the glowbulb, thus allowing the light to fall on the Countess's face, after which he said, "Well, my dear Whitecrest, our arrival seems to have been timely."

"I am convinced I have heard that before, too," murmured Tazendra.

"How, you know me?" said Daro.

"Indeed," said Pel, and turned so the light fell on his face (the glowbulb, we should add, was only now moving into place above the ensemble, so quick had been all of the action). "You are without doubt one of Her Majesty's maids of honor, and are called Daro, are you not?"

"Indeed, and I recall your face, yet I cannot think where I have seen you."

"I have been at court," said Pel, "though in other garb than this. Perhaps—"

"Ohhhhhhh," moaned Srahi.

"Help," suggested Mica.

"Countess, is that your voice I hear, or am I dreaming?" said the Captain. "And why is it so cold?"

"Perhaps," said Pel, "we ought to bring everyone inside, and tend to that unfortunate length of steel which seems to have embedded itself in your stomach, Countess, and attend, as well, to anyone else who is wounded."

"Which appears to be everyone," agreed Tazendra. "But who are they? Was that, indeed, Khaavren's voice?"

"It is I," said Khaavren. "But why am I on the ground? And—"

"Questions later, my dear," said Pel.

"Who else is here?" said Tazendra, looking around.

"I am, Baroness my master," said Mica.

"Mica, is that you?"

"Most of him," said Mica.

"How, most of him? What then is missing?"

"Just about a foot," said the servant. "I hope I will not be less useful to you on that account, however."

"Well, well, we shall see. Who is this?"

"I do not know, but he was killed by sorcery from that woman whose head you have just parted like a ripe melon."

"I see," said Tazendra.

"No doubt the coachman," said Pel. "But who is this? Could it be Srahi?"

The reader will note that the above conversation had taken only two minutes, yet this was time enough for Srahi to have recovered sufficiently to say, "Who else might it be, do you think? Here, after saving my brave master from the Gods know what sort of violence, and him helpless, are we thanked? Are we even assisted indoors? No! The good Mica lies bleeding and freezing on the cold street, and—"

"By the Gods," said Pel. "It *is* Srahi.

"It could be no one else," agreed Tazendra.

"Let us bring them all inside, Khaavren first of all."

"Cha!" said Khaavren. "I am the healthiest present, save

for you late arrivals. Attend to the Countess, then send for a physicker."

"Ought we," said Pel, "to move her at all before the physicker arrives?"

In answer, Tazendra at once bent over and conducted a brief but thorough inspection of her wound. She then, using bits of cloth from Laral's costume, stanched the bleeding as best she could and said, "We must be careful, but we ought to move her at once to a place where she can be kept warm; I cannot tell what damage this weapon has done, yet I fear . . . come, Pel, help me bring her inside."

The Countess was too weak from pain and shock to object to this plan, and allowed Pel and Tazendra to carry her inside. When she had been set on the sofa, they returned to find Khaavren standing up, and even assisting Srahi with Mica, who still had his bar-stool clenched in his hand. They replaced both Khaavren and Srahi, and sent the latter off to find a physicker, which she claimed she could do in two minutes. Mica seemed unhappy at seeing her leave, but he bore his loss, like the pain of his wound, as an old campaigner.

Soon they were all settled in the parlor in this fashion: Daro lay on the couch with cloth all about the knife which was still in her stomach, and with her head near the grey arm-chair, upon which, we should add, was Khaavren, his feet propped up before him and his head tilted back. On the floor near him was Mica, sitting on several spare blankets, and using his master's pillow, while Pel and Tazendra occupied two of the chairs (that is, one each). Even as Tazendra stretched out her legs, tossed her hair, and opened her mouth to make a pronouncement on some subject or another, Srahi came in.

"Well?" said Tazendra. "And the physicker?"

"He is behind me," said Srahi, "and will be here before you can draw a breath—he stopped only to pick up those supplies he pretends he might need." She then seated herself before Mica, with her legs crossed netmaker-fashion and her face set in a stern, forbidding look that discouraged questions about the physicker, requests for potables, or discussion of any other sort.

The physicker, a resolutely cheerful Chreotha with a Serioli name that was all but unpronounceable (wherefore we shall refer to him as "the physicker," trusting our readers will not object), did, in fact, arrive in scarcely more than the time Srahi had mentioned—at any rate, few breaths were drawn and no more conversation took place before he arrived. Srahi sent an imperious glance around the room, but said nothing except for giving the briefest greeting to the physicker (whose name she massacred without apparent embarrassment), to which he responded by affable nods to all present, and after which he went around the room inspecting the patients, beginning with Daro, then Khaavren, and lastly Mica. No one spoke while he made his examinations, but, rather, everyone watched his face, hoping for a clue to the condition of the patient in question. No such clues were, however, forthcoming—he remained cheerful, and said nothing until he had examined all three, then, without consultation (which consultation would necessarily have produced an argument) he began his treatment first with Mica, saying, "There is no question, my friend, but that you must lose that foot and a portion of the leg, but we shall certainly save the knee, which ought to be a comfort to you."

Mica closed his eyes tightly and did not seem especially comforted.

By chance, the physicker was not entirely unskilled, and had brought along dreamgrass oil to ease pain, which he carefully measured out and administered on thin wafers. After urging two of these on the poor Teckla, who was so frightened he could scarcely swallow and had to be assisted with long draughts of water, most of which he spilled, the physicker commanded that a room be set aside for his surgery, with clean sheets and a bucket ready. By the time the room was ready, the dreamgrass had taken effect.

It is not our intention to pander to those of our readers who delight in blood; moreover, it is the belief of the author that there has been enough blood already in this chapter of our history to satisfy all but most depraved of readers; we will, then, content ourselves with saying that the remainder of

Mica's foot and ankle were removed without mishap, and after the stump was neatly tied, the physicker checked all of the Teckla's vital signs and pronounced him out of danger.

Daro's wound, though shallow, was, as Tazendra had observed, the most dangerous, because the knife had come near to cutting open her intestines, which must surely have resulted in death unless extreme measures were taken. But fortunately, after examining her, the physicker announced that, in fact, no serious damage had been done, and after dosing her with dreamgrass, he drew forth the knife in one easy motion; then, after cleaning the wound, he quickly closed it with five stitches, which Daro bore quite complacently, the dreamgrass having done its work.

After giving Khaavren a quick inspection, and announcing that he required nothing more than rest, the physicker collected his fee, which was generously contributed by Tazendra, and departed. By the time he left, all three patients had been moved back to the parlor, and all of them were able to speak without moaning, although, to be sure, two of them—by which we mean Daro and Mica—at times had to struggle to concentrate on what they or their companions were saying.

Khaavren, upon hearing the door close, wasted no time in asking what had happened, with the result that several voices attempted to answer him at once. After some few moments of this, he asked for and received silence, and required the stories to be told simply, clearly, and one at a time. The next several hours, then, were taken up in sorting through what had happened and attempting to reconstruct it and put it into some kind of coherent order, beginning with an account from Pel and Tazendra of their recent activities (with which the reader is already familiar, except to say that, upon reaching the Imperial Palace, they discovered that Khaavren had been taken ill and sent home, and they had hastened there as quickly as they could), including Srahi's explanation of how she and Mica came to be there at that time (which, likewise, the reader has already heard except for certain portions which we are confident the reader can fill in himself), and concluding with an effort on all sides to piece together exactly who had been wounded how and when, and, in turn, who had done exactly what to the assassin (whose body, we should add, still remained on the sidewalk, next to that of the coachman, because Khaavren felt too weak to subject it to his usual scrutiny). In all, these activities continued (with, we should add some measure of success) far into the night.

"Well," said Khaavren, when at last he understood the sequence of events, "it seems that, once again, I've been saved by the arrival of my friends—in this case several of them. Moreover, this time there can be no doubt that the true heroes are Mica and Srahi."

"For my part," said Tazendra, giving Mica a fond glance, "I could not agree more."

"Bah," said Mica, blushing and wondering if he could contrive to be killed for both Khaavren and his master at the same time and resolving to do so as soon as a means could be found, "we were only too happy to be of any small service we could, were we not?" He addressed this last to Srahi, who sniffed disdainfully, but also smiled—a task to which the muscles of her face seemed unaccustomed.

Khaavren suggested they allow the servants a glass of wine, and, moreover, offered to drink to the health of the two of them, and this proposal was promptly put into action—they were honored the more in that it was Pel who went to fetch the wine and Tazendra who poured it into the cups, waiting upon the servants, as it happened.

After draining his glass, Khaavren said, "And now, my friends, I must sleep, for I can scarcely keep my eyes open, and to-morrow promises to be a day of unusual interest."

"What of to-morrow?" said Pel.

"Indeed," said Khaavren, who sounded (and was feeling) more than a little drowsy. "What of to-morrow?"

"Will you be able to rise in the morning?"

"I must," said Khaavren. "There is something I must do. It is very important and, wounded or not, I must go at once to the Palace."

"What is it?" said Pel and Tazendra together.

"I do not remember," said Khaavren, "although, no doubt,

I will when I wake up. For now, I believe that I can hold my eyes open no longer. Good night to you, my friends, and to you, Countess."

They all, in turn, expressed their wishes that Khaavren would sleep well and comfortably, except for Daro, whose eyes were closed and who was breathing evenly and deeply, and Srahi, who was audibly wondering who was going to clean up the blood that had soaked into the floor, the sofa, three good sheets, and, it would seem, every towel in the house.

We must, at this point, apologize to the reader, for we are not unaware that this would be a good time, with everyone drifting off to sleep, to end this chapter of our history; yet it is our desire to inform the reader of all of the significant events before allowing the next day to begin with our next chapter, wherefore we must go back in time to when Khaavren was unceremoniously leaving the Palace, which was at just about the same moment that His Majesty was ceremoniously closing up the Palace, by which, be it clearly understood, we mean that he was doing the rounds, after which he retired to his bedchamber, which he did at about the same time that Khaavren and his friends were being placed in chairs and sofas about the house, and settling in for the evening's conversation which we have already had the honor of summarizing for our reader. His Majesty, too, was settling in for an evening's conversation, but, there being no one there to converse with, he perforce spoke to himself.

"It is not," he began, lying on his side, "as bad as it seems. Though there is rebellion, there is also an Imperial Army. Although there are conspiracies about the court, there is Jurabin. Although my Captain is injured, the good Navier believes he will recover fully, and soon at that. Moreover, I have my health, and my hand is strong upon the tiller of the Empire, and I have Noima, my Consort, a consolation in time of trouble—although, in fact, I really *ought* to see about a replacement for old Wellborn; I am unused to being without a Discreet.

"But leave that—let us dwell on what we have, rather than

what we do not have, for that way lies contentment, and the other way lies unhappiness. Yet, to the left, among the possessions we have been pleased to enumerate we must included an admirable memory, which reminds us that Wellborn was wont to speak of contentment in the most disparaging of terms, pretending that contentment was stagnation, and that it was the lot of Man to struggle ever higher.

"All of which is well enough, but what, then, ought I to be struggling against? The rebel Prince, certainly; but I have done all I can as far as he goes. What else?

"Bah! What an occupation for a grown man, and an Emperor no less! To lie awake attempting to find something to worry about! Next I shall come to mistrust the Warlord and the Captain, than which there are no more loyal souls in the Empire, even as I mistrust Jurabin, who . . ."

He stopped in the midst of this soliloquy, shifted onto his back, locked his hands behind his head, and repeated this last phrase to himself. "What have I said? I mistrust Jurabin? Now, how did that thought come to take root? I have always trusted him before. Well, but there can be no question but that he has changed, although I cannot fathom precisely in what manner he has changed."

He folded his hands on his stomach and stared up at the ceiling. "No, now that I think, I *do* know in manner he has changed—he is no longer so devoted to Noima as he was. It is, to be sure, an odd thing for a husband to consider (for I am a husband as well an Emperor), yet, after those devotions which, long years ago, gave me a certain unease (and of which I was once so jealous that I spent an entire day with Wellborn speaking of nothing else), to now be disturbed that those small attentions—which I was never certain existed—are now entirely absent.

"And what of Noima herself? Has she noticed the change? Of course she has—why else would she be so angered at the Lady Aliera? This, then, is the answer to that mystery. But the first question still confronts us, and in as forceful a manner as ever: Can Jurabin still be trusted?

"For that matter, though it pains me to even ask the question, can Noima be trusted? Not her heart, of which I have never had cause to doubt, but her judgment? If not, and I fear that to ask the question is to answer it, I must be less hasty in agreeing to her wishes—my own words to her, in which I counterposed the needs of Empire to the desires of the husband, were prophetic. No, I must do what is best for the Empire, and Jurabin certainly will agree; indeed, it was he who argued against the arrest of Aliera, which would have solved the domestic problem, at the cost of—"

His Majesty broke off abruptly, sat up in his bed, and cried, "The Gods! Of course Jurabin argued against Aliera's arrest! He is in love with her, and this is coloring all of his decisions, as, indeed, his reaction is coloring all of Noima's! What, then—is the court nothing more than a playground of romance, and the policies of Empire nothing more than tools of intrigue? This cannot be allowed. I will not allow it. If I have to dismiss every councilor in the Chambers and live like a celibate, I will not allow it. I will not. Whatever pain I condemn myself or even my loved ones to, I will not."

And repeating this phrase over and over to himself, he lay down once more, turned over onto his side, and at last, and at much the same time as those in Khaavren's house, drifted off to sleep.

# Chapter the Twenty-fourth

---

*Which Treats of the Philosophy of Conquest,*
*The Conquest of Philosophy,*
*And Several Instances of Pride.*

B Y THIS TIME, WE DO not doubt, the reader is beginning
to wonder about Aliera and Sethra, who were last seen
in the Imperial Palace, where they learned that
Khaavren had been ordered to arrest Adron. The reader might
presume that, in fact, they reached Adron, warned him, and
that Adron had therefore broken camp at once, leaving a pa-
trol of three warriors to either stop Khaavren should he appear alone, or give warning should he appear in force. The
reader who does make these presumptions is, we should say
at once, correct on all counts. And, as it is well known that
the Breath of Fire Battalion was famous, above all, for its
speed, it should come as no surprise that, as red dawn broke
over Dragaera, the battalion should be found encamped a
good forty leagues from the city, having covered this distance
in a single night and still had time, after making camp according to Adron's particular code, to get a good night's sleep
(except for those who had guard duty, which was, under the
circumstances, a fair number).

Aerich was awakened at dawn, and Fawnd, a good servant,

woke even before his master and hastened to help him dress, while making certain that klava was available and determining if any messages had arrived during the night. On this occasion, in fact, one had, and Fawnd hastened to present it to the good Lyorn, who read it at once, frowned, and said to himself, "I am to breakfast with His Highness this morning, as well as certain others to whom he refers as guests—I assume these will include his daughter Aliera and, no doubt, Sethra Lavode; therefore I ought to present myself in a fashion that will show the esteem in which I hold them."

To Fawnd, then, he said, "Ribbons for the belt, silver medallion, vambraces."

"Yes, Venerance," said the servant, and immediately set out the named items.

Aerich was not easily deceived, nor was he on this occasion—he arrived in Adron's tent to find Adron and Aliera already awaiting him; Sethra appeared even as Aerich was greeting the first two.

We must, in all conscience, pause for a moment to utter yet another brief apology to our reader; during what follows, which, we give our word, is entirely necessary to our history, we shall be spending time with four persons, three of whom, we admit to our sorrow, have names which begin with the same sound and are, moreover, of roughly similar length, and even contain similar sounds within. We are not insensitive to the difficulty it may cause some readers to keep track of when a passing symbol refers to Adron, when to Aliera, and when to Aerich. We shall, of course, do our best to help the reader by making reference, from time to time, to some characteristic by which the individual may be told from the others: "His Highness," for example, or "the Lyorn," or "Adron's daughter." Yet, it cannot be denied that a certain amount of confusion is inevitable under these circumstances, and we therefore tender our apologies, offering as our only justification that, in the event, these people were there, and to change their names for them would be to take liberties which no historian could justify, and for which those involved, some of whom live even as we write these words, would hardly thank us.

This said, let us pass on to consider the breakfast to which His Highness had determined to treat his daughter, the Lyorn, and the Enchantress of Dzur Mountain.

It was not large, as such breakfasts go—it was Adron's opinion that he, and, by extension, his troops, would fight better if not weighed down by a large meal, although some sustenance was certainly required. Hence, each guest was given warmed bread and butter, a ration of potatoes, a piece of dried whitefruit, and a slice of roasted kethna. There was also blood-tea in good quantity (Adron, being superstitious about the name, had forced himself to enjoy the acrid tang) and klava.

"So does Your Highness believe," said Aerich toward the end of the repast, "that His Majesty will attack today?"

"It is not unlikely," said Adron. "It is what I would do. The longer he delays, the more horses we will be able to move into position, and the faster and more efficiently we will be able to strike. Rollondar cannot be unaware of this. In all honesty, I am surprised that the attack did not come during the night, although we would certainly have had the advantage in any battle in darkness."

Sethra looked at him sharply. "Your Highness cannot, even with all of your skills and all of your forces, expect to defeat the Imperial Army in open battle."

"I do not fight in order to lose battles," said Adron quietly.

"Your Highness must perceive," said the Lyorn, "that, once battle is joined, I cannot support it—however much I revere Your Highness, I cannot countenance rebellion."

"It is not rebellion if the cycle has turned, my dear Lyorn."

"On the contrary," said Aerich. "Rebellion is exactly rebellion, until it succeeds, which is how one knows the cycle has turned."

"A pretty dilemma," agreed the Prince.

His daughter shrugged. "It is all well and good to discuss such matters of theory, but soon enough the battle will be joined and such arguments will no longer matter, being replaced by arguments of a more convincing sort."

"And you," remarked Sethra dryly, "are so impatient for the slaughter to begin that you can barely contain yourself."

"Well," said Aliera sharply. "And do you condemn me for this?"

"I have seen too much blood, too many battles, to take any joy in them."

"I," said Aliera, "have not."

"With the Favor, you never will."

"If you can find an honorable way to prevent this battle, my dear Sethra; you are welcome to do so—moreover, I will even help you."

"Will you? Well, I have been considering exactly this question."

"Have you then?"

"Indeed I have."

"And?"

"It may be that I know a way."

Aerich studied her, but said nothing. Adron leaned forward in his chair. Aliera said, "Well, let us hear it, for I am convinced it must be a good one. And, moreover, a quick one, for I do not doubt that the Warlord is, even now, advancing with all of his forces."

"It is unlikely," Sethra pronounced.

"Unlikely?" said father and daughter with one voice.

"You are, neither of you, as aware as I am of the state of the Imperial forces. Rollondar will not be able to attack before to-morrow's dawn at the soonest, unless he chooses to launch an attack in which he will be outnumbered in both men and horses, and I promise you he will not do so."

"The Imperial Army is not gathered?" said Adron.

"Not in the least."

"And yet, Jurabin and His Majesty must both have realized—"

"Jurabin," said Sethra with a smile and a covert glance at Aliera, "has been distracted these past few days, and is not thinking clearly. And as for His Majesty, well, the reins of government are too new in his hands for him to yet feel the subtleties."

"Yet the Warlord—"

"Will not have called for a general arming and preparation without explicit orders. It is never a wise move, and after several hundred years of a Phoenix Reign, with the Dragon over the horizon, no Warlord would risk giving such advice unless asked in the most explicit of terms."

"That is true," said Adron.

"Well then," said Aliera. "Let us hear this famous plan. And if I think it a good one, well, I will subscribe to it as I promised."

"Then listen," said Sethra.

"We are listening," said the others.

Sethra quickly described her plan, while the others listened attentively. When she had finished, Adron blinked and said, "That is it?"

Aliera said, "That is your plan?"

Aerich said nothing.

"That is my plan," said Sethra.

"You will be arrested," said Adron.

"You will be killed," said Aliera.

Aerich said nothing.

"I will be neither killed nor arrested," said Sethra.

"His Majesty—"

"Knows that I am Captain of the Lavodes. He will not like it, but he will take no action against me. And if he does—"

"Yes," said Adron. "If he does?"

"He will discover that he is unable to move against me."

"Well," said Aliera, "that may be true, but your plan cannot succeed."

"I will not dispute with you," said Sethra. "Yet, nevertheless, I will make the attempt, for it is the only way to avert civil war—and that on a scale that I am not ashamed to say frightens me, who have seen such wars come and go for more years than you, Aliera e'Kieron, can imagine."

Aliera seemed about to object, but evidently thought better of it. Adron, for his part, nodded slowly. "It would, indeed, solve the problem, although I cannot believe it will work. Still, if it did, think of all the bloodshed we would avoid."

"So will you support me in this attempt?"

"With all my heart," said Adron, "though I think you are doomed to fail."

"And you will agree to your rôle in the plan?"

"Entirely, my friend, and without a second thought."

Sethra nodded, then turned to Aerich, saying, "And you, my good Lyorn?"

"I believe with His Highness that it cannot succeed, yet it is worth the attempt—none of us knows all the subtleties of the Orb, or of His Majesty's character."

"And you, Aliera?"

"If you try, well, I will accompany you as I agreed."

"You? Never in life. The risks which I do not run, you most certainly will."

"And what of that? Do you think I care a thimble for what His Majesty might think to do to me?"

"And yet, I cannot protect you."

Aliera rose to her feet, her hand upon the hilt of her sword. "How, did I somehow convey the impression that I desired your protection?"

"Aliera!" said her father. "Not at breakfast!"

Aliera bowed and sat once more.

Sethra shrugged her shoulders. "You may accompany me, if you will permit. I do not think it wise."

"Nor do I," said Adron.

"I consider the entire affair unwise. Yet, if Sethra will have it so, I shall accompany her."

"When will you set out?" said His Highness.

"At once," said Sethra. "The sooner begun—"

"Indeed. Then allow me to call for two horses."

"Very well."

Adron sent for two of his best horses, which, upon being delivered, were given over to Sethra and Aliera. Sethra mounted at once. Adron stood before Aliera, took both of her hands and looked her in the eyes.

"Daughter—" he said.

"I know, father," said Aliera. "I will be careful. And you—"

"Yes?"

"Do nothing that you needn't."

"Of course."

"Then fare well."

"Fare well."

Adron and Aerich watched until the two riders were out of sight, then they returned to Adron's tent. Adron walked over to his mosaic of purple stones, studied it, and sighed. Aerich stood next to him.

"I do not know what Your Highness is constructing," he said, "yet it frightens me."

"And well it should," said Adron. "It is now complete, and, should I draw power through it, it would embody the most powerful spell this world has seen since the lost ages of the Jenoine."

Aerich looked at him. "So much?" he said in a whisper.

"So much," said the Dragonlord.

"But what use can you have for a spell so powerful?"

"I face a powerful foe," said Adron. "The most powerful of my life, or, indeed, the life of any sorcerer."

"Would Your Highness care to tell his servant of what foe he is speaking?"

"Who else, my friend? The Orb."

"Your Highness would set elder sorcery against the Orb itself?"

"I would."

"For pride?"

Adron turned to the Lyorn sharply. "So it may seem," he said. "Yet it is not so."

The Lyorn raised his eyebrows and waited. For a while, he thought the Dragonlord had nothing more to say, but then Adron seemed to sigh. "My dear friend, you must consider, first of all, the state of the Empire. Then there is the state of the court. Then there are those signs and portents by which one can, sometimes, receive hints about what the Gods and fate have in store for us. All of these must be taken into account, yet of none of them can we be certain. Therefore, we must allow ourselves every possible option, until the moment of crisis, when our choices are necessarily narrowed, and the only possible action becomes clear."

"Well," said Aerich, "I understand what Your Highness does me the honor of telling me, yet I do not comprehend—"

"I will explain, Duke, for I value your friendship, and, even if you think I am choosing wrong, well, I would still wish for your esteem, and thus I would have you informed of my thinking in this matter."

Aerich bowed and signified that he was listening.

"I am in rebellion against the Empire," he said.

"Well, that is true."

"I have decided that I cannot suffer the insult he has done me, and therefore everything that follows must follow."

Aerich nodded.

"Yet, there are several possibilities from which I can choose, and several ways in which events may play themselves out in spite of any choices I may make."

"Your Highness is as clear as the water of Libedu."

"In the first place, it is possible that I shall simply win against His Majesty—a military victory brought about by mistakes on the part of the Warlord Rollondar, or on the part of His Majesty, or by circumstances unforeseen. Do you know what this would signify?"

"That the cycle has turned, and Your Highness is meant to have the Orb."

"Exactly."

"Well, I understand."

"Next, I may be defeated militarily, which would result in either my death or my capture—and, as I am certain you know, capture would mean death, only somewhat delayed and more ignominious, being upon the Executioner's Star rather than on the field of battle. What, then, would this signify?"

"That the cycle has not turned."

"We understand each other perfectly."

"Well?"

"Well, Duke, I give you my word that, in the latter case,

I should accept defeat, and the decrees of fate, and not risk unleashing the powers of elder sorcery against the Orb."

"How, you would not?"

"Never in the world."

"But then, if I may do myself the honor of putting a question to Your Highness—"

"You may."

"Why create the spell at all?"

Adron nodded, as if this question were not unexpected. "To begin, I built it in anger—I have been studying these patterns for more years than I can count, yet the idea that such power could be a weapon even against the Orb only occurred to my thoughts when I learned of the insult His Majesty had offered my daughter. I constructed the spell, and then, as it were, I came to my senses; or my rage cooled, as you would have it; and I realized that, insult or no, I would not use such means to take the throne."

Aerich bowed. "That seems well thought, Your Highness."

"I have not finished."

"Well?"

"Consider the issues I first mentioned, those being the state of the Empire, the state of the court, and the signs and portents with which one might be acquainted."

"Yes, I am considering them, Highness. I am, in the first place, not sufficiently familiar with signs and portents."

"Well, leave them. What next?"

"The Empire is troubled: The Council of Princes is due to meet, and there is no agreement among any of the Houses about the Imperial Allotment; there are food shortages in the city such that fortunes are being made smuggling grain past the gates, while food sits rotting in the harbors; there is such discontent in the city that the Guard have been alerted to prepare for riots at any time; in the North, the mines—"

"That is sufficient, Duke. What of the court?"

"His Majesty is attempting to rule his own court, but assassinations and conspiracies have deprived him of much of the knowledge he requires to make decisions. Furthermore, he allows the Consort to influence him in matters regarding the welfare of the Empire."

"Well, we are in agreement regarding the state of the Empire and the state of the court."

"I am pleased to be in agreement with Your Highness."

"What can this mean except that the cycle has, indeed, turned, and I must take the throne?"

"It could mean that we must do our best to rally behind the Emperor in this time of trouble, Your Highness. And it may mean nothing at all."

Adron sighed. "Both true," he said. "And exactly my point. That is, you perceive, the difficulty: There are too many possibilities. And yet—"

"Yes? And yet?"

"One possibility, and one that I cannot overlook, is that everything is just as it seems, no more, no less."

Aerich stared at the Prince, waiting for him to continue. After a moment he did.

"The appearances are that the Empire is in a shambles, the court is in confusion, and His Majesty is turning into the worst sort of tyrant—for it is a tyranny built on ignorance and foolishness, rather than selfishness or even malevolence. If things continue as they are there will be famine in the city while food rots in the harbors of the South, there will be war in the East and rebellion in the West, there will be division and strife in all layers of society, the Imperium insulting the noble, while the noble suppresses the bourgeois, and the bourgeois cheats the commoner. That is the direction in which we are heading, and all evidence that the cycle has turned is speculation, and perhaps nothing more than desire turned to belief. Do you understand what I am saying, Duke?"

"I understand, but—"

"Then consider what it means that I have the power to prevent all of this—that circumstances have worked so that I can prevent great evil—if evil is to come. Or if catastrophe looms—and, Duke, with the anger of the people, the fear of the bourgeois, and the pride of the noble all mixing in the pot which no hand stirs, can you doubt that catastrophe looms?—might this not be the working-out of fate, that I have the chance to prevent it? Could it not be that I am fate's tool in this?"

"Has Your Highness considered," said Aerich slowly, "that your efforts to prevent catastrophe may bring it about? For fate, as Your Highness knows, cannot be denied."

"Fate cannot be denied, but what has ever been accomplished, that is worth the accomplishment, except in spite of or against fate? The struggle is always worthwhile, if the end be worthwhile and the means honorable; foreknowledge of defeat is not sufficient reason to withdraw from the contest. Nevertheless, what you say is true; it may be that the nobler act is to have this power and not use it."

Aerich said, "I think I understand."

Adron nodded. "So, to summarize, if the cycle has turned, the spell will never be used, except insofar as it can be used as a threat—which use is not inconsiderable. But if the cycle has not turned, then I shall not use this spell in any case, unless—"

"Yes, Your Highness? Unless?"

"Unless matters become so desperate that I must *force* it to turn, because one man, Emperor or no, cannot be permitted to cause such destruction as I foresee if it can at all be stopped; and, Duke, I apply this rule to myself as much as to His Majesty—more so, in fact."

"Will Your Highness then allow yourself to be defeated, without using those powers?"

"I will," said Adron, looking steadily at the Lyorn.

"Yet Your Highness will keep this spell in readiness against a circumstance scarcely subject to definition, and which, if it occurs, will cause Your Highness to unleash a spell which might risk the existence of the Orb itself?"

"I will."

"Will Your Highness deign to explain why? For I do not yet understand."

"It is because I fear, Duke. I fear that this Emperor, unable to face the consequences of his actions, and his inactions, will threaten such tyranny that any risk will be justified, and, moreover, he will do so with such strength and determination that great effort will be required to prevent his success. If, at the moment of decision, I have seen no evidence, than I shall not use the spell, even if it means my own death."

"Do you truly think him so evil?"

"I fear he is so weak."

"But who will decide when the petty injustices of a monarch become the evil of a tyrant, or when circumstances have reached the point where such desperate measures are required?"

"I will," said Adron. "I can trust no one else."

Aerich looked at the round, neat, glossy purple stones, and said, "Pride."

Adron looked at him for a long moment, then turned his own eyes to the mosaic. "Perhaps," he said.

These purple stones were also the subject of a brief discussion between Aliera and Sethra, as they rode, knee to knee, toward the Imperial Palace. They had just left the first post-station when Sethra said, "You are aware of the mosaic of purple stones your father has constructed?"

"I am indeed."

"Do you know how they work?"

"I am not unacquainted with elder sorcery."

"Do you know what the spell is intended to do?"

"Yes."

"Very well."

"How, that is all you have to say?"

"Yes. That is all."

They rode at a good speed to the next post-station, where, after exchanging signs with the officer, they were given fresh horses, and so continued.

"Ahead of us," remarked Aliera, "is the Flower Road, though I've never seen any flowers on it. In any case, it leads to the Gate of the Dragon, and so we are nearly there."

"You do not know how the road came to be named?"

"Not the least in the world."

"If you like, I will tell you."

"I should like nothing better."

"Here it is, then."

"I am listening."

"It is said that in the Ninth Reign of the Issola, the War-lord, Markon e'Lanya, had just won a decisive battle upon the Lockhair Plains, through which we have just passed, during the Smallflute Uprising. The people of the village of Lockhair lined this road and covered him with flowers to mark his passage. He slowed down to acknowledge them, which gave other citizens of the region time to gather flowers with which to perform the same courtesy, so that he was addressed in this manner all the way to the gate of Dragaera City, which was, by the way, then named the Dragon Gate in his honor."

"It is a good story."

"Is it not?"

"But I heard you say, 'It is said.' "

"Well, and if I did?"

"It makes me wonder what truth there is in the story."

Sethra smiled. "Very little. In fact, there was a cart of flowers on the road, and, in trying to move it hastily, the owner, a Jhegaala whose home had been saved by Markon's army, tipped it over, and to cover his embarrassment he made some remarks about how honored he was that Markon should ride over the flowers—remarks that would have served better had he not stuttered so horribly in delivering the speech. Still, it is true that Markon did win the battle—and cleverly at that—and that the Dragon Gate was named in his honor. The road did not change its name for some years, until the story had grown enough that even those who had seen the event believed the story rather than their own memories."

Aliera smiled. "He won the battle, you say—and yet, in truth, did he do so without your help?"

Sethra laughed. "Entirely. I was on the other side, though in no important capacity."

"How, you took arms against the Empire?"

"I've taken arms against the Empire, my love, nearly as often as I've taken arms *for* the Empire."

"Well, then, why will you not help my father on this occasion? You could do so, you know. It may be that the Lavodes would decide the issue."

Sethra was silent for some few minutes, then she said, "It is true that I have taken arms against the Empire, but I have never taken arms against the Cycle."

"I do not understand the difference."

"I am not certain I do either, Aliera e'Kieron. Yet I know that, in this case, I cannot but oppose him. If that makes me your enemy, we can now dismount and settle matters, as we have come close to doing so often this last five-day."

Now it was Aliera who fell silent, and so they rode for some distance, until she at last said, "No, for my part, this is no cause to quarrel. When you make a remark that annoys me, or when you laugh at a time that displeases me, or when you give me a look that seems to hide a sneer, then I can fight you, and still might. But I cannot fight when you speak of your duty and your willingness to act in the way that seems right to you. But come, are there not an appalling number of Teckla on the road? What does this mean?"

"They are not only Teckla; I see some bourgeois. It means, I think, that all is far from well in the city—you perceive how many wagons there are? Many of these citizens consider this a good time to be away from the city; and, come, do you think them wrong?"

"Not in the least. Is that not the post-station ahead? The last one, I think, which means that we shall be in the Imperial Palace in an hour, and see what we shall see."

We will allow Sethra and Aliera to continue their ride, while we turn our attention back to Khaavren, who is, just at this moment, arriving at the Palace. We should note that we have no rigorous policy regarding chronology—that is, having decided to relate this history, we have determined to do so in a way that, without ever compromising the truth, makes for as pleasurable an experience for our readers as possible. If, therefore, we are required by the logic of our history to move about in time, well, we are perfectly willing to do so. To the left, however, we must insist that when it happens that events fall out in such a way that we can relate them precisely in the order in which they occurred, nothing in the world will prevent us from doing so.

We have exactly such an occasion here, for Khaavren, upon waking up at his accustomed hour, still felt a certain weakness caused by the blood he had lost, and, moreover, he recalled Navier's orders—yet not his intention to arise early in order to address His Majesty on certain subjects; wherefore he at once went back to sleep.

He awoke a second time some hours later and only then recalled that there was something upon which he ought to speak to His Majesty, and so, hastily throwing on his clothes and buckling on his sword (which Srahi, to her credit, had placed in exactly its proper place, that being on a peg at the top of the stairs), he rushed to the Palace as quickly as he could, not even entering through the Dragon Wing, but, rather, passing directly into the Imperial Wing, where he found His Majesty while the latter was sitting down to break his fast.

His Majesty looked up, and his face glowed with pleasure. "Ah, ah, Captain! You are well, I perceive?"

"Indeed, Sire, though shamefully late, for which I hope Your Majesty can forgive me—I plead my recent wounds as an excuse."

"A worthy excuse, without doubt, good Captain, and you are forgiven."

"Thanks, Sire. But I have not interrupted Your Majesty's breakfast without cause—on the contrary, there are issues that will not wait."

The Emperor, who was eating a smoked fish which had been covered with whipped and fried hen's eggs, put down his utensils, wiped his chin, and said, "Speak, then, for I am listening."

"Your Majesty may remember that I was ordered to arrest Lord Adron, and that, moreover, I was ordered to ensure his safety after his presumed arrest."

"Yes, I remember that, Captain."

"Your Majesty may also remember that I failed to arrest him."

"That is not something I am likely to forget."

"Yes, Sire. Well, Your Majesty must understand that, although I did not arrest him, I did make preparations for ensuring that, if I had, he would remain in captivity."

"Well?"

"Sire, nearly all of my guards are dispersed around the Iorich Wing, and in other key places around the city, and have been on duty with little or no sleep most of a day."

"Then they ought to be recalled, don't you think, Captain?"

"I am entirely in accord with Your Majesty on this point. However—"

"Yes, Captain? However?"

"If Your Majesty is contemplating military action against His Highness—"

"Action you recommended," recalled the Emperor.

"Yes, Sire. If Your Majesty *is* contemplating action of this sort—"

"I am more than contemplating it, Captain, I am resolved upon it."

"Then Your Majesty ought to be aware we are in no position to oppose the riots in the city that must necessarily accompany any such action."

"How, riots?"

"Yes, Sire."

"Among the people?"

"Exactly, Sire."

"Why is this?"

"For several reasons, Sire. First of all, Lord Adron is extremely popular—indeed, the people, and those in the city most of all, perceive him as their protector, because of his daughter's action at the bakery, and because he is the Heir, and Your Majesty is not, at this time, popular with the masses because of the food shortages and the taxes, and—"

"Captain! How could such a state occur and I remain ignorant of it?"

"Sire, it is because some of those with a duty to keep you informed have been assassinated, and others have been distracted, and yet others—by this last, Sire, I mean myself—have been, first busy, and then wounded. This has all happened suddenly, and much of it bears the marks of conspiracy."

The Orb had darkened steadily to the point where Khaavren feared an outburst, but Tortaalik, barely master of the Empire, scarcely master of his house, was able this time to master his emotions. He said, "How much time will be required for you to make arrangements to keep order in the city?"

"A day, Sire. It cannot be done in less time."

"Well, Rollondar will not be setting out after Adron before to-morrow's dawn."

"That is true, Sire, but the army will be gathering, and the army will know why, and so the people will learn why, and, Sire, I cannot be responsible for the next thirty hours if the people learn that Your Majesty intends to send the Imperial Army after His Highness."

The Orb darkened again, and His Majesty glared and said through clenched teeth, "What, then, do you propose, Captain?"

"Sire, Your Majesty must at once cancel the attack on His Highness."

"Cancel it, you say?"

"Yes, Sire."

The Emperor's mouth worked, and he said, "His Highness is a friend of yours, is he not?"

Khaavren bowed and said coolly, "I have the honor of calling him a friend, yes, Sire."

The Emperor met the Captain's gaze, then dropped his eyes. "Very well," he said. "I will suspend the attack until such a time as we believe it to be safe."

"Sire—"

"I will announce to everyone—including Rollondar—that it is to be canceled. But we will maintain the army in the city.

I assume that, should there be disorder, you would have some use for the army?"

"Yes, Sire."

"Then it will be so. And yet, Rollondar said that each day that passes allows Adron to move more horses into position."

"Sire, the Breath of Fire Battalion cannot face all the forces Lord Rollondar commands, however much preparation His Highness has."

"You are certain of this?"

"Entirely, Sire."

"Well then—what is it?"

This last was addressed to a servant who appeared suddenly at the doorway.

"Sire, Sethra Lavode and Aliera e'Kieron beg the honor of an audience with Your Majesty."

The Emperor looked at the Captain, as if expecting an explanation from him, and then looked down at his unfinished breakfast with an expression of distaste, and said, "I shall see them in the Portrait Room."

"Yes, Sire," said the servant.

# Chapter the Twenty-fifth

<hr/>

*Which Treats of Two Very Different Persons,*
*Each of Whom Reveals Plans*
*For the Benefit of a Very Different Audience,*
*And for the Reader.*

HIS MAJESTY ARRIVED IN THE Portrait Room and took his seat (by which, be it clearly understood, we mean the throne, for, insofar as there was a throne in the Imperial Palace, it was the tall, soft, gilded chair which sat at the head of the Portrait Room on a slightly raised dais). Khaavren took his position at the Emperor's elbow, after which His Majesty commanded that the visitors be admitted.

He had arrived, as it happened, only two or three minutes before the time normally set aside for meeting with High Lords and Princes, which allowed him to pretend that he was not, in fact, making an exception to established protocol—it was important to Tortaalik that everything at court appear to proceed normally; that no sign of the turmoil beneath the surface should show in the functioning of the court or in his own countenance. Therefore, when Jurabin entered just before tenth hour was signaled, and glanced in surprise at the already-occupied throne, the Emperor responded by giving him a look of reprobation, as if it were Jurabin who was late rather than himself who was, in fact, early.

Jurabin, detecting this comedy, bowed as if in apology, and took his position behind the throne just as Sethra and Aliera, having been announced, made first their appearance in the Hall, then their way to the throne.

They both executed deep courtesies, as befit nobles come before their Emperor; courtesies which His Majesty graciously acknowledged with lowered head and sweep of hand and which he punctuated with the words, "We welcome you both to our presence, and hope that you have had a journey hither that was neither too tiring nor too difficult, and that, moreover, you will both enjoy your visit to our home and that your errand, if any, will have a satisfactory conclusion."

Sethra, speaking for both, said, "The journey, Sire, was not tiring, and was only difficult when we confronted the throngs at the Dragon Gate itself. Yet, Sire, we came with all speed, and we thank Your Majesty for the alacrity, as well as for the kindness and courtesy, with which we have been received."

"You came, you say, with all speed," said Tortaalik. "From this, then, may we presume that you have an errand to us?"

"We have the honor of coming before Your Majesty with certain proposals," said Sethra. "Proposals to which we humbly beseech Your Majesty to condescend to listen."

"I shall indeed be only too happy to listen to any proposals delivered by two such messengers—one famous through all of history, the other a High Lord of the most esteemed line of the House of the Dragon. But tell us, first—on whose behalf come these proposals?"

As Tortaalik gave this speech, Khaavren, standing in his accustomed place next to and slightly behind the throne, stroked his cheeks with his hand. If, as he suspected, the "proposals" they were about to hear came from Lord Adron, then he might have work to do at once. (We should note, for those who are worried about guardsmen still uselessly on duty, that, as they walked to the hall, Khaavren had written out a note to his corporal, Thack, in which he commanded that the extraordinary forces he had called out be relieved at once.) Aliera, we should note, had still not said a word, but rather had remained mute, and had looked at His Majesty with a gaze that only barely indicated the respect due her Sovereign.

"Sire," said Sethra, "I come on no one's behalf but my own. The Lady Aliera accompanies me from choice, and to indicate support for the proposals I am about to have the honor of laying before Your Majesty."

"Very well," said the Emperor, who seemed to Khaavren a little disappointed with the answer, as if he had expected to hear Adron's name, and had prepared a scathing reply should this name be pronounced. "We are ready to listen; let us hear these proposals. What is it they address?"

"They address many issues, Sire."

"Well?"

"Among them the food shortages in the city, the taxes upon the merchants, the rebellion on the part of His Highness, Adron, the Dragon Heir—"

"Ah!" said Tortaalik. "Pardon me, but I believe you have pronounced the word, rebellion."

"Yes, Sire, that is the very word."

"And you, Lady Aliera—do you also use this word?"

"I do, Sire, for it describes the case admirably. Your Majesty ought to note, however, that in my mind, I do not condemn the act by so naming it, but, rather, I only identify it accurately."

The Emperor looked at her carefully, as if undecided whether to become angry, but the Orb didn't change from its neutral, placid, pale rose, and His Majesty merely said, "Very well, continue."

"Yes, Sire," said Sethra, after a brief glance at her companion.

"I wonder what it is they are doing," said Khaavren to himself. "Have they true proposals, are they about to effect an elaborate insult, or is it part of some deep strategy? And, whatever they think they are doing, how will it be received? Cha! What point speculation? I will find out soon enough, I think."

Sethra continued, saying, "These problems, in addition to those I have already had the honor of enumerating, include the confusion, assassinations, and conspiracies at court which were the reason I was first asked to temporarily forsake my home in exchange for taking up residence in Your Majesty's."

"Very well," said His Majesty. "Those are the problems you wish to address. To be sure, they are no small issues, but, rather, are deep, broad, and powerful. And yet you say you have proposals which will cure all of these ills?"

"To cure all of these ills, Sire, is too much to ask of any-one, or any one idea. Yet I believe that, should Your Majesty take the step I have the honor of suggesting, it will make a good start to finding remedies for them all."

"In that case, I can hardly contain my impatience to learn of what this step consists, and I beg you will do me the honor of informing me this very instant."

"I am about to do so, Sire."

"Well?"

"This is it: I suggest that Your Majesty at once abdicate the throne and give the Orb to the House of the Dragon, accept-ing that the Cycle has turned and the House of the Phoenix has honorably fulfilled its destiny."

His Majesty stared at her, as if unable to believe what he had heard. Meanwhile, Sethra continued speaking as coolly as if she were explaining to His Majesty the best weather in which to hunt the brightbird.

"I have reached agreement with His Highness Lord Adron that, should Your Majesty agree to step down as Emperor, he will at once step down as Dragon Heir, so that no rebel will sit upon the throne, which I know may cause Your Majesty some concern. Moreover—"

*"That will do,"* cried His Majesty. The Orb was a bright, pulsating red—so bright, in fact, that Khaavren found that he was squinting against its glare. The Emperor's hands gripped the ornate gold filigree on the arms of the throne, and Khaavren, though he was behind His Majesty, could imagine the flared nostrils, and the eyes that managed to widen and narrow at the same time.

"You *dare*," said His Majesty. "You dare to suggest that I—that I step down from the throne? That the way to treat with rebels is to give in to their demands? And to give in, moreover, when I have the power to crush them? You dare to suggest that I will be so weak, so cowardly, as to run from the first hint of trouble in the realm? You dare to say that the rebel will be willing—*willing*—to relinquish his claim, when with a single order I can cause him to relinquish his head?"

Sethra remained mute; the Emperor continued.

"And come to that, Sethra Lavode, are you aware that I can perform this same service for you and your companion? What you have suggested amounts to treason—can you give me a reason why you should not both be arrested forthwith?"

Khaavren, standing behind the throne and reckoning that he could, by stripping the Palace of everyone with a guard post and emptying the Sub-wing of the Red Boot Battalion, have produced perhaps a score of guardsmen, could have found several good reasons why Sethra Lavode and Aliera e'Kieron ought not to be arrested just at that moment, but, as he was not asked for his opinion, he did not venture to speak.

Sethra said, "I had expected no other answer from Your Majesty, wherefore I am not disappointed."

"Disappointed? Your disappointment, or lack, is not at issue. The question is whether the two of you are to be arrested."

At this point, Sergeant (who, as we recall, was not, in fact, a sergeant) entered the room looking both nervous and tired (he, as it happened, was one of the unlucky ones who had not yet had a chance to sleep); being on duty, he was able to ignore both protocol and His Majesty, which he did in the course of making his way around the side of the room, clearly intending to speak to Khaavren.

Meanwhile, Sethra said, "That is Your Majesty's decision, and, as Your Majesty has not deigned to listen to my advice on matters of far more importance, well, I shall offer no advice on this question, but, rather, leave it to Your Majesty's best judgment."

As the reader might imagine, this did nothing to calm Tortaalik's temper; he turned to Aliera and said, "Well? And what have you to say, daughter of a rebel?"

Aliera gave him deep courtesy, smiling the while, and said, "I am pleased, Sire, to see everything my father has said confirmed, and to know that I now have an easy conscience regarding the choices he has made. Your Majesty may, of course, arrest whomever Your Majesty wishes to arrest; and, Sire, I am convinced that Your Majesty needs no lesson from me on living with consequences."

As she was speaking, Khaavren had noticed Jurabin, who, in turn, was staring at Aliera in rapt fascination—fascination so obvious that Khaavren became embarrassed for him. He was considering the implications of this unhealthy and possibly dangerous obsession on Jurabin's part when Sergeant reached him, and whispered in his ear, "Captain, there are some nineteen or twenty persons gathered outside the several doors of the hall, all of them wearing black, armed with sword and dagger, and carrying the sort of rods one might associate with wizards. The group seems to be of no one single House, though many of them appear to be Dzurlords, and one or two are without doubt Dragonlords."

"Very well," said Khaavren.

"But, Captain, what shall we do?"

"Nothing," said Khaavren, who understood that, should the Lavodes descend in force to rescue their leader, nothing that the Red Boot Battalion did could make any difference in the fray. He looked at Sethra, speculating.

Sergeant said, "Nothing, Captain?"

"Exactly. Continue with your duties. They will leave presently."

"But, Captain, they have picked up Sethra's weapon, and Aliera's, and seem ready to enter the Hall of Portraits, where weapons are forbidden."

"Should they attempt to enter the room, you will allow them to do so, but, in any case, they will not, I assure you—soon they will put down the weapons they have picked up and walk away, peaceful as monks, silent as Discreets."

"Yes, Captain," whispered Sergeant doubtfully, and went back the way he'd come. Khaavren, meanwhile, was thinking, "If they *do*, in fact, just go away, I shall improve my reputation among my command for wisdom, coolness, and perspicacity; if they do not, then I shall at least have saved the lives of several guardsmen who would have fallen trying to arrest Sethra and Aliera; and for my own task, that of protecting His Majesty, I have, at any rate, the Orb on my side, and that is no ally to take lightly."

As these thoughts were flitting through the Captain's head, the Emperor had been ranting at Aliera—a rant of which Khaavren had perforce missed the bulk, although he did not believe there was likely to have been any vital information contained therein—and he had not yet, in any case, been given the order to make the arrest. Aliera, for her part, appeared to be listening to the Emperor with great attention. His Majesty was saying, "I shall not arrest you now, either one of you; but if you have any wisdom, you will remove yourselves from my presence, from the Palace, and from the city, for I warn you that I am holding my temper in check only with great difficulty, and you have both set your feet upon the road that leads to Justicer's Square."

Aliera said nothing, acknowledging His Majesty's words with only the slightest bow of her head.

Sethra said, "Sire, Your Majesty cannot believe I am frightened, wherefore I am not worried that Your Majesty will take my words in any but the manner in which I mean them: Because Your Majesty has not attempted to have us arrested, and in spite of Your Majesty's attitude toward my suggestion, in the coming confrontation, which my experience tells me will entail the greatest threat to the Cycle and to the Orb our Empire has ever seen, I, as Captain once more, offer the Lavodes to the Empire during the crisis. I do this, not for Your Majesty, but for the Empire; and if Your Majesty believes I make this offer for any reason but conviction that it is in the best interest of the Empire, Your Majesty makes a grave error.

"Sire," she continued, "I shall be remaining here, in the Palace, in those quarters in the Dragon Wing that were lately occupied by Gyorg—should Your Majesty take it in mind to arrest me, well, it is there Your Majesty shall find me. Should

Your Majesty wish to accept my offer, it is still there that Your Majesty shall find me. I leave this choice, with my respects, at Your Majesty's feet."

With this she bowed respectfully, as did Aliera, and they backed away from the throne, still bowing; then, after seventeen steps, they turned and walked coolly together out of the Hall of Portraits.

Khaavren remained where he was, saying nothing. Jurabin, said, "Sire, Your Majesty ought to consider—"

"Keep still, Beespatch," said His Majesty. "I shall ask for your advice when I require it."

Jurabin straightened with a start, started to speak, sputtered, and ended by saying, "Yes, Sire," in a small, choked voice.

At this point, we can almost hear the reader saying to himself, "How, that was it? That was Sethra Lavode's plan, to ask His Majesty to abdicate? Impossible! There was something deeper concealed within that calculating mind, and we shall see, by and by, what it was."

Lest we leave the reader with false expectations, we must, with all the authority of the historian (who is, after all, relating this history, and thus has control of all the knowledge the reader has available, at least during the process of reading), assert that, in fact, there was no deep plan within the mind or heart of the Enchantress; she believed that the Emperor deserved a chance to step down on his own, before he was forcibly removed, which she suspected would happen soon.

But, if she so believed, why did she then give him her loyalty, rather than giving it to Adron? Because it was only a belief—she was in no wise certain that the Cycle had turned. Let those who, even today, pretend expertise on that great wheel of destiny recall that Sethra Lavode, most powerful of wizards, deepest of seers, and wisest of sages, in that great moment of crisis that occurred in the five hundred and thirty-second year of the Eighteenth Reign of the Phoenix, did not know if the Cycle had turned; and, in her doubt (which, in the event, proved well-founded, for, as the historian writes these words, the Eighteenth Reign of the Phoenix has only just come to a close with the peaceful and well-ordered beginning of the Eighteenth Dragon Reign) chose preservation of the Empire over her personal loyalties and the vicissitudes of fortune.

Sethra had made a difficult choice, but she had made it with her eyes open—she would, insofar as she could, work to preserve the Empire and the Cycle, but she would first give His Majesty the chance to step down, knowing that, if he did, it would be proof that the Cycle had turned, and that, if he did not, it would mean either that the Cycle had not turned, or that Adron was right on all counts—His Majesty had overstayed the welcome of the fates, and catastrophe beckoned if he maintained his grip on the Orb. She did not know how she would determine which of these possibilities was true, but she knew that she would know best if she remained near him, which is why, after making her proposal, she then offered the Lavodes to defend his reign.

It had never occurred to her (or, in fact, to anyone else, with the exception of certain mystics to whom no one listened) that, of the two possibilities—the Cycle still pointing to the Phoenix, and Tortaalik guiding the Empire toward disaster—both could be true.

Certainly, this possibility, or, in fact, any of the possibilities, were of no concern to Greycat, who sat in the common room of the cabaret in the Underside where we are accustomed to see him—he was filled only with his own plans and schemes, tending and nurturing them as a deranged gardener might tend and nurse a noxious weed, with no thought of those around him, or of the broader consequence of his actions.

The cabaret was nearly empty, save for a sleeping drunk and the host, both of whom were at the far end; with the house so empty, Greycat saw no reason to use the private room. Dunaan entered, found him at once, and sat beside him.

"Well?" said Greycat. "Does fortune smile upon us?"

"She smiles," said Dunaan. "And she frowns."

"How, at the same time?"

"Yes."

"Fortune has a very flexible countenance."

"That is well known."

"Well, let us hear from fortune, then."

"Do you wish first to know how she smiles, or how she frowns?"

"Tell me first what causes her to smile, which will make her frown the more bearable."

"Very well, this is it:"

"I am listening."

"The assassin is recruited, is ready, and awaits but your word to strike."

"Excellent. You answer for him?"

"He is skilled, brave, and too trusting—he will do all you wish."

"Excellent. Well, then, it but remains to let me know in what way fortune frowns on our endeavors."

"It is quickly done; two words will inform you."

"Let us have them."

"Laral has failed in her mission."

"How, Laral has failed?"

"Exactly."

"Was she caught?"

"She was killed."

"By the Captain?"

"No, as far as I can learn, by nearly everyone in the city except the Captain."

After a moment's consideration, Greycat said, "What of her body? For he was able to learn far, far, too much from Chalar, and could learn, perhaps, even more from Laral."

"He will learn nothing from Laral. Her body was left on the street, and is now gone."

"That is something, then."

"I hope so."

"But, Dunaan, what happened? How did she fail?"

"She trusted her spells against a sorcerer and her blade against a swordsman, while trusting her sense of timing against that of a very punctual lackey."

"You observed all of this?"

"I observed the scene after it was over, and I questioned those who lived nearby and heard the sounds, and I spoke with those in the Palace who knew what had become of Khaavren and who, for various reasons, will speak with me."

"Well, but Dunaan, you should know that Khaavren, if not dead, is, at least, wounded."

"So I learned from my friends in the Palace. Who wounded him? It could not have been Laral."

"No, another performed that service for us."

"Ah, another. Who?"

"Soldiers of His Highness, Adron." Greycat smiled, as if he thought this a great jest.

Dunaan, who rarely jested, gave a slow nod and said, "What then?"

"When can your assassin act?"

"At once, if you so decide."

"At once, meaning—"

"He will be in place within an hour, and will strike—if we may call it that—on this very evening."

Greycat nodded, considering. "Everything seems to be working in our favor," he said, as if to himself. "The Emperor could not be doing a better job if he were part of our plan, and the same is true of Adron—indeed, I believe this is working better than if we had succeeded in killing him. And the decision to leave Jurabin in place has also proven a good one—Aliera's arrival at court has rendered him entirely useless. The only problem is—"

"Yes. The Tiassa, Lord Khaavren. You ought to have let me solve that problem myself."

"Well," said Greycat. "If you wish—"

"Of course," said Dunaan.

"Yet, he is now alerted."

"That is of no consequence."

"Very well. And your pay will be what I paid Laral. There is, fortunately, no lack of funds."

"That will be satisfactory."

"And, as for your assassin, you may tell him to be about his task, for nothing else is needed."

Dunaan nodded, but, instead of rising at once to his feet, he remained where he was, contemplating the nail of his right thumb as it rested on the table. After allowing the Jhereg a few moments for this contemplation, Greycat came to the conclusion that there was, in fact, nothing inherently interesting about the nail, but, rather, Dunaan had something on his mind which prevented his directly being about his business, wherefore he, by which we mean Greycat, said, "Come, is there something about which you have some questions? If so, you need but ask, and I will do all I can to answer you."

"You have," said Dunaan, "spoken of all the factors aligning themselves in our favor."

"Well, that is true, I have said that. What of it?"

"Those factors you have outlined speak of an Empire in turmoil and a court in confusion."

"That is very well expressed," said Greycat. " 'An Empire in turmoil and a court in confusion.' Yes, they speak of these things—they even shout of them, so that one must be deaf not to hear."

"I am not deaf," said Dunaan, "and I hear."

"And then?"

"Your plan is to present to His Majesty solutions to these problems, with the aim of being placed into a powerful position at court."

"That is exactly it. Do you see a weakness in the plan?"

"I see one way in which it might fail, and yet another way in which, even if it does not, there may be some cause to worry."

"Let me then hear these ideas, and I will answer them if I can, and if I cannot, then we will consider what is to be done."

"I ask for nothing else."

"Then I am listening."

"In the first place, will your ideas on how to solve the problems facing the Empire convince His Majesty?"

"That is one question, and it is a good one. What is the next?"

"If they serve to convince His Majesty, and they are then put into practice, will they, in fact, solve the problems? And if they do not, will you not be dismissed as easily as you were accepted, and, moreover, must you not suffer, as everyone else, from the disruptions in the Empire and the court?"

"That is another good question."

"I am pleased you think so. Can you answer them?"

"To answer them requires that I reveal my plan for solving the problems of the Empire."

"And are you willing to do so?"

"To you, Dunaan, I am, for your cooperation is important, and you must be convinced that I know what I am about, both now, and after the plan has succeeded."

"Very well, then, if you will tell me, I am listening."

"In the first place, we need not worry about His Highness."

"How, we need not?"

"No, for the Imperial Army will remove him handily. He has made himself a rebel, for which he deserves our thanks. Nothing more need be said."

"Very well," said Dunaan after some consideration. "I agree about His Highness. But what of the disorder in the streets?"

"His Majesty will not see this as a problem, because His Majesty thinks of the populace as mindless rabble, and cannot believe there is any threat from them."

"Well, you may be right about His Majesty. But you and I, my friend, know this is not the case. How, then, do you propose to solve it?"

"I have, in the first place, certain connections among the people, which can do no harm. In the second, I have a force at my command which will, when added to the Imperial Guard, know how to deal with 'rabble.' In the third, where there is an uprising, there are leaders. Where there are leaders, there are weaknesses—with your help, and that of your friends, my dear Jhereg, we will subvert whom we can and kill whom we cannot subvert."

Dunaan nodded slowly. "Yes, that will work—if you have, indeed, these forces of which you speak."

"I have sent for them, and they are even now making their way to the city."

"Very well. But what of the disruptions at court?"

"If I have His Majesty's ear, half of these disruptions can be solved with dismissals."

"Well, and the other half?"

"For the other half, the Emperor's ear will not serve—but the Consort's bed will."

Dunaan stared. "How, you think—"

"There are pressures, my dear Jhereg, of which you have no idea. But I know things about the Consort which will have her doing what I wish her to do—in all matters. You need have no fear of a disturbed court, my dear Dunaan."

Dunaan swallowed carefully, as if this idea shocked him—hardened killer that he was. But he said, "But what, then, of the Meeting of Principalities and the Imperial Allottment, which I assure you has His Majesty more worried than anything except, perhaps, the rebellious Prince?"

"I shall have an answer to make him on that score at once, my dear Jhereg—indeed, I count upon this answer, more than anything else, to secure for me the post I seek."

"Tell of what this answer shall consist, for you perceive I am most anxious to learn."

"This is it: I will tell him I have arranged an agreement between the House of the Jhereg, the House of the Dragon, and the House of the Dzur, whereby they agree to pay the bulk of the assessment; with this done, the others Houses can hardly fail to agree, don't you think?"

Dunaan shook his head. "It is a pretty story, but what makes you think His Majesty will believe it? I, for one, assure you that it sounds entirely unconvincing to me."

"Does it?" said Greycat with a smile. "That is odd, my friend, for it is true—or, rather, it will be true before two days have gone by."

"Impossible!" cried Dunaan so loudly the host turned to look at the two gentlemen in the corner who had hitherto been so quiet. Dunaan glared at him, and he quickly returned to wiping mugs with a dirty towel. "Impossible," repeated Dunaan in a softer voice.

"Not in the least," said Greycat with utmost calm.

"How, the Dragon come to an agreement with the Jhereg? The Jhereg with the Dzur? The Dzur with the Dragon? Any two of these seem impossible—how will you manage all three?"

"I am not inexperienced as a diplomatist, though this may startle you."

"Well, so you are experienced. Nevertheless—"

"Attend me."

"I am attending."

"We conclude the arrangement with the House of the Dragon in the simplest way—we tell them that, far from needing to pay anything into the Imperial Treasury, they will be sent to attack the Pepperfields, and will, furthermore, use it as a staging point for an invasion of the East, in which they may keep whatever they wish."

"Bah! We have an agreement with the Easterners over the Pepperfields."

"A score of generations of Easterners have lived and died since that agreement was made—they will not remember it."

"But His Majesty will."

"His Majesty will not be told until it is too late—he will be presented with the agreement among the Houses, and that will be that."

"I would assume," said Dunaan, who did not yet appear convinced, "that you will require something of the House of the Dragon in exchange for this service you will be rendering them?"

"Oh, yes, indeed," said Greycat. "The House of the Dragon will aid the Imperial Army in putting down the rebel, Adron, and selecting a new Heir; as well, of course, as agreeing to the proposals put forward by the Jhereg and the Dzur, who between them will be paying the bulk of the allotment— the House of the Dragon will agree."

Dunaan nodded slowly. "Very well. But what of the House of the Dzur?"

"They will agree to anything I say."

"How is that?"

"Do you know who Princess Sennya is?"

"Of course: the Duchess of Blackbirdriver, Dzur Heir to the Throne."

"Then you know she has not appeared."

"Many delegates have not appeared."

"In her case, it is by my orders."

"How, your orders?"

"Exactly."

"You give orders to the Dzur Heir?"

Greycat nodded.

"How can this be?"

"Does it matter? She'll do what she is told, and she will be told to support our bargain."

"Yet, I cannot believe—"

"Pah! It is easy to control a Dzurlord—no one is more sensitive to appearances; threaten to publicly shame one and he is yours."

Again, Dunaan nodded. "Well, I am convinced about the Dragons, and even the Dzur. But I will not believe you have a hold over the House of the Jhereg, my friend."

"The House of the Jhereg, as you know better than I, is a fiction. That group of entrepreneurs of which you are a member controls the House, and runs it like a business."

"Well? What of it?"

"Through you, my friend, I shall make the Jhereg a business proposal."

"Well, let us see; but I warn you, it will have to be a good one."

"It is."

"I am listening."

"And remember, there is no need for His Majesty to ever learn the details of our transaction—he need only see the documents which attest to the agreement among the Houses."

"Yes, but if you have any illusions of cheating the Jhereg—"

"I assure you, I do not. I will make a bargain, and hold to it—the more so because I know what will become of me if I do not."

"Very well, then, let us hear this proposal."

"We find a pretext—"

"A pretext is easily found. What sort of pretext?"

"What does it matter? Some popular and innocent person will die accidentally—"

"How, accidentally?"

"Yes. Perhaps a Dragonlord. Aliera might do, if she survives the coming events. Or Tuorli, if she does not become Heir—perhaps even if she does; she is popular."

"Well, then, an innocent dies accidentally."

"Yes, from a mishap caused by dreamgrass."

"These things happen," said Dunaan.

"Yes. It clouds the perceptions, and causes accidents. We have all seen it any number of times. Perhaps a fall from a tower, or during a swim—"

"This can be arranged. Yet I do not—"

"There will be great sorrow at the loss of this person, who was so popular."

"Very well."

"I will direct this sorrow through the same means I will be using to help put down the riot, and I will turn this sorrow into outrage."

"How, outrage? At whom?"

"Not whom, my friend—what."

"At—?"

"Dreamgrass."

"Outrage at dreamgrass?"

"Exactly."

"But I do not see—"

"With pressure from the masses, and from me, and from the Consort, we will then prevail upon His Majesty to pass edicts forbidding the growth, sale, or use of dreamgrass anywhere in the Empire."

Dunaan stared at him, his eyes growing wider. Eventually, when he spoke, it was in a whisper. "The prices . . ."

"Indeed. And, not only the prices, but consider that all of the honest merchants who sell it will be forced into other lines of work, so that—"

"Yes! Only the Jhereg will be selling it!"

"Exactly. And, of course, we need not stop with dreamgrass. There is freeze-powder—"

"Leads to public brawling."

"—murchin—"

"Highly addictive, eventually fatal."

"—luck drops—"

"A fire hazard in the preparation."

"—wine—"

"Clouds judgment."

"—bear's teeth—"

"Causes madness. The Gods, my friend! That such a thing should never have occurred to us!"

"Well, can you answer for the approval of the Jhereg?"

"Answer for it? I nearly think I can!"

"Well, then, you know the entirety of my scheme; what do you think of it?"

Dunaan, his eyes dripping gold, said, "It is an excellent plan; I've never heard a better."

"Well then, nothing more need be said. Commence the entertainment we have arranged for His Majesty, dispatch our annoying Tiassa, then make contact with those in the Jhereg with whom we must treat."

"Yes, yes," said Dunaan, speaking as if in a dream. "The Emperor, the Tiassa, the Jhereg."

"Exactly. I will see you soon."

Dunaan stood up, still appearing to be in a daze, and walked out of the cabaret without another word. When he had gone, Greycat stood and retired to the private room, where he sat down and said, "Well?"

"I heard," said Grita from the shadows.

"And?"

"There are times when I am ashamed to know you."

"How, you refer to my plan to appease the Jhereg?"

"No."

"Then you refer—"

"Yes."

"I had not known you cared."

"I do not."

"Well, then?"

"Nevertheless, that you would use—"

"I have not asked for your opinion."

Grita laughed—a laugh in which there was little humor, and no humanity—and stepped out of the shadows. The two of them looked at each other, as opposing commanders will study each other for weaknesses. At last, by some means which would have been unfathomable to anyone else, they seemed to agree that the contest, if so it was, could be ended without resolution.

Grita spoke as if nothing had passed between them, saying, "I attempted to carry out the mission you assigned me."

"And?"

"I was able to gain entrance, but the battalion moved out before I could strike, and I was unable to match their pace. Therefore I returned, and, from what I have just heard, you are even pleased that Adron still lives."

"It is true, I am."

"I did learn something, however."

"Oh, and what is that?"

"He has a guest."

"That being?"

"The Duke of Arylle."

Greycat's eyes narrowed, and he said, "Indeed. You saw him?"

"With these eyes."

"Well, well." He paused to consider, then said, "I do not see that this changes anything—on the contrary, it may simplify certain matters in the future. But for now, though it is good to know, there is nothing that needs to be done as far as Adron or his guest are concerned."

"Well, what then?"

"Can you arrange another riot for the evening of the day after to-morrow?"

"Perhaps."

"How, perhaps?"

"It may be that I can."

"And yet, on the last occasion, there was no uncertainty."

"That was before."

"Something has, then, changed?"

"You are perspicacious."

"Your irony is useless. What has changed?"

"Before it was a question of starting a riot at a certain time—now it is a question of preventing an uprising from breaking out beforehand."

"I see. Then you think—"

"The entire city but awaits a spark, and who knows when it will come?"

"Hmmm. Well then, if it comes early, so much the better. If nothing has happened before the time I have named—"

"Then I shall provide the spark."

"Excellent. Then, I believe, there is nothing more to be said."

"On the contrary," said Grita. "There is a great deal to be said, but I do not believe we will say any of it. I have no wish to, at all events. Have you?"

By way of answering her, Greycat stood and walked out of the room and out of the cabaret, where he studied the street and the faces that seemed, for a moment, to float above it, unattached to any bodies. He watched the crowds, who seemed to be running about faster and in greater numbers even than usual. After a moment, he realized that many of these were people who had chosen this moment to take a journey away from the city, as if afraid what they might find if they woke up here to-morrow. Yes, Grita might very well be right, he decided. It could be that the city was close to detonating—he could almost see it himself.

But that was of no moment; indeed, it might work to his advantage; everything appeared to be working to his advantage. He permitted himself a small chuckle and walked easily about the Underside, which had almost become home to him; he wondered if he would miss it after he began dwelling in the Imperial Palace.

# Chapter the Twenty-sixth

═══◆═══    ═══◆═══

*Which Treats of Dzurlords.*

S O THIS, THEN, WAS HOW matters stood at the Imperial
Palace: Sethra returned to the Dragon Wing to take possession of the chambers left vacant by Gyorg Lavode;
Aliera accompanied her. His Majesty, still seething, sat upon
his throne biting his lips until they bled and waiting for the
hour of relaxation, which would allow him a certain respite—
which hour, we should add, had still some few minutes before
it began. Khaavren stood at His Majesty's elbow, considering
the several problems that faced him, with the disharmony in
the city, the rebellion of Adron, and the evident conspiracies
within and around the court. Jurabin stood on the other side
of the throne, unable to speak, and wishing desperately for a
pretext to leave. Unfortunately for the Prime Minister, he was
stuck in his spot as thoroughly as a jhegaala in a chreotha's
net—as, in fact, were His Majesty, Khaavren, and those few
courtiers who had chosen to make an appearance in the Portrait Room that day.

It could not but be a trial for the reader to sit with these
persons until the longed-for stroke of the bell should signal

that all present might take their ease; we shall, therefore, leave them, confident that they will be doing nothing that could excite our interest; instead we will follow Sethra and Aliera through the Dragon Wing and toward the room where Sethra had chosen to take her quarters. They had not, in fact, gone far into the wing when they saw two familiar figures coming the other way and perforce stopped to greet them.

In order to explain how these figures, who were none other than Pel and Tazendra, came to be at the Palace at that time, we must go backward in time a few hours, trusting the reader to recall the warning we have just recently advanced regarding our willingness to engage in such time-hopping whenever the appropriate occasion shall arise.

Tazendra, then, upon rising, had been rather surprised to discover that Khaavren was not at home. Upon questioning Srahi (who resented the questioning, but submitted to it under urging from Mica) she learned that the Tiassa, when he had appeared an hour ago, had seemed to be in a great hurry, and had rushed out the door, yelling for a coach.

"I am pleased, at any rate, that he took a coach," said Tazendra.

"And yet he was rushing," said Pel.

"What of it?" said Tazendra. "He has duties. You remember that he mentioned last night——"

"I remember that he said he would arise early and leave for the Palace."

"Well?"

"Well, he did not, as it happened, leave early, but rather late; which indicates that he still felt some fatigue. In truth, I did not think he would leave at all——I had thought he would be overcome by his wounds, and must therefore sleep."

"Bah! And yet you have known him these five hundred years."

"That is true."

"I do not see any reason to worry."

"And yet, he has been wounded."

"Well, that is true, he has been wounded."

"I am worried about him."

"Bah! You were worried yester-day."

"Well, and was I wrong to be?"

"Come to think of it, Pel, you were not. Do you fear another attack?"

"Not so soon, I think. But, considering his health, I should be glad to see him, and glad, too, to return to the Palace and learn what is afoot there."

"And, no doubt, to return to your normal attire."

"Bah, as you would say. I find I am well suited to the garb I am now affecting. The robes of a Discreet are too constricting in their looseness; I prefer something that binds tighter in its freedom. And besides, why listen to another's gossip, when one can become gossip?"

"I do not comprehend—"

"It is unimportant, my dear Tazendra. I was speaking in hyperbole."

"Ah! Well, that explains it, for I have never had a head for foreign tongues."

"But you agree, at any rate, that we ought to check on our friend?"

"Oh, entirely. But what of the Countess?" The Countess, we ought to add, had not yet risen.

"What of her?"

"Might she also wish to know what has become of Khaavren? Perhaps you did not notice—"

"I noticed, my dear Tazendra."

"Well, then—"

"You must know, however, that she is banned from the Palace."

"How, banned from the Palace? I've never heard of such a thing! Oh, do you mean barred from the Imperial Wing? For, if so—"

"No, I mean, in fact, that she has been exiled from the city."

"How, exiled from the city? Impossible!"

"Not in the least."

"Why was she exiled?"

"She was one of Her Majesty's maids of honor, and quarreled with her mistress over some issue or another."

"Come, how can you know all of this?"

"Tazendra, you know that I hear many things."

"Well, that is true."

"Then believe me."

"Very well, I believe you."

"We will, in any case, write her a note in which we will explain that we have gone off to visit Khaavren, which will ease her mind."

"You are very thoughtful," said Tazendra.

"Then let us be off, my good friend, for time waits for no one."

After this profound reckoning, then, Pel wrote a carefully worded note for Daro which he entrusted to Srahi's care, after which he and Tazendra walked out to the Street of the Dragon, hailed a coach which happened to be passing by, and directed the coachman to bring them to the Dragon Wing, where they expected to find Khaavren in his offices and where they could, therefore, reassure themselves as to the state of his health.

The coach delivered them to the Sub-wing of the Imperial Guard, where they were admitted at once upon claiming business with the Captain, but they discovered, to their surprise, that not only was Khaavren absent, but he had not yet been seen that morning. As the reader can imagine, this filled our friends with worry, although the reader is well aware that Khaavren is entirely safe, and standing comfortably, if nervously, at the elbow of His Majesty.

"Where can he have gone?" said Tazendra as they stood in the hall once more.

"Perhaps," said Pel, "his business did not take him to the Palace. Or perhaps it took him directly to His Majesty."

"Well, then, what should we do?"

"It would seem to me," said Pel, "that if we were to go to the Imperial Wing, we might inquire of the guardsmen on duty if they have seen their Captain, and we should be almost assured of an answer, for there cannot be any reason for them to dissemble to us."

"Well thought, my dear friend," said Tazendra.

Without another word, then, they set off for the Imperial Wing, and had nearly reached it when they were confronted by two familiar figures—which familiar figure of speech ought to alert the reader that we are now, albeit from the opposite direction, returned to the very time and place from which we departed when we left Sethra and Aliera.

"Well met," said Sethra, bowing, "clever Pel and brave Tazendra."

"And well met to you," said Pel, returning her courtesy, "wise Sethra and noble Aliera."

Tazendra and Aliera also added their own greetings, and they spent a few moments in polite conversation, discussing the exodus from the city and other such matters, until Pel, who had not for an instant forgotten his mission, said, "You appear to have come from the Imperial Wing."

"Well, that is true."

"Have you, then, seen our dear Khaavren? He has been wounded, you know, and we are concerned for him."

"Khaavren, wounded?" said Sethra.

"Indeed," said Aliera, "he was there with His Majesty, with whom we have just concluded a visit, but the Captain seemed entirely healthy so far as we could see."

"So much the better," said Tazendra.

"How did he come to be wounded?" said Sethra. "Has there been another attempt on his life?"

"That is to say, yes and no," said Tazendra.

"How, yes and no?" said Sethra.

"There was an attempt on his life," said Pel.

"But that is not how he came to be wounded," added Tazendra.

"It would seem," said Aliera, "that there is a tale to be told."

"Indeed," said Pel. "And one that, in fact, I am surprised that you do not know, for, at the time he was wounded, you could not have been two steps away."

"I?" said Aliera.

"Indeed," said Pel.

"Is there a hint of reprobation in your words, my good Discreet?"

"Not in the least," said Pel. "If you would hear all of the details, you may come with me while I look in on my friend Khaavren, and I will explain it to you—I give you my word that I hold you blameless in the affair."

"I should like nothing better," said Aliera, a certain tension going out of her voice. "But I have just seen Khaavren in the audience chamber with His Majesty, and I should not care to make another appearance there—if for no other reason," she added, laughing slightly, "because it would soften the impact of a truly grand exit." She bowed to Sethra as she made this remark, then added, "I will, however, walk with you as far as the doors, if you will have it so, and listen to your story—and then I can tell you of our interview with His Majesty, which I promise will amuse you."

"Nothing would please me more," said the Yendi.

"Sethra, I shall meet up with you later, no doubt, either in your new quarters, or elsewhere."

"Very well," said Sethra. "If you, my dear Dzur, would be so good as to accompany me, perhaps you could inform me of these circumstances even as Pel is explaining to Aliera."

"I will do my best," said Tazendra, who was, in fact, doing her best not to be intimidated at the thought of a one-to-one conversation with the Enchantress of Dzur Mountain. "Although I am not good at explanations."

"I am certain that we will get along together splendidly," said Sethra.

"Come then," said Aliera, taking Pel's arm. "Sethra and Tazendra, until later."

"Until later," said Tazendra and Sethra.

In the event, it took Tazendra very little time to explain, with the help of Sethra's astute and precise questions, what had befallen Khaavren. Sethra appeared to be saddened by the events, but before she had a chance to make any comment, if indeed, there were a comment on her mind, they had reached the third-floor room where Gyorg Lavode had had his quarters. The first thing Sethra did upon opening the door was to stop on the threshold and slowly exhale.

Tazendra said carefully, "Had you thought it would already have been emptied of his possessions?"

"No," said Sethra in an unnaturally harsh voice. "I had thought that I would not mind so much." She entered the room; Tazendra held back for a moment out of respect either for Sethra's feelings or for the dead man she had not known. Sethra did not speak, but rather looked around the room, carefully studying the decorations, possessions, and artifacts that had remained undisturbed since his death.

Tazendra cleared her throat and, said, "My lady, would you like to tell me about him?"

Sethra turned and studied the Dzurlord, noting the discomfort on her countenance, and noting as well the sympathy that lay beneath it. "No," said Sethra. "Come, you tell me about him."

Tazendra opened her mouth, closed it, and said, "My lady, comprehension is not—"

"There has never been a stupid sorcerer who has lived past his five hundredth year. Come in."

Tazendra obediently stepped into the room, where she said, "I don't—"

"Look," said Sethra with an intensity that Tazendra found surprising, intriguing, and even disturbing. "Look about you," she said. "Who was he?"

Tazendra gave a bemused glance about the room, filled as it was with various articles of black clothing in discreet piles as if plugging up holes in the floor; occasional works of art depicting outdoor scenes and done in soft colors; scribbled notes stuck up on walls with such notations as, "too far frwrd mks r slid off end," or, "12 factd crstl not engh, try 16 and cvr w/gel—WATCH FOR FLASH!!!" three potted plants near the window, all of which seemed to have been dead for years; and a disheveled bed with pale yellow sheets which were still stained with blood. Once again she started to speak, stopped, and instead walked slowly through the chamber, occasionally stopping to look more closely at something that caught her eye.

Presently, Tazendra realized that she was crying.

"What is it?" Sethra asked softly.

Despite her tears, Tazendra spoke in an even, unbroken voice. "It is the watering pail beside the flowerpots."

"What of it?"

"There is still water in it, yet the plants—"

"Yes," said Sethra Lavode. "What else?"

Tazendra gestured with her chin toward the bedside table, upon which rested a notepad, quill, ink, and blotter; on the notebook were scrawled several lines, unevenly, as if written when coming out of sleep. "He was not . . ."

"That is true," said Sethra. "He was not a skilled poet. What else?"

"Who is Diess?"

"A lady who occupied his thoughts for some years. Does the poem mention her?"

"No, no. But there is a note from her glued to the lamp near his bed."

"Yes, I see it. What does it say?"

"That she values his friendship."

"Ah. Which means, of course, not his love."

"So I would take it. And yet—"

"And yet it is glued to the lamp by his bed."

"What else?"

Tazendra pointed to a grey chair in the corner, a stuffed chair that seemed to be falling apart; one leg was missing and was propped up by books, while the stuffing on one side had burst from its bounds and the headrest was loose on the other side. "That is where he would sit betimes," she said, "and look at that picture," here she pointed to the opposite wall, "and contemplate the ruined side of the castle, and how he would someday repair it, for," she indicated the painting again, "that cannot be other than his home, and," here she indicated a whetstone by the side of the chair, "he would, I am convinced, sharpen his sword as he did so. I believe it must have been a form of meditation; I, myself—" she broke off abruptly, and blushed.

"Of course," said Sethra. "You are a Dzurlord, as was he. To the Dzur, there is a ritual to the sharpening of the sword—so warlike and yet so soothing; a preparation for the future, a defiance, a threat, and, at the same time, it is rhythmical, and, while so engaged, one is given to dream, and to think about the blade, its history and destiny; and to contemplate and wonder, above all, for what one strives—and always one finds answers to this question, for finding those answers is what it means to be a Dzur.

"Sometimes," she continued softly, staring at the painting which Gyorg must have himself spent so much time gazing upon, "those of other Houses laugh, or call the Dzur foolish, stupid, or blind, and there is no good answer to such charges, for to kill for such an insult is often beneath the Dzurlord; yet there is always the sword, whose sharpening breathes of the future, and the glory which is not only in being remembered, but in knowing one has defied the entire world, and pitted one's self against the impossible, and proven, to all who are not Dzur, that there is value and glory in the battle, regardless of the outcome. All of these thoughts come to mind when the Dzurlord sharpens his sword, and looks upon some token of the past until he can feel the wind that blows to the future."

For some time, it had seemed as if Sethra were speaking to herself, but at last she fell silent. "You understand," said Tazendra in a whisper.

"I have lived a long time, comrade," said Sethra, smiling. "And moreover, he was my friend; he said to me things a Dzurlord would not ordinarily tell someone of another House."

"I believe that," said Tazendra, looking upon the Enchantress of Dzur Mountain as if for the first time. "Yes, I believe that he would."

Tazendra paused, then, and, after a moment, she said, "I'm sorry I didn't know him."

"Yes," said Sethra. "You would have liked him. Come. I have seen what I came to see, and must now have the servants pack away his belongings, which his kin may want. Then I will have the room cleaned, and fresh bedding put in, after which I shall take up residence, and remember him when I go to take my rest. We shall find the servants, then see if we can rejoin our friends, who are no doubt in the Imperial Wing with the good Lord Khaavren."

"My lady," said Tazendra, bowing toward the door.

"My lady," said Sethra, also bowing toward the door.

Tazendra went out first, and they walked down the hallway together, even as, not far away, the assassin, Mario, set foot in the Imperial Wing of the Palace.

# Chapter the Twenty-seventh

*Which Treats of Regicide,
For the First, But Not the Last Time.*

SHOULD ONE TAKE THE TIME to look at Volume Four of Dentrub's *Imperial Wing of the Old Palace*, one would learn that there were ninety-one entrances to the wing; and for each of them one will find cataloged its location, size, function, uses, and history. If, instead, one should peruse Burrin's *Overview of the Architecture of the Old Imperial Palace*, one will find reference, in the third chapter of volume eight, to "The ninety-four entrances to the Imperial Wing," although only a few of these are discussed in detail. Kairu, to pick still another example, in the sixth volume of his *History of Doors and Windows*, which can be found in manuscript in the Vallista Library of the Imperial Palace, points to no fewer than one hundred and six doors into the Imperial Wing, and, indeed, describes each one with the passion of a connoisseur.

We need not worry about the precise number for two reasons: First, because G'aereth, in certain letters, makes reference to the need to guard six different means of approach from the outside world to the areas where His Majesty might, at different times of the day, be found, and this is the number in which we are interested; and second, because we know how Mario entered, and that is what is most important to our history.

It is worth noting that, in fact, it would have been absurdly easy for Mario to have gained entrance on that day because of the condition of the Guard—Khaavren's command were tired to a man, and any number of ruses, tricks, or bluffs would have sufficed to get past them. Yet Mario, in formulating his plan, had not known of this circumstance, and when he learned of it he did not choose to deviate from his intentions. Therefore, some three hours before noon, he arrived at the main entrance to the Imperial Wing dressed in a dirty brown woolen tunic, loose pantaloons that smelled of offal, plain boots, a sort of cap, and even a pack over his shoulder; and, in this garb, looking as if making the request took all of his courage, he demanded to see His Majesty. The guard on duty, though tired, out of sorts, and disposed to send the beggar on his way with a beating, knew perfectly well that this beggar was within his rights, and knew, furthermore, how the Captain felt about guardsmen administering casual beatings; therefore he gave the clapper the particular pull associated with this request—a request which had been used to occur some two or three times a month, but which had lately become a daily event.

"Someone will be with you in a moment," said the guard.

"Thank you, my lord," said Mario in a tone of great humility.

Soon, there appeared a minor functionary named Dinb, who held the position called, "Master of the First Gate," and whose task, among other things, was to admit those of the lower classes who wished to exercise their right to an audience with His Majesty, and attempt to discourage them. It must be denied in the most emphatic terms that Teckla were beaten, as many claimed was the case; there has never been a good reason to believe such tales, and every reason to believe that beatings were, in fact, unnecessary—the methods actually used were sufficient to discourage nearly all of those who appeared, and if His Majesty had to face the one or two

Teckla or tradesmen in a year who were able to pass through all of the intimidation, well, this was not considered too irksome by those who determined who would and who would not have the privilege of a face-to-face meeting with the Emperor.

Dinb was well-suited to the task, both physically and, if we may be permitted the expression, spiritually; he was a burly Iorich, with the rippling muscles of his upper arms visible through the thin blouses he affected, and a large head of curly light brown hair which concealed his noble's point as well as concealing most of his forehead, but left revealed his cold, dark eyes. He had previously been employed by the notorious publisher, Lord F——, in the task of meeting with authors and answering any questions they might have of His Lordship concerning publication schedules and payments. In spite of his imposing looks, and his ability to assume a threatening demeanor, he was in fact a cold, emotionless man who, with the exception of certain fishes he kept in a glass bowl in his chambers and to whom he spoke often and at great length, was not known to have any affection for or interest in anything except his duty, which he pursued with an uninspired rigor.

He escorted Mario to the room which had been set aside for this purpose—a very large, imposing room with no furniture at all, and decorated only with oils depicting prisoners in chains, prisoners being executed, and His Majesty looking entirely regal. Here, as was his custom, Dinb asked the supplicant his business, and, upon being informed that it was His Majesty's ear that was sought, proceeded to lecture the visitor about the importance of His Majesty's time and the vital nature of the matters with which His Majesty was currently contending. After this he added, in a tone suggesting that he was revealing secrets, that His Majesty was not well-disposed to anyone to-day; that a previous visitor, who had slipped on a minor point of court etiquette, had been hauled off at once to the Justicers; and that another day would certainly be preferable.

Should the supplicant, though by this time undoubtedly

displaying signs of fear, insist that he was adamant about seeing His Majesty to-day, Dinb would turn his palms up as if to say that he acquitted his conscience in advance, and then would proceed to inform the supplicant in gruesome detail of the search of his person that would necessarily take place to insure His Majesty's safety, and that the supplicant would be summoned when it was time. After this, Dinb would walk out of the room by the great double doors that, Dinb implied, would lead to His Majesty. The other door, the small, friendly door through which the supplicant had arrived, would remain invitingly open, and it was the rare Teckla who would not slink away during the three- or four-hour wait that invariably followed.

We should note that there were other means of handling those who did wait, and that the road to see His Majesty was by no means as simple as we have implied (or, in fact, as the law required), but we shall have no cause to follow these procedures any further, for Mario did what was expected—he slipped out of the door he had entered by, which put him, all alone, in a short, narrow hallway which let out into the anteroom where Dinb had first appeared, and where a guard still waited. This hallway, we should add, had no features except doorways on either end, and a window high on either side.

Mario, now that he was alone and unobserved, wasted no time in scaling the wall with the help of certain hooks that he fastened to the wall and ropes with which he scaled it—the reader ought to understand that he had carried these in his satchel, from which the reader may correctly deduce that Mario knew exactly what he was doing, and had planned out every step. Once he reached the top of the wall, Mario pried open one of the windows to which we have just alluded and slipped through it, thus landing in a small, rarely used garden that was entirely enclosed by the Imperial Wing, and was, in addition, completely unguarded. He contrived to remove his hooks and to close the window—no simple task in that it had to be done quickly while he perched atop a wall—and then dropped down to the garden.

He hastened, then, to divest himself of his too-conspicuous

clothing, leaving only plain, tight-fitting garments of black and grey and a leather harness about which were hung the weapons and tools of his trade, all of which he had carried in his satchel. The satchel now being empty, he concealed it, along with his discarded clothing, behind a heart-pear bush. He then checked the time, and having discovered that he was nearly a minute early, he waited where he was, moving no more than one of the statues that dotted the garden, until the minute had passed, after which he made his way along the wall, keeping to the shadows, until, after having turned a corner to his left, he reached the third window, which, being opened, admitted him to an old room that Tortaalik had turned into a clothes-closet, and which contained a small key-hole. This keyhole, when the lock was carefully and silently removed, provided him with a good view of the well-guarded door to the Hall of Portraits—the door through which His Majesty, if on schedule, ought, according to Mario's calculations, be passing out of in the next two minutes.

His Majesty, as we know, had no intention of remaining in the Hall of Portraits an instant longer than he had to; in fact Mario had barely time to take a breath before the doors opened and His Majesty came forth, preceded by Khaavren and followed by Jurabin, as well as by the two guards who had been watching the door but who now, their task completed, set off to be at hand wherever His Majesty decided to spend the next hour and a quarter.

At just about this same time, the guardsmen Mario had first seen ought to be relieved by another; in the unlikely event that Dinb had left word of the "Teckla" who was expected to slink away from the Palace, each guard would assume the other saw him leave—the chances that Dinb or anyone else would make a careful check were almost nonexistent; Mario, at any rate, reckoned this one of the safest of the necessary gambles he had to make in order to effect the assassination of His Majesty, followed by a safe escape.

An instant after His Majesty, His Majesty's Guards, and the courtiers had left the room, they were replaced by the omnipresent and inconspicuous Teckla who entered to ensure that the room was clean, polished, and stocked with whatever His Majesty might require when he returned later that day. This process took some forty-five or fifty minutes, after which time the room was locked.

It took Mario only a few seconds to defeat this lock, and scarcely more to lock it again, after which, alone in the Portrait Room and with nearly an hour at his disposal before His Majesty would return, Mario carefully made his preparations.

That there be no confusion later, when time and place will assume greater importance, let us now—while there remains yet a certain amount of time before the speed of events will catch up, and even overtake, the urgency of the historian to record them—take a moment to consider the precise placement within the Palace of the principal actors in this unfolding drama, at the point when it yet lacked fifteen minutes of the thirteenth hour of the morning.

To begin, as one ought, at the apex of our social pyramid, His Majesty, after changing his wardrobe to a martial costume, reclined in the small Lounge of Furs only a few steps from the Portrait Room. Khaavren, as was his custom, inspected the room carefully; his recent wound in no way hindered his ability to use his eyes. Upon being certain that there was no danger, he then took a position outside the door to await those who would replace him. His Majesty gave no thought to these precautions, for he had become quite used to them, and they seemed as normal to him as breathing. He sat himself down, then, in a comfortable chair and read from a book of traditional stories from the Kanefthali Mountains which had been collected and transcribed by Baroness Summer and was a book of which His Majesty had been fond since childhood.

Her Majesty was in her chamber. After the ordeal of her morning bath, she was resting by playing quions-of-fours with several of her maids of honor.

Jurabin, after escaping the Portrait Room, retired to the Seven Room where he caused the fire to be lighted. He then stared into the fire, and went over the events of the last few days in his mind, attempting to ease the turmoil therein, and, if possible, to discover what he could and should do to re-store to himself Their Majesties' favor—unfortunately, he found he was able to think only of Aliera's eyes, which was of no help in this instance.

Khaavren, as we have indicated, stood outside of the Lounge of Furs, until, after some few minutes, Menia appeared to take his place, which gave Khaavren the chance to make his way to His Majesty's kitchen, where he gorged himself in good style. The staff, we ought to say, looked upon him suspiciously, recalling the last time he had eaten there, but as he seemed, this time, to have no intention of collapsing before them, they eventually relaxed into their accustomed good humors. After finishing the meal (which consisted of bread and a large portion of a certain cold fowl which had been prepared in the Elde Island manner, with a sauce of tart fruit and handshoot seeds), he set about personally inspecting each guard post in the Imperial Wing, pausing to have a few words with each guardsman to make certain no one was about to fall asleep.

Sethra and Tazendra were making their way from the Dragon Wing to the Imperial Wing, walking slowly, and stop-ping to look at the scenes of battles depicted on the walls—Sethra would describe the inaccuracies of the depiction and point out for her companion's benefit where Dzurlords ap-peared, or where they did not appear but, to be accurate, ought to. For her part, Tazendra had quite forgotten that she was in the company of the Enchantress of Dzur Mountain and chatted on merrily, speaking of battles she had fought and ad-ventures she had had, and of certain spells she had been at-tempting to duplicate from certain ill-kept notebooks handed down from her family. Eventually they reached the Imperial Wing, and began to conduct an unhurried search for Pel and Aliera.

Pel and Aliera had begun a discussion of Khaavren's injury and Sethra's proposal, which discussion had become so ab-sorbing that they had forgotten their intentions, and had wan-dered aimlessly about the Imperial Wing until, by chance, they came upon Khaavren, who had just completed the inspection of his guard positions and was about to return to his offices in the Dragon Wing to see if anything had occurred which required his attention.

"Well met, my friends," he said.

"And to you!" cried Pel. "I had worried about you, and upon my oath it gives me joy to see your firm step and hear your strong voice."

"How, you had worried about me?" said Khaavren.

"Your injuries," said Pel.

"What of them? You know that we soldiers are made of rednut wood, and, should our bark be punctured, we may lose a little sap, but we will send out our full complement of leaves nevertheless, while digging our roots a little deeper."

"I am pleased, too," said Aliera, bowing. "The more so because I know how you came to be injured, and I assure you that I regret the fate that has placed you and my father in opposition to one another."

Khaavren turned his palms up. "It is an honor to have a good enemy, and old friends make the best enemies. But come, where are the two of you bound?"

"Why—I hardly know," said Pel. "In fact, we were conversing, and letting our feet carry us where they would—is that not so, Aliera?"

"It is exactly the case. And what of you, Khaavren? Whither are you bound?"

"I have no urgent destination," said Khaavren. "In fact, for the next twenty or thirty minutes, why, I am entirely at your service."

"Then," said Pel, "let us find a place where we can sit comfortably and converse."

"I should like nothing better," said Khaavren.

"An admirable idea," said Aliera.

"Then let us walk this way, for I know a place where His Majesty is wont to hold conversations, and, although the walls, as I have learned, are sufficiently thin that no secrets ought to be told, well, I am certain we will find a great deal to say to one another of matters about which we need have no fear of being overheard."

Aliera and Pel at once agreed to this plan, wherefore Khaavren led them to the Seven Room which, as it happened, was not far from where they had met; they reached the room in good season, and were about to clap in order to ascertain if it was in use, when the door saved them this trouble by opening, as it were, in their very faces and revealing the troubled countenance of the Prime Minister, who looked on Khaavren's expression, which, because the Captain had been startled, appeared even more stern and forbidding than usual, which caused Jurabin to blanch and cry out, "What, has it come to this already? Am I then to be arrested and forgotten, like poor Bellor? There is no cause, I assure you, I give you my word as a gentleman, my dear Captain, that I am innocence itself! Why—ah, is that the Lady Aliera behind you? Alas! Then all is known. It is too late! I am undone!"

Khaavren, although surprised, felt a certain amount of pity for the Prime Minister, who had changed in such a sort time from being the true decision-maker of the Empire to a weak, vacillating courtier desperate to hold favor; wherefore Khaavren was on the verge of explaining that they were only there to make use of the room for conversation, and had even opened his mouth and drawn breath to make this explanation when he felt a grip on his arm and heard Pel whisper in his ear, "Silence, my friend—let him speak, let him speak!"

But Jurabin seemed to have done with speaking, and wished to do nothing except kneel before Khaavren and entreat him with sounds from which no distinct words could be discerned. Khaavren looked at Pel, wondering what the clever Yendi had on his mind. In answer, Pel stepped up and said, "Come, come, it it not as bad as all that, my friend."

"How," said Jurabin, looking up at hearing the strange voice. "Who are you?"

"What does it matter?" said Pel mysteriously. "What matters is that it is not too late to save yourself from disgrace and arrest."

"How, it is not too late?"

"Not in the least," said Pel. "We merely wish to ask you a few questions, and, should you answer them honestly, well, it may be that no more need be said on this, and you will return to His Majesty's side none the worse for having spoken with us."

Jurabin frowned, rose unsteadily to his feet, and appeared to be thinking. Pel, however, urged him back into the Seven Room, sat him in a chair, and said, "Come now, let us waste no time. You know what we wish to discuss. What, then, have you to say?"

"How, I? You pretend I have something to say?"

"You perceive that we are here," said Pel.

Jurabin looked at Aliera, then at the others, and, though he made certain sounds, some of which approximated words, nothing he said could be construed to be an answer.

Khaavren leaned over to Pel and said, "What are you trying to find out?"

"Everything he knows," whispered Pel.

"Cha! He is the Prime Minister; why should he know anything?"

Pel glared at him.

Let us say, at this point, that we sympathize with the reader, who is very much aware that there is an assassin hiding in the room where His Majesty will be appearing in a very few minutes, and, no doubt, the reader would very much wish to discover exactly what will happen. As we have already had the honor to say, we sympathize with this desire, but we must insist that if the reader is to *understand* what happened, as well as merely *know* what happened, (and by "what happened" we mean both in the Portrait Room and for the duration of our history), then the reader must be informed of the events in the Seven Room that occurred among Khaavren, Pel, Aliera, and Jurabin.

This said, we will continue, and mention that Pel—secretive, careful, aloof Pel—was frustrated. Once he was informed that someone was conspiring at court to impair its efficiency, he at once set himself the task of discovering who, and why. He did this, we should add, for several reasons: for one, he was sincerely Khaavren's friend and was pleased to do his friend a service; for another, he enjoyed the challenge of discovering who was pulling the ropes that made the court dance; for yet another, there was a certain measure of genuine worry for the Empire—he knew how fragile were the threads of policy, and how, at times, the smallest slip could have repercussions that would last for generations. But, above all, his own schemes had been dealt a severe blow by the decision to cut the funding for the Institute of Discretion, because it was through the Institute that he reckoned on moving up through the ranks of society as part of fulfilling his own ambition—Pel was nothing if not ambitious. Both the reduction of funds, then, and the general disorder around the court, made Pel realize that the stairs he had planned on climbing were, in the first place, covered with ice, in the second, cracked and pitted in unlikely places, and, in the third, unstable at their foundations. Therefore, before he could continue with his own schemes, so long in the design and so precise in the execution as they had been, he must be certain of the balance of influence and power at court, and it was exactly this balance that had gone awry as a result of the conspiracy that Pel had detected, but was unable to track down.

Khaavren, though he did not know most of this, realized that Pel was frustrated, and this knowledge shocked him as he had scarcely been shocked in all of his years—of everyone he knew, it seemed, Pel was the one who always had a plan, and always knew exactly what was going on, or, at any rate, how to find out. Khaavren, himself, was perfectly comfortable turning over every rock he came to until he discovered the one under which someone had buried a key, and then trying every lock he came to until he found one it fit; but Khaavren was disturbed, and even frightened to realize that Pel was working in just this way.

This discovery effectively silenced Khaavren, who could only stare at his friend with all the expression of a wall from which the lone painting has just been removed. Aliera, though clever, did not know Pel; she did not, therefore, realize what was going on. She was convinced that the Yendi was playing some sort of deep game, and resolved to help him in any way she could, for, although she did not trust him any more than she would ever trust a Yendi, she nevertheless felt that his interests coincided with her own, at least on this occasion.

Jurabin was far too confused to have any opinions on anything; he simply knew that his love for Aliera had been discovered, and that he was facing ruin. To a man such as Jurabin, who, as we have endeavored to show, was, in fact, a conscientious administrator and one who took sincere pleasure in seeing the Empire function as smoothly as it could be made to, and who was, moreover, the sort of administer who gloried in crises, because then more than ever was his presence required, removal from his position was no small matter. He had been, he thought, making the best of a difficult situation when the assassination of Smaller had led to such confusion in the finances that it had become necessary to dismiss the Superintendent, appoint another, and hope accounts could be made to balance so that the state of the treasury would at least be known. And then, with Aliera's arrival, it had been as if he were thrown into a maelstrom, and for a while he could not see where to plant his feet, but, rather, he found himself pushed hither and yon by his overwhelming urge to attract Aliera's attention while simultaneously keeping his passion hidden from the Consort, who reckoned him her ally in the court and who would turn from him if she could not count on his affection, which translated to his support.

And, as if all of this were not bad enough, there was the outbreak of rebellion conjoined with His Majesty suddenly waking up, as it were, and taking control of the Empire itself. Had the Prime Minister been in full possession of his faculties, he could have either convinced His Majesty to allow him, Jurabin, to continue guiding matters, or at least have made certain His Majesty was fully informed about all of the significant issues; in the event, however, Jurabin effectively collapsed, and now to be confronted with Aliera, a representative of His Majesty, and (for so he assumed) a representative of the Consort, left him weighted down by the double burden of fear and of his own guilt—that is, his conviction that he deserved ruin and disgrace. And, if this wasn't enough, by having all three parties represented, as he thought, he did not dare attempt to play one off against the other; which he assumed was the reason for sending them, and further proof that all was known.

That, then, was the situation when Pel turned back to Jurabin and said, "Come, the court is in a shambles, and His Majesty is acting with neither reliable knowledge nor dependable advice, and this is because you, who have these duties, have failed in them. Is this not true?"

Jurabin could only nod miserably.

"If you would save yourself, then, your only hope is to tell everything."

"I will do so," said Jurabin in a hushed voice, for, under the circumstances, he could not think of holding anything back.

"Then tell me this: Who is behind this conspiracy?"

Jurabin looked up in amazement. "Who is behind it?"

"Yes, you must tell us at once. The assassinations, the disruption, the hastily-made decisions—who has planned all of this, and, moreover, for what reason?"

This question so surprised Jurabin that, for a moment, he could only stare in wonder. Then he said, "But, I assure you, I have no idea in the world, and my only wish is to find out."

"But you—"

"I? I have hardly been working with a conspirator—I have been helplessly engulfed in love such as no man has ever before known. It has bent my mind, and turned my muscles to water, and—"

"How, love?" cried Pel. "For Aliera?"

Jurabin looked down again, for he could not look upon Aliera, and he nodded.

Pel shook his head. "Could someone plan on him falling in love? It is hardly credible. It must be coincidence. Unless—"

He paused, considering, and turned to Aliera. "Could he be the victim of a love-spell?"

"How, I?" cried Jurabin, outraged. "You think what I am feeling could be—"

"Be quiet," said Pel. "You annoy me."

Jurabin, however, was far too angry to be silenced so easily. "It is preposterous," he said. "And absurd on the face of it—how, a victim of a spell, who stands under the Orb every day, and the Orb not detect it?"

"The Orb," said Pel, "would not have been looking."

"No," said Aliera suddenly. "He is right. The Orb would know if anyone nearby was acting under the influence of magic—it is part of the system for protecting the Emperor that was built into the Orb. Sethra told me so."

"But," said Pel, who did not wish to abandon his idea so easily. "Could not the Orb have been tampered with?"

"It is unlikely," said Aliera.

"But is it impossible?"

"It is unlikely," she repeated.

At this point Khaavren seemed to wake up, and he said, "If there is even a small possibility of it, we must discover at once if it has happened."

Aliera began, "And yet—"

Khaavren shook his head. "This falls within my duties, and I say it must be investigated."

"Well, but how?" said Aliera.

"His Majesty will, in a very few minutes, be entering the Portrait Room. We shall meet him there, and you will inspect the Orb."

"Who, I? I have no part in this. Moreover, I have not the skill to do so."

"Well, but who does?"

"Nyleth, the Court Wizard, perhaps. And certainly Sethra Lavode."

"Well, you and Pel find Sethra and have her meet us there."

"I will do that," said Aliera.

"As will I," said Pel. Then, as an afterthought, he turned to Jurabin and said, "For now, resume your duties as if nothing had happened."

"Very well," said Jurabin, to whom anger had restored poise, allowing him a modicum of dignity in spite of all that had befallen him.

"Come," said Khaavren. "We must hurry."

He and Jurabin, therefore, made their way back to the Portrait Room, Aliera went back to the Dragon Wing to look in Sethra's chamber, and Pel set off on a search through the Imperial Wing in case Sethra had returned.

It so happened that Khaavren and Jurabin reached the Portrait Room just at the same time as His Majesty, and so, after Khaavren looked over the room, in which he saw nothing wrong (Mario had been careful), His Majesty entered and took his throne, after which the doors were opened to admit any courtier who wished to speak to or be seen with His Majesty. The first to be admitted was Sethra Lavode. Upon seeing her, His Majesty's countenance darkened, but Khaavren said, "Sire, she is here at my request—there is an issue of Imperial security."

"How, is there a danger?"

"Sire, I do not think so, and yet I am loath to take the chance."

"Very well. What must be done?"

"Sire, we must inspect the Orb, to be certain that it has not been tampered with."

"How, the Orb tampered with?"

"Sire, it is unlikely, yet I should feel better if Sethra were allowed to ascertain."

His Majesty looked at Khaavren, as if wondering what the Captain knew or suspected that he was not saying; but then he said, "Very well, carry on."

"Thank you, Sire." Then bowed to Sethra and said, "My lady, did Aliera find you?"

"No, it was Pel who said you desired my presence, although he did not explain why. Yet, having overheard your discussion with His Majesty, I now understand."

"And are you willing to help?"

"Most willing, although I think it unlikely that an enchantment could have been placed on the Orb itself without every sorcerer in the Empire being aware of it. Indeed," she added in a low voice, keeping her back to the courtiers, "the Orb will always protect itself by protecting His Majesty; the reverse is true as well. Therefore—"

"Yes?" said Khaavren. "Therefore?"

"The only way to disrupt the working of the Orb is to hide His Majesty from it—that is, to make His Majesty invisible to the Orb."

"Could this be done?"

"Zerika was clever," said Sethra, still speaking softly and, moreover, keeping her back to the room, so that no one behind her could overhear. "It can only be done by, in turn, psychically hiding the Orb from His Majesty—in other words, by severing the psychic link between Emperor and Orb."

"That sounds impossible," said the Emperor, with a glance up at the Orb—which was still placidly revolving around his head, now emitting a rosy glow—and seeming not at all self-conscious.

"Very nearly," said Sethra. "It would require an immense amount of energy—an almost inconceivable amount to break the connection between Your Majesty and the Orb. And even then, I think it would fail."

"Why would it then fail, if sufficient power were used to penetrate its defenses?"

Sethra smiled. "Zerika, as I said, was clever; when the Orb detects enough energy in its presence to be a threat, well, it will, in a sense, pull into itself—that is, it will close itself off entirely."

"Well," said Khaavren, "but that would break the connection with His Majesty."

"True," said Sethra. "But, you perceive, it could not be tampered with; it would remain in that state as long as it felt the energy in its vicinity. And if this were to happen—"

"Yes," said Khaavren, paying the strictest attention. "If this were to happen?"

"Then, as I said, every sorcerer in the Empire would know it at once, so that His Majesty would be alerted, as would you, and you would then be able to guard against it."

"Well, I understand," said Khaavren. "It would, therefore, be impossible to plant a spell within the Orb ahead of time."

"I can think of no way to do such a thing—the Orb was designed to prevent exactly this. Now, if it is the case that someone has circumvented the Orb's defenses in this way, well, I should like nothing better than to meet the wizard who could do so, and until I have met him, or seen the results of his work, I shall continue to believe such a thing impossible."

"And so," said Khaavren, "it is unlikely that we have anything to worry about on that score."

"That is precisely the case."

"Nevertheless," said Khaavren, "to be certain, I would be happy if you could reassure me that all is as it ought to be."

"Yes. If Your Majesty will allow me?"

His Majesty would, and Sethra approached the Orb. She reached out her hands and seemed to cup the Orb without actually touching it; and she stared into it. Khaavren watched her closely, but was able to see nothing on her countenance except great concentration, and, after a few minutes, some beads of perspiration. The Orb maintained a light brown color during this time, which lasted for some few minutes. At last Sethra, frowning, said, "There is no spell upon the Orb, and yet—"

"Yes?" said Khaavren.

"There is something."

"How, there is something? What can this mean?"

"I do not know. And yet, there is sorcery present—a strong spell, and one of a type I am unfamiliar with; and, moreover, it is, if my skills have not utterly deserted me, only a potential—nothing has been done, but there is magic present, waiting to be released." She frowned, and Khaavren took a step closer to His Majesty, while looking carefully around the room. He saw nothing out of the ordinary, and yet he looked again, and this time his eye fastened on the wall behind His Majesty, which was, as we have had the honor to mention, covered with a large tapestry. This tapestry, as it happened, depicted Zerika the First and Kieron the Conqueror clasping hands amid slain Easterners while the victorious army cheered, jhereg sat on nearby trees, and a Phoenix flew overhead.

Khaavren's eyes had fastened on one of the trees, which seemed to him to contain a flaw he had not noticed before. He drew his sword.

"Captain, what—"

"Bide a moment, Sire. It may be nothing, and yet—"

And yet it was, indeed, something—for, at that instant, Mario, realizing that fate had played him a cruel trick, and realizing, moreover, that his choices were to stay where he was and be captured or to move at once, moved. The first thing he did was to drop the pearl and crush it beneath his heal, thinking that he would have sufficient difficulty with Khaavren and Sethra Lavode, and at least, he thought, he could prevent the Orb from coming to His Majesty's aid. At the same time, he sprang from his position behind the tapestry, in which he had carefully cut a slit that was nearly invisible, and leapt out at Khaavren holding a sword in one hand and a dagger in the other.

Sethra, for her part, had noticed the crushing of the pearl, and, although she did not know what sort of spell it was, nevertheless put forth her power to prevent it from taking effect. Khaavren stood between the assassin and His Majesty and prepared to cross blades with the small, wiry man wearing grey and black. Mario, wanting to reach Tortaalik, attempted to force Khaavren back with a fury of thrusts and cuts, but the Captain, not retreating a step, parried each attack, and, after just a few passes, forced the assassin up to the wall, at which point Khaavren said, "If someone will send for a few of my guards, well, I believe we will have this fellow chained up and safe in good time."

The assassin still held his sword and his dagger, but Khaavren had both of these locked against the wall, rendering him essentially helpless. To Khaavren he seemed a quiet, almost uninteresting sort, without even the cold, heartless eyes that usually mark those who kill for pay—although, as he stood backed up to the wall, he allowed no trace of expression to cross his countenance.

Sethra, who had finished her work, remarked, "A peculiar spell to use in an attack."

His Majesty had stepped from the throne, and discovering that he had no weapon, had contented himself with standing up and glaring at his attacker. Now he turned to Sethra and said, "What was it intended to do?"

"Sire, it is nothing I would wish to have done if I were launching an attack—now that I have defeated it, I have also identified it, and, had it succeeded, it would have done nothing except destroy the memory of him who released it—that is, of this Jhereg."

Khaavren, who had not taken his eyes off the assassin, noticed something like shock cross the Jhereg's features, to be quickly replaced by the empty, stony look he had been affecting before.

"Certainly," said His Majesty, "it is an unusual spell for an assassin to carry, unless he is a fanatic of some sort. But we shall find out soon enough, I think."

"Your Majesty," said Khaavren, "is correct on that score, for here are the guards come to help take him away. Do you, sirs, each take an arm, removing the weapon as you do, while I—the Gods!"

This ejaculation was caused by Mario suddenly striking out with a foot and catching Khaavren's leg below the knee, which, in turn, caused Khaavren's leg to buckle; it may be that, had the Captain been unwounded, the trick would not have worked, and who can know how history would have been different? But, for whatever reason, Khaavren's grip on the assassin's right hand loosened, and Mario brought the hilt of his rapier down on Khaavren's head, momentarily stunning him.

It is to the credit of the guards that their first thought was for His Majesty—they at once stepped between the assassin and the Emperor. This, while certainly their duty, left a clear path to the door—a path which Mario lost no time in taking; he was gone before Khaavren had regained his feet.

Khaavren, for his part, said coolly, "Raise the alarm—we must catch him. Turn out every guardsman who can be roused. Seal the Dragon, Athyra, Iorich, and Imperial Wings at once."

Menia, one of those who had arrived to take Mario away, rushed off to carry out the Captain's orders. Khaavren, meanwhile, picked up his sword, bowed to His Majesty, and said, "Sire, I have business that will not wait. If my Lady Sethra will consent to guard Your Majesty—"

"Gladly," said Sethra.

"—I will be about my task, knowing that Your Majesty is in good hands."

Without another word, then, he turned and was out the door in pursuit of the assassin.

More than once the historian has read such words as, "The deplorable state of Palace security," or, "No one had ever thought of the need to protect the Emperor," in works that discuss the events that occurred around this time. None of these mention Khaavren by name, without doubt because none of the authors know the name of Tortaalik's Captain of the Imperial Guard. Yet his name and his deeds are matters of public record, even if, perhaps, the motivations behind his deeds, or the information that can lead one to discern the motivations behind his deeds, requires a certain amount of effort to discover. What could cause an historian (and, in many cases, an historian who is otherwise not incapable) to engage in such inept work? This we cannot say. Happily, it is not our duty to explain the errors of our brothers, but, rather, to insist upon the truth—which, in fact, we are now about to do.

Thought had, indeed, been given to His Majesty's safety— G'aereth had demanded it, being all of his life suspicious of the Orb's abilities in this regard, and Khaavren had inherited this duty with the shoulder-pin that identified him as the Captain; and we have been inexcusably remiss in our duty if we have not given the reader to understand that our Tiassa was not one to take duty lightly.

But there are additional points that ought to be made. In the first place, whereas in our own happy era, under such circumstances the Captain need only wish for more guardsmen, in effect, and they would arrive, there was no such instantaneous communication then, or, at any rate, very little. Hence, when Khaavren gave the urgent command for help in securing the assassin, the only guards who were nearby were those guarding the door—to have sent for others would have taken, at the least, three or four minutes. The reader (and any future historian who wishes to address this matter) also ought to remember that, because of his wounds, he was not at the peak of his powers that day; and, for the same reason, most of his command were either sound asleep, or on duty even though they *should* have been asleep.

To be sure, Mario had found, and exploited, a true weakness in Khaavren's defenses, and even without the wounds and weaknesses, there can be no doubt but that the assassin would have gained entry to the throne room; but it is likely—in fact, it is all but certain—that, had there been better means of communications, and had Khaavren's troops been better rested and more numerous, and had Khaavren himself been uninjured, Mario would either never have escaped the Portrait Room, or, having escaped, would have been caught at once.

But with circumstances as they were, it was not so easy. Mario led them on a chase throughout the Imperial Wing, while Khaavren, after sending a messenger for more guards, directed the search, using two score of messengers to inform himself of the progress of the search, and deploying his forces as best he could.

Who can follow Mario's path through the Imperial Wing? From the reports of cooks, we know that he passed through the kitchen; from the reports of gardeners, we know he passed over one of the low roofs near the Athyra Wing; from Menia, who took a thrown knife in her left thigh and a severe knock on the head, we know that he ventured into the tunnels connecting the Imperial Wing with the Lyorn Wing; from a report by Brudik, Lord of the Chimes, we know that, wearing Menia's stolen cloak, he walked boldly and calmly into the Dragon Wing—the last place anyone would have expected; and that he was nearly out of the door of this wing—would, in fact, have escaped by simply walking out of the Sub-wing of the Guard, had he not been seen by Thack, who knew everyone who belonged to the uniform, and who, upon seeing the back of a head that he did not recognize above a cloak that he did, gave the alert in an instant.

Mario was almost captured then and there, but, it seemed, the assassin knew the wing better than any had thought—better even than many of his pursuers, and entered what looked to be a closet on the second story of the Warlord's Sub-wing but which actually opened in back, putting him near a stairway up to the third level, which housed the Lavodes—who, having been alerted by Sethra, were none of them there, but were all off searching for him.

By this time he had abandoned the cloak, and was dressed simply in his tight-fitting black and grey garments, hung about with weapons, and he was also bleeding slightly from his left arm where Khaavren had nicked him, when he stepped out of a hidden doorway, into the hall, and practically into the lap, as it were, of Aliera e'Kieron.

They stared at each other for a moment, Aliera appearing not at all worried by the naked sword, and Mario not certain if such beauty as he was seeing could actually exist, or if perchance he had been killed during the chase, and was now meeting his reward in the Paths of the Dead—in fact, for an instant, he rather hoped he was; but then he recalled that he had matters to finish that required he live a bit longer, so, on reflection, he hoped he was not.

Aliera said, "You are a Jhereg."

Mario said, "You are the most beautiful woman who has ever lived, or ever will live, in the Empire or anywhere else."

"Well," said Aliera.

"I am," remarked Mario, "confronted by a difficult decision."

"Life seems to be full of them," agreed Aliera. "What is yours?"

"Whether to continue running for my life, or to stay here and look at you."

Aliera allowed herself a smile. "Were it I," she said, "I should choose life."

"And yet—"

"Who is after you?"

Mario laughed. "Ask rather, who is not?"

"Well, what have you done?"

"They believe I tried to kill His Majesty."

"Kill His Majesty?" said Aliera, her eyes widening. "That is an excellent thought; His Majesty ought to die."

"How, you think so?"

"Entirely. And yet you said, 'they think.' "

"And so I did."

"Is it not true?"

"Oh, it is true in part."

"In part?"

"Yes."

"Would you care to explain?"

"I thought I was to kill His Majesty, and, in my own mind, I even attempted to do so."

"Well?"

"But those for whom I made the attempt—"

"You made the attempt for others?"

"For money."

For an instant Aliera's face darkened, then she said, "Well, but you are a Jhereg."

"That is true. And you are beautiful."

"You have already said that."

"And you have already—"

"Yes. But, then, continue with your history."

"It seems that I was not to actually kill him, only to appear to make the attempt, after which my mind was to be destroyed so that I could not identify those who had instigated this plan."

Aliera frowned. "They must be paying you an exorbitant amount of money."

"Not enough."

"But then—"

"They have betrayed me, you see; it is clear that someone wanted an unsuccessful attempt on His Majesty's life, and I was to be used to carry it out, and then I was to be thrown away."

"Ah. Only—"

"Yes. Only I have lived, and my mind is not destroyed, and I may yet escape."

"And if you do, will you attempt once more to kill His Majesty?"

"I will not."

"Oh," said Aliera, sounding disappointed.

"But I will certainly speak with those who gave me this mission, and I will speak to them in terms which allow for no doubt about my opinions."

"Well, I understand that. But if, as you say, they are searching for you, ought you not to be on your way?"

"It is, as I have said, a difficult choice."

"What, can you be serious? To escape with your life or to stare at me? A difficult choice?"

"Yes."

"You are mad."

"Certainly I am mad, in a particular way."

"And yet—"

"Well, I have chosen."

"And what is your choice?"

"I will stand here and look at you until they take me away, for each second more than I can absorb every nuance of your form will be hours of pleasure in the future, so that—"

"Come with me."

"How, where are we going?"

"First, around this corridor, then down these stairs."

"Well, and then?"

"To this window, which we will open, like this."

"And yet, I do not—"

"After that, into this room, which, as daughter of the Heir, is still mine. Do you stay here while I stand by the doorway, so that if anyone should attempt to gain entrance, well, I will kill him."

Mario swallowed. "But you are a Dragonlord," he said at last.

"Yes," said Aliera. "And you are beautiful."

The effect these words had on Mario can scarcely be exaggerated. He took two steps backward and ended, fortunately, by sitting in a chair, after which he sat in a daze, not really hearing Aliera's conversation with Thack, who, in the company of two other guardsmen, arrived in time to see Aliera staring at the window at the far end of the hall.

"My lady!" they cried.

She said, "Are you looking for a slender man in grey and black, bleeding slightly from the arm?"

"We are indeed; has he been here?"

"I nearly think he has," said Aliera, still staring intently at the open window.

The guardsmen thanked her profusely and went through the window themselves, following the only possible path, which led over some roofs toward the Lyorn Wing, while Aliera returned to the room and shut the door.

"What is your name?" she said.

"Mario, my Lady."

"I am Aliera e'Kieron. You will remain here for an hour, after which time I will show you how to escape the Palace."

"My lady—"

"Well?"

"I don't know how to thank you."

"I know a way," said Aliera.

For Khaavren, the next two hours were among the most active in a life filled with activity—he spoke with thirty-one people who had, or may have, seen Mario; he studied the marks around eleven pried-open windows; he consulted six drawings of the Palace; he found blood stains in three places where he did not expect to, and failed to find them in another four where he suspected he would; he also gave orders for more searchers here or for abandoning searches there, and, in the end, he discovered a significant footprint, followed the most obvious path, and was forced to conclude that his quarry had escaped.

This, however, did not end his activities, for there were certain puzzles that he was determined to solve: a window left open where Mario had not gone, a window that was closed through which he seemed to have gone, and the lack of marks and signs, especially the blood stain we have already mentioned, where there ought to be some. He therefore spent yet another hour questioning and cross-questioning witnesses, until, at last, a suspicion began to grow.

He spent still another hour, much of it on his hands and knees on the grounds outside of the Dragon Wing or squinting over diagrams of the Palace, until, although he disliked the conclusion he had perforce reached, he could no longer deny it. It was then that he came to His Majesty (once again interrupting his dinner), and explained what he had discovered and how he had proved it.

His Majesty gave the only orders possible under the circumstances, and, on this occasion, Khaavren, even to himself, had no objection to make. And so it was that, at the fifth hour after noon on the sixteenth day of the month of Vallista, in the five hundred and thirty-second year of the Reign of His Imperial Majesty Tortaalik the First, Khaavren, his face pale with fury, presented himself at the chamber of Aliera e'Kieron and, upon being admitted, said, "Madam, I have the honor to arrest you in the name of the Emperor; please give me your sword and come with me at once."

Aliera bowed her head slightly and handed him her sword. "What delayed you?" she said.

# Chapter the Twenty-eighth

⊰═══◆═══⊱        ⊰═══◆═══⊱

### Which Treats of the State of the Empire On the Very Eve of Crisis.

W<small>E MUST NOW TURN OUR</small> attention back to Adron's encampment, which was filled with soldiers ready to ride, to kill, or to be killed at the least wish of His Highness, Prince Adron e'Kieron, Duke of Eastmanswatch and Dragon Heir to the throne. The camp was in such a state as anyone who has been a soldier will recognize at once—a camp ready to move, to attack, or to defend at the first word or the least sign of trouble. The call to action had been sounded, without an official word being spoken, by yester-day's sudden departure from the city, and now, again with no orders issued, everyone knew that battle was coming, and would not be long delayed.

Some whispered that His Majesty had unleashed an army, and it would be arriving over the crest in moments. Others claimed to have heard Adron order his daughter and Sethra Lavode to steal the Orb from over His Majesty's head, and that Lord Adron would be taking possession of the city as soon as he received word that this had been accomplished. Still others insisted that Adron was waiting for intelligence indicating that the exact moment was right to launch an assault on the city. In any case, the horizon was scanned constantly for signs of spies or messengers, and, as there were a good number of spies (Adron's) and messengers (again, Adron's) each day, there were also a good number of false alarms; yet it should be clearly understood that these in no sense discouraged those who watched.

The messenger who arrived from the Palace at around the seventh hour after noon, having ridden by the fastest post, was, therefore, watched eagerly and assisted even more eagerly; and when he was admitted to Adron's tent, the tent was itself then watched with the greatest possible eagerness, in hopes of learning somewhat from Lord Adron's countenance whenever he should emerge.

Within the tent itself, Aerich, who had been conversing with His Highness when the message arrived, watched Adron, who was staring at the yellow parchment in his hand as if willing it to burn—although he could not really be doing so, because had he actually so willed, it would have. One might say that, rather than the note, it was the Lyorn who burned—who burned, that is, to know what was written upon it that had caused His Highness to at first pale, and then flush, and now merely stare fixedly at the parchment, reading it over and over again. Aerich, though uncharacteristically impatient to know what it contained, would certainly not ask.

At last Adron looked up at him, and at first it seemed that he had mastered his emotions, but, on a closer look, Aerich saw that this was not the case. The reader may be familiar with the peculiar smelters that fill some of the towns along the Twindle River with their stenches; these smelters use a method of generating heat that requires an attendant to regulate the air flow into the furnace in such a way that the fires do not become so hot as to melt the furnace, which would cause a general conflagration, and yet enough air is let out so that the entire furnace does not explode from the heated air trapped within. In the parlance of that profession, this is called, "stroking the vent," and requires a gentle touch combined with nerves that resemble the exact sort of high-grade steel the furnaces produce. We mention this because it seemed to Aerich that this was exactly what His Highness was doing—attempting to release enough of his anger so that he would not erupt into irrationality, yet not so much as to unleash the very fires he sought to control. In this context, we hope the metaphor, striking as it was to Aerich, is also sufficiently clear to the reader.

Adron, without a word, handed the note to Aerich. The note took this form: "Your Highness is informed that Aliera e'Kieron has today been arrested for High Treason, and is confined to the Imperial Prisons in the Iorich Wing to await trial." That was all, except for the signature, which was the mark of Liseter, the Court Scribe, and contained the appendix: "By the wishes of His Majesty, Tortaalik the First, Emperor of Dragaera."

Aerich wordlessly handed the note back to His Highness, unable to find anything to say.

"Well, Duke?" said His Highness.

Aerich said, "I should wish, above all, Highness, to learn the details."

"And so I shall, Duke," said Adron. "I shall go to His Majesty and inquire after particulars. But I shall bring my army with me."

"Your Highness—"

"For now, I will give orders that the spell wagon be loaded with the argument I have prepared for His Majesty."

"Sire—"

"The army will set out in the morning. The city will be mine in the afternoon. The Orb will revolve around my head before nightfall."

"Then Your Highness has made up his mind?"

"Irrevocably."

Aerich bowed. "Your Highness perceives, no doubt, that I cannot remain."

Adron nodded. "May the best of fortune be yours, Duke."

"And Your Highness's as well."

"Perhaps we shall meet again."

"Perhaps we shall," said Aerich. And so it was Aerich, not

Adron, who emerged at last from the tent. At first, this was disappointing, for nothing could be learned from the Lyorn's countenance; yet, in only a short time, he and his servant were mounted, and were departing the encampment at a good speed, which led to endless speculation: Some believed that Aerich was a diplomatist, attempting to reconcile His Highness with the court; of these, a few believed his departure signaled success, but most were convinced that he had failed. Still others believed that Aerich was a powerful sorcerer, who would be in advance of the battalion when the attack was launched. A few maintained that he had offered His Highness an army to help them against the Imperial Army. Some suggested that he was a close friend of His Highness's, but that, being a Lyorn, he would not take arms against His Majesty (these last were, we should add, essentially correct).

In any case, speculation ended just a few minutes later when Lord Adron emerged and ordered his spell-wagon prepared. It was not his custom to announce his decisions, or even to let his troops know that action was planned, but, from the orders he gave, and from the meeting he held with his officers far into the night, there could be no possible doubt this time.

Aerich informed Fawnd that they would be leaving at once and traveling quickly; such was the Lyorn's expression, communicated by voice and gesture, that his servant, although just lately recovered from the first such journey, and although dreading another as he dreaded fire, allowed neither whimper nor sigh to escape his lips, and allowed neither frown nor scowl to cross his countenance.

Aerich and Fawnd rode fast and hard, using the Imperial posts, Fawnd keeping up the rugged pace of the journey without complaint; and so they reached the Dragon Gate shortly after dark. Aerich wasted no time by stopping at the house on the Street of the Glass Cutters, but, rather, gave certain explicit instructions to Fawnd, after which he turned at once toward the Imperial Palace.

Fawnd was warmly greeted by Srahi and Mica, who were speaking in low tones near the fire that Srahi had built, pretending that Mica's injury required warmth; she was also making certain that he drank Covaath cider in great quantities, both to ease his pain and to help him gain strength. Neither of these treatments, we should say, had been particularly recommended by the physicker, but Srahi insisted upon them, claiming that they had been used by her family for generations and had never failed. Mica, for his part, had no thought of resisting her ministrations, although he was careful not to allow the cider to intoxicate him.

Fawnd appeared, then, in this domestic scene, and, addressing both of them, said, "Pack."

They looked at him, understandably startled. "I beg your pardon," said Mica, imitating Tazendra as best he could. "But I do not understand what you do me the honor of telling me."

"Pack," repeated Fawnd.

"Well," said Mica. "But, pack for what?"

"To leave."

"How, we are leaving?"

"Yes," said Fawnd.

Srahi turned a worried look upon Mica, and said, "But you are not fit to travel."

"Nevertheless," intoned Fawnd. Then he added to Srahi, "You, too."

"How me?"

"Yes."

"By whose orders?"

"My master's."

"I—" Srahi stopped before certain words were out of her mouth, remembering, in the first place, how intimidating the Lyorn could be, and second, realizing that, if Mica were to be traveling, there was good reason to be traveling with him.

"But why?" said Mica.

Fawnd shrugged.

At this point, Daro appeared, leaning on the nearest wall, and looking pale, for she, of them all, was in considerable pain, and after having read the message thoughtfully provided by Pel and promptly delivered by Srahi, she had returned to her bed and remained there until this moment. Now she said, "What is this I hear?"

Fawnd bowed low to this woman, who, though he did not know her, and though she was dressed only in a housecoat, was clearly a noblewoman. "My lady," he said, "I have been instructed by my master to see to it that we—by which I mean Srahi, Mica, and I—leave the house, and the city, and even the district, within the hour."

"Within the hour!" cried Srahi and Mica together.

"Yes," said Fawnd.

"But," said Daro, "who is your master?"

"Duke Arylle," said Fawnd.

"I do not know him," said Daro suspiciously.

Mica said, "My lady, the Lord Khaavren speaks of him as Aerich."

"Ah, yes," she said. "I have, indeed, heard him pronounce this name, and that with the greatest respect and affection. But, has he given a reason for these strange orders?"

"No, madam, he has not."

Daro made her way to a couch and eased herself into it. After breathing deeply for a moment, she said, "Have you, yourself, any guess about why he gave these orders?"

"No, madam."

"Well." She pondered for a moment, then said, "Was he at the Palace before issuing these orders?"

"No, madam."

"But then, where was he?"

"At Lord Adron's encampment."

"Oh," said Daro. "That may explain everything." She frowned, then, and said, "Well, you had best be about it."

"And yet," said Srahi, "if my master returns, and I am not here—"

"I will explain," said Daro.

"Thank you, my lady."

"But there is something you must do for me."

"Yes, my lady?"

"You must pack quickly, and you must, in addition, pack up everything of your master's which he would want preserved, and that you can put on a wagon in the time you have. Do not waste a moment."

"I will do so, my lady," said Srahi, who was beginning to understand that the matter, whatever it was, was entirely serious.

"You," said Daro. "What is your name?"

"Fawnd, my lady."

"You must nearly be packed already, for you have come from a journey."

"That is true, my lady."

"So you find a wagon—here, take this purse, pay whatever you have to. A wagon with a good team—can any of you drive a team?"

"I can," said Mica.

"Good. Find a wagon and a team and bring them here at once."

"My lady," said Fawnd, "I will do all you ask."

"Where are we to go?" said Mica.

"Bra-moor," said Fawnd.

"Which is?" said Daro.

"My master's estate, near the Collier Hills."

"Very well," said Daro. "You had best be about your business, then."

"Yes, my lady," said Srahi and Mica. Mica then looked at the heavily bandaged stump of his leg and scowled, but said nothing. Srahi gifted him with a tender look, which he returned in full measure.

"We must," remarked Srahi, "be certain to bring your barstool."

The reader may be wondering about Tazendra, who was last seen in the company of Sethra, but who did not, in fact, appear in the Portrait Room with the Enchantress. When Sethra had been summoned, Tazendra thought it a good time to attend to certain matters, wherefore she took herself to the Dzur Wing of the Palace—that great, lofty, dark, empty hall where hung oils of only the greatest of the great and which was dominated by the mammoth dzur sculpted in the depths of time by Pitra himself; from there she followed one of the side wings, along the passage where the Lists were kept, stopping, from time to time, to find the name of a relative. On each side of this hall were sitting rooms done each of them in stone, and each featuring a different weapon made famous by some great warrior, and named, in some cases for the warrior, in others for the weapon. Eventually, she chose one that was named for Arylle, who had led the expedition which had discovered, among other things, Tazendra's homeland; Arylle was also renowned for being the lone survivor of an ill-fated foray against a pirate stronghold on an island in the far west (this was unusual, because, to get one of these rooms in the Dzur Wing named after one, it was generally a requirement that the hero not survive).

Tazendra, after assuring herself that the room was empty, sat in front of the fire, removed the necessary items from her pocket, and began to sharpen her sword, where we will leave her with her sword and her thoughts.

Khaavren, upon receiving Aliera's sword, made her his accustomed offer—that is, that she might pack a valise.

"I have done so," she said. "I am ready."

"We may," said the Captain, "arrive at the Imperial Prisons by any reasonable route you choose. Have you a preference?"

"Not in the least," said Aliera. "Everyone will know of my arrest in any case, and I am hardly ashamed of it, so it matters not the least in the world."

"Very well, then if my lady will follow me."

"I am at your service, Captain."

Other than this, there was no conversation between them, for Khaavren was still too angry, and Aliera too proud; as the rest of the walk was conducted in silence, we see no need to inform the reader in any great detail of the hollow sounds their boots made on the Ringway Stairs, or the odors of fresh paint in the Blue Corridor, or the startling, almost painful light that struck their eyes as they passed by the window above the Warding Gate into the Iorich Wing, or any of the other details of their journey. Suffice it to say that, in due time, Aliera was turned over to Guinn and his jailers, and Khaavren returned to tell His Majesty, who was playing at shereba (for, we should add, stakes that were so small as to be only tokens) with certain courtiers, that his mission had been accomplished. His Majesty responded with a simple nod, and Khaavren repaired to his offices to see if anything of moment had happened during his long absence.

He looked through the correspondence that had accumulated during his absence, and had not gotten far when he stood and called for Thack, who presented himself at once, appearing, thanks to a brief nap, to be somewhat refreshed. He bowed upon entering and said, "Yes, Captain? Is there some matter upon which you desire to speak to me?"

"I nearly think so," said Khaavren.

"What is it, Captain? For you perceive I am entirely at your service."

"This," said Khaavren, waving a note about.

"The note, Captain?"

"Yes. Unless my eyes have failed me at last, it has your mark upon the bottom."

"Why, so it does," said Thack. "Have I erred in some way? For I observe from your countenance, Captain, that something his displeased you."

"Never mind that," said the Captain. "Are you aware of what it says?"

"Yes, Captain, it speaks of a certain movement among the population—"

"Movement! You say, movement?"

"Why, yes, Captain—"

"When every Gate to the city is filled with a constant stream of people—and people of all classes, I might add—desperate to leave the city, so that fights have broken out, and Baroness Stonemover has been forced to activate her reserves, and some citizens have been trampled to death in their urgency to leave, well, you call it *movement*? And if the entire Palace were on fire—which is not as hard to imagine as you might think—would you then say, 'there is a certain warmth'?"

"Well, Captain, I—"

"I should very much like to ask why I was not informed of

this before, but I cannot, for I know very well why; it is because I have been wounded, and, moreover, because I have been seeing to the aftermath of the attempt against His Majesty."

"Captain, I—"

"No, I am not blaming you, Thack; it is only that I am annoyed, and now I must decide what action to take."

"It would seem, Captain, if I may be permitted an opinion, that Baroness Stonemover is doing what has to be done."

Khaavren shook his head. "Thack, have you spent any time in forests where there are dangerous animals, such as dzur, or tiassa, or bear, or wolves, or even dragons?"

"Why, yes, Captain, I have."

"Have you ever seen all of the birds fly away suddenly, while the smaller animals are seen scurrying into their holes, or in some other direction?"

"I am familiar with this, yes, Captain."

"Well, and if you were to make certain that these birds escaped safely, and the small animals reached shelter, well, would you then feel, as you seem to feel about the exodus from the city, that nothing more needed to be done?"

"I take your meaning, Captain."

"I am glad you do."

"But, Captain, have you any orders for me?"

Khaavren sighed. "None yet, my good Thack, for I will not know what to do until I have finished reading all of these cursed reports. But be prepared for anything."

"Yes, Captain."

Khaavren read the reports, forcing himself to take his time so as not to miss any detail, and, at the same time, allowing himself to build a picture of the city as it stood; and, more important, to attempt to feel how it was moving. The change in the mood and character of the city even from that morning, when he had come to the Palace, was shocking; and again he cursed his wounds, which had forced him to take a coach— what he would have seen walking, instead of driving by, would have told him a great deal that he could not deduce even from the most accurate of reports.

As he worked, the notion began to grow that, if things were falling out as they seemed to be, there was nothing to be done. If the full force of the Imperial Army were called in, then, perhaps, a semblance of order could be kept in the city; but, failing that, he could find no plan, even one involving all of his forces, Baroness Stonemover's, and even the Lavodes, providing they could be persuaded to help, that would, in the event of a fully fledged riot, have any chance at all of preventing an equally fully fledged conflagration. His only choice, as he saw it, was to concentrate his forces around the Palace, with the idea of protecting His Majesty, while simultaneously hoping His Majesty would find a way to appease the populace.

He sighed. When word got out that Aliera had been arrested, well, this would not ease the situation.

However, Khaavren had not reached his position because he was one to give up easily; on the contrary, he sat and racked his brains, going over and over the reports, for several hours. He was still thinking when it came time to escort His Majesty on his rounds, which occurred just before the twelfth hour after noon. As they went through the familiar ritual, Khaavren took a certain pleasure in pacing out the path through the quiet Palace, as if the troubles they faced were, at any rate, over for the day.

His Majesty said, "Captain, I have received word that Lord Adron is preparing to move against me in the morning."

"I am surprised, Sire."

"How, you did not think that, with his daughter arrested, he would attack at once?"

"No, Sire, it is not that."

"Well?"

"I am surprised that he would give warning. The Breath of Fire Battalion moves so quickly that it would seem that, to attack in the morning, he needed do nothing before the very moment of the attack."

"Well, that is true, except, according to Lord Rollondar's intelligence, he has made certain magical preparations, and these require time to bring into position."

"Ah. Magical preparations."

"I have alerted those Athyra wizards on whom we can depend."

"Yes, Sire."

"Are you still worried about the populace?"

"I am, Sire."

"Well, do not."

"How, do not?"

"I have given the problem over to Baroness Stonemover."

"And, yet—"

"You will have another task on the morrow, and one that will allow no time to concern yourself with rebellious Teckla."

"Sire?"

"In the first place, you must protect Noima."

"I understand. And Your Majesty as well."

The Emperor shrugged, as if he could not argue, but was not pleased to consider himself in need of protection.

Khaavren said, "Your Majesty has done me the honor of mentioning one task; what, then is the second?"

"You must arrest Lord Adron."

"Yes, Sire," said Khaavren.

"You perceive that it is your duty."

"I believe, Sire, that I had the honor of informing Your Majesty some days ago that this was my opinion; I am pleased that it coincides with Your Majesty's."

"Have you any questions?"

"No, Sire; everything is clear to me."

"That is good, Captain, for I am tired, and it seems we have arrived at the end of the rounds for this evening."

"Yes, Sire, and allow me to wish Your Majesty a good night."

"And a good night to you as well, my dear Captain. I will see you in the morning."

"No, Sire, another will be here; for to-morrow I must prepare to carry out Your Majesty's orders."

"Ah. Yes. Then I will no doubt see you later in the day."

"Yes, Sire. No doubt Your Majesty will."

In spite of his coolness when answering the Emperor, Khaavren was certainly surprised by these orders, although, he reflected as he walked back to the Dragon Wing, he need not have been—what could be more natural than to assign the Imperial Guard the task of protecting Their Majesties? And what could be more natural than assigning their Captain the task of arresting the rebel?

To the right, the task annoyed him, for he was not convinced that Baroness Stonemover was equal to the task. Yet, to the left, he felt a certain relief, for in his considering the exodus from the city, and all it implied, he had realized that there was no way to reliably keep order in the streets—not with Adron attacking from without as the forces of disorder had their way within; Khaavren was pleased to cede this task to Stonemover. And, as for protecting Their Majesties, well, there were certain steps to be taken, and that was that—if they were overwhelmed, then there was no more to be said, except that each guardsman must do his best. As for arresting Lord Adron, well, that was a mere formality. If the Imperial Army were victorious, all he need do was find Adron and take his sword; if the Imperial Army were not victorious, there could be no arrest.

Although, to be sure, it would be something to be remembered if, while the battle raged, he could penetrate the lines and lay hands on His Highness, carrying out the arrest of the general while the troops fought on. As he had this thought, he smiled, and within him the Khaavren of years ago whispered it was just such chances as this that he had longed for.

He shrugged. The Khaavren of years ago may have longed for such chances, and, to be sure, would have gone through fire and blood for just such an opportunity; but the Khaavren of today was older, perhaps wiser, and, above all, without his friends—indeed, was not Aerich even now keeping company with His Highness? No, thought Khaavren, the chance for such heroics comes, at the most, but once in a lifetime, and he had had his five hundred years before, and had taken it, and there was no more to be said on the subject. These, at any rate, were his thoughts when he stepped into his office.

"Ah, my dear Khaavren, there you are! I have been awaiting you."

"Aerich!"

"Yes, it is Aerich. Why, what is it? What accounts for that look on your face?"

"I have been thinking, Aerich, and you were very much in my thoughts."

"How, I? Well, I cannot but be pleased to be thought of by my good friend. What were you thinking?"

"Tell me first, Aerich, where are Pel and Tazendra?"

"Pel was here with me for some time, but has now returned to the house, where he awaits us."

"And Tazendra?"

"She spent an hour in the Dzur Wing, and has now gone to join Pel. Why, is there something for us to do?"

Khaavren laughed. "I nearly think there is. Go now and join them, my friend, and tell them to sharpen their weapons, for to-morrow we shall have a task to perform."

"Very well. You know I never ask questions."

"I know it well. And, Aerich, we ought to send the servants out of the city."

"I have done so."

"How, you? You know what is going to happen to-morrow? Ah, but I have forgotten; you have just come from His Highness. Apropos, has he your loyalty?"

"He has my friendship, but if he had my loyalty I would not now be here."

"Good, good," said Khaavren.

Aerich smiled. "It is a pleasure to hear you laugh."

"It is a pleasure to have again something about which to laugh. Go now, my friend. The morning will see blood, but to-night will see scratches on parchment; I will be hard at work for some hours."

"Till to-morrow, then."

"Till to-morrow."

# Chapter the Twenty-ninth

### Which Treats of Khaavren's Peculiar Interactions with An Assassin or Two.

EVENTUALLY THE LAST OF KHAAVREN'S instructions were written out—and written out, we should add, so clearly and precisely that he had no fear of a lieutenant misinterpreting them. He made certain each document was signed and placed in its proper receptacle, after which, rubbing his eyes, he permitted himself to make his way home.

It was, by this time, quite late, yet the streets were still alive—more than alive, it seemed to Khaavren, they were awake and aware. There were, in the first place, more people out than he was accustomed to see at such an hour. In the second place, many of these people were clearly abandoning their homes—taking what possessions they could and leaving as quickly as they could manage by foot, horse, wagon, or coach, depending on the person's wealth. In the third place, there was an attitude among those who remained—an attitude of watchful expectation, and of alertness, and of fear, and even of anger. Indeed, there were some who openly sneered upon seeing the Captain's uniform, although none of these were close, and, after giving him such a look, sometimes accompanied by a gesture, each one at once took to his heels.

As he passed the Avenue of Seven Swans Park, he noticed a figure huddled against a store advertising preserved fruit. Realizing that there was something familiar about this figure, Khaavren looked; looking he recognized Raf, the pastry vendor. "My dear Raf," said Khaavren, approaching. "How do you fare?"

"Ah, ah," said Raf, looking up bleakly. "Is it you, my dear Captain?"

"Indeed it is, my friend, indeed it is. But come, what accounts for the sorrow I read upon your countenance?"

"You ask me that!" cried Raf.

"Yes, I ask you that; I even think I ask you twice. What is the matter, my friend?"

"Ruined, Captain! I am ruined!"

"How, ruined? And yet, it was less than two weeks ago that you were flourishing!"

"That has ever been the fortune of man," agreed Ruf. "From the highest to the lowest in an instant."

"But come, what has happened? Will no one buy your pastries?"

"Buy my pastries?" said Raf. "And what pastries have I to sell?"

"How is this, no pastries?"

"Indeed, none."

"But, it seemed to me that you had a cart, and—"

"The cart is gone," sobbed the Teckla. "Destroyed by ruffians, who pretended they could use it to pack their belongings so they could leave the city."

"Cha! In truth?"

"But what of that?" continued Raf. "For the last three days I have been unable to afford the flour my pastries require, and so I have made none."

"You could not afford flour, my dear Raf? How can this be? I had thought you near to being a wealthy man!"

"The price of wheat, my dear Captain, it is abominable.

And if no one can afford bread, well, can anyone afford pastries? And my wife—"

"Well, your wife?"

"There is no one to buy her pottery. We may lose our home because we cannot pay the note, if, indeed, it is not destroyed outright."

"How, destroyed?"

"Everyone speaks of marching on the Palace, Captain."

"Everyone? Who is everyone?"

"Everyone! And if they march on the Palace, well, the Palace will march back, and what will be left of our city?"

"Come, come," said Khaavren, "it cannot be as bad as that. There is always hope."

But the Teckla would not be reconciled, and, after trying for some few moments, Khaavren gave him a few silver orbs to help him over these trying times. Raf was tearfully grateful, but Khaavren still left a sad and bitter man behind him as he continued on his way home.

Khaavren was considering the implications of this conversation, as well as thinking of his plans for the morrow, when, as he stepped onto the Street of the Glass Cutters, he was attacked by Dunaan.

We apologize if this seems abrupt, but, as history is a recapitulation of life, and as the history we are relating is Khaavren's and not Dunaan's, it seems appropriate to allow our narrative to reflect, as it were, Khaavren's reaction to the event, as opposed to Dunaan's, for, in fairness, as far as the Jhereg was concerned, there was no trace of abruptness whatsoever. On the contrary, he had, having learned Khaavren's route home, spent many hours in picking his spot, and then, not knowing precisely when Khaavren would be there, had spent several more hours waiting. He had three assistants who, on the one hand, were to warn him of Khaavren's approach, and, on the other, were to make sure there were neither police nor friends of Khaavren nearby when the Captain approached.

We should add that, although these three nameless assistants performed their functions, they were not expected to be

in sight when the attack took place, nor were they ever informed in so many words what was happening; this was by
invariable Jhereg custom, and was done so that, should any of
these three be caught and forced to testify under the Orb,
each would be able to state that he had not seen Dunaan kill
anyone, nor had he known that Dunaan was going to do so—
the Orb would recognize these as truths, which would make
it more difficult to convict, not only Dunaan, but the assistants as well.

On this occasion, Dunaan waited between two buildings
next to which Khaavren invariably walked, and had, moreover, disabled the one glowbulb that operated in the vicinity
(otherwise, of course, it would have helpfully lighted him up
and alerted everyone in the area that someone was crouching
in an alley). He was informed by certain signs that the Captain approached, and was informed in a like manner that there
were neither police nor agents of the Captain anywhere in
sight. Khaavren then stepped past the narrow gap between the
buildings and Dunaan, utterly silent, and with a long, wicked
poniard naked in his hand, glided up behind him.

Khaavren, guided by some warrior's instinct, or perhaps by
the half-heard sound of Dunaan's heartbeat, turned in time to
see the knife flashing down for his throat, and to feel the annoyance that he had, again, been taken by surprise, and even
(for the reader ought to understand that the mind works much
faster than the body in such circumstances) to berate himself
for lack of caution, after surviving no fewer than three earlier
attempts. This time, there could be no reprieve; this time the
assassin was in perfect position, and Khaavren's friends,
though scarcely a hundred meters away, might as well have
been at Redface for all they could help the Captain.

Khaavren had only time to begin a curse before the knife
flashed down, continued past his shoulder, and hit the ground
with a clang an instant before Dunaan, gasping and stumbling, landed on his knees. At this point Khaavren's body reacted faster than his mind, for, before he had time to realize
he had somehow been given exactly the reprieve he could not
expect, his sword was in his hand.

Dunaan fell face first to the ground. The Captain noticed an object, such as a dart or a small knife, protruding from the exact center of the assassin's back; there was, in fact, very little blood, yet the effect on the Jhereg seemed profound. "I cannot move my legs," he said conversationally.

"Well," said Khaavren.

"I believe I have been poisoned."

Khaavren endeavored to keep an eye on his assailant, who could have been only feigning an injury (although for what purpose, when he could have easily killed Khaavren, wasn't clear), and at the same time look around to find his deliverer, who, for all Khaavren knew, might have only accidentally struck down the assassin. The Captain remarked, "If you have indeed been poisoned, my dear fellow, I give you my word that it was not my doing. Come, let me ask you a few questions."

"Ask your questions to the air, if you wish; you'll get no answers from me—at least, not until I have learned who has so treated me; for I cannot imagine how you could have struck me in the back while I was facing you."

"Were you asking about me, my good Dunaan?" said someone who could not be seen, but whose voice appeared to come from the same shadows the Jhereg had lately quitted.

Khaavren's eyes strained in that direction, while the assassin remarked, "I do not know who you are, for I am no longer able to turn my head. I believe, in fact, that I shall soon be unable to talk, and, no doubt, an inability to breathe will follow shortly."

"You are perspicacious," said the unknown.

"You have killed me, then," said Dunaan.

"Exactly."

"How did you find me?"

"I found the location where you would necessarily kill the Captain, for I knew you intended to do so, and then I waited until you revealed yourself. Come, what do you think?"

"An entirely admirable plan, I tell you so. But I cannot help but wonder—"

"Yes?"

"Who are you, and why have you done this? I confess that your voice sounds familiar, and yet—"

"How, you ask who I am? And why I have killed you? Come, your mind is not yet paralyzed; a moment's thought should answer your question. Whom have you lately betrayed?"

"The Gods! Are you Mario?"

"None other."

"But you were taken!"

"Obviously not; you ought to have assured yourself on the success of your scheme."

"And yet, I heard an attempt was made on His Majesty, and that, in fact, there had been an arrest."

"I cannot speak to that," said the unknown, still hiding in the shadows. "But, well, here I am."

"Captain," said Dunaan, "you should be ashamed of letting a dangerous assassin loose—how is someone to be able to make an attempt on His Majesty and yet walk the streets? You are only a poor sort of officer after all."

"Maybe," said Khaavren. "Maybe I am as poor an officer as you are an assassin. Yet consider that His Majesty yet lives, and that so do I, whereas you—"

"Well, I cannot dispute you there. Ah! When I consider the chance that was before me, the opportunity that is now gone, it is enough to make me gnash my teeth, yet they will scarcely respond to commands. I perceive my speech is slurring. My breath is going. I cannot speak! I die, I die."

"Well," said Khaavren.

"Well," said Mario.

Khaavren stood over the one called Dunaan, and discovered that, indeed, he was no longer breathing. He addressed the shadows, saying, "I perceive from certain things you have said that you, who seem to be called Mario, are the very one I spent so many hours looking for today."

"Indeed I am. But what is this about an arrest being made? Have you taken the wrong man?"

"Hardly. I have taken the right woman."

"The right woman? Come, sir; I have just saved your life. In exchange, tell me what you mean."

"That is only fair," judged Khaavren.

"And so?"

"I today arrested the Lady Aliera, who, for reasons I cannot guess, helped you to escape from the Palace, while I and all of my guardsmen were searching for you."

"How, you have arrested Aliera?"

"I had that honor."

"My dear Captain, having saved your life, I confess that I am now of a mind to kill you."

"My blade is out, my dear assassin, and I am ready. You may try your best."

"Oh, my best is sufficient, I promise you, for you are not protected by the Orb. If you are not convinced, you may ask Dunaan there."

"As you would, then. I am ready."

"Well, remain ready, then, and let us speak for a moment."

"As you wish; you have, indeed, saved my life, and, though I long to get my hands on you, well, I cannot deny you a few minutes of conversation, at least."

"Then tell me this: What is the charge against Aliera?"

"High treason."

"And the evidence?"

"Irrefutable; the more so because she has made no effort to deny it; she pretends she hates His Majesty, and that anyone attempting to kill him has her favor."

"She does not deny it?"

"Not in the least."

"Will there be a trial?"

"A mere formality, unless she changes her mind and chooses to deny what she did; but even in that case there can be little doubt that His Majesty, who was, I assure you, displeased by the attempt on his life, will surely find her guilty."

"And then?"

"And then, I'm afraid she must be executed."

"Executed!"

"Yes."

"By what means?"

"She will be taken to the Executioner's Star, and there each of her appendages will be removed, in order, by a single blow of the ax. It may be that His Majesty will be kindly disposed, and will thus order the executioner to begin with her head; but it may be otherwise."

"Well, I understand. Tell me, Captain: If I let you go, will you pursue me? For I must admit that I am inclined to let you live, if for no other reason than to avoid giving Dunaan's shade the satisfaction of knowing that you were killed, should this shade come to hear of it. And yet, I will not allow myself to be arrested—I have matters to attend to and issues to resolve."

Khaavren shrugged. "You have, as I said, saved my life, even if you did so for your own reasons, so I will tell you this: I will not now pursue you. And to-morrow my time will be so taken up that I will not have a moment to spare. But, beginning the day after that, I will bend all of my efforts to tracking you down."

"Agreed. Perhaps I will see you again, Captain."

"Perhaps so, assassin."

"For now, farewell, Khaavren."

"And fare you well, Mario. When we next meet, one of us will die."

Khaavren heard no sounds, but somehow he knew that Mario had vanished into the shadows. He bent then, to inspect the body as well as he could in the dim light that emerged from the buildings across the way. He made as good an inspection as he could, although, in truth, standing alone on the street where he had lately been attacked caused him a certain amount of worry; still, he finished his investigation in good order (the results of which investigation we will spare our readers, as they play no material part in our history) and then walked the hundred meters to his house, where, as he lighted a lamp and poured himself a small glass of wine and sat on the couch, he was pleased to see Daro appear next to him.

She seated herself with some effort, which Khaavren noticed. "Madam, are you still in pain?"

"I confess, I do feel a certain discomfort when I endeavor to move."

"And yet, was there not a dose?"

"Perhaps I will take it later; for now I wish my mind entirely clear. Do you know that your friend, Aerich, has ordered the servants out of the house, out of the city, and even out of the district?"

"Yes, so he told me. I was going to do the same, but he acted first, Apropos—"

"Yes?"

"You should leave the city as well, madam."

"How, I? You think I am in some danger?"

"The city is going mad and Lord Adron is attacking, and a madman believed he could assassinate His Majesty in spite of the Orb, only I am convinced he was not mad; yes, madam, you are in danger, as is everyone who stays here."

"And you pretend that I should run from this danger?"

"You pretend that, wounded as you are, you can fight?"

"Well, there is some truth in what you say, yet this very wound makes travel unlikely."

"A coach—"

"How, is there a coach to be found? Aerich's servant, Fawnd, took every minute of the hour he was allotted to find a mere wagon, and he returned covered with blood and bruises, so that I do not believe he had an easy time of it."

"I can find you a coach."

"His Majesty's?"

"What of it?"

"I no longer hold the position at court I once did; hence I no longer have a right to ride in His Majesty's coach, my dear Captain."

"Would that stop you from doing so?"

"It would."

"Hmmm. You are stubborn."

"Well, I am a Tiassa, and moreover, I am from Adrilankha, where each day we must contend with the sea; we must give

way now and then, it is true, but we learn to always return to
our position, and to build our walls the stronger for the bat-
tering they must endure."

"I take your point, madam. And yet, to merely use one of
Their Majesty's coaches, and a coach which otherwise—"

"No, Captain."

"Well, I have a thought."

"Then share it with me."

"If we were affianced, that is, if you were to consent to
marry me, well, then you could ride in the Coach as the
fiancée of the Captain of the Guard and no one could have
reason to object; what do you say to that?"

Daro had nothing to say to that for some few seconds, after
which she said, "I will admit, Captain, that, in the first place,
marriage had never occurred to me."

"Well, and in the second place?"

"If it had, I do not believe I should have anticipated a proposal such as you have offered."

"Is it any the less welcome for that? Come, you know that
I love you, for I have said so; do you love me a little?"

"You know that I do."

"Will you permit me to kiss you?"

"Willingly."

"Well?"

"Here, then. Ah!"

"Yes?"

"Be careful of my wound."

"Oh, Countess. I am sorry."

"Think nothing of it. Once more, but carefully."

"There."

"That was better."

"What, then, is my lady's opinion?"

"You kiss well."

"Cha! You are laughing at me; you know that was not the
question."

"You wish to know my opinion?"

"Yes, that is exactly what I wish."

"Very well, here it is."

"I am listening."

"I believe, in the first place—"

"Yes, in the first place?"

"That we ought to get married, and have some number of children."

"Yes, we shall make boys as pretty as their mother."

"And girls as brave as their father."

"How, you deny you are brave?"

"Well, you deny you are pretty?"

"You confuse me, Countess."

"Does that make me less attractive?"

"Not in the least."

"Well, then."

"But what about the second place?"

"Oh, in the second place, I believe that, marriage or no, I wish to stay here with you, whatever may happen."

"Madam, I am going into danger to-morrow."

"I know. I wish—"

"Yes. But you cannot. You know that your wounds prohibit it. And, moreover—"

"Yes?"

"You know that I love you."

"Yes. Take my hand."

"Here it is."

"When then?"

"If I go into battle to-morrow worried about you—"

"Ah, my brave Captain, that is unfair!"

"I know. Yet, it is true; I would be worried for you, and, worrying, I—"

"Well, I understand."

"And then?"

After an interval of silence large enough to hold a small conversation, Daro sighed. "Where shall I go, and for how long?" she said.

"Follow the servants to Aerich's estate, and I will join you there when this is over; I shall request of His Majesty a leave of absence, which he cannot fail to grant me, and then we shall be married."

"Very well. When must I leave?"

"To-night."

"How, to-night?"

"I shall send for the coach, for, if you are to leave, you must be out of the city before the first light breaks."

"If anything happens to you—"

"I think that nothing will."

"Why do you think so?"

"Because I love you, and you will be waiting for me, and we will be married; nothing will happen to change that."

"Do you promise?"

"I promise."

"I take you at your word."

"You may do so."

"Then send for the coach, and we shall spend the time until it arrives in holding hands, and speaking of the future."

"That is an admirable plan, Countess."

"I am glad you think so, Captain."

As they put this plan into practice, we trust the reader will not need to intrude on these few moments of privacy, but will allow us to follow Mario as he walks through the streets toward the small hotel where he makes his home. He did not, in fact, arrive at his destination.

Contrary to any expectations this phrasing might give the reader, it was not because he, in turn, was set upon an assailant; rather, it was because he was set upon by an idea. No doubt the reader, whether because of a familiarity with history, or because of a close reading of this very work, is ahead of the historian—that is, the reader knows already the idea that has just occurred to Mario as he makes his way toward home after killing Dunaan and choosing not to kill Khaavren. If so, the historian is rather pleased than otherwise; while there is, without question, a certain joy in surprising the reader with a revelation, we cannot fail to take pleasure in knowing that we have provided the reader sufficient clues to remove the possibility of surprise. Or, to put it another way, whether the reader at this moment knows what Mario intends to do, or whether the reader will only discover this when the

time comes to reveal it, in either case, we beg to submit that
we have done our job.

To return, then, to Mario—he stopped at a particular street
corner upon being struck with this sudden notion, paused for
some few minutes, during which time the idea, dropped some
minutes earlier on ground which had been tilled in the Palace,
sprouted at that moment and grew like a veritable jumpweed.
When it had matured, a process which took, as we have implied, only a few minutes, he abruptly turned on his heel and
went off in an entirely different direction from the one he had
been taking before. This brought him, after traversing streets
still relatively crowded with those who were, because of pre-
science, gossip, or just good sense, fleeing the city, to an un-
prepossessing leather-goods store, and through it, to a door in
back, where he at once clapped.

Soon enough the door was opened a crack, revealing a
small woman of about a thousand years, with close-cropped
light hair and the round, pleasant face of a Teckla, save for
the excessively dark eyebrows and large nose. She wore the
grey and black of the House of the Jhereg.

She said, "It is late; what do you want?"

Mario wordlessly held out a small piece of paper. The
woman, whose name was Cariss, studied the paper carefully,
her eyes growing somewhat wide, then opened the door fully
and stood aside for Mario to enter. The apartment, though not
spacious, was cluttered with cut glass, strands of jewels, and
small sculptures done in ivory or bronze, as well as plush furniture, and the whole of the floor was covered by a thick,
dark carpet—the room spoke of comfort, luxury, and wealth.
Wealth, as it happened, was the subject that was first discussed after Mario had been seated in a soft chair near a
burning lamp, so that the light made his face appear to glow
in its luminance.

"I perceive," said Cariss, "that you are in funds."

"The bill," said Mario, "is negotiable, in whole or in part,
and can be drawn on the Jhereg treasury."

"So I perceive. It is not a small amount."

"I require but a tenth part of it; the rest can be yours."

Cariss nodded slowly. "I will not pretend that I am uninterested. What do you want?"

"First, you must answer me a question or two."

"Very well. Will you have klava?"

"It would keep me awake."

"Tea? Wine?"

"Have you water?"

"I have a well; the water is sweet."

"Excellent."

"A moment."

She returned with the water, sat, and said, "Now, ask your questions."

"How much power can you summon?"

"Power?"

"Yes."

"The question is meaningless."

"Excuse me, it is not."

"But ... power to do what?"

"Nothing."

"Power to do nothing?"

"Exactly."

"I do not understand."

"I am not surprised, for it is unlikely anyone has ever before asked such a question."

"Then you must explain."

"Attend me."

"I am attending."

"The pure power through which sorcery works, the power which the sorcerer shapes and controls in order to work the changes in matter that the sorcerer desires—that is the power I wish to summon at a certain time and a certain place. But it is important that there be a great deal of it, hence, I wish to know how much of it you can cause to be summoned."

Cariss considered. "Well, you want to know how much undirected power can be pulled through the Orb—"

"Not through the Orb."

"Not through the Orb? But how else—"

"Elder sorcery, of course."

"Elder sorcery?"

"Exactly."

"You know more than I would have thought, young man."

"It is necessary for me to know a little of everything. Yes, I am speaking of elder sorcery."

"Such a thing would be illegal."

Mario gave her a look impossible to describe.

"If," she said at last, "you would explain exactly what you are trying to do—"

"No," said Mario.

A look of impatience crossed Cariss's features; Mario touched the pouch into which he had put the bill; Cariss shrugged.

"I will tell you this much," said Mario. "I need to be able to summon an immense amount of power, using elder sorcery, and I need to put it into a certain area and keep it there, though only for a few seconds."

"You speak of power as if it were a glass of water that you could simply put somewhere."

Mario set his glass on a table near his elbow. "Well?" he said.

"This power will do nothing," said Cariss, shaking her head.

"That is what I wish."

"And you want to do it yourself?"

"Exactly."

"Even more difficult."

"I am not offering a small sum of money," said Mario. "Nor are you unskilled."

"Are you attempting to flatter me?"

"No, madam, I am attempting to purchase your services."

"To do what?" she said, beginning to sound a little vexed.

"To fill an area with power," said Mario, who was, himself, becoming annoyed at having to repeat himself. "Is it possible?"

"Possible? Anything is possible. There would need to be a medium, and—"

"A what?"

"Something upon which to lay the power."

"Would the air not work?"

"Too insubstantial—too thin."

"What then?"

"Thick air."

Mario frowned. "I do not understand."

"Fog. Mist. Air with a great deal of water mixed in, so that the energy can attach itself to the water."

"How much energy can you supply?"

She shook her head. "You still do not comprehend—it doesn't matter how much, because it won't be *doing* anything."

"Good," said Mario. "Then I wish for a great deal of power. A *great* deal."

"If your wish is to attract the attention of every sorcerer in a thousand-mile radius, well, I assure you there are easier ways to go about it."

"That is not my wish."

"It will happen, nevertheless."

"Then let it."

Cariss stared at him, as if trying to see into his mind to discover the use to which he intended to put this unusual spell. Then she sighed and said, "Does it matter what form it takes?"

"I do not understand."

"The spell must be invested into an object if you, rather than I, are to use it. Does it matter what object?"

"No. Something small."

"Will you be setting it off, or will another? If it might be another, I will instruct it to release upon a word or a sign. If it is to be you, then we can arrange for it to respond to your will. Or, if you prefer, I can arrange it so you simply open it like cracking an egg."

"That would be best."

"That is how it shall be."

"Then you can do it?"

"I can do it."

"How much power?"

"There is no limit to the amount of power available, only to the amount one person can control. When the energy isn't doing anything, it need not be controlled."

"And so?"

"And so we will summon more power than, I think, has ever been seen before in one place—and all of this power will do nothing except to exist, alerting ever sorcerer for a thousand miles in all directions, and then it will be as if it had never happened."

"Excellent."

"How long do you wish it to hold together? A few seconds is easy; after that, I must find power to hold it together, and this power can only come from the Orb, or from itself; and I have no wish to attempt to control that sort of power even for something trivial—especially for something trivial."

"Ten seconds would be good, five seconds may well be enough."

Cariss considered for a moment, then said, "Eight seconds, then; or perhaps a little more. I can do that safely enough."

"So be it. Eight seconds. How, precisely, will it work?"

"It will be a small glass ball. You will shatter the glass, and the area—how big an area?"

"A fifty-foot diameter will be sufficient."

"Very well. The area will fill with fog—"

"How long will it take to fill?"

"Do you wish it to happen quickly?"

"Yes."

"Less than the drawing of a breath, then."

"Very well."

"It will fill with fog, and each particle of this fog will be charged with immense power, which will do nothing, and everyone within the circle will be bathed in power, which will do nothing, although," she frowned, "it may feel a trifle odd, I don't know. In any case, after eight seconds, the power and the fog will dissipate, and nothing will have changed."

"Good. That is what I wish. Apropos the fog—"

"Yes?"

"Can it be made thick, so that a person might hide in it?"

"That is easily done. It can be made so thick you will not be able to see your hand, though it be six inches in front of your eyes."

"Perfect."

Cariss shook her head, as though resigning herself to remaining mystified. "When do you need it?"

"When can I have it?"

"You can have it in an hour."

"Then that is when I need it."

"It will be ready."

"I will wait here."

"Very well. Oh, have you a preference for the mist?"

"A preference in what way?"

"Its color. Black, or red, or grey, or—"

"Grey," said Mario. "The color of death. Let it be grey."

"It shall be grey," said the sorceress.

# Chapter the Thirtieth

*Which Treats of Dawn
On the Day of Battle.*

THE MORNING OF THE SEVENTEENTH day of the month of the Vallista of the 532$^{nd}$ year of the Reign of Tortaalik the First was cool if one considered it to be late summer, but warm if one thought of it as early autumn. Even before dawn, while the Dragon Gate, with its high stone walls and strong iron bars, stood open to the world, there was a promise of a breeze from the east, bringing with it the sweet aroma the last of the blossoming late-apples, and a promise, as well, of that perfect weather where one is comfortable in a heavy cloak if one is standing still, in a lighter cloak for those walking about, or in a simple jerkin for those engaged in heavy exercise.

Should the reader realize with sudden dismay or annoyance that the weather has been all but ignored by the historian, we will point out that, according to our almanac, the weather had remained, with the least variation, slightly warm, but not forbiddingly so, with a little wind, and only a sprinkle of rain upon one or two of the nine days which comprise our history; there has been, in a word, little of interest about the weather, and therefore no reason to take up our reader's valuable time by describing it.

Indeed, the only reason for mentioning it upon this occasion is, as the astute reader has no doubt realized, by way of making an ironic contrast between the conditions of the day and the events destined to take place upon it—a comparison that may be unnecessary in a strictly historical sense, but which, because of its appropriateness, the historian finds irresistible. Moreover, as great events are about to unfold, we consider it a pleasing device to begin with facts which are, in essence, unimportant—that is, to turn our reader's attention to matters unrelated to our history, after which, the reader may be assured, we will gradually begin to reveal those momentous events, as well as the no less interesting personal events, the reader's interest in which has, no doubt, caused him to remain with us to this point in our history.

The Dragon Gate, as we have already said, was built of iron and stone; the stone was in the form of a pair of towers which were built as part of the city wall itself; the iron consisted of bars three-quarters of a meter in thickness and separated by half a meter. It was, we should add, very difficult to see through these bars when the gate was closed. Should it happen that the Warlord wished to close the gate, this could be accomplished by releasing the single massive rope that worked an intricate series of wheels, gears, and pulleys which held the grid poised above the gateway. Dragons' heads adorned each tower (or, rather, a sculptor's rendering of such heads—to use real dragons' heads would have been disrespectful).

Some few hours before the first light of morning filtered through the overcast the streets had emptied themselves of citizens—all of those who wished to leave had either done so, or realized, now that the Warlord had had the gates of the city closed against the expected attack of His Highness, they would be unable to do so; and those who remained tucked themselves into their homes where they hoped they would be safe. Daro, the Countess of Whitecrest, was, in fact, among the last to leave. We should add, as an aside, that this, while true for the district near the Dragon Gate, where we have placed ourselves, was not true everywhere—the Underside, for example, was quite active, and many historians place the beginning of the Uprising as during the night we have just skipped over; to be sure, there were isolated fires, and some shops had been broken into.

All of which is not to say that the streets near the Dragon Gate were empty—we were careful above to say the streets were empty of *citizens*; in fact, had we wished to indulge in low humor, we might have made a remark to the effect that there was a veritable army of people within the Gate, the supposed humor being found, of course, in the fact there *was* an army within the Gate—to wit, the Imperial Army, which flooded the square to overflowing with the regiment of the Calivor Pike-men led by Lord Tross, followed by the cavalry regiment of Sorett, led by Lady Glass, which was almost contained in the square, and filling the streets around the square on both sides was the cavalry brigade of Lookfor, still commanded by the Duke of Lookfor who had founded it. In the streets behind them, awaiting their command to move into place, were remaining infantry divisions too numerous to mention.

The Warlord was mounted in the middle of the Sorett Regiment; on one side of him was Lady Glass, on the other was Nyleth who commanded the Wizards of the Imperial Army. Other soldiers and wizards had manned the towers, awaiting the command, should it come, to lower the gate, and waiting as well to give word that Adron's army had been sighted.

"Upon you," said Rollondar to Nyleth, "falls the chief burden. You must, first of all, evaluate the threat contained by this spell-wagon he is reported to have; you must determine if it is a real threat. You perceive, if it is a bluff, I will close the gate and we will defend it, while I disperse the troops to the other gates of the city, and we will fight defensively. If the threat is real, we must make destroying it the center of our strategy, wherefore we will leave the gate open and attack them through it, with the intention of leading you and your assistants against the spell-wagon."

"I understand," said Nyleth, an Athyra with large, brilliant eyes and a perpetual smile, giving him the appearance of a madman, which some thought he was. "But what if Lord Adron appears at another gate?"

"He will not," said Rollondar. "Oh, he may end by attacking another gate if it looks best to him, but the Breath of Fire Battalion will appear first at the Dragon Gate—Adron would die rather than miss an opportunity for such theatrics. I give you my word that he hopes to give battle here and enter beneath this arch."

"I understand, my lord."

"Do you then, my good Nyleth, understand what your task is to be?"

"Yes, but—"

"But?"

Nyleth continued smiling, as he leaned forward; Rollondar resolutely reminded himself that, mad or not, the Athyra had proven himself in a score of battles. The wizard said, "If the threat does prove real—and, my lord, if there is elder sorcery involved it is almost certainly real—I will need a guard of fighters to help reach the spell-wagon."

"You will have one," said Rollondar, "for, should it prove necessary, and should nothing else present itself, I will send my personal guard to aid you against those who guard the spell-wagon."

Nyleth looked around him at Rollondar's legion of grim, powerful fighters, and his smile grew broader. "That will certainly do, my lord."

"You understand, then?"

"Entirely."

"Very well. Then no more need be said; now we await Lord Adron's pleasure." He did not seem entirely happy as he said it, for one rarely enjoys time spent waiting for another's pleasure—certainly Greycat did not, as he paced the floor of the cabaret in the Underside, occasionally stopping to look outside to see if the one for whom he was waiting was arriving, or if violence had yet erupted in the streets. By chance, in that area, there had been as yet neither looting nor burning, and so Greycat returned to his pacing.

The cabaret was nominally closed, but one would not have guessed it to look upon it, for it appeared to have a sizable contingent of patrons—no fewer than a score of men and women were there, sitting, drinking, talking quietly, and occasionally glancing at Greycat with expressions of trust and confidence. They all of them affected garb that would have been appropriate in the mountains, and they all of them had the look of those who spend a great deal of time out of doors; for these were none other than the advance guard of the army of brigands of whom Greycat had earlier spoken to Dunaan; they had arrived the day before, and been told to meet at the cabaret in the early hours of the morning. Now they were here, armed head to toe, and they awaited Greycat's orders, while he waited for someone who, unaccountably, was late.

The door opened, but it was Grita who walked in. She glanced at the assembled brigands, appeared to dismiss them with a glance, and said, "We must speak."

"Well, speak," said Greycat, who, though surprised to see her, did not wish to acknowledge this fact.

"In private."

"Very well. In back?"

"Outside."

"If that is your desire," said Greycat, shrugging.

"I will."

"Here we are, then."

"Yes."

"Well, what have you to say?"

"He for whom you are waiting will not appear."

"How, Dunaan will not appear?"

"That is correct."

"What could keep him? He knows that I but await word of his mission's success before going to His Majesty."

"His mission did not succeed."

"What? The Jhereg refused?"

Grita frowned. "I know nothing of any Jhereg refusing anything."

"But then, of what do you speak?"

"I assumed he was to kill the annoying Tiassa."

"Yes, yes. And then, afterwards, he was to go to the Jhereg and—"

"There was no afterwards."

Greycat stared. "How, he failed to kill the Tiassa?"

"Exactly."

"Are the Gods protecting this guardsman?" Greycat, we should add, pronounced the word *guardsman* in a tone of utmost contempt.

Grita shrugged. "In this case, it seems an assassin was protecting him; or, at least, that is how it seems from what I was able to learn."

"An assassin? Do you mean—"

"Yes. Dunaan is dead."

"Dead!"

"Killed by a Jhereg assassin."

"And the Tiassa yet lives!"

"Exactly."

For the first time, Greycat's eyes now held doubt and confusion.

"Well?" said Grita. "Do we continue?"

"How, you mean continue to His Majesty? Not for the world! We can do nothing until we have killed the Tiassa."

"But still, one man—"

"He will denounce me to His Majesty."

"Well, but does not His Majesty know you already?"

"I know how to play to His Majesty's weaknesses; I cannot do so while the Tiassa lives, for he has His Majesty's ear."

Grita shrugged. "What then?"

"We must kill him ourselves."

"What, you and me?"

"You and me, and our friends in there." He gestured toward the cabaret where his band of cutthroats waited.

"Do you think there are enough of us?"

"Do not jest; it is no laughing matter. Yes, I think there are enough of us."

"Then let us be about it."

"We must find him, first."

"That is taken care of," said Grita with a peculiar smile.

"Taken care of? How?"

"He is at home, and I have set spies there; when he leaves, we will be informed."

Greycat smiled for the first time—a smile reminiscent of Grita's. "Excellent. Then we must return to waiting, but now, at least, I know why I am waiting."

"Shall we go inside?"

"By all means."

"After you."

"I am leading."

The first haze of morning light, so deceptive and ambiguous, had still, perhaps, not quite touched the Palace walls when Sethra stood in the hall which had once borne her name but which was now, after the Lavode Scandal, called the North Room, high in the Dragon Wing. The hall was not overly large, being crowded when more than a hundred were present, and the hearth, which filled most of the west wall, seemed almost absurd for such a small room. There was now a fire upon it, however, and the two score or so assembled there were grateful for it; the furnaces which heated the Palace had not yet been tested for the season, and none were ignited—and the high reaches of the Dragon Wing were but ill-heated at the best of times.

All of those assembled, including Sethra, affected black garb without a speck of color anywhere, save for the chance gleam, here and there, of a weapon's hilt, or a red or blue jewel that might glitter from a sheath or a belt. There were hard wooden chairs in the room, set in a large circle, and every chair was occupied. Sethra's voice was not loud, but it was penetrating. "Our task," she said, "is the protection of the Imperial Wing, and especially of His Majesty. We will be aiding the Red Boot Battalion, but not working with them. I have chosen this course because, while it may be that the Imperial Guard have the skill to protect His Majesty from throngs of rioting citizens, we cannot depend on them to protect His Majesty from well-formed and -trained Dragon warriors; furthermore, while I cannot support the rebellion, neither do I wish to attack Lord Adron, and, so far as I can see, duty requires no such attack. Has anyone anything to say?"

"I do," said a thin woman who, to look at her, one would think too retiring to ever speak in a gathering of more than three; yet her voice was strong and confident.

"What is it, Dreen?"

"My sympathies, such as they are, are with Lord Adron; this Emperor is a fool, as I think we all know, and he is only reaping what he has sown, as the Teckla say. Why do we not support him entirely?"

"For my part, Sethra," said an older man named Tuvo, "I agree with Dreen. I have no respect for His Majesty; why should we defend him?"

There were nods around the room, and some looks of doubt. Sethra said, "Good questions, to be sure. The reason is that Lord Adron has been studying elder sorcery—studying it deeply, and, more than studying it, has been working with it. To my knowledge, he is prepared to invoke powers that threaten the Empire, even the Cycle itself. This causes me some unease, but it would cause me more to consider him as Emperor. He would make a gifted Warlord, but I cannot countenance him as Emperor—not a man who would use such means either to gain the throne or to gain revenge—or, indeed, for any other reason."

"And yet," said a short, attractive woman with curly dark hair, "you will not directly oppose him?"

"I cannot, Roila Lavode," said Sethra. "He is too close a friend."

"Well," said Tuvo, "then do you, Sethra, remain here and defend His Majesty; the rest of us, under some captain upon whom we will agree, will go find His Highness and attack him on the spot. Come, what do you think of my plan?"

"For my part," said Roila, "I am entirely in accord with Tuvo; if there is a chance His Highness may employ elder sorcery against the Orb—"

"He may indeed," said Sethra.

"Then who better to face him than us?"

"There is a great deal of truth in what you say, Roila, and your plan is good, Tuvo, but I will not stay behind. If the will of the Lavodes is to attack Adron, well, my place will be to lead the attack."

"Not in the least," said a woman called Nett. "Why should you be asked to do battle against a friend? We all know what that means—and, in truth, it is to have the choice to refuse such battles that many of us, who desired military service, have accepted the black garments of our corps. Moreover, Sethra, there is no need for you to be there. Consider that His Majesty does, indeed, require protection, and who better to supply it than you? And consider that, though it may be that your presence on the field could be decisive, it is just as likely that your presence in the Palace could save His Majesty's life—unlike Dreen and Tuvo, I should like to see His Majesty preserved if possible, for the continuity of the Orb; I do not feel the Cycle has turned. No, Sethra Lavode, follow your heart, and we will follow ours; you to the Palace and His Majesty's side, we to the gate and His Highness's flank."

There were murmurs of "well spoken" about the room, and Sethra nodded. "If that is the will of the Lavodes," she said, "so be it. I recommend Roila to lead you into battle; does anyone object?"

There were no objections.

"Very well," said Sethra standing. "If you are to reach the gate before the battle commences, there is no time to lose. Go with the Favor, and I hope to see you all again this side of the Falls."

The Lavodes stood as one, presented their compliments to their Captain, filed out of the room and, stopping only to secure their weapons and tools, out of the Palace and so out along the Street of the Dragon toward the gate.

They arrived as the first, tentative, very faint light began to drape the city in morning. They worked their way to the gate itself (annoying no few of Lady Glass's cavalry) in time to hear, "A rider!"

The rider, who was in fact a lookout placed by Rollondar

to watch Adron's movements, came to the gate in good time, and a path was opened to the Warlord. Roila Lavode, while too far away to hear the report, was able to determine that Lord Adron had been spotted and would soon be over the hill. She worked her way close to Rollondar, and said, "Warlord, the Lavodes are ready to help you."

Rollondar looked at her, forcing aside the soldier's instinctive distrust of such an undisciplined corps, and said, "Good."

"Have you instructions?"

"Will you follow them?"

"If they suit us."

Rollondar scowled but said nothing. He had the authority to order them away from the battle; anything else he must convince them to do. As he was considering this, he learned that the Breath of Fire Battalion, though moving uncharacteristically slowly, was now in sight, and a great battle-wagon had been sighted behind the waves of horsemen.

"What do you think, Warlord?" said Nyleth.

"I think that, as things stand, we can crush the Breath of Fire Battalion like closing our hand."

"Well?"

"Well, Lord Adron is not one to put himself in such a position."

"Therefore?" said Nyleth.

"I think the spell is real."

"You do not think they will turn and attack the other gates?"

"It will be no small task for them to break the gates that are closed—they cannot do it before we reach them; I have troops keeping the paths clear, and our road is shorter."

"Well, Excellency?"

Rollondar stared grimly out of the open gate. "As we said before, you must discover what the spell is and if, as I am now convinced, it is a threat, destroy it."

"Very well."

Rollondar turned to Roila. "Have you been listening?"

"Yes."

"Can you beat a path through the battalion to reach the battle-wagon? Which is, I am certain, actually a spell-wagon."

"Yes."

"Then that will be your task."

"Very well," said Roila, and she returned to where the Lavodes waited, and said, "We have our task."

Even as she spoke, a scant two hundred meters away Lord Adron e'Kieron, the rebel Prince, drew his forces up before the Dragon Gate and watched the approaching dawn. He stood before his spell-wagon—a wagon so large that it could, and, in fact, did, contain his tent; so large that sixteen horses were required to pull it. His officers were assembled before him, and he addressed them in these terms: "We cannot, in fact, achieve a direct victory here, but, fortunately, we do not need to. Now that we have stopped, and are within the correct distance, I will begin working my spell, which will take control of the Orb—in effect, making me Emperor, though we ought not to depend on our enemies laying down their arms upon this occasion."

He accompanied this remark with a grim smile—a smile that was echoed by all the officers. He then continued, "Unlike His Majesty, I shall not be afraid to use the power of the Orb in battle, and I shall begin to do so at once. For, even as the Orb comes to me, bursting through walls in the Palace, flying over the city wall, I will be able to turn its power against our enemies—the closer the Orb comes to me, the more of its abilities I will be able to use. By the time it reaches me, the battle will be over."

He took a breath. "There is some danger, to be sure; that is why the battalion must be ready, for we will be attacked the instant the enemy sorcerers realize what I am doing, and, if I am disturbed while I am working, we will lose everything."

"How dangerous is it?" asked an officer.

Adron paused, as if considering whether to answer this question, or how much he ought to tell his officers. At last he said, "I have studied a great deal, and I know what I am doing, though, to be sure, there are always unknown elements in a spell of this magnitude. Yet I do not believe the spell itself will be dangerous—the energies of the spell will be directed at the Orb, which is, as you all know, a device designed, more than anything else, to accept and direct immense energies; indeed, the very method by which I hope to take control of it requires directing great energy straight at it, rather than at His Majesty or around the Orb, and so I will get past the defenses built into the Orb; in the same way, then, there will be, I believe, little danger from the spell itself.

"Yet that is not the only danger, for should the battalion fail, and should I be distracted before the spell takes effect, it will mean defeat for us, and capture and execution for me and, perhaps, for you as well, my officers. You perceive that I do not disguise the risks." He shrugged. "Beyond that, unless something unexpected happens, well, I do not believe there is grave danger.

"But," he added, "there is always the possibility of the unexpected happening, wherefore we must necessarily keep our guard up at all times. Do you all clearly understand what I am saying?"

They all did.

He took another breath. "Good. Are there, then, any more questions?"

One of the younger officers cleared his throat.

"Well?" said Adron.

"How long must we hold them?" said the officer. "That is, in order for you to have time—"

Adron frowned. "You must hold the enemy as long as possible. How could your task be anything else?"

The officer looked uncomfortable. "And yet—"

"Very well," said Adron, giving forth a sigh. He calculated briefly, and his glance strayed to the battle-wagon behind him. At last he said, "Before the spell is ready, I shall need, I think, four and a half hours, or perhaps less."

The officers looked uncomfortable, and many of them allowed themselves significant looks at the Gate where Rollondar's forces waited. Adron, seeing this, added, "It may be that they will not attack us before that time."

"Your Highness thinks not?" said one of the older officers.

Adron shrugged. "Rollondar is cagey and wise, but he does not know what I am doing. He may wait and try to discover what I have here, in which case there will be no attack until the spell begins to take effect."

"Well, and then?" said another officer.

"And then it will already be too late. Perhaps half an hour, perhaps more, until all is over."

"That is not so long," said the officer.

Adron shrugged. "Any more questions?"

There were none.

"Then let us form ranks," he said. "When all is ready, I shall begin the enchantment."

At about this same time, Tazendra said, "It is demeaning to have to make one's own klava."

"How," said Aerich, frowning. "Demeaning?"

"She means," said Pel, "that it is humiliating."

"I do not comprehend," said Aerich.

"It is humiliating," said Pel, smiling, "because it has been so long since she was required to do so that she has forgotten how."

Tazendra grunted. "Well, that may be."

"However," added the Yendi. "I have not, and so if you will permit me—"

"Gladly," said Tazendra.

As it happened, it was Aerich who ground the beans while Pel boiled the water. Some time later, then, Khaavren came down the stairs to the smell of good, fresh klava. For a moment he was confused to find no one there, until he realized from the soft sounds of conversation above that his friends were gathered in what had once been Aerich's room.

"Hullo, my friends," he called. "I will join you when I have poured a cup of klava."

"Bah!" said Tazendra. "We have the pot warm up here, and a cup ready for you."

There could be no answer to this argument, so Khaavren at

once went back up the stairs to Aerich's room, where he gratefully accepted his cup and sat in the chair that, by custom, had been his in the old days. He said, "My friends, do you know that it has been five hundred years since we have all been gathered together in the same place?"

Aerich nodded, "Let it not be five hundred years before we are so gathered again."

Tazendra said, "These pleasantries are all very well, but I am burning to hear Khaavren's plan."

"How," said Khaavren, "you pretend I have a plan?"

"You always have a plan," said Tazendra sagaciously.

"And moreover," said Pel, "Aerich indicated that you had one when he returned last night."

"It is impossible to fool our Aerich," said Khaavren.

"Well?" said Tazendra.

"Yes, I have a plan."

"Ah, so much the better," said Tazendra.

"Then let us hear it," said Pel. "For I confess that I am as anxious as Tazendra to know what you wish us to do."

Khaavren nodded, then paused for a moment to gather his thoughts. At last he said, "There will be a battle this morning."

"Of this," said Pel, "I am not unaware."

"Nor am I," said Aerich.

"Nor I," added Tazendra.

"Well, that is where I wish to go."

"That is your plan?" said Tazendra. "To fight in a battle? Well, I am entirely in accord with this idea. Yet, as a *plan*, I hardly think—"

"Hush, Tazendra," said Pel amiably. "That is not Khaavren's plan."

"Oh," said Tazendra, sounding disappointed.

Aerich maintained his habitual silence.

"What are you smiling about?" said Pel.

Khaavren shook his head, "It seems as if five centuries have simply vanished, and we are here as we always were."

Aerich gave the smallest smile, Pel saluted, and Tazendra threw her head back and laughed.

"But go on," said Pel. "Let us hear this famous plan."

"Yes, yes," said Tazendra. "Let us hear it."

"It is very simple," said Khaavren. "In the first place, you must know that Lord Adron is a rebel."

"That is clear," said Pel.

"And that, if he is defeated, he must be arrested."

"That follows naturally," said Pel.

"As Captain of the Guard, it is my duty to arrest him." They all nodded.

"His Majesty, in fact, has told me that I am responsible for this."

They waited.

"What I do not understand," said Khaavren, "is why it is necessary to await the end of the battle before arresting our friend the Prince."

"Bah!" said Tazendra. "Does one arrest one's friends?"

"Sometimes," said Aerich.

"And yet," said Tazendra. "To make an arrest, well, it is not much of a plan."

"Tazendra does not comprehend," pronounced Pel.

"My dear," said Khaavren, "I speak of arresting him in the midst of a battle. That is, of finding a way past the lines of fine Dragonlords bent on slaughtering one another, and Teckla waiting to be slaughtered, and then meeting up with Lord Adron, and taking him away."

"Oh," said Tazendra. She considered. "That is rather different."

"Indeed," said Pel. He smiled. "It will certainly make an adventure, if we can do it."

"If we can do it?" said Khaavren. "Cha! We are all of us together. What could stop us?"

"Well, I nearly think I agree with you," said Pel.

"Come, Aerich, what do you think?"

"In truth," said the Lyorn, "it does not please me to arrest His Highness, a man I revere, and a friend for whom I have no small regard. And yet—"

"Well, and yet?"

"For reasons that I cannot speak of, even to you, my friends, I think we not only should, but must get to Adron, and arrest him, before he can—that is, as soon as possible. Indeed, I'd have proposed something like it myself, only, as I am no longer a guardsman, I have no authority to make arrests. But in Khaavren's company, and with Khaavren as our Captain, well, I no longer have any objection to make."

Khaavren nodded. Though he wondered at the dire hints contained in the Lyorn's speech, he knew better than to ask about matters concerning which Aerich preferred to remain mute. He said, "And you, Tazendra?"

"How, me?"

"Yes. Do you like the plan?"

"My dear Khaavren, five hundred years ago, the four of us were near to facing an army of Easterners. Do you remember?"

"Why, yes," said Khaavren. "As it happens, this event has not escaped my memory. What of it?"

"Well, since that time, I have often regretted that we did not have the opportunity to fight that army; it would have been a glorious thing."

"And then?"

"This time, instead of an army of Easterners, it is an army of Dragonlords—moreover, an army of His Highness's crack troops."

"And so you are for it?"

"With my whole heart."

"Then we are agreed?" said Khaavren.

"Agreed," said Aerich.

"Agreed," said Pel.

"Agreed," said Tazendra.

"In that case," said Khaavren, standing, "we must be on our way at once. It is dawn, and we must be past the wall before the battle is joined."

As the Breath of Fire Battalion forms its ranks, we will turn our attention to a district of the City called Catchman Tower; so called because it was dominated by the slender spire of a tower built during the Twelfth Chreotha Reign by Lord Catchman. The tower, in fact, served no useful purpose, but, made of pale white stone polished smooth as glass, it was not unattractive. The district was not, in fact, in the Underside, but was rather just to the east, bounded by the Street of the Tsalmoth, and it was a short distance from the Street of the Tsalmoth that a group of urchins from the Underside, having ventured out of their district in the excitement of the night, were amusing themselves by throwing stones and other objects at a squadron of four guardsmen of the White Sash Battalion. We are not unaware of the ironic resonance that the contrived riot and the real uprising were instigated similarly—that is, by young people throwing things at the police. Yet it is significant that, in one case, it was the humiliation of rotten vegetables, while in the other, it was the far deeper humiliation of death, for, by chance, one of these stones, thrown by an unusually burly Teckla youth with a good eye, struck a guardsman named Heth square in the forehead with such force that he was killed on the spot.

Without consultation, the other three guardsmen left him there and set off in pursuit of the urchins, who had begun running upon seeing Heth fall. The guardsmen were faster and the distance was not great, but, turning into an alley, the urchins ducked into the first house they came to, which was shared by six families of Teckla, who worked at the clothing mill by the canal. It happened that the clothing mill had been shut down two days before, and so all of the Teckla were both frightened and angry. Upon hearing the commotion, they opened their door in time to see, not the urchins (who were hiding in a basement storage room) but three guardsmen with weapons drawn and blood in their eyes.

The Teckla, as will happen on occasion, were angrier at the intrusion than they were frightened at the guardsmen, and moreover, counting only those of a reasonable age, they outnumbered the guardsmen by some twenty-eight to three— they greeted the guardsmen, then, with sticks, brooms, kitchen knives, and whatever else was to hand.

The guardsmen, chased into the street, called for help, and

it happened that help was available, for there were two other squadrons of four within earshot.

The Teckla called for help as well, and there were some hundreds of Teckla, as well as no small number of tradesmen of other houses, who were also within earshot.

The Five Hour Uprising had begun.

# Chapter the Thirty-first

*Which Treats of Uprisings
In General and Specific
With Special Emphasis on Their Effects
On Heroes and Brigands
In Providing Distractions, and
In Making It Difficult to Cross the Street.*

IT IS COMMONLY BELIEVED BY the shallow and the ignorant that human attitude, character, and opinion is immutable. Even those who, in their own lifetimes, observe the wearing away of stone, the eroding of mountains, and the shifting of rivers, will go so far as to say that an entire group of people—a thousand times more volatile than our stone, mountain, or river—is this way or that way, holds these opinions or subscribes to those beliefs; thus not only committing the error of seeing a populace as an organism not made up of countless and vital divisions and differences, but also failing to see that the opinions of masses of people, when subjected to sudden changes in their circumstances, can alter more quickly than the color of the Orb can respond to a change in the spirits of the Emperor. Needless to say, such people have only the most absurd and foolish explanations for the Five Hour Uprising that occurred on the seventeenth day of the month of the Vallista in Dragaera City and her surrounding districts.

For example, we have heard from one that it was a vast conspiracy on the part of the Jhereg—certain proof that that historian, who shall remain nameless, has yet to become acquainted with the Cycle. Another has suggested certain intoxicants accidentally making their way into the water supply—which gives us to wonder: Where exists this water supply unanimously drunk by Teckla and tradesmen, yet never tasted by the nobility? We have even heard it suggested that Adron himself deliberately worked for this end—Adron, be it understood, who had only the vaguest notion that there even was such a thing as a populace.

But leaving aside such theories, it is certainly the case that to see such a drastic change occur so quickly, and with so little warning, will, no doubt, surprise many readers; in fact, we should not be surprised to learn that some readers have thought that we ought to have better prepared them for so shocking a revelation, and that there are facts of which we have kept the reader ignorant, and that, in effect, we have ill-used the reader by withholding these statistics. To any such reader we tender our sincere regrets.

Yet those who hold these opinions ought to remember, in the first place, that nearly to a man, all of those who dwelt in the city at that time, even those who had—like the drops from the two-minute clock-fountain in the Lyorn Court—been predicting exactly such occurrences for centuries—and predicting them, be it understood, always for some day in the nebulous future—were taken entirely by surprise. Khaavren, in fact, who made it a matter of policy to be in touch with the pulse, as it were, of the city, had not expected the eruption as soon as, or with the violence with which, it actually occurred. The one exception, in fact, was Grita, who lived in the worst area of the city and consorted with all manner of shady characters, and had been working for some time to bring about exactly this result; although, as the reader will discover, even she was amazed at the suddenness and ferocity of the spontaneous outburst against order and decency that took hold of the minds of the population.

In the second place, we beg any of our readers who may be annoyed to remember that we have, in fact, been forecasting exactly this occurrence; beginning with Khaavren's first conversation with the pastry-vendor, who discussed the effect of the wheat-tax on the citizens, to his latest discussion with this same pastry-vendor, who spoke of the collapse of his hopes in terms that Khaavren, at least, understood to be symbolic of the collapse of the world around him.

These, then, are our excuses, should the reader feel himself to have been misled. As for those who were involved in the Five Hour Uprising, either attempting to quell it or adding fuel, as it were, to the fire, no one was as befuddled as the participants; which circumstance is, in fact, inevitable. There are some historians who, even to-day, lay the blame at the feet of the short-lived leaders; yet according to all of the evidence, these leaders, as amazed as anyone, were catapulted to the top of the Uprising as it progressed, because, like Plumtree, they expressed themselves in public a little better than their compatriots; or, like Tibrock, they had been expressing themselves in writing and were thus in the public eye; or, like Hithaguard, they made one or two suggestions that were well-received by their fellows and thus were called upon to make more. Certainly, none of the leaders had planned on such an Uprising, or, indeed, had the least idea of where it ought to go; it had, as it were, its own mind, and there was little anyone could do once it had been set on its destructive, and ultimately futile course. To lay the blame on such "leaders" as these is to blind one's self to the logic of the Uprising.

What was the logic of the Uprising? Or, if the reader prefers, who was actually to blame? Pleasant as it might be, for the value of surprise if for no other reason, to lay the blame at anyone's feet but Tortaalik's, it is difficult to do so. That is, though others may have erred, certainly it was His Majesty's failure to address the problems of the very city in which he lived that was the direct cause of the people's exasperation. And yet, one might fairly ask: What could he have done? It is an inarguable fact that, with every day that passed, wheat became scarcer. To replace the wheat with rice from the South would have meant unblocking the harbor and providing the pirates of Elde Island with choice targets upon which to practice their trade; and, even if the Orca had taken it upon itself to rid the seas of these pirates, the cost in transport of the rice would have been greater even than the wheat; all of which does not even consider whether the populace would have been willing to substitute rice patties for bread, a proposition the historian finds dubious at best.

The price of wheat is, then, as much a culprit as anything, and for this we can lay the blame on—the weather, for had the drought broken, the prices of wheat, flax, maize, harbrand, and lockbean would necessarily have fallen. But, then, why was not the end of the drought brought about by sorcery, as even then lay within the skills of wizards of the House of the Athyra? And here, once more, we are forced to conclude that His Majesty erred—erred in remaining ignorant too long, erred in requesting rather than requiring the Athyra to address the problem, and finally, erred in placing so much import on the Imperial Treasury that he allowed the Athyra, the Dragon, and the Dzur to intimidate him into requesting, rather than requiring, action which he ought to have known was necessary.

In any event, however, the people of the city began to fear that they were abandoned; that their daily bread was, more than threatened, actually denied to them. As their fear grew, so did the degree to which they listened to the least rumor which offered a hope, or a hero, or, failing these, at least a culprit. Aliera's action at the bakery had provided a hope; the rumors of Her Majesty siding with the greedy merchants to artificially raise prices (which was never true) provided a culprit. The rebel Prince, through his grievances, in point of fact, had little to do with the danger of famine in the city, became another hero. And thus when rumors abounded that the Emperor was sending the Imperial Army against him, the Emperor became another culprit.

The day before the Uprising—that is, the 16th day of the Month of the Vallista, matters reached a certain height; it was impossible to walk half a league anywhere in the city without seeing someone on a street corner declaiming loudly, and publicly, against His Majesty, against Her Majesty, against Jurabin, and against the Guard, who arrested those who so declaimed, which arrests became fresh grievances. Some, frightened by these demonstrations, left the city that day; others left for fear of Adron, whom they were afraid might, in his justified (so they thought) wrath against His Majesty, slaughter every citizen without regard for politics (indeed, among those who stayed, many put up placards with crude drawings of Adron's seal, hoping to convince his supposed hundreds of thousands of troops to leave them in peace, and it was these placards, as much as anything else, which drove the fatigued and harassed Baroness Stonemover to such harsh measures against the least sign of disloyalty); still others left out of vague, ill-formed notions that all was not right in the city and would only get worse.

These last were, we must insist, exactly right, as the events of the 17th proved, although, in two different ways, it was that very panic that indirectly provided what Grita had called "the spark," as we now propose to demonstrate.

In the first place, with such a sizable portion of the population gone (and estimates have ranged as high as ten out of every hundred citizens), undisciplined youth, especially Teckla, felt free to roam the streets and engage in mischief in a way they would never have dared if the population had not been so diminished.

And in the second, the final impetus that exasperated the population beyond endurance was the closing of the gates of the city before dawn on the 17th. To be sure, there was no other choice—Rollondar knew what he had to work with, and knew the speed of the Breath of Fire Battalion—by leaving any gate open except that within which his army assembled was to invite the Prince to attack the Imperial Army's flank. But, to the people, this was not seen as a military maneuver, but, rather, as a petty, tyrannical gesture intended to prevent them from leaving the city where they faced conditions of starvation and repression. Does the reader wonder that they reacted to this development with either rage or panic—which two reactions, we should say, were indistinguishable by dawn? Here, again, we find the curious inevitability which seems to have followed the Uprising from its beginning to its tragic conclusion.

Does the reader wish to know details of the Uprising? Does the reader wish to know how much of Dragaera burned that day? Which buildings were looted? Whose homes was invaded, and what became of the dwellers therein? In fact, there were not as many incidents of this type, nor were they as destructive, as many believe; certainly any institution representing the Empire in any way was attacked, and many counting-houses looted and burned; and of course some areas of the Palace, especially the Jhegaala Wing with its long exposed neck, and the isolated pagodas that formed part of the Yendi Wing, were burned and battered. But for the most part, it was the worst portions of the city, such as the Underside, which both provided the berserkers and took most of the damage.

In all, the Five Hour Uprising went through most of the stages of a normal uprising in a compressed time—the sudden, uncontrolled riot, the rising of leaders, the refusal of the Empire to treat with those leaders, the consolidation of the insurgents and their leaders into what Lord Mikric has termed an "alternate Imperium"—a second, but almost equally effective ruling body, which took as its home, instead of the Imperial Palace, the short, elegant, and practical Pamlar University Administration Building—a fact which some historians have attempted to make symbolic. The Uprising, we should add, was spared the inevitable quarrels over power and policy that accompany success, just as it was spared the inevitable executions and repressions that accompany failure; yet, for all of that, it was a full-scale uprising, complete in nearly every detail and carried through in just under five hours.

We have said this to be certain that the reader has some understanding of the situation in which those we have been following throughout our history found themselves—the background, if we may, against which our history is painted. The precise details of this Uprising, as we hope we have shown, are an endless source of fascination and speculation, but we have no intention of actually spending the reader's time on any of it beyond this point—in other words, it is only to the degree to which the Five Hour Uprising has an effect on our history that we have chosen to introduce and give a brief synopsis of its life and death.

For our purposes, then, it is sufficient to say that, as the light of day grew on the morning of the 17th a haze of smoke was already beginning to form over the city. It was beneath this haze, in the first hours of dawn, that Mario made his way once more to the Imperial Wing of the Palace. This time his methods were different—faster, less elegant, but just as effective. It is not hard to imagine where he found one of the uniform cloaks of the Phoenix Guard—he removed it from a corpse. Whether he found the corpse or whether, if the reader will permit, he *created* the corpse, we cannot know, but certainly with a few dabs of dirt cleverly applied to his face to both conceal his identity and make his features appear more Dragon-like, and with the uniform cloak of the White Sash Battalion, he had no difficulty presenting himself as a guardsman just come from facing the angry rabble; and when he claimed to have an urgent message from Baroness Stonemover to His Majesty, he was treated with every courtesy, and asked, moreover, if the message could not wait until the Palace was open, some two hours hence.

"How," said Mario, pretending dismay, "two hours? And yet I am told the message is urgent."

"Well," said a well-meaning guardsman, "you must convince me it is urgent enough to disturb His Majesty, who is only now rising from his bed."

"That decision," said Mario, "I am loath to make. But come, perhaps I can explain to Lord Khaavren; surely he will be able to advise me."

"He would," agreed the guardsman, "but he is not here, nor will he be here today."

"How, not here?" cried Mario, pretending surprise, although he had determined already that the Captain must, of necessity, be near to the battlefield. "But then, who is in charge of your corps?"

"Who else but Thack?"

"Well, and where do I find him?"

"Do you know the Sub-wing of the Red Boot Battalion?"

"Know it? I nearly think so. Is not my own brother married to a Redboot's sister (although, come to that, I do not recall the guardsman's name)? Nevertheless, I have been there on two occasions, and know it well."

"And can you, without help, find your way to the sub-wing from here?"

"Well, I can indeed, for in my youth I ran messages from Jurabin to Khaavren, in hopes of learning the routes and paths, for, I freely confess, it was my hope to have your uniform, rather than that of a mere policeman."

"Well," said the guard, giving him a friendly smile. "Do not give up hope; who knows, it may be, after all of this is over, that the Captain and His Majesty will decide to expand the guard, and you may yet effect a transfer, and I will call you comrade."

"Ah, ah! I promise you, nothing would make me happier."

"Well, until then, if you know the paths, you need but take them, and ask after Thack."

"I will do so. But might it be that I cannot find him?"

"That is true, for his duty takes him about the Palace, and he must perform His Majesty's rounds this morning, as the Captain is away."

"Well, but then?"

"Bah! You are a good sort; if you cannot find him, seek him in the Imperial Wing."

"I will not fail to do so. And yet—"

"Well?"

"Is it not true that I will need a safe-conduct to pass through the halls?"

"Not in the least, unless you venture into the Imperial Wing itself."

"But might my errand not take me there, as you have just said?"

"Well, that is true. Here, take mine, only promise to return it to me when your business is completed."

"I will not fail to do so; and yet, between looking for Thack, and awaiting His Majesty, it may be some time."

"Well, what of it? I am on duty until the first hour after noon."

"Shards and splinters! A long watch!"

"It is the day for it."

"That is the truth; I have only just barely escaped with my life from a crowd of ruffians, and the day promises to become warmer before it cools. In truth, I confess I was not sorry to be given this errand, if only to be for two minutes off the streets, which is to say, off the front lines of battle!"

"Given the errand?" said the guard with a conspiratorial smile. "Come, the truth now: Did you not, in fact, request the errand?"

"Ah, well, I don't say that I didn't. But come, consider: There are monsters out there; they hate the uniform and they do not know rules of combat, but attack in any numbers and with whatever comes to hand. In all honesty, do you blame me?"

"Not the least in the world, I assure you, and to prove it, here is your safe-conduct."

"You are a good fellow!"

"Allow me to pin it on your cloak."

"Very good."

"There it is."

"I thank you."

"Good luck on your errand."

"And the Favor to you; I will see you when my errand is complete."

With this, Mario gave a humble bow, turned, and walked past the guard post, down a short corridor toward the Dragon Wing, through which he continued coolly, as if having no fear of being recognized, and, from there, he came to the Iorich wing, his first destination. There he asked after Guinn, the jailer, who happened to be present.

"Greetings," he said. "We shall be bringing a good number of citizens to their new homes here."

"Well," said Guinn. "We can accommodate them."

"Are you certain? For, you perceive, the Baroness insists that we ascertain how much room you have before we bring them in."

"Well, to be sure, we cannot contain them all. But should they be common citizens, we can certainly take another two or three score."

"And noblemen, by which I mean a count?"

"Another four or five will present us with no difficulty."

"Excellent. But, forgive me, what of the accommodations? We are dealing with matters of High Treason by an aristocrat, and thus we must be certain, on the one hand, that the cell is secure, and, on the other, that no disrespect is shown by treating the prisoner as if he were common."

"Well, I understand, and, I assure you, this is a matter upon which we pride ourselves. Come, if you like; we happen to have a prisoner now, a certain Dragonlord who has been arrested for High Treason exactly, and, if you like, we will visit her, and you will see for yourself what the accommodations will be like for those with whom the Baroness chooses to honor us."

"How, you have such a person here?"

"Indeed, we do."

"And convicted on a charge of High Treason?"

"Oh, no, not at all."

"Pardon me, good Guinn?"

"Arrested only; there are other quarters for those who are convicted, where they are shown every possible comfort while awaiting execution. Yet the chambers for those who are merely awaiting trial on such charges are, while entirely secure, perfectly comfortable, so that, however nice an aristocrat's sensibilities, he shall have nothing of which to complain."

"I think the Baroness will be pleased, if the arrangements are as good as you say."

"Let us then go and look," said Guinn.

"I should like nothing better," said Mario calmly.

It was, by the this time, ten minutes after the seventh hour of the morning.

A few minutes later, Khaavren, Aerich, Tazendra, and Pel left the house, and began making their way toward the Dragon Gate, which was not far away. It was, in fact, so close that they soon realized that they would have to fight their way through ranks of infantry to reach it.

"Bah!" said Tazendra. "There must be another way."

"There may be," said Pel, stopping as if to recall something.

"Indeed?" said Khaavren doubtfully. "I do not know another way."

"I did not either, but I have recently heard that, if one takes the Toehold Bridge from the Paved Road, one arrives at the Gate of the Seven Flags, which is, as you know, not far from the Dragon Gate."

"Ah," said Khaavren, considering. "That may be true; I had not known of it."

"But," said Tazendra, frowning. "Will not the Gate of the Seven Flags be closed?"

"Khaavren is Captain of the Guard," said Pel gently.

"So he is," said Tazendra in wonder. "I had forgotten that circumstance."

"Well, what do you think, Khaavren?" said Pel.

"I do not know," said Khaavren. "Let us, at any rate, attempt it."

"Certainly," said Tazendra, "if it allows us any more room."

"Indeed," said Khaavren; "we could even risk horses on the paved road, and perhaps all the way to the gate."

"Let us then do so," said Aerich calmly. "For I believe there is no time to spare."

They at once ran to the Hammerhead Inn, where horses were always stabled. Khaavren suggested the others see to equipping the horses, while he, Khaavren, arranged matters with the landlord. They at once agreed to this plan, and Khaavren entered the inn.

"Greetings, Tukko, old friend," he said.

"And to you," said the aged Jhereg. "Is there something you wish?"

"Certainly, for you perceive I am on duty."

"Of that there can be no question. Come, what do you wish to know?"

"Simply this: Were all of your horses stolen during last night's festivities?"

Tukko smiled. "I am a Jhereg," he replied.

"So I had thought. But have they been used?"

"Not all of them; I still have six that I have been holding back against my own desire to escape or someone so rich and so desperate to leave that one horse might mean my fortune."

"Ah, I knew I could count on you."

"What, then? Does His Majesty require a horse?"

"Four of them," said the Captain. "I will return them when I can."

"The Imperial treasury, I have heard, is in dire straits; nevertheless, I am convinced it can withstand the cost of four horses, should it come to that."

"Indeed it can," said Khaavren.

"Very well, then."

Khaavren gave the Jhereg an imperial for his trouble and repaired to the stables, where he found that Aerich, as skilled as any groom, was just completing, with help from Pel, Tazendra, and the stable-boy, the work of equipping the horses. Khaavren tossed the stable-boy an orb.

As they mounted, Khaavren addressed Tazendra, saying, "This reminds me—"

"Well?"

"I have here two flashstones; do you have any similar arguments? And have you any for Pel and Aerich?"

"I have one," said Pel.

"I have three," said Tazendra.

Aerich shrugged, and accepted one from Tazendra, which he put into his pocket.

"And then?" said Tazendra.

"Let us ride," said Khaavren, and they rode from the inn as if the Breath of Fire Battalion were behind, rather than before them.

As they rode, Pel said, "Have you a plan?"

"But, didn't I tell you my plan? And did you not agree to it?"

"Not in the least," said Pel. "You told me an *intention*, and I agreed to it. But have you a plan for carrying out your intention?"

"Ah, you argue like a casuist."

" 'Tis true, I mark things into discrete categories."

"A touch," said Khaavren.

"Well?"

"No, I have no plan."

"Ah."

"Does that worry you?"

"A little, perhaps," said Pel.

"You, Tazendra?"

"Oh, if you wish to have a plan, well, I do not mind."

"Aerich?"

The Lyorn shrugged.

Pel said, "Consider that we are, after all, about to, in essence, attack Adron's army—just the four of us; I do not think that a plan would do us any harm."

"Well, I agree. Have you one to offer?"

"As it happens, I do not."

"Then let us get as far as the Gate of the Seven Flags, past it, and see how matters stand; then we can discuss plans."

"With this, I agree," said Pel.

"Bother," said Tazendra suddenly.

"What is it, my dear?" said Khaavren.

"The battle has begun without us and I am vexed at it."

"How, it has begun?" said Khaavren, straining his eyes toward the Dragon Gate, which was obstructed by buildings and distance. "Do you think so?"

"Well, look you. Do you not see the smoke?"

"Why no, in fact, I do not."

"Bah, you do not? But look, there it is! No, where I am pointing."

"I see it now."

"I am glad you do."

"But, Tazendra, that is not the battle."

"How, it is not?"

"No, the Dragon Gate is that way."

"But, what is that way?"

"The Imperial Palace, the Underside, the Morning Green, the—"

"How, you mean, the city?"

"Exactly."

"But, then, why is it burning?"

"I believe the citizens are rioting, Tazendra."

Tazendra's eyes grew wide. "The Horse! Are they?"

"So it would seem. Do you not agree, Pel?"

"Entirely, my dear Khaavren."

"And you, Aerich?"

Aerich looked sad, and nodded.

"But, what should we do?" said Tazendra.

"Continue," said Khaavren. "And hope, if we defeat Adron, that there is still a house to return to. Or, for that matter, a Palace."

They continued further, and discovered that either they had reached the Uprising, or the Uprising had caught up with them, for they found themselves among gangs of Teckla and merchants of various Houses, who were busying themselves in the most destructive of ways—the few glass windows in the area were soon all smashed, and two or three buildings were burning; indeed, the entire area would certainly have gone up in flames (as, to be sure, certain other areas did) had there not been a good amount of stonework that would not burn.

Khaavren's uniform, to be sure, attracted a certain amount of attention from the angry populace, but his martial air and his calm demeanor made those who looked upon him think that perhaps there would be better targets upon which to vent their frustration. And moreover, there rode next to him a woman with a large sword slung over her back, and the colors of a Dzurlord in her clothing, and with a haughty, challenging gleam in her eye; as well as a man wearing the costume as well as the cool countenance of a Lyorn warrior; and a cavalier upon whose fierce, angry eye none could look—in other words, they were not set upon as they rode through the crowd.

It was, nevertheless, a crowd, and they were on horseback, so it took them some time to reach the Toehold Bridge, although after they had passed it there were no more delays, and soon they arrived at the Gate of the Seven Flags, which was built of thick mortar and had a single tower from which the gate could be worked—which gate, we should add, was, in fact, three separate slabs of hard, lacquered wood, each one eight or nine centimeters thick. And which gate was, as Tazendra had predicted, closed.

"Well?" she said.

Khaavren shrugged. "Open the gate," he called.

There were ten or twelve soldiers on duty, as well as a mounted messenger who remained on the alert to run for help in the case of trouble. "How, open the gate?" they called back. "Impossible."

Khaavren shrugged and rode forward so that, when he spoke, they could not fail to hear him. "I am," he said in a conversational tone, "Khaavren of Castlerock and, by His Majesty's will, Captain of the Imperial Guard, Redboot Battalion. Some of you should recognize me. My friends and I are required to pass through this gate on Imperial business. If, therefore, this gate is not open in one minute, I will open it myself, treating any who oppose me however I must. Those who survive will be reported to His Majesty, with what results I am certain your imagination will tell you. The minute," he concluded, "begins now."

It took perhaps twenty seconds to open the gate. They rode through and heard it close behind them.

"The Dragon Gate," remarked Khaavren, "is this way."

"I hope the battle has not yet started," remarked Tazendra.

"Well, in fact," said Khaavren, "though perhaps for a different reason, so do I."

It was twenty minutes past the eighth hour of the morning as Greycat, standing before his score of cutthroats, remarked, "I had no idea they would attempt to take horses through the throng of soldiery."

"Well," said Grita, "but they did, and we have lost them."

"Unless," said Greycat, "we can determine whither they are bound, in which case, you perceive, it matters not in the least if we are following them or not, for we will nevertheless be able to arrive where they are."

"But can you make this determination?"

"Perhaps. Consider, they are not going toward the Palace."

"Well, that is true, they are not going toward the Palace."

"And neither are they going toward where the Uprising is at its peak."

"That is also true. What then?"

"Well, where else could they be going?"

"Only to the battle."

"Exactly."

"But—"

"Yes?" said Greycat.

"The battle, when it begins, and if it has not already begun, will be at the Dragon Gate, and we saw them riding *away* from the Dragon Gate."

"That is only natural; they could not have ridden horses through the infantrymen assembled on the street."

"Well, but what then?"

"They must have another means of arriving at the battle."

"What means is that?"

"I do not know. Perhaps they think to arrive by way of the Gate of the Seven Flags."

Grita shrugged. "It is near to the Dragon Gate, but it will be closed, or Rollondar is a fool."

"It will not be closed to the Captain of the Guard."

"Maybe," admitted Grita. "And yet, even if they open it to him, well, we have no Captain of the Guard with us."

"But do you agree that this is how they have gone?"

"It seems not unlikely."

"Then we know that they have gone, for some reason, to the battle, perhaps to assist the Warlord. So much the better for us."

"How?"

"Because, should his throat be cut in the midst of battle, no one will think anything of it."

"Well, that is true. But how do we get there? The gate they are using, as I've said, must be closed, and the Gate of the Dragon is filled with soldiery."

"Ah, that *is* a question. Let me think."

Greycat considered for some few moments, then called, "This way!" His troop, if it may be dignified by such a term, followed him, although they did not do so in anything like a military fashion. Still, they followed.

After a time, Grita said, "We seem to be approaching the Gate of the Seven Flags."

"You are perspicacious."

"And yet, it is closed."

"I will convince them to open it."

"How?"

"You will see."

When they reached the gate, which had been closed behind our friends, Greycat paused some distance away to study the situation. He turned to Grita and said, "Do you see the fellow on the horse?"

"Well?"

"Kill him."

Grita shrugged. "Very well," she said.

She walked over to him, calling out, "My dear sir, a moment of your time please, for there is trouble in the city and I am worried."

As he turned to consider her, Greycat turned to his band and said, "Take the tower."

The brigands charged the tower. The soldier on the horse

turned, startled, and then was startled yet again as Grita grasped his saddle and, using it as a handhold, vaulted up and neatly cut his throat.

The battle at the tower lasted scarcely longer than it had taken them to open the gate to Khaavren's command. A few more minutes, and the gate stood open.

Grita said, "Should we not close it behind us?"

"A good idea," Greycat acknowledged, and gave the order. The rope was cut by one of the band who was skilled at scaling walls, after which he rejoined them.

"What now?" said Grita.

"We have just sealed ourselves out of the city," said Greycat. "And yet, I confess this does not worry me overmuch, for soon I will be able to send to His Majesty to bring me an escort to the Palace. But first—"

"Yes," said Grita. "First we must kill the Tiassa."

"This way," said Greycat.

It yet lacked a few minutes of the ninth hour of the morning.

# Chapter the Thirty-second

### Which Treats of the Meeting
of Khaavren and Greycat,
And the Discussion Which Took Place
Between Them.

KHAAVREN DREW REIN AT THE top of Flag Hill and looked down at the scene spread out below.

"They are not attacking," remarked Tazendra.

"Who?" said Khaavren.

"Why, neither of them are attacking," explained Tazendra.

"That is true," said Khaavren. "But I wondered which of them you had expected to attack."

"Ah. I see." She frowned. "Both of them, I should think."

"Well, that is not unreasonable."

"I am glad you think so."

"What now?" said Pel.

"In fact," said Khaavren, "I am uncertain. Aerich?"

"The Tiassa asks the Lyorn for an idea?" said Aerich with a smile. Then he shrugged. "We must find Adron. He is, no doubt in the battle-wagon."

"Spell-wagon," said Tazendra.

The others looked at her.

"What is the difference?" said Khaavren.

"A spell-wagon carries spells into a battle," said Tazendra.

"Well," said Khaavren. "And a battle-wagon carries battles into spells?"

"Not in the least," said Tazendra patiently. "A battle-wagon carries spells intended to be used in battle against the enemy, whereas a spell-wagon may carry any sort of spell whatsoever; that is, a battle-wagon is necessarily a spell-wagon, while the reverse is not true. Do you see?"

"In truth," said Khaavren, "I do not; the difference appears to be trivial."

"Perhaps it is," said Tazendra doubtfully. "And yet, it seems to me—"

"I beg your pardon," said Aerich. "Tazendra is right; it is an important difference, and one we ought to bear in mind."

"How, do you mean it?"

"I have never been more serious."

"And yet—"

"Were that—" said Aerich, indicating the large wagon below, "a battle-wagon, it would hold sorcerers and artifacts and would be used against Lord Rollondar's troops."

"Well?"

"Well, I can say little more, for some of what I know was told to me in confidence."

"But," said Pel softly, "you, Tazendra, say the spells in the wagon are not to be used against the Imperial Army?"

"Oh," said Tazendra, confident now that she had unexpectedly been supported by the Lyorn. "I don't say that at all."

"But then, what are you saying?" said Khaavren with some exasperation.

"That we don't know what spells it contains, and that, therefore, we ought not assume—"

"Ah," said Pel. "I begin to comprehend the difference. Should we attack with the notion that it is a battle-wagon, then we might—"

"Yes, yes," said Khaavren impatiently. "I understand." He looked down at it, and, moreover, at the grim warriors who stood around it. "In any case, we must climb onto the wagon, and enter the tent, for there can be no doubt that Adron is there." He sighed. "Why do they not attack?" he murmured.

"Who?" said Tazendra.

Some hundreds of yards away, Rollondar said, for the seventeenth time, "Why do they not attack?"

Lady Glass, who stood next to him, shrugged. "He wishes to fight a defensive battle, that is all; he wants you to attack, so that he can use his greater mobility."

Rollondar shook his head. "What is your opinion?" he asked Roila.

"I haven't one," said the Lavode, but she was frowning and looking out at the neatly formed lines of the Breath of Fire Battalion.

Nyleth appeared at the moment, returning from the front ranks. "Well?" snapped the Warlord.

Nyleth shook his head, "I can tell you nothing," he said, smiling as if it were the greatest joke in the world.

"How, nothing?"

"Exactly. Counter-spells, illusions, blinders, cloaks, baffles—whatever it is, if it is anything, more work has gone into concealing it than I have seen go into the actuality of most spells."

At this moment, a messenger, wearing the livery of the Imperial Army, rode up the Warlord, saluted, and said, "Your Excellency."

"Well?"

"There has been a massacre at the Gate of the Seven Flags."

"How, a massacre?"

"No one is guarding it, Excellency."

"Is it open or closed?"

"Closed."

Rollondar nodded grimly, then frowned. "A clever maneuver, but why does he not take advantage of it by storming the city through that gate?"

The messenger said, "Excellency, it may be that he had nothing to do with it. The streets—"

"Well?"

"The streets are filled with rioters."

"Rioters?"

"Everywhere, Excellency."

"Then there are no longer clear paths to the other gates?"

"I fear there are not—certainly the streets between here and the Gate of the Seven Flags is not clear."

Rollondar stared once more through the Dragon Gate, as if trying to find his enemy and read his mind. "So," he said, as if to himself. "His spell is either a bluff or not, and he is either behind the rioting or not, and he either intends to assault another gate or not."

"This lack of intelligence is insupportable."

Rollondar fell silent, scowled, and took counsel with himself. After a moment he then straightened up. "I must gamble, it seems," he said. "It is an elaborate bluff, or a profound threat. If it is a bluff, it is intended to make us attack him and leave the gate undefended. If a threat, he wants time to prepare it. I believe the threat is real, and so I make my throw. But I will hedge in these ways: First, I will send a brigade of infantry to each of the other gates, who will sweep aside any opposition on the way; second, because our forces are thus reduced, we will not attempt to surround them, but will attack on three sides, and Lookfor will hold a division ready to defend the gate should Adron charge it. Oraani," he added, addressing his commander of infantry, "attend to the gates as I have said."

This order was acknowledged, and Rollondar continued looking forward, but his countenance was clear and strong, and there was even something like a smile upon his lips, now that the waiting was over and the time for action had arrived. "We attack at once," he said. "Glass, prepare to charge them. Tross, pike-men behind. Lookfor, you will guard both flanks as well as the gate behind us when it clears. Lavodes, go with Nyleth, break through, and destroy Adron's spell."

There were echoes all around as officers acknowledged orders. Lady Glass said, "Well?"

"Now," said the Warlord.

Glass gave the signal to charge. It was, at this moment, almost exactly the tenth hour of the morning; and, at the Palace, His Majesty had just refused to treat with, or even to see, the delegation headed by Plumtree. His schedule now called for him to be in the Portrait Room, so that is where he took himself, still refusing to deviate from his agenda. Thack walked before him, Sethra Lavode behind.

We will now turn our attention to the other side of the wall, a scant minute later, where Molric e'Drien poked his head, threw the entry flap of Adron's tent and, with some hesitation said, "Highness?"

"What is it?" snapped Lord Adron, not looking up from his work.

"They are charging."

"Well?"

"The Lavodes are in the vanguard, and seem determined to push their way through."

Adron looked up, then, and a certain doubt appeared in his eyes. "Is Sethra there?"

"No, Highness."

"Ah." He returned to his work. "Stop them," he said. "Hold them for an hour."

"Yes, Highness."

At this same time, Khaavren said, "There!"

"Where?" said Pel and Tazendra together.

"Between the near flank, and the file headed by the woman with her head shaved."

"Well," said Pel, "I see the place; what of it?"

"When battle is joined, the flank must move that way, while the long file has to go forward."

"Why is that?" said Tazendra.

Khaavren, who had seen more than a few battles, just shook his head. "It must be that way."

"What of it?" said Pel.

"That will allow us to slip past the lines and reach the battle-wagon."

"Spell-wagon."

"Yes, the spell-wagon."

"They clash!" cried Tazendra. "Ah, what are they doing?"

"Rollondar," said Khaavren, "is hoping to use his pike-men to make the horses shy, so that his cavalry can find pur-chase against their line—clever, but I do not believe it will work against warriors—and horses—trained by His Highness."

"Time presses," said Aerich.

"We must wait until the line—ah, there, you see how that division is moving? Let us dismount at once, our chance is coming soon."

"Very well," said the others.

They dismounted, and, in fact, it was only a short time later that Khaavren, calculating carefully how long it would take them to close the gap, said, "Now is the time to move."

"I am forced to disagree," said someone behind him.

Khaavren and his friends turned.

"In fact," continued Greycat coolly, "I think it is time for you to stay where you are. You perceive, you cannot flee without being cut down as you run, so you may as well attempt to nick a few of us with your sticks, which will, no doubt, provide you some consolation in the Paths of the Dead."

Khaavren looked at the assembled ruffians and cutthroats, and, having had time during Greycat's speech to recover himself, said, "I am glad that you have allowed us the chance to have this pleasant conversation, sir, before I spit you like roasting fowl."

The other bowed. "I am called Greycat," he said. "This is Grita, and these are my friends. If you wish, you may draw; it all comes to the same thing, but, no doubt, you shall feel better holding a weapon when the end comes."

"When the end comes," said Khaavren, drawing and placing himself on guard, "I have no doubt I shall be holding a weapon, but I think that, to bring about this end, it will take someone more skilled than you, Greycat, or Garland, or whatever you are pleased to call yourself."

"Garland," said Tazendra, frowning, as she also drew her weapon. "It seems to me I know that name."

"It has been a while, my dear," said Pel. "Think nothing of it." He carefully removed the grey gloves from his belt and deliberately drew them on, after which he took his sword into his hand and cut the air once or twice before saluting his adversaries and taking a guard position.

Aerich did not speak, nor had he yet drawn his blade.

"It has, indeed, been a long time," said he who had been Lord Garland and who was now called Greycat.

"It would seem," said Khaavren to Aerich, "that there are five of them to each one of us. I do not consider this a problem, especially when we recall the games we played near Bengloarafurd. And yet, should you choose not to fight, well, then it is closer to seven to one, which I confess would worry me a bit—I might be scratched."

Aerich barely smiled. "I will fight," he said. "But first, Lord Garland—"

"Call me Greycat," said the other, with a glint of hatred in his eye. "I renounced my name when you ruined me. I shall take it back when I have restored myself to His Majesty's favor, which should happen soon after we have dispatched you. Wherefore, as much as I am relishing this conversation, I wish to make a quick end of it so I can be about my business."

"Restore himself?" said Tazendra. "In fact, I believe I begin to recall the cowardly fellow."

"And I," said Pel, whose polite demeanor began to turn grim, "believe I know who is behind the riot of last week, and the assassination of Smaller, as well as the death of Gyorg Lavode, and—"

"And Captain G'aereth," finished Khaavren, in whose eyes the light of anger was beginning to burn. "Yes, I nearly think you have the right of it, Pel. But, Aerich, I believe you were doing this gentleman the honor of speaking to him. Come, complete your thought, then, when you have finished, why, we will begin the slaughter."

"I merely wish to know," said Aerich, bowing, "if—Greycat—is entirely certain he wishes to begin this battle, which, I promise, can have only one result. For, I give you my word, I hold no more animosity toward you, and should you choose to give over—"

Greycat smiled. "Of course you hold no animosity toward me; you won last time. Yes, I am certain."

"Very well."

"Bah," said Tazendra. "This conversation wearies me. Let us begin the game."

"As you will," said Khaavren.

Aerich now drew his sword and his poniard, and took his accustomed guard position, arms crossed near the wrists, both of which faced him, and vambraces guarding his upper chest and neck. Expecting to be surrounded, the four friends put themselves into a position to guard each other's backs, thus forming a circle in which they all faced outward: Khaavren faced the distant battle; Aerich waited at his right hand; Tazendra stood at his left; Pel was at his back, facing Greycat and Grita, who stood a little apart from the others. Pel leaned back and whispered to Khaavren, "It may be that, with my flashstone, I can dispatch Lord Garland, as, I believe, we ought to have done five hundred years ago."

"No," Khaavren whispered back. "I think we ought to save those for making this fight a little more even; besides, at such a distance you could miss, and that would be an embarrassment to me."

"So be it," whispered Pel, shrugging.

The brigands, indeed, formed a circle around them, staying just a fraction out of reach of their blades. As the cutthroats took their own guards, Greycat laughed. "This should be short work," he said. Then, addressing his troop, he said, "Have at them, and an imperial to everyone for each of them who dies screaming."

"Do you know," remarked Tazendra, "I live for moments like this."

The historian might, in order to build tension in the reader, the release of which would provide a certain aesthetic pleasure, claim that our friends were, even apart from the discrepancy of numbers, in a bad place, for Khaavren had not fought a duel in more years than he could remember; Aerich had hardly touched a blade, even in practice, since he had left the Guard; Tazendra's efforts had been mostly given over to sorcery; and Pel had been training, of all things, in the Art of Discretion.

But such a statement, while literally true, would be, in essence, dishonest; for Khaavren had never stopped training, and, moreover, had fought in a score of pitched battles; Aerich had learned in the traditional school of the Lyorn warrior, and so could not, even if he wished to, lose the skills so acquired: He practiced each day simply by walking, breathing, and moving; Tazendra was a Dzurlord in every sense, and, sorcery or no, would never consider leaving off her practice with the blade; and Pel, of them all, had fought perhaps a hundred times since entering the Institute of Discretion. Moreover, they knew each other of old, so that hardly a word of gesture was needed to know when one might move, or to indicate an opening or warn of a fresh attack.

And yet, the odds were, indeed, five to one, and the four friends knew they could not afford a mistake. And so, when Tazendra dropped her dagger, took out her flashstone, and discharged it with such authority that three of the enemy fell at once, one of them, indeed, being dead before she landed, Khaavren said, "My dear, you ought to have waited."

"Bah," said Tazendra, throwing the now-useless stone over her shoulder (luckily missing Pel) and quickly picking up her poniard. "I have another." Several of the enemy, upon hearing these words, turned pale. Indeed, one of them, who stood in front of Aerich, allowed his concentration to drop, which proved an error: before he was aware, Aerich had darted out and delivered a blow which very nearly separated his head from his shoulders, after which the Lyorn returned to his guard position before anyone could react.

"What now?" said Pel. "It is only four to one. Come, I like this game."

"Time presses," reminded Khaavren.

"Well, that is true," said Pel. "And so?"

"Shall we make it three to one?"

"That would be better."

"On my call then. Ready—now!"

On the call, as their enemies flinched, they dropped their

daggers, took out their flashstones, and discharged them at the nearest of their foes. It happened that each had been charged carefully, and so, in all, four more of the enemy dropped, one of them dead, the other three merely injured, but certainly taken out of combat.

"Now!" called Greycat. "Quickly, attack them!"

Had the entire band done so at once, there is no doubt the issue would have been quickly settled—but in the mountains they had had little experience with determined, skilled, and organized resistance, still less with seeing eight of their number fall in as many seconds, and at that all without having so much as scratched the enemy; in short, they were demoralized, which, as anyone experienced in melee knows, is more than half the battle won. What happened was that, of the twelve who remained, seven of them attacked, while the other five held back for a moment. It happened to fall out, then, that for that instant, Aerich had three opponents. Tazedra had three opponents, Pel had one, and Khaavren had none at all.

Pel parried the attack of his enemy easily, and, though he counterattacked, did not score a hit; Aerich contented himself with parrying all three attacks with his vambraces—he, of them all, had no real use for his poniard except as an extra attack—and did not attempt a riposte. Tazendra, like the others, had not had time to pick up her dagger, and she might indeed have been wounded by one of her attackers—for three, all attacking at once, might well have been beyond her abilities—had not Khaavren, realizing in an instant that he had time, lunged to his left and driven his rapier through the heart of one of Tazendra's foes, who responded by dropping his blade and sinking to his knees, in which position, oddly, he remained for the course of the battle.

Khaavren's movement, however, had been seen by those whose duty it was to attack him, and they both did so at once, with such haste, driven, perhaps, by a certain guilt at not having responded to their leader's order with more alacrity, that, in fact, they interfered with each other for just long enough that Khaavren was able to return to his position, although he still, like the others, was without a poniard.

"Oh, now, that was well done," remarked Tazendra.

"You think so?" said Khaavren. "Cha! You've saved me often enough."

"Perhaps I shall again," said the Dzurlord.

Khaavren's two attackers recovered, and, without delay, struck at him simultaneously. There are certain schools of swordplay practiced among Easterners (we will not dignify their practices with the word "fencing") which teach an empty-handed parry. It is, by all accounts, a difficult and dangerous maneuver, yet we daresay there was never a better time for it to be put into practice. Unfortunately, Khaavren had never heard of any such technique, and so, while deflecting one of his enemies' blades with his sword, all he could do about the other attack, which took the form of a thrust for his neck, was to slice at the blade with his left hand, using the hand as if it were a knife, which, in point of fact, it was not; the move could, therefore, have no other result but to give him a deep cut on the outside of his left hand; although, to be sure, he did deflect the thrust and prevent his throat from being cut.

Khaavren winced, which caused his enemy, who had just cut him (or rather, who had just allowed Khaavren to cut himself), to believe that he could end the fray at once by making an instant attack on the injured Captain. Khaavren, however, was not one to allow a wound to distract him; he noted the too-hasty attack, and seeing that it was a wild cut aimed at his head, took the opportunity to fall to his knees while giving his enemy a good cut in the side. The brigand, a quick man with dark eyes somewhat reminiscent of Pel's, cursed and brought his blade at once down at the top of Khaavren's head, while his comrade, whose thrust had also missed thanks to Khaavren's abrupt loss of altitude, attempted to cut at Khaavren's head. It happened, however, that, when Khaavren dropped, his injured hand landed on the poniard he had earlier dropped; without taking time to adjust his grip (he was, in fact, holding the knife on the forte of the blade) he drove up and forward, avoiding the head cut, and stuck his dagger into the neck of the already-injured brigand, who, apparently, considered two wounds sufficient cause for him to leave off the engagement; he stepped back and spent the remainder of the battle (and, as it happened, his life) holding his neck and wandering aimlessly about the field, gasping and choking.

By now the fray was general—Khaavren, again with both weapons, and determinedly ignoring the pain that throbbed from his maimed hand as the blood positively spurted from it, had all he could do to hold off two attackers; Aerich was engaging three at once, and, with the skill of which only a Lyorn is capable, was contriving to force them to get in each other's way, so that, although he still had not managed a counterstrike, he was solidly holding his own. Pel's fierce expression, as much as anything, counted for keeping two of his attackers at bay, yet the third would certainly have scored against him except that Tazendra, who was veritably dancing with her two opponents, took a step forward, then a step back, and said, "Do you know, I have forgotten my third flashstone," and raised her stone at one of those who was attacking Pel.

The burly ruffian froze in place for an instant, and an instant was all that was required before the nimble Yendi had given him a good thrust through the eye, which caused him to drop to the ground without a word or a sound.

"Perhaps," said Tazendra, as she turned back to her opponents, "I was wrong about the third flashstone; it seems I gave it to Aerich."

"Such a mistake," remarked Pel.

"I am ashamed," said Tazendra, aiming a cut at one of her enemies, which the brigand only avoided by a hair's breadth.

"However," she added, "this one has a second charge," at which point she proved that she did not always bluff, by laying one of Khaavren's opponents full length upon the ground.

"Blood of the Horse," said Pel. "So does mine!" His opponents quickly stepped back as Pel raised his empty hand (he had, in fact, dropped his useless flashstone), but he took the opportunity to recover his poniard, which lay at his feet, proving that, since the first pass, they had exactly held their ground.

Khaavren, already wounded, felt himself begin to grow faint from the blood he was losing from his left hand; however, he now had only a single opponent. He drew himself up, smiled, raised his weapon, and said, "What is your name, my friend?"

The brigand, a young man of perhaps three or four hundred, who appeared to be a Jhegaala, looked at his dead comrades. Seeing the Tiassa's cool smile and reddened sword, he now carefully licked his lips, cleared his throat, and said, "I am called Theen."

"Well, Theen," remarked Khaavren, "Perhaps you had best leave now, for if you remain you will die."

Theen did not need to be asked twice; he took to his heels, heading away from the battle and the city as fast as his feet could carry him.

Khaavren took a breath and turned to help Aerich, who was still holding his own against three determined brigands.

"This is insupportable," said Greycat, drawing his blade.

"Well," shrugged Grita, who, not having a sword of her own, took a long, curved saber from one of the dead men.

"My dear Tiassa," said Greycat. "Come, I will dispatch you myself."

Khaavren, who had been about to engage one of Aerich's opponents, turned to Greycat and Grita; he wordlessly took his guard, although he felt his knees trembling. He clenched his teeth, and saw, rather than felt, the poniard drop from his weakened hand.

"A shame," remarked he who had been Lord Garland, and took a guard position, while Grita, next to him, raised her sword. Khaavren felt himself weaving as he stood. Aerich was still closely engaged with three of the enemy, Tazendra and Pel each with two; there was no help for him.

Khaavren stepped forward, half stumbling, and, as Grita and Greycat smiled, the Tiassa swept his left hand at them, covering their faces with his own blood. Both of them winced, and both attempted to wipe the blood from their eyes, and, before either of them could react, the Tiassa's sword had exactly pierced Garland's heart. Khaavren at once drew his sword from the wound and took a guard position, facing Grita; Garland stared in amazement, then fell heavily and began clutching the ground. Grita, upon clearing her eyes and looking around, screamed, dropped her saber, and fell to her knees at Greycat's side.

At the same time, one of Aerich's opponents, startled, dropped her guard for an instant—and an instant later her head was swept from her body, which motion, in turn, distracted one of those fighting Pel, who paid for this error with a wound in the thigh that caused him to fall to the ground, holding his leg. Tazendra's opponents both stepped back, watching.

Grita, taking Greycat's hand in hers, screamed again, and then began sobbing noisily.

Tazendra took a quick look around, and said, "Your leader has fallen, but you are still five to four; come, what do you say? Shall we have at it? Ah, you are useless," this last because the five of them, as if by consensus, turned and followed Theen, the one of Khaavren's enemies who, if the reader recalls, had been allowed to run. At about this time, the brigand who had been kneeling during the entire contest at last sighed and pitched forward onto his face.

Khaavren's friends gathered around the Captain, who stood, panting and watching Greycat and Grita. Not a word was spoken among them, but Khaavren was made to sit while Tazendra poured water into his mouth and Pel bound up his hand.

Aerich cleaned his weapons and sheathed them, then knelt next to Grita, who was now crying silently, and said, "Your father?"

She nodded.

"You are a half-breed, aren't you? He was a Tsalmoth; of what House is your mother?"

She didn't answer, but she didn't have to; when she

glanced up at the Lyorn, he was able to see. "A Dzurlord," he remarked.

"How!" said Tazendra, standing up and approaching them. "Her mother a Dzurlord?"

"Look at her chin, at her eyebrows, at her ears."

· Grita said nothing.

"Who?" said Tazendra. "Who is your mother?"

Grita did not speak.

Greycat, or, if the reader prefers, Garland, opened his mouth as if to say something, but only blood came forth. He then glanced at Khaavren, giving him a look of hatred impossible to describe, looked up at Grita, and, after coughing for a moment, took his last bloody breath and died.

Grita dropped his hand, stood up slowly, gave a long, slow, careful look, as full of hatred as her father's had been, and then turned and walked away. She took one of the horses upon which Khaavren and his friends had arrived, untethered it, mounted, and rode quickly away in the same direction as the brigands.

Tazendra took a step toward her, but Aerich held out his hand. "We don't need them; let her go."

Tazendra shrugged. "Very well," she said.

"Khaavren, can you walk?" said Pel.

The Tiassa took a deep breath and rose shakily to his feet. "Yes," he announced. "Of course I can walk. I have an arrest to make."

# Chapter the Thirty-third

*Which Treats, Once Again, of Regicide,*
*With Special Emphasis on Its Consequences.*

THE READER OUGHT TO UNDERSTAND that the entire battle took less time in the event than it takes to read it—and, indeed, far, far less time than it took the historian to set it down; all of which is to say that it was but a quarter of an hour after the tenth hour of the morning, which is when we should, once again, look in upon His Majesty.

Tortaalilk set about his business with a high hand, first rejecting yet another entreaty to meet with a representative of the citizens, then ordering the representative, Hithaguard, summarily thrown into the prison of the Iorich Wing; and he had given orders for the Guard to be issued flashstones to use against any gathering of citizens.

When Jurabin attempted to dissuade him, he ordered Jurabin from the hall. When Sethra attempted to speak on Jurabin's behalf, she was also told to leave. Even as she stormed out of the Hall of Portraits, Brudik, the Lord of Chimes, intoned, in one breath, "Messenger from Lord Guinn the jailer," and, "Messenger from Baroness Stonemover."

"Ah, ah," remarked His Majesty. "What is all this? Out of

room in the prisons to the right, and another defeat for my Guard to the left? Well, bring them both in anyway, and we shall hear yet more messages, and may they bring better news than we have heard hitherto."

The first messenger was dressed in the colors of the Iorich Prison Guards; the second, a man in the cloak of the White Sash Battalion, looked as if he had seen battle that day. Each, upon showing his respective safe-conduct, was admitted in to the presence of His Majesty.

From his position in front of the gate and just behind the front lines, Lord Rollondar e'Drien sat upon his horse and directed another cavalry division to attempt to breach Adron's line of defense, noting that, while his pike-man had been cut to pieces, and each infantry division he engaged seemed to break almost at once, the Lavodes were having some success on their own in escorting Nyleth ever closer to the spell-wagon.

"It is taking too long," he murmured, and studied the battlefield, his ears deaf to the clash of steel, the discharge of flashstones, and the cries of the wounded.

Roila Lavode had spent most of the time too busy to think—spell, counter-spell, thrust, cut, parry; indeed, it was undeniable that Sethra had created the Lavodes, taking the name from a Serioli word that meant "versatile," or, pronounced slightly differently, "of mountains," for just such occasions as this. Yet Roila and her comrades were unused to being checked; the more effectively her efforts were resisted, the more convinced she was that the entire battle had been arranged by Adron with nothing more in mind than to keep wizards and warriors away from his spell-wagon. This thought, as the reader can readily understand, filled her with fear about what the wagon might contain, and this fear, in turn, redoubled her urgency to reach the wagon at all cost. When a chance breathing space in the fray allowed her to look at the tent, she wondered if she had erred in not accepting Sethra's suggestion to accompany them; if Sethra had been there, surely they would have reached it by now. She wondered what Gyorg would have done, then, cursing herself for vacillating, discharged another ferocious spell of the sort that only the Lavodes knew, hefted her blade once more, cried to her comrades, and continued.

She pressed on, often over bodies; as she did so, she tried not to dwell on the fact that sometimes they were the bodies of Lavodes.

Close enough now to see Roila and her compatriots fighting, Khaavren, Aerich, Tazendra, and Pel watched events unfold, and waited.

"Stay low," said Khaavren.

"Bah," said Tazendra. "This sneaking around is—"

"Necessary," interrupted Pel. "Did you not see that even the Lavodes were not able to penetrate? And yet, they have the same destination that we do. If we are seen—"

"I know, I know," grumbled Tazendra. "Yes, yes, I shall crawl. But still—"

"How are you, Khaavren?" asked Aerich gently.

"I shall not slow us down," said Khaavren, though his voice sounded weak.

"And your hand, how is it?"

"It is not bleeding as much."

"So much the better," said Pel.

"I should like another flashstone," remarked Khaavren. "For then we could quickly remove that annoying fellow who seems to be the only one watching in this direction."

"But," said Tazendra, "the sentry would be spotted as he fell."

"Indeed," said the Tiassa. "Yet, while the sentry was being replaced, there would be nearly a minute during which a path from there, to, do you see? there, would not be observed; a minute, then, during which we could cross this last cursèd forty yards that separates us from the line, and once inside the line, well, we can simply walk to the spell-wagon."

"The noise would attract others," said Pel.

Tazendra said, "What have you been saying? I cannot hear for this battle."

"I said—but it is of no moment," amended Pel. "Come,

Aerich, they must know you, can you convince them to let us past?"

Aerich looked at him, but gave no other answer.

Pel shrugged, "Have it so, then. But I wonder—look!"

None of them required this suggestion; a chance spell from Roila Lavode, of what sort none could say, had caught the sentry, who was flung backward, and lay—senseless or dead—on the ground. Now Adron was not careless in anything he did; he was certainly not careless in the placing of sentries; each could be seen from two other positions, and the instant one fell, another was dispatched to take his place. But it would take a certain amount of time for the new sentry to reach the proper position, and, during that time, by working from rock to tree to gully, they could make it.

Without a word needing to be spoken, then, the four of them raced across the open ground, past a line of riderless horses, and found they were within the perimeters of Adron's defenses. "It is as well," remarked Khaavren, gasping, "that Rollondar did not attempt to surround them, or we should never have gotten through."

"Come," said Aerich, and indicated the way to the spell-wagon.

In an instant they were behind the wagon, and only two Dragonlords stood guard there to watch against exactly such attacks. Their eyes fell on Aerich, and for an instant they hesitated; an instant was all they had, for Pel dispatched one with a good thrust, while Tazendra's blade nearly split the other's head. Aerich looked unhappy, but said nothing as they assisted Khaavren onto the bed of the wagon. Khaavren gasped, teetered, and nodded.

Pel drew his poniard and, with three quick slashes, had opened up the back of the tent. Khaavren entered first, sword in hand, followed at once by the others.

Adron, hands outstretched, was before the array of purple stones that Aerich had seen so many times, only now the stones were glowing, and lights were rippling back and forth among them. As they entered, Adron turned, and his eyes seemed to gleam to match the stones, and dance in time to the flickering lights that raced among them—indeed, it seemed to Khaavren, who was faint and befuddled, that the glow originated within Adron, rather than from the board.

Khaavren paused only a moment, before stepping forward and laying his hand, still leaking blood despite the bandages, lightly on Adron's shoulder. He spoke carefully and distinctly, saying, "Your Highness, I have the honor to arrest you in the name of His Majesty; please give me your sword and come with me."

Tazendra, who knew no little about sorcery, gazed at the board with growing understanding, accompanied by growing horror. Adron smiled, and his eyes gleamed even more. "I'm sorry," he said. "You have, no doubt, performed heroically, and your project was as well conceived as it was, I am certain, brilliantly executed."

"Well?" said Khaavren, staring at him fixedly.

Adron shrugged, attempting—and we say it to his credit—to conceal some of the triumph he felt. "But you are two minutes too late; the spell has taken effect."

The Orb told them, and any who thought to ask, that in ten minutes the eleventh hour of the morning would be upon them.

Strictly speaking, Adron was not telling the truth. That is, the spell had begun its work, but it had not finished. Indeed, there was nothing any of them could have done to have interrupted its working, which is what Adron meant; the spell would continue shaping itself for twenty or thirty minutes, and, when ready, it would, without warning, strike out over the leagues that separated the spell-wagon from the Imperial Palace and seize the Orb, wrest it out of His Majesty's control, and put it under the control of Adron—this would happen, whether Adron or anyone else now wished it. But, for the moment, the Orb still responded to His Majesty's commands; in fact, there was as yet nothing outside of Adron's tent affected in any way, wherefore we can say that the spell had not, in reality, "taken effect."

The Orb, then, entirely unaware of the powers about to be directed against it, still circled His Majesty's head, and was emitting an icy blue as His Majesty heard, now an arrogant demand from the "Provisional Government" headquartered at the University of Pamlar (by which, be it understood, we mean the old Pamlar University, in Dragaera, not our fine institution of the same name in Adrilankha), now a report of the undecided battle outside of the Dragon Gate, and now word of another district of the city into which the Guard dared not go.

We should say, for the sake of completeness, that the Provisional Government, while failing to impress Baroness Stonemover or Rollondar with its legitimacy (Stonemover had arrested the messengers and Rollondar had refused to even accept the message), it had, in its own name, arranged for certain shipments of wheat to enter the city (once the gates were reopened) and was speaking to a representative from Elde Island on the subject of permitting certain ships to pass freely; moreover, the Provisional Government had created up its own militia, which militia had re-established order in the Morning Green district and the Clubfoot area—neither of which Stonemover had been able to do, and all of which, as the reader can no doubt understand, exasperated His Majesty more than Stonemover's failure to quell the disturbances in the rest of the city—Tortaalik did not understand why the rioters were still not either dead or imprisoned.

His Majesty, then, looked upon these latest messengers—from Guinn and from Stonemover—with a barely concealed scowl, wondering what fresh annoyance he would have to contend with. The messengers advanced together, the jailer nervous, eyes averted, the guardsman humble, head bowed.

"You first, jailer," said the Emperor.

"Sire, it grieves us to report an escaped prisoner."

"What?" he said, wide-eyed. "Who has escaped?"

"The Lady Aliera, so please Your Majesty."

"Aliera!" cried the Emperor, springing out of his chair, and nearly turning white. "Aliera? It does *not* please me. Where is Guinn? Why did he not come himself, rather than send a messenger? That such a thing should happen to-day, why, it is enough to . . ." he did not finish his sentence, but merely sat down again.

"Sire, Guinn is injured, for he was wounded during the escape. The Iorich Wing, the Dragon Wing, the Athyra Wing, and the Imperial Wing have been sealed so that none can escape, and—"

"That was what I was told about the assassin," said the Emperor bitterly. "Come, how did it happen?"

"I do not know, Sire. Guinn could only say two words to send to Your Majesty; it is doubted that he will live through the day, and—"

"Never mind," said His Majesty. "We must find her, that is all. Let me hear the rest of the bad news first."

He addressed this to the other messenger, who had not moved from his bowed position, kneeling before the throne. "Well, what is it?" snapped His Majesty. "I haven't an eternity to wait."

Something fell from the messenger's hand, which His Majesty at first thought to be the message. He glared at the messenger in the uniform of a guardsman, who was no longer bowing his head, but, rather, was now staring into His Majesty's eyes with an expression of cold ferocity.

The Emperor recognized the assassin, even as the glass broke and, before the Emperor had time to speak, a thick, grey mist filled the room, flooding the chamber with energy, flooding the Orb with energy, and breaking, for a moment, the Orb's connection with His Majesty. And yet, as quickly as the mist filled the room, something happened even more quickly—so fast, in point of fact, that every courtier was able to see it: The Orb lost all of its color and became a plain, clear, crystalline globe; and at the same time, it fell to the floor, hitting with a sharp, dreadful *crack* that sounded through the room and in the heart of every guardsman and courtier present.

And in that instant, Mario struck—the first thrust from his needle-sharp poniard went directly into the Emperor's heart; the next, an instant later, cut his throat. Only a second passed before the last assault, which afterward became known as the "blow to the Orb," a phrase used so extensively that its origin has been all but forgotten—the third and final knife wound, this time the edge of a heavy woodsman's knife to the back of Tortaalik's neck, severing his spine.

It was, perhaps, fortunate for Roila that she was not engaged in combat in the instant when Mario's spell took effect in the Palace—for, though she did not know what it was, she knew that something was very wrong, somewhere. She tried to ignore the clamor in her brain and continued pressing forward to the tent, afraid that she was already too late.

Sethra Lavode, standing, furious, outside the Hall of Portraits, turned and ran back. She saw the area around the throne filled with thick mist, but did not at first understand its significance—did not understand that it was her own careless words which had told the assassin how to strike.

In the tent, Tazendra and Adron jumped at the same moment, each crying, "What was that?"

Then Tazendra looked at Adron; and Adron, looking back, said, "It was none of my doing."

Seconds passed like an eternity. Sethra gazed around the room, seeing nothing but grey, but surrounded by inconceivable amounts of energy—energy filling the room, covering the Orb. . . .

The Orb!

In an instant, then, she realized what had happened. With a cry she ran to the throne, but, at that moment, His Majesty Tortaalik the First, Eighteenth Phoenix Emperor, died. Sethra looked around for the assassin, and as the mist began to dissipate, as suddenly as it had occurred, she caught a glimpse of Mario even as he slipped out of the room. Into her hand she took her dagger, Iceflame, and though no doubt many of the courtiers thought that it was she who had filled the room with fog for her own purposes, and some of them, who were even now screaming at the sight of His Dead and Bloody Majesty must have thought her guilty of his murder, none dared step before her—she was Sethra Lavode, the Enchantress of Dzur Mountain, and Iceflame was in her hand like vengeance personified; the living embodiment of the mysterious, terrible power of that mysterious, terrible mountain whence she came.

She didn't see the assassin, but was convinced that he could not have gone far. She stood there, outside of the room housing the dead Emperor, and reflected.

For those readers too young to have experienced it, when an Emperor dies, it is not at once apparent; to be sure, everyone will feel, more or less, according his nature, a certain emptiness or hollowness; and so when, perhaps days or weeks later, he learned that the Emperor passed away on thus-and-such a date, he will say, "Ah, that is what it was." But there is no trumpeting of the event within the mind, no reason to be certain, and, thus, there was no reason for Adron to feel the sudden sense of foreboding that came over him as he stood in the tent, marching stares with Tazendra, while Khaavren, Aerich, and Pel looked on.

He shook his head, and said, "It is gone; I don't know what it was. Yet, I fear—"

"What have you done?" said Khaavren, who, though not a sorcerer, had felt distant echoes, as it were, of the sensation that Tazendra, Nyleth, Sethra, Adron, and others had felt upon the release of Mario's spell.

Adron blinked, as if he'd forgotten the Captain was there. "I fear—"

"What have you done?" said Khaavren again, and dropped his sword, which fell to the wooden floor of the wagon with a dull thud. Khaavren would have followed it, but Aerich and Pel caught him and helped him to a seat.

"Are you all right?" said Aerich.

Khaavren nodded dumbly and reached for his sword. Pel put it into his hand. "I do not," began Khaavren, choked, and said, "I feel weak."

Adron leaned his head out of the tent and called for his physicker, who appeared at once, stared at the hole in the back of the tent, and said, "What has—"

"Tend to this man," said Adron.

"Your Highness is kind," said Aerich.

Adron shook his head, stared at the flashing lights on the

mosaic of purple stones, and frowned. The entire shape of the board appeared to be changing now—to grow in three dimensions, as if the ominous power of the spell were reaching out, growing, taking on a life of its own.

The physicker unbound Khaavren's hand, *tsk'd* at its condition, and said, "He will need stitches. I have everything here." He addressed Khaavren kindly, saying, "With the Favor, sir, we shall save your hand." Khaavren, for his part, only heard the words, as it were, from a distance.

Sethra did not have to wait long to find the assassin; in fact, she did not even have to look; she had been standing outside of the Portrait Room but a short time when, his face now cleaned of grime, and dressed in simple Jhereg colors, he walked around the corner toward where Sethra was standing. On his arm was Aliera.

"You!" cried Sethra.

"To which of us are you speaking?" said Aliera sweetly. "And are you waving that around because you intend to use it, or merely to emphasize a gesture?"

"What have you done?" said Sethra, in a voice as cold and hard as ice.

"Come and see," said Aliera, and, still holding Mario's arm, they walked into the Portrait Room. The mist had, by now, entirely dispersed. Without a pause, Aliera strode up to the throne; ignoring the body which had slid to the ground, three knives still protruding from it, and around which courtiers and servants stood, remaining a good distance away, but unable to keep from staring.

Someone said, "The Consort must be informed," to which someone else replied, "You may have the honor."

The Orb was once again floating—only now above the Emperor's body, emitting grey for mourning while it interrogated the Cycle and searched, in its own way, for the new Emperor; Aliera disengaged her arm from Mario and took the Orb into her hands, saying, "I claim the Orb and the throne in the name of my father, Adron e'Kiéron. The Reign of the Phoenix is over, and the Reign of the Drag—" she stopped, and a puzzled look crossed her features. The Orb began to emit red sparks. Aliera let go, but it stayed where it was, only now there were blue and green sparks as well, and these became brighter, larger, and more frequent. Then, abruptly, it stopped, and became the Orb again, glowing white and angry.

Aliera looked at Sethra and said, "What have you done?"

"I?" said Sethra coldly. "I have done nothing, more's the pity. I would suggest that you take the matter up with your father, but I very much doubt you will have the chance."

"What do you mean?" said Aliera.

But Sethra only shook her head. Iceflame was still in her hand, though, and, knowing she had but seconds to act, she raised it and called upon the power of Dzur Mountain.

Inside Adron's tent, the physicker looked up and said, "I've done what I can, we shall have to—what is it, Your Highness?"

For a look of confusion was spreading across Adron's features; in fact, more than confusion, it was almost as if, without actually growing, he was becoming larger.

"I do not know," said Adron. "The spell cannot have worked so quickly."

But the effect continued, until Adron had almost the aspect of a minor deity, and yet it continued, and then, abruptly, his expression changed. "By all the Gods," said Adron. He did not cry it loudly, but conjoined with the look of terror on his face as he stared at the mosaic, the soft oath was all the more stirring. Even Khaavren opened his eyes and seemed to take some interest in the proceedings.

It was Aerich who said, "What is it?"

"The Emperor," whispered Adron. "Someone has killed the Emperor."

Khaavren, for his part, blinked; surprised, in fact, at the sudden swelling of emotion in his heart. But the others frowned and said, "What of it?" by which they meant, not that they were not concerned, more or less, at the idea of someone having managed to kill His Majesty, but, rather, that this news did not by itself account for Adron's extreme reaction.

His Highness said, "Don't you understand? My spell was

intended to fight its way into the Orb, wrest control of it away from the Emperor, and put it under my control. But someone has killed the Emperor, and so—"

"You," said Tazendra, startled "are now the very Emperor that your spell is attempting to win control away from in order to give it to you. How peculiar."

"I believe," said Adron, attempting to laugh, "that I shall be remembered as having the shortest reign of any Emperor in history." Then he shook his head. "Too fast, too fast. I cannot control—"

He broke off and began to tremble.

Outside, shouts indicated that the Lavodes had broken through, and were coming to stop Adron's spell; too late, too late.

Adron looked at those in the tent and said, "You, my friends, do not deserve to die. Moreover, someone must be left to tell history of my folly."

"How," said Aerich, standing suddenly. "Someone left?"

"How," cried the physicker, who was, in fact, a Vallista, not a Dragonlord. "Die? I have no wish to die." He bolted from the tent without another word.

"It is too late," said Adron, "but I still have some seconds to act, and more power at my disposal than any sorcerer has ever had. Come, Duke, you have been my friend; if you love me at all, give me your hand that I might save you and those who are dear to you."

"Here it is."

"Ah, my daughter!" cried Adron with sudden pain. "The Orb itself! Sethra, can you hear me? You must save the Orb, and you must save my daughter!"

Adron now seemed to glow like the Orb itself. The purple stones on the board flashed like cold fire, racing around the pattern so fast they appeared to flicker; and the pattern itself, now, seemed to fill the room, enveloping them all in its presence; indeed, Tazendra began to feel an odd sensation, as if she were actually inside the Orb.

"You others, take the Duke's hand if you value your lives. Yes, like that."

"I do not believe I can stand," said Khaavren.

"You can," said Aerich simply. "You must."

The Tiassa looked into his friend's face, nodded, and with help rose to his feet. He was still unsteady on his feet, but there was no question, from Adron's tone and Aerich's look, that the matter was serious, and so, supporting himself by leaning on Pel and Tazendra, gripping Aerich with his bandaged hand, he remained standing.

In the Portrait Room, Sethra said grimly, "I hear, and will do as Your Highness asks. If I can."

She still held Iceflame high, but now she walked toward Aliera, who waited next to the Orb. Aliera felt Mario tense suddenly; she said, "Bide. I do not understand what is happening, but do not attack her."

"Very well," said Mario.

"What did my father want?" said Aliera.

"He wants me to save you," said Sethra. "I will try, but I must, above all, save the Orb, and that is not easy."

"Can I help?"

"No, little Dragon," said Sethra, something like amusement crossing her features. "You cannot help." Sethra placed her left hand on the Orb; her right still held Iceflame pointing up at the sky.

There was a flash, so that Aliera, Mario, and the assembled courtiers were momentarily blinded. Mario felt that he was slipping away in a direction he had not known he could move, and he reached out for Aliera; Aliera felt a sudden wrenching she could not describe, and she reached out for Mario. Sethra reached out for them both.

In the tent, Adron looked into Aerich's eyes and said, "Remember me, Duke."

"I shall not forget Your Highness."

"And you others, do not fail to tell what happened to any who ask."

"We shall not—Your Majesty."

"Then farewell and—"

"Yes?" said Aerich.

Adron smiled for the last time. There was a single bloody

stain on his shoulder where Khaavren had touched him, and his face was glowing with power and, indeed, majesty.

"Don't tell them that I meant well."

Aerich found no words to say, and in that instant it seemed to him that the world around him ceased, for a moment, to exist.

# Chapter the Thirty-fourth

---

*Which Treats of Adron's Disaster,*
*And the Fall of the Empire.*

E VIL, HEROISM, DISASTER, TRIUMPH, HORROR, and love—
these together represent the summit of human emotion, and the apex of our tale.

We ought to assure the reader that, except in a very limited
way, the work he holds in his hands has no pretensions of being a history of Adron's Disaster and the Fall of the Empire.
We are following the lives of certain personages, and some of
them, indeed, were involved in these great events, but it is
only in the course of following these characters that we are
witnessing the Disaster; at the point when we began this tale,
in fact, we, knowing where we would end, made the decision
to summarily omit any references to children, babies, or even
pets (with the exception of certain unimportant fishes) who
may have come to our attention—it is possible that the reader
noticed this omission. Yet we do not apologize. It is our contention that to have included such pitiable characters, knowing they were destined only for destruction, would have been,
historically accurate or not, to have given in to the basest,
lowest form of literary theatricality; readers who wish to in-

form themselves (or, indeed, torment themselves) by reading of such horrors are directed to entire rooms in the Adrilankha Public Library which are filled with such accounts.

What we wish to make clear, in other words, is that we do not consider ourselves required to detail, nor will we indulge ourselves by detailing, building by building, person by person, horror by horror, all that was entailed in this, the mightiest catastrophe in the history of the Empire.

Is it not sufficient to contemplate the Imperial Palace, with all her history, character, and beauty, gone forever in the drawing of a breath, with all of her nobles, princes, guards, discreets, jailers, and servants vanishing beneath a tidal wave of amorphia to become, in fact, this selfsame amorphia, and so lose every semblance of structure, humanity, and personality they once possessed?

There can be no doubt of the speed with which it occurred, for there were innumerable witnesses—witnesses who became refugees, with their own stories to tell of racing against the growing flood of amorphia which not only threatened to engulf them, but did engulf, according to each witness, at least one friend, lover, or family member—that is to say, no one close enough to see the destruction of the city escaped by more than a hair's breadth; thus none failed to see others who, for lack of speed, lack of alertness, or lack of fortune, did not escape.

Fittingly, it was Adron himself who died first—whether the mosaic of purple stones destroyed him, or whether, grim as such a thought might be, he destroyed it; they nevertheless went together, dissolving into the component energy of all matter: amorphia. We have called this fitting; is it, then, the judgment of the historian that Adron was evil? To be sure, he perpetrated the most profound tragedy since the mythical catastrophe which freed man from the enslavement of the Jenoine (which later was a tragedy, of course, only from the point of view of these Jenoine, or those who feel all life of equal value); but was he, in fact, evil?

The historian believes he was; for what can evil be but the willingness to cause untold misery for one's own desires?

Were we convinced that his motives were as selfless as, in the last instant, he claimed to Aerich they were, we might, instead, consider him a fool; yet this historian at least believes that central to his actions was rage—rage so strong that it overrode all of his concern and his caution; rage so strong that it destroyed the Empire.

The reasons for this great anger, that is, how much of the mixture was for the ill-treatment of his daughter and how much for the ill-treatment of the Empire, we cannot know, nor do we care; his caution abandoned him and he acted, not from thought, but rather from his own hatred, and so destroyed, first himself, then the city, then the Empire.

The first thing to happen, an instant before the dissolution, was: The Orb vanished. In the long, complex, and mysterious history of Sethra Lavode, the historian doubts that she ever performed an act more courageous, more difficult, and more vital than, with full knowledge of what was about to happen, standing in the Portrait Room and sending the Orb to the one place in all the world where she knew, however all-encompassing the impending disaster proved, even should it destroy every speck of life on the world (which, in fact, she was not certain was not the case) the Orb, at least, would be safe; in other words, to the Paths of the Dead.

That, having accomplished this feat of unheard-of skill and daring she then, for no reason other than friendship, remained where she was long enough to collect Aliera and attempt to also bring her along to a place of safety is to know that out of all the heroes with which history is here and there dotted, there is at least one, and here we mean Sethra herself, who has proven before the very eyes of history that her reputation is not undeserved—that is, she consistently proves, ever and anon, that she still has all of those facets of character which won for her the renown she enjoys.

Nevertheless, however much skill she displayed in this last action before the fall of the Empire, however much courage it took to carry it out, it was not, at least in the most complete sense of the word, entirely successful.

To teleport—that is, to transfer from one place to another,

arriving whole and well—was not, even then, entirely unknown in the annals of sorcery. To be sure, there had never been a certain, confirmed case of its being done successfully, but there were, in the first place, rumors; and, in the second, enough close failures to make the rumors believable (as well as to permit anyone who witnessed the gruesome results of such a failure to drink without paying for a score of years). As recently as the past Athyra Reign, in fact, a mere seven hundred years before the events we have had the honor to relate, the wizard Tigarrae of Plainview published a three-volume work on the subject, in which he claimed to have successfully teleported himself from one end of his test chamber to the other. To be sure, an attempt, after the publication of his work, to repeat the experiment before witnesses resulted in failure and death for Tigarrae; yet the work stands, even today when such uses are commonplace, as an excellent manual for students in the magical sciences.

And, we should add, it was far from unknown then for small, inanimate objects to be transferred from one place to another—indeed, as long ago as the Sixteenth Dzur Reign, the Warlord, Shenta e'Terics, while engaged in a campaign far to the southeast, speaking to the Court Wizard through the Orb, received by this method certain maps which he later claimed to have been decisive in bringing the campaign to a successful conclusion.

The notion of teleporting someone *else* from one place to another had only been seen in the most outlandish of popular ballads and plays; certainly no sorcerer or wizard, even the great Norathar the Sorcerer, Court Wizard during the Seventeenth Dragon Reign, had ever seriously discussed such a thing. That, under the most adverse of conditions, and the greatest possible press of time, Sethra managed such a thing even in part stands as one of the greatest tributes to a wizard of whom, even then, it was said, "She redefines the possible each day of her life."

Even such a triumph cannot remove the sorrow engendered by the tragedy—indeed, nothing ever can as long as man's memory shall endure. Yet, even the awful destruction and suffering, the memory of which will always haunt us, cannot detract from the honor Sethra Lavode deserves from us all. Similarly, that today she has vanished from sight, perhaps for all time, does not detract from the honor. And that she is now, again, seen by many as a figure of horror or evil is as great a shame to us as Adron's Disaster is—or ought to be—to the proud e'Kieron line of the House of the Dragon.

The Disaster—

Even as Aliera vanished, and Sethra with her, the overwhelming power of the amorphia devoured the Dragon Gate, scarcely noticing as it destroyed the ten thousands of souls before the gate. Nyleth the Wizard, Rollondar e'Drien, Lady Glass, Roila Lavode even as she set foot onto the spellwagon—all were utterly destroyed. Did Roila frown as she saw the countenance of the unhappy physicker as he rushed from the tent to his doom? We do not know. For her, for the assembled Lavodes, it was over in an instant; Molric e'Drien, Adron's loyal chainman, lay bleeding from several wounds pinned beneath his fallen horse, proud that his father was triumphant, ashamed that he had not fought better for his commander; he would never meet his brother.

In what was, by all reasonable reckoning, the same instant, it ended for those in the Palace, whether Guinn the jailer, fighting a futile battle against death from the wounds Mario had inflicted when he rescued Aliera; or Brudik, Lord of the Chimes, staring in horror at His fallen Majesty; or Noima, the Consort, not knowing that the sudden sorrow filling her was because of her husband's death and still, perhaps, weaving her schemes; or Jurabin, alone in the Seven Room, wondering if he had fallen forever out of favor; or Thack, wondering if he were on his way to earning a promotion from his revered Captain and thinking, perhaps, that there was a certain warmth; or Sergeant, standing helplessly among the courtiers wishing someone would tell him his duty; or Ingera, Lord of the Keys, resting quietly while awaiting the hour when duty would call her again, and idly wondering whether the uprising represented any real danger; or Dimma, on his knees, weeping bitterly and realizing that he, too, had loved Tortaalik, for all his faults; or Erna, planning ways to convince His Majesty to restore funds to the Institute of Discretion; or Bellor, in the Imperial prisons, speculating on her ultimate fate; or Vintner, reading quietly in the Lyorn Wing and wondering what the Council of Princes would ultimately decide about the Imperial Allotment.

As the Palace was devoured, so, then, was the city. Raf, the pastry-vendor, died hiding from the upheavals he did not understand and hoping his new home would be safe; Cariss, the Jhereg sorceress, fingering the bill she held on the Jhereg treasury as she felt the effect of Mario's spell and wondering, but never knowing, why he had wanted it; Tukko, at the Hammerhead Inn, wondering if the Captain needed the horses in connection with the uprising or with the battle; Wensil, in the Silver Shadow, hastily putting boards up in front of his beloved glass window in hopes of preserving it; Tibrock, at the University of Pamlar in Dragaera, attempting to find the words that would convince His Majesty to receive another delegation from the people; the Count of Tree-by-the-Sea and the Baroness of Clover, together on his wide bed in the Dzur Wing, she wondering if she would see him again, he wondering how to go about learning from her the whereabouts of the Baroness of Newhouse, to whom he found himself attracted.

In a flash, in an instant, all were gone, as was the Palace, and all of the landmarks and buildings by which the city was known and for which it was loved, as well as those others, all but unknown, yet landmarks in their own way—the Silver Exchange, the Nine Bridges Canal, Pamlar University, the nameless cabaret in the Underside where Lord Garland had conspired with his daughter, the equally nameless inn where, upon entering the Guard five hundred years before, Khaavren had killed a man named Frai. All of these were now gone forever, preserved only in the memories of those who had seen them, or in such works of art as happened to depict them—of all the buildings and artifacts by which the city was known, only the Orb itself was preserved.

Yes, indeed, the Orb, as every child knows, reached the

Paths of the Dead; inert, quiescent, and useless except in potential; but it survived.

The same, in fact, might be said of Aliera, for she, too, reached the Paths of the Dead, only not, as Sethra had intended, as a living woman, able to return. In concentrating her powers on sending Aliera after the Orb (thinking that this would ensure at least one potential Emperor of the Dragon Line, which she had thought would immediately take the throne), Sethra had only managed to bring Aliera's body; Aliera's life-essence, or soul, was ripped from her body in the maelstrom of elder sorcery which was even then beginning to cascade through the city, and her soul found its way no one knew where. Indeed, Sethra herself thought for many years that it had never escaped the fall, but had been destroyed along with so many others. It is not impossible that the belief that she had failed accounts for Sethra's vanishing from human intercourse, if, indeed, she has not met her fate in some awful battle or tragic mischance.

We now know that Aliera's soul survived, but was lost to all knowledge until a time that exceeds the scope of this history.

Aliera's soul survived, but so many others, as we have shown, did not. Yet, what of those who, thanks to distance from the city, survived the first catastrophic effects, yet could not survive the following moments? For, indeed, most of the city was consumed in an instant, but after this instant, the effects of the spell spread at blinding speed: The dwellers in the small communities that existed outside of the walls of the city (or, at any rate, those to the north and west) heard a low, continuous rumble which brought them from their homes in time to hear the rumble become louder and louder, and to see a great red and black cloud descend on them in the drawing of a breath, and then—oblivion.

Others, further away, had time to run, but not to escape. Indeed, no one who was closer to the site of the explosion than five leagues survived; but there can be no doubt that many who were closer had time to realize their fate, to run helplessly, or to grasp their children to their bosoms and cry to the heedless Gods. Of the following days, weeks, and years of the plagues, the invasions, the starvation, this history will not speak; but of all the facets of the Disaster, none captures the horror so well as the consideration of those in the floating castles of the e'Drien line of the House of the Dragon. The reader, then, is invited to think of those proud Dragonlords, masters of their particular (although, perhaps, decadent) sorcery, who, upon realizing that, inexplicably, the Orb had vanished from awareness, then realized that sorcery had abruptly become useless, and then that they were falling.

The magnitude of horror accompanying the Disaster is such that it seems almost profane to give more than passing reference to that upon which we have concentrated—that is, to Sethra's ironic success. The irony to which we have just made reference, and which consists, as much as in the backdrop of horror against which it occurred, in the Enchantress's conviction of failure, is augmented when we consider that the assassin, Mario, through on one's planning, even his own, was caught in the spell, and thus he, too, was teleported. No one knows where he went either, but many believe that he, body and soul, arrived in the same place as Aliera's soul—arrived bewildered, perhaps without his memories, but alive. It is believed by many, especially among the Jhereg, that he still lives, practicing his grim trade and always searching for the one woman he ever loved, Aliera e'Kieron, daughter of the man who brought down the Dragaeran Empire.

What could be more ironic, yet what could be more beautiful? The cruel assassin, who, as much as Adron himself, was responsible for the Disaster, saved himself, by accident, because of his overwhelming love for Aliera—the very love that caused him to commit the act which, conjoined with Adron's, destroyed a city and an Empire.

If Aliera and Mario ever found each other again after the disaster, no one knows of it, and we will not demean ourselves by indulging in speculation. But, yes, Aliera and Mario, Srahi and Mica, Daro and Khaavren had all, amid catastrophe, found love which endured the fall of the

Empire. In the opinion of the historian, this is no small matter.

The greatest evil, the greatest heroism, the greatest disaster, the greatest triumph, the greatest horror, the greatest love—what could better summarize, and bring to a close, the history we have had the honor to humbly lay before the reader?

# Conclusion

H AVING SAID, AND WITH THE best of intentions, that we
have finished our history, we find that we cannot in
good conscience leave the reader without letting him
know something of the fate of those with whom he has traveled so far; it is our opinion, moreover, that dramatic effect
must necessarily take its proper place behind justice—
whether justice to the accused and accuser at court, or justice
to the reader of history; and those to whom we have gone for
counsel and advice have convinced us that justice absolutely
forbids such an abrupt ending as we had at first contemplated.

Let us, then, wasting none of the reader's valuable time
with further explanation, bring ourselves to Aerich's home of
Brachington's Moor, where, several hours after the events we
have just related, we find Aerich prostrate amid a grove of
trees; we find him, in fact, frowning at a certain confusion in
his mind, as if the sight before him—a lush green meadow,
a pond, and certain familiar formations of vegetation, were at
once expected and surprising.

After some few minutes, the reason for his confusion became apparent to him: He had, in his last conscious moment,
been thinking of nothing else but this, his home, and wishing
fervently to be there; yet he could not imagine how such a

thing had come to pass. But we have failed utterly in our depiction of the character of our Lyorn if we have allowed the reader to believe that he was the sort to doubt the evidence of his own senses; that is, Aerich realized that he *was* home, and accepted it at once, resolving to put off until another time consideration of how it had happened.

He sat up slowly, feeling a certain lassitude coupled with disorientation, and looked around. Khaavren lay next to him, his eyes closed; Pel was just beyond, and appeared to be awakening, while Tazendra was already sitting up, although she did not seem entirely aware of her surroundings. Aerich caught her eye, and she said, "I am reminded strongly of the occasion some years ago when I caused an explosion while working with certain spells. Either I have done it again, and had a monstrous strange dream while doing so, or there has just taken place an event of no small importance and no few repercussions."

"I do not think you have been dreaming," said Aerich. "Although it is possible, for we have been unconscious for—" He paused in order to find the time, and realized that the Orb had vanished from his awareness. He said, "The Orb—"

"So I have noticed," said Tazendra, and only then did Aerich notice that the Dzurlord appeared to be distraught, and was only with difficulty managing to speak in an even tone.

"Well," said Aerich. "No doubt . . ." but he fell silent, frowning, and left his thought incomplete.

"We ought to bring our friend inside," said Pel softly.

"Yes yes," said Tazendra, springing to her feet as if delighted to be active. She assisted Aerich to rise, then Pel. The three of them then half-carried the ailing Khaavren into the manor. For his part, the worthy Captain said nothing except, "Daro," which name he called or moaned once or twice as he was brought to bed, assisted by Steward and certain other servants, whom our unwillingness to introduce new characters at such a late stage of our history prevents us from giving the attention they perhaps merit. During this time Steward, who appeared disturbed, and, indeed, alarmed by the sudden disappearance of the Orb, as, in point of fact, was the case with everyone else, contrived to inform Aerich of all that had happened during his absence, none of which, we should add, requires our attention, for we have no reason to believe that the reader has any wish to learn about the "peasant's duel" between Loch and Handsweight, which resulted in the former's broken arm; nor the elegant lyorn the artisan Smith engraved into the hinges on the lower door; nor the number of fish caught by certain peasants in Aerich's pond; nor the number of poachers apprehended by Warder who were now awaiting Aerich's justice; nor the riot of miners in the Shovelful Market; nor any of the other details with which our Lyorn was forced to contend.

In the same way, we will not discuss Tazendra's experiences when she returned to her estates except to say that she had rather less to contend with, and even less interest in contending with it, wherefore her sojourn was of only the briefest character; she came back to Bra-Moor within three hours after leaving.

Khaavren slept, although not well; he woke from time to time, sometimes calling for Daro, at other times speaking as will those who are delirious, the details of which remarks we will withhold out of respect for our brave Tiassa. Pel spent a great deal of time with him, as did Aerich when he was not attending to his estates; Tazendra, after returning from home, returned also to Khaavren's bedside. From time to time, we should say, his eyes opened, but they rarely focused, although once he looked directly at Aerich and named him before falling asleep again.

The next morning's dawn—that is to say, the dawn of the first day of the month of the Jhereg in the first year of the Interregnum—saw no improvement, and we may state with confidence that it was worry over Khaavren, and, indeed, over Mica, Fawnd, and Srahi (and, at least on Khaavren's behalf, over Daro), that kept our friends from dwelling too much upon what had become of the Empire herself, although, to be sure, this was not a matter that could keep itself from their discourse. And yet, when the subject of the Emperor, or the Empire, or the Orb presented itself, they all of them shied away from it, as if each entertained thoughts he did not wish to express.

On the second day of the Interregnum, Khaavren awoke in truth, although only long enough to take a bit of soup and water brought by Steward and fed him by Aerich himself. After eating what he could, he slept again, and, awakening a second time late that night, said, "Daro?"

"She has not yet arrived, my dear," said Pel, who now sat alone with Khaavren in the darkened room.

"Ah. Yet, no doubt she will," said Khaavren in a quivering voice.

"No doubt," said Pel. "No doubt she will. How are you feeling, my friend?"

But Khaavren was asleep once more. He was still asleep, and appeared pale and drawn, when, late the next morning, the three of them gathered again to discuss his condition, and to determine if, in the absence of a physicker, anything could be done.

"I am not," remarked Tazendra, "especially skilled in the healing arts, yet, could I but reach the Orb, I do not doubt that I could be of some help to our poor friend."

"I don't doubt it," said Pel. "Nevertheless, we must not give up hope; no doubt the confusion will be resolved, and the new Emperor, whomever he may be, will put things in order quickly. Do you not agree, Aerich?"

"I do not know," said Aerich. "Yester-day I should have agreed with you, and yet, I have never heard of an entire day passing with no sign of the Orb's existence, much less three; but, if I am not mistaken, it is very nearly ninety hours since we were abruptly transported, or, if I may, *teleported* here."

"That is true," said Tazendra. "Nevertheless—but what is that?"

"Someone has arrived," said Aerich, glancing at the door with an expression in which he could not conceal a certain degree of disquiet.

An instant later Steward, upon clapping, was admitted, and said, "Fawnd has returned."

Aerich shrugged, meaning, "And was he alone?"

"There are two Teckla with him, one of whom is being carried on a sort of makeshift stretcher, for he appears to have left part of his leg behind him on his journey."

Aerich shrugged once more, this time to indicate that they had made good time. Tazendra leapt to her feet and rushed down to greet her loyal servant, while Aerich and Pel remained by Khaavren's bedside.

"I am pleased they survived," said Pel.

Aerich nodded. "I have grown accustomed to Fawnd, and should have missed him; and Mica has become—dare I say it?—nearly a member of the family."

"Do you know," said Pel. "It is true—we are nearly a family. Is it not strange how our friendship has survived all of these years and trials?"

"Strange?" said Aerich. "Call it so, if you will."

"And you? What would you call it?"

"Tell me, do you believe everything Tazendra says of herself?"

Pel laughed. "Not the least in the world, I assure you."

"Well then, you must not believe everything you think of yourself, either."

Pel frowned, and there was a glint of something like anger behind his eyes. "I do not understand the answer you have done me the honor to make."

"Do you not?" said Aerich. "Well then, let us only say that we have this friendship that so sustains our spirits because, very simply, we have earned it."

Whether Pel would have made any rejoinder to this observation we cannot say, because at that moment Tazendra entered the room, a wild look in her eyes, saying, "The Gods! The entire city is gone!"

Pel stood at once. "What is this you tell me?"

"I have it from Mica that not one stone is left standing upon another in Dragaera."

"Impossible," said Pel.

"They were, he tells me, overtaken by any number of people fleeing the downfall, and they all speak of catastrophe beyond imagination. Fawnd and Srahi," she added, "agree with all he says."

Pel and Aerich looked at one another, then said, "Let us go and interrogate them ourselves."

"Pray," said Khaavren weakly, "rather bring them here, so that I may listen, too."

"My friend!" cried Aerich. "You are awake!"

"Well," said Khaavren.

"How are you feeling?"

"If you please, let us hear this story."

The three friends interrogated one another with looks, punctuated by one of Aerich's most eloquent shrugs, after which, with no words needing to be spoken, they brought Mica's bed up into Khaavren's room along with Srahi and Fawnd, and they spoke for several hours, questioning each of the servants carefully. The scope of the disaster gradually unfolded before them in the second- and third-hand accounts taken from those with whom the Teckla had spoken. Mica spoke quietly, eschewing the bombastic style of oration he usually affected in imitation of his master; Srahi, when she added a detail or two, was more quiet than anyone had ever seen her; and Fawnd, though he spoke as always, appeared from his countenance to have been deeply shocked by what he had witnessed.

And, if this were not enough, from time to time, as they spoke, refugees would arrive to be given a meal and a place to sleep in one of the outbuildings, and Steward would convey their tales of woe as they arrived. Aerich made occasional sounds of sympathy, Tazendra would, from time to time, gasp in horror, and Pel would ask questions in his quiet voice—questions that, most often, had no answer. Khaavren spoke no word during this time, but seemed to sink deeper into his pillow.

There is no need to try the reader's patience by relating for a second time what he has already learned, and in far more detail, in the preceding chapter; we will instead say that, as the day darkened, so, then, did the spirits of our friends as they drew closer and closer together in horror and fear.

At one point, Aerich, as he watched Srahi and Mica, who were shamelessly holding one another's hands, turned to Khaavren and said, "Do you fear for the Countess?"

Khaavren swallowed and, with great difficulty, in a voice scarcely to be heard, said, "I should know if anything had happened to her. There can be no doubt, I should know." It need not be added that Khaavren's tone belied his words.

And yet, it is not our intention to torment our reader (as, indeed, our brave Tiassa was tormented) by wondering about Daro. We will, then, at once dispel any fear the reader may have by asserting that she arrived at Bra-Moor even as the last light of the day was receding in the direction of broken and vanished Dragaera; she was shown in to the room where were gathered Khaavren, Aerich, Tazendra, Pel, Mica, Srahi, and Fawnd, and, with no word needing to be spoken, she came to Khaavren's bed and took both of his hands in her own, and reverently kissed them.

"I feared—" she began. Then she said, "And yet I knew—"

"And I," he whispered, and it seemed to those around him that life returned to his eyes even as he spoke. "I knew, yet I feared."

"Well," she said, attempting to laugh. "We are together, and nothing else matters."

"Nothing else matters," agreed Khaavren.

As the end of one tale is always the beginning of the next, and as the line between one and the other is more often as vague as the edge of the Sea of Amorphia than sharp as the edge of Khaavren's sword, the reader ought to understand that this was the beginning of the Interregnum, and that, even as Khaavren and Daro partook of the joy of their mutual survival, the first seeds of the Great Plagues were beginning in Adrilankha, Candletown, Northport, Branch, and Tirinsar. The Easterners were strong, and some of them had made no treaty with the Empire. The Dukes were strong, and would soon realize that there was no Empire to limit their desires. In a word, then, the most horrible, deathly, and fearful era since the downfall of the Jenoine was only beginning. And, in fact, we are fully aware that, if we have lost sight of Grita, the reader has not forgotten her, as perhaps he forgot Garland once before.

And yet, we insist upon our right to leave the reader here, because as adulthood is the end of youth, so, then, can marriage be seen as the end of life as a single man. Certainly, Khaavren, the soldier, the Captain, the bachelor, was no more. If there is a tale to be related of Khaavren and Daro, or perhaps of some of the others of our confraternity, well, that does not change our opinion that, if an end must occur somewhere, this is where it must fall.

As we humbly ask for our recompense, whether in gold or in esteem, we do not do so with the arrogant conviction that there is no more to tell, for, as Master Hunter has pointed out, the end, where it is possible to determine it, can never be expressed—yet, if more is to be told, then the historian, we believe, has the right as well as the duty to demand both that his work be appreciated, and that he be permitted, insofar as his judgment and his conscience allow him, to place both the beginning and the end where he will.

We cannot but be grateful that the audience—that is, the reader—has trusted us to invade his mind with our gentle weapons of word and image, and, moreover, we do not fail to understand the obligation under which this places us. Therefore, in the interest of the satisfaction of our reader as well, we must insist, of honesty, and although we have not forgotten enemies, plagues, invasions, wars, and famine, we nevertheless direct our reader's gaze to calm Aerich, happy Tazendra, and smiling Pel, who, in turn, are looking upon Khaavren and Daro, who stare deeply into each other's eyes with the happy, tender, and even joyful expression of fulfilled love, and it is here that we choose to take our leave of the reader.

# About the Author

Brust: Allow me to say, in the first place, that I'm delighted we've actually had the chance to meet.

Paarfi: Well.

Brust: The first thing I would like to know, and I'm sure many readers are also curious, is this: Do you write like that on purpose? I mean, is that your natural style, or are you deliberately playing games with auctorial voice?

Paarfi: I am afraid I do not understand the question you do me the honor to ask.

Brust: Never mind. I've noticed that you have gone through a considerable number of patrons. Would you care to comment on this?

*(Paarfi cares to do nothing except look annoyed.)*

Brust: Well, then let us discuss admission to what you call The Institute. Do you still hope to achieve it?

Paarfi: Sir, are you deliberately trying to be insulting?

Brust: Sorry. Well then, uh, are you married?

Paarfi: I fail to comprehend why the reader ought to concern himself . . . herself . . . it . . . curse this language of yours! How do you manage?

Brust: I use "he" and "him."

Paarfi: Preposterous! What if—

Brust: Let's not get into that, all right?

Paarfi: But how did you address the problem in my work?

Brust: I used "he" and "him."

Paarfi: That is absurd. In some cases—

Brust: I'd really rather not discuss it.

Paarfi: Very well.

Brust: Now, what were you saying?

Paarfi: I was saying that I fail to comprehend why the reader ought to be concerned with such questions as my matrimonial state. Moreover, it is entirely personal in nature, and I am uninterested in such discussions.

Brust: Some readers like to know—

Paarfi: Are *you* married?

Brust: . . . I see your point. Well, are there going to be any more books about Khaavren?

Paarfi: It is not impossible.

Brust: I take it that means maybe.

Paarfi: Well.

Brust: Is it a question of money?

*(Paarfi declines to answer)*

Brust: Have you any opinions about music?

Paarfi: I do not understand why you wish to know.

Brust: To find out whether you've heard any of my music, such as *Reissue* by Cats Laughing (tape), *Another Way to Travel* by Cats Laughing (tape and CD), *Queen of Air and Darkness* by Morrigan (tape), *King of Oak and Holly* by Morrigan (tape), *A Rose for Iconoclastes* by Steven Brust (tape and CD)—all of which may be ordered from SteelDragon Press. For a catalog, one could send a stamped, self-addressed envelope to P. O. Box 7253, Minneapolis, Minnesota, 55407. The cost is a mere—

Paarfi: That is insupportable, and I have no intention of sitting here while you shamelessly—

Brust: All right, all right.

Paarfi: Well?

Brust: What do you want to talk about?

Paarfi: We could discuss literature. For example, its creation. Or we could even discuss the particular work in which a transcription of this conversation is destined to appear, by which I mean, of course, *A Discussion of Some Events Occurring in the Latter Part of the Reign of His Imperial Majesty Tortaalik I.*

Brust: I've . . . uh . . . I've actually given it a different title.

Paarfi: You've what?

Brust: Trust me.

Paarfi: The proper title, Sir, is—

Brust: Look, I know publishers, okay?

Paarfi: Are you proud of that fact?

Brust: Well, then, uh, would you mind explaining why you have sometimes used feet, inches, yards, miles, and so on, and other times meters, centimeters, and kilometers, as well as leagues, and even furlongs and like that?

Paarfi: You ought, in my opinion, to stop asking questions to which you know the answer, and to which, moreover, any intelligent reader could determine the answer.

Brust: Say it anyway, all right?

Paarfi (*looking pained*): Very well. There were, at the time in which this work is set, six completely different systems of measurement in use throughout the Empire. Your translation of these into terms with which the reader is familiar is an attempt to capture some of this complexity. There. Does that please you?

Brust: Thank you. Would you like to give the reader a hint about where to find Devera in this volume?

Paarfi: As it happens, she does not appear at all.

Brust: Huh? But I *told* you—

Paarfi: It would have been inappropriate, not to mention dishonest, to have simply "put" her somewhere, when, in fact, I was able to learn nothing of where she may have appeared, or, indeed, whether she appeared at all.

Brust: *(Inaudible)*

Paarfi: I beg your pardon?

Brust: Nothing.

Paarfi: Would it be possible for you to find a question that requires some degree of thought to answer?

Brust: All right, then, for whom do you write?

Paarfi: I beg your pardon?

Brust: Do you have an audience in mind when you write? Are you writing *to* someone, or just to please yourself, or what?

Paarfi (*looking interested for the first time*): Ah. I see. I write for those who love to read.

Brust: Well, of course, but—

Paarfi: I believe you have failed to comprehend what I have said. I do not mean that I write for those who simply like a good tale well told, or for those who use the novel in order to explore what your critics are pleased to call "the human condition," or for those who treat a story as a distraction from the cares of the day, but, rather, I write for those who take joy in seeing words well-placed upon the page.

Brust: Typesetters?

Paarfi: I believe you are attempting jocularity. I believe you are failing.

Brust: In fact, I think you know what you mean: Your reader is the one who doesn't rush on to see what happens next, but relishes the way the sentences are formed. Is that right?

Paarfi: Substantially.

Brust: That's interesting.

Paarfi: And, you, sir?

Brust: Me?

Paarfi: For whom do you write?

Brust: Uh ... I think I'd like to please all of the above.

Paarfi: I beg your pardon?

Brust: All of those in the list you mentioned—those who like a good story, those who—

Paarfi (*ironically*): A worthy goal, no doubt. And yet, do you not write in what is called a *genre*, or, more accurately, a *marketing category*, where it is assumed that one cannot create works of lasting importance?

Brust: Let's not get into that.

Paarfi: Very well. Tell me, then, what do the initials "PJF" after your name indicate?

Brust (*annoyed*): I said I don't want to get into that.

Paarfi (*stiffly*): I beg your pardon. But if you are going to go so far as to insist on having obscure initials after your name on the very title page of a novel, I should think the reader would have the right to know what these initials indicate. Is it an elaborate joke? Is it a statement of what you hope to accomplish? Come, sir. Here is your chance to explain to your public.

*(Brust declines to answer.)*

Paarfi: As you wish. Name some of your favorite writers, please.

Brust: Well, Alexander Dumas—

Paarfi *(ironically)*: I should never have suspected.

Brust: Twain, Shakespeare—

Paarfi *(sniffing)*: You would be doing me an inestimable service if you stopped trying to impress me, and, instead, named writers of the time in which you have the honor to work.

Brust: You mean contemporary writers?

Paarfi: If you please.

Brust: Oh. Well. Zelazny, Yolen, Wolfe, and Shetterly, to start at the back of the alphabet, or maybe Bull, Crowley, Dalkey, Dean, Ford, and Gaiman to start at the front. Or—

Paarfi: I do not comprehend.

Brust: Never mind. I'm awful fond of Patrick O'Brian and Robert B. Parker. Diana Wynne Jones is wonderful. I shouldn't mention Megan Lindholm, because I've written a book with her, but—

Paarfi: You perceive that none of these names are familiar to me.

Brust *(stiffly)*: You asked.

Paarfi: And, moreover, I do not believe that one can be "awful fond" of someone.

Brust: Deal with it.

Paarfi: Then, if you please, name some of your colleagues of whom you are not "awful fond."

Brust: Huh?

Paarfi: Name for us the bad writers in what is euphemistically called, "the field."

Brust: Oh, yeah. Right. And maybe monkeys—

Paarfi: I take it you decline to answer?

Brust: That'd be a yes.

Paarfi: Well. Would you care to speak of any works in progress?

Brust: I'm thinking of writing another story about Vlad Taltos.

Paarfi (*yawning*): Indeed?

Brust: Yes. In this one, he is paid an immense amount of money to kill an annoying, stuffy, pretentious historical novelist, but ends up doing the job for free, and, in the course of the book, he discovers he enjoys torture, and—

Paarfi: I believe this discussion is at an end.

Brust: Damn straight.